HIDE AND SIDHE

BOOK II OF A CENTURION IN THE LAND OF THE FAE

J. E. BRUCE

BooksForABuck.com
2012

BooksForABuck.com
August 2012
ISBN: 978-1-60215-187-1

One should rather die than be betrayed. There is no deceit in death.
It delivers precisely what it has promised.
Betrayal, though... betrayal is the willful slaughter of hope.
~ Steven Deitz

PART ONE: LATRONES

— I —

*"**We're** soooo screwed,"* Aetius groaned softly as he plopped himself down beside me.

And we *were* so screwed—so *sincerely* screwed.

What to the untrained eye appeared as nothing more than the dazzling starry sky reflected in the dark, still water of some tranquil mountain lake was in fact a vista that was anything *but* idyllic: the perfect mirror of heaven was in reality the pinpoint glow of thousands of campfires rivaling the thickly seeded stars above in their vast numbers.

So in fact we weren't just so sincerely screwed, we were so *super* sincerely screwed.

"Lady Ainiaan did mention the Faoimhuir weren't to be trusted," I whispered, as if that was justification enough for the unhappy discovery that there were more campfires scattered across the valley below than I had soldiers, and I seriously doubted the Faoimhuirian troops were so well off each man had his own personal bonfire, much less each had *multiple* fires.

Wood was exceedingly scarce—in fact everything was scarce on this misbegotten wasteland of saltpans, high desert and even higher mountains. What little vegetation managed to grow was stunted and any that happened to grow around the periphery of the pans was poisonous to eat, laden with the same salts that turned any standing water into a soupy pink brine which blistered the skin of anyone foolish enough to touch it—gods only knew what happened if you tried to drink it—facts I somehow knew, facts we *all* somehow knew.

I had to assume this life and death tidbit had been instilled into our memories without us being aware of it—a collective *'listen to me'*—akin to Turan's wordless command, and for that I was grudgingly thankful.

Otherwise the foolhardy and impulsively curious among us—and sadly there were more than a handful—would've found out in short order and by the most expeditious of means. But this warn-off was no act of compassion—it was pure self-interest. The Tuatha needed every able body to fight their war. Losing men to poisoning only increased our chances of losing, *period.*

As far as I'd been able to determine there was no animal life hereabouts—not that I could blame the gods for refusing to squander any more lives on this sad experiment; plants, in my opinion, were waste enough. I hadn't seen any bugs—no small relief as I had little liking for any creature with more than two legs, and I held those with more than four and who also had a tendency to earn a dishonest living in the absolute lowest regard possible.

Of course this meant that all my hard work in training my soldiers in proper foraging techniques was largely for naught—what provisions we'd brought were all we had—anything else was at best chancy, at worst deadly. Once the food and water ran out… well, no reason to belabor the point. Still, it would have been nice if someone had bothered to mention that this 'Earth-like planet,' upon which two human armies were to slug it out to determine the ultimate fate of humanity, was something akin to hell.

Latrunculi. That was the name my troops had bestowed on this forgettable world. A grim joke among soldiers all too well aware that *this* game of strategy was for keeps; losers—assuming any on the losing side survived, were to be left here, abandoned by their masters while the victors were to be granted passage home. Call it an added incentive—not that we needed any. Having a limited amount of food and water was yet another enticement to not dally about.

In truth I no more trusted the Tuatha to hold up their end of the bargain—assuming we were victorious—than I'd expected the Faoimhuir to live up to their word, and we all knew how honest the Faoimhuir were: all the evidence you could possibly want was spread out below us, glittering in sinister frankness. Maybe the Tuatha would just leave any and all survivors for the Si'aafu—those massive scorpion-like creatures Lady Ainiaan had described to me in such skin-crawling detail, creatures who considered human flesh a delicacy—now *that's* a cheery thought…

Perhaps, before I go any further, I should introduce myself: my name is Arrius Marcus Niger—Arri to my friends and '*Oh fuck, not you again!*' to my enemies—until recently Hastatus-Posterior, Centurion of the Fifth Century, First Cohort of the Ninth Legion Hispana, under the command of Quintus Petillius Cerialis, and now Legate of the First Legion Spartoí—yes, *those* Spartoí.

And yes again, in case you were wondering, that is a *huge* leap in rank and not one I would have ever considered possible for someone of my truly humble origins. But don't think for one instant this was an honor or a career advancement I would have sought out. I'd set my goal somewhat lower, that of Primus Pilus—not just any Primus Pilus, but the youngest Primus Pilus *ever*. So, yes, I'm ambitious, *very* ambitious—never once claimed otherwise. I've just learned the hard way never to bite off more than I can swallow in one gulp, and going from Hastatus-Posterior to Legate could, justifiably, fall into that category; it was akin to biting off the rear end of a mule and getting kicked in the teeth as an added bonus. And of course since the Tuatha were involved, it wasn't like I'd been given a choice in the matter—all right, fine. I *had* been given a choice as to what rank I would now hold, or should I say my men had decided what rank I would now hold, and they'd collectively decided on legate—with the encouragement of the aforementioned Lady Ainiaan. The First Legion Spartoí couldn't possibly go into battle without a commander, *a legate*, she argued. And my men believed her.

I'd gone into battle plenty of times without a legate telling me what to do. In fact I'd gone into battle plenty of times without the legate being anywhere near where the actual fighting was going on. But I digress…

I could have said no; I could have kept my centurion status—I'd been led into battle plenty of times by centurions, in fact every time, and once I was a centurion myself, I'd happily, and in a few cases, not so happily led others into battle. Say what you will about us centurions, we rarely shirk our duties when it comes to the actual slash and bash and blood everywhere fighting. But my troops had their hearts set on legate and I was loath to disappoint them—or Lady Ainiaan. So, legate it was.

Months back I'd been taken prisoner by the Tuatha—literally snatched from the jaws of death—for the specific purpose of leading an army against their sworn enemy, the Faoimhuir. I'd been told that the result of this battle, which would take place on what the Tuatha claimed was an Earth-like planet, would decide the fate of all of humanity—including barbarians. To that end we'd 'arrived' in this predicament—*er,* I mean *on this planet*—three days before, but exactly where we were, or, perhaps more importantly exactly *how* we got here, how long the trip had taken I cannot tell you.

My last trustworthy memory before finding myself here was of sitting astride my very restless warhorse, Wushah, with Felix beside me and aboard his glossy black mount, Tuzun. While I was now legate, Felix, ironically, held my long-coveted rank of Primus-Pilus, and we were watching as the centurions called their soldiers to order and the men responded by immediately drawing themselves up into neatly ordered columns of shiny armor and scarlet, standards at the fore of each century and glinting in the dawning sun—it was an all too familiar sight, and one I truthfully never thought I'd see again.

That was the morning of our departure, a bright and balmy mid-summer dawn and the climax of all the months of preparation. But instead of feeling my usual sense of eager anticipation, of excitement at the battle to come, I felt only gnawing dread. I'd said my farewells to Hanni and Boian the evening before; both asked—begged in fact to accompany us, Hanni as added muscle as he was an ogre after all, and Boian as a cook, but while both had proven themselves as worthy allies—and Boian was a damned fine cook—I'd told them no. This was not Hanni's fight, and bringing along only one woman, even a woman of Boian's well-known willingness... well, that was a recipe for disaster. Hanni, in response to my gentle refusal had sworn a blood-oath to protect Boian from any repercussions once we'd left.

I'd assumed Lady Ainiaan would come to see us off, but no; I kept my own disappointment to myself so my men, all of whom had grown quite fond of her, wouldn't consider this a rebuff. Perhaps her father had refused to let her come, perhaps it was just too painful for her. Perhaps. But I'd grown fond of her too and had hoped to see her one last time, to thank her for all of her help, her willingness to share her knowledge with my soldiers and me.

In fact no one had come to see us off, Boian and Hanni because I told them not to, but the others? You'd have thought Rasaben would have been there, if nothing more than to make sure we actually took our leave. It was all rather anticlimactic, and as irrational as it was, I resented the fact that the Tuatha didn't feel my men deserved a suitable send-off to battle. If my soldiers felt the same, they didn't show it. Then again, they were former Kellesuf; maybe they were in fact as relieved to be done with the Tuatha as the Tuatha were relieved to be done with them.

I remember glancing to my left, past Felix to Taskim's Keep and the massive wood and stone fortifications that blocked any view of Turan's apartments and perhaps one last parting glimpse of her and my infant son—and them of me; of realizing with a deep ache that it was probably for the best—we'd already said our goodbyes.

It was time to go.

I remember turning Wushah's massive head, of Felix and Tuzun instantly mirroring our actions, followed by a deep, undulating wail from the chorus of *buccinas*: the long-awaited signal to usher us on our way.

Taskim had told me to head towards the rising sun, a very curious order that at the time seemed perfectly reasonable in its utter simplicity and one that I, just as curiously, did not question.

I glanced at Felix and at his grinning nod, I clicked my tongue and Wushah started off, his massive, flax-feathered hooves treading lightly on the dew-damp and sparkling grass, the damned beast eager to get on with it. It took all of my strength to keep him in check; had I given him his head he would have raced ahead to meet the sun before it fully cleared the distant line of trees.

With a muffled clatter and rustle, the columns of infantry, supply wagons, engines and finally the cavalry, like some gigantic, multi-legged beast, fell into step behind us, the far end having to wait as movement slowly rippled down its immense and muscular length.

The next thing I knew, I found myself still astride Wushah, Felix close beside me and the two of us staring out at a barren, mountain-ringed desert awash in a deep ocher glow, our long, inky black shadows stretching out before us like so many skeletal fingers.

The air was chill; it prickled my exposed skin, and it had an odd smell to it. No longer the pungent fragrance of pine and the earthy scent of summer-warmed grass, this air strangely—ominously—held the same coppery taste as blood.

Wushah whickered nervously and tossed his head. Felix's mount snorted and pawed the ground. Behind us other horses replied, sharing their unease as men's whispered voices echoed the sentiment all the way down the column.

I gathered my loosely billowing cloak around me and twisted in the saddle to cast an over-the-shoulder glance past the ranks of my equally startled men and anxious horses and oxen, past the eeling dragon-headed banners and the veritable forest of cavalry lances held aloft, pennants fluttering in the breeze. What I saw confirmed that we were *here*, the place—the planet—chosen by the Faoimhuir as the field of battle: a suitable arena for combat with an angry red and bloated sun hanging just above the crags of the far distant, dagger-edged peaks that completely encircled us like the crumbling walls of a long-abandoned coliseum. And the red sun wasn't alone: another, smaller and brilliant blue star was held in its grasp by long, dazzling white tendrils, like lovers—or, more likely, mortal enemies in a death grip.

My open-mouthed, wide-eyed stare compelled everyone else to turn—all fifteen hundred men in perfect unison, accompanied by a metallic rustle of armor and groan of leather—towards the sight; drovers rose from their benches, cavalrymen turned in their saddles, foot soldiers and their centurions glanced over their shoulders and like me, gaped at the bizarre and, I have to say, unnerving spectacle of a battle on such epic proportions—a celestial version of *pancratium*.

More anxious whispers rippled down the column as men clutched their weapons; others reached for protective talismans, some did both, as if either could protect us against the actions of such unearthly foes.

So, seemingly one minute we were *there*, and now we were *here*—but how we got from there to here was a complete mystery, an absolute blank.

While holes in my normally faultless and, dare I say it, *gapless* memory had become all too common since I'd fallen into the hands of the Tuatha, it was still damned annoying, and, yes, I admit it, deeply unsettling to stumble across another one, and one so obviously wide and deep, encompassing the collective memory of a legion.

And this time it went beyond memory lapses. I'd never thought to ask exactly *where* we were going, how long it would take to get here, *how* we would get here—I hadn't even asked how long we would remain here, how long we had to wage this proxy war, although the provisions provided suggested no more than three months and only if we very carefully rationed ourselves—and now, as I thought about it, three months seemed an excessively long time to do what we came here to do.

It wasn't because I didn't care or was so confident of victory; it certainly wasn't because I was so trusting that I accepted Taskim's promise that the Tuatha would in fact come collect us once we'd secured victory.

Such questions just never occurred to me—until now, when if course it was too damned late to ask—ostensibly a *huge*, potentially fatal oversight on my part, but one I knew was a *coerced* oversight as the Tuatha had the ability to deny a man his common sense, his volition—I'd certainly experienced this first hand with Turan, and on more than one occasion.

Perhaps I *had* asked, had demanded to know, perhaps they'd even told me, only to later wipe that memory, wipe the reasonable desire to know these essential facts from my mind.

I *had* foolishly believed I held the upper hand once I'd gained control of the Kellesuf, the Tuatha's army of slave soldiers. I'd even gone so far as to challenge Taskim, bait him and his fellow Sidhe Lords; I'd reveled in treating them with the same sneering contempt they'd shown me. I knew now that that had been a lie as well; they'd manipulated me into doing their bidding by playing on my obvious vanity, my arrogance while tampering with my usual prudence when it came to life and death decisions. *That* was the harsh truth. They knew me, knew my weaknesses, my personal failings far better than I knew myself and they'd exploited them—*and me*—masterfully.

On that bitter thought, I leaned forward and from our rocky aerie and scanned the valley far below.

What if it's all a feint? What if a goodly number of those campfires are unattended—a bit of visual trickery intended to cripple morale among my men?

What if they don't realize we're here, maybe they think we're still en route?

I'd been told once—by Gnaeus Domitius Corbulo himself—that it's the uncertainties, the nagging 'what ifs' that will kill you as easily as any sword thrust, any arrow barrage. Prophetic words indeed.

My eyes desperately sought the telltale flicker of movement—tangible proof of my worst fears or my faintest hopes—but if enemy soldiers were moving around down there, they were smartly doing it in the dark. Most were probably sound asleep—resting up for the battle to come, toasty warm by their fires, the damned lazy bastards—while we'd spent a goodly part of the night scrambling up the side of this barren mountain with only the stars above to light the way, freezing our damned butts off, in order to get a measure of their strength.

As I gazed down at the glimmering encampment and my mind mulled over all the possibles—all the 'what ifs'—I felt someone settle down next to me, opposite Aetius, shoulder and knee pressed to mine in the tight and precarious squeeze of our mountaintop perch.

I didn't need to look to know it was Felix, this fair-haired, close to perfect reincarnation of my closest and now very *dead* friend. This man, *this* Felix, had, sometime in his previous life, been stabbed in the throat and as a result had this odd wheeze when he exerted himself or breathed in cold or especially thin air—exactly like what one would expect to find on the same said freezing mountaintop.

It was a former life of which he had no memory, a life he would never remember, taken away by force and, later, a new life with its own set of memories—*my memories*—forcibly imposed. But along with this new life came the keen awareness that he had, at one time, been someone else.

You'd think he'd hold a not unreasonable grudge about this awful, compulsory exchange, but he, like all of my soldiers, each and every one former Kellesuf—men whose minds had been washed clean and thus in the exact same situation as he—accepted this complete identity swap as if it was his due. Most had even gone so as far as to express everlasting gratitude at having an identity again even if was not truly theirs, and all, even those like Rufinius who openly voiced his resentment of his appalling treatment at the hands of the Tuatha did their utmost to live up to my expectations, to my memories of those who, through me, had unwittingly donated their souls to these men.

As Kellesuf, they'd never questioned their Tuatha masters; they'd been rendered incapable of speaking unless spoken to and did and died at the direction of the Tuatha. But men who will follow orders without question do not in fact make good soldiers; it was a critical blunder the Tuatha discovered almost too late and at the expense of countless Kellesuf lives.

There were, however, two highly personal attributes the Tuatha had not erased from these men: the first were physical scars, old wounds and in some cases tattoos or deliberate scarification, mute testament to a prior existence, to unremembered experiences and lost beliefs that marked the body yet left no record in the mind—like the ugly pucker-mark on Felix's throat.

Desperate to fill in any remaining holes in their newfound personalities, the soldiers had made a game of creating elaborate, of course hugely heroic and, on some occasions, exquisitely gruesome explanations for the scars almost all of them bore—all in good fun, but always with an undercurrent of profound loss, a loss of such proportions I freely admit I cannot even imagine. In fact I'd rather not even try.

The second attribute was sadly transitory: their native accent. While Kellesuf, each man retained some hint of a regional intonation, perhaps because they so rarely spoke—only when spoken to and then rarely more than a 'yes, sire', 'no, sire'—the Tuatha saw no need to wash this taint from their tongues. Some I could readily place as I happened to be nearby when a Tuatha deigned to speak with one, prompting an always softly worded, deferentially laconic reply: the occasional Sicambriian twang, the distinctive sing-song pitch of an Isaurian, or a clipped Dacian, others were a complete mystery, such as an oddly cadenced burr vaguely reminiscent of those damnedable Hermunduri and yes, the Marcomanni. But unlike the scars, these traces all too quickly vanished into a shared accent—*my accent*, a provincial 'Mauri' brogue with the underlying Massaesylian rolling 'r', an inflection my friends, officers and troops had always attributed to me spending my formative years in Egypt, which wasn't far from the mark.

Felix, Rufinius and Aetius were the exceptions—each one had been hand-picked for the roles of my closest friends because of their close

physical similarities to the originals and to cement the ruse, each had to
sound like his predecessor as well as look and act like him; if I closed my
eyes, I could almost believe I was hearing the first Felix, the first Rufinius
and Aetius speaking. *Almost.*

All in all, these shadowy connections to former lives left a rather eerie
result.

For me, when I walked among my soldiers, there was this odd,
disjointed and more than just a little macabre mélange of familiarity and
foreigner: of a facial expression, a nervous gesture, a verbal tic, a
distinctive hitch to the gait that immediately brought to mind an
acquaintance, a friend, even an rival but worn by an entirely new face and
used by a vastly different body. It was as if they were ghosts who hid their
true selves behind masks of the long dead, while I alone walked about
barefaced, whole and truly alive—

Wheeze… wheeze… wheeze.

Yup. Felix.

"We're soooo screwed," he whispered after a momentary silence to
analyze the situation laid out before us.

So, so, so. It was unanimous.

The remainder of our ten-man reconnaissance squad was hunkered
down behind us, well hidden among the boulders that made up this bare
and freezing outcrop, which in turn provided an unparalleled view of the
valley.

In order to reach this vantage point undetected we'd opted to wear
only our leather tunics, woolen undertunics and breeches, a reasonable
precaution against the occasional warning flash and constant glimmer of
starlight on armor—and not just any armor, but Tuatha armor, which had
its own damned eerie luminescence even in the dark. We'd also forgone
socks and sandals during the actual climb, preferring the guaranteed
silence and better purchase of bare feet on loose scree, even at the risk of
stubbed toes, not to mention rock-bruised and cut soles. We'd even
smeared soot on all exposed skin and those fair-haired among us, like
Felix, had covered their heads in their neckerchiefs.

There were enemy pickets about—so, while they vastly outnumbered
us, they wisely weren't being cocky about it—we'd caught glimpses of two
sentries lower down on the mountain, and overheard unsuspecting voices
of others on our cautious climb, which necessitated a hasty, albeit
soundless retreat and then a time-consuming search for another, safer
path through the rockfall to where we could overlook almost the entire
valley below.

Pity about the view.

Weary of staring disaster in the face, I lifted my gaze.

I will give Latrunculi grudging praise for one thing: it had the most spectacular sky—the handiwork of a bored-stiff Coelus or his local equivalent, or so Nestor, one of our physicians, maintained. In daylight the bowl of the heavens was pale ocher shading down to dusty deep lavender and streaked with saffron and vermilion-colored clouds, while the bloated star, dubbed Romulus by my troops, blazed a dazzling orange-red and its corresponding, yet diminutive companion unsurprisingly named Remus, shone an equally dazzling azure.

However, just after sunrise and just before sunset the combined and low-angled suns' light had a brief, but very odd effect of intensifying certain colors: at dawn anything tending to red or yellow, such as our crimson undertunics and cloaks or the gold on our insignias burned bright as if lit from within, while anything blue or green were muddied almost black. At dusk, it was the reverse: cool colors blazed like foxfire, while anything red was turned to a deep, dirty, purplish-brown. It was as if the planet was giving warning, a visual clue as to what was to come: scorching days and chill nights. However, during the long hours of day, when both suns filled the sky, colors returned to a truer shade.

At night points of light in every hue imaginable glimmered against a faintly glowing backdrop stained a faint ocher from the dust, and the entire western sky was filled with a massive, luminescent whirlpool—a celestial Charybdis—that looked, in the still night air, close enough to touch.

Eye-popping beauty aside, nighttime made for concealment little better than daytime. It was as if the world was perpetually bathed in the glimmer of a full-bellied desert moon and speaking of, Latrunculi in fact had not one moon, but three: *Bellator, Latro* and *Miles*—more wry humor from men who, as former Kellesuf, had seen little to laugh about as each "moon" was barely more than a pebble, insignificant in the greater scheme of things, visible only in the halflight of dawn and dusk when most of the stars had faded or had yet to come out.

From what little Taskim had told me—what I'd been permitted to remember—was that Earth, *home*, was somewhere out there in that sparkling vastness—too far away for the human eye to see, a distance too great to far a human mind to grasp. And yes, I understood that Earth is a *planet*, a world, just as Latrunculi is. I understood that Bellator, Latro and Miles were *moons* that circled Latrunculi, and that in turn Latrunculi circled Romulus and Remus in an endless cycle. I understood that there were huge, empty spaces between worlds, an immense dark sea in which planets like Earth and Latrunculi and thousands of others sailed along like ships, some in flotillas, others singly, each carrying their precious cargo of life, while creatures such as the Si'aafu patrolled these deep waters like celestial sharks, gobbling up the weak, the unwary.

Turan and Lady Ainiaan had taught me these things, believing such an education would hold me in good stead, and because I understood and accepted them, so did my men. But the old beliefs, the old ways aren't so easily shoved aside, much to Lady Ainiaan's chagrin I might add, because in truth they made far more sense—I mean, who kept the planets and moons in line? Who commanded the suns to rise, and just importantly, to set each day? So maybe the suns weren't burning chariots drawn by flaming horses. There was still the niggly question as to exactly *how* they moved across the sky, how they remained aloft on their daily travels. So, my men and I still believed that gods and goddesses controlled things like that—what other explanation could there be?—controlled our fate and appeasing them was every bit as critical to one's continued wellbeing as breathing and eating.

At times this hybrid view left us collectively scratching our heads, but for the most part it worked for us by preserving our sense of who and what we were—our standing in the world, so to speak—and that there was in fact an explanation for everything, no matter how bizarre, it's just that as mere mortals we weren't in on the joke. The gods were well known pranksters, after all. And so were the Tuatha—a people who, if one believed Turan's veiled remarks, were close kin to gods, if not gods themselves.

So, as I stared at the night sky, I found myself dearly wishing I at least knew where Earth was in that vast and shadowy cosmic sea, even if I could not see it. As it was I had no place to affix my gaze when my thoughts turned, as they often did since arriving here, to Turan and my infant son, Neshoue.

I had no idea how much time had passed since I'd bade them farewell. It seemed like just a few days ago, but something told me that time, with the aid of the Tuatha, was again playing its nasty tricks on me, leaving me in the dark, so to speak, while it continued on its lumbering, unerring path. It had taken well over a year to march from Egypt to the hinterlands of Parthia, granted, doing a lot of fighting along the way, but even couriers, if unimpeded, took months to travel the same distance.

If Earth was so far away, had Turan had time to recover? She'd looked so ill, so desperately frail when I left.

Was Neshoue walking yet? Was he fully grown? And if the latter, would he be a man I would be proud to call my son, or would he be another Rasaben, another Tistriya?

I forced my eyes back to the valley but too late to stop the inevitable answer from rushing to the fore: I'd likely never know. That was the bitter gist of it. I'd never know their fate, never know my son, just as they would likely never learn my personal fate. All they would know is if I'd succeeded, if my soldiers won the coming battle, or—

A hand lightly gripped my shoulder and I flinched then glanced towards its owner. Despite the icy glow of starlight I was barely able to make out Felix's youthful, handsome face behind the soot.

He stared at me for a moment then whispered, "With the gods' favor, you'll see them again—you'll get us home, Arri. I know you will."

I dropped my watery gaze to my lap just as another hand alighted on my other shoulder: *Aetius*.

"Felix's right." The hand let go, replaced by an unusually restrained elbow to the ribs—anything more robust risked a fatal plunge. "You'll get us home, Legate. Never doubt that. We certainly don't."

I wanted to say it wasn't up to me as to whether we ever saw home again; I wasn't even sure if it was up to our gods—I speak of good, solid Roman gods—perhaps none even realized we were here as I wouldn't put it past the Tuatha to have simply 'forgotten' to pass that important tidbit of information along to the higher ups. I wanted to say I was having serious doubts as to whether we had any chance at winning this battle, decisively or not. But I didn't—there was nothing to be gained by burdening these two with the true depth of my fears.

For a moment no one spoke, then from somewhere behind us I heard a softly grumbled, "Legate, are we going to sit up here all damned night? My damn butt's turning to damned a block of ice."

Duccius. Yes, I was again in the company of a man everyone referred to as 'that mad Marcomanni' because he was both, and in this case he was also right. We'd seen what we'd come here to see—as disconcerting and demoralizing as it was. Time to return to camp, report what we'd seen and catch a little sleep before the suns rose and the day heated up.

Latrunc̆uli had one small advantage over Earth: it had longer nights. Of course the downside of that was that it had likewise longer days—each almost half again as long as on Earth. Which meant we still had plenty of time to retrace our steps—*carefully*—back down the mountain, down and then back up a narrow gorge and onto a wide swath of saltpans, out onto the mountain-ringed high desert proper—the presumed site of the upcoming battle and where we'd found ourselves that first day—across a dry riverbed that looked like it hadn't seen running water in a thousand years, then, finally, a quick scramble up to our camp atop a flat topped and steep-sided hillock not far from a range of high, extremely rugged mountains. While the hillock was more exposed than the mountain valley chosen by the enemy it was far more easily defended, with a completely unobstructed view of its surrounds—and heeding Lady Ainiaan's warning it was *solid* rock.

No one was going to sneak up on us and catch us unawares—not even the damned Faoimhuir. Damned if they would.

We had the near range of crags at our back; far enough away that that strategic high-ground couldn't be used against us yet close enough for a hasty retreat if needed, a bastion for survivors if our forces were indeed overwhelmed on the field, a place fit for ambush, where our archers could pick off the enemy one by one and bleed them to a draw, assuming the Faoimhuirian soldiers were too eager or too stupid to sit back and let this natron-mummified corpse of a planet do their dirty work for them.

To the fore of our hilltop camp was the riverbed, which wound its languid way almost completely around the hillock, but its innocuous appearance was deceptive. While there was little chance of a flash flood, it was still a dangerous ally and as serviceable as any proper Roman ditch, with the added benefit of no proper Roman ditch-digging: under its thin, sun-baked crust lay powdery sand so soft and deep if you weren't careful where you trod you could easily sink up to your waist—as I can personally attest—and an army rushing an enemy stronghold is rarely that careful, especially when making a mad dash across open ground. It was the perfect killing field for any direct assault on the hillock as men crossing the riverbed would be completely exposed, and again within bow-range of our archers, not to mention tower-mounted scorpios.

A forty foot wide gap, hidden behind the hillock and the only place not defended by the encircling oxbow course of the ancient, soft-bellied river was now guarded, day and night, by a hidden battery of deadly ballistas; it was also going to be our route off the hillock, to avoid being ensnared ourselves by the extinct river, not to mention the only safe path for the engines that would otherwise founder on soft ground.

And if the enemy attempted a surprise attack on the hillock, this hidden pathway would also serve as the route our cavalry would take, their presence, or at least their true numbers concealed until they'd formed up then came out of hiding at a full, galloping charge at the enemy's flank—a startling sight I hoped would shock and confound the enemy into a confused and panicky retreat... right into the sand pits of the riverbed and the sights of our now very gleeful archers.

But the first line of defense were the saltpans with their veneer of sharply pointed, poisonous salt crystals—natural caltrops—which rimed vast puddles of pinkish-red, skin-blistering brine that were scattered across the flats: sludgy, shallow ponds that had instantly reminded me of the low desert south of Alexandria and its scattering of equally noxious natron pools.

Early in my military career, and because of my ability to blend into the native Egyptian population, I was often dispatched to distant Roman encampments in Cyrenacia and upper Egypt, carrying messages of the utmost urgency and secrecy from Lucius Antonius Vallus, Commander of the Alexandria Garrison. In one such instance—this was several months before my ill-fated trip to Oxyrhynchus—I'd been sent to the settlement of Terenuthis and on my way back I was forced by slavers in search of merchandise to quit the heavily traveled waters of the Nile and take a long and dangerous detour through the low-lying desert and its shallow lakes of toxic brine.

I'd grown up in the desert after all, knew how to survive in such wastelands, whereas my pursuers were men of the river, of its dirty, squalid settlements huddled against its shores like so many mud swallows' nests, and who wisely and quickly gave up their chase once they lost sight of the life-giving Nile. Clearly the going price of a young, lighter-than-Nubian skinned and physically attractive male—even in the high-end niche markets that catered exclusively to wealthy households—was just not worth the personal risk.

I'd learned, one could say *first-hand* the foul nature of the strangely beautiful and colorful liquid that made up the natron pools—the inflamed skin of my curious fingertips had taken days to stop throbbing—so I guess you could reasonably argue that I wasn't quite so wise to the ways of the desert as I'd assumed, either. But I never repeated my mistake, in fact never thought I'd be in a position to repeat it. Yet here I was, confronted by a strikingly similar phenomenon—so incredibly far in distance and time from my first introduction and despite the unpleasant memory, the sight sent a jolting pang of homesickness through me.

I'd given orders to Rufinius, who over the previous months I'd come to discover was a damned good engineer, rivaling any military engineer I'd worked with, and Jotia, who excelled at organizing the troops in to efficient work gangs, that while we were gone those left behind—fourteen hundred and ninety men in all—were to fortify our position. One benefit of the night's ghostly luminescence was that men could work just as easily and safely as if in the full light of day, perhaps more so as they wouldn't have to contend with the strength-sapping heat, not to mention the daily afternoon dust storms.

As I mentioned earlier, there was little wood, but Latruncŭli had rock in abundance. It was my hope that by the time we returned, the soldiers should have a good start on a dry-stone circuit wall.

Marcus Polycleitus, Centurion of the Cavalry, was tasked with securing proper accommodations for the two hundred and two horses, four hundred and twenty one oxen, one hundred and fifty goats, a hundred odd chickens, nine dogs, four trained hunting hawks and yes, even three cats that had the ill fortune of accompanying us.

The horses' comfort and care came first as the cavalry was, I hoped, our secret weapon. The oxen were, from the get-go, on a one-way trip, draft animals that would also serve as food just as the supply wagons, once unloaded, were designed to be cannibalized for their wood, rope and canvas. The goats would supply milk and cheese and yes, as provisions ran low, fresh meat. The chickens were to supply eggs and failing that, stock for the soup kettles. The dogs had been camp pets, taken in by the soldiers as strays, found half-starved in the forest wilds surrounding Taskim's Keep during foraging trips and which had been smuggled along, hidden in the supply wagons.

While I have no love of dogs, had I known ahead of time of the soldiers' plans, I wouldn't have denied them these creatures even though they were extra mouths to feed. Dogs did have their uses and I knew Aetius and one of his men, Ocelus, had been training them to serve as trackers and watchdogs—tutored in the skill by Taskim's very own master of hounds, or so they'd told me. I'd never seen, much less heard a dog while a 'guest' in his Keep, but...

And of course war dogs were excellent terror weapons, almost as unnerving as cavalry.

The hawks were gifts from Lady Ainiaan and she'd trained four of my men as their handlers. Had there been any birds—aside from the aforementioned chickens—or hare about I could see reason for their inclusion, but since I'd seen, shall we say, neither hide nor um, *hare* of either, their purpose was little more as a source of wagering entertainment for the men.

Now as to the cats—while I wasn't avid fancier, I didn't actually dislike cats as I did most four footed creatures. I'd grown up in Carthage and Alexandria after all, and while Romans preferred dogs as companions, the citizens of both cities kept cats. I'd quickly learned that the benefits to having a cat went beyond simple companionship. Like dogs they served a valuable domestic service: in the case of cats, they kept their owner's homes and storage rooms free of vermin as well as snakes and scorpions. Carthaginian and Egyptian mothers often kept a cat in the nursery for just such a purpose and I strongly suspect many a babe owed its life to the ever-watchful family cat.

Lady Ilissia's villa was overrun with at least a dozen cats at any given time, but these were fat, lazy beasts whose sole purpose, as far as I could tell, was as decoration and to that end spent their days stretched out in the sun on a balcony or tile floor, or idly gazing at the colorful fish that darted here and there among the papyrus and rushes in the courtyard's large pool, perhaps bestirring themselves occasionally to dip their paws into the water in a blatantly spurious show of trying to catch a snack.

I'd always been secretly envious of their languorous attitude towards life—and their mild contempt towards us, their supposed keepers. As far as I was concerned, cats had discovered the meaning of true happiness… but cats being cats, they were not about to freely share their hard-won knowledge with those they considered inferior—they would, however, permit us to learn by observing them—*if* we had the patience, which, I freely admit, I didn't.

And, as it so happened, Rufinius and another of my centurions, Baculus, prized the creatures. The two steadfastly maintained that they'd brought the cats along to protect our grain stores from pilferage by rodents—nonexistent rodents as it turned out. Only later did I learn the truth: at these cats, while still kittens, had, with Lady Ainiaan's involvement, befriended Rufinius and Baculus while the two were confined to Mabog's surgery, recuperating from close to fatal injuries bestowed upon them by a drunken Rasaben during one of his many 'sparring' contests. The cats had remained steadfast to the two men even after they'd been given my memories, willingly following them from the barracks to our camp despite it being the middle of winter, and so the two men remained steadfast to the three cats. So, one muscular gray stripped named Leonidas, a tiny black and white, Thisbe, and a very fat and fluffy orange, Xanthus, would now share Rufinius and Baculus' fate. Like us, they faced a sad reward for their unflinching fidelity.

At my whispered, *"We've seen enough,"* Aetius lurched unsteadily to his feet, followed by Felix, who then offered me a hand up which I gratefully accepted. In the time I'd been seated, cross-legged on the rock ledge, my joints had stiffened up and my left leg had still not recovered from the rigorous climb.

I motioned for Duccius, *this* Duccius, who like his predecessor was wild-eyed and wild-mannered, but also as sure-footed as any mule I'd ever met, to take the lead, knowing if anyone could bring us safely down the mountain it would be this mad Marcomanni.

As Felix and then Aetius carefully made their way back into the surrounding rockfall to fall in line with the others, I chanced one last glimpse at the distant enemy camp.

Enemy… and yet not. *Human.* Like us, so far, *far* from home. And just like us pawns of greater beings, about to fight their war, about to kill and be killed for reasons not fully explained, possibly even beyond our human comprehension.

Perhaps all based on a lie.

The Tuatha unquestionably had the capacity to completely control our fate while manipulating us into believing our actions served our purposes when in fact they served theirs, often as not to our lasting detriment—one might argue that this *is* the pithiest definition of a god.

Had we *ever* had free choice, free rein over our destinies? Were gods in fact truly nothing more than deified slave owners in search of ever-increasingly bloody entertainment? Had I'd traded one set of gods for another? Was this nothing more than gladiatorial combat on a global scale?

I've never been a devout man, having learned the bitter lesson at a very tender age that the gods only listen to those who could pay in advance and in full for the privilege of an audience. Nevertheless I still found myself deeply disturbed by these less than pious thoughts—and even more disturbed that I hadn't had them earlier.

I tore my eyes off the Faoimhuirian encampment and with a sigh and a shake of my head, started trudging after my fellows. We had an hours-long and perilous trek ahead of us and I should have kept my mind on where I was putting my bare feet; instead it kept churning with other worries, far less immediate but deeply personal and intensely nagging: I'd fathered a son by Turan—not an impossible act if one believed the words of priests. There were plenty of examples of such assignations, but in most cases the father was a god, the mother mortal, not the other way around—the only exception I could remember was, by ironic happenstance, Aeneas.

I'd certainly never once contemplated the possibility that one day I might contribute my humble seed to this rare population of semi-divine beings—which prompted another, equally unsettling question: would Neshoue share Turan's abilities? Would he—assuming we did chance to meet—even look upon me as his father or would he show me, a mere mortal the sneering derision of the Lords of the Sidhe? Aeneas *had* honored his mortal father along with his goddess mother, so there was some hope of similar expectations, I suppose.

I heaved a sigh, shook myself loose of these troubling thoughts and turned my full attention on following the man ahead of me and a good thing too as footing suddenly became a precarious mix of sloping shale with a skittery overlay of sharp pebbles. Several men stumbled; one, Burrus, slipped but was saved a fatal fall to the rocks far below by Aetius's timely grab.

Once back on his feet, Burrus shivered in fright at his close call while the rest of us glanced about, looking for an easier way down. None was to be had, so after a few moments to allow Burrus a chance to reclaim his nerves, we resumed the descent but now all of us were on edge—*literally*.

We managed the rest of the way without serious mishap and paused at the lip of gorge for a quick meal of the ubiquitous hardtack, eaten while standing and in total silence while our weary eyes nervously scoured our starlit surrounds for any sign of pursuit. No one dared sit, as tempting as it was, for fear he'd be unable to rise and have to be helped back to his feet by those who were less foolish but every bit as tired.

After a welcome pass-around of our last full waterskin to wash the cloying dust from our throats, we were off again, but at a more deliberate pace with the risk of detection lessened by distance and terrain, down another steep and even more tortuous incline, our bruised and bleeding feet protesting each step, our minds painfully aware that for every potentially ankle-twisting step down, there was going to be an equal, potentially ankle-twisting step up the opposite and even *steeper* side of the gorge.

The chasm was so deep and narrow only a thin and meandering ribbon of starry sky was visible at the very bottom. Looking up, I was struck by the unpleasant resemblance to some massive, be-speckled snake slithering silently overhead. Others saw the same and murmured uneasily amongst themselves; it was *not* a good omen, especially with us, literally, in the belly of the beast.

The climb out was a burning torment on lungs and limbs alike, each step gained by sheer force of will, and for every man who stumbled, there were two to steady him and help him on his way. By the time we topped the far lip of the gorge we were all breathing hard and shaky and many of our party were clearly suffering terribly from their injured feet—one, Aulus, had taken a bad fall and his chin bled profusely, soaking his tunic collar.

No one complained, no one made a sound but their wincing expressions were visible, as were their limping, stumbling steps as they leaned on each other for support, like drunkards staggering their way home before dawn and their irate wives caught them in their painful and incensed glare.

I had no idea how long we had before what little darkness we enjoyed fled the twin sunrise, and I had no desire to be caught out in the open once that happened—exposed not only to the fierce heat but the sharp eyes of the enemy, who, like us, had to have scouting parties afoot. They too might have horses—I hadn't seen or heard any evidence of it, but that didn't mean we alone held that advantage and we wouldn't have a ghost of a chance to reach the natural moat of the riverbed, much less our own camp if pursued by mounted soldiers, or, gods forbid, chariots.

When we'd set out, shortly after dark, I'd looked upon that immense and radiant whirlpool, knowing I could use it as a reliable timekeeper, just as I'd used the familiar denizens of Earth's night for the same purpose. This foreign sky held no recognizable and obliging guideposts; the whirlpool would have to suffice and to that end I'd spent many sleepless hours of the previous two nights staring up at it, both fascinated and yes, a little frightened by it as I'd experienced, while serving aboard the merchanter, *Aequitas,* what a whirlpool could do and this one was of a size to swallow entire worlds, of that I had no doubt—a true monster of the deep.

I marked in my mind one particular feature, a tiny but especially dazzling spot of celestial flotsam trapped half way down its outer-most eastern edge. When we'd started off the previous evening the bulk of the whirlpool, along with the brighter spot were almost directly above us, but now, as we slowly, wearily trudged our way back across the flats, the spot touched the peak of a distant mountain that lay almost directly ahead of us. Once it disappeared, the suns would rise in their perpetual pursuit.

I reluctantly called a halt, ordered everyone to finish what little food and water we still carried, hoping that would be enough to sustain us for the last, and due to our exhaustion, most dangerous leg of the trip. I also made sure that every man had donned his canvas-wrapped sandals—no need to muffle our passage now, nor was there any risk of slipping on smooth rock—to protect injured feet from the scattered saltpans' vast evaporation rings that turned the flats into an obstacle course of tiny, poisonous and near invisible spikes.

Once the last of the hardtack was stuffed into mouths almost too tired to chew, and the last of the water was swallowed by throats almost too parched to notice, I motioned for Felix to take the lead while Aetius and I took up the rear—to conceal from the others the sudden, excruciating leg cramps that would catch me unawares—while Aetius kept tabs on our dog-tired men, quietly urging them on and keeping them together as they were wont to wander apart in their blind weariness.

I clenched my teeth and squeezed my eyes tightly shut as Cleander, chief of our four physicians, worked a foul-smelling and stinging salve into the painful cuts and stone-bruises on my feet and with what seemed like utterly unnecessary vigor.

"You should have listened to me, Legate," he grumbled, for what was, I swear, at least the fifth time, each word punctuated by his fingers as they poked and squeezed and kneaded my abused flesh. To make matters worse, my feet had always been terribly ticklish. "I told you—we *all* told you that you're just too damned valuable, to critical to the mission to go gallivanting about—"

"And I already told you I *wasn't* gallivanting," I interrupted softly but irritably, not wanting to wake Felix, who was fast asleep on his cot in our shared command tent, although in truth anything short of a bucket of ice-melt tossed across the shoulders wouldn't have awakened him, and maybe not even that. He'd barely stirred when Cleander had attended to *his* injured feet. When Felix slept, he *slept*; of course I suspected the lozenge Cleander had insisted Felix swallow prior to his ministrations had helped. He'd demanded I swallow one, too, which I had, but only to get Felix to follow my example without too much bellyaching.

For some inexplicable reason the lozenge hadn't helped me one damned bit; of course Felix wasn't ticklish, either. "I was leading a reconnaissance squad—"

"Then leave the leading of reconnaissance squads to others—need I remind you of what happened to Marcus Claudius Marcellus?"

He didn't—the ignoble end of the famous general was a cherished incident among legionaries who found themselves, for one reason or another, disgruntled with their commanders, just as it was considered a cautionary tale among officers. Marcus Claudius Marcellus foolishly insisted on accompanying his scouts while they looked about for a suitable place to teach the upstart Hannibal and his ragtag army a lesson they would not soon forget. Needless to say, Hannibal got the last laugh as Hannibal often did. But what Cleander didn't mention was that Hannibal's Numidian horsemen were involved, as they usually were; in fact Numidians, on horseback and on foot had been a thorn in Rome's side, off and on, for a very, very long time, often as not while we were supposedly their allies. I'd always believed that if Rome had made the effort to differentiate Numidians, then perhaps we wouldn't have felt the need to poke the empire at every opportunity. Fair's fair after all. Just thought I'd mention that.

"Jotia for one," Cleander continued, "who I must add was mightily put out you didn't task him with the job, or Felix," he jerked his chin towards the snoring lump in question, "both perfectly capable men— you've told me so yourself at least a dozen times and *you're* no longer Centurion, *remember?*"

I stared down the length of my supine body to where he squatted beside my mistreated feet—squinted quite angrily in fact, for his immaculate aim at one of my soft spots—and I'm not referring to my ticklish soles. It only added—excuse me—*salt* to the wound that he was also right, and right on so many angles of the matter: I *was* no longer a centurion; I *was* critical to the mission; worse, I'd taken my second in command, Felix with me, not to mention Aetius, leaving Jotia and Rufinius in charge of those who remained behind—no offense to either man, but I'd been *stupid, stupid, stupid!*

I took a deep breath, braced myself for a smug response and admitted, "You're right." I didn't say just how right he was. I felt that would just be gratuitous.

Instead of grinning, instead of saying, 'Of course I am,' he simply nodded, a surprising and graciously concise acceptance of my equally surprising, humble admission.

Unlike his namesake predecessor, who, while a halfway decent surgeon, wasted few if any words on his patients—'stitch 'em up and send 'em back for more of the same' seemed to be his motto—*this* Cleander was, by comparison, a veritable chatterbox—who sometimes said *too* much. He was also one of a handful of older Kellesuf, Cleander himself in his early forties, while the vast majority were in their twenties, with a few, a sad few like Carus, my aide-de-camp, in their late-teens.

Cleander was a balding man, every bit as tall as Felix, a man who'd never been handsome even in his youth, with hollow, pitted cheeks— evidence of some long ago malady—a sharp, angular face with deep-set brown eyes, gangly body and long, slender fingers—*skilled* fingers. He was a very capable surgeon; Taskim's own physician Mabog had declared such, a perfect choice, he said. Cleander *was* the perfect choice, as was Iulius, Nestor and Tigidius—all had what the casual observer might ascribe to an inborn affinity for the medical arts, but Mabog and I both suspected from the start that these four *had* been physicians once—as had their namesakes—or they'd served in a similar capacity at some time during their previous lives, due to expedience or desperate need as combat surgeons were always in short supply, highly skilled ones were even more hard to come by.

Aetius had privately voiced his own theory about this Cleander's past: he believed he'd been a knackerman in his prior life, rarely elevated to apprentice butcher if Aetius was feeling particularly charitable. But then Aetius, who seemed to attract injuries in the same proportions that he attracted trouble—just like his namesake—had been forced to suffer Cleander's brusque manner and painfully thorough ministrations more than anyone else, which probably explained his less than complimentary opinion of the man.

It was much the same with those who had gravitated towards our cavalry unit, or had willingly, one might even say happily taken on the otherwise rather thankless task of field cooks, Florianus chief among them, a man who, I quickly learned, could make dirt soup taste... well, if not tasty than at least tolerable. In each and every case, it was apparent that while these men's minds did not retain the hard-won expertise of their missing past, their hands had somehow held onto the ability, as if drawing on some whispered instruction only they could hear.

"I'd strongly urge you stay off your feet for a day or two—a week would be even better."

I scowled at him.

He stared back, unfazed. "Just my advice, Legate, which I know you won't heed any more than you heed anyone's advice."

As senior-most among the physicians, he was the only one of the four who dared speak to me like that. Even the chronically foul-tempered Nestor kept his less than complimentary opinions of me to himself. Then again, maybe it had nothing to do with rank, or, that like me Nestor was clearly from Numidia, possibly Cyrenacia, and so was loath to criticize a fellow Mauri—which, when I think about it, is pretty unlikely as we Mauri are infamous for stabbing each other in the back, figuratively *and* literally. Maybe with Cleander it was the decade plus age difference. Maybe it was just Cleander, who knew he was too damned valuable himself, too critical to the undertaking to be trifled with, even if the potential trifler was the legate.

That didn't stop my scowl from puckering into a downright baleful glare.

"I've done what I can for now." He checked my left leg, shook his head as he rose, wiping his hands on the same damp rag he'd used to scrub the dried blood and grit from my feet, then he pulled a small vial from a leather bag that hung from his belt. "Here. Give me your hand."

I did as he asked and he shook out two small white tablets onto my palm. "For the leg spasms and the pain."

I had thought about refusing—on principle, but my feet, despite, *or in spite* of the damned lozenge, still throbbed painfully and my left thigh kept cramping. My eyes darted to Felix, then back to Cleander, curious as to why Felix had somehow escaped both the pain and more of Cleander's noxious potions.

As if sensing my thoughts Cleander said with a hint of conceit, "He's Kellesuf," as if that was explanation enough, and perhaps it was. While physical pain had been a novelty to them at first, and the discomfort of minor injuries had left them startled and deeply distraught—like small children—most had gone on to demonstrate a tolerance for pain and injury that would have left me grimacing and swearing profusely, if not completely incapacitated. This ability to endure such had its benefits—it also had its drawbacks, as you can well imagine.

"Go on," he urged, drawing my attention back to the tablets in my palm by pushing my hand closer to my mouth. "They'll even help you sleep." At my hesitation, he added, "It's just you and me, Legate, so don't be brave—*or* stupid as I won't be impressed *or* surprised. And there's little your two eyes and two ears can add to the fifteen hundred sets of each that surround us."

I was tempted to stick out my tongue; instead I looked around for something to wash them down. "Water?"

"No need—they'll melt in your mouth."

Squinting at him, I tossed them into my mouth and yes, they did in fact melt, and even more surprisingly, they did so almost immediately, leaving behind a rather unpleasant bitter taste, akin to the lozenges Turan had forced me to swallow shortly after my capture.

I made a face.

He was unmoved. "I'll have Florianus bring you food and drink. Then you need to rest, better, take Felix's example and sleep if you can. I'll be back to check on you both in a few hours—"

"How are the others?" By my order, he and the others had seen to the immediate medical needs of the rest of the reconnaissance squad, *first.* I was to be last. Strangely, Cleander didn't argue that point—I suspect he wanted me to suffer as long as possible, without appearing to leave me to suffer, the bastard.

"About the same as you. Gods' favor to us, none worse, fortunately—
"

A shadow passed in front of the tent flap, accompanied by the sharp glint of sunlight on armor briefly visible through the gap between flaps.

"You apparently have a visitor," Cleander said as if genuinely surprised anyone might want to speak to their legate. "Do you feel up to some company?"

"Depends on who it is, I suppose—and what he wants." I dearly hoped it wasn't Titivillus, a man who took his role of centurion just a wee bit too seriously for my liking. Of course the original Titivillus had been, not surprisingly, the same and then some.

I was too tired to deal with even this watered-down version and his desperate need to discuss everything to do with camp life, from where and how deep to dig the latrines—I personally didn't give a damn as long as my tent wasn't downwind—to who needed a good talking to about the corrupting influence of fistfights on discipline, which invariably meant Aetius, because if fists were flying, there was a damned good chance two of those fists were firmly attached to Aetius.

The original Titivillus had also loathed the original Aetius, and for the exact same reason: Aetius' penchant for fighting with anyone over anything at any time was bad for morale. And to that end *that* Titivillus had jabbered about why would I want to spend my leisure time in the company of such a scalawag?—it didn't look good to consort with such obvious malefactors and as such it reflected badly on the centurion ranks as a whole. The simple fact that the first Aetius was an exceedingly brave and loyal soldier, albeit with one or two glaring flaws, not to mention he was a hell of a lot of fun to be around, with his grandiose yarns and very unique take on life seemed utterly lost on the original Titivillus. In fact I think the whole concept of 'fun' had been lost on Titivillus—his only joy came from listening to camp gossip and damning others.

While *this* Titivillus was far less inclined to act on rumor, he was, in a word, a *prig*. A damned good centurion when it came to keeping order, but still a damned prig. He always gave me a serious headache.

"Shall I make up a guest list?" Cleander replied snidely.

"Just show whoever the hell it is in then go torture someone else."

He smiled, a slow drawing back of the lips to expose his clenched teeth. He unclenched them just long enough to reply, "Of course, Legate. Your wish is *always* my command." He grabbed the flap and jerked it aside.

It wasn't, thankfully, Titivillus. It was Marcus—Marcus *Polycleitus*, Centurion of the Cavalry specifically, as there were one hundred and thirty-eight Marcuses amongst us—and the dark look on this Marcus' equally dark face did not bode well. Aper, his second in command, was, not surprisingly, at his side.

Aper, whose features and coloring suggested he'd probably come from Parthia, possibly Scythia, either one explanation enough for his affinity for horses, was Marcus' constant shadow, a raw-boned, serious-faced and silent young man who, according to the rumors I'd heard, tolerated no abuse of his four-legged charges—even the oxen—clearly preferring their company over his two-footed comrades. He'd been Marcus' choice as second, not mine and the cavalrymen loved him—presumably the horses too—just as they adored Marcus. From what Marcus told me, Aper possessed a keen military mind, so I had no reason to interfere. In fact I'd encouraged my officers to choose their immediate subordinates from among the ranks, promising them I wouldn't second guess their decisions while warning them if their choices proved unwise, or hinted at partiality at the expense of proficiency I'd have no choice but to revise my choice of them.

I got my elbows under me—and Cleander, who was still standing in the doorway, shot me a warning look. Not that he really needed to: I had no intention of actually getting to my feet—feet, which, despite the damned lozenge *and* the magically melting tablets, still throbbed like hell. The last thing I wanted to do was put my weight on them, but Marcus looked too serious, too damned unhappy not to make a show of showing him and his frame of mind due and serious respect.

"Please, Legate, stay where you are," he said, and I happily flopped back on my cot and tugged my rolled up cloak under my head.

He gestured with his chin to one of the two folding field chairs in the tent, next to the folding field table—both a luxury here as everyone else was relegated to sitting on their cots or on the ground—and I nodded. He picked it up then set it down next to my cot. Aper, for his part, took up a parade-rest stance behind his senior once Marcus had seated himself.

"What brings you to my bedside, Marcus? You look worried."

"We are, Legate—about the horses." His eyes darted to my feet, back to my face. "How are we to cross the saltpans if the need arises? Those crystals will render them lame before we travel more than a few paces and poison their blood in short order."

"Do what we did: wrap their feet in cloth—leather would be even better."

"But where are we to find enough leather for the job? Two hundred and two horses, sir, each with four feet."

"I'm well aware of how many feet a horse has, Centurion," I grumbled—as someone who'd been repeatedly stepped on by horses I'd gotten *very* good at counting. Besides, my head ached; my body ached. My throat was raw; my empty stomach was growing impatient for the promised meal and, damn Cleander, my feet *still* felt as if they were on fire.

I was, simply put, in a foul mood, but not without reason. While we'd been back in camp for several hours and it was well into morning, I'd yet to be granted the luxury of even an hour's nap—unlike the rest of the exhausted squad, including Felix—Cleander and Jotia and now Marcus had seen to that, first with Jotia's long and painfully detailed report of all that had transpired while we'd been gone, including the welcome news that the circuit wall should be finished by the end of the day.

Felix *had* tried—I'll be extremely generous here and say he tried *manfully*—to stay awake and listen; instead he just stared at Jotia with watery, heavy-lidded eyes and droopy head nodding—not in agreement, just nodding. Since he hadn't offered any input, except the occasional, loud and protracted yawn, and was clearly too muzzy-headed to offer up any useful ideas, neither Jotia or I realized he'd actually fallen asleep until he ever-so-slowly toppled sideways, shoulder landing softly on his cot, blond head following, one foot still on the floor, the other left dangling.

Jotia stopped his report long to enough to scoop up Felix's legs and place them on the cot then draw his blanket over him. Felix mumbled his thanks as he oozed over onto his back. At least I think he mumbled his thanks. It might have been a snore.

We also hammered out the logistics of dispatching another reconnaissance squad as soon as night fell—one that would remain sequestered in our well-hidden mountain aerie, this time with enough provisions to last a week, to watch the enemy, keep an eye on their movements and send runners back with any news. Our first trip had been done in haste, each man carrying only enough supplies to last the night. We had no assurance, after all, that the telltale glow on the bellies of the clouds that hung on the distant peaks *was* evidence of the enemy's location instead of some natural, nightly phenomena.

Aetius, we both agreed, was the man to lead the return visit; the choices as to who accompanied him I left up to Jotia and Aetius. I also ordered another squad to the near mountains, the ones to our backs— lead by Duccius—to watch for any developments from on high.

Then came Cleander on his last stop; he shooed Jotia from the tent, leaving me alone to suffer his tart remarks and his equally nasty salve.

I had, at least, had the chance to bathe, with Cleander's help, and rid my skin of its irritating rime of camouflaging soot but that was not enough to brighten my otherwise black mood, and horses, even when I was in a good mood were not a favored topic. I abhorred the beasts—with the sole exception of my own mount, Wushah, who, I am equally loath to admit I'd become rather fond of despite him stepping on my feet on more than one occasion—unintentionally, I'm sure—and breaking several toes. But neither did I want the animals to suffer needlessly. Lame horses were worse than worthless. And the cavalry was, I hoped, my secret weapon, to be held in reserve and sprung on the enemy just when they thought they had victory in their grasp and had gotten damned cocky about it.

A massed cavalry charge—even better a *surprise* massed cavalry charge—in my considerable experience with this shock tactic, was always good for knocking the initial cockiness out of foot soldiers, although there is a well-kept secret about massed cavalry charges we legionaries were taught early on: horses aren't stupid. While their riders might be hell bent on suicide, the horses under them rarely feel the same and so will refuse to actually run into a stalwart and rather prickly block of equally massed infantry with the hopes of breaking the line, trampling men under hoof and scattering the rest. More often than not, the horses will realize what's about to happen and stop so abruptly they'll successfully launch their now very startled riders right onto our awaiting pila. If you didn't know better and if you were observing the goings on from some distance you might reasonably assume you were actually watching some sort of innocent gymnastics competition involving vaulting. Close-up you'd realize all of said gymnasts were now little more than skewered meat and their mounts looking innocent of any involvement.

But Marcus and Aper had other, even more unnerving surprises in reserve than simple charges—tactics I'd never seen before, much less heard of, and therefore had not been passed along via my memories—again, more proof of previous lives bleeding to the surface in unexpected ways. I wouldn't have believed some of the maneuvers Aper described were even possible... until I witnessed them for myself while the two put their unit through its paces, practice after practice, in a large open area to the east of Taskim's Keep, an area cleared of trees just so the cavalry could rehearse until these moves had become second nature to man and mount alike.

"You have my permission to take some of that extra canvas we brought, use that to make a tent, then take one of the regular tents and use its goatskin to make your horses their boots." Canvas was the option I'd chosen for my command tent—the celebrated, or if you were an unpopular general involved in an unpopular campaign, the infamous *praetorium* from which equally unpopular orders issued forth. Canvas was more than adequate for shelter against the all-pervasive dust as well as the chill of night and yet in the heat of the day not as damned stuffy or smelly as the traditional goatskin.

"It might take more than one tent, Legate. It might take a number, with eight hundred and eight hooves to boot—and you know that extra canvas was brought for a specific purpose. I'd rather keep it for that."

"Then have the centurions readjust the tent assignments and tell anyone who complains about doubling up to come see me—*after* I've had a few hours of sleep," I added irritably. It was annoying to be this tired and in this much pain and still have to deal with a steady stream of people demanding my undivided attention, but the capper was to have to suffer all of this while also having to listen to Felix *snore*. Damn the man!

Marcus got the hint. "I'll have *my* men triple up, Legate—they'll not complain about it, even among themselves and that should be enough goatskin to do the trick." With that he gathered himself up and with a curt nod to Aper, followed by a crisp salute to me, he strode out of the tent.

Aper replaced the chair beside the table, clearly using that as an excuse to linger.

I was reluctant to ask him why he was hesitating, fearful it might take a prolonged explanation when I was this close to finally being allowed to sleep. I eyed him with a warning look of 'this better be short and sweet', and: "You find fault with my plan?"

"No, sir."

"*You* think your men will complain?"

He shook his head. "No—"

"Then...?"

His dark eyes flicked to the tent flap, then back to me and in a low voice said: "I've heard rumors, sir, we've all heard 'em—"

Ah, so Fama—Titivillus' patron goddess—was about, stirring up trouble with her double-edged sword. Soldiers' camps were always targets of her meddling, damn her.

"*What rumors?*" I replied, realizing too late I might've just opened Pandora's box, this one overflowing with camp rumors. Where *was* Titivillus when I needed him?

Aper again glanced at the doorway, as if this time measuring its distance in case he needed to make a very hasty escape; indeed he might, if he kept me from the beckoning arms of sleep much longer. "That the enemy outnumber us ten to one?"

I stared up at his gaunt face. I'd seen him in practice, in mock combat and he was good, *damned* good, both on foot and on horseback, with sword and lance, but it was impossible to tell if he'd ever seen real combat, and even if he had, it was impossible to predict if any of *that* ghostly experience might resurface, triggering once honed reflexes when confronted with a *real* enemy with *real* intentions of doing *real* harm.

Simply put, he was scared.

Of course so was I—damned scared in fact—not that I could admit it to anyone but myself and I was reluctant to let even me in on the secret. Bad for morale you see. So instead I said, "Nothing so dire. At *most* four to one."

He stared at me with his intense eyes, clearly unsure if I was joking... or deadly serious.

"*Truth*. The Faoimhuir *lied*." Okay, I was lying too; it seemed the only decent thing to do under the circumstances. He'd find out the real truth soon enough—when it was far too late to panic.

He exhaled, shook his head. "We're still screwed—if you don't mind me saying so, sir."

"I've fought against worse odds, much worse, *and won handily*. And besides, we have horses. They *don't*." I said that with a certainty I really didn't feel as I wasn't sure if they did or not, but this man needed reassurance he wasn't facing his own imminent and violent death—or, knowing Aper, the imminent and violent deaths of his beloved horses. "I'm not even sure if they've ever *seen* horses, much less armored horses. Could come as a hell of a shock—especially," I grinned a knowing grin, "armored horses materializing out of thin air."

That prospect clearly cheered him—my tactic worked!

"You'd best go help Marcus make those boots. Battles don't wait for our convenience, Centurion, and once the enemy realizes we're here, I have no doubt they'll come looking for us, hoping to use their superior numbers to overwhelm us. I want to be waiting for them, show them Roman discipline and tactics can overcome just about anything, least of all numerical superiority—and a full-on cavalry charge is pretty damned hard to ignore, even if *your* line *is* packed ten deep."

He nodded, saluted smartly, then spun on his heel and hurried out of the tent.

I stared after him, *hoping* the enemy would advance on us ten deep. Not only did we have two hundred and two warhorses, and with luck the enemy hadn't been let in on the secret that massed cavalry charges might disintegrate short of actually engaging when the horses decided they'd had enough of all the foolishness, we'd brought along ten onagers—siege engines to be sure, but since we didn't know what we'd be facing, I felt it best to err on the side of prudence—fifteen ballistas, sixty scorpios, and my all-time personal favorite, hundreds and hundreds and *hundreds* of caltrops. They were wicked little beasts, easily carried in enough numbers by individual soldiers to make for serious trouble and which, while designed primarily to cripple horses and war elephants, could be almost as effective against massed infantry charges as the men crowded up behind the first line wouldn't see the nasty little buggars until it was too late to avoid impaling their feet.

Just in case there was any lingering doubt, I do *not* believe in half-measures.

— III —

A hand alighted on my shoulder, followed by a whispered, *"Arri...?"*

I was on my stomach, head pillowed on the crook of my left arm, my right arm flopped over the edge of the cot, my relaxed knuckles resting lightly on the dirt floor—in other words my absolute favorite sleeping position. So, I *had* been sound asleep *and* comfortable. And now I was awake and not particularly happy about it.

I irritably opened one eye a crack, forced my slitted gaze up the length of the person standing over me until I reached the face. *Felix*.

"Why are you whispering?" I grumbled as I slowly, wincingly, eased myself over onto my back. "'Fraid you'll wake me up?"

"Didn't want to startle you—you *do* have a tendency to come out swinging." He rubbed his jaw for emphasis.

"True." And it was; I'd unintentionally knocked him on his ass several times when he'd tried to wake me by more, *um*, energetic means—until he learned not to be quite *so* energetic, not to mention a little quicker in stepping back, out of reach.

I lifted my head, peered at the gap between the tent flaps and was startled to find the ribbon of sky visible was a decidedly dusky purple hue. Had I really slept the *entire* day? It certainly didn't feel like it; it felt like I'd just nodded off—clearly I needed to revisit my opinion of Cleander's magically melting tablets.

I gave my gritty eyes a quick knuckle rub. "You shouldn't have let me sleep so long."

"Why not? You certainly earned it."

"So did you—but you've obviously been up for some time."

Felix, always a stickler for sartorial elegance, was in his highly polished banded armor—he, like many of my men, had opted for this style early on, rather than my preferred ring-mail as each type had its advantages *and* disadvantages—minus only the helmet, his pale blond curls ruffled by the cooling twilight breeze that blew through the gap in the tent flaps. More worrisome, he was grinning, a decidedly smug grin—*with dimples*. Have I already mentioned he has dimples? So did the first Felix; it drove women wild—don't ask me why. I've never figured it out, perhaps because I'm not so blessed. I do have to say that I do, however, *more* than make up for this deficiency in other far more, ahem, *substantial* ways.

Speaking of women, there weren't any here—absolutely no chance of any women here, more's the pity as just thinking about women made me suddenly crave a woman's company—Oxyrhoë instantly came to mind, not Turan surprisingly, or even Sifrie, but Oxyrhoë, a slim, flaxen-haired whore from Lindum who had a true gift for making a man forget his troubles. Her expectations were simple, straightforward and completely expected. You didn't have to think when you were with Oxyrhoë; you just did what came naturally—after first paying in full.

Damn, why did I start thinking about these things? I forced the thoughts from my mind before they could take physical form and focused on something far more immediate: my feet, which were swathed in salve-soaked cloth and yes, still quite painful, but less so than this morning. Felix, who'd suffered as much as anyone, seemed oblivious to his own bandage-wrapped feet—ably demonstrating the knack of most former Kellesuf, under certain circumstances, to disregard physical pain.

"Didn't need much sleep as you," Felix replied, "*much* younger you see."

I got an elbow under me, growled: "I'm what, *at most*, four years older than you?"

The age of each Kellesuf was, curiously, the only personal fact the Tuatha had recorded about these men. Not how long they'd been Kellesuf, not where they were originally from, not where or when or why they'd been taken prisoner and sold into slavery—yes, Taskim had willingly divulged what I had long suspected: the Tuatha actively shopped the slave-markets of the Empire and far beyond, selectively purchasing men who were in relative good health in order to then turn into Kellesuf—of course they had other sources too, namely those unfortunates who the Faoimhuir had, for whatever reason, left behind.

Taskim had even rationalized this horrendous deed by arguing that in sparing these men the awful fates usually imposed upon captured soldiers or criminals—a brutal life as a slave, death by sacrifice or in a gladiatorial ring—the Tuatha had actually performed an incredibly humane act. All right, so yes they were still slaves, he'd said, and yes, at the total mercy of their owners' whims, but on the upside, as Kellesuf they didn't realize it.

I had had to physically stop myself from strangling him after this smug revelation and the accompanying insight into the Tuatha mind-set, that destroying a man's mind so as to make him a blindly obedient slave-soldier was, to them, an act of supreme benevolence.

But I digress…

The Tuatha had to have questioned each and every man destined to be Kellesuf as it's not a simple task to judge a man's age just by his look, most especially a soldier or brigand, both grueling professions, which, if they didn't kill a man outright, certainly aged him prematurely. So, the Tuatha had asked each man his age, just as Turan and Taskim had gone out of their way to ask me mine—then wiped all memory from his mind.

As I said, *curious*, but not an altogether unfamiliar habit: Romans—I speak of true Romans, not someone like me who had been born in the provinces and of questionable parentage and only claimed citizenship, an assertion which thankfully for me was never seriously challenged—were also fixated on age. I'd known many a legionary who was obsessed with the worry that the stone-carver might chisel a wrong age on his grave-marker; some had even gone so far as to have his companions swear a blood-oath to make sure it was done correctly, vowing to return as a feared Lemure if the trusted friends failed to live up to their pledge.

I'd never known my exact age, something I'd never personally been troubled by, but an ambiguity many of my fellow legionaries found very odd. I'd always made the excuse that my parents had been killed while I was still very young—truth, at least as far as my mother's death was concerned; I never knew my father or his fate—and that seemed to satisfy them.

I seriously doubt if the Tuatha picked up this custom from Romans as they claimed they despised everything about the Empire so I chalked it up to some perverse quirk appreciated only by the Tuatha. Nevertheless I imparted this seemingly inconsequential tidbit, along with source of their original accent, assuming that by pure accident I'd overheard it—these shattered fragments of a man's former life—to their rightful owners; each man, in turn, clutched them to his heart as if they were priceless jewels, proof that each *had* been someone else, once.

Felix took the potentially touchy reference in philosophical stride, as he did most things. "If *you* say so."

He stepped back as I very carefully dropped my feet to the floor, then he offered me a hand up, which I gratefully accepted, even if by doing so I added more evidence to his blatant insinuation that at twenty nine—or thereabouts—I was already old and feeble. It didn't help that I *felt* particularly old and feeble this fine evening. It was also no secret that I didn't trust my left leg, especially on first rising and while the terrible slash wound I'd suffered at the hands of some damnedable Iceni had healed, thanks entirely to Mabog, I'd lost a significant amount of muscle and I'd developed a slight limp, which became even more noticeable when I was overly tired or had done something strenuous—like, say, an hours-long hike in the dark over very treacherous terrain. My left shoulder too became stiff in cold or damp weather, another legacy of that accursed bog and a well-placed Iceni spear.

In those rare moments when I was alone with my past, usually in the middle of the night when the throbbing ache of the old injuries or the recurrent nightmares awakened me and couldn't get back to sleep, I risked reminiscing, risked wondering, 'what if...' and invariably I found myself wondering *if* my century had somehow survived the Iceni ambush and *if* we'd somehow made it back to camp *if* I wouldn't have found myself facing *misso causaria*—an honorable discharge through debilitating injury received during battle as my reward for my years of loyalty and sacrifice. Probably. Not exactly the glorious retirement with the generous pension of a highly-decorated Primus Pilus I'd envisioned, but...

Fortunately for me, damp was not a worry here—nor was being cashiered. Retirement, of any stripe, was not an option here on Latrunculi.

But I digress. These old injuries were, after all, one of the reasons—a major reason—why my troops had urged that I ride into battle rather than walk. Besides, most felt it just wasn't proper and fitting for a legate to engage the enemy on foot—even if that legate was an *infantry* legate who also happened to be scared spitless of horses.

I'd worried my leg might give out at very inopportune time and sparing myself a possibly very long hike to the field of battle—letting a horse do the honors—lessened that embarrassing possibility significantly. Besides, I looked damned impressive atop Wushah.

But in light of wanting to spring horses on the enemy, I realized I just might have to walk after all. Then again, one horse, two if Felix rode Tuzun—and if I rode Wushah he'd insist on riding Tuzun—did not necessarily give away that we had a whole damned armored cavalry unit ready to charge at my signal. The two of us riding to the front could in fact work in our favor—the enemy might, when they saw the cavalry galloping towards them, realize that while two armored warhorses were damned daunting, *two hundred* coming at them at full speed, lances leading, was fucking terrifying. Just the noise alone, the thunder of hooves, the bellows of men, and the trailing cloud of dust obscuring their true numbers was deeply unnerving, even to soldiers well used to dealing with cavalry—I speak from harrowing personal experience.

Felix knew my limitations, knew the history attached to the disfiguring scar, knew I found this obvious debility—which, unlike my shoulder was always visible unless I wore breeches—maddening, and while sympathetic, he also never wasted an opportunity to get in a dig—not surprisingly, just like the original Felix would've done, given the chance. This time he only shook his head sadly and clicked his tongue as I straightened up, wincing and groaning softly as every muscle and joint I'd abused the night before got their cruel revenge.

I fixed him with an annoyed stare. "Stop that."

He did, only to only to grin and murmur, *"Old man."*

He'd clearly awakened me for a reason, damn him, and it wasn't to make light of my sore muscles and my abused, rapidly aging body. He was just waiting for me to ask what that reason was, so I obliged him: "Is there some justification for rousing an *old man* from his death bed?"

The smug grin widened, threatening to split his boyishly handsome face in half. "The men have a surprise for you."

Uh-oh. I did not like the sound of this, not one damned bit. I wasn't a man fond of surprises. I'd had far too many unpleasant and potentially deadly ones sprung on me over my life to find *any* enjoyment in being caught unawares. "Care to give me a hint?"

"Nope."

Then I had a horrible thought and flicked him a sidelong, worried look. "Are Aetius and Rufinius in any way—*even remotely*—involved?" It was a wise precaution as the two shared penchant for elaborate practical jokes just like the original Rufinius and Aetius.

"Nope."

I eyed him as I considered the remote possibility that he was in on the prank and so was sworn to secrecy, then I snatched up my leather tunic, tugged it over my head, and once I had it settled into place, I turned to him. "Is this a formal affair or can I go like this?"

"Formal. *Definitely* formal. Full kit. Even the helmet—*on* your head, Legate, if you please."

I was disliking this more by the minute. I still hadn't gotten used to the helmet, with its high arching sagittal plume of alternating blocks of black and blond horsehair, with a long, trailing tail and bracketed on either side with two long white goose feathers no less, each feather held upright in its own socket, just above my ears. While I was familiar with the fashion as it had been very popular among certain higher ranks, I'd always felt the embellishment of feathers to an already elaborate helm simply gratuitous. Besides, head-on the combination was instantly—at least to me—reminiscent of a startled donkey. While that was all just and fitting when the commanding officer in question acted little better than a startled donkey on the battlefield—Cerialis immediately comes to mind but maybe that's just my enduring enmity at the man for abandoning us in that bog yet again rearing its ugly head—I did not count myself among that illustrious assemblage of anxious asses.

Felix steadfastly maintained the plume and feathers made me look even taller—a blatant appeal to my vanity but even he was known to mimic a high-pitched bray when he felt the need to tweak me, damn him.

That said, I was now the legate and like it or not I needed to wear what my men had been convinced by Lady Ainiaan was a legate's distinctive headgear. On the upside, the Tuatha armorer had outdone himself: all of our helmets, made out of the same strange luminescent material as our armor, had been silvered, giving them an extra gleam, especially in bright sunlight, but mine went even further, with elaborate, appliqué brass designs that adorned the crown along with the cheek pieces and neck-guard. My phalerae too had been silvered and made a very impressive display, not that it cheered me up at this point.

I sighed, gathered up my armor and began to dress. Formal dress no less—whatever this 'surprise' was it better be damned good to make up for this supreme inconvenience. And if it *was* a prank... I'd have the prankster's ears for supper.

A few minutes later and now fully attired in my legate's finery—*including the damned helmet*—I turned back to him, narrowly avoiding dumping lamp oil all over me as the plume had come perilously close to the small, thankfully *unlit* lamp suspended from the tent's roof support. "Sure you won't give me just a small clue?" I asked, angrily tying the cheek-pieces in place under my chin—a necessity, I'd quickly learned, as the high horsehair plume did act like a sail if the breeze was strong enough. The one benefit in the plume and feathers was that they *did* make me appear much taller than anyone else, even Felix, who, minus his helmet, was taller than me.

He paused, as if truly giving my appeal serious consideration then he shook his head. "Nope."

I squinted at him. *You fucking bastard.*

He grinned then turned smartly on his heel and strode out of the tent, holding the flap aside for me.

I ducked and stepped out of our shared abode to find our twilight surroundings much changed just since morning: it had taken on the familiar orderliness of a Roman camp, with eight-man tents lined up in neat rows, each row of ten demarcating a century. The circuit wall was almost complete—an impressive task in itself—and was now easily taller than three very tall men, one standing on the next man's shoulders. Small watchtowers—stacked slate topped with wooden planks salvaged from emptied supply wagons—had popped up at regular, strategic intervals. So had larger firing platforms, which now bristled with deadly scorpios. Each tower and platform even had a canvas canopy, to provide welcome shade to the crews who stood watch.

Rufinius and his second, Dulcitius, had gone all out, with a truly imposing result. Anyone who tried to approach our camp without a proper invite was doomed.

"This way," Felix said, drawing my pleased attention away from what were damned outstanding fortifications.

I trudged after him, away from the center of the camp, annoyed and at the same time hoping he was leading me to the nearest mess wagon—I hadn't eaten since early morning after all. The tantalizing fragrance of cook fires permeated the camp and my stomach reacted to the enticing smells by growling, *loudly*.

To my dismay we walked right past a mess wagon and its expectant cooks, who then followed me and my puzzled shrug with their equally disappointed, deflated stares as Felix and I continued on, in the general direction of the single, heavily fortified gateway to our hilltop camp.

Ahead of us one of the damned dogs was barking frantically—that briefly drew my annoyed attention as I'd actually forgotten all about them. My officers were well aware of my aversion to the beasts and had passed the word along to keep them out of my sight, while the cats, I must mention, were regular and not altogether unwelcome visitors to my tent, coming and going as they pleased, sometimes demanding to be picked up and petted, other times just making a quick visit to check on me—or, more accurately, checking to see if I had any food or goat's milk to share—before moving on in their camp rounds.

The soldiers had found the perfect solution for keeping the dogs as far away from me as possible: they routinely took them with them on patrol and one had notably warned his human companions of a patch of quicksand by becoming mired in it himself, saved only by being dragged to safety by his long tether; they'd also proven themselves decent goat herders, so perhaps their inclusion was not such a foolish indulgence after all as they all were earning their keep—unlike the cats, who, through no fault of their own, had yet to find a single rodent, snake or scorpion for that matter.

I shrugged irritably and turned my attention back to Felix, thinking he was taking me to see the stables. No. The latrines? No *again*. Pity too, as I realized I had a serious need for a visit.

As we rounded a row of tents, I saw what he'd brought me to see: a half-naked, bald-headed and bloodied man trussed up like a sacrificial animal and ringed by grinning soldiers along with one of the dogs, the shaggy white one Aetius had mentioned had turned into quite a good watchdog—and the source of the barking as it turned out. The man was seated on the ground not far from the wooden, double-doored and now shuttered gate that only a few days before had been the sturdy beds of two supply wagons, his arms tied behind his back, ankles likewise bound and legs folded under him—a very precarious and painful position—I speak from first-hand experience.

I stopped, crossed my arms and stared unsympathetically at what I first assumed was some camp ne'er-do-well who'd just tasted the rough justice of his fellows. It was dusk, the deep lavender sky already thickly strewn with stars—not the best light for judging faces and familiarity.

But as he lifted his bruised eyes to meet mine, I realized he was *not* one of my men. He looked at me in a way none of my men would, even one who'd done something really, I mean really *bad*.

And this, logically, meant only one thing: my soldiers had somehow captured themselves a Faoimhuirian.

Was he a scout? A member of an advance party, probing our defenses? If the latter, I was going to have sharp words with my dimple-faced Primus-Pilus as I should've been awakened the instant someone realized our camp's defenses were being challenged.

Then another possibility came to mind: was he an envoy, a courier sent with a message from his commander?

I took a step closer; he flinched back, terrified, as well he should be, no matter his reason for being so far from his own.

I irritably motioned to the soldier holding the now snarling dog at bay to silence the beast then I squatted and looked over our prisoner. It was obvious, even in the deepening shadows of twilight that he'd been badly beaten; his nose looked to have been broken and blood flowed freely from his nostrils, soaking the gag in his mouth and liberally coating his throat and bare, sand-coated chest. One eye was almost swollen shut and his breeches were torn in several places and spotted with more blood—I couldn't help but flick the dog a sidelong, accusatory look and it had the good graces to wag its feathered tail at me as if to proudly acknowledge its toothy handiwork.

The man was also *not* bald-headed as Cleander and a handful of my soldiers were, hence my mistaken assumption he was one of mine—his head had been completely *shaved*; a fine stubble had regrown, just enough to give his scalp a downy appearance. His face too had a visible shadowing of beard under the blood and grime.

I had to stop myself from visibly reacting to what I was feeling in my gut; it was as if I was looking at myself after Turan and her men had captured me, after Kyrou had beaten me senseless: the same exhausted, bleak stare, the nonstop quiver of muscles kept taut too long... *pain.* Pain in every joint, pain everywhere and to the point of hazing out, body and mind overwhelmed by it. And not surprisingly he was clearly having some trouble breathing, whether the result of the paralyzing fear that he was about to be executed now that the soldiers' commanding officer had made his appearance, the broken and bleeding nose, the gag or all of the above.

I lifted my sharp gaze to the ring of expectant, dare I say gleeful faces. "Send for Cleander." By my tone and expression I clearly *wasn't* pleased. In fact I was furious. But then again, I had no one to blame but myself for my soldiers' actions. I'd never instructed them on what to do if they actually captured any of the enemy—a major oversight that was *all* mine; no blaming the Tuatha for this one.

Faces instantly lost their pleased grins; even the dog began to whine, sharing the soldiers' startled bewilderment.

"And remove the damned gag before he strangles on his own blood!"

Several soldiers lurched forward to obey which of course panicked the Faoimhuirian even more and he tried to kick, to fight back but there was just no give in the bindings and all he succeeded in doing was toppling over, face-first into the dirt, which made him struggle all the more and set the damned dog barking again until its handler risked his fingers by muzzling it with his hand.

It took three men to finally subdue the prisoner long enough for a forth to jerk the gag free of his mouth, but once they'd released him, instead of screaming, he just lay there, glassy-eyed and sucking in breath—again, an eerie replay of my own harrowing experiences as a prisoner of the Tuatha.

My life, especially early on, had been spared on many occasions, a few at the last possible instant and by purely chance meetings. I'd always felt a foolish need to repay the debt whenever I was given the chance, often as not to my great regret—and in this case I also felt a deeply uncomfortable sense of empathy for this bloodied and beaten man, no matter who or what he was—that was for me to find out, and, hopefully, without having to lay another hand on him.

Keeping my expression, my voice as bland as possible, I rose and turned to Felix. "Once he's been seen by Cleander, have him brought to my tent."

Felix, equally taken aback, and yes, clearly disappointed by my response, only nodded.

"I leave him under your care until he's delivered to me."

That prompted another sober nod from Felix, unhappy acknowledgement that any new marks were going to be his and his alone to explain.

I swept my gaze around the now silent group of soldiers and said quietly, "Pass the word: prisoners are *not* to be mistreated. There'll be no punishment this time as none of you knowingly acted against orders, but henceforth anyone who engages in such behavior will receive the *exact* same treatment, and if the prisoner dies as a result, well..." I paused, leaving the obvious unsaid. "Do I make myself clear?"

There was the requisite, albeit puzzled murmur of agreement; no one dared question this unexpected and to them inexplicable order, no one dared to take responsibility for what had been done to this man in my name and I was not about to ask for someone to step forward.

While my soldiers were no longer Kellesuf and each was fully able to think for himself, all retained the Kellesuf penchant for fixing on one objective to the exclusion of all else. They'd actually showed remarkable restraint by not killing him on sight as they'd trained tirelessly for months and with one goal in mind: *kill Faoimhuirians*.

So, my men had found themselves one... and beaten him severely— perhaps he'd even provoked it by attacking one of them, *first*—I hadn't thought to ask, I'd been too taken aback, to startled by the ugly and highly personal comparisons. And in truth I had no knowledge of how Faoimhuirian soldiers behaved—even Taskim was ignorant, he freely admitted such. Like Iceni? Dacians? Parthians? *Picts...?*—gods forbid!

All I knew, all Taskim knew was that they were blindly loyal to their masters, generations born into service with no concept of any other way of life. *Slave-soldiers*, Taskim warned me—just as Kellesuf were... until the Tuatha realized the fatal error of their ways—*or had they?*—I shoved that disturbing thought aside, focused on the matter at hand. I'd been given to understand that the Faoimhuir were not quite so enlightened.

That said there was something in the look this man gave me as he was dragged to his feet that said he was anything but a blindly obedient slave who would calmly walk into the jaws of death if so ordered.

This man wasn't just scared out of his wits, he was pissed—*murderously* pissed.

So maybe he *had* been the one who'd attacked first—and it wasn't like he was out on an evening stroll and just happened upon our camp. And if he knew where we were, others likely did too.

"Where'd you find him?"

After an awkward moment of sidelong, prompting stares among the most culpable, one of the soldiers—Marius was his name and the burliest of the lot—reluctantly pointed. "Out there, sir, on the far edge of the riverbed."

I raised my brows, recalling my discussion with Jotia over the urgent need to send a reconnaissance squad into the nearby mountains, to watch for enemy movement from the rugged heights, to map out escape routes and search for possible hideouts, if it came to that—and perhaps, if fortune favored us, even a source of fresh water. On our first-day trek to the hillock we'd been forced to cross and crisscross a tangled skein of streambeds—all dry—but unlike the river, these streambeds had held water in recent months—the soil beneath their hard-baked sands was still damp and the horses and oxen could smell water; their excited pawing at the ground was as clear as any human-voiced discovery.

I'd assumed it was this scouting party who'd found him. Not so. *"So...?"*

"I was on watch," replied the soldier who was holding the white dog in check, "up on that watchtower," he pointed, "about to be relieved. That's when I spotted him chasing a goat. I assumed it was Hardalio..."

Hardalio. I might have known he was somehow involved. Hardalio, like his namesake, was a man clearly hailing the Baleares or some hard-baked like-land; short of stature with sinewy muscle sheathed in swarthy skin; dark, curly hair, deeply set black eyes and the ever-present leather slings wound about his forearms, his belt laden with sacks of lead pellets, each small missile as potentially deadly as a sword thrust. And since every pellet had been carefully, not to mention colorfully inscribed with an obscene message for the recipient, one could say that each strike added insult to fatal injury.

The first Hardalio had been little better than a stranger to me, an auxiliary hastily assigned to my cohort on our ill-fated march to trounce the Iceni. He'd been a man who much preferred the solitude of his own company to that of his fellows. The equally aloof Rufinius had known him best of any; Rufinius always spoke highly of Hardalio's unflinching bravery, his deadly aim—Hardalio had died in that bog too, defending the empire, defending his centurion, his sling bolts little match for the blizzard of Iceni arrows.

This Hardalio had been one of Lord Tistriya's complement of Kellesuf; Tistriya himself had been the last holdout among the Sidhe Lords, reasonably disinclined to hand them over to my control, my command, but his belated acceptance, when it finally came, had cost his Kellesuf dearly: as latecomers, they were left to pick over the scraps of my memories, having little choice but to dress themselves in ghostly, half-done personalities others, given greater choices and of more substance had wisely passed over, like tattered clothing, more hole than whole.

Of all the Kellesuf, this group had the most trouble adapting to their newfound autonomy. It took much longer for the implanted personalities to take root and grow and so they kept to themselves, an uneasy knot of quiet, wary-eyed men who had been loath to let go of their Kellesuf habits, just as a drowning man is fearful to let go of a sliver of flotsam even when shore is within reach.

Hardalio had been the first among his fellows to immerge from this self-imposed segregation, overcompensating for his earlier reticence by thinking just a little too much for himself. I'd had to discipline him on one occasion for wandering off on his own, to 'explore the wilds' around Taskim's Keep he'd said by way of explanation when he'd been forcibly returned to camp and delivered into the path of my frustrated gaze. Innocent enough, one might suppose, perhaps even expected of someone who was putting himself together, piece by piece, desperately trying making something whole of what had been nothing but fragments and using the world around him as a sort of glue, but I'd suspected he was in truth following some deep-seated urge, trying to find his way home even though he had no idea where that home was, if it was his true home or a false memory, a fragment of the real Hardalio's shadowy past I'd picked up along the way.

I sighed, turned my attention back to the soldier who was still speaking.

"…earlier heard Hardalio mentioning he was looking for one of the goats that had somehow managed to escape its pen and slip through the gate while the engineers were hanging the doors and had strayed off. He'd asked those of us in the watchtowers to keep an eye out for it."

I did not like where this was going, and certainly not with Hardalio involved. If Hardalio had gone looking, alone, as was his damnedable inclination, in the process leaving the protection of the camp and putting others at risk, he was going to have some serious explaining to do. This was not the forested wilds of Taskim's holdings after all. This was Latrunculi, where a man alone and unschooled in the planet's dangers could easily come to an unpleasant end and leave no trace of it to warn others not to repeat his mistake. I then turned back to the soldier—*another* Marcus, Marcus *Antonius* if memory served. *"And...?"*

His eyes cut to the prisoner, then back to me. "The moment I got off duty, sir, I asked permission from Centurion Baculus to leave the camp to assist—I took a squad," he motioned to the others, "and Aëllo with me..."

I looked at Felix and whispered out of the corner of my mouth, *"Aëllo?"*

Felix gestured to the dog.

"...just as you ordered, Legate, not to venture out alone, only it *wasn't* Hardalio... it was *him*." He glared furiously at the Faoimhuirian. "He was trying to make off with our damned goat!"

I again rolled my eyes towards Felix who again stared back, this time with lips tightly pursed against the almost overwhelming desire to burst out laughing, despite the underlying gravity of the matter.

"And...?" I prompted.

"As we approached," another volunteered, "asking if he needed help, he let go of the goat and came at us with a knife, which is when we realized he wasn't Hardalio..."

I swept my eyes across the group; none, to my immense relief, looked injured, not even the dog.

"...so we set Aëllo on him. He mustn't have ever seen a dog— because he panicked and tried to run but she had no trouble catching him. He began kicking her so Aëllo began biting him and he fell down into the riverbed where he got himself thoroughly *stuck*," the man continued with audible disgust.

I eyed the prisoner. It certainly explained his thick coating of sand, and his bloody, tattered breeches. I glanced at Aëllo, smiled and murmured, *"Good dog,"* and damned if she didn't wag her feathery tail in reply.

"So we went down after him," a third soldier added—suddenly everyone was overflowing with helpful information and eager to talk, "and pulled him out and the minute we did, he attacked us again— managed bash Attius in the head with a rock before we could stop him— *can you believe it?"*

So there was a casualty; I again looked at Felix.

"He was seen by Tigidius, who patched up the damage and sent him to his bed. Nothing serious, just a lingering headache."

Well, it certainly explained why they'd beaten the Faoimhuirian to a pulp. I would've probably done the same thing, given the provocation. "So what happened to the goat?" With limited provisions, even a single, obstinate goat was important.

"Took off," another soldier grumbled disgustedly. "By the time we managed to get *him* back up here, it had already found its way home and was bleating at the gate, asking to be let in."

I'd say everyone looked rather sheepish at the admission that a goat had outsmarted all of them, but... "And Hardalio?"

"Turns out he'd never ventured outside, sir," Marcus Antonius replied, "suspecting the goat would come back when she got hungry."

So, at least everyone was accounted for and in one piece—including the goat—and even more importantly, I wasn't going to have to make an example of Hardalio. The man had a history of giving me serious grief and I was pleased for once that I would not have to repay the favor. "Any sign that our guest here had company?"

"No, sir," a fifth man, Fabius Marius, spoke up. "We took Aëllo and searched the full length of the oxbow as we returned to camp—the only tracks she found were *his*," he motioned to the prisoner, "and the damned goat's."

If only it were so. "Post extra guards tonight." I gave the sorry object of everyone's undivided and now *very* aggrieved attention one last look then shifted my stare to the dog, adding, "And give Aëllo an extra ration tonight—she's earned it."

The man holding her tether grinned with pride and gave the dog a scratch between the ears; I would have done the same except, as I think I've mentioned before, I'm deathly afraid of dogs.

With that I walked away, back the way we'd come—with one diversion for a tour of the latrines, which I found very satisfactory indeed.

— ii —

I swallowed the last spoonful of stew—stew one of the cooks assured me actually contained some meat, although a thorough search of my bowl had not turned up a scrap—chased it with a gulp of wine, then sat back, my belly content, my feet less so but no longer throbbing and watched as Carus, who, some months before had attached himself to me as my personal aide, refilled the mug.

With his assistance, I'd shed my armor *and* the damned helmet. I was now wearing only my leather tunic, woolen undertunic, breeches, socks and sandals. Latruncŭli's nights thankfully didn't have a bitterly icy edge— at least this time of year—but the night air that blew down from the mountains did have a noticeable bite. I'd be thankful for the undertunic, socks and breeches, not to mention my heavy cloak, when I finally took to bed.

"Enough," I murmured and Carus lifted the decanter, but no sooner had he set it back on the table when we both heard a shuffle of feet outside the tent: my order had come back to me, arriving on multiple feet.

I sighed, having temporarily forgotten I had an appointment.

I accepted a scrap of damp cloth Carus offered me and wiped my greasy lips and chin just as Felix poked his head through the tent flaps. "Legate?"

I nodded permission to enter.

He did so, followed by two soldiers who were holding the Faoimhuirian, keeping him on his feet as they crab-walked him into the tent, through the narrow opening while Carus hastily gathered up the empty bowl and cloth, clearing the table for the unpleasant business at hand.

The man looked marginally less terrified, but only because he was clearly drugged to the gills. While I didn't question my physicians' reasons for this, it was going to make questioning him far more problematic.

Taskim had told me that the Faoimhuir and Tuatha had agreed on one exception to the rule that only the technologies, the knowledge of the time period chosen could be employed by the combatants and that exception was medical care for the wounded, the injured and the sick. I had no way of knowing if the Faoimhuir had lived up to their end of this agreement—in truth I didn't give a damn. I could only vouch for the Tuatha, who had, but rest assured this was no startling act of compassion on their part. An incapacitated soldier was a serious liability; not only was he a mouth to feed who otherwise contributed nothing, he also needed to be protected by other, able-bodied men, thus costing even more, draining the ranks in rapid order, making it that much more difficult to fight and yes, win.

Fighting was the reason we were here. Winning, in light of our unpleasant discovery of the night before, was clearly up for grabs.

While Cleander's surgery was nowhere near as sophisticated as Mabog's, the outsized supply wagons that served as mobile field hospitals were a *huge* advance over anything Rome's legions had had at their disposal—so were the medicines at my physicians' disposal, which included painkillers—no explanation needed there—special 'fluids' that could stave off death from blood loss, potions that could put a man into a deep sleep while surgery was performed—a vast improvement on the accepted but not necessarily very effective methods of either drinking an elixir of poppy juice or getting blind drunk prior to having a wound cauterized or a limb hacked off—the preferred choices, or the far less favored option of passing out once well into the procedure with the accompanying risk that you might *not* pass out, or you might come 'round well before it was over—and something called 'anti biotic', a strange name for something that in fact *saved* lives, and a huge advancement over the widely held belief that rubbing a puppy over a man felled by sickness had a curative effect—for the man. The puppy not so much.

All I knew was that these magical tonics could and did save lives otherwise doomed because I'd seen their miraculous effects *for* myself *on* myself.

I motioned to the other chair at the small table, Felix's chair when we shared our meals together, or when he or one of my other officers came to discuss strategy. This time Felix knew the invitation was not his, but rather the man who was sagging heavily in the grip of his guards, causing them to constantly readjust their hold on him.

The Faoimhuirian was urged to step forward by one of the guards' well-placed kick to one heel; he tried to move but his legs weren't working right so he was hauled over to the chair, then, under my watchful eye, carefully placed on it while Carus took up a defensive stance beside me, his hand resting on the pommel of his sheathed gladius, ready to repel any attack, not that the prisoner could have mounted one, at least not an effective one in his present gelatinous state—and oh yes, *with his damned hands tied behind his damned back.*

Don't get me wrong—I appreciated Carus' solid concern for my safety but in this case it was utterly unnecessary.

The Faoimhuirian, for his part, stared dully at the tabletop, swaying slightly and precariously as the narrow, armless and rather rickety folding chair was not designed for someone who'd lost this much control over his body. Without me saying a word, the two guards reluctantly shuffled forward and placed themselves tightly on either side of him, effectively wedging him in place. It made for a *very* crowded table.

Then I noticed our captive had fixed his blood-shot gaze on the mug of wine. He licked his bruised and swollen lips—a *stitched* lip, I noticed. Somewhere along the line his lower lip had been split—*and* repaired. I immediately recognized Iulius' work; Cleander might've used six or seven stitches to draw the split together. Iulius had used four. It was an efficient technique greatly appreciated by the recipient—stitches really hurt, going in and coming out, even more so on something as sensitive as a lip—not that I suspected for one minute that this man would be grateful for anything we did for him or to him.

I shot Felix a querying glance.

"He tried to bite Iulius; Iulius punched him in the mouth him before I could stop him. I accept full responsibility."

And clearly Iulius was a man who tidied up after himself. Another plus.

"Any other 'new' injuries I need to know about?"

"I think I broke a finger."

"Yours or his?"

Felix affixed me with a suffering stare. *"His.* When I tried to pry him loose of Cleander's throat after Cleander reset his nose."

I seriously wondered at this point why Felix had not handed this clearly unappreciative patient over to Nestor's particularly well-suited brand of ministrations; Nestor would have probably used ten stitches on his lip, maybe even twelve.

While Cleander was always at the ready with a calmly worded, yet stinging comeback to any grievance no matter how well-founded, he rarely lost his composure. Nestor on the other hand, just like his predecessor, was forever foul-tempered and had been known to knock a man senseless if he was given any cheek, sometimes doing more damage than the damage that had brought the man to him in the first place.

Realizing I'd just answered my own question, I turned my arched stare back to the man. "My physicians were just trying to help you…"

He met my gaze, blinked slowly and again dropped his bruised gaze to the mug.

"…and I'd be most appreciative it if you'd cease provoking people. You're not doing anyone, least of all yourself, any favors by it."

I waited for some sort of response. Nothing. Not even a flick of the eye.

"I don't think he understands us," Felix said.

I fixed my exasperated gaze on my second in command; it was usually Aetius who just had to state the patently obvious as if it was burning a hole in his tongue. Felix usually knew better.

"He hasn't spoken," he continued, oblivious to my pinched stare, "hasn't reacted as if he grasps what he's being told—"

"Like let the fuck go," one of the soldiers muttered under his breath, eyeing his charge in a very unhappy way.

I glanced up at the man. Tullius Maximus was his name, a thickset, reddish-haired man with an infectious laugh—he'd not been part of the group who'd captured and beaten this man, yet there were fresh bruises on his forearm, *his* throat and he was well on his way to a seriously impressive black eye. I sighed again, looked back at our Faoimhuirian. He was still staring at the mug.

He might not understand us, he might not speak, but he was making his desires apparent, loud and clear.

I reluctantly pushed the mug across the table then motioned for Tullius to bring it to the Faoimhuirian's mouth so he could take a sip.

No sooner had the mug met his lips when he lurched into it and took a large, frantic gulp then promptly spewed his mouthful, splattering me, my leather tunic and woolen undertunic in the process and his guards instantly reacted, jerking him up and back, the chair toppling beneath him and snarling itself in his rubbery legs, not to mention theirs; Carus too started for him, but I grabbed his sword arm and pulled him back.

"Stop!" I snapped and the soldiers, who'd been trying to subdue him, froze.

The Faoimhuirian, who was under no such constraint, continued to struggle, to get his feet under him, all the while wheezing and coughing explosively.

"He's not fighting you—he's choking, dammit!" I rose, circled the table and pulled the chair free of the tangle of their feet, then righted it. "Sit him back down!—and untie his hands."

He was still coughing so violently he seemed unaware of having the bindings cut even though once free he immediately and reflexively brought one hand to his throat while the other gripped the edge of the table.

Finally the frenetic coughing stopped, replaced by a tight, high-pitched wheeze each time he inhaled, but at least some of the color had returned to his round, piebald face.

Keeping my eyes on him, I warned, "Wine, *not* water—don't guzzle," and again pushed the mug in front of him.

He stared at it, clearly tempted but also just as clearly reluctant to repeat what he'd just gone through. Or maybe he thought I was deliberately offering him something to make him choke—I wasn't sure. Either way he made no move to touch the mug.

"What's your name?"

He kept staring at the mug and as he did so, I stared at him and noticed for the first time that his chin was tattooed: a single, faint vertical bar, topped and footed by a dot. His left upper arm was identically marked, albeit a little darker, with the addition of a small triangle to the right and left of the bar. I'd seen similar tattoos before: Scythians sported them on their backs, necks and yes, occasionally, on their faces; some of the Germanic tribes too engaged in this sort of body adornment. The backs, arms and legs of more than a few of my soldiers were likewise festooned, and a handful, including Marcus Polycleitus, bore facial tattoos or deliberate scarifications, all less than subtle hints of their true heritage. The original Duccius had a number of geometric tattoos that ran down the length of his spine as well as on his right hip and both shins—a shaman's work he'd told me, to cure a fever that had once almost killed him, admitting that given a choice he would've preferred dying of fever to the pain of the prolonged tattooing and worst of all, he'd added tetchily, it hadn't even spared him future fevers!

Curiosity satisfied, I rapped my knuckles on the table, this time drawing the man's flinching and blood-shot gaze. *"Name.* What's your name?"

He blinked; his jaw muscles twitched. The drug was clearly wearing off, perhaps purged from his blood by the brief but violent struggle.

I pointed at myself. "I'm Arrius Marcus Niger, Legate of the First Legion Spartoí." I then pointed at him. *"You?"*

He continued to stare—a very opaque stare.

"Tuatha," I said, again pointing at myself. "Faoimhuir," I added, leaning across the small table and poking him in the chest. That garnered another blink.

I lifted my annoyed gaze to Felix. "Did any of our famously meticulous physicians bother to check if his tongue's been cut out?" That *was* a tactic used by some of Rome's more barbaric neighbors: send a spy who was incapable of speech and if he got caught… oh well. It certainly would explain why he'd choked on the wine.

Tullius' much younger partner, Roscius, taking this as a proposal to investigate, grabbed the man's jaw and turning his head, tried to pry his mouth open. In his eagerness to impress the legate he'd sadly forgotten the Faoimhuirian's hands were no longer bound—until the Faoimhuirian, in one deft movement, grabbed Roscius' wrists and sank his teeth into the soldier's forearm.

The situation, not unexpectedly, swiftly went downhill from there.

Screaming in agony, Roscius tried to wrest his arm free while Tullius, Carus and Felix grabbed the prisoner and tried to pull him the other way—not the best tactic when one person has his teeth deeply embedded in the flesh of another—while the lit oil lamp, caught in the confusion of flailing limbs, lurching bodies and bobbing heads swung wildly, its light and harried company of shadows darting and dipping around the tent like things alive and desperate to flee the rapidly expanding chaos.

I tried to intercede by grabbing the Faoimhuirian's wrists, hoping to at least break his handhold on Roscius, if not his bite-hold and got a knee in the groin for my troubles—I was spoiled for choice as to *whose* knee actually did the dirty deed but I promptly decided each party to the toothy tug-of-war was on his own. I had my own issues now, which I staggered clear of the mêlée to attend to.

The racket drew others—rescue came running from all quarters of the camp and within a moment or two the prisoner was flat on the ground, six men on top of him—amazingly enough, the struggle had not collapsed the tent on top of us. Perhaps there were just too many soldiers packed inside for the tent *to* fall.

To add to the general confusion, Tullius was now holding onto his partner for all his worth as Roscius, having just had a large chunk of flesh ripped from his arm and unwilling to let bygones be bygones, was desperately trying to kick his now fully subdued attacker in the head while screaming some truly creative obscenities.

I couldn't really blame Roscius. *I* wanted to knee the man in the groin and see if he enjoyed it as much as I had—even if his knee had not been the culprit. Yes, I can be that small-minded—hard not to be under the circumstances.

"I'll call for Cleander," Felix said before I could—which was good, because I wasn't sure what my voice would sound like. Personally, I would have opted for Nestor, but...

"*May I kill him, Legate?*" the bitten guard snarled, clutching his profusely bleeding arm with his other hand, using the rag Carus had handed him to staunch the flow. "*Please?*"

I took a deep breath, slowly released my protective hold on my crotch and tugged the leather tunic and its disarranged pteruges back into place. "*No,*" I managed without, thankfully, anyone realizing I sounded remarkably like a startled version of Lady Ainiaan.

"But—"

Fortunately, Cleander took this moment to appear, pushing and shoving his way through the anxious throng that had crowded the doorway of tent. Clearly he'd already been on his way, warned by the fact that the entire camp was descending on my quarters at a dead run, as the man Felix had sent to collect him had just exited the tent, the two almost knocking each other down in their mutual haste.

Cleander looked at me, he looked at the bleeding Roscius, he looked at the wrecked interior of the tent and finally, at the squirming, grunting and cursing heap on the floor.

"Yes?" he asked, unflappable as always.

I jerked my chin toward Roscius, who by now had stopped trying to kick the prisoner. Now he was staring, glassy-eyed at his arm as if he hadn't realized just how much damage had been done and his normally swarthy face had gone a decidedly pasty hue. Clearly he was one of the minority of Kellesuf who reacted to such an injury as any normal man would—as I would.

Cleander blew out his cheeks then casting me, specifically my still very pinched face, a sidelong look, asked, "Are you injured, Legate?"

"Got kneed in the balls," I managed tightly.

"May I check for damage?"

All eyes swiveled towards me, and then dropped to the aforementioned and abused parts of my anatomy.

"*No,*" I replied through clenched teeth.

'Sure?"

I nodded, emphatically, still not fully trusting my voice to do the honors.

Cleander, with an annoyed shrug, turned to the injured guard and Tullius, who was holding Roscius' elbow, lending discreet support as Roscius, despite his best efforts, had begun to wobble noticeably. He'd stopped dripping blood everywhere but only because his arm was wrapped in the now blood-soaked rag. "Take him to the surgery, ask Iulius to stitch him up."

Tullius nodded and carefully guided his newest charge out of the tent.

All eyes now fell on the cause of this mayhem.

The Faoimhuirian had finally stopped fighting—six large men sprawled on top of him, his arms and legs pressed firmly into the ground and spread eagle had clearly proven just too much, even for him.

"*Up,*" I gestured to the six and they quickly untangled themselves and scrambled to their feet, dragging the Faoimhuirian with them and holding him tightly in their grasp, arms pinned behind his back. His face had acquired a few new scrapes and cuts and Cleander's efforts at resetting his nose had gone for naught.

I stepped close—but not *too* close. While the Faoimhuirian looked like he'd finally exhausted himself, I was not about to risk finding out that I'd seriously miscalculated his stamina—or his knee's reach and hoping my voice wouldn't betray me, said, "I've had just about enough of you…"

He managed to lift his head at that, met my exasperated and yes, furious gaze with a glazed one of his own, but thank the gods my voice sounded, at least to my ears, only a little huskier than normal.

"…I've apologized for your rough treatment; I've had you seen by my physicians and had your injuries tended to. I've tried to reason with you." I took a deep, ragged breath. "And what do you do? You attack my men—you attack *me*. And oh, yes, this all started by you trying to make off with one of *our* damned goats!"

The glazed stare melted away, replaced by a look of grim satisfaction.

Maybe he understood me—or maybe he was just reacting to my clearly frustrated tone. Either way that smug smirk was just begging to be knocked clean off his bloodied and dirty face. "*Can* you speak, goat-thief? A simple nod will do." I gave him a moment to reply and when he didn't, I turned to Cleander and growled, "Is he mute?"

"Strange as this may seem, Legate, I just never found quite the right opportunity to engage him in conversation."

I scowled.

"I can talk—"

I jerked my eyes back to the Faoimhuirian, to the lilting and strangely cadenced accent.

"—I just don't care to talk to you, *Tuatha-filth*." He punctuated the remark by spitting a mixture of blood and saliva in my face—

—and I roundhoused him, my left fist meeting his jaw with a loud and, for me, decidedly gratifying meaty *THWACK!*

His head snapped back, my knuckles following.

I knew how to throw a punch, damned if I didn't, and in such a way my knuckles usually avoided my opponent's teeth—that's surefire way to give yourself a truly nasty wound, worse, if a tooth or two end up embedded in your flesh. I learned *that* the hard way early in military career—I also learned how to throw a punch in such a way my opponent's teeth ended up firmly embedded in *his* flesh, be it lip or tongue, leaving him with a lingering reminder never to annoy me again.

Even better—for me—the Faoimhuirian's jaw was not quite as hard as Rasaben's and I was able to quickly conceal my wince; besides, everyone's eyes were on him as he crumpled into the arms of his startled captors.

Cleander stepped close, grabbed my left hand before I could jerk it away and carefully checked it for injury. Seeing only a skinned knuckle, he fixed me with his brown, and for once—and I must say to my *immense* satisfaction—decidedly flustered eyes.

He, like all of my men, had never known me as a centurion, much less a common foot soldier, had never actually seen me in the thick of tavern brawls and street fights. While Aetius was famous for starting fights, I was equally well known as a man who *finished* them, and finished them in such a way that my opponent didn't get up right away. On a few notable occasions he didn't get up, *period*.

I shrugged. "I did warn him."

Cleander cleared his throat, regained his composure. "So now what do you want to do with him?"

There was a chorus of truly inspired suggestions from the surrounding soldiers, one or two of which I readily admit I seriously entertained for an instant or two.

"I want him awake."

"Then *you* shouldn't have struck him so hard," Cleander replied with a hint of testiness.

I clenched my now throbbing fist, growled, "*Wake. Him. Up.*"

Cleander took the not-so-subtle hint and muttering to himself, stepped close as the guards hoisted the unconscious man back to his feet and held him there. He gave the prisoner's shoulder a shake, which only served to make the Faoimhuirian's head wobble, followed by a not so gentle slap across his face. While Cleander and the guards were preoccupied, I took the opportunity to discreetly suck on my abused knuckles—I never said punching a man in the face didn't entail some hurt. It did, damned if it didn't. It's just that in most cases, if done properly, the lasting reward far outweighed the temporary ache—and in this case, the truly disconcerted look on Cleander's normally imperturbable face was definitely worth the transitory discomfort.

The Faoimhuirian groaned and groggily raised his shaved head at Cleander's not so gentle bidding. I was pleased to note that my fist had resplit his stitched lip and it was again bleeding profusely and now his misshapen nose, which had effectively stopped my upward swinging fist, was bubbling with each exhaled breath—maybe Nestor would have his turn after all; I doubted Iulius or even Cleander would again volunteer their services and Tigidius was *always* willing to defer to his seniors.

"Are you a spy or just a common goat-thief?"

The man's bruise-swollen eyes narrowed in a feeble attempt at bravado.

"I can have the truth beaten out of you."

Don't ask me how he managed it, but he *laughed*. He actually laughed, although the effect was somewhat spoiled as he briefly choked and coughed on his own blood, but as soon as he recovered he rasped, "No... no you can't." He jerked his blood-slick chin towards his captors, took a sniffing inhale of breath, then bubbling again, said, "They already tried... and... and failed."

"Maybe they didn't try hard enough."

Hands that held him tightened their painful grasp on his limbs and he winced. Sniffle; bubble. Repeat.

"As much as I'd like to hand you over to my men for them to do what they see fit—maybe let our dogs have another go at you?—I find I have a far better use for you than an hour or so of after dinner amusement."

He continued to glare defiantly at me, but as I stared into his blood-shot and bruised eyes, I saw a flicker of unease. He'd come here expecting one of two outcomes: either to get what he'd come for, which something told me wasn't a damned stray goat, *that* had just been lucky happenstance, or to be captured and die in a most unpleasant way—so, once he realized capture was inevitable, he'd done his damnedest to incite a quick and relatively painless death, which, too bad for him, hadn't happened, thanks in large part to Aëllo. That I was suggesting a third alternative clearly left him off balance.

Still keeping my eyes locked with his, I said, "First thing tomorrow morning I want our goat-thief here physically able to make his way back to the Faoimhuir camp."

That garnered a collective gasp; even Cleander looked appalled. The Faoimhuirian looked down right stunned.

"You're to deliver a message to your leader, goat-thief: High desert. Daybreak. Three days from tomorrow—"

That earned a collective cheer from the soldiers present and a blink from the Faoimhuirian as he continued to alternately sniff and bubble.

"—unless of course he'd rather surrender to me and spare himself and his troops the embarrassment of being thoroughly trounced."

A slow grin spread across the Faoimhuirian's battered and misshapen face, exposing a bloody mouth and some freshly broken teeth. "When *we* finish with *you*, *filth*, there'll be nothing left but your rotting corpses."

I shrugged. "Better a rotting corpse than perpetual slavery my friend, or being handed over to the Si'aafu whole and very much alive."

For an instant—just an instant—his grin tightened and his eyes widened ever so slightly before he reclaimed his earlier bluster, but I had him now. The threat of the Si'aafu was no abstract worry for this Faoimhuirian, it was a very tangible fear.

"You mean you *haven't* heard?" I replied, my fingers briefly covering my lips in feigned horror. "Oh. Dear." I shook my head, added, "Well, I am *so* sorry to be the bearer of such disturbing news but you see your masters far oversold what they could deliver to the Si'aafu. The Si'aafu were, to put it bluntly, *not* amused and made ugly threats, *very* ugly threats, so in order to spare themselves ending up on the dinner menu, your masters have been supplementing their shortfall in humans they've been 'harvesting' from Earth with *your* people."

He stared at me for a moment, digesting that, then stammered, *"You... you LIE!"*

I held up my hand, stopping Felix's fist just short of cuffing him in the head.

"Believe me or not; it's none of my affair—they're *your* masters, thank the gods not ours, but believe me when I tell you that I have *no* intention of allowing any of *my* men to be taken alive by Si'aafu, even if it means I personally put each one to the sword." I noticed more than a few furtive glances from those soldiers present, including Felix and Cleander, but no one said a word or raised an objection. I was deadly serious, so to speak, and they knew it.

"But do yourself *and* your people a favor," I continued, "when you get back to camp, ask around; see if anyone's heard of people suddenly gone missing—close relatives perhaps? I've been given to understand Si'aafu find children particularly tasty. Not so... *chewy.*" I clicked my teeth together, which garnered some truly shocked stares from the soldiers, along with a few startled, uneasy snickers. A pure fabrication on my part to be sure—I had no idea, but it seemed like a good gambit to get this Faoimhuir riled up.

"IT'S NOT TRUE!" he snarled, having reclaimed his wits along with his abused rage.

See? My ploy worked. Call me many things—and I'm sure you, like most who have met me have—but you can't deny I'm a damned good provocateur.

"We're too—"

"Valuable?" I interjected, suspecting where this particular argument was going. Oh, yes, I'd heard it before, countless times with other fiercely loyal slaves; I understood their way of thinking, sad to say, misguided as it always was when things got ugly. "You truly believe your people are more valuable to the Faoimhuir than the Faoimhuir themselves? Your children are more precious to them than theirs? Unlikely," I chuckled, "and of course along with pissing off the Si'aafu, your masters have gotten themselves into a nasty squabble with the Tuatha.

"My, my, my. Enemies coming at them from all directions… they must be quite desperate by now, and that level of desperation can make otherwise unthinkable choices not so unthinkable, in fact I suspect the level of desperation your beloved masters have brought down on themselves can make *anything* thinkable—short of sacrificing themselves and *their* children, that is—"

"So you're an expert on the Faoimhuir, *Tuatha filth?* You can read their minds?" He lifted his chin, stared down his badly deformed nose at me, which kind of defeated the whole purpose. It's hard to look snooty with a freshly broken, bleeding nose. "You're bluffing!"

All right, he was starting to piss me off again because the last remark was said in such a way as to splatter my face and tunic with his bloody saliva, which in turn caused me to blink and step back, then angrily wipe my face with the back of my hand. But rather than punch him again as I was sorely tempted to do because that would mean I'd again have to wait for Cleander to revive him, I decided instead to give his trust in his masters another shake, rattle that blind-faith of his and see what might fall out.

"I don't have to read their minds—I just need know what I'd do if I were them."

He snorted in contempt, which unfortunately only set his nose to bleeding again.

"I *do* hope you're right… for the sake of your kin." I shrugged again, casually, as if the matter was of little concern to me when in fact it was of paramount importance—I *needed* to know what motivated this man and his fellows to fight; I wanted to seed doubt, doubt this man would spread like plague once back among his own. Cripple *their* morale. So I tried another approach: sudden and explosive anger. *"Maybe all this,"* I gestured furiously around me, *"maybe starting a war with the Tuatha is in fact one huge distraction, win or lose, to catch the single-minded attention of the human-hungry Si'aafu while your masters go to ground—"* I stopped in mid-sentence, mid-tirade.

To the Faoimhuirian and my soldiers it probably looked like a dramatic pause for effect, but in reality it was because it suddenly hit me like an unexpected and viciously hard punch to the gut that this very well might *be* the absolute truth, the awful reality behind all the political maneuvering, stumbled upon purely by accident, blurted out in a fit of frustration… *shaken loose.*

Maybe the Faoimhuir had, in fact, *out*-out-maneuvered the smugly clever Tuatha.

Gods….

I quickly gathered myself up, continued a little less confidently. "Worth the terrible risks—and the equally terrible costs to your people *and* mine, yes?" With that I hastily stepped back. "Rest well tonight, goat-thief. You have a long walk ahead of you." I angrily jerked my chin towards the tent flaps and the soldiers dragged the now stammering and spluttering man outside.

Cleander, with a sidelong, decidedly unsettled glance at me, followed.

"Felix."

He'd started after Cleander, but stopped and turned to me, eyebrows raised in query.

"Make sure he's safely housed for the night. I want *no* mishaps to befall him, or us for that matter."

"Yes, Legate." He reached for the tent flap and started to step outside.

"And Felix…?"

He turned, half in, half out of the tent.

"Pass the word: daybreak, three days from tomorrow."

"Yessir."

"But to anticipate attack at any time. I don't expect the Faoimhuir to honor our invitation, but rather try to get the jump on us."

He nodded grimly and as he ducked out, I turned to find Carus putting to rights the interior of the tent.

I exhaled, shook my head, then eased myself back onto my chair and picked up the mug, forgetting that most of its contents had been spewed in my face and on my tunic.

Carus appeared at my side unbidden, wine decanter in hand. At my nod, he refilled the mug then stepped back, dutifully waiting my next command.

"Go get your supper, then get yourself to bed."

He reluctantly nodded at the dismissal, set the decanter on the table as he produced another rag from a pouch tied to his belt and placed it beside my mug, then he picked up the empty bowl and with one last look around to make sure everything was back in order, he stepped out of the tent, leaving me seated at the table, staring bleakly at the replenished mug.

I took a deep swallow and then arching my head back, closed my eyes and exhaled slowly while I tried not to succumb to total panic at what I'd said in haste, in frustration… *in anger.*

What if this was all some huge smokescreen, designed to keep both the Si'aafu and Tuatha preoccupied while the Faoimhuir dug themselves some deep dark hole in which to hide, perhaps for a very, *very* long time? It made sense—a whole lot of *very* unpleasant sense.

On top of that, I'd just committed us to battle three days hence—by doing so most likely precipitating a preemptive strike by a much larger force and too late now to change my mind—unless I went back on my word to release the Faoimhuirian.

No. We'd come here to fight; we'd spent months preparing. There was absolutely nothing to be gained by delaying further and much to lose. And if beings greater than us were impatient for a show, I was damned well going to give them one, even if by doing so, I gave the Faoimhuir exactly what they wanted—not that I had any choice. If I didn't initiate hostilities, the enemy would and on their terms.

Count on it.

But—there's always a damned, nagging *but*, isn't there?—this was the first time I'd led an army into battle, the first time every single soldier's life was depending solely upon my decisions—and if the Tuatha were to be believed, not just the lives of my soldiers, but the very fate humanity itself hinged on my choices from here on out.

Up until now I'd been responsible for my century—eighty men, tops, not a whole damned legion, even if this legion was not actually the full complement of a Roman legion, far less in fact, which I suppose was in some ways a good thing—fewer lives on the line, but also precious few to meet the overwhelming numbers of the enemy, to decide the fortune of humanity: life or death on a global scale.

Fifteen hundred men, each one my responsibility, each death mine and mine alone. I could only hope Roman discipline could and *would* be the tipping factor. It was, in truth, our only hope.

As I gazed at the mug, I found myself gripped with sober misgivings as to whether I was up for the job—the first time in my career that I can honestly say this. I'd worked hard, *damned hard*, to get to where I'd gotten—I'd spilled a lot of my own blood in the process, suffered unbelievable hardships. That being said, I'd always had this unshakeable belief in myself, in my ability to do whatever I set my mind on, to get over whatever or whoever had gotten in my way, and get on with it. That belief had kept me alive as a child, a teenager, a legionary and finally, as a very successful and well-respected centurion.

Without realizing it, my hand sought out the comfort of my chest harness, replicate it might be—the reassurance of the phalerae, the torcs—tangible proof that my rise through the ranks had not been by chance or luck, but the harness was on the cot, next to my mailed shirt.

So instead I wrapped my hand around the handle of the mug.

Maybe that was it—a simple matter of believing in *myself*, not some gods-given talent that had gotten me so far.

Now I was faced with the frightening possibility that I might have neither to draw on when the outcome was never more critical.

I exhaled, forced my fingers to relax their death grip on the mug, brought it to my lips and took a sip, hoping that might help ease the sudden tightness in my throat, the knot in my gut, then I set it back down.

As the only man the Tuatha had left with his memory, my intimate knowledge of war craft intact, I'd gone from Hastatus-Posterior to Legate in one leap, in the process cleanly passing over the rank that had been my goal in life, that of Primus-Pilus—a rank Felix now held—along with sidestepping all the hard-won experience, the intrinsic, well-aged wisdom that went with a steady, step-by-step climb up through the ranks.

One could say that in the proverbial blink of an eye, I was anointed—or, more precisely *doomed*—to lead these equally doomed men.

The worst of it was that I *had* refused at first, only to later change my mind, convincing myself that fighting the Tuatha's war was no different than campaigning for the Emperor, that some things you just had to take on trust. In truth it wasn't my pragmatism at work here. It was my vanity, my pride that wouldn't let me walk away from this ultimate challenge. I'd told myself, told Turan and Taskim and Rasaben, boasted to *everyone* that I could lead these former Kellesuf into battle and come out victorious. I think at the time I actually believed it, but now…

On top of this nagging uncertainty was the unwelcome but not altogether surprising realization that the Faoimhuir had flat-out *lied* about the size of their army, along with who knows what else—maybe we would be facing those terrible fire-birds Rasaben had mentioned—combined with the cold apprehension I couldn't shake that there would be *no* passage back home, even if we were victorious.

And that too was completely my fault, my sole responsibility: I'd goaded Taskim, tormented Rasaben, humiliated the other Sidhe Lords in the incredibly stupid and arrogant belief that *I* was the one in control—*fool!* They had no reason to come collect us, in fact I'd *provided* them with a damned solid reason not to! I'd done exactly what they wanted; I'd stepped into their neatly laid trap, taking fifteen hundred men with me to our certain deaths, whether in battle, through starvation or capture by Si'aafu—

"Enough!" I tossed back what remained of the wine, slammed the mug down on the table and lurched to my feet. There was nothing to be gained by sitting here, winding myself up into a full-blown panic. There'd be plenty of time for that, later, when I was facing down an army that vastly outnumbered my own.

I looked down at myself, at my wine- and blood-spattered tunic and angrily snatched up the cloth Carus had left then furiously rubbed my face, my throat, as if in doing so, I could wipe my mind clean of its disturbing thoughts. Then I made an equally vigorous attempt at wiping the drying stains from the oiled leather of my tunic, and as I did so my fingers happened across the small bulge that was the snakestone amulet— a 'gift' from Turan that I'd come to realize was more than a token of fealty, far more than an adornment marking my servitude—without it, it would have been difficult if not impossible to freely converse with my soldiers, much less the Tuatha.

Turan had never explained its strange powers—and I'd never thought to ask, not even Lady Ainiaan; only later did I discover that all Kellesuf— not to mention Hanni… even Kyrou, Perus, Boian and Jaro, in fact all of the Tuatha's servants wore similar amulets and for the same reason. Without them, we'd be reduced to simple gestures—easily misunderstood—to make our thoughts known.

Just above the puzzling snakestone was a circlet of small, irregular lumps, the cherished collection of faience, tigers-eye and glass beads, and a raw silver, four-pointed star, all strung on an aged leather thong, and behind them, a replicate signaculum—an updated version of the one that had disappeared under suspicious circumstances. While I was never able to prove it, I'd never shaken the belief Kyrou had been responsible. I'd insisted each of my men also wear one of these small tablets, and for the same reasons the empire's legionaries were required to wear them: it provided a simple and relatively accurate way to identify one's badly decomposed or horribly mutilated corpse. And as someone who'd often been tasked with such an odious job, I can attest that a little extra effort in the physical attribute description department makes all the difference between being given proper burial by your surviving friends and being left for someone else to deal with. And by someone else, I mean the worms and the crows.

I tossed the rag onto the table, slipped my hand into the neck-slit of my undertunic, carefully tugged the necklaces from their hiding place, then stepped under the tent's single suspended oil lamp, into its warm glow and gazed down at them as my fingers, by long and loving habit, toyed with the beads, prodding loose their always consoling, soft tinkling sound.

While the tigers-eye beads were my own, later additions to the necklace—each denoting an extremely close call, a hard-won victory, the primitive star and the equally crude slave beads of glass and faience had been a gift from the man who'd also bestowed upon me the name I've borne for now over half my life, *his* name: *Niger*. It was a name no one had ever questioned, a name everyone presumed was a good, solid Roman name—and it *was* a good solid Roman name—while Niger himself was a former slave from the distant, legendary kingdom of Nok with wrinkled, sloe-black skin the hue of Nile soil after the yearly flood.

I'd never reached Nok; I'd always hoped I would, hoped if I did I might locate some of his family, those lucky enough to have escaped the shackles and whips of slavers, so I could tell them I'd left him in good health, that he'd gained his freedom and was a wise and generous man.

I have no doubt he was now dead and probably had been dead for many years. He'd been a very old man when I, a youth, knew him, his thin and wiry body bowed from a harsh life, his shoulders and back crisscrossed with the cruel marks of his past, while his mind was as sharp as any. He was always smiling, his large teeth dazzling against his leathery black skin.

He'd told me to make the name Niger proud. I hoped in some small way I had.

My fingers lingered on the star, thumb and forefinger going through the familiar motions of rubbing it, as if by doing so I could conjure up a different fate than the one I now faced. Niger had told me such stars were given to the boys of his people when they reached manhood, a symbolic gift of the four corners of the world—and a potent reminder that, as his people said, one cannot know where one will die.

I'd always wondered if the star might also be a guidepost, a map for the soul, pointing the way home, so it could eventually find its way even if the body did not.

If so, would mine eventually find its way back to Turan? Perhaps back to where it truly belonged, to Simitthu and the abandoned barracks to join with the host of Lemures? Those same Lemures who'd kept the child Arri unwelcome company after the soldiers had left and who still paced its crumbling passageways, waiting patiently to be reunited with their physical forms, not knowing that their bodies had long ago turned to dust? Or was this asking too much from a crudely shaped piece of raw silver? Was the distance just too great, the separation too profound?

And, if given a choice, would I willingly abandon my soldiers, leaving their souls to wander this strange world while mine returned to ours?

No.

If it was our fate to die here, with no hope of rescue, no hope of ever seeing home again, then that was that. Either we all left or we all stayed.

I stared down at the star, signaculum and snakestone, all cupped in my palm, each embodying the salient chapters in my life, I found my gaze blurring. *Is this truly our fate?*

Worse, *had* Turan known ahead of time we were to be abandoned, just as she'd known ahead of time that Taskim was about to forcibly rip my memories from my mind? Perhaps *this* was the explanation why we'd come here well supplied to survive for several months rather than only a week or two. At the time I hadn't given the matter much thought; I simply attributed it to a morale boost on the part of Tuatha, sending us off to do their bidding by making sure we were amply supplied with provisions. A well-fed army is an enthusiastic army after all.

Perhaps the true reason *was* a far darker one; perhaps Turan knew there was no plan to bring us back, that we had been collectively condemned to the Tuatha version of the Roman *damnatio memoriae*, with all memory of *our* existence "officially" wiped from *their* minds. Perhaps she wanted to give us—*give me*—a fighting chance not only against the Faoimhuir but against an entire planet.

We'd been given enough horses, oxen, chickens and goats—even dogs, hawks and cats of each sex to provide breeding stock if it came to that, *if* we realized our truly dire predicament in time and adjusted our needs accordingly. We had innate knowledge of what to avoid on this world, possibly even innate knowledge of what was safe although we'd yet to find reason to test the latter, knowledge that could have only come from the Tuatha, from Turan. Perhaps she'd demanded such in trade for not giving me forewarning—had I known ahead of time I would have surely turned my forces on the Tuatha—something they had to have realized... and greatly feared might come to pass.

Perhaps these few advantages were Turan's way of assuaging her guilt, her complicity in this final betrayal, for sending me into oblivion, deliberately forgotten, making me yet another man of the void, a Kellesuf in everything but name. *Perhaps—*

I felt a tear roll down my cheek and watched it drop onto the snakestone, briefly turning its pearly gray surface a glossy black.

Turan… help me—help us!

I folded my fingers tightly around the three amulets, bit my lip and squeezed my eyes shut, hoping to shut out the memories, the pain…the sudden, intense longing, but it didn't work. There was no reassuring, voiceless '*Listen to me*' reply to my silent plea.

Utterly alone in my self-imposed darkness, I saw things more clearly—*too clearly*—as thoughts bubbled to the surface, unbidden.

I was suddenly back on the *Sulaviae*, looking down into the slick, star-speckled black of a becalmed, nighttime sea, trying to screw up the courage to jump, to kill myself, to be done with it… to join my friends. But I couldn't and Turan, still smarting from my rebuff to her advances, had her revenge by humiliating me, leaving me utterly defenseless and questioning my own sanity.

And I forgave her.

Thoughts turned, and I was in her chambers, only the ruddy glow of the banked fire giving shape to my surroundings. She'd told me she was willing to give me all the time I needed in order to trust her so that I could love her as she loved me…and then she betrayed that nascent trust in the most deeply and horrifically personal way, by being a party to the awful plunder—*the violent rape*—of my memories.

And I'd somehow managed to forgive her for that, too, because I so desperately wanted what she offered: to trust, to love someone in my own time and on *my* terms, not those imposed on me. No one had ever offered me that; no one had ever cared enough.

Then another wrenching shift and I was again in her quarters, beside her bed, months later, and I was staring into her hollow, shadowed eyes, confronted by the reality that she was dying—that the child she was carrying, *my* child—was slowly poisoning her, just as she was poisoning him, and if that had not been enough, there was her startling admission that by getting herself pregnant by me, although *any* Roman, *any* human would have done, she said, she'd derailed Rasaben's plans to marry her off to one of his chieftains in hopes of regaining his lands and his place among the Sidhe lords. So, she'd used me in the most intimate and degrading way; I'd been a means to an end—in this case a foil to her brother's aspirations—nothing more.

And I forgave her for that, too, because she said she loved me.

She made me *believe* it, made me believe in myself in ways I'd *never* believed. Made me believe in the impossible, that I could actually love someone, fully and completely, with nothing held back, nothing shielded. And perhaps most importantly of all, that she truly loved *me*, loved the *real* Arri, the abused and fearful child, the deeply flawed man, not the conceited, supremely confident and self-centered façade I showed to the world.

And when I prepared to take my leave that fateful morning, she said, "Come back to me," and I'd *believed* her, truly believed there was a chance, possibly even a good chance that I might return, might see my son grown, see Turan well again, find comfort that I hadn't, in my own ignorance, my own desperation to satisfy my physical needs, killed her by getting her with child.

I still wanted to believe her, wanted to believe she was still alive and waiting for me; I so very much wanted to believe she hadn't been a willing participant in this ultimate desertion.

Turan loved me—she told me so, countless times; she and she alone wouldn't have willingly abandoned me as everyone who'd ever mattered to me had done, but… if she had, then maybe, just maybe I could forgive this, too—

I swallowed against the hard lump that had formed in my throat, unfurled my fingers and smiled tightly down at the snakestone as I murmured, "I will always be your faithful servant, m'lady," then brought it to my lips and kissed it. I then slipped it and the other necklaces back under my tunic, where they settled against my bare skin—familiar and comforting, tangible surrogates for her unspoken, *Listen to me.*

I took a deep breath, wiped my eyes, my cheeks and looked around me, suddenly realizing I didn't want to be alone with my thoughts, my fears—my personal host of Lemures—so I turned on my heel and strode out of the tent and into the fire-lit camp, into the welcome and welcoming company of my soldiers.

I shifted my weight from one foot to the other, inadvertently betraying my unease to anyone who bothered to notice, and when I realized what I'd been doing I stopped, hoping it was still too dark or if someone had noticed, they'd assume it was just my left leg bothering me. But Felix wasn't fooled, neither was Rufinius. Out of the corner of my eye I caught the telltale eye-glitter of their furtive, knowing glances and as my gaze caught theirs, Rufinius immediately looked away while Felix replied with the faintest of commiserating smiles.

The other four soldiers present were too preoccupied with the goings on far below, watching for trouble, for ambush, their eyes scanning the desert, using the predawn icy glow of starlight to catch any unexpected movement, the glimmer of armor perhaps, any hint that our prisoner had not come alone and his companions had lingered, hidden from view by the high bank on the far side of the riverbed. One had even notched an arrow and was holding his bow at the ready, just in case.

We were standing on one of the firing platforms, a platform made to accommodate two bowmen along with a scorpio and its two-man crew, a platform which was now obligated to hold seven, and in full armor no less—along with the scorpio, a touchy weapon that discouraged unnecessary contact even by its handlers.

The breeze that softly gusted up and over the steep sides of the hilltop had finally driven off the night's chill, replacing it with a pleasant predawn warmth, its languid, heaving breath alternately raising the platform's canvas canopy then letting it gently settle, like some massive bellows. The whirlpool confirmed sunrise was on its way—the telltale spot of flotsam was falling ever closer to the ragged western peaks to our backs.

While everyone else's gaze was on the starlit desert below, watching as a small, well-armed force escorted the Faoimhuirian to the dry riverbed, my eyes were on the heavens—what wasn't blocked by the canopy— looking for some sign, some… *omen* if you will, anything that might lift me free of my growing anxiety.

All I saw were stars, thousands upon thousands of twinkling stars…and a tiny, fast-moving speck almost lost within the background glow, curiously fading and brightening as it arced high overhead.

I'd seen such messengers before, although usually much brighter and even quicker; Massaesyli believed boys born on those rare nights when the sky was set alight by volleys of fiery arrows were particularly blessed—obviously I had not been one of the so fortunate. My mother had told me I'd entered the world in the midst of one of the worst thunderstorms she'd ever experienced, which I suppose should have been a clue my life was to be equally tumultuous—but in my travels I'd come to learn that other peoples had other views and most looked upon these flaming missiles as augers of ill.

So, possibly another bad omen. My lips pinched into a glower. *Fucking wonderful.*

We'd arrived here five days before—three days from now we'd be out on that very desert, awaiting the arrival of dawn as well our enemy, assuming our adversaries were agreeable and would kindly reply to my polite summons by showing up ready to do battle at the appointed hour and at the appointed spot. Preparations were well underway, had been underway since each side had arrived on this gods-forsaken planet—I hadn't needed the terse report Aetius sent by night-runner to know this. Nevertheless I'd always found this an odd situation: both sides methodically readying themselves for battle, cognizant, even complicit with the enemy doing the same thing.

Scouts sent up into the mountains behind us had seen no sign of enemy movement, of reconnaissance squads—no sign of human presence except ours. But the enemy were up there, in their mountain stronghold, doing what we were doing, thinking what we were thinking, everyone aware that inevitably we'd meet, out there, on that natural arena of high desert.

I did have to wonder what the Faoimhuirian soldiers were using as motivation, what promises they'd been given. What would be their reward if they won? Their freedom? Taskim had said that they'd been born into slavery, generations upon generations who'd known nothing but service to their masters—so would they even know what to do once free? And in my experience, people don't ask for things they don't know exist. Perhaps even more germane to the matter, had their masters told them if they lost they'd pay not just with their lives, but those of their wives, their children?—frantic, retreating offerings to appease the insatiable, advancing Si'aafu?

That would certainly motivate *me*, even more than the promise of manumission.

I'd been told by a veteran centurion, a man by the name of Silvanus Julius Vulso, that to conquer an enemy you first must understand him, know what motivates him, what he wants, what he fears. He said by doing so there's always the possibility that you might avoid bloodshed, perhaps even find some common ground, thus turning an adversary into an ally, rather than a subjugate who demanded constant watching.

This was an unexpected insight into the power of diplomacy for me; that the sword was not the only answer to a threat, real or imagined.

I wasn't even dissuaded from this practice by the cold-blooded murder of Vulso by several Canenefatae posing as peace envoys while he was the midst of a parley with their arch rivals, the Frisii—in fact I often called upon this knowledge, thus honing my skills at the word as well as the weapon, giving each its chance, its place, in Germania, in Gaul, and most of all in Britannia with the Corieltauvi and Regni, the and yes, even those damnedable Iceni, sharing a meal at a chieftain's fire, walking with him among his filthy and wary-eyed subjects, admiring his slat-ribbed horses and cattle as I ferreted out what he really wanted, what he really needed, in the process convincing him that only the empire could provide these things—and of course more, much, much more.

I knew nothing of this enemy, these Faoimhuirians, knew nothing of their masters, unless one could take the Tuatha as a valid comparison. Not even that conjecture was helpful as I'd spent almost a year in the company of the Tuatha, one might even say *intimate* company yet I was still utterly baffled by them, by their motives, their methods and yes, their ultimate goals, which an inner voice warned me was not the deliverance of humanity.

Vestrum noscite hostem—know your enemy.

If only.

I sighed, dropped my gaze and quickly spotted the small group of men. While I'd been lost in thought, they'd reached the rim of the riverbank. As I watched, one hastily detached himself from the rest— more like roughly expelled from the rest—and without a backwards glance started down the crumbling slope and quickly vanished from view. The rest remained where they were, following their orders to the letter: stand watch until the Faoimhuirian had made it safely to the far bank and was well on his way.

As I stared at the knot of men who milled around on the near bank— at one of the very few crossings that afforded firm ground as I wanted the Faoimhuirian to believe this was the norm, rather than the exception—I found my thoughts returning to the approaching battle. I'd done all I could; my men had done everything they could to give us every advantage possible, but would it be enough?

I could only hope that the clash, when it came, would be quick and decisive; no drawn out skirmishes, no back and forth, over and over, each side bashing at the other until we exhausted ourselves, each side slowly bleeding the other to death. Even if it was our fate to lose, which I have to admit was not all that farfetched, I'd prefer it to be over with quickly, rather than a protracted conflict where the end, while inevitable, was only delayed.

"There he is," Rufinius murmured, drawing my distracted gaze.

Sure enough, the Faoimhuirian had reappeared; he was now standing on the far bank, staring back at his former captors and breathing hard.

I had to wonder what he was thinking—was he confused? Grateful? Pissed as hell? I'd made sure his injuries had been rechecked, his wounds re-stitched, his nose reset and his belly full before he was hustled out of the camp, blindfolded and his ears muffled to avoid any chance of him seeing or hearing things I wished to keep secret for as long as possible. I'd even ordered that he be supplied with a full waterskin and pouch of dried fruit—more than enough to last him, assuming he didn't dawdle—or take a foolish chance that the she-goat was still on the loose and would go willingly with him this time.

That almost made me smile. *Almost.*

Felix put two fingers in his mouth and let loose a sharp whistle, signal for the escort to make their return.

Helmeted heads turned towards the keen report, armor glimmering eerily, a combination of its own peculiar luminescence and the abundant starlight; a hand thrust a sword aloft, made a quick, circular slice through the air, acknowledging the signal and the escort formed up then began trotting back the way they'd just come. On the far bank the Faoimhuirian, realizing he was in fact free—or suspecting a trap—took off at a run.

"Looks like a scared rabbit making for its hole," Rufinius added with a note of disgust.

The man, clearly eager to put as much ground between himself and our camp as quickly as possible, promptly caught a foot on a sand drift and went sprawling.

I couldn't help but wince in sympathy, as did Felix. Rufinius shook his head, muttered, "A rather inept rabbit," and stifled a chuckle.

The scorpio crew and archers, taking their lead from Rufinius, laughed softly amongst themselves with a noticeable lessening of tension.

The Faoimhuirian rose ungracefully, staggered several steps in the deep, loose sand, stumbled and fell to his knees, again lumbered to his feet, risked a quick glance back at us as if checking to see if anyone had noticed or if anyone was following, then took off again, this time managing to get clear of the deep drift without falling again.

So, it was done. My summons to battle was on its way, conveyed by two fast albeit rather clumsy feet.

"Maybe he'll trip going down that gorge and break his neck," one of the archers muttered, his eyes darting to me in clear hopes of garnering an approving nod or smile. Aulus was his name, a smallish, gaunt man with keen, feral eyes and reflexes to match. He'd been part of our reconnaissance squad and had his own unpleasant experiences with that treacherous cleave in the earth, the stitched up gash on his chin and darkly bruised cheek lingering reminders of his own near fatal misstep when exhaustion had trumped reaction.

I responded as Aulus had hoped, a quick, nodding grin, not because I wanted the gods' damned Faoimhuirian to break his gods' damned neck, but because my soldiers needed something to hang onto, even if it was the forlorn hope that the enemy as a whole would somehow, by proxy, come to a similar ignoble end.

I clapped Aulus on the shoulder, smiled at the other three, then with one last glance and spotting our Faoimhuirian, who had finally found his stride and was making relatively good time across the open desert, I started for the ladder that gave access to the platform.

Rufinius beat me to it then flicked me a look: silent appeal that he go first, just in case my damned leg gave out on me.

I was in no mood to be coddled and the set of my jaw made that clear. He hastily stepped back and allowed me to descend without further delay, and once back on the ground, I looked around. The camp was awake, had in fact been awake for hours. While we'd taken full advantage of the longer days, spending the time between dawn and dusk with the normal chores of soldiers, none of us had adapted to the equally longer nights. Aside from those tasked with standing watch or manning the firing platforms during the night and who, in many cases, had just found their beds, the rest were up and about, already hard at work.

Aware that Felix and Rufinius had stopped behind me, awaiting my pleasure, I glanced over my shoulder, grumbled, "You'd best get something to eat before it's all gone," and waggled a finger in the general direction of the nearest mess wagon.

They knew a dismissal when they heard it; they knew I wanted to be alone. With an understanding nod from Felix and a forced smile from Rufinius, the two walked away, whispering to each other. About me, I have no doubt, damn them.

I thought about heading to the stables. I'd only checked on Wushah once since we'd arrived, trusting his care to Aper, but I had nothing suitable to offer the warhorse in apology for my lapse. I glanced after Felix and Rufinius, briefly thought about joining them—*no.* I was in no mood for company, be it two or four legged. I considered returning to my tent, where I knew I'd be left alone, at least for a little while, long enough to reread Aetius' somewhat cheering report of the enemy camp in apparent turmoil, presumably over the realization that we were here. And if they hadn't, they'd know for sure soon enough—good, let *them* panic. I even thought about polishing my own armor and in the process work off some of my fretfulness before it began to wear off onto my officers, my men—

"Le... g... g... gate...?"

I swore—silently mind you—then grudgingly turned towards the breathless voice and saw a very grimy soldier limping wearily towards me, bringing Felix, who was now carrying a lit torch, with him. I rummaged through my famously accurate memory for his name. Quintus...I think, but I wasn't one hundred percent sure. Maybe ninety, ninety-five tops. *Fifteen hundred men*—I think 'ninety-five percent sure' of one man's name is pretty damned good.

"Yes, Quintus?" I went for broke, figured if I was wrong, his lack of reaction—or quizzical stare would give it away.

He stopped before me, bent over and grabbed his knees as he gulped hungrily for air.

Of course maybe he was so winded he hadn't heard me.

I crossed my arms and stared irritably at him as Felix placed himself at my side and followed my lead—minus the arm crossing. He was holding a lit torch after all, with the other hand now firmly affixed to his hip, but the effect was the same: annoyed impatience.

Finally the soldier straightened up and between gasps said, *"My... my ap... ap... apologies... Leg... Legate—"*

"Catch your breath, Quintus," Felix chided.

The man nodded, took several more heaving gulps.

So I was right. *Hah.* I struggled not to flick Felix a triumphant grin—let him think I was positive I had it right all along...unless, of course,

Felix was yet again following my lead, assuming I knew when he didn't have a clue.

"Centurion Duccius sent me…"

I felt my gut instantly twist into a knot, fearing the worst possible news—

"…we found water, Legate. A spring! Good water, too, *sweet.*" He quickly untied a waterskin—a relatively plump waterskin I might add—from his belt and held it up as proof as my startled mind struggled to swivel on its bearings.

Felix accepted the skin, took a measured sip then swallowing, turned to me and nodded.

That was good news—*excellent* news in fact as it was pretty obvious to everyone that despite twelve of our wagons being little more than gigantic water barrels on wheels, we were going to run out of water far faster than we were going to run out of food, as it was truly astonishing just how much water fifteen hundred men, two hundred and two horses, four hundred and twenty one oxen, one hundred and forty nine goats, a hundred or so chickens, nine dogs, four hawks and three cats could drink in a day. If you were wondering, yes, the one hundred and fiftieth goat, by peculiar happenstance the very one that had gone exploring had given her all to the previous evening's meal. One damned she-goat—fifteen hundred men—*and Aëllo.* Let's not forget the damned dog who, based on *my* damned order, had likely gotten more than her fair share—no wonder I hadn't found a shred of meat in my stew. Florianus had probably thought I meant for him to give her my portion.

"How hard's the climb?" Felix asked, his penchant for the practical taking the fore, and took another wincing swig from the waterskin. He swallowed, wiped his lips. "Could the horses and wagons make it?"

"Wagons? No." Quintus strongly shook his head for emphasis. "Not sure 'bout the horses—there's a lot of loose rock, tricky footing…" he paused long enough to brush his dusty and scabbed-over knees, drawing our eyes to the scrapes and gravel burns that also discolored his shins—along with his palms, elbows and chin. "But there might be a safer route—Centurion Duccius said he saw a gap in the mountains several leagues further north…"

As he turned to point, I couldn't help but notice that the seat of his breeches had taken a severe mauling too, and I had to wonder if he felt the draft.

"…maybe a pass, and on the way up we spotted several trails—"

"Trails?" I asked, my startled eyes darting to Felix.

"Game trails—so says Caepio—he and Lamia went to check one out. He said the one they followed for a short distance was really old—no fresh tracks and no sign of what might have made them, and we looked, believe me sir, we *looked*, but from what we could see the trails look just wide enough an armored horse could be led, I suppose, oxen maybe, if we had a mind to take them, but not the wagons or engines for that matter— I didn't take any of the paths on the way down sir, just in case I met up with whatever made them."

That was indeed a smart move and I nodded my approval for him taking caution over the temptation of an easier, less hazardous descent, a decision that had clearly cost him a fair amount of skin, not to mention clothing.

"And there's more, sir—as the rest of us set about making camp at the spring, Centurion Duccius and Caepio used what remained of the day to scale a nearby peak, thinking it might give us an even better view, and the centurion said to tell you he caught a glimpse of what lies to the west, beyond the mountains. He said he saw a vast expanse of what looked like *grasslands*—well, it was gray-green, like steppe, he said, whatever it was, and rippling, as if blown by the wind. And he saw a flowing river, no doubt about *that* he said. Water, fast moving and lots of it, he said."

I almost smiled. Maybe this world wasn't so dead after all—maybe the desert had been chosen because of its innate likeness to an arena, high-walled, its floor covered in sand to soak up the blood. And *if* the planet wasn't dead and *if* any of us survived the coming battle and *if* our masters failed to come collect us then we weren't necessarily dead, either— granted, a lot of 'ifs' but still, better odds than I'd have given you only a few minutes ago.

This also meant that maybe my efforts at teaching my men how to forage had not been a waste of time—it might in fact hold them in good stead.

"Did the centurion or Caepio spot any trails leading down the other side?" That might be critical, if we truly wanted to escape. Of course this also meant that our enemies could just as easily use the trails to pursue us, but with our luck—along with the strategic placement of booby-traps— and their misfortune, maybe *they'd* meet up with whatever made them and not us.

He shook his head. "No, sir. Centurion Duccius said the light was fading by then and he and Caepio didn't linger, wanting to return to camp before night fell—rather than them."

I couldn't help but chuckle, and the soldier grinned through his mask of grime, dried blood and rivulets of sweat.

All in all, it was better news than I could have possibly hoped for, despite the lingering unease of what had made the trails—or that they could be just as easily used against us. As I've mentioned before, we hadn't seen any sign of life beyond plants, and scarce few of those. Hopefully the trails *were* very old—thousands of years old. Maybe. But it did make me wonder if perhaps we weren't the first to make this surprising discovery—maybe the Faoimhuirians had reasons beyond the obvious for making their camp high in the mountains, where water and possibly game was plentiful.

"I almost forgot the best part!" Quintus stuffed his hand down between his dusty, ring-mail shirt and sweat darkened tunic and began fishing around.

I looked at Felix; he looked back, then we both turned our intensely curious gazes on the soldier as he continued to search for something secreted within his clothing. What could top a spring with drinkable water, mountain trails our horses could traverse, possibly even a pass and the possibility of a lusher, life-sustaining landscape beyond?

My hopes soared—had he perhaps stumbled across a map that could lead us home? A lost civilization comprised only of desperately horny women…? Okay, maybe that one was a wee bit farfetched. He was fishing around inside his mailed shirt after all; hard to secrete a woman under his armor—not that I haven't seen soldiers try.

Finally, after a fair amount of bodily contortions, Quintus withdrew his hand and held out something that looked like a crab, or perhaps more like a shrimp, blotchy brownish-yellow in color, with a flattened, crescent shaped and segmented body covered in what looked like tiny feathers and just slightly larger than his palm and outstretched fingers. "The spring… it's crawling with these." He stepped closer, offering me the squashed creature and my soaring hopes came plummeting back to earth, hitting with a loud, gut-twisting *splat.*

As I may have mentioned before, I'm not fond of anything with more than two legs, four, max. I'm *not* squeamish. I just have standards and simply put, more than four legs just isn't right and proper; in my humble opinion it's an unjustifiable extravagance.

This particular specimen had seven appendages—*furry* appendages I must add for accuracy's sake—presumably it originally had eight, as there was a stub where the eighth should have been, the missing fuzzy limb perhaps squished within the folds of Quintus' ring-mail shirt—*ugh!*—just the thought sent a fresh shiver down my spine. So much for no bugs—

"It's *edible,* Legate." He stepped even closer and again offered it to me, having somehow totally misread my appalled reluctance as delighted, *famished* astonishment.

I again looked askance at the creature. *Edible bugs?* My stomach, my mind, recoiled at the thought. It didn't look edible—or the least bit appetizing, with its sickly color, furry legs, feathery body and a row of what I had to assume were beady black eyes that formed a line that extended halfway down the length of its body. In fact it was downright hideous looking and an hours-long trip down a mountainside, squished and squeezed inside the man's sweaty armor had not helped one whit. I had to assume in life it was not quite so flat—presumably Quintus had fallen on it, repeatedly—although I had nothing to prove that assumption.

"How do you know?" Felix asked, voicing my own concerns as my stomach continued to squirm.

"We ate a bunch of 'em," Quintus replied proudly.

I blinked, revolted and yes, now more than just a tad queasy. I took a step back, just in case as it just wouldn't do for the legate to vomit on one of his soldiers no matter the provocation.

"How long ago?" a new voice asked before Felix could: *Cleander.*

He walked up to us, briefly eyed the creature Quintus still held in his outstretched hand, plucked it from his palm and studied it. Without warning he gave it a vigorous shake, presumably to startle it, see if it *was* still alive. It certainly startled *me* into jumping back another step, but if the bug was still alive, it wisely wasn't letting on. So possibly a smart bug too. Oh joy. Plus one of its spindly, fuzzy legs came flying off, narrowly missing me only to hit Felix smack in the chest and I couldn't help but flinch.

Felix eyed it disdainfully then using two fingers like tweezers slowly peeled it off his otherwise pristine band armor and handed it back, murmuring, "Yours, I presume?"

Cleander accepted it without comment and looked as if he was considering how to reattach it.

"Last night...?" Quintus replied slowly, his eyes darting from me to Cleander, then back to me and by his suddenly uneasy tone it had suddenly occurred to him that he might, at any moment, keel over stone dead.

"Stomach upset?"

"Yes," I said, realizing too late and by Cleander's sidelong, annoyed glance that he wasn't speaking to me.

"No," Quintus replied then recovering himself, added, "We cooked 'em real good."

Cleander looked at me and arched his brow. In truth there was nothing else to say. That look said it all.

"All of you ate them?" I asked—clearly the concept of foraging had been taken a little too eagerly to heart; one rule I *thought* I'd successfully drummed into all of them was when dealing with an unfamiliar, potentially edible item was to have an expendable volunteer try it—like one of the dogs or a goat, only they hadn't taken one with them, so barring that, the lowest ranking among them—and if said 'volunteer' failed to have *any* adverse reaction after a few hours then it was possibly— *not probably*—safe to eat. But then again, we all somehow knew what to avoid, what was poisonous—like the plants that grew around the edges of the saltpans—so perhaps I'd been right, perhaps what was safe to eat had been instilled in us as well. It seemed only fair.

He nodded, smiling, oblivious to my less than pleased tone.

"And none of you got sick," Cleander added, dispensing with the loose leg by tossing it aside.

Quintus shook his head, the smile turning into a downright smug grin.

"How do they taste?" Cleander asked, taking a much closer look at the small corpse he held in one palm. Felix handed the torch to Quintus, who obliged Cleander and brought the torch even closer, but as far as I was concerned better lighting didn't help.

"Just as they look like they'd taste—"

"And what, pray tell, is that?" Cleander replied, lifting his intense gaze just long enough to make eye contact with Quintus.

I held my breath, not to mention my stomach, awaiting his answer.

"Like... shrimp?"

Despite the feathery down that covered its back and its row of eyes even I had to admit it did remotely resemble a shrimp—a really big, really *ugly*, smashed flat shrimp.

"Really? Because this creature looks to be more closely related to a spider."

Oh, gods... My stomach did a back flip and Quintus, who up to that instant looked quite pleased with himself and his gastronomic find, abruptly—to his credit—didn't look quite so pleased.

"Spider...?" he asked, his voice having suddenly gone high pitched and thin.

Cleander nodded.

Now Quintus looked like he wanted to throw up, yet even he knew at this point it was pointless as his meal was just too far down to want to come back up, even at his intense pleading.

To everyone's surprise, Cleander snapped the hapless creature in two, then brought one of the halves close to his nose, took a sniff, followed by a small, tentative nibble of the exposed green flesh. He chewed thoughtfully then wiping his lips with the back of his hand, said, "You say the spring is full of them?"

Quintus nodded, slowly and now quite unenthusiastically. "They hide under the rocks, but they're pretty easy to catch—there are also things that look sort of like fish—"

"Sort of like?" Felix asked.

"Well, more like bright blue eels? About twice as long as your arm and about the same size around—they're too fast to spear or shoot with arrows, though, or we'd have tried them too."

Cleander turned to me, offering me the other half. "It's actually not bad tasting."

I eyed it then him. "I'll take your word for it, thank you all the same."

He shrugged, said, "Well, if none of the men who ate these get sick or die by this evening, I'd say we can assume they're safe to eat."

"It isn't a matter of safe or not," I muttered, eyeing the now torn asunder creature with a look of utter revulsion.

"Beggars can't be choosers, Legate," Cleander replied. "And the men, not to mention the dogs will certainly benefit from the extra meat in their rations—we can feed the shells and legs to the goats, hawks, cats and even the chickens," he added as we all noticed that Xanthus had suddenly appeared from nowhere, as Xanthus had a habit of doing, and was now investigating the discarded leg.

Xanthus was always the first on a potential meal, and sure enough, after a few tentative pats with a paw, she snatched up the limb and trotted off to be alone with her furry prize.

I gave myself a shake then turned back to Quintus, said, "Go with Cleander. He'll want to watch you for the next few hours."

He saluted then he and Cleander walked away, thankfully taking the revolting creature with them.

I stared after them and slowly shook my head. A spring, passable trails, maybe even an actual *pass* through the seemingly impassable mountains, grasslands, maybe, and a river, definitely. Plus edible bugs— don't forget about the bugs. I know I won't.

Felix chuckled at my expression and rubbing his hands together, said, "I don't know about you but I'm suddenly famished."

I wasn't. But I also realized that I might not get another chance to eat until the midday meal was served, which was many, many long, hot and hardworking hours away and I knew I'd regret it if I didn't eat something.

"I guess I could eat," I replied then clapping him on the shoulder, added, "as long as it isn't spider stew."

— ii —

If Quintus was a fair example, the scouting party suffered no ill effects from their impromptu feast and by late-afternoon Cleander had cleared him to return to duty, which meant another grueling scramble back up the mountain. But this time he was joined by two others, along with three of the dogs, just in case they happened come across whatever had made those trails, along with adding their strong backs, including those of the dogs, to the arduous task of transporting heavy rucksacks stocked with provisions for the food caches and supply dumps Duccius had already set up, well hidden among the crags. The two were then to return the following morning with news of any further discoveries, good or bad, leaving the dogs behind with Duccius and his party; it was my hope the dogs could sniff out whatever had made the trails—or warn the soldiers of its approach, assuming whatever it was hadn't died off millennia ago.

Before the men left, Cleander warned them not to indulge in any of the creatures—we'd all agreed to refer to them as 'shrimp' rather than the far less appetizing but more accurate alternative—just in case there was some sort of delayed reaction. That went for the eels as well. And the same was true for those still up on the mountain—Quintus was to pass along Cleander's directive than everyone was to stick with the rations they'd already packed in, even when it came to water—and that included the dogs. I concurred, reinforcing the order with one of my own; I was not about to think I had eyes up there, an early warning system only to later learn, *if* I lived to learn, that they were all dead of delayed spider poisoning and therefore unable to inform us that we were about to be set upon and massacred.

And yes, Xanthus, who was kind enough to volunteer as taste-tester for the four-footers among us appeared no the worse for her indulgences, either.

For my part I spent the day oiling my tunic and polishing my armor— yes, I said *polishing* as there was no sand available to toss into an empty barrel along with the ring-mail, then roll the barrel about using the sand to clean all the nooks and crannies of accumulated dirt and dried gore—a time-saving trick I'd learned long ago; yes, there was ocher *dust* in abundance, but using it kind of defeated the whole purpose as it left the armor clean, but it also left it a less than manly orangey-pink and looking as it if was about to rust away.

One of the notable advantages of Tuatha armor was that unlike Roman steel armor, it didn't actually rust. Here on Latruncŭli it just looked as if it was rusting if it wasn't polished regularly, so in fact the advantage was rather moot. On the other hand, one of the glaring disadvantages of ring-mail, be Tuatha or Roman, was that shy of using the aforementioned sand in barrel technique, it was a bitch to polish.

I visited Wushah—even riding him around the camp to give him some exercise and at the same time offer words of encouragement to my troops—and later hashing out contingencies with my officers over our midday meal of hardtack and cheese, with Felix jotting down notes on the writing tablet he was rarely without—problematic during the day as Latruncŭli's stifling heat tended to soften, if not outright melt the wax.

I'd then spent an hour or so watching the falconers put their birds through their paces—chasing lures, responding to directional whistles— and was suitably impressed. While the sport had never caught on with Romans, I'd seen the like in Egypt and Parthia and was amazed that the hawks always returned to their handlers rather than fleeing once released. I'd have been more impressed with our hawks if there had been birds or hare to catch, game that could have been added to the meager ration of meat in our cook pots.

I'd even made the time to write down my thoughts, a habit I'd started while still on Earth, a practice encouraged by Turan and Lady Ainiaan and which had quickly become less a diary and more a chronicle of my life— the good *and* the bad—a legacy for my son in hopes that through my words he might come to know me, his father, as someone who was more than just the name of his long absent sire, a man who was all too human.

I'd continued it here, having brought several rolls of the finest vellum, iron-gall ink and a quill, all neatly rolled up and tucked in one of Wushah's saddlebags, for what purpose I cannot tell you. Each of my men could read and write, Latin *and* Greek, as well as speak a number of tongues fluently because I could, and by the same token they knew everything I did, experienced Latruncŭli, its wonders and its woes as I did. There was nothing I could commit to the written word that they didn't already know for themselves and if we were to be abandoned here it wasn't like there would be a generation after us—when the last of us died, so would our presence on this misbegotten world.

Maybe it was my last link to my son, to Turan, a very tenuous thread that somehow stretched all the way home and one I just could not force myself to sever because deep down, and as irrational as it seemed, I desperately hoped Neshoue would eventually come looking for me. If he did, chances are all he'd find would be the scrolls, but if he read them he'd realize that unlike me, he had a father who never forgot about him, who longed to be reunited with him and only death had the power to intervene. *Perhaps.*

By late afternoon the bustling and at times boisterous camp had fallen abnormally quiet; men, weary from the heat and the long hours of what had become little more than make-work to keep minds and hands busy, their throats raw from the cloying dust, had gathered in small groups, some seated around the campfires. All were patiently, hungrily awaiting the evening meal by talking hoarsely to each other, making feeble jokes or just gazing into the firelight, preferring to be alone with their thoughts, their fears.

I did have to wonder what former Kellesuf thought about when they were alone in their own minds—did they recall fond memories, relive experiences, remember long-lost friends and family as any man would do who was facing his death? Did they do this all the while painfully aware that these sketchy reminisces weren't truly theirs, that they were little more than unwilling voyeurs, or did they just allow themselves to be lost in someone else's past, filling in the yawning gaps with pure fabrication, happy to be anywhere but here? I couldn't imagine it—I didn't want to imagine it.

Felix and Rufinius had no sooner joined me in the command tent, Felix seated across from me at the table, Rufinius perched on the edge of my bunk, to wash the dust from our throats with some wine while we awaited the arrival of our dinners when we heard a commotion—distant at first, but getting louder by the second. Startled, we hastily rose as one; Rufinius was the first to reach the tent flap and jerk it aside to see what was approaching with such a clamor of dust-raspy yet excited voices.

We quickly stepped outside as men surged towards us, an armored tide coming at us from several directions at once, funneled down the passages between the orderly lines of tents, and swept along in their midst was one of the soldiers Aetius had taken with him—Bassaeus—no one needed to remind me of his name; he was the same man Aetius had sent the previous night, the man whose unexpected late night arrival had startled me out of a sound sleep.

And now he was back; I couldn't make myself believe this was good news.

Bassaeus staggered forward, separating himself from the rest as the others instantly fell silent and absolutely still, like statues—something only Kellesuf could do in such eerily perfect unison—an unyielding ring wall of armor eerily glittering and glimmering in the cool-hued late afternoon sunlight.

"Legate," he murmured hoarsely and dipped his ocher-dusted blond head.

I motioned for Rufinius to fetch one of the folding chairs from the tent as Bassaeus looked as if he was about to drop in his tracks. He was well known among the troops as someone who could sustain an easy lope for miles, even in full rig including pack. That was the reason Aetius had picked him as the message runner and as a former Kellesuf he very well might have pushed himself far past a sane man's endurance to maintain that dogged pace the entire way—just as Quintus had done, only with Bassaeus it would have been coming and going, and coming back again, eight miles, at the very least—*each way*—and the last relay done in the full heat of day. "Bring water—*and food,*" I said to no one in particular and several men broke away to do my bidding.

Bassaeus gratefully sank down onto the folding chair Rufinius held steady for him, accepted a mug of wine from Felix, took a deep, wincing gulp then looked up at me. "We got a good look at the enemy today, Legate, I mean a *real* good look—"

I felt my entire body tense in preparation for hearing the worst of possible news—news heard by my men as I heard it and there was simply nothing to be done about it.

"—more than half are women and children, sir."

If the crowd around us had been quiet before, it was like a tomb now. Hundreds of thunderstruck eyes met mine. I glanced sidelong at Rufinius; what thoughts this news stirred behind his black eyes he clearly planned to keep to himself, so I dropped my gaze to Bassaeus as he took another, even deeper gulp from the mug.

At this point I wouldn't put anything past the Faoimhuirians, even going as far as to dress their soldiers up as women, suspecting we were watching them and trying to throw us off—the children, well…maybe they were pigmies or dwarves. I'd seen both in the royal houses of

Egypt—they didn't look much like children close up, but at a distance? *Maybe.* "Are you absolutely certain?"

Bassaeus nodded, took another loud gulp, empting the mug, then gladly exchanged it for one full of water and a heaping plate of food a soldier offered him. He placed the plate on his lap as he said, "Must be over two thousand of them—maybe more. We weren't sure at first as their heads are shaved…"

As he paused to take a swallow of water, I looked at Felix, eyebrows raised. "Faoimhuirian fashion?"

He shrugged, "Not a particularly attractive one," and lightly touched his own curly locks.

Bassaeus exhaled tiredly, continued, "All of 'em, shaved, just like their menfolk, but then Gaius and Libius managed to get themselves close to a pool at the edge of the Faoimhuir camp and got a good look, I mean *real* good at a group as they were bathing. Absolutely no doubt, Fabius said…" He held his cupped hands in front of him, mimicking holding large breasts then he began shoveling the food into his mouth with little delicacy.

I again slid my gaze to Felix, then back to Bassaeus. "And soldiers? How many?"

He swallowed then shrugged, "Hard to tell, sir—but Aetius said to say he believes not a lot more than us."

I flicked Felix another glance. He raised his eyebrows, every bit as startled by this revelation as I was, as startled as learning more than half their number were women and children—or dwarves.

It didn't make sense. I knew what I'd seen, what we'd all seen—thousands of campfires. Then a more worrisome thought came to mind: *what if they'd already dispatched the bulk of their army, leaving the women and children behind, guarded by only token force?* The sidelong look my second in command gave me suggested the same had occurred to him.

Bassaeus, oblivious to our silent conversation, wiped his greasy lips with the back of his hand then scooped up another handful. He shook his head, muttered through a mouthful, "Odd bunch."

I crossed my arms. "How so?"

"They all look… *kinda scruffy?* Beat up, maybe's a better description—and their camp's poorly organized—not easily defended the way they've got it set up, like they don't know what they're doing. Far too spread out. Of course the whole damned valley floor's dotted with pools, not to mention the streams that feed them—"

"Pools?"

He nodded. "Lots of 'em—in and among the boulders that is. One big enough I suppose you could call it a small lake."

This had the potential of being very good news on several levels: what if what we'd assumed was firelight was in fact *starlight* reflected on still water? The dusty night sky tinged everything a faint reddish-gold, including the brightest stars and the air, even at night, quivered, easily mimicking the shifting glow of fires. What if Aetius' calculation of the number of enemy was accurate after all? And what if surface water—*drinkable* water—at least up in the mountains, was truly abundant? Perhaps we could in fact survive here, *if* any of us survived the approaching battle.

Bassaeus again filled his mouth, swallowed, and filled it again, washing the food down with a large gulp of water. "We could've grabbed several of the pickets, even slipped into camp and set fire to some of their outlying lean-tos and set off a panic if we'd had a mind to—we could have probably grabbed ourselves a few women too, but Centurion Aetius said no, said we weren't there to stir up trouble, just watch."

I nodded, pleased, not to mention relieved at Aetius' restraint. Then again women and children were involved. Aetius—I speak of the original Aetius—had lost his entire family, a local woman he'd planned to make his wife the instant he retired, along with their five children to a plague, a plague he'd come very close to succumbing to as well. This unspeakable tragedy had happened several years before we—*literally*—struck up a friendship after I came to his aid in a brawl; it was a loss that always weighed heavily on him and despite all of his bluster and bullying, his penchant for pummeling the crap out of other soldiers for scant little provocation, I'd often find him, on his free time, carving wooden toys for the children of the garrison; he'd even been known to get down on his hands and knees and act the part of a horse for the smallest children to ride. Few of his fellow legionaries were stupid enough to ridicule this soft spot in an otherwise very fearsome man—and on the rare time one did, he only did it once.

This Aetius carried the same heavy burden, grieving the loss of a family that he'd never in fact known—part and parcel of fully becoming the Aetius I'd committed to memory and in such detail; an unwelcome endowment to be sure.

I risked another glance at Felix, suddenly regretting my decision not to remain longer in our aerie overlooking the enemy camp, at least long enough to get a better look by daylight—if I had, and if by doing so I'd come to the same startling conclusion as Aetius, I might've opted for a surprise attack on their supposed stronghold, using the valley's natural defenses against them. But again, maybe this was all a feint, a trap. Maybe they knew we were watching them and were hoping to play us for fools. Maybe the bulk of their army *was* secretly encircling us.

Bassaeus continued to wolf down the food, pausing only long enough to hand off the now empty plate for another that was just as full as the first.

"So, the Faoimhuirians hadn't lied… exactly," I muttered, watching him tuck away an astonishing amount of food at an equally astonishing rate.

"But why send women and children?" Felix asked.

"Motivation."

"Their side?"

"*And* ours," I replied, unable to keep the chill from my voice, and with a shake of my head, turned back to Bassaeus—and happened to notice Marcus Polycleitus and Aper among the circle of men. "Any evidence they have horses?"

Bassaeus shook his head, muffled through another mouthful, "No, sir. Not even draft animals. No animals at all—at least none that we could see, or hear for that matter." He swallowed, added, "Just children, and women, lots and lots of 'em…" He managed a weary grin. "More than us, certainly, a hell of a lot more."

That remark sent an ugly stir through my troops. I could feel it. It raised the hairs on the back of my neck. Kellesuf or not, they were still men with men's well-known wants, wants that for most had been left unsatisfied once free of their Kellesuf mind-set.

Felix noticed the mood too, leaned close and whispered, "If that was the plan, then it appears to have worked—perhaps a little too well."

I nodded. Women and children had always been victims, the hapless booty of men's wars, the sometimes not so innocent bystanders swept up in the mêlée, given even less regard than the enemy and rarely any quarter. A noble adversary deserved respect; women garnered little, children even less.

To order my men not to take full advantage of this unexpected windfall would be unwise, offering the enemy a weakness I had no doubt they, given half a chance, would exploit.

It did, however, explain why our prisoner had reacted the way he had. It also added a new twist: if we were to be abandoned here—and at least some of us survived, it would certainly make life more tolerable to have women as company, assuming we could persuade the Faoimhuir to part with some of them.

I looked around. "You heard Bassaeus. The Faoimhuir have brought their women—"

A deafening roar went up and hundreds of swords and pila thrust suggestively at the darkening sky.

I waited, letting the soldiers loose their reactions, their glee, foolishly believing this increased our chances of winning—with unexpected spoils to boot.

Finally I motioned for quiet and they settled with only a few lingering murmurs to be heard within the ranks.

"Which means their soldiers will fight even *more* tenaciously. Meaning berserkers—count on it."

That silenced everyone; even Bassaeus stopped eating, his hand halfway to his open mouth, his suddenly uneasy eyes fixed on me.

Now that I had their undivided attention, I continued, "This news does *not* guarantee victory, it only complicates defeat—for both sides." I swept the ring of faces with my suddenly and deliberately fierce gaze. "These Faoimhuirians are *not* barbarians—and I have no intention of leaving them with the impression that we *are*. Do I make myself clear?"

The soldiers looked at each other, at first bewildered, then, as each man thought about it, they began to nod and mutter unhappily amongst themselves.

I then turned back to Bassaeus. "Do they appear to be making ready?"

"Yessir. We spotted squads being dispatched—maybe scouts, maybe to set up ambushes," he shrugged, "impossible to tell. The rest were preparing to move—"

"Clearly our rabbit managed to return safely to its burrow," Rufinius grumbled; I nodded in reply.

"*Including* the women and children, sir," Bassaeus added, drawing my arched gaze, not to mention Rufinius' and Felix's.

If this in fact was the case, then it made it even more certain that what Aetius had seen was in fact the enemy's true numbers, not a camp of those left behind. "Are you absolutely sure?"

"Yessir, or, should I say Centurion Aetius was."

"Perhaps they fear we might circle around and attack their unprotected rear," Felix offered up.

"Maybe they're overconfident of victory and wish their wives and children to witness their triumph," Rufinius countered irritably—that had certainly been a glaring tactical error in many an Iceni attack, to the point I was often left to wonder if the men would indeed fight as ferociously as they did if they hadn't had their even more fearsome and bloodthirsty womenfolk urging them on. There was a damned good reason Roman troops feared being captured only to be handed over to the women. *Damned* good reason. Thinking I was about to meet this fate had utterly undone me, I freely admit it.

Bassaeus looked at Rufinius, Felix, then at me. "Centurion Aetius believes they plan on moving out tonight, once darkness has fallen." He pointedly glanced up at the deepening lavender sky.

Felix exhaled, smiled a relaxed smile. "And with that lot trailing behind it should take them at least two full days to reach the desert, if not longer."

Bassaeus shook his shaggy head. "I dearly wish that was so, Primus-Pilus. You see, there's a narrow pass further up the valley—Geta and Maenius went for a look-see. They reported it'd give 'em a straight shot to the desert several miles south of us. Maenius estimates they could make the desert by daybreak tomorrow, baggage train and all, if they take that route, and it looked like they had every intention in doing so."

"Which would leave their rear *and* flanks exposed once out on the desert," Rufinius replied.

"A trap?" Felix offered, turning his arched gaze on me, "hoping to spread us thin, using their kin as bait?"

"I wouldn't put it past 'em," I replied, "I wouldn't put *anything* past 'em. But my bet is they're hoping to catch us unawares, or at least be waiting for us on ground of their choosing, when I'd much prefer to be waiting for *them* on ground of *our* choosing."

That garnered a reserved murmur from the soldiers, a ripple of unease mixed with relief: time was running out, the anxiety of waiting was almost over.

"It looks like it'll be a lovely evening for a horseback ride," I murmured as my gaze again fell on Marcus, "yes?"

Marcus grinned, his teeth dazzling against the deepening shadows and his black skin. He saluted, then turned and vanished into the crowd with Aper on his heels. Other men—those who made up the cavalry—quickly followed. The rest shifted to fill the sudden holes in their ranks.

"Prepare the ox—we'll sacrifice it at sunset," I said, "and once we've paid proper tribute, go about your business just in case *we* have watchers that are not our own," I jerked my chin to the crags of the hinter range, to where Duccius and his men were hunkered down—hopefully *without* unexpected and wholly unwanted company, "make as if this evening is no different than any other evening; eat your suppers, clean your armor—and once it's dark, go to your tents as if you are off to your beds—get some sleep if you can. And once the cavalry is well away, be ready to move out on my order."

My softly worded command sent another ripple through the soldiers: armor creaked and glinted in the strange cold glow of the unhurried approach of twilight, nervous feet shuffled, eyes glittered.

"Go," I murmured, motioning with my hands and the tightly packed crowd began to disperse.

Bassaeus lurched unsteadily to his feet, awaiting my orders.

"Rest," I said, grasping his armor-clad shoulder. "I'll send another runner back to Aetius."

"I'd much rather go myself, sir."

"I need strong legs, Bassaeus, sound lungs—eyes that can spot any enemy pickets and ears that can warn of enemy scouts."

"I have them, Legate. And besides," he paused to grin, "the Faoimhuirians aren't the only ones who've found themselves a shortcut—I can be back at Centurion Aetius' side, overlooking the valley in no time."

I grinned and clapped his shoulder. "Good man. All right—go get some sleep and once you're refreshed come back to my tent. I'll have a message for Aetius waiting for you—but understand, you'll not be going alone this time, too much is at stake."

He looked disappointed, unhappy perhaps that I did not fully trust his abilities but knew better than to question my order. He nodded, turned and walked away in search of his bunk.

I took a deep, mind-settling breath of the smoke-tainted air then glanced at my two silent companions.

"Women," Rufinius murmured, wiggling his thick black eyebrows.

"Motivation," Felix countered softly, his full lips drawing back into a leering grin.

"Nap," I replied flatly, startling them both, and with that I stepped back into the tent, intent on catching at least an hour or two of shuteye before I was called upon to officiate over the ritual sacrifice.

PART TWO: HOSTES HOSTIUM

— V —

It was hot, with every indication that it was going to get much, *much* hotter. The suns had yet to show their faces above the blood-tinged distant mountains but I already felt their fiery breath on my skin—not the best weather to fight a battle while wearing armor, even if that armor was Tuatha armor.

The desert before us quivered; illusionary pools of quicksilver danced and slithered over its ocher sands, giving false life, the appealing likeness of shimmering water to the otherwise barren and bone-dry flats.

Felix, who was standing beside me, squatted and scooped up a handful of the powdery grit then rose and let it sift through his fingers and the ocher dust wafted to our right, away from the sunrise as if wanting to make good its escape. But once the suns rose and the desert heated up, the wind would shift—in our favor, I hoped.

Far to the south pillars of dust were boiling up into the pre-dawn sky only to blow westwards, also away from the coming sunrise: the enemy was approaching, slowly, en mass and on foot—no horses, not even draft animals, just as Aetius had reported—our scouts had told us that lagging behind the main force was the imprudently spread out and rambling baggage train of their followers who labored in the predawn warmth, pulling hand carts and herding uncooperative, exhausted and if they were smart, *very frightened* children. If they kept up this rate of speed the leading line would be almost within artillery-range soon after the suns had fully cleared the far peaks.

I expected to be nervous, tense. I had been, during the late hours of the night, but once I'd given the order to armor up, and Felix and I had saddled up, the nerves calmed and the muscles relaxed. It was all over but the fighting now, and oh, yes, the dying.

We'd sacrificed a pure white bull brought specifically for the purpose at sunset the previous evening and collected its blood for a libation to appease the gods of Latruncŭli, just in case there were any lurking about, watching to see which side showed them proper deference. I've never been a pious man as I think I've mentioned, but I was damned if I was going risk any local deity's petty ire, not to mention our own gods' indignation at this point, not with so much riding on divine favor—and speaking of gods, our self-appointed soldier-priest, Gratian, had even gone so far as to perform the rite of *evocatio,* in hopes of enticing the Faoimhuirians' gods into switching sides, strongly suggesting it wasn't too late and if they did, we wouldn't hold their past loyalties against them, not at all, we would in fact welcome them with open arms...

...of course if I was right about the Tuatha being gods, or at least semi-divine, then logically the same would hold true for the Faoimhuirians, no? And if this were true, what incentive would they have to ally themselves with us? Besides, if I was right about what was really going on here, the Faoimhuirians were long gone. But why spoil an extremely well executed *evocatio* that gave everyone else a last-minute morale boost?

The bull's blood, mixed with a special wine also brought for this use alone was poured over the improvised altar the troops had erected in the center of the camp the very first day. It was the sort that always sprung up in temporary Roman encampments, attention heaped on it every bit as fickle as the camp was impermanent.

This one was no exception: it had quickly become festooned with private offerings: small handfuls of grain, pieces of hardtack and dried fruit mostly, reserved from each man's rations, along with thin strips of crimson undertunic, covered in scribbled prayers for divine protection—and, I must note, one extremely thread-bare sock with a note politely requesting a replacement—anchored with pebbles to flutter like ribbons in the breeze, taking their messages skyward.

The libation complete, Gratian then cast the ox's entrails onto the clean sand that had been spread about the base of altar and studied the pattern—yes, his chosen specialty as a priest was a 'gut-gazer'—looking for signs of good or ill. After several tense minutes, he straightened up and declared to the assembled troops that the gods indeed favored us, his deep, booming voice rolling over the deathly still ranks and echoing off the surrounding circuit wall as if the gods themselves answered. That done, the ox itself was parted up, the entrails gathered up and dusted off and every edible bit was then roasted over the cook fires, providing satisfying, if not filling meal for everyone—Gratian heartily agreed as he helped himself to a piece that the gods couldn't possibly begrudge us this.

One can hope.

And later, shortly after darkness fell a brilliant shooting star hissed and crackled overhead, fully, albeit briefly illuminating the camp as well as the surrounding desert in its flickering icy glow, only to disappear behind the very mountains that had shielded the enemy—a fiery javelin hurled at our foes by unseen fingers.

Its sibilant passing startled everyone, waking men from their uneasy sleep, drawing everyone from their tents at the strange fizzling noises, frightening horses, goats and oxen and setting the dogs to frantic barking—everyone at first fearing an artillery attack—but alarm quickly turned to absolute stunned awe once everyone realized this was no attack, just a spectacular display of celestial fireworks. Even Gratian followed its blazing path with a decidedly contented, bordering on smug grin.

A good omen then. In fact a *very* good omen I decided, flung earthward by the hand of Mars himself. Or perhaps the gods of Latrunculi were so pleased with our offerings they in turn were offering to light our way to the enemy's very heart? The Greeks had mentioned such in their writings after all, so it wasn't a totally novel concept.

Bassaeus and Lusius, the soldier I'd tasked with accompanying Bassaeus, had accompanied Aper and half the cavalry, briefly sharing the backs of two horses as the group silently rode down the backside of the hillock, hoof-beats muffled by goatskin boots, and, gods' favor to us, not even a gentle night breeze to stir up a dust trail as they came around the hillock and out onto the desert proper.

The horsemen had been in the process of mounting up when the shooting star flew overhead, and had been every bit as terrified as their mounts, but once assured its passing was a good sign, not a portent of disaster, and calming their nervous horses, they began laughing, teasing and elbowing each other as to who among them had been most afraid.

At Marcus' whistled signal, they then headed out of our camp two abreast, Aper and Pictor in the lead, each man saluting as he passed me, passed Felix and Marcus and Rufinius as we stood at the open gateway to see them off.

Once the last of the column cleared the gate and started down the backside of the hilltop, the doors were closed and barred and I, along with Felix, Rufinius and Marcus then hurriedly scrambled up the nearest ladder to watch their progress.

The horsemen stopped some distance from the hillock, and from my vantage point on the southernmost firing platform I watched as Bassaeus and Lusius slipped from the backs of the horses, waved their farewells to their mounted companions, then together took off at a leisurely, but easily sustainable lope, heading for the riverbed's nearest safe crossing. The knot of riders remained where they were for a few minutes, a veritable serpents' nest of restless horses and men, armor well hidden under cloaks of ocher-stained canvas.

Once Bassaeus and Lusius reached the far bank, an upraised hand signal from Aper sent the riders off at a leisurely canter, and once they'd dispersed and fanned out, I was hard pressed to spot them, even with the star-glow. One hundred horsemen, each no more than a moving shadow-speck, were quickly lost as they disappeared into the tangled skein of dry washes and meandering stream channels to the south.

Ocelus, our resident master of hounds, along with Hardalio and another of Tistriya's former Kellesuf, Marius, had earlier vanished into the hinter hills, taking remaining dogs with them, to warn Duccius of the dramatic change of plans—and with the equally startling news from Aetius. They and the dogs also carried packs stuffed tight with medicines, dried meat and grain to add to the already well provisioned caches dotted about the high mountains, along with as many goats as they could safely manage—sixty or so in all, a lifeline for survivors, for Duccius and his men if the worst befell the rest of us.

Then it came time for us to move out, a slow, deliberate march down the backside of the hillock, myself and Felix leading and again in total silence—not quite twelve hundred men, two horses and our battery of ballistas and onagers, the engines' wheels wrapped in leather and their axles generously greased… all moving with barely a whisper of noise.

Left behind on the hillock were men enough to crew the firing platforms, Cleander and his fellow physicians and of course Marcus and the rest of the horsemen.

The oxen had been boxed up near the gate, held in deliberately close quarters. If the enemy somehow managed to get past us, past the cavalry, past the scorpios, those left behind were to toss lit torches into the enclosure then throw open the gates and let the panicked animals loose, to pour out the only escape route and with luck trample or gore anyone in their path as Cleander and the others used the chaotic diversion to set fire to the rest of the camp, leaving nothing behind the enemy could use then make their escape to the mountains and meet up with Duccius. The remaining goats, the cats, hawks and chickens would be set free and by necessity, on their own. I didn't give the chickens much of a chance, especially with hawks and cats on the loose. The goats… well, goats usually find a way to cope.

Cleander had my order that if this dire event indeed came to pass, he was to take command then head for the grasslands. Aetius had been sent a matching order via Bassaeus and Lusius: if the legion was destroyed, he was to take his men to safety and regroup with Cleander and Duccius. What they did after that I'd left up to them; I trusted Cleander's temperament would be a good counterweight to Aetius' and Duccius' and between the three they'd do what they needed to do to keep the others alive until the Tuatha returned… or even if they didn't.

And now we were here, at the appointed spot, waiting for the suns to rise, waiting for the enemy to engage us. Waiting to kill and be killed.

Wushah and Felix's mount, Tuzun, stood on either side of us, nervously tossing their massive heads and snorting; they knew what we were about and were eager to get on with the business of war. And behind us: row upon row of soldiers, for maximum effect two hundred and forty columns stretched across the desert, each column five men deep or thereabouts—a bit of visual trickery on my part as the quivering and shifting air would double, perhaps triple our true numbers—and lined up in perfect order, pairs of pila held erect, loosely encircled by fingers, upright shields resting against armored bodies, eyes staring straight ahead with the fixed concentration only Kellesuf could master.

The columns were so perfectly still our feet stirred up no dust, providing no warning to the enemy of our position, our true numbers and the eerie gleam of our armor lost within the shimmer of the dawning air and hidden behind shields. Even the war engines, with their coating of ocher dust had taken on the look of the surrounding desert at any distance, utterly unremarkable to the casual or untrained observer.

The advantage we held was only transitory. In a matter of minutes, as Romulus cleared the crags, the wind would shift and the approaching enemy would suddenly find themselves facing a standing army that would appear to have materialized out of thin air, its armor ablaze in the dazzling, blood-red sunrise—a suitably unnerving sight. And if things went as planned, this would be only the first of many unpleasant surprises the day held for the Faoimhuirians.

I handed Wushah's reins to Felix, made sure my damned helmet was properly seated and secured then I turned to my troops and as I walked the foremost line, I nodded and smiled, murmuring words of encouragement to my centurions, reassurance to the troops—but for whose benefit? The stares that met mine were calm and confident without being cocky. There were a few nervous smiles and furtive glances to be sure. Kellesuf they were, but they were also men, men who knew as well as any that they might not survive the day, or even the hour. But they were sure of their training, fully trusting the rigid discipline I'd pounded into them to hold them in good stead: each and every man knew his job, knew what was expected of him and what to expect of his fellows—what to expect from me.

I was immensely proud of all of them, of what they'd accomplished... and yes, what *I'd* accomplished. Together we'd succeeded in forging and fielding a force as skilled, as disciplined as any Roman legion. What it lacked in numbers, it more than made up for in the sort of cohesiveness only Kellesuf with their largely shared mind-set could attain, much less and perhaps even more importantly, *sustain.*

First Legion Spartoí, a suitable name indeed.

I lifted my gaze to the standards, then stared down the perfect leading line of rectangular, curve-bodied scutums bearing the legion's emblem, a rampant, gilded dragon surrounded by a ring dragon's teeth—Lady Ainiaan's fancy—along with our legion's motto and private joke, *Ad idem,* of the same mind, and all on a deep scarlet background. Lady Ainiaan's hand was just a evident in the design of the legion's standard held aloft by our burly and properly intimidating standard-bearer, the appropriately named Tullius Maximus: not an eagle, in recognition that this was not an officially recognized Roman legion, but another gilded dragon—and not just any dragon but a *wyvern,* she corrected me on several occasions— wings spread, talons gripping the standard's crossbar and its scaly tail coiling down the pole as if to keep it steadied and aloft on its perch.

And strategically scattered among the ranks were more dragons: gilt-headed pennants with toothy mouths agape to grab the wind and fill their colorful fabric bellies—yes, another of Lady Ainiaan's fancies. She adamantly claimed the Roman cavalry used such; I for one had never seen the like, but even I had to admit they made a splendid and yes, intimidating display once unleashed. For now their long tails were held captive against their staffs, their handlers awaiting the signal to release the dragons to snap and snarl at the enemy, their bodies writhing above the heads of my troops like hundreds and hundreds of schooling eels. Yes, as I already mentioned, these dragon pennants were supposedly cavalry accessories, but this was *my* legion, dragons were *our* mascots and as legate *I* could do what I damn well wanted, so for us they were infantry embellishments; besides, pointing out where our horsemen were hiding, using colorful wind-socks to mark the exact spots would have been rather counterproductive. The cavalry in fact had their own pennants—attached to the very pointy ends of their lances.

I made eye contact with Rufinius; he tapped his forefinger on the brow guard of his centurion's helmet and smiled, his black eyes sparkling. There was nothing to say beyond that all too familiar gesture, that all too familiar look: *Good luck and may the gods favor you.*

I knew this man, knew him better than he knew himself—*far better.* But no matter what I did, not matter how much time I spent with him, how much time I spent with all of my men, there remained this strange disconnect, as if at times I was seeing double: in this case the real Rufinius—the long-dead friend—and his very much alive twin.

I realized I'd never fully get used to it and maybe that was all for the best.

Maybe.

I smiled and returned the gesture. *You too, my good friend. May the gods favor us all.*

As I pivoted on my heel, I happened to catch the blue-eyed gaze of Gnaius Flavius, who was standing just behind Rufinius and holding one of the dragon pennants captive. He and Carus were two of our youngest members—each no more than sixteen. His eyes held an extraordinarily serene gaze, especially on someone of his age and considering what we were facing, but then again, this was what he'd trained for, what they'd all been trained for—why they'd been turned into Kellesuf, only to be turned into someone new and yet not.

I acknowledged him with a dip of my head, then I made the return trip in silence, my eyes not on my men this time, but on the enemy, on the thick cloud of dust that seemed to cover half the desert, like a gathering thunderstorm, unnerving in itself.

I stopped again beside Felix, dug into a small pouch on my belt, withdrew two gold bells and tied them to Wushah's brindle, just below his ears as Felix repeated the ritual with Tuzun. It was a technique Aper had been taught by one of Taskim's men, a practice all of our warhorses had been habituated to. Horses in battle often panicked at the terrible and sudden sounds, the screams of man and horse alike, but the bells were a constant, comforting presence.

I'd heard of the practice of course, had, in fact seen with my own eyes—and heard with my own years—as the use of such bells by Scythians, Parthians and even Egyptians, for cavalry and chariots was common. I'd never been entirely convinced of the underlying theory, but was willing to go along with it. I figured the worst that could happen is that I'd have musical accompaniment while being trampled to death by my own damned panicking mount.

I no sooner secured the second bell than Wushah shook his massive bronze head as if to test them before battle; satisfied, he snorted, champed at his bit and rolled his white-rimmed eye towards me, as if to say, 'What are you waiting for, fool? Let's get on with this!'

I patted his muscular neck, gathered up his reins and then at my nod Felix stepped close and cupped his hands for my knee. I reached up, grabbed the near front and rear pommels, placed my left knee in his hands and in one fluid movement he heaved me up and onto the saddle.

Months before we'd left Earth Marcus had convinced me to adopt a proper Roman saddle and it didn't take long for me to recognize the less than obvious virtues of this saddle over the more enclosed Tuatha model: it was far better for fighting as it gave the rider much better maneuverability, it was less likely to entrap a man if his horse was struck down in battle—which even I knew wasn't a rare event—and while as minimal as minimal can be, the saddle was far more comfortable for both man and mount, especially during a long ride. Its only drawback: no stirrups.

Marcus, when I questioned this, replied snootily that a real horseman didn't need stirrups, that good balance and a feel for the horse under you was enough and as proof offered up the Parthians, Scythians and even my own people as examples. Stirrups, as far as he was concerned, were for rank amateurs. Of course he also had a tendency to refer to the Tuatha saddles as men's cradles—more often than not when Rasaben was within earshot.

So, after a moment of getting my thighs and butt properly wedged against the pommels, I settled, secure, as Wushah tossed his head and whickered, pleased to feel my weight on his back.

Felix then hurriedly circled Tuzun and followed suit—without the aid of a heave up I might add, a skill I'd never mastered. I'd like to blame it on my bad leg and arm, but in truth I just didn't have the grace... or the height. Maybe it if had been Lady Ainiaan's roly-poly pony, Mugwort, rather than Wushah I might have managed. Maybe. I'm not saying for certain.

From behind us came the faint, corresponding rustle of shields being lifted from their rest and balanced on arms, the soft click as fingers tightened around pairs of pila shafts, and the low, ominous groan of rope as the ballistas and onagers—the onagers loaded with our secret weapon—were readied. These all too familiar and portentous sounds, while barely audible, still sent my heart thumping, just as they always had.

At my signal the engines were then rolled slowly, carefully and silently forward, well beyond the front line of soldiers to limit the risk of injury to the troops behind them, only to stop as they came abreast of our warhorses and the already established line of scorpios.

The onagers were to be the first to deliver an uncompromising message to the Faoimhuirians, a barrage of incendiary missiles, followed by a simultaneous volley of bolts from the ballistarii and arrows from the scorpios and sagitarii, a shocking assault that should take out a goodly number of the first few lines of the enemy before they even knew what hit them and, I hoped, throw the rest into total panic.

I held up my hand, signaling total silence, absolute stillness. Tuzun and Wushah, taking their cue from the soldiers, held fast, muscles taut, ready for the slightest touch of the heel to charge, fearless and headlong at the enemy.

The suns were almost clear of the mountains and the wind had begun to shift and to my relief we still held the gods' favor as the wind started to blow towards the enemy. They'd have a moment or two to see us as the dust cleared and blood-red Romulus rose and caught our luminescent armor and the rippling, jewel-colored dragon pennants in its dazzling light and realize what was about to happen before all hell literally broke loose.

I glanced at Felix. Sensing my gaze, he looked at me and grinned, his handsome face framed by the polished cheek-pieces of his centurion's helmet and awash in the blood-red glow of dawn, the crimson, transverse plume stained an even more dazzling vermilion. I started to grin back; instead I was struck with the awful memory of the *same* steady look, the *same* eager grin, but on a different face, the face of the original Felix—*my* Felix, as we readied ourselves to meet the Iceni—of seeing that same face twisted in agony and awash in real blood—*his blood*—as he was hacked to pieces, of his desperate screams, the screams and agonized cries of the rest of my century, of me watching, utterly helpless as men I'd considered my closest friends—*my only friends*—die in the most hideous and excruciating ways.

A cold shiver ran down my spine—Wushah reacted, his withers quivering under the saddle, against my legs.

I risked a glance over my shoulder at the rows of men patiently, *willingly* standing behind me, then my eyes darted to the left and right, to the engine crews, all quietly, unquestioningly, awaiting my order... just as Felix and my century had done that fateful morning in that accursed bog. Each trusting his centurion's orders to lead him to glory, to victory—orders that in fact had cost every man his life and cost Rome and the

Ninth Legion a stunning, ignoble defeat; orders that cost me my freedom and perhaps even my sanity. Orders that had, unerringly, led me here, to this far, far distant world, to face an all too similar situation with a replacement army made up of replicated men and with the very real possibility of an all too similar and equally horrific ending for each of them.

I looked at Felix again, this time out of the corner of my eye, the cheek-piece of my helmet offering some concealment for my taut-lipped expression, my sudden and almost overwhelming sense of panic at the realization that I was about to see Felix die *again*, see Rufinius die *again*, see other men die *again*... and for what?

My guilt and grief over the death of the first Felix had come close to driving me to suicide, had in fact driven me into the dark of madness only to pulled back by Turan. If I survived, yet again, and Felix did not, what would I do? With any other survivors of this battle depending upon me, I couldn't sink fully into madness, couldn't escape into death by my own hand. I couldn't abandon them any more than I would have willingly abandoned the originals.

And if *this* Felix, *these* men died today, I would bear an even greater responsibility than I had with the originals, because I'd created them—my memories had fashioned them, granted not by choice, but for this purpose and this purpose only: men who would fight and die and do it because they knew nothing else. *Kellesuf.* Men of the void. Blood currency for the Tuatha in their ten thousand-year feud with the Faoimhuir.

Expendable.

I'd come to love this Felix as much as I'd loved the first—perhaps more so because I now knew the true value of such friendships as well as their ephemeral nature. I loved my men—each and every one, as much if not more than they loved me... and I was about to get us all killed.

I swallowed hard against the excruciatingly painful knot in my throat and fixed my slitted, watery gaze on the approaching column.

Did I really want to die for the Tuatha? Moreover, did I want my men to die? Did I want the Faoimhuirians to die for their masters?

The answer came swiftly enough. No. Absolutely not!

I squeezed my eyes shut, struggled with the terror, the gut-twisting dismay that I'd waited too late, that I'd committed my soldiers—committed the enemy—and there was simply no backing out now, no way out, but... one.

Me.

I opened my eyes to find that the flaming head of the blood-red Romulus had just appeared above the distant peaks, signal to let loose the dragon pennants which now free writhed and wriggled in the stiff, hot breeze and snapping loudly as if truly alive. And just as I'd hoped the sun's intense ruby light streamed through the clefts in the rugged peaks and over the desert, setting my Tuatha armor and the armor of my men ablaze—if the enemy was an approaching thunderstorm, we were a wildfire, a conflagration spread across the desert by the scorching dawn wind.

In the distance the advancing column lumbered to a halt as if not quite believing the appalling spectacle before them. Dust rose and cleared, blown away by the heaving breath of the rising suns, leaving our two armies to stare across the barren desert that separated us, no more than a palisade of quivering air and a moat of rippling mirages to keep us apart.

I took a deep breath and committed myself—and my men—again, by using an upraised hand signal only they knew and would honor: *hold position.*

Behind me I sensed the sudden shift, from the expected anxiety of men facing an approaching enemy, every muscle drawn taut, ready for the order to charge, to utter bewilderment as the order to stand fast rippled down the ranks. Shields were slowly lowered, again coming to rest on the earth; fingers reluctantly loosened their grip on pila.

Engine crews, equally baffled, carefully eased off the tension on the ropes, just enough.

Felix cleared his throat, hoping to draw my gaze, to see in my eyes what I'd seen, to understand what had prompted me to stop the preemptive and, presumably, devastating artillery attack that had the potential for ending the battle right there.

I swallowed against the tightness in my throat and turned to face him. "I beg your forgiveness, Primus-Pilus."

He stared back at me, even more puzzled, his intense blue eyes desperately searching mine, searching for understanding in my cryptic words.

"There will be no battle today. Not if I can stop it."

He blinked, blinked again. Beyond him, the crew of an onager overheard my remarks and fixed me with their equally stunned stares.

"If the Faoimhuir choose to kill me rather than listen to my offer of a truce, as they very well might, I ask you to seriously consider your options before committing yourself to what to do next. And since I might not have a chance later, I tell you now I'd prefer you not avenge me, but rather quit the field if these Faoimhuir allow it, return to the camp, gather up the others and go find those grasslands Duccius spotted. In other words, Felix, *choose to live.*

"This is not my fight or yours, neither is it theirs." I jerked my chin towards the silent line of the enemy then again fixed him with my gaze. "When I die, Felix, I want it to be for something I believe in, such as stopping this battle, and in doing so end the stranglehold these Faoimhuir and Tuatha have on us, not just for today, but *forever.* I don't want to die to satisfy the bloodlust of some Sidhe Lord, I certainly don't want you or anyone else to die for them—gods' favor *not* that."

He continued to stare at me with the same deeply wounded expression he'd worn the night we'd first met, when I told him then I wanted no part of the Tuatha's plans, no part of their war: 'But that's why Kellesuf exist, why I exist,' he'd said, and so it was.

He and the others were no longer Kellesuf, hadn't been for many, many months, but the old ways, the old fears still had their grip on them.

"Find another reason to exist, Felix. Help our men find another, far more fitting reason—like conquering this world."

He swallowed convulsively, then: "Permit me to accompany you, Legate. It's not fitting—"

"No," I replied softly, my voice equally strained. "Not this time, good friend. I'm sorry."

He blinked several times, briefly looked away, and then again met my gaze. Frantic. "Then take someone else—Rufinius, Baculus... Jotia, anyone—*I beg you!*"

I shook my head, my throat gone excruciatingly tight. If I was about to die, I wanted to be alone, suffer the consequences of my foolishness alone. I'd been the sole survivor of the Iceni ambush; it seemed only fair that I be the sole casualty of this battle, if that's what the gods willed, if that's what it took to finally end this madness.

I clicked my tongue and Wushah stepped forth, a steady walk at first, until I was well clear, then I gave him a little more of his head and he began to prance, accompanied by the bells' rhythmic jingling, flaxen tail held aloft, muscular neck arched, his massive, scale-armored body angled in such a way as to make the most of the spectacular sunrise—a horse in every way as vain as me. A fitting pairing, man and mount.

The enemy had drawn to a halt at the confluence of two of the larger dry streambeds. The ground was relatively flat—when water had flowed it had slowed here and spread out only to be swallowed up by the ever-thirsty desert.

It looked to be a good position to take a stand, but looks can be very deceiving and I was desert-born. I understood this land as if it was my own: they'd come to a halt in the absolute worst possible spot for them, the absolute best possible for us.

A tangled system of feeder streams, deep, narrow channels that carved their way through the sun-hardened sand along with their even deeper, dry wash kin were all around us. Together they created a maze of tortuous, soft-walled cuts in the earth that effectively boxed in the Faoimhuir. For them it was either forward or backward and backward, if done in haste, or, say, in a panicked retreat, meant backing over their own baggage train, which had bottled them up from behind.

So, effectively only one way: *forward…* right into the awaiting arms of my soldiers.

Perfect. Now, gods, if you will just bear with me just a little longer, I promise I'll make it worth your while…

I kept my eyes on the Faoimhuirian line as I approached, searching for someone who appeared to be in command among their ranks. No one immediately presented himself, which was worrisome in itself and the closer I got, the more worried I became.

This was no formal armed force drawn from the many worthy rivals of Rome, past *or* present: it looked nothing like what the Carthaginians in Hannibal's day had fielded with its disparate ranks of foreign mercenaries mixed in with regular troops; it wasn't even a decent copy of the Cheruscis and their bloodthirsty allies. Best of all, it bore absolutely no resemblance to Mithridates's imposing armies, with their characteristic weaponry. This was nothing more than a motley collection of men and arms—just as Bassaeus had described them: scraggly, haggard… beat up looking.

And scared. Very, *very* scared.

Some carried spears, others swords and from what I could see, no two weapons were quite the same and many looked to be very crudely made. None wore armor, at least none I could see. And while they clearly meant business, none seemed to really know quite what to do with the weapons they held.

The whole lot looked more like a rabble of villagers roused from their beds by the approach of marauding barbarians and desperately hoping a token display of force would be enough to keep their cattle and their grain stores safe—or, in this case, their women and children safe. If only for their sake we were marauding barbarians—they'd stand a better chance if we were, because if we engaged it was going to be a slaughter, a straightforward and wholesale slaughter and most of those who faced me were clearly coming to grips with that awful, stomach-wrenching truth.

Hostes hostium: the enemy. *Our* enemy.

We expected to meet a creditable foe but what I was now facing was in fact little more than a wretched mob.

I gave the silent line of bruised-looking men another careful study, searching for concealed bows, hidden war engines among their ragtag numbers, but saw none. Just in case, I drew Wushah up just out of accurate bow-range. He promptly swung his rump around, presenting his scale-armored side to the enemy, just so. A gentle tap with my heels and he instantly froze in place, only his flaxen tail and ears remained animated, haughtily flicking this way and that.

By the expressions on the Faoimhuirians' sweat-streaked and dusty faces, clearly none had ever seen a horse—perhaps had never even *heard* of a horse; I suspected they weren't exactly sure what we were: half man, half… who knows what? An armor-clad monster with two heads and a hyperactive tail?

It was tempting to dismount, show them I was every bit as human as they and at the same time send a clear signal that I'd come to parley but if I did, there was no way in hell I could get back up on Wushah's back without help and something told me no such help would be forthcoming, at least from the Faoimhuirians.

So, I remained safely ensconced atop Wushah, knees tucked tight against the front pommels, butt wedged up against the back, just in case someone did something really stupid and Wushah had a mind to make good our escape before things got really ugly and without bothering to ask a by-your-leave. I had a brief image of him wheeling around and bolting for safety and me, taken by surprise, tumbling backwards over his broad rump only to land on my ass, all done in front of the entire damned Faoimhuirian army—now that would be an impressive sight indeed, at least for a minute or so, until they set upon me and bashed me to death.

I pushed that lovely picture out of my mind and cleared my suddenly dry throat that had little to do with the damned dust and the heat.

"I've come to parley," I said in my best Centurion's—er, I mean *Legate's* Voice, one that would carry across the separating distance and a voice that had always held me in good stead when I wanted to get people's undivided attention. "Who speaks for you?"

I waited, my narrowed eyes scanning the silent line of very frightened men.

And waited.

And waited some more.

"Are you all mute?" I added irritably, my tone causing Wushah's ears to flick back and forth in a sign of annoyed solidarity while he champed on his bit. His four massive and feathered hooves, however, remained firmly planted on the ground. He knew his job, his part in this performance, damned if he didn't. "I know at least one of your number can understand me, so have the goat-thief show himself."

Nothing. They just continued to stare, slack-jawed, as if we were some bizarre apparition they just could not get their heads around. Most were clearly still fixed on figuring Wushah and me out. Were we one creature? Two?

Great. Just... great. I come parley and what do I find? I find a bunch of blithering idiots entranced by a damned bit of horseflesh and glitter.

On the upside, if they'd never seen a horse then most likely they'd never seen a donkey either, so little chance of them seeing any similarity between that humble creature and my helmeted self. Or maybe the amulet's curious translating abilities only reached so far? Maybe they hadn't reacted because they couldn't understand me? That would certainly put a crimp in my plans if true. Difficult to parley when you cannot easily understand each other. Difficult, but not entirely impossible.

Maybe they needed an inducement, shake them out of their stunned silence—like me turning my back on them and walking Wushah casually, snootily away?

Would they continue to just stand there, gaping like fools and do nothing?

Or would I be playing into their hands and the instant my back was turned they'd start firing arrows and lobbing spears at me?

Appearances aside, I was not about to trust my life to the estimation that they didn't know how to use the weapons they were holding. That too might be a ploy, hoping to lure me a little closer... just a little closer still... then *wham!* I'd be a good as dead and doubling for a hedgehog. Uh-uh. I'll pass. Thank you all the same.

I could, with a whispered command to Wushah, have him turn tail and bolt and he very well might outrun any arrows, but that wouldn't be particularly dignified. And having him back-step until we backed our way right back to beside Felix where I'd pretend my gambit at singular heroics had never happened was definitely a nonstarter.

I'd come here to stop a war which now seemed would be more like a massacre and damn it, I was going to at least have someone pay me the courtesy of listening to me, even if they refused to talk back. And I did appear to have a captive audience.

I took a deep, steadying breath. *Here goes.*

"The Tuatha lied to me, lied to my soldiers, just as your masters have lied to you. How do I know this? Look at you—you're no match for us. We were promised a *fair* fight—equal numbers with equal weaponry, may the best side win. But this is clearly not the case. You certainly outnumber us..."

That caused a minor stir among the ranks that faced me—which meant they *could* fully understand me. Most excellent.

"...but we're *far* better equipped and much, *much* better trained. If we engage, you will kill some of us, no doubt, but understand this: we *will* utterly destroy you—*all of you.* We're Romans—and we Romans are famous for our discipline, our tenacity, but above all else, we are *infamous* for our willingness, our ability to *kill* without hesitation or discrimination if ordered to do so. In battle it means *nothing* to my men to run their swords through another person, be it a man, woman *or child."*

I let that harsh truth put down roots in their minds before I continued, "Our stock and trade is war and have no doubt, we are very, *very* good at it. We have artillery..." I pointed to the line of gleaming armor far behind me, "...that can lob missiles that can reach you *here,* right where you stand, from *that* distance and spread fire among you, fire that will cling to your clothing, cling to your skin and burn all the way to the bone..."

That garnered a soft, collective and very uneasy gasp. So, they weren't *entirely* stupid, either. Good. Stupid enemies were far more impulsive than smart ones.

"...and I could have ordered my artillery to fire the instant you came into range, along with my archers..."

I saw the line heave back, like a retreating tide, as if by doing so they could put themselves just beyond reach of those deadly missiles and hail of arrows. So, not particularly heroic-minded enemies either—even better.

"...but there's simply no need for this, no need for anyone, on either side to die—I come in good faith, *alone,* to parley, to stop this madness here and now."

"We don't believe you," came an all too familiar lilting voice, followed by a commotion within the ranks. Faoimhuirians hastily stepped aside to allow an equally familiar looking man, wearing a grubby, belted tunic and tattered, bloodstained breeches, to roughly elbow and shove his way free from the rest.

I couldn't help but laugh out loud. *"You're* their commander, goat-thief? Gods protect you all if you are!"

"I'm no thief, Tuatha-filth!"

"Indeed? You mean the goat my men caught you fornicating was *yours?"*

There was dead silence for a heartbeat or two then one Faoimhuir, a short and square-faced man burst into startled laughter, others immediately joining in.

"I wasn't fornicating!" the goat-thief snarled, glancing over his shoulder at his companions, instantly silencing them, which only meant what I said next was heard by all:

"It certainly looked that way to my soldiers."

"Maybe because they're all a bunch of butt-fuckers just like you, Tuatha-filth, so you assume everyone else is, too!"

I looked suitably aghast. "Now what would leave you with that impression?"

"I didn't see a single woman in your camp—what am I supposed to think?"

"That unlike you, *we* don't drag *our* women and children into our wars?" My unruffled contempt must've gotten through because many within the line began to whisper furiously to each to other while fixing me with their sidelong, anxious gazes, so I decided to hammer home the point in hopes of escalating it to a full blown panic: "That *we* don't use them as shields or bargaining chips because *we're* civilized—"

"Civilized? You're nothing more than a bunch of bloodthirsty barbarians!"

I raised my brows in mock offense. "You don't happen to know a Sidhe Lord by the name of Rasaben, do you?"

That confused the goat-thief for a moment then he recovered and snarled, "You fight with swords and spears!"

Is there any other way? I looked past him, a little confused myself. "We're not the only ones, it would appear."

"Not by choice!" He spat on the ground.

I eyed the spot, watched the parched ground swallow the spittle whole then I lifted my gaze to again look at the rest of this roughscuff 'army' while doing my damnedest to look haughty, cultured and yes, incredibly handsome—the epitome of a dashing military commander. Fine, I didn't have to *try* looking incredibly handsome. I *was* incredibly handsome, damned if I wasn't—the glittering armor certainly didn't hurt; neither did the silvered helmet with its high arching plume and trailing tail of horsehair. I was, in a word, *magnificent*.

And let's not forget there were women about—hard to tell if any were nearby with everyone wearing baggy clothing and their heads shaved, but astride the equally resplendent Wushah I was clearly visible even to those towards the back, and if I couldn't sway these men by logic, then maybe I could sway some of the women, and yes, perhaps even a few men, with my looks, my seemingly supreme self-confidence. Not like it hadn't worked before: steady-nerved bluff with a healthy dash of masculine puff was a tactic not to be underestimated: men wanted to be led by officers like me; women just as eagerly wanted to bed men like me.

I lifted my gaze, swept the gaunt and dirty faces of the motley crowd and motioned expansively to myself. "I ask you good people, do I *look* uncivilized?"

That earned me some chuckles, a few more nervous grins—and *not* at my expense.

I smiled, my absolute best, most charming smile and saluted them in time-honored Roman fashion, right fist to armored chest—my wrist deliberately pressed hard against the snakestone to muffle my voice— followed by a dip of my helmeted head as I said in a softly muttered, mannerly Latin that wouldn't carry to anyone but the gods, assuming they were eavesdropping: *"Victurus te saluto."* He who is about to win salutes you—my private joke that was, in fact, no joke at all.

Their self-appointed speaker, annoyed that I no longer seemed to be paying him any attention took another step closer and cleared his throat.

I very reluctantly dropped my gaze and arched a disdainful brow, as if surprised to find him still standing there and replied in a clearly weary tone, *"Yes?"*

"I am Isem. I speak for our leader."

Now both brows shot up. "Why," I asked, truly incredulous—no faking here because I was truly incredulous, "when you're clearly so utterly unqualified for the job?"

That garnered outright laughter from within the ranks and another quick and angry backwards glance by Isem, but this time his pinched stare wasn't quite so effective in silencing the mob. He then swiveled his furious eyes back to me. "Did you come here hoping to frighten us with talk of your murderous habits, Tuatha-filth? Save your breath—we're not afraid of you, your weapons or," he briefly glared at Wushah then lifted his eyes again to me, "your alien machines!"

I patted Wushah on his arched neck as I stared down my nose at Isem. "You think Wushah here is a machine? A fancy wind-up toy perhaps? Wushah is a *horse*—a living, breathing animal, like the goat you were trying to—um, *steal.*" I tapped Wushah lightly with my heels as I gave his reins a sharp tug and he reared, an explosion of churning hooves and glimmering armor, whinnying his damned head off while I calmly kept my seat and my gaze fixed on Isem. It was a trick we'd spent hours practicing to perfection for just such a need—well, in truth I'd desperately wanted to impress Turan with my expert horsemanship and never got the chance—at the cost of my dignity on more than one occasion I might add, not to mention a very sore ass. Thankfully this wasn't one of those occasions.

Wushah came down with a resounding *thump!* that sent up a cloud of dust and another startled undulation down the already imperfect line of men.

Hah! I thought. Isem looked as if he'd soiled his tattered breeches; he'd certainly scurried back several steps.

"I don't want to frighten you." All right, actually, I did—I wanted to scare the crap out of these men and might have actually succeeded with Isem. I've found fear can be a very useful tool, hugely effective in winnowing the superfluous chaff of bluster and leaving only the essentials, like, say, life and death?

"Then why come?" Isem snarled, taking a step closer, trying to regain some of the figurative and physical ground he'd lost. "Why threaten us with your weapons, your... *horse.*"

"I wasn't threatening you." I patted Wushah's armored neck. "Wushah wasn't threatening you—"

Wushah took that moment to wuff his breath and stamp one massive, feathered hoof, as if to say, "Hold on there, not so fast," and Isem hastily backed up again.

"—we just wanted you to understand—"

"We understand *you* well enough, *Tuatha-filth.*"

I massaged the bridge of my nose with my fingertips, took a deep, steadying breath and exhaled, slowly. This was not exactly going to plan—so, time for a new plan. I gave Wushah a firm pat on the withers, then returned my hand to the sun-warmed and sweat-damp leather pommel and said wearily, "I'd really rather you stop calling me that. My name's—"

"Butt-fucking Tuatha-filth," Isem interrupted and turned to grin at his fellows. Others laughed, granted, a forced laughter, but still... damned annoying.

"Isem." I said it quietly, almost a whisper and he jerked his eyes back to me, startled by my tone; Wushah for his part began to fidget, shifting his massive weight from one hoof to another and tossing his head, the bells tinkling in response. This wasn't nervousness on his part. It was a deliberate contrivance; at my secret signal he was now sidestepping, bit-by-bit, away from the ragtag line of men that had begun to shift and break up; some had moved closer, in grudging, fearful curiosity or with malice in mind it was impossible to tell and I was not about to find out by having them suddenly rush us and drag me from the saddle.

I'd much rather draw them, each and every one, slowly, without them noticing, away from the baggage train. Put some space between the armed men—I'll not dignify this mob by calling them soldiers, they were a seriously frightened rabble, nothing more—and the noncombatants. That way if they rushed me, and I had time to get off a signal to launch the attack, the volleys of incendiary missiles and arrows would fall upon the men, obliterating their numbers, while leaving the women and children largely unscathed. I had no quarrel with them, at least not at the moment. Now this Isem was another matter altogether...

"Do you *want* to die Isem? I can oblige you." I lifted my gaze, briefly, to the others. "My men and I will happily oblige any and all of you who wish to die today. Or tomorrow. Or the next. Or the week after. But I have to ask, to what purpose? Your masters have abandoned you here, just as ours have abandoned us—"

"THAT'S A DAMNED LIE!"

Wushah turned his massive head towards Isem, and tonguing his bit, fixed him with his baleful, white-of-the-eye rimmed gaze as he continued his slight of hoof—*sidestep... sidestep... sidestep*—with the Faoimhuirians slowly following, like bewildered sheep.

Satisfied Isem got the point of etiquette driven home by Wushah's sharp stare and would allow me to finish this time, I continued but kept my voice soft, forcing the men to keep following, in order to hear me. "The Tuatha have abandoned us here because they're rightfully afraid of us, afraid of how powerful we've become—entirely my fault I must confess, due to my arrogance, my stupidity. I caused the Tuatha to fear us, fear *me*—I thought I was in control, thought I could control the Tuatha but they played me for the vain fool that I was."

Isem was now grinning, that same damned annoyingly smirking grin that had so rankled me back in my tent.

"And I *was* a fool, Isem. I freely admit it. *I'm not one now.*"

The grin faded, just a bit.

Then in a louder voice, one that would carry: "Your masters have left you here too, Isem, left all of you, as *bait* for the Si'aafu. We're *all* bait."

The grin almost disappeared.

"And the Si'aafu *are* coming. *Bet on it.*"

The grin vanished completely.

"I wouldn't even be surprised to learn that your masters have told the Si'aafu exactly where to look so they won't have to waste precious time searching, time I'm sure the Si'aafu would much prefer spending feasting, *savoring* their fortuity, one could say."

Isem immediately glanced skyward, as did a goodly number of the others, suddenly fearful of the unseen, the potential, the possible truth in my words. Men began to whisper worriedly to each other, eyes darting to me, to the sky, to Isem.

Good. Now I've got you all good and rattled…

Of course I had to stop myself from following suit and look to the heavens as well. Instead I used the Faoimhuirians' brief distraction to glance over my shoulder at my troops. They had to be wondering what the hell was taking so long. To them the matter of a parley, an offer of truce should boil down to a simple yes, please, or fuck, no. Kellesuf were not prone to long-winded debates on anything, not even on something this critical, fully Romanized Kellesuf even more so.

But these people *weren't* Kellesuf with all the good and yes, *bad* that came with being Kellesuf. I'd be well advised *never* to forget that.

I again looked past Isem, to the others, said, "I propose we stop all this dangerously foolish posturing and work together and maybe, just maybe survive this, perhaps even make this place a passable place to live out our lives—finally free of our masters' shackles, free to live our lives as *we* see fit, not as others demand." I dropped my gaze back to Isem, in the process drawing everyone else's gaze to the man as well. "Or we can do as your masters want, as *you* clearly want, Isem, and provide a diversion—not to mention a hearty meal for the Si'aafu—while *they* find a place to hide."

That set off an ugly mutter within the mob, instigated by the square-faced man.

Isem felt the mood shift and turning to them, yelled, *"SHUT THE FUCK UP!"*

I again swept the faces of haggard looking men who now stood clumped together, their earlier, pathetic attempt at a precise leading line having completely disintegrated into a milling, disorderly crowd, a crowd that was clearly beginning to think about what I'd said, put two and two together and not like the result.

Wushah continued to his sideways retreat, the maneuver lost in the restlessness of his shaggy hooves, in the dust he and hundreds of pairs of nervous, shuffling feet were kicking up.

"That's what this is all about," I continued, motioning expansively around me, "a *diversion*, so they can get themselves and *their* families to safety while *yours* feed the Si'aafu." I looked past Isem and scanned the grubby faces of the loosening mob. "Something to think on, *yes?*"

The ugly grumbling began to spread.

"And to show you I come in good faith, I'll tell you what I can offer you. I offer you a highly trained, highly disciplined fighting force—"

"For what?" Isem snorted with laughter. "To battle the Si'aafu? Using what, *your swords?* You have no idea, do you, you piece of shit, absolutely no concept whatsoever of what you're proposing to fight."

I smiled, a slow, arrogant smile as my eyes locked with his. "I'm not suggesting we could obliterate the Si'aafu—while I might be a barbarian in your eyes, Isem, a piece of shit, I'm *not* stupid—but we can certainly bloody their noses, make them realize they're going to have to work, and work damned *hard* for their suppers. My men could do that—would, on *my* order, do all within their power to *protect* your families even at the cost of their lives—you, Isem, on the other hand, could, and probably *would* not."

"And *why* would they do that?" Isem fired back. "Why would you order your soldiers to protect us?"

I honestly didn't remember suggesting I'd order my men to protect Isem at the possible cost of their own lives, but I figured saying that might be counterproductive at this delicate stage. "Because there are women and children involved?" I replied slowly, as if stating the patently obvious to an imbecile because in truth I was. "Because we're human and the Si'aafu are not?" I lifted my gaze, stared past him to the others, effectively dismissing him. "To the rest of you, I also offer engineers who can build homes to withstand the cold of winter, the heat of summer, dust storms, the rains and the snows that will surely come, men who can build bridges to span rivers and chasms, who can build more weapons to repel the Si'aafu and anyone else who comes looking for an easy meal, or perhaps slaves—I understand we humans are quite the item in the galactic slave trade?" I paused, saw more than a few heads nod in unhappy reply.

"My engineers can also build fortifications that can protect us from whatever animal life dwells on this planet, and if you think it's lifeless, *think again*—my men have come upon trails up in the mountains." I jabbed a finger at the crags to the east—a calculated slip for those smart enough to catch it*: I have more soldiers up there—where you just were, so I wouldn't suggest going back.* "Trails. Not some natural phenomena, but paths *made* by someone or something. Something or someone rather large, going by the width of the trails—" All right, a complete fabrication on my part, call it artistic license to drive home my point. "In other words, we're *not* alone here."

Unease rippled through the ranks, following the anger and leaving more frightened whispering and heated muttering in their combined wake.

"I offer highly skilled physicians who can treat your injuries, medicines for your ills and those of your women and children—"

That definitely garnered some interested, almost hopeful stares.

"—just ask Isem, who *thanked* my physicians by trying to strangle them. And in case any of you're wondering, his injuries were the result of him *attacking* us, not the other way around."

Hundreds of pairs of startled eyes swiveled towards him.

"Or did he lie to you about that? Did he paint a picture of a heroic escape from the clutches of bloodthirsty barbarians? *Hardly!*" I snorted. "We caught him with one of our goats—what he was doing with it is obviously up for debate—but when we tried to peaceably reclaim our property he attacked my men and brained one with a rock.

"My soldiers roughed him up a bit for that—I'd have done the same, considering the provocation. He then attacked my physicians who were trying to treat his injuries. And what did we bloodthirsty barbarians do in retaliation? We gave him food to fill his belly and a bed for the night, then we escorted him to the edge of the desert, made sure he was safely on his way…"

More angry murmurs and chary sidelong looks. Pieces were definitely starting to fall into place for these men and the picture taking shape was not a pleasant one… for Isem.

"…and oh yes, we also provided him enough water and provisions to make it back to you—"

"Only so I could pass along your message, Tuatha-filth! And I did! As you can see." He waved his hand about. "We're here, aren't we?"

I smiled. "And for that I thank you, *most kindly.*"

He blinked.

"I've grown very weary of you, Isem. I again ask to speak to your leader and if he's indisposed, I'll settle for anyone who will do me the simple courtesy of addressing me *by* name and not calling me names. A woman perhaps? Even a sensible child will do. Anyone but *you.*" I lifted my gaze and scanned the grubby faces, looking hopeful. "Any volunteers?"

I found myself searching for the square-faced man, the one who laughed at Isem but before I could spot him within the dust and the shifting the mob there was a sudden disturbance towards the back which slowly made its way towards me; men shuffled aside as a small knot of people pushed their way through the crowd. Finally an older man, barrel-chested, with sunburnt skin and tattoos on his chin like Isem stepped free of the others and started towards me. He had the purposeful stride of someone long used to carrying more weight on his now gaunt frame. Hungry, just like the rest. Beat up looking, just like the rest.

Wushah continued his slow sidestepping, drawing the man, and the others who trailed after him, further away from the baggage train, opening a small, almost imperceptible gap between them.

I watched the man, one hand resting easily on the leather pommel, the other loosely holding the reins.

I thought he was going to stop when he came abreast of Isem, but he kept coming while Wushah continued: *sidestep… sidestep… sidestep.*

The raggedy gap between the men and the baggage train widened a little more.

He kept coming. *Now* he was making me uneasy; he was definitely making Wushah anxious. The others followed and soon flowed around Isem, swallowing him up in the trailing rabble. I risked a quick glance around me to make sure none of them had circled around without me noticing. It was starting to feel like a trap, like a noose that was tightening, that instead of us encircling them, cutting them off from their baggage train, they were encircling me, cutting off escape.

I let go of the pommel and wrapped my fingers around the grip of my sword. Wushah had sensed my growing worry and his entire body was now tensed, ready at the slightest tap of my heels or tug on the reins to explode into a gallop.

The man abruptly stopped, motioned for the others to stop, glanced over his shoulder and murmured, "Remain here, you're making him nervous." He then started walking again towards me; thankfully the rest did his bidding and stayed where they were.

He again stopped, no more than ten feet from me—far, far too close for my comfort. "I am Borzu."

"I am honored to meet you, sire." I tipped my head, released the sword grip just long enough to tap my forefinger against the helmet's browridge before I resumed my hold on the weapon. "I am Arrius Marcus Niger, Legate of the First Legion Spartoí."

"I am very honored to meet you, too, Legate." His grubby, sunburnt and tattooed face stared up at me for some time, his bright blue eyes taking me in, taking in my armor and Wushah with another kind of hunger: intense fascination.

Then: "I am unarmed." He held out his arms. It was impossible to tell if he was telling the truth. As with the rest, he was wearing a loose fitting, belted tunic, baggy breeches and knee-high boots, any one of which could conceal a dagger.

"I *am*, sire."

"I assumed you were—a perfectly reasonable precaution on your part. May I approach?" He started to take a step.

"I'd rather you remain exactly where you are, sire. Apologies."

He stopped, smiled. "Of course." He gave Wushah another lingering stare. "I've heard of horses. Never seen one before." He met my gaze. "Of course I've heard of Romans too—read all about your empire—fascinating stuff, simply fascinating." He shook his head, adding, "Never, in my wildest dreams, did I ever think I'd actually *meet* a Roman though, and a Legate no less."

I suddenly realized I was sweating; I hadn't noticed before. My armor was heating up in the sun; I could feel rivulets of perspiration trickling down my back, my legs... my face, and I was instantly reminded of the less common name for armored cavalry, *clibanarii*—a far from flattering appellation derived from the Greek for a camp oven because a horseman could easily bake inside his armor on a hot day. Tuatha armor only made it a slower process, but the end was the same.

It was still early morning yet I was well on my way to medium-rare and it showed in the heated tone of my voice: "Are *you* in command, sire?"

"I am, or, should I say I was until very recently the *ceann feadhna* of the *Fihroon*," he said by way of explanation, not that that helped me one damned bit.

I squinted at him, wondering if he was trying to confound me. I was definitely in no mood to be confounded. "Sire, you have me at a disadvantage."

"Allow me to explain. A *ceann feadhna* is a rank similar to that of legate, although from what I've read, a legate is in command of far more men than I had under my command, and the *Fihroon* was our ship."

"A ship's *captain*."

"Yes." He nodded vigorously and smiled, with a hint of condescension—or maybe I was just that hot and bothered.

I gave my sweat-soaked neckerchief an annoyed tug. "A warship?" It seemed highly unlikely, but I decided to give him and his men the benefit of the doubt.

He shook his head. "A planetary survey ship."

When I only stared at him, he pointed upwards. "Space—she sailed between the stars, studied worlds like this one. And these are my crew and their families." He motioned expansively to the now deathly silent rabble behind him. "Not quite four thousand all told. A little shy of a full Roman legion."

"Most of whom are women and children," I replied coolly despite the heat. "*Not* soldiers."

"None of us are soldiers, Legate, as you've already surmised." He broke our uneasy staring match and gazed past me, to my troops. "Fifteen hundred I hear."

So, Isem had not come alone—there had been others, watching us, or perhaps one of my men had let that fact slip in the hopes of rattling Isem and there was simply no point at this point in denying it. "Yes."

"Horses? Besides this truly marvelous specimen I mean." He smiled warmly at Wushah; Wushah tossed his massive head and snorted in response, every bit as unmoved by his flattery as I was.

I clamped my lips shut, refusing to play into his hands by answering this time.

He stared up at me for a moment, sighed audibly and shook his head, then said, "I propose we go for a walk, Legate—to a point half way between your people and mine. Would you feel more comfortable if we did that?"

"If I wanted to be comfortable, sire, I'd have found some way not to be here. I'd have stayed at home, fathered sons who'd care for me when I was old and feeble and look forward to dying in my sleep in my own bed… *if* I wanted to be comfortable."

"Indeed," he chuckled, an unexpectedly easy, affable chuckle, then: "Would you be more at ease—let's put it that way. You've made an interesting proposal as well as some very serious accusations. I'd very much like to hear more, of both—"

POP!—

—followed by a fierce punch to my lower back and I was suddenly face down and scrambling for a grip of Wushah's armored neck.

"STOP!" I heard Borzu bellow. "STOP HIM! NO! YOU'RE GOING TO GET US ALL KIL—"

POP!—

—Wushah lurched sideways, stumbled and fell to his knees, almost toppling me from his back.

Blood. I saw blood as I tried to get myself balanced again but as Wushah fought to get back to his feet I found myself slipping from the saddle, unable to get purchase on leather suddenly gone slick beneath my knees.

I grabbed a pommel, somehow managed to land on my feet only to be knocked flat as Wushah fought wildly to get up, screaming as he tried to get his legs under him.

I scrambled back to my feet, staggered well away of him as I jerked my sword free of its scabbard then I wheeled around, looking for my unseen attacker within the swirling dust thrown up by Wushah's panicked struggles and the now scattering, shrieking mob.

I could feel blood running down my arm, down my leg. I pressed my right elbow against my side, clutching my belly with my hand, hoping to stanch the flow.

POP!

Something whizzed past my nose and startled I stumbled back several steps; I almost fell again as I turned towards the source of the sharp report, sword at the ready.

Faoimhuirians were now running in every direction, screeching in abject terror and as the curtain of dust briefly parted I saw why as my ears and eyes were drawn to the all too familiar chorus of bridle bells, barely audible within the screaming and wailing.

The maneuver Marcus and his cavalry had practiced and practiced and practiced under my gaze and yet I still didn't quite believe was possible was now unfolding before the Faoimhuirians in horrifying reality: Aper and his horsemen had been hiding in the dry washes since well before dawn, armored horses laying on their sides, their armored riders laying along their backs, one leg hooked over the saddle, an arm draped over the horse's neck and fingers around its muzzle to keep it calm, to keep the bells silent, both man and mount absolutely still and covered with ocher-stained canvas and looking like nothing more than drifts of sand within the deep, shadow-filled gullies—if anyone had bothered to look at all.

Felix must've ordered the attack and I just hadn't heard the blast from the buccinas amid all the high-pitched screaming and in response horses had lurched to their feet at their riders' signal and as the men swung up onto saddles, horses scrambled up the banks: one hundred armored horsemen, seemingly erupting out of the very earth itself—the legend of the Spartoí come fully to life but on four legs and at a full gallop no less, riders roaring, lance tips dropping and coming to bear on targets, horses thundering across the desert from the right and left with the clear intent of cutting off the men from their baggage train, from their families, a variation on the classic pincer movement.

It had been intended as a shock tactic, one employed only *after* my infantry had drawn the Faoimhuirians away from the baggage train and had engaged them. The cavalry was to then rush their unguarded flanks, go right for the women and children, the feint causing the enemy's lines to break, the front lines having little choice but to stand and fight, the rest retreating, intent on protecting their families as the horsemen then turned their attention and their lances on their true objectives: the armed men at the rear of the panicked formation.

Separate and slaughter, or, if you prefer, the more prosaic 'divide and conquer'—yes, yes, yes, I *realize* that phrase has been attributed to both Julius Caesar and Phillip of Macedon and you'll pardon my obvious favoritism if I say it was definitely Caesar. But no matter who said it, he was grossly misquoted and presumably by someone who felt the need to soothe any guilty consciences as divide and conquer comes across as far less... um, messy? But trust me, no one with the cold-blooded reputation of Caesar or Phillip for that matter is going to mince words. War *is* messy, damned if it isn't and whichever way you prefer the phrase it's a cliché, but still a damned good way of winning a battle—insuring maximum losses for the enemy, minimum for you. Always a good thing...

...except the two front lines *weren't* engaged. Which meant Felix must've seen something I hadn't, something that had caused him to radically adjust strategy. Meanwhile, Faoimhuirians were scattering with no thought as to direction as long as it was away from the pointy ends of the onrushing cavalry and kicking up a thick pall of dust in their haste to escape.

And now, as the wind briefly changed directions I *clearly* heard a chorus of warbling blasts from our buccinas over all the screaming and roaring and yelling and bells jingling and thundering of hooves, with their strident, blood-curdling call to arms, not just to the infantry, but the remaining cavalry still back on the hillock.

I glanced over my shoulder, fully expecting to see whirling missiles, trailing smoke and flames, streaking across the early morning sky, followed by an arcing swarm of arrows and bolts.

Instead I saw Felix now leading a full running charge, bellowing at the top of his lungs, replacing the roar of the buccinas, the soldiers behind him also screaming at the tops of their lungs, and far behind them, but catching up fast, the rest of the cavalry, presumably also screaming at the tops of their damned lungs.

I felt a sudden flush of startled rage. *They've started the gods' damned war without me!*

Then a second thought: I was on foot, wounded—how badly I had no idea—presumably presumed dead, *murdered* in fact, my extremely pissed off soldiers now hell bent on revenge, and oh yes, I was in the very midst of a very sensibly panicking enemy.

Oh, shit...! I instantly let go of the anger and briefly succumbed to a bit of panic myself. At any moment I expected to hear an ominous warble, warning of the oncoming barrage of hurled pila as my troops closed with the enemy, pausing only briefly to hurl the javelins, freeing their hands for close-in fighting with their shields and swords before they actually engaged. But the pila salvo also failed to materialize... perhaps for the same reason the artillery had failed to launch their deadly burning missiles: fear of killing our horsemen and their mounts in the dust-thick chaos.

I dropped to one knee, glanced around and realized with some small relief that I appeared to have been completely forgotten about in the sudden and dramatic turn of events, or, more to the point, I'd been lost in the clouds of dust kicked up by all the fleeing feet which was then quickly carried aloft by the hot dawn breeze.

Then another unexpected stroke of good luck: over the tumult I heard a bell tinkle, softly, which meant it had to be very close by. Following the familiar noise I turned and peered into the swirling murk and to my immense relief spotted Wushah standing not far from me. He had a bleeding wound in his shoulder and he was staring at me with a look of absolute reproach, as if to say, "Well, this is certainly a fine mess *you've* gotten us into," but he *was* standing, his weight on all four thick legs.

I clicked my tongue, motioned to him and as he started limping for me, I began staggering drunkenly towards him, clutching my sword. I grabbed his bridle, managed to snatch a trailing rein, and good thing too. People darted past us, shrieking, some so close they actually brushed Wushah or me and one actually ran smack into me, and if it hadn't been for Wushah's bulk I'd have been knocked down; it was hard enough to knock the breath from me as I was bashed into Wushah's armored withers without even so much as a 'pardon me' from said basher. Others were dragging or carrying screaming and wailing children: terrified and terrifying apparitions whipping past only to vanish in the swirling eddies of thick ocher dust.

Wushah started to back up, tugging the rein, rolling his eyes and whickering fearfully, not that I could blame him one damned bit. We were, to put it mildly, at the epicenter of all the deadly mayhem.

I stumbled after him, keeping a death grip on the rein—I couldn't remount, but I could use his huge body to protect me if only I kept him close. If he bolted I was in big trouble, a choice between letting go fending for myself in the midst of a massive, man-made dust devil that made it near impossible to tell friend from foe until too late, or holding on and being dragged and trampled under his hooves—to musical accompaniment. Let's not forget about that.

Out of the corner of my eye I caught a glimpse of onrushing armor before the thick, swirling dust again enveloped me: the infantry was closing fast. It was only a matter of minutes now before they'd start to hack their way through the churning mêlée, maintaining the discipline I'd taught them—discipline that would save their lives and cost the Faoimhuirians dearly.

Wushah was now barely more than a looming shape beside me. My eyes burned from the blowing grit, my vision blurring and my grip on the rein was slipping, lubricated by the blood that now coated my arm, my hand and dripped off my clenched fingers in appalling quantity.

A hand grabbed my left elbow to steady me.

I flinched from the unexpected touch and peered into the murk but couldn't recognize my divine-sent helper was the dust was so thick.

"Come, Legate... hurry," a hoarse male voice urged, barely audible over the din. *"We need to get the hell out of here!"*

"Then help me up," I rasped as I patted Wushah's blood-wet shoulder with my blood-and-grit sticky fingers. "Easy, *easy.*"

Wushah snorted loudly in reply and shivered, every bit as scared as I was, depending on me to get us out of this maelstrom of swords and spears, of murder-minded and terrified people.

It took me two tries, but I somehow managed to re-sheath my sword, then I grasped the pommels, said, "Up... I can't get up on my own—*dammit, man, give me a boost up—hurry!*"

I bent my left knee, felt hands grab it just as Wushah started shifting sideways, forcing me to hop on my right foot, but I kept my hold on the pommels—if I let go, I'd never manage it again. *"Hold still, dammit!"* I snarled and my helper froze.

"Not… not you! I'm talking to the damned horse! UP!" And up I went. I threw my leg over the saddle, somehow managed not to go toppling over the other side, even managed to get both knees tucked against the pommels. Then I felt someone scramble up behind me, and Wushah staggered sideways at the unexpected passenger on his rump.

"How the hell to you steer this thing?"

I whipped my head around. I'd assumed my rescuer was one of my men, but it was Borzu seated behind me, his body pressed to mine, one arm now firmly wrapped around my blood-soaked waist.

"Get… get the fuck off!" I tried to give him the elbow.

He tightened his hold to the point I thought he was trying to squeeze the life out of me. At the very least he was squeezing the air out of me.

"I'm trying to save you, don't you see?"

I felt like telling him I couldn't see at all. I could, but what I could see was really nothing more than a blur of rapidly moving shapes. *"Off…!"* I grunted as I began to wobble in the saddle, my knees losing their grip on the blood-slippery leather.

"You're an idiot!" he snarled in my ear.

"Been told that before…"

"I can see why! Tell me how to control this horse of yours or we're all going to die!"

I couldn't speak for Borzu or Wushah, but I *knew* I was definitely about to die no matter what—I was losing blood at an alarming rate and there was simply no hope of getting to Cleander and his life-saving fluids in time. The only question now was if the gods would kindly give me the time I needed to bleed to death—a few minutes, give or take—relatively painless, or so I've been told—of course not by someone who knew first hand—or would some other, far uglier and painful fate intervene? Being skewered on a passing cavalryman's lance was a definite possibility, or I could be thrown off a panicked Wushah and trampled… even chopped up by my own men, mistaking me for the enemy in the thick curtains of dust.

I figured what the hell, as my last act in this life I'd humor this Faoimhuirian, so I dutifully handed the single rein back to him. *"There you go. Enjoy."*

He snatched it, snarled, *"That can't be all of it!"*

"All I got." My vision went completely. I felt myself sagging forward, felt him jerk his arm tight around my waist, keeping me upright, heard him cursing as he yanked desperately at the single rein and Wushah seeing no other way but to walk in a circle until the imbecile on his rump realized we weren't getting anywhere.

More cursing. The rein went slack. Wushah dutifully stopped.

Most annoying of all, I hadn't died yet.

Borzu leaned close, rapped his knuckles sharply on my helmet. *"Hey! You still with me?"*

My reply was cut off by a thundering crash… followed instantly by furious yells and replying, horrified shrieks.

The infantry had arrived. Perfect damned timing.

"Order your men to stop!" he snarled in my ear.

I really wanted to say, 'The hell I will!' Instead I did the next best thing. *"You… first—"*

Another explosive epithet—a surprisingly accurate précis of my life—then: *"THIS IS BORZU—I ORDER YOU TO STOP! DAMN YOU, STOP!"*

Then only slightly quieter, a shout apparently for my ears only, *"Your turn!"*

"Have… have… yours stopped?" My speech was getting thick, even I could hear it—never a good sign. I was scant moments from losing consciousness, from dying—and I was damned if I was going to die for nothing, or, in this case worse than nothing: as the very cause of the very massacre I'd stupidly tried to prevent. The Fates do so enjoy irony and this was certainly a prime example of their biting wit, but I wasn't in the mood for irony. Damned if I was. I was pissed. *Damned* pissed.

"They can't until yours do—now order them to stop!"

I gave my head a sharp shake, found my vision had come back, briefly, saw what I wanted and leaned forward to grab it.

Borzu clearly thought I'd passed out and tried to stop me from falling.

"Lemmmmmego!" I slurred and after several wild flails of my arm, managed to snag Wushah's other dangling rein, almost losing my helmet in the process. I somehow managed to sit up, pushed my helmet back and off my face, shouted, *"Hang on!"* then with a hard jerk on the reins, I wheeled Wushah around to face what I had to assume by the blood-curdling screams and deafening clangs to be the heart of the fighting.

Taking as deep a breath as Borzu's near stranglehold on my waist would permit and bracing myself for what I knew was really, I mean *really* going to hurt and quite literally be the death of me, I kicked Wushah hard in the belly and as he took off at a mad gallop into the fray I screamed, *"THIS IS THE LEGATE—STOP THE GODS' DAMNED FIGHTING YOU FUCKING IDIOTS!"*

And you know, they did.

I opened my eyes. At first my surroundings were little more than a shifting blur of light and dark, but slowly, *ever* so slowly my vision cleared and I found that I was staring up at a fabric ceiling, so I watched in curious detachment as it rose and fell, rose and fell with each gentle puff of breeze and soon I found myself matching my breathing with it... in and out, up and down....

I had no idea where I was, no idea how I got here—all too familiar and frightening territory for me, which meant I wasn't sure I really wanted to know, to be honest. My experiences with the Tuatha, with Turan, had taught me to be careful what I asked for. Very, *very* careful. Maybe I was dreaming... maybe I was dead.

I was sure of one thing: I *really* had to pee.

I tried to ignore the urge, telling myself if I was dead, I shouldn't have to pee. I mean it goes to reason, right?

In... out, up... down. In... out...

Nope. I had to pee and that was that, so I wasn't dead—not that that truth was at all reassuring. There remained the niggling facts that I had no idea where I was—and that I really, I mean *really* had to pee. So rather than lay where I was and pee on myself I tried to sit up, got a sudden, stabbing pain in my side as a reward and inhaled sharply.

"So."

My startled eyes sought out the voice, an unfamiliar, lilting voice. *Close.*

I heard a scrape of a chair behind me, followed by approaching footfalls. I tensed as I watched as a person—a total stranger—walk into my limited view.

Shaved head; tattooed chin.

Faoimhuir! My mind reacted in instant recognition and horror and the shock shook loose other, fragmentary memories, of me riding to out parley, of talking to a line of haggard men, of Isem—

"Are you in pain?"

Another shock: despite a belted tunic, the Faoimhuir was *female*.

She placed her hands on her broad hips and stared down at me in pitiless appraisal. "I know you aren't deaf and I know you can speak and quite eloquently when it suits you, so how 'bout you answer me?"

I slowly wet my gummy lips with an equally gummy tongue and rasped, "Who are you?"

"If you please."

"If I please *what?*"

"Who are you, if you *please.*"

"You know who the hell I am!" I winced, squeezed my eyes shut, then, as the gripping pain eased off just a bit, I reopened them just as she heaved a sigh, as if I was a willful child.

"I meant try being more polite by asking *nicely.*"

I squinted at her, jaw muscles twitching. Realizing she wasn't going to budge until I did, I finally replied hoarsely, "Who are you, if you *please.*"

"See? How difficult was that." She grinned at my pinched scowl. "I'm your babysitter—"

"The hell!" I grabbed the blanket that covered me, tossed it aside and tried to sit up, which was a mistake. Actually, two mistakes. Two really, really *big* mistakes. The stabbing pain now felt like a red-hot iron had just been shoved into my side and I instantly lost all interest in sitting up and promptly fell back on the cot. And I was naked. *Of course.* So I was in agony and stark naked, unable to move, unable to retrieve the discarded blanket without making the blinding agony even worse, with a shave-headed, tattoo-chinned, tunic-belted Faoimhuirian woman staring down at me. *All* of me.

She suddenly chuckled. Yes. Chuckled—*at me!*

"What's so gods damned funny?" I hissed through clenched teeth.

"You."

I couldn't help but blink in surprise. I wasn't used to women laughing at me, especially when I was naked. Blink in astonishment, yes. Grin and lick their lips, definitely. But chuckle? No, absolutely not!

"Cleander said you were a handful. I didn't fully appreciate what he meant until now."

I wasn't sure if she was insulting me outright, or that was intended as a backhanded compliment. I decided on insult, going by her expression. Then I realized she'd said, 'Cleander,' and I had a horrible thought that maybe like me, he'd been captured, because if he had, then—

"Impressive."

I blinked, jerked my mind back to the moment and followed her still very amused gaze—*oh, shit!* "I have to pee."

"Oh." She sounded disappointed, as if there was another explanation she would have preferred, like—*oh, hell no!*

As if reading my thoughts, she snatched the blanket off the ground and without further ado—or any more chuckling, draped it over me—but not without, I must note, taking one more peek. "I'll see what I can find to… um, accommodate you." She started for the back of the tent.

"Where is he?" I resisted the temptation to lift my head and look around.

She stopped and turned back, eyebrows raised. "He?"

"Cleander—I demand to see him!"

She walked back to my bedside and again placing her hands on her hips, stared down at me. "You honestly believe you're in any position to demand anything? You're alive and largely in one piece, which is more than I can say for many of my fellow crewmen—I strongly suggest you show your gratitude by behaving yourself and not act the fool you claimed you weren't any longer, all right?"

I squinted up at her. She might have been pretty once, years and years ago. She wasn't now, with deep set, icy blue eyes and a hard and dirty face. The shaved head, now covered in dark brown fuzz, didn't soften her looks one bit and neither did the chin tattoos. Three vertical bars this time, rather than Isem's one, and topped by a horizontal bar.

"Who the hell are you?"

She crossed her arms and gave me that long-suffering look again. "What happened to your manners?"

"Name. Tell me your gods' damned name!"

She arched a brow.

I looked away, took a deep breath—or as deep as I dared with my side aflame. Then I looked back at her, eyes flashing but my voice when I spoke was as sweet as sweet could be: "May I please ask your name?"

"Much better. It's Maisoh…"

And here I'd have guessed nasty fucking bitch.

"…there. Happy now?"

"Faoimhuirian."

She shook her head. *"Adranii.* The Faoimhuir are our masters." She jerked her chin towards me. "Tuatha."

I thought she was going to say, 'Tuatha-filth', but she stopped at Tuatha. She *looked* like she wanted to say "Tuatha-filth' though, damned if she didn't.

I shook *my* head, prefect mimic of her gesture. "Roman—Tuatha *were* our masters."

"But *fighting* for the Tuatha."

"Brought here to fight for the Tuatha—just as you were brought here to fight for the Faoimhuir—"

"That *was* the plan… until *you* decided to play hero."

"I was trying to stop a gods' damned massacre!" I grimaced then managed to get a ragged gulp of air into me.

"So you were." She looked away then back at me. "Thirsty?" She didn't sound like she really cared one way or another.

I was, now that she mentioned it; my mouth and throat felt as if they were coated in dust, but I didn't want to say so. Hell if I wanted to be beholden to this… this *Ah-dran-hee,* or whatever the hell she called herself, in any way. Playing hero indeed! I'd show her!

My expression must've given me away as she shook her head and walked away, to the head of the bed; I followed her with my eyes as far as I could go, then I clenched my teeth and forced myself onto my side only to find her standing at the rear of… *my tent, with my folding table, my folding chairs!*

Worse than I'd imagined. Far, far worse. These Faoimhuir—'cuse me, *Adraniis* if you please—had clearly overrun our encampment, which meant—

"I strongly suggest you not move around—you'll risk reopening your wounds."

I fixed my horrified gaze on her to find her holding a decanter in one hand, a mug in the other. She sloshed some water into the mug, poured more on a grimy cloth she pulled from her equally grimy breeches pocket, set the decanter back on the table, then walked back to me as I *very* gingerly eased myself back onto my back while keeping my eyes on her.

She knelt, held out the wet cloth. "You're a damned mess, *hero.* Wipe your face."

Don't ask me why but I did as she asked and when I was done, I offered it back to her. It was even filthier than before. "You might take your own advice."

She snatched it out of my hand, offered me the mug, none too happily I might add, and at my very wary nod, brought it to my lips, said, "Water…" and as I took a sip, she added, "…with just a hint of poison."

Startled, I choked, coughed explosively. This of course shot another agonizing jolt through my body and I couldn't help but wet myself. I coughed again, peed again, coughed, peed… and finally, having emptied my bladder, finished up by gasping loudly for breath.

She stared down at me, holding the mug and cloth in one hand, the other hand on her hip until I'd gotten myself back under control then said, "Idiot."

I squinted up at her, up at this 'babysitter'.

"If I'd wanted you dead, I'd have simply smothered you while you slept."

Now that was just what I needed: to be reminded of just how helpless I was, how damned vulnerable—memories of my brutal treatment at the hands of Turan, shortly after my capture suddenly rushed to the fore—memories whose sting of humiliation and griping fear hadn't faded in the slightest over the months. I immediately fixed my slitted gaze on the gap in the tent flap as my mind tried desperately to reassemble events that had led to this all too horribly familiar situation.

I remembered riding out alone, remembered speaking to the shifting line of Faoim—'cuse me, *Adraniis*—remembered being hit hard by... *something*, finding myself on the ground in the midst of utter chaos. My last firm memory was of someone helping me remount Wushah—beyond that was a swirling murk every bit as opaque as the thick dust that had choked air of the battlefield and the now throbbing pain in my side made it difficult to push beyond that.

I gave up and set my mind loose in hopes once left to its own devices it would pick up more bits and pieces in its wanderings. I focused instead on my surroundings—what little I could see and did my best to ignore the unpleasant and spreading dampness of my bedding. The tent's lamp was unlit; the only illumination was coming from the dusty streamer of light pouring in through the slit in the flaps. It was impossible to tell if it was mid-morning or mid-afternoon by the ribbon of sky visible.

I heard the scrape of a chair and assumed—*hoped*—she'd returned to the table, leaving me alone now that she'd had her fun at my expense. Instead she placed the chair next to the cot, sat down and offered me the now empty mug. "Use this."

I looked at it, then her.

"Need help?"

Realizing she meant I was to urinate in the mug—and she was offering to 'help'—*gods!*—I looked away, muttered, "My coughing fit took care of it—thank you," which of course drew her curious gaze.

"Oh." She offered me the wet rag. "Here."

I very reluctantly accepted it, but I was wet enough already, thank you, so instead of doing as she expected, I roughly wiped my gritty, stinging eyes, my throat, then resting my hand on my bandaged wrapped torso, tightened my fingers into a fist around the rag and squeezed my eyes shut. *Felix. Rufinius. Aetius… Carus.* I desperately wanted to ask; I was just as afraid to learn that with the possible exception of Cleander, I was yet again the lone survivor of a self-made folly. And on top of this, *if* I asked about anyone, and *if* they were, by some miracle still alive, I'd put them at even greater risk. And this woman, this 'babysitter' was clearly not of a mind to volunteer any information, to ease my mind about anything.

She pressed her palm to my forehead; I flinched at her unexpected touch but kept my eyes tightly closed, kept my fingers clenched around the filthy rag.

She got the message and withdrew her hand, murmuring, "Fever's finally broken." Then: "Can I get you anything?"

My friends?

"Dry bedding perhaps?"

Her idea of humor? I gave my head a quick, sharp shake, muttered aloud, "Just leave me the hell alone… *please.*" There. Polite enough, bitch?

I heard her exhale, heard her rise and walk away. Through my closed lids I saw a brief flare of light—she'd done as I'd asked and then some by stepping outside.

I took a deep breath, settled myself to wait for whatever would come next. I could hear voices, muffled, a distance away. Some even fainter still and high pitched—*children?* And others hushed—those were right outside. My eyes snapped open just in time to watch a shadow pass along the canvas wall of the tent only to stop by the flap. More whispered voices—a stifled chuckle.

I braced myself, unsure if I should pretend that I'd fallen back asleep, or stare down whoever was standing outside, presumably about to enter.

Before I could make up my mind, the tent flap was jerked aside, a person entered, briefly silhouetted against the daylight; another followed. I struggled to get an elbow under me, all the while knowing if they meant me harm there was damn little I could do about it—

"Don't try to get up, Arri."

Felix…? I squinted into the glare as my heart began pounding against my ribs. "Felix?"

"Hear you're still making trouble—big surprise there, eh?" He stepped close, into the streamer of dusty light and grinned down at me. "Did you really piss your bed?"

I grabbed his hand, tightly, jerked him closer. *"Felix?"*

His grin vanished and he sank down onto the chair. I kept my stranglehold on his wrist, terrified this was a dream, a hallucination, that at any moment he'd shift through my fingers, like so much ocher dust.

He searched my frantic, glistening eyes for a moment then the smile slowly came back, dimples and all. "Yeah, it's *me*, you crazy bastard."

"You're alive...?"

"Did you think I was a ghost?" Then realizing his remark had hit a little too close to the mark he added, "You're the one who almost died, damn you."

"And by risking his life—almost losing his life, saved the rest of us," another voice added. I'd forgotten Felix had not come alone and I squinted at the person who still stood by the entrance.

He stepped closer, out of the glare and I blinked in surprise as I realized he was an Adranii. Even more surprising was that he looked familiar.

I turned back to Felix. He was wearing only his leather tunic, undertunic and breeches, no armor, but... he *was* armed, his sheathed gladius hanging from his baldric and his dagger from his belt. He noticed my furtive glance to the weapons then gave me an odd look. "What are you thinking?"

"I'm not sure what to think to be honest."

"Don't you remember?" he asked, definitely worried now.

"Remember?"

"What's the last thing you do remember, Legate?" That was the Adranii. He squatted beside Felix, eye level with me.

"Trying to shove someone—*you*," I amended because I suddenly realized why he looked so familiar, "the hell off my horse."

Borzu chuckled. "Almost succeeded, too."

"Ah," Felix replied, looking marginally less worried. "Cleander said you probably wouldn't remember much of what happened—you've been delirious, talking a lot, yelling in fact, fighting with us—"

Cleander was right—I had no memory of that... although I did have a dim memory of calling someone a fucking ugly bitch and to get her gods' damned hands off me—*Maisoh... perhaps?* It would explain a few things, such as her winning attitude.

"—suffice it to say, a lot's happened since you tried to push Captain Borzu off your horse."

At my anxious stare, he added, "Feel up to us filling in some details?"

I nodded, reluctantly released my hold on his wrist and grimacing, managed to get myself up onto both elbows.

Felix motioned for Borzu to bring the other chair as he grabbed my rolled up cloak off his cot and stuffed it under my shoulders and head. I settled back, thankful for the support; thankful too that neither had commented further on the large damp spot on the blanket.

Borzu set the chair down and sat next to Felix. Borzu, I noticed, *wasn't* armed. Felix caught that glance too and gave my bare shoulder a reassuring pat. "Everything's all right, Arri. Trust me."

I looked at him, at Borzu, then back at Felix, clearly unconvinced, still *very* wary. I really wanted to believe what I was seeing, but it seemed just too good to be true: Felix, alive and seemingly unharmed... maybe I was still delirious, maybe this was all a hallucination—

"It's over, Legate," Borzu began without preamble.

"Over?"

"The battle, the war, whatever you want to call it. Over before it really got started, thanks entirely to your timely, and I must say impressively bellowed order, we were able to get the sides to disengage before more people were killed. A goodly number of injuries, unfortunately, and some of them quite serious, but only eighty seven dead..."

"Eighty seven?"

Felix and Borzu nodded in unison.

"Eighty two men, four women, one child... and a horse," Felix added.

"Astonishing," Borzu said, "when you consider the utter mayhem and all the weapons flying about."

And it was astonishing. Truly.

"Three of the dead are yours, Legate, the rest mine, including the man who shot you."

"Shot...?" I pulled my eyes off Borzu, fixed them on Felix, but it was Borzu who answered,

"With a projectile." He dug into his breeches hip pocket, fished around for a moment then produced a small lumpy ball and held it out for me. "This was fired from a weapon using an explosive charge."

I raised my brows in begging interest.

"The loud popping sounds? That was the weapon discharging."

My mouth formed a silent 'O'. I remembered them, clear as day.

At his urging, I reluctantly took it from his broad palm.

"That's it—damned thing passed right through you, got tangled in your mail on the way out. A little to the left or a little higher and you wouldn't be here talking to us. You wouldn't be here, *period*. Centurion Aper cut another one out of your horse. A third killed one of my men— by accident I have to assume; a forth killed one of your horses."

I stared at the small metallic slug, and using my thumb, rolled it around in my palm.

"I had no idea anyone had a projectile weapon on them, Legate. Sakahar *did*. He was thrown in with the rest of us shortly before we were dropped here, said he was a life support tech. Kept to himself, didn't talk much, seemed all rather dazed by the situation—no reason to raise suspicions—many of my people had reacted similarly, but in light of his attempt on your life, using such a weapon and based on things my crew have since told me, I have a suspicion he wasn't one of us, meaning he *wasn't* Adranii, but rather a Faoimhuir plant—a Faoimhuirian himself."

"Your masters."

He nodded. "I've been discussing this with Centurion Felix here." He grasped Felix's shoulder. "We think it's very possible he was sent along to keep us from doing exactly what you *succeeded* in doing: meet, talk, and come to the realization that we're all in the same boat, so to speak."

"Isem?"

"A Faoimhuir plant?" Borzu shook his head and snorted, "No. Just a fool. A damned fool and a troublemaker—I'd been trying to get him transferred off my ship for over a cycle. It was his misfortune that he was still aboard—he'd been transferred off a number of ships at the request of the commanding officer, knew another such request for transfer would go very badly for him and his family, so he was fighting the request, which meant a final decision was delayed."

"Then why did you send him out to speak to me?"

He smiled, rather ruefully. "I thought it was a trap, we all did—we'd been warned about you, told you'd try to trick us, entrap us and once we dropped our guard we'd be massacred. Isem volunteered, said he'd dealt with you already, knew 'how to handle you'." He grinned at my slitted gaze. "I figured if I had to lose someone, sacrifice someone, better him than anyone else. But when it became clear to me, clear to all of us that you were, um, *deadly* serious, that you really had come to parley, that you didn't want to fight any more than we did, well… that's when I made my appearance." He motioned to my bandaged torso. "I'm truly sorry, Legate. The last thing I wanted, the last thing *any* of us wanted was bloodshed… largely because we knew if it came to that, you'd hack us to bits."

"Then why did you come in response to my… *invitation?*"

"What choice did we have? Isem told us you'd said if we didn't show up, you'd bottle us up in that valley and set it to the torch. That didn't seem like an idle threat in light of the fact that one of the two envoys I'd dispatched never returned and the other was found horribly mutilated—"

"What envoys?" I looked at Felix then back at Borzu, eyebrows raised. "We never received any envoys."

"Centurion Felix told me the same thing and I have no reason to doubt either one of you. Pity one of your horsemen lopped off Sakahar's head with his sword—not that he didn't richly deserve it, especially after shooting the man's horse out from under him—I suspect if he was still alive he could enlighten us as to our missing man's fate."

"I could order my men to search—"

"The two were dispatched as soon as we realized you'd arrived and when they failed to return we made our own search—as far as we dared, which is when we found Sallis." He winced, continued, "Isem was in fact part of the search party and decided on his own to stray a little further afield than he was supposed to—ignored the recall order—the damned fool, maybe hoped he could collect some valuable intelligence on you, improve his standing in my eyes... or Sakahar's—"

"And thought he'd grab our goat when he saw it."

"As I said, he's a damned fool." He exhaled forcefully, continued, "If Sakahar truly had no hand in the disappearance of Viri, which, in light of the brutal murder of Sallis seems unlikely, then some other tragedy has surely befallen him as this planet, as I'm sure you've come to realize, has little tolerance for mistakes and I'd be the last person to want to risk more lives searching for a body. When we found Sallis, we assumed they *had* made it to you and you'd kept Viri as a hostage while returning Sallis's body to us as a very clear message—but Centurion Felix has assured me this is not so, that neither man ever reached you.

"And you might like to know that with Sakahar dead, Isem has recanted his 'heroic tale of escape' as you put it, and told me the truth about what happened—the whole, *ugly* truth, which matches what you said, and what Centurion Felix told me about his 'visit'—he now claims Sakahar had threatened to kill his wife and children if he told the truth. Of course who knows if he's telling the truth about that as he's never seemed particularly concerned for their welfare, only his."

Borzu sighed, shook his head. "What you all must have thought of the rest of us, using Isem as a guide. Of course you can well imagine what we thought of you, after finding Sallis. He and Viri were well-liked, highly respected officers—seeing what was done to him... it sent my people into a frenzy of panic and rage and of course Sakahar was telling anyone who'd listen that this proved that there would be no negotiating with you—that the only way we could possibly win was to get the jump on you and pick a place to do battle where we'd hold the advantage. Clearly we failed at both."

I shrugged. I didn't know what else to do, or say for that matter. Each side had a lot of rethinking to do.

"Up for making an appearance?" Felix asked, clearly wanting to change the subject. "It's been five days and the men are getting anxious—"

"Five days…?"

He nodded, continued, "You were deemed stable enough to leave the medical wagons and be brought back here only this morning—word got out and as we carried you here on a litter all the men wanted to see you, touch you, help carry you, assuring themselves you were alive, but despite actually seeing you and being told you were doing well enough you could recuperate in your own tent, rumors continue that you might not make it.

"Cleander's done his best to cut that off by giving the men regular updates on your condition, but I tell you, it's not enough. They need to *see* you, Arri, prove to everyone you're on the mend. You looked like death when we got you back to camp—I actually thought you *had* died on the way." He shook his head, blew out his cheeks and roughly wiped his suddenly watery eyes with his fingers. "Damn, it was close—*too damned fucking close*. If it hadn't been for Maisoh you'd have bled to death for certain."

"Maisoh…" My eyes widened. "You mean—"

"The woman who was just here?" Borzu nodded. "Yes—luckily for you she'd served as a medic early in her career and still served in that capacity on the rare occasions when we were forced to make planetfall in order to complete our surveying. She volunteered to sit with you, freeing up—"

"You owe her your life, Arri," Felix interrupted, "she kept you alive, don't ask me how, until Cleander and the others arrived with a medical wagon—she didn't tell you?"

I squinted at him as if that was answer enough. So I *was* beholden to her—and in debt for something far more valuable than a damned sip of water. "She has the demeanor of a damned crocodile," I muttered. Then, sensing I didn't have a very sympathetic audience, even from Felix, I promptly changed the subject—to something I could reasonably be unreasonable about. "I distinctly remember giving you a direct order not to engage if I was killed."

"But you *weren't* killed," Felix countered. "And besides, I don't remember any such 'direct' order. I remember you telling me that that was your *preference*. A preference is *not* an order, certainly not a direct order. It's a... *preference*. When we heard the explosion, saw you fall, saw your horse go down..." He shook his head again, swallowed convulsively and fixed his glistening eyes on his knees. "After that some of the Adraniis appeared to be charging us—so I ordered the attack. I didn't realize until it was too late that they were actually just fleeing in panic." He lifted his head, took a deep, unsteady breath then fixed me with a surprisingly even gaze. "I take full responsibility, Legate."

I met his stare. I fully appreciated the agony behind his outwardly composed expression and tone; I recognized the second-guessing that was still going on and would go on, possibly for the rest of his life, the recriminations, the doubts—I was still questioning my role in the battle of the bog after all, and on a daily basis, despite knowing it was well past changing the outcome. And it was then that I realized what a terrible legacy I'd thoughtlessly bequeathed on my closest friend through my actions—just as Cerialis had callously bequeathed to me.

"We'll talk about it later," I replied tightly, to which he only nodded. This was a matter that required careful handling and not something I wished to discuss in front of strangers.

Borzu abruptly stood and grasped Felix's shoulder, drawing his pinched stare. "I agree with Centurion Felix—your men need to see you, Legate. So do mine. Knowing you're on the mend will put a lot of minds at ease, lessen the understandable friction between my people and your soldiers—there's a helluva lot of mistrust and some outright hatred on both sides, I'm sorry to say—it's going to take a lot of work on everyone's part to overcome our entrenched opinions of each other."

"You're certainly nothing like I expected a Faoimhuirian to be."

"Adranii," Borzu corrected with a smile. "And it can't be any worse than what we thought of you. And now we're all going to have to somehow get past all of that and work closely together, to, as you so eloquently said, make this planet a passable place to live if it turns out we have in fact all been marooned here. And not just that—I agree with you, the Si'aafu are coming, and sooner rather than later, I'd wager—possibly *very* soon."

I raised my brows.

"One of my spotters thought she saw a ship pass overhead six nights back. Unlikely it's Faoimhuir. Might be Jaglavak, come to watch—curious creatures the Jaglavak—"

"Watch what?"

"Watch us, watch you... watch the Si'aafu, see what all the fuss is about—but don't count on the Jaglavak to intervene if the Si'aafu make planetfall. So we'll need to be ready for them. And the first step is to assure everyone that you're going to be all right—no hard feelings and all that. Do you have any idea how fiercely loyal your men are to you?"

"Yes." I met Felix's intense stare. "Yes, I do."

"I can honestly say I've never seen the like—speaks volumes about Roman training."

"And the man who leads us," Felix said quietly, giving my badly bruised shoulder another cautious squeeze.

"Indeed, indeed." Borzu stepped back. "If we help you, Legate, can you get dressed?"

I nodded when in truth I wasn't at all sure I could even get up, much less dress... and there was that niggly issue of walking. So I decided to take one thing at a time.

On the upside I wouldn't be lying in my own piss, so I started to accept Felix's proffered hand then realized I was still clutching the small metal slug.

I looked up at Borzu. "What happened to this... projectile weapon?"

"I have it," Felix said, rose and turned for his own cot. He slipped his hand under his rolled up cloak, withdrew a rather ugly looking item, dull gray, with an offset grip attached to a long tube.

"It was found near Sakahar's body," Borzu added, eyeing the weapon as Felix resumed his seat, "while we were recovering the dead. In light of events, I felt it was probably best to hand it over to your people, but to avoid any potentially fatal mishaps, I made sure it was unloaded, first."

Felix offered it to me; I accepted it very gingerly, found myself surprised at just how ungainly, how unbalanced it was—and oddly feather-light—nothing like a perfectly balanced sword or well-crafted pilum where substance and solidity were welcome allies. "Unloaded?"

"Of more of those," he pointed to the slug cupped in my other palm. "The weapon can discharge unexpectedly if improperly handled—that's why I was so shocked to realize Sakahar had one in his possession—you can imagine what would happen if someone fired it inside a starship."

Felix and I both stared at him, eyebrows raised.

"Oh, yes, of course you wouldn't." Borzu smiled uneasily. "Suffice it to say it would be catastrophic if a projectile such as that ruptured the skin of the ship."

"And what about a Si'aafu?" I asked, dropping my gaze back to the strange weapon I still held in my open hand. Ships weren't my concern. Si'aafu were. "Could this kill a Si'aafu?"

"Undoubtedly," Borzu replied. "They do have a tough exoskeleton, but—"

"A what?" Felix interrupted.

"Plate armor-like skin. But yes, a projectile such as that," Borzu pointed to the slug, "could definitely penetrate it at relatively close range, just as it penetrated your armor."

"Then we'll need more of them, lots more," I said as I handed the weapon to Felix. "Have Rufinius study this with an eye to replicating it." I fixed my hard stare on Borzu. "We'll need the projectiles as well… and someone who knows how to use the weapon in order to teach my men."

"Legate," Borzu began and, I might add, with, I noticed, a slightly patronizing tone to his voice, "in all due respect, this weapon is a very complex mechanism, requiring very exacting standards and specialized tools, not to mention the right mix of alloys and the need for explosive chemicals to fire the projectiles."

"Captain," I replied in kind, and yes, I used the term captain because I couldn't recall the phrase he'd used, plus Felix had referred to him as captain, so… "in all due respect, you do not know Rufinius, and we cannot afford to dismiss any advantage, no matter how seemingly unfeasible it might be."

Borzu stared at me, clearly unconvinced, perhaps suspicious this was nothing more than a ploy to get my hands on the rest of the slugs, then with a nod, dug into another pocket and withdrew nine small metallic ovoids. "These are all of them."

I stared at them; they looked nothing like the one I held.

"It flattened and deformed as it passed through your armor and your body," Borzu explained.

I couldn't help but make a face at the thought. *"Oh."*

He handed the projectiles to Felix. "I'll ask Maisoh to assist your man Rufinius. Perhaps between the two of them they can come up with something."

I fixed him with a quizzical stare. "Why Maisoh?"

"She's the *Fihroon*'s chief engineer, or should I say she was, until we were brought here—didn't I mention that?"

I kept my startled bordering on appalled reaction to myself, having learned that my less than favorable opinion of this woman did not set well even with Felix. *But still... a woman engineer? Gods! What is civilization coming to? But, it might explain the male attire...*

Aloud I said in as bland a voice as possible, "Is she any good?" I could only imagine the look on Rufinius' face when he heard the news: Oh, we need you to work side by side with the Adraniis' chief engineer to fabricate this exotic weapon in mass and in a real hurry... and oh yes, by the way, their chief engineer is a woman dressed as a man and with the demeanor of a damned crocodile—*enjoy!*

Now, if it had been Nestor, I might have found some irony, perhaps even some glee in the pairing, because, like Nestor, this Maisoh had demonstrated a knack for expressing some small regret for her unprovoked nastiness without *precisely* apologizing, but Rufinius? Gods' favor... he'd done nothing to deserve this, and even if he had, he still didn't deserve this.

"She's *very* good."

"For a woman," I added helpfully, thinking he'd accidentally left that bit off.

Borzu gave me an odd look. "She's very good. *Period.*"

I glanced at Felix, hoping for support but he only stared back at me with the same strange expression, as if *I* was in the wrong for questioning the competence of a woman doing a man's job! Just dressing like one didn't mean you were one.

"Good," I grunted, deciding that was the safest thing to say as I struggled to sit up. Felix placed the weapon and the projectiles on his bed then slipped his hand behind me and gently boosted me the rest of the way.

I waited a moment, and once my head had stopped spinning, I slowly swung my legs over and dropped my feet to the floor. I hadn't puked, I hadn't passed out despite wanting to do so, so... so far so good.

I cautiously felt the bulky dressing that encased my torso, from armpits to hipbones—a noticeably damp dressing.

"Cleander's assured us you'll recover fully," Borzu said, "*if* you do what he tells you, that is, and I understand that might be a problem?"

I fixed my increasingly annoyed stare on Felix. "Why does everyone always believe Cleander?"

"Because he's telling the truth?"

I eyed him.

He shrugged, knelt and slipped my right foot into a sandal, then the left. He quickly laced them, rose, then he and Borzu offered me their hands, which I took, and with their help, I slowly, carefully and trying not to groan or grimace, rose only to stand there, wobbling.

"*Ooooohhh... crap,*" I mumbled and squeezed my eyes shut.

Felix and Borzu each immediately latched onto an elbow, held me steady until the almost overwhelming urge to pass out... well, passed.

Satisfied I wasn't about to fall flat on my face, Felix let go and grabbed the filthy rag from the bed and gave my lower half a quick and welcome rub down, then he tossed the rag aside, snatched up my bloody and tattered undertunic and helped me get it over my head. Next came the leather tunic, projectile holes, back and front, bloodstains and all. I toyed with the one in the front, stuck two of my fingers into it and whispered thinly, "Big damned hole."

"Yeah," Felix replied. "Got one in the back, too." He poked his finger through it, just in case I had any doubt. "But smaller."

As if that observation offered some comfort. Although it did raise a question: why would the hole in the front be bigger than the hole in the back? I looked at Borzu, then down at my tunic. "Didn't hurt that much at the time—for such a damned big hole." And it was true. I'd been stabbed on countless occasions, with swords, knives and spears. And each time it hurt like fucking hell. Being 'shot' felt more akin to being punched, *hard*, or kicked by a horse—again, I speak from experience—followed by a brief but intense burning sensation.

"Well," Borzu replied, "I guess that's something to be thankful for."

I nodded then looked at Felix and by his disdainful stare at the ruined tunic, I thought he was going to tell me this 'appearance' demanded full kit—armor to conceal the damage at the very least, and probably the damned helmet as well.

"This'll have to do," he said, much to my relief. "Carus hasn't finished repairing your mail. Besides, the troops just want to see you, Arri, make sure you're on the mend. Ready?"

At my very unenthusiastic nod Borzu walked over to the flap and drew it aside.

I blinked in the glare, then started walking, one very unsteady step at a time, Felix supporting me all the way. When I reached the doorway, I glanced at him, managed thickly, "Don't think I can walk very far."

"Don't have to." Handing me off to Borzu, he stepped out first then turned back, ready to grab an elbow if I faltered. I followed, steadied from behind by Borzu.

I stopped, looked around at the encampment, at our fortified settlement. Things *had* changed dramatically—and *not* for the better. Tents and makeshift lean-tos were packed cheek-by-jowl; the once orderly rows were now more like the cramped, tortuous passageways of a rabbit warren, barely wide enough for one person to negotiate. Baggage carts—those now infamous baggage carts—were everywhere, strange looking contraptions with the sum of people's lives billowed over their lips and scattered on the ground around them like so many abandoned refuse barrows.

Simply put, it was no longer a clean, orderly Roman camp. In an incredibly short space of time—five days, according to Felix—it had become something akin to a slum. Stank like one, too. Clearly the latrines, which had been built to accommodate fifteen hundred men weren't capable of coping with almost four times that number.

Felix, painfully aware of my stunned rapidly turning to openly disgusted reaction, hastened to say, "We all agreed that for everyone's safety, no one should remain outside of the fortifications—"

"You did say we should join forces, Legate," Borzu interjected and I glanced at him, wide-eyed.

Fine. I vaguely remembered suggesting something of the kind—I'd never anticipated *this* result.

"So things are a tad crowded," Felix continued.

A tad? That's an understatement!

"We've been too busy tending to the wounded, convincing the Adraniis they were safe in our company, burying the dead and setting up living quarters, along with retrieving everything of possible value that was left on the battlefield. First thing tomorrow we'll set to work, make things right—"

"There's no damned room to make things right," I replied softly, still in shock at the truly abysmal state of affairs. "There's no damned room, period." And there wasn't. The circuit walls had been built at the very edges of the hillock—the camp was as big as it could possibly be.

Felix persisted: "The engineers are doing what they can—"

"We won't be able to stay here," I said flatly. "Too exposed, and with the crowding, things could get unpleasant really quickly." Actually, they already had. The cloying stink, in combination with my lightheadedness and the throbbing pain was making me queasy.

I looked around again, now that my initial shock had begun to wear off. To my right was a ring of soldiers, quietly playing a game of latruncŭli using pebbles and a game board hastily drawn by fingers in the fine, all-pervasive ocher dust. Further down the rambling aisle was a cluster of very grubby children being tended to by several equally filthy Adraniis, male, female, impossible to tell with the shaved heads, except—*gods, one looks to be heavily with child*—and beyond them, more soldiers, their backs to us, backs to the Adraniis, talking amongst themselves.

No mixing. *Definite* boundaries. Not even curious gazes. Everyone was keeping to their own, Adranii with Adranii, Roman with Roman. Not a good thing in such tightly packed space—someone was bound to step on toes. Add to that the presence of women and things could get very ugly very quickly.

I decided first thing in the morning I was going to put my soldiers to work... doing *something*. Resume the daily combat drills for one—presumably the Adraniis, by accepting our hospitality now expected *us* to defend *them* against the Si'aafu and gods forbid any of *my* men not be fit for the job—shoring up the fortifications just in case we were attacked and oh yes, building more damned latrines. Anything to keep them busy and out of trouble. One incident could derail everything.

Borzu, sensing my thoughts said, "We thought about segregating the camp, your people on one side, mine on the other but after discussions with your officers and mine, we agreed it was best to let our people intermingle."

"Hasn't worked, has it?" I growled—in a mood to state the damned obvious.

"Not as well as we'd hoped, no, but perhaps when everyone sees you up and about, that'll change."

Doubt it, I thought as my eyes continued to take in the horrendous conditions.

To my left squares of canvas had been draped on ropes run from the top of the circuit wall to the ground below to form a long, sloping sun canopy and underneath were people, *lots* of people, covered in blankets, some on cots presumably scavenged from the soldiers' tents—which I suspected meant my men were occupying them, others lying on the ground—presumably Adraniis. Then again, maybe medical need dictated who got a cot and who didn't. Gods' favor *that* be true—to show blatant preference based on anything other than severity of injury was a surefire way to stir up trouble.

I spotted Cleander, Iulius and Tigidius too; the three, along with two Adraniis—one looked to be Maisoh although I wouldn't swear to it—were wandering among the wounded, stopping occasionally to check on individuals.

Tigidius at that moment happened to look our way, saw me and stared in open-mouthed shock, then he started towards me, yelling, "*LEGATE! IT'S THE LEGATE!*"

Head snapped around, soldiers near and far turned to stare at me as if not quite believing it was really me—even a few heads on cots and others on the ground lifted and turned towards me—then the able-bodied started towards me, also yelling, suddenly cheering, their voices drawing more... and more, soldiers running towards us from all directions, sending Adraniis scuttling out of their way, grabbing children and ducking into their lean-tos, out of sight.

I began to tremble and Felix and Borzu tightened their hold on my elbows, effectively supporting my full weight.

The oncoming crush of men stopped at Felix's barked order to halt and quickly formed up into a solid semicircle around us, dozens thick, a wall of silent, anxious faces, dust streaked, weary and bruised, many with obvious injuries, some bandaged, others not. I caught a few furtive, bordering on blatantly menacing glances at Borzu, but thankfully Borzu appeared utterly unfazed by it as if he fully understood their accusative reactions and I was suddenly very thankful he was at my side, clearly helping me stay on my feet—that alone would send a much needed signal to everyone that we simply had to support each other—figuratively *and* literally—there was no other reasonable choice if any of us hoped to survive. Even better, a few Adraniis had cautiously reemerged from their hovels to witness the goings-on and while they kept their distance, they too could see me, see Borzu at my side.

Rufinius suddenly appeared as he managed to squeeze his way through the tightly packed throng. He was stripped to the waist, his left upper arm wrapped in a bulky, blood-soaked bandage and his sunburnt skin coated in a rime of sweat and dirt. He did his best to knock the caked ocher grime from himself, from his hands, then meeting my gaze, he smacked his clenched fist to his bare, notably bruised chest, winced then said, "Hail to the legate!"

A roaring echo of the salutation went up from the soldiers—I could only imagine the intimidating effect that had on the Adraniis as the booming chorus reverberated off the circuit walls, multiplying the thunderous homage tenfold.

Rufinius grinned, stepped close and, giving me a cautious squeeze on the shoulder, waited for everyone to settle, then said loud enough for all to hear, "You're one crazy bastard, you know that, Legate?"

"Hard not to know with everyone telling me that," I replied, my voice having gone quite thin and raspy.

He chuckled and stepped back, allowing others to come forward, in ones and twos, in small groups—all done without any jostling, to touch me, gently grab my hand, carefully pat my shoulder... or, like Tigidius, just smile and nod, as if all his prayers had just been answered and to his immense satisfaction.

More soldiers came, running pell-mell from all corners of the camp—sending the few curious Adraniis darting back into their lean-tos—crowding close, every one of my men wanting to see me, ask how I was, did I need anything?

Florianus and one of his cooks arrived, presumably alerted by the cheering, bringing food and drink, roughly pushing and elbowing their way through the boisterous, happy crowd, yelling, "Make way!"

Beside me Felix whispered something to Caius, who'd appeared at his side some minutes before and the soldier nodded and slipped past us, into the tent while I kept a frozen smile on my face, kept trying to make eye contact, recognize everyone, acknowledge each of them, but it was getting harder and harder with my vision blurring and my legs shaking.

"ENOUGH!" Felix finally bellowed in his best Centurion's Voice. "You've all seen what you came to see—pass the word—the legate's on the mend, so be off with you! And be quiet about it! The legate needs his rest."

The men immediately began to back away—again in good order, nodding, casting sidelong, relieved smiles at me and mumbling their thanks to the gods that I was alive. Even Rufinius departed, but not before giving my shoulder another squeeze, as if to reassure himself that I was real—or perhaps reassure *me* that he was alive. I responded in kind, lightly touching his injured arm, to which he shrugged and smiled.

Then, with the tap of his forefinger to his brow—*gods favor you*—he stepped into the retreating tide of soldiers just as Caius reemerged with my wadded up bedding in his arms and at Felix's sidelong look, nodded then hurried off with his burden.

"Let's get you back to bed," Felix said and with Borzu's help I was assisted back into the tent with Florianus and his aide following.

It was a welcome relief to sink back down onto my freshly remade cot—by now the shaking in my legs had spread to my entire body and I'd broken out in a cold sweat.

I dropped my head into my hands, tried to collect myself, tried to calm the shakes, the overwhelming emotions—*all those faces, my men… alive*—that surged through me and realized I was actually shivering.

Felix noticed and snatched up his cloak, drew it tight around my goose-pimped shoulders.

"Thanks," I muffled, not raising my head from its cradle.

I heard Borzu say he was going to get Cleander, heard Felix's murmured agreement, heard Florianus whispering to Felix. Then more whispers, scuffing footfalls… and then:

"You doing all right?" Felix asked, worried, drawing a chair close. He sat down, facing me and used his knees to brace mine.

"Yeah."

"You look like death."

I lifted my head as I continued to shiver, met his stare with a watery one of my own and managed to say without stuttering, "Feel like death if you want the truth."

"You scared me, Arri, damned if you didn't. I thought you'd been killed outright, or trampled in the chaos—then we all heard what sounded like your bellowed voice, ordering us to stop fighting. So we stopped, shoved the Adraniis back, using the our shields and swords to get the message across we wanted them to keep their distance, opening up a gap between us while we sorted out what had just happened.

"Of course our first priority was to find you—we couldn't at first—all that damned dust that had yet to settle, all the confusion. Overturned baggage carts and their goods strewn everywhere, the wounded, bodies. Children screaming for their mothers, women sobbing, calling desperately to their children and all of them staring at us like we were monsters.

"I was in a panic, I can tell you—I was afraid they had you—or, truth, your corpse—and hoped to use it for ransom, maybe to trade for their injured and dead who'd fallen behind our line." He stopped, a forced wan smile. "Then Wushah appeared out of the dust, like some gods-sent apparition, with you and Borzu on his back—*gods, Arri*. Everyone started cheering… even the Adraniis when they realized it was *over*, that we weren't going to butcher the lot of them for murdering you."

"Wish I'd been there to see it," I replied and managed a half-hearted smile.

His expression, however, was suddenly very sober. "It wasn't until after I reached your side that I realized you'd lost a lot of blood, that you'd passed out and it was only Borzu keeping you upright and in the saddle." He paused, heaved a breath then continued: "You're not doing as good as the troops have been told—you probably guessed that. You're going to have to take it easy—do *exactly* as Cleander tells you. If you don't, he says you could start bleeding again and this time he might not be able to stop it."

"He's always coddling me, Felix. I sneeze and he panics. I fart and he starts planning my state funeral. Everything to do with my health is doom and gloom with him. I think he does it just to annoy the hell out of me—"

"It's my job to 'coddle' you, Legate…"

I looked up to see Cleander standing in the doorway of the tent, Borzu behind him. *Oh, shi—*

"…annoying the hell out of you is an unexpected bonus." With that he walked over to me, jerked the blanket off my shoulders just as I was starting to feel warm, then sat down next to me and began poking and prodding at my bandaged torso.

I winced, flinched, twitched, and when my visual clues weren't enough, I finally snarled, *"That hurts, dammit!"*

"It's supposed to."

I dropped my head back into my hands, which did not stop his deliberately painful exam—not that I really expected it would. "Lemme know when… when you're done," I managed to force out through clenched teeth.

"Done."

I very slowly lifted my head, just enough to look at him out of the corner of my eye. "Verdict?"

"You're going to live. But… and this is a *big* but, you are going to have to *stay* in bed for the next few days at the very least, sleep as much as you—"

"Have you seen the camp?" I jabbed a noticeably shaky finger at the tent flap. *"I can't lounge around in bed while things get even worse!"*

"I can have you tied down if you ask nicely."

I grabbed the cloak and jerked it around me. *"I'm fine, dammit!"*

"You are *not* fine, Legate. You came exceedingly close to bleeding to death—"

"Fine. So I wasn't so fine five days ago. But I'm quite fine now."

"You *are* not fine, you're *far* from fine."

"Yes I am!"

"Fine! Have it your way—"

"Fine! I will!"

Cleander looked up at Borzu. "You see what I have to work with, Captain."

The look Borzu gave me left me with the distinct impression that he *agreed* with Cleander.

"Fine," I growled. "I'm still not altogether fine. But I'll be fine by tomorrow, you'll see. *Now off!"* I gave Cleander an elbow.

He surprisingly took the hint and abruptly rose, unbalancing me and I toppled backwards, sprawling crosswise on the cot. I lay there for a moment, extremely uncomfortable with the back of my head resting on the cot's wooden stay as the three stared down at me, clearly aware of my predicament and just as clearly waiting for me to admit that I was too gods damned weak to rearrange myself properly before they lifted a finger to help.

"Can someone please get my legs for me?"

Cleander did the honors by none-too-gently scooping them up and dumping them on the cot as Felix took my shoulders and tugged them towards him, centering the rest of me on the narrow bunk. Then Cleander set about removing my sandals—again, done with as much jerking and tugging as possible. That done, he snatched the blanket from Felix's bed and drew it over me. "You need to eat."

"Later," I grumbled as Felix lifted my head—*gently*, I might add—and placed it on my rolled up cloak.

"Fine. Later. Just *eat*. Felix—make sure he eats, all right? And he needs to drink as much water—*not wine*—as he can hold."

"I'm not using the latrines, that's for damned sure."

"Then piss in the corner, or hell, on yourself again for all I care." With that he left, muttering angrily to himself as he did so.

Felix waited until the flap had fallen back into place, as if the canvas provided complete privacy from eavesdropping then fixed me with a blatantly irritated stare. "Can you *please* make an effort not to infuriate Cleander at every opportunity? You might find you have urgent need of him, especially if you refuse to listen to what he says."

Borzu for his part kept his eyes fixed on his booted feet, like a guest caught up in an ugly family quarrel.

"Tomorrow send scouts over the mountains," I said abruptly, angry and taken aback by Felix's less than respectful tone, and in front of strangers—very recent enemies no less. "Check out those grasslands Duccius says he saw. Have them look for a suitable place to build a better encampment, more protected... not as visible. Take some horses if Marcus is willing—see if they can safely make the trails."

"Already done, Legate," Felix said, clearly just as annoyed with me as I was with him. "Joint teams were sent to the mountains first this morning. A unit of the cavalry was also dispatched to search for a more suitable route for the wagons and engines."

I stared up at him, growled, *"By whose damned permission?"*

"By your leave, sir," he replied with uncharacteristic frostiness. "We didn't know how long you'd be—"

"Conveniently knocked out cold?" I wasn't sure why I suddenly felt so angry, why I felt so betrayed, but I did. Damned if I didn't, as irrational as that was… or, maybe it *wasn't* so irrational. Felix was clearly very angry, furious *with* me, scared *I* might do something *he* deemed reckless—me, *the damned legate!* Reckless—like stopping a war and saving how many damned lives? If I hadn't been so gods damned reckless, he'd most likely be dead—Rufinius… Marcus, Cleander… the lot of them, dead or injured— most if not all the Adraniis too. *Reckless indeed!* He'd questioned my orders before, yes, but *never* in such a blatantly insolent, bordering on patronizing tone, *never* with an audience—and now in front of a gods damned Adranii? And *that* made me even angrier—

"Legate," Borzu said in an appeasing tone and drawing my black expression, "Felix and I agreed we must act and act quickly…"

So it's Felix now, not 'Centurion Felix'? My slitted eyes darted to Felix, back to Borzu, *his* slip of the tongue leaving an extremely bitter taste in *my* mouth.

"…we also agreed it would be best to include some of my men, which, aside from the obvious benefits of greater numbers, they'll be quite helpful in choosing our next camp as we've had some experience with the Si'aafu—Felix here tells me you haven't."

I flicked Felix another sidelong, extremely reproachful stare. He stared back, unblinking, arms crossed. *Defiant—gods damned defiant!*

"Legate," Borzu said, painfully aware of our heated, albeit silent exchange, "we must be completely honest with each other—freely admit our weaknesses, our knowledge gaps. I've had the honor of meeting most of your officers—

To discuss the usurpation of my command?

"—impressive lot, *damned impressive*, with solid on-planet experience, invaluable experience since we are all now, and for the foreseeable future, if not permanently, *on-planet*. In return for this expertise of yours, I offer you ours, on the Si'aafu, which I freely admit is not as comprehensive as I would wish it was."

What he was saying sounded reasonable… but I wasn't in a mood to be reasonable, nor was I at all comfortable, furious in fact with the idea of Felix—or any of my officers for that matter—being so willing, and without first consulting me, to freely divulge what we knew… and, more importantly, what we *didn't* to strangers and I made a mental note to speak to them about it first chance I got—assuming I was given that chance. We might be allies of expedience, but Borzu was still Adranii…and we were still Roman and not all of our interests overlapped—quite the contrary.

Borzu grabbed the other chair, pulled it close, eased his large frame down onto it then fixed me with his penetrating stare. "Things clearly cannot remain the way they are—you yourself said as much. We *cannot* stay here. Nerves are already frayed, tempers running on a knife's edge…"

I squinted at him. *Like mine, you mean? Like I don't have damned good reason to be furious? My camp's a stinking pisshole, my damned naïve second in command has taken it upon himself to ally himself far too closely with someone who just five days ago was our sworn enemy, trusting* you *to be trustworthy, while I'm conveniently kept out of the way, watched over by one of* your *trusted subordinates? Like the one who almost murdered me? Gods, if those weren't reasons enough to be in a temper, I don't know—*

"…so by giving your men and mine something constructive to do, and do *together*, we greatly lessen the chance of some incident occurring that can throw us back at each other's throats."

"What else has been done in my name," I asked coldly, too furious to even consider the truth in his point, "while I've been… *indisposed?*"

Felix stood his ground despite the baleful look I was giving him. "We've combined our food supplies and put it under joint control, thus assuring everyone that all will get an equal portion for as long as it lasts. And we've sent a group to the spring Duccius found, to collect water in whatever containers we can spare and bring it back to camp. We were already running perilously short with all the horses and such, and now… well, we'll run out of water in less than a day or so without resupply. Our combined food stocks should keep everyone fed, if not full for at least two weeks, maybe three if we're extremely careful, but not much more—"

"Three weeks?" I gasped, taken aback. Last time I'd spoken with Florianus he'd assured me our supplies could last three *months*, longer if we carefully rationed ourselves… but that was before our camp was overrun with Adraniis—*starving* Adraniis, little better than gods damned rats! I turned my appalled, accusative stare on Borzu.

"I'm afraid we were left here with very little in the way of supplies, Legate," he replied apologetically, the truth of his claims etched into the hollows of his cheeks, the shadowing around his eyes and prominent bones in his hands. "We were already running out when you arrived, and with children to feed…" He left the rest unsaid, clearly hoping to play on my conscience, my compassion.

I glared at him, long and hard. He was right of course, damn him—and damn me for continuing to voice opinions that he and Felix could openly, and, yes, all right, *rightfully* oppose. Maybe Felix was right—maybe I was more badly injured than even I was willing to admit to—I certainly wasn't thinking clearly, suddenly suspicious of everything and everyone—yes, including my closest friend.

That said, I'd known people like Borzu, plenty of them in my life, people with the ready hand for the gimmie, the other hand holding nothing but empty promises. "And what do you propose to offer in trade, Captain Borzu? I know what my men would say was fair trade for their bellies going empty."

Borzu stared back at me; he knew what I was suggesting without me saying it out loud. "I'm painfully aware that you and I come from vastly different cultures, Legate, and in yours I'm sure what you're suggesting is commonplace, but *not* in mine. Women are equal to men in my society, not chattel to be offered up in trade. And even if some of our women *were* willing—and I must say none, to my knowledge, have voiced such a view—do you honestly believe this would ease tensions? Quite the contrary."

"Perhaps some will have a change of heart, once we get to know each other," I replied coolly. While he might be right—all right, he *was* right—I was already primed to be insulted by his remark that none of his women had expressed any interest in my men—men who were a hell of a lot cleaner, not to mention in far better physical shape than Borzu's scraggly, dirty and shave-headed lot. His women should consider themselves lucky indeed if any of my soldiers expressed an interest in *them*—

"Perhaps so, Legate, and I truly hope this will happen, *eventually*, for everyone's sake, but it's for the women to decide if they wish to consort with your men; it's not up to you and me, and certainly *not* up to your soldiers."

"They *won't* press the issue," I replied, even more irked at his suggestion that my men were no better than a bunch of sex-deprived brutes. They *were* sex-deprived, but they *weren't* brutes, hell if they were. "They might ask, politely, but that's as far as it will go, I can promise you that. And since we're on this rather, um, *th-horny* issue, I strongly urge that you speak to your men, warn them *not* to flaunt their good fortune by making it obvious they're having sex while right next door sit a tent full of my men, having no choice but to listen, eh?"

"I've already done so, Legate—not that it was really necessary. Sex, I believe, is the last thing on my people's minds right now."

I wish could say the same about my men; they'd had sex on their minds ever since they'd learned there were women about—okay, *fine*, they'd had sex on their minds ever since they'd shed their Kellesuf mindset. Having women around only rekindled those yearnings. I nodded, petulantly, turned to Felix and growled, *"What else, Primus-Pilus?"*

"The horses and oxen... we'll need to find them pasture. They'll both be critical to our survival and Captain Borzu and I have agreed that the oxen are not to be slaughtered for meat unless there's absolutely no alternative to keep us alive as they could provide a *sustainable* source of food, along with draft animals.

"As for the goats, Hardalio had the foresight to make sure we brought along four males and several of the she-goats were pregnant when we left. And Marcus says that mares outnumber stallions almost twenty to one, and with the oxen a greater percentage of cows to bulls, which is unexpectedly fortunate for us—"

But hardly accidental, I thought bitterly to myself, but I was in no mood to thank Turan, either, even if it was only a mental nod to her 'thoughtfulness'.

"—there have even been a number of unintentional matings—your Wushah appears to be one of the major perpetrators in this by the way..." he forced a grin as if I should be proud, or perhaps even satisfied, by proxy? "...making good use of the times the horses have been allowed out of their stables to mix freely in the pens—so again, we have a good start on a steady population of horses... but only if we can find them proper grazing."

That started the two off on an animated discussion about basic animal husbandry.

Felix, clearly aware I was still very angry and angry with him and why, latched onto the topic, an excuse to talk about something I could not find immediate fault with—something in fact I'd already given some thought to, just as the Tuatha, perhaps at the urging of Turan, had clearly taken into account—meaning I could not find continued fault with *him*. It was also a topic Borzu clearly knew nothing about, but was willing to go along with in hopes it eased the escalating tension. Felix had come by his impressively vast knowledge through Lord Taskim's stable boys and grooms, his cowherds... and of course, the font of all wisdom when it came to the proper care of anything with fur and four legs: Lady Ainiaan.

As I listened, finding I had nothing to add, not even a pissy aside, I realized the two had already spent a good deal of time talking over other things, thinking of contingencies that while blatantly obvious now that they'd brought them up had not occurred to me. Not now, not when we first arrived. *Not at all.* And I thought I'd thought of every possible possibility—in fact I'd prided myself on having thought of every *possible* possibility... except, of course, our camp being overrun by starving Adraniis.

Felix and Borzu had come up with the same ones I had, sure enough... as well as a host of others.

And suddenly: *they* don't *need me.*

And then another thought, even more unsettling: *I'm the only real human here.*

The Kellesuf were made-men as Turan was wont to call them, with no memory of who and what they really were and no true connection to Earth except through me. The Adraniis had no link to Earth except through some long distant, long dead ancestor; they were as ignorant of their home planet as each Kellesuf was ignorant of his own past.

I was the only one who had a strong bond with Earth. Worse, I was the only one who had any reason to want to return. My men would go where I went, because that's what they thought they should do. But they had to have begun to wonder what would become of them when—*if*—we returned. Would they be allowed to keep their new personalities, or would they be forced back into being Kellesuf?

The choice was obvious, to the Tuatha, to me, and probably to my men as well.

Borzu was now speaking of long-term plans, of making this world ours, of hard work and turning it into something where everyone would be free, no one would be under the yoke—using my own damned words, those I'd spoken to his people—to make his point. Clearly he had no desire to go home, either, to return to his feckless masters—assuming he could even find them.

And now they didn't need me. None of them needed me.

I felt utterly useless, unnecessary, and in my present state possibly even an encumbrance in what by anyone's best case estimation was going to be a hardscrabble existence at least for the first few years, if not for decades.

Self-pitying? No doubt. Realistic? Very possibly.

I tried to tell myself I should be pleased, I'd trained an army of Kellesuf to think for themselves, to be self-sufficient; I'd trained Felix to lead if I was killed, Aetius and Rufinius and all of my centurions, too—taught them all how to survive, and each and every one had far exceeded my wildest expectations.

And I'd accomplished what I'd set out to do when I rode out, alone, to parley with the Adraniis: I'd successfully out-out-outmaneuvered the Tuatha *and* the Faoimhuir and forged nascent alliance that given some time might, just *might* be strong enough to repel even an attack by the Si'aafu.

I'd saved my friends; my actions had spared the lives of all but three of my men.

I *should* be proud and intensely relieved.

Instead I felt a loneliness so profound that I couldn't help but shiver. *Old man...* That's what Felix had called me. And I was. At twenty-nine I'd outlived my usefulness, even to myself. I should have done everyone a favor and died—

"*Arri...?*" Felix grabbed my shoulder, drawing my distant, unfocused stare. "Are you all right?"

I blinked, mumbled, "Get... get Cleander...."

Felix shoved the chair back with such force he knocked it over, said, "You'll stay with him?" and at Borzu's quick nod, and with one more frightened glance, he bolted from the tent.

Borzu stared at me, really stared; I could feel his gaze on me but I refused to look at him, kept my blurring vision fixed on the tent's fabric wall instead.

"Tell me what's happening, Legate, perhaps I can help."

I didn't want to talk to him; I certainly didn't want his 'help'. He'd more than helped enough already—driving a wedge between myself and the man I considered my closest friend.

"Felix's a good man, Legate, a very capable officer," he continued, clearly feeling the need to reassure me—*but of what?* That they didn't need me? "You've trained him well. You've trained all of your men very well. He and they can do what needs to be done—just as you need to rest, get your strength back."

Go away. I squeezed my eyes shut, grit my teeth. *Leave me the hell alone.*

The small silence stretched into a longer, decidedly uncomfortable silence that clearly began to gnaw on Borzu's nerves and he shifted in the chair, shifted again, then finally: "We're criminals..."

I couldn't help but open my eyes at that startling and wholly unsolicited confession.

"…condemned to die," he continued as he touched his shaved head. "I've already told Felix this, told your officers, so they would understand us better, realize we pose absolutely no threat to you and your men, that we truly welcome this alliance and how grateful we are to them and especially to you, Legate, for what you freely offered us.

"And now I will tell you what I told them in full: according to the Faoimhuir, we're mutineers… and as such, we were all scheduled to be put to death. And because the Faoimhuir subscribe to the belief that any miscreant Adranii's guilt extends to his family, wives, husbands, children… even grandchildren, they were to be put to death as well—and as is custom, they were to executed *first*, so we, the most culpable, could witness the awful result of our evildoing."

This wasn't an unheard of punishment—we Romans engaged in it, punishing the entire populace of a town whose leaders had recklessly resisted us—but we at least had the good sense to usually spare the women and children, and in some cases even enemy soldiers who surrendered—granted, by sending them to a lifetime of slavery but for some life was everything, free will, such as it was for most, was… *negotiable*; unlike barbarians who killed wantonly, we Romans only resorted to slaughtering everyone if we needed an example of what happened to those who stupidly persisted in testing our patience until it ran out. Case in point: Carthage.

"You wonder why Adraniis are blindly loyal to the Faoimhuir? Now you know why—to disobey carries a terrible cost, a cost too much for most to bear. And our crime? We ran from a scheduled encounter with the Si'aafu that smelled more like an ambush—the *Fihroon*, my ship, I told you about her…"

I nodded, very reluctantly, unwilling to be drawn out but the name did sound vaguely familiar.

"…she's a planetary survey vessel. By strange coincidence we mapped this very planet some seventeen cycles ago—equivalent to twenty two of your years—and as such we carry only minimal armament. On our last voyage we were ordered to divert from our intended destination and instead rendezvous with a Si'aafu courier in order to deliver a communiqué too politically sensitive to be sent by the usual route, at least that's what we were told and there was nothing particularly unusual in that—we'd done it before, many times but this time, instead of meeting up with a single courier, we found ourselves facing several of their warships. When they stated they intended to board us, I decided to run, save my crew, my ship—I thought I was doing the right thing. Our masters saw it differently.

"They said that my failure to deliver a very important message to the Si'aafu had had serious diplomatic ramifications—that I'd panicked when the Si'aafu demanded to board my ship and accept the message in person, which is something they'd never done before. The Faoimhuir called me a coward and when I refused that label, they called me a mutineer, called my officers, my crew mutineers. I tried to take the blame all onto myself, tried to convince them that my officers and crew were innocent but by then our masters were so enraged by my 'blatant defiance' as they called it, they ignored my pleas and ordered our families to be brought to join us.

"I truly believed I was about to be the cause of the deaths of not just my crew but also their families—three thousand, eight hundred and seventy eight people in all—more if you count each of the sixty eight women in varying stages of pregnancy as two. All because I'd heard those same rumors about the Faoimhuir handing over Adraniis to the Si'aafu and I feared *we'd* been 'offered up', sent to the Si'aafu under the pretext of delivering a message when in fact we were delivering ourselves.

"That the Faoimhuir reacted so harshly, rather than weighing the merits of my actions that saved not just the crew—a highly trained and experienced crew—as well as our ship, well, that made me even more of a believer in this 'rumor'.

"Worse was finding out that instead of the usual fate of mutineers, of criminals, which was to be spaced—akin to being suffocated," he added quickly at my blank stare, "we *were* to be handed over to the Si'aafu—ironic justice, the Faoimhuir said—*all of us*, and very much alive, because, as we were told, the Si'aafu prefer to butcher their own meat as they needed it."

I couldn't help but shudder at that.

"We were kept in cramped detention cells for well over a month, ten, fifteen of us packed into a cell not much bigger than this tent—time enough for three of the women to give birth. The Faoimhuir had already taken all of the children and infants elsewhere, 'for safekeeping' they said, until we were handed over, rightly believing we'd kill them rather than let the Si'aafu have them.

"They'd also taken the pregnant women, returned the three once they'd given birth while they kept the newborns, kept the women separated even from each other to avoid any chance of them finding some way to abort, keeping those who were at high risk of miscarrying due to the stress, or who were suicidal, sedated, as the Si'aafu consider pregnant humans a supreme delicacy—"

I suddenly recalled the heavily pregnant woman I'd spotted and shuddered again.

"—in fact anyone who began to fail, stopped eating, tried to kill themselves was taken and forcibly fed, kept alive... for the Si'aafu they said—some refused to believe this, they kept telling everyone the Faoimhuir would never do such a thing, that we were too valuable..."

I privately recalled Isem's protests to that effect—the same argument so many doomed slaves had used, believing it to be true right up to the end.

"...that it was all just to frighten us, to teach us the errors of our ways, but others, like me... we knew it was no idle threat. Then, finally, the day came for us to be shipped out. Amidst all the chaos and panic of being herded from the cells, of being reunited with our children, believing we were about to be loaded aboard a Si'aafu ship... we were instead brought to a large audience hall. There we were given an unexpected reprieve of sorts. Or, should I say, a stay of execution.

"We were offered a choice: be handed over to the Si'aafu, or be brought here, where we were told we'd meet a smaller force of Tuatha soldiers—a terrifying thought I must admit—almost as terrifying as being handed over to the Si'aafu. Tuatha are rumored to employ all manner of intelligent yet undeniably fearsome creatures in their dealings with Faoimhuir, so we had no reason to assume this army would be a *human* army.

"We were told if we agreed to the latter, we were agreeing to fight you—to settle a long-standing dispute between the Faoimhuir and the Tuatha, and if we managed to defeat you, we'd be pardoned—*all of us*, or should I say any who survived would be pardoned and those who were killed would have their criminal records expunged.

"It was obvious to everyone that our chances of defeating a Tuatha army, even one of lesser numbers, were slim to none—none of us are fighters as you so rightly deduced. And there were pregnant women and children among us. But, if we chose this option, we at least had had some chance, hair-slim as that chance might be—as I said, we'd mapped this planet, knew its environment was not entirely hostile to human life. Granted, your masters and ours deliberately placed us in one of the least hospitable locales, but..."

He smiled, briefly. "I thought the best I could hope for myself, for my crew was a death marginally better than waiting to be butchered, piecemeal by hungry Si'aafu, to see our children, our grandchildren taken…" he heaved a breath, wiped his suddenly watery eyes then continued, "that perhaps some of my crew might even escape the carnage and go on to eke out a living unnoticed by the Si'aafu or our masters for that matter—who would reasonably assume we were all dead—or as good as dead.

"I never thought we'd meet a human army, never believed I'd meet someone of your caliber; never imagined I'd be sitting and talking with the 'enemy'; never even entertained the possibility that we could form an alliance and maybe, just maybe, turn the tables on what are clearly our common enemies.

"And yes, I agree with you: I think the plan all along was to use us—your people *and* mine—as bait for the Si'aafu so that the Faoimhuir could take advantage of their distraction to hide—almost fifty five hundred humans, essentially free for the taking, even if over half were barely more than skin and bone—a *very* tempting lure for the Si'aafu. And yes again, I wouldn't be surprised to learn that our *beloved* masters even told the Si'aafu *exactly* where to look—which planetary system I mean, not exactly which planet. This system has several that could support human life and I seriously doubt they'd want the Si'aafu to find us *too* quickly. The Si'aafu on the other hand will be desperate to find us before we do what we were told we were sent here to do, and that's to fight and kill each other.

"Fortunately this is a truly huge planet—three times the size of Earth—and its atmosphere is highly reflective to orbital scan. It caused us a great deal of problems when we did our survey—we ended up launching multiple unmanned probes, but now this phenomena, combined with the fact that we possess no advanced technology that could give the Si'aafu something to home in on, will work in our favor because they'll have no choice but to search, grid by grid, and using low-flying scouts—an extremely tedious and time consuming task, time we can use to our advantage."

"But an advantage that is by no means accidental," I grumbled, speaking for the first time.

He shook his head and briefly stared down at his folded hands before again meeting my wary gaze. "I am grateful beyond words that you've taken us in, Legate, that you've offered to protect our families, share your knowledge, your own dwindling foodstuffs with us. I beg you, please understand what the women in particular have gone through—why they shouldn't feel as if they are being pushed, or worse, treated as chattel.

"The Faoimhuir were always pressing us to have more children—any woman who circumvented the usual method of getting pregnant often enough to draw attention was either given over to a Faoimhuir to forcibly impregnate or was artificially inseminated—"

"Artificially... *what?*" He'd said a number of things I didn't follow and I strongly suspected he'd done it deliberately, so I was damned if I was going to let on that I didn't grasp what he was saying, but now he'd hit on something that genuinely piqued my curiosity, and piqued it enough I was willing to admit my ignorance.

"*Inseminate*—a technique to induce pregnancy without a man being, *um*, directly involved."

I blinked, blinked again, wondering how that was possible, or why it would even be desired—by *either* party.

"As I said, women in Adranii society *are* equal to men—but because Adraniis are a form of wealth to the Faoimhuir, we're expected to produce children, *lots* of children, and if we fail to do so...well, not to bore you with the details... the Faoimhuir force the issue—and women are not the only ones forced to submit...."

Loath as I did to admit it, his words struck a nerve—

"...on top of that, while we were being held... well, I'm dismayed to say some of my men took out their frustrations, their fears, their sense of helplessness on the women in ways they never would have even considered under other circumstances, encouraged, I was later told, by the guards who told them they'd be spared in trade for getting a woman pregnant. They weren't of course, despite a number succeeding—"

"Are these men among us?"

"Yes—"

"And they go unpunished? What about this equality you speak of? Even in my unequal society such crimes don't go punished." Fine. That wasn't entirely true—it all depended upon who the rapist was, who the victim was, but I was not about to quibble over such details, at least not at this moment.

"It was decided that retribution would gain us nothing—"

"Decided?" I interrupted coldly. "*By whom?*"

He shifted, clearly and intensely uncomfortable. "By me, Legate, by my top officers, two of whom *are* women."

"Were they among those who were raped?"

He didn't answer immediately, then reluctantly, "No."

"How you mete out punishment among your people, or fail to mete it out is your decision. But understand this: you and your people are now in *my* camp, under my aegis and I want *none* of your troubles spilling over onto *my* soldiers, otherwise the wrongdoers will fall under *my* justice and I am nowhere near as enlightened as you Adraniis—*do* I make myself clear?"

"Perfectly clear, Legate." He paused, looked away, then continued, "My crew, they're *good* people." He again fixed his pleading eyes on me. "They want to earn their way—"

"Would your women's sensibilities be offended if they're asked to help with the cooking? You're right, my culture and yours are vastly different, and our values are every bit as important to us as yours are to you. It will take my men some time to accept what your people take for granted, accept this... *equality*—cooking is something your womenfolk can do in the meantime—without offending *us*, assuming they're willing. I won't demand it."

"I'll speak to them—I'm sure they'll understand—"

"We're *not* children, Captain," I snapped and wincing, clutched my side. "We're just not you. Not only that, we don't *want* to be you. Fail to grasp that simple fact at your peril."

He took a deep breath, nodded. "Point taken—" He glanced over his shoulder as we both heard a commotion approaching: Felix returning with Cleander, drawing others along in their wake.

He rose, lifted the chair out of the way. "Please think over what I've just told you, yes? If you do, I think it will ease some of your reasonable concerns."

I only stared up at him, then turned to watch Felix and Cleander enter... and, a few seconds later, an Adranii followed. Felix was wheezing; Cleander was breathing hard and clutching a small leather satchel to his heaving chest. The flush-faced and loudly gasping Adranii appeared close to done in, presumably trying to keep up.

I fixed my eyes on him only to realize he too looked vaguely familiar.

"I... I apologize in... in the delay getting here," Cleander gasped, drawing my uneasy gaze, "Khouri here," he jerked his chin towards the Adranii, "and I were... were with Nestor on the... far side of the camp— a watchtower railing gave way and a couple of men took... took a bad spill, broke some bones." He looked me up and down as he caught his breath, then he tossed the satchel on the bed, knelt in front of me and very carefully palpated my flank as he stared into my eyes, looking for a flicker of pain, a grimace, I suppose.

But the pain I was feeling was far, far deeper—beyond his reach... or so I thought.

After a moment of mutual scrutiny, he glanced over his shoulder and motioned to Borzu and Felix. "It's all right, you two can leave now."

Borzu started for the flap then hesitated when Felix remained where he was, still wheezing, a very worried expression on his sweat-streaked face.

"I said you can leave," Cleander said, snatching up his satchel as he rose. *"Now*, Captain Borzu, and take the centurion with you."

Felix gave me one last rather confused glance, then reluctantly followed Borzu out of the tent, but he didn't go far. He just stood outside, still wheezing. Borzu may have stayed with him, the two waiting to eavesdrop on whatever Cleander said to me, I couldn't tell, and to be honest, I didn't damn well care.

The Adranii, however, remained. I briefly met his intense gaze with an unfriendly stare of my own then I looked questioningly at Cleander.

"Khouri was the *Fihroon*'s physician," he said by way of belated introduction. "If it hadn't been for him and Maisoh and a handful of others who had some training in the medical arts, we'd have lost a lot more than we did."

I again looked at this man, this Khouri—now I was sure, I *had* seen him before. He was short with a square face and wide-set eyes... and had been among that ragtag line of Adraniis—the one who'd been the first to laugh at my insinuation as to exactly what Isem had been doing with the goat.

I had other more hazy memories of him leaning over me, talking—calling to me? To someone else? I remembered he looked and sounded scared. And another dim recollection of my hands around his neck, of people yelling and Nestor frantically trying to pry loose my stranglehold.

The Adranii still looked scared as he smiled nervously at me—and yes, there were indeed days-old, purpling bruises on his throat. So, so, so.

"I'm honored to finally meet you, Legate."

He didn't look the least bit honored; he looked intensely afraid, clearly for good reason and I was in no mood to dissuade him of that apprehension.

I squinted at him, hoping to drive home the point that I didn't want him anywhere near me, then as he took the hint as well as an uneasy step back, I shifted my narrowed stare back to Cleander, not at all happy to find that yet another of my trusted officers had closely aligned himself with an Adranii.

"I think it might be a good idea for you to spend the night in one of the medical wagons," Cleander said, to which the Adranii nodded his wary agreement. "Clearly I was too hasty in discharging you."

It wasn't like Cleander to admit fault in anything. But I wasn't about to agree with him. I knew what he—what both of them were thinking. "I'm staying here."

Cleander exhaled as he flicked Khouri a sidelong glance, then, shaking his head, he walked over to the table, placed his satchel on it and began rummaging through his supplies.

I could feel Khouri's worried gaze on me; I pointedly ignored him and his damned 'concern' as I growled, "Just give me one of those sleeping drafts of yours."

Cleander stopped rummaging long enough to look at me. "Think you need it?"

"And here I thought you'd be ecstatic I was finally asking you for one of your nasty potions, rather than refusing what you've offered."

"I *am* pleased, Legate, of course I am, but I'm also concerned about this very much out of character request—afraid the pain might keep you awake? Or is it something else?"

I squinted furiously at him. *You damn well know it's something else—and you damned well know what that something else is.* "Everyone tells me I need my rest, everyone tells me I need to stay in bed, everyone tells me not to worry, that they'll take care of everything! I'm *fed up* with being told what to do! So to shut everyone the hell up I've decided to stay in bed for the next damned week—*hell, maybe even longer and let everyone else do the damned worrying, all right?*"

He crossed his arms. "I don't believe you."

"Then never the hell mind, all right? *Leave!* Go on, *go!*" I motioned angrily to the tent flap with my hand, a hand that was now visibly shaking. *"Go, damn you, and take that gods damned Adranii with you!"* I hurled the blanket aside, tried to stand, got part way up and immediately sat down as the ground was suddenly yanked out from under me.

Khouri reflexively lurched forward to grab me then wisely thought better of it; Cleander just stood there, watching as the shakes spread to the rest of me—this time I wasn't cold, I wasn't shivering. I was just shaking uncontrollably.

I dropped my head into my hands, chattered, "Jjjjjjusttttt gggggo awwwway…"

"I think it best you do as he asks," Cleander said, then a moment later, he sighed and added, "He's a decent physician you know—when Felix came to get us, we both thought you'd started to bleed again and if you had, I would've needed his help."

I ignored the remark and kept my head cradled in my hands.

"Here."

This time I slowly lifted my head out of my hands and looked up. He was holding a mug.

"A sleeping draft. You're right, Legate. You definitely need it. You're utterly done in and not thinking at all clearly." He again offered it to me. "We'll talk—just the two of us—tomorrow about what's really bothering you—assuming after a good night's sleep it's still an issue, all right?"

I nodded, the gesture barely visible within the shaking and reached out to take the cup but my hands were trembling so violently I knew if I did, I'd spill it all over me.

He eased himself down beside me, wrapped his arm around me, steadying me and brought the mug to my lips and I took a gulp, then another, eager to get as much down as fast as possible all the while fully aware that the moment the drug took effect, Cleander could and probably would have me carried back to the medical wagon where I could watched, very closely and not out of concern of renewed bleeding, maybe even kept in a drugged stupor, or worse, tied down, maybe both—*safe*, and out of everyone's way.

I took another deep gulp then as I swallowed with a grimace, he took the mug away.

I made a futile grab for it. *"Mmmmore—"*

"Trust me, that's *more* than enough." He rose, pointedly tossed what remained on the dirt floor then placed the mug on the table. "Now let's get you out of that tunic before what I just gave you knocks you on your ass. I need to check the dressing, just to make sure this is all just a matter of simple exhaustion and nothing more."

I'll give it to Cleander; the liquid concoction stopped the damned shaking. It also left me suddenly and strangely disinterested in everything—aside from sleep—that was now an irresistible draw. I no longer cared about the loss of command, loss of trust, of friendship, loss of... *everything*. Even my deeply rooted terror of being tied down evaporated.

Nothing mattered except sleep.

My eyelids fluttered; I began to droop. I could feel my muscles turning to mush, my bones showing every intention of following in short order.

Cleander grabbed a fistful of my tunic collar as I started to topple, gave me a shake. "Up, Legate, damn you, get up!"

I didn't want to get up—wasn't at all sure I could get up even if I'd wanted to, which, as I already said, I didn't. I wanted to lie down—why didn't he understand that? *Wait.* This was Cleander after all—of course he'd want me up on my feet right after he gave me a potent sleeping draft; it wouldn't be Cleander without him throwing in some measure of perversity—with his insistent voice, his equally insistent tugging on me, on my tunic, which made my head snap this way and that on a neck that felt as if it was nothing better than jelly.

"We need to get you undressed," he said and gave my collar another, not so gentle jerk. "Come on, Arri, be a bit of a help will you?" That request was followed by a more violent shake of my collar, and, since even that wasn't enough, a painful slap across the face that briefly brought me, blinking, back to semi-wakefulness.

"Up!" he said again and I somehow managed to stagger, rubber-legged, back to my feet, managed after a brief struggle and with his 'help', to rid myself of the ruined tunic, and at his damned insistence, even managed to take off the blood-stained undertunic. He then helped me back down onto the bed—well, not so much help, more like just let me drop like a stone back onto the cot. No sooner had my bare butt hit its surface than I sprawled out, only to stare muzzily at the canvas roof as he poked and prodded and clicked his tongue.

"Meant to mention this earlier: don't panic if you see blood in your urine, all right?"

I somehow managed to shift my bleary stare from the ceiling to his less than sympathetic face and slurred, "I... I woooon't... if yooooo doooon't."

"Deal. But if lasts more than a few days, you *tell* me, all right?"

"Suuuure..."

Satisfied, he covered me with several blankets, tucked them tight around me then straightened up and crossed his arms. "What I just gave you should help you sleep through the night, if not a little longer—I'll stop by, or send one of the others, every hour or so, to check on you. But if you do happen to wake and find you can't get back to sleep, send Felix for me. Agreed?"

I snuggled down in the blankets and closing my eyes, mumbled sleepily, *"Yaaaaahhhhh..."*

I heard him walk to the table, gather up his satchel then softly walk back to stand at the bedside, watching as the draft took me willingly by the toes and pulled me into the warm, dark void.

— VII —

I was sound asleep—or should I say I'd *been* sound asleep, only to be drawn out of a deep, blessedly dreamless slumber by the odd, tickly sensation of something lightly tugging and toying with my hair. At first, in my dim awareness, I tried to pass this off as nothing more than a stiffer than usual breeze blowing through the tent flaps, ruffling my sweat-stiff hair, or possibly even one of the cats. Xanthus in particular was prone to playing with our hair—or in one notable case, toying with an accidentally exposed piece of male anatomy—while we slept, a way to wake us up so we could offer her something to eat, in other words a bribe to leave us the hell alone. Thisbe liked to lick our hair while we slept, or tried to sleep, but in her case no reward was necessary for the impromptu grooming session. She did it gratis.

I vaguely remembered Felix stirring sometime well before dawn, of him stumbling blindly around the tent, bumping into things in the dark and cursing softly, the noise drawing me close enough to full waking to tell him to damn well light the fucking lamp so he could see what he was doing before he fell on me, of him muttering his profuse apologies as he struggled to light the lamp and after a few moments finally succeeding. Of me blearily watching him as he dressed; of him urging me to sleep all day if I could, then muffling through a hasty mouthful of dried fruit that he'd posted guards even though Borzu had assured him that his people meant me no harm.

I replied, 'One can hope', although maybe I just thought it—that being said, I had damned good reasons for being more reserved in my option than he was. Felix was perpetually the optimist, gods knows why, considering what had been done to him. Of course he hadn't had his flank recently ripped to shreds, a fact that might've encouraged him to be a little more suspect of these Adraniis' heart-felt well wishes made right after an attempted assassination by one of their number—an accused assassin who, conveniently, had been killed shortly thereafter, thus taking any claim of innocence to his grave. For all anyone really knew, the real culprit might still be very much alive.

That said, whether this newfound regard for the legate was strictly true was moot, whether the real villain in my close to successful murder was dead was moot. The high-walled and heavily fortified encampment was now packed, chockablock with Adranii women and children along with their anxious, overly protective menfolk; any attack on my person would be countered with a very ugly response by my men and every Adranii had to know this—if not by common sense, then by recent experience. The guards were just an added precaution, a less than subtle visual cue to keep one's distance—and, presumably, keep one's voice down. I was therefore presumably safe as safe as could be, permitted to sleep undisturbed for as long as I wanted… or so I'd been promised.

So I was, yet again, in my favorite sleeping position—flat on my stomach; I'd forgone my rolled up woolen cloak in preference for the more familiar, less scratchy crook of my arm as a pillow.

The odd tug came again.

I groggily opened my eyes and turned my head, flinching and instantly wide awake as I came face to face not with Xanthus, Thisbe or even the broad-faced and green-eyed Leonidas, but with a very grubby, sunken-eyed child, wraith-like in the dusty shaft of light that streamed through the narrow slit in the flaps. With the shaved head, loose, tattered clothing and all the dirt, it was impossible to tell if this shriveled waif was a boy or a girl—not that it really mattered. I had a thoroughly unwelcome visitor and that was that.

I cleared my throat, carefully eased myself onto my back, drawing the blankets, which had become tangled around my hips and legs while I slept up around my chest. "What are you doing in here?" I rasped as I managed to stuff the rolled cloak under my neck while glancing at the tent flaps. Felix had been good to his word: they were tied shut, with only the narrowest of gaps between them. So, the child had somehow slipped inside unnoticed.

I looked back at this filthy apparition and whispered, *"You're not supposed to be in here—shoo!"*

The urchin only stared at me as it reached out with clear intent of again touching my hair. I didn't move. The thought of having this child's dirty fingers in my hair was only marginally less unpleasant than the thought of frightening it and having it cry out, drawing its parents along with a host of ugly misunderstandings.

I suffered its sticky, curious touch, tolerated the fingers tugging and curling my hair only to let go and watch with fascination as the sweat-stiff locks fell back into place. Had this child ever seen hair?—I'd always kept mine slightly below shoulder-length, a personal choice that in truth cost me a lot of good-natured and some not-so-friendly ribbing as I climbed through the ranks—*acersecomes* I'd been called, the unshorn boy, a reference to a common custom among Romans as well as Greeks of not cutting a youth's hair until he became a man. But the term also carried a more suggestive meaning, and so you might imagine it was with no small amount of wry humor on my part that many of my troops naïvely adopted the same habit, assuming it was the norm rather than a personal affectation and like me, they kept theirs clean, combed and well-oiled, even here on Latrunculi where small indulgences had been encouraged to keep up morale. It was a small vanity after all.

All Adraniis were shaven-headed, although all of those I'd seen were now showing signs of growth, with downy fuzz on their scalps and the shadow of beards on the men, which only added to their disheveled appearance. I'd not thought to ask Cleander, or Borzu for that matter, if the strange style—or perhaps a mark of the condemned as Borzu's self-conscious gesture had suggested—extended any further and after what Borzu had told me the night before about the women I doubted I'd be finding out any time soon.

"I hear your mother calling to you—you'd better go before you earn yourself a paddling."

The brat shook its head, its intensely interested gaze now fixed on the black stubble on my cheeks, my chin and I couldn't stop myself from flinching back as its smelly fingers came close to touching my lips. Grimy, stinky fingers touching hair, especially hair already in need of a good wash was one thing, but lips? No, that was *just* too much.

"Please don't do that."

It stared at me with an expression of aggrieved innocence only a very young child can carry off with any hope of being believed, but thank the gods its fingers sought out another lock of hair on my forehead to toy with.

"Your mother must be getting very worried about you—hadn't you best go now?"

Another, more adamant shake of the head.

All right. *Now* I was getting annoyed. I'd earned by rest, damned if I hadn't. And whatever Cleander had given me to help me sleep, to knock down the burning pain in my side had been startled out of my system.

I had no idea when Cleander might return to check on me—for all I knew he might have left shortly before the child arrived, leaving me, he rightly believed, safely cradled in the arms of Somnus—maybe the child slipped in, unnoticed while Cleander was tending to me and remained hidden in the shadows until Cleander left—

"Anachie…!"

I jerked my head towards the soft voice—a woman's whispered and very worried voice.

"Anachie… where are you?"

The child glanced over its shoulder then back at me as a shadow flitted across the far wall of the tent, followed by another softly voiced, *"Anachie?"*

I stared at it, willing it to leave under its own power. *Go… shoo!*

Instead of doing as I was silently pleading with it to do, it resumed its fingering of my hair.

Perhaps, I thought, I should feign sleep—that way if the woman peeked into the tent, all she'd see was her precious little darling playing with my hair and the legate apparently fast asleep and therefore oblivious.

"Anachie…?"

I tore my eyes off the child, looked at the slit in the tent flap and saw the silhouette of someone directly outside. *Gods!*

I closed my eyes, hoping it wasn't too late to appear sound asleep as I heard the woman's fingers desperately tugging at the knotted flap ties while I furiously wondered where the damned guards were—then a flash of light as a flap was drawn aside.

"Anachie!" she hissed. *"Come here—"*

"What do you think you're doing, woman?" came a stern male voice—an all too familiar voice. *Felix.* "Away with you!"

"But my boy's in there!" the woman cried. *"Please, we meant no harm!"*

Through my slitted eyes I saw other silhouettes hurriedly approach, all much taller, heavier than the woman.

"What do you mean your boy's in there?"

"Please, he's only a child!"

Felix jerked the flap aside and clutching the blankets to me, I squinted into the glare, feigning startled grogginess.

"Legate?" He stepped inside, the Adranii following, grabbing the child and jerking him against her. "Are you unharmed?"

I nodded and looked at the woman—she was staring at me with large, terrified eyes, clutching the child to her as if we were Si'aafu about to make a snack out of them both.

"Anachie meant no harm, sir—*please, I beg you!* Let us go and he won't bother you again, I give you my word—"

"Damned right he won't bother the legate again," Felix growled, having drawn himself up to his full and quite impressive height, arms akimbo and a very menacing glower on his face. "I'll be speaking to

Captain Borzu about this—expect a visit from him. I'd have your explanations ready if I were you—"

"Felix," I said, finding my voice, "it's all right—no harm done."

Felix looked down his nose at the woman. "You see that our legate is an extremely tolerant, understanding man—pass the word, yes?"

She nodded vigorously, then glanced at the tent flap and to the two grim-faced guards now standing just outside, one holding the flap aside—and where they hell had they been?—then back at me, silently pleading for me to give her permission to take her child away. Not that I could blame her. She was in a tent, *our* tent, with two strange men, one of whom was wearing only a bandage and a blanket and her only exit was blocked by more men—*armed* men who did not look the least bit sympathetic to her current predicament.

From what Borzu had suggested, what the Adraniis believed, based on what they'd been told by their masters, by Isem and the alleged Faoimhuir spy and further cemented by the mutilated remains of one of their officers was that we were little better than those damnedable Iceni and not enough time sharing close quarters—even sharing our food and water, the protection of our camp—had passed to prove to any of them that that opinion was utterly unfounded.

I should have given her leave right then and there, but she intrigued me, as did Anachie, who stood behind the bastion of his mother's thin, grubby arms, staring back at me with a look of eager curiosity that had clearly not been satisfied. This Adranii, the antithesis of the coldly aloof Maisoh, was, aside from the aforementioned Maisoh, the only woman of her kind I'd seen close up. I suddenly found myself as curious as her child, and was loath for her to escape so quickly.

"Manners, Felix. Fetch our guests a chair. And perhaps some water for Anachie—and wine for you?"

The woman swallowed convulsively, her eyes darting between Felix and me and the guards as Felix placed a chair next to her and motioned curtly for her to sit down. She clearly wanted to bolt but knew better than to try.

I motioned to the guards to leave us in hopes that alone might prove to her that we meant no harm and in response to their unhappy departure she cautiously eased herself down in the proffered chair, her arms still firmly locked around her boy.

"I believe we might even have some dried fruit," I continued, and at Felix's nod, I added, "Anachie, would you like something sweet to eat?"

He nodded eagerly and fought against his mother's hold, quickly squirming free despite her efforts to keep her grip on him. He trundled over to where Felix now stood, beside the table. Felix was in the process of lighting the lamp and didn't notice him as Anachie stared up at him in wide-eyed awe, astonished by Felix's fire-starting prowess—as, I must add, did his mother. It was as if neither had ever seen someone light a lamp! Had I known she would react as if this was some amazing, magical skill, I'd have offered to do the honors.

Once the lamp was lit and the fire-making display was over, Anachie immediately began tugging at one of pteruges that fringed Felix's leather tunic. *"Please?"*

Felix, despite his best efforts to look every bit the stern Roman centurion, couldn't help but smile at the small, pleading face. He re-hung the now lit lamp, said, "Of course," and squatted, offering the child the plate of fruit. "Here. Just one piece, all right? But you can pick which one."

Anachie took his time deciding, frequently glancing up at Felix for direction.

Felix pointed. "Perhaps that one—it looks like it's the sweetest."

Anachie snatched it and stuffed it in his mouth as if fearful Felix might suddenly renege—as if he was used to adults reneging when it came to food.

I knew that feeling, damned if I didn't. I knew what it was like to watch adults fill their bellies while I went desperately hungry—to be beaten senseless when I got caught snatching a morsel meant for someone else's mouth.

The woman stared at this exchange, large eyes brimming with tears, as Felix rose and returned the plate to the table.

"Felix…?"

He glanced over his shoulder at me.

"Arrange it so the children—*and* pregnant women and those who've recently given birth always have enough to eat, even if the rest of us must go without."

The woman fixed her startled, watery-eyed stare on me.

Felix gave me an arched look then with a nod and a murmured, "Of course, Legate, I was just about to suggest the same thing."

Like hell you were, you lying, dimple-faced scoundrel!

If sensing my thoughts, he shrugged, utterly innocent as always, then he picked up the decanter and began to fill our two mugs with wine.

I turned my attention back to the woman. "We don't mean either of you any harm, we're just… *curious*. Just as your son was curious. Please, share some wine with us. We're not rude company, I promise you—well, I'm not. I can't speak for Felix here."

He fixed me with a wounded look as he handed me my mug, then he smiled warmly at her and yes, of course his damned cheeks dimpled—usually a surefire introduction when it came to the opposite sex—as he offered her the other mug.

She accepted it, clutched it tightly in both hands and in a voice barely above a whisper said, "If… if I do this, will you let my son go?"

I took a deliberately slow, measured sip from my mug, swallowed, wiped my lips with the back of my hand and replied, "If you do *what?* Share our wine while your son eats his fruit?"

She licked her lips, murmured, "You know," then motioned to me and I looked down and realized I was exposing far more of me than I thought I was. *Damn!*

I quickly jerked the blankets over me, said, "You mean have sex with me—have sex with *both* of us?" Out of the corner of my eye I caught Felix's unguarded and decidedly intrigued reaction: *'At the same time?'*

She visibly flinched at my voicing of her worst fears, then, I'll give her credit, managed a quick nod as she lifted her chin to stare at me directly in an attempt at putting us on an equal footing, as if to say, 'I have what you want and I'll give it you but only on *my* terms.'

I looked at Felix, as did she. "What do you say to that, Primus-Pilus?"

"I'd be lying if I said I wasn't interested." He sighed, a *very* frustrated sigh and shook his curly-blond head. "But that's not what the legate meant."

Startled, she looked back at me.

"Felix's right. I meant no such thing. We… we just haven't had any women to talk to. Surely you can understand that. We *won't* touch you—I give you my word. We'd just like… some female company for a little bit. But if you'd rather leave, then you and your boy are free to do so." I motioned to the flap.

She surprised me and mightily surprised Felix when she remained where she was. "May Anachie have another piece of fruit? He's very hungry."

"Of course," Felix replied, then, "and you?"

She nodded, "Please."

He offered Anachie the plate again, and once the boy had picked another piece with Felix's expert guidance, Felix stepped close then dropped to one knee and offered her the plate. "M'lady."

She smiled—*she actually smiled*—and plucked a piece from the remaining selection.

"We have some cheese as well," he offered.

"This will be fine, thank you," she replied and began to nibble on the fruit as her eyes darted between the two of us.

"My name's Arri," I said then jerked my chin to Felix, who was still kneeling beside her. "He's Felix, if you hadn't already guessed."

She nodded to Felix, then me. "I'm Eithne."

"That's a beautiful name," Felix said an instant before I could, *damn* him.

She caught my exasperated expression as I snapped my mouth shut and giggled, albeit with a nervous edge to it.

I grinned as I slowly, very carefully, dropped my feet to the floor, keeping the blankets tucked tight between my legs—the last thing I wanted to do was to accidentally expose myself again—she might assume this time it was no accident.

"You're *very* impressive in your armor," she said, giving me—*all of me*—a long, decidedly appraising look.

Then again...

"But out of it he's exceedingly plain, as you can see," Felix said as he rose, motioning to himself, his leather tunic, tooled baldric and belt and the elaborate scabbard of his gladius with a graceful sweep of his free hand. "Not at *all* like me."

She looked at him, then back at me, her face breaking into a genuinely relaxed grin. "Actually, you're both *extremely* handsome."

"*Really?*" we asked in unison and perhaps just a wee bit too eagerly—gods, we sounded like damned Kellesuf!

She nodded. "You've both caught the eye of a lot of us—you on your... *horse...*"

Presumably before I was shot? It was a reasonable guess—even I had to admit that I looked bloody-awful afterwards.

"...and you, Centurion," she looked up at Felix, "walking around the camp with Captain Borzu."

"It's the hair," Felix replied, running his fingers suggestively through his shoulder length, light blond curls.

"Well, that certainly doesn't hurt—gives all of you a *very* exotic look," she agreed and lifted her hand. "May I?"

He hurriedly placed the plate on the table then again dropped to one knee and leaned close and as she ran her fingers through his soft, flaxen locks he gave me a sidelong triumphant grin and wiggled his eyebrows.

I sat there, my own usually glossy blue-black, wavy hair stuck to my scalp in stiff clumps, a damned blanket wrapped around me and a now quite rank, bloodstained bandage encasing my torso. While Felix looked thoroughly the part of the Roman officer, I looked and smelled like something hacked up by one of our camp cats—worse, I knew it. Even worse: Felix knew it and was using it to his advantage, damn his mangy hide.

Anachie took that moment to plop himself down beside me. I looked down at him and sighed pathetically. "No dimples you see," I said, pointing to my own dimpleless, beard-shadowed cheeks as he made quick work of what was stuffed in *his* cheeks. "Not fair, but… that's the way it is."

He grinned up at me, and damned if *he* didn't have dimples.

I threw up my hands. "I give up!"

Eithne laughed and rose, prompting Felix into hurriedly getting back to his feet as well. I thought she was about to make her excuses to leave—Felix clearly thought the same and was desperately looking around for something to tempt her to stay; instead she walked over to me. I stared up at her, not quite sure what she was going to do—not even sure what to hope she'd do.

She ran her fingers through my filthy hair then she leaned down, caressed my stubbled chin and kissed me on the lips in such a way it sent my heart thumping wildly against my ribs.

I remained frozen in place, not sure what had prompted her to do this. Pity? A desire not to provoke jealousy between Felix and me? Or was she playing us off against each other?

"Thank you," she murmured in my ear as she gently wiped a sweat-stiff lock of hair away from my eyes and tucked it behind said ear.

"For what?" I croaked, genuinely perplexed, hoping she didn't see me shiver—hoping she didn't notice other responses her feather-light touch, her suggestive kiss had elicited.

"For being kind to Anachie… for making me," she touched her own downy scalp, "feel… attractive."

"But you are," we said, and again, a bit too quickly and yes again, in perfect unison.

"It's been a very long time since a man's made me feel desirable."

I winced. "I'm sorry." It wasn't the most inspired thing to say, but I didn't know what else to offer. I *was* sorry. Women needed to feel beautiful—needed to feel desirable. That's what men were for, and clearly her menfolk had fallen down on the job and fallen down badly because she *was* attractive, even with the shaved head and dirt, not to mention *damned* desirable—and I had to fight the urge to toss the blankets aside and show her just how damned desirable she was.

"What's there to be sorry about? I have two extremely handsome men flirting with me—I'm certainly not complaining." She paused, looked Felix up and down, clearly intrigued with what she saw, then repeated the same process with me, as if revisiting what she thought I'd suggested earlier and this time coming up with a very different reaction to the whole idea. *"Definitely* not complaining, in fact..." She dropped her gaze to my lap, ran her tongue suggestively over her lips then shifted her gaze to Felix.

He grinned—dimples, not to mention his hopes, on full display.

Then her eyes darted to Anachie, who was seated beside me, as if she'd momentarily forgotten he was present. "I... *oh*, ahh... um. I'll... I'll let the others know that you... well, let's say you'd be interested if any of them decide to visit."

Felix's grin dissolved and his shoulders sagged.

I must say I felt a bit... deflated myself. That said, I said, "I do truly appreciate the offer, it's been quite some time since I've... well, enjoyed what you're suggesting, but I ask that you not say anything..." I pointedly ignored Felix's strangled splutter, "...as Felix and I cannot accept anything that isn't freely available to our soldiers as well, and something tells me your kind offer to pass the word doesn't extend to them."

She stared at me for a moment. "Maybe not right away. But there are many of us who are uncommitted, partnerless—"

"Fifteen hundred?"

She blinked and shook her head.

I glanced down as I felt Anachie's thin arms encircled me. I wrapped my arm around him and he reacted by snuggling even closer—*damn the boy*. I blinked, lifted my gaze back to her. "Then we have a problem, a *serious* problem. Now, I can personally vouch that any one of my men would make a damned fine husband—take Felix for example..."

She looked at him and he immediately drew himself back up to his full, and yes, quite impressive height—and puffed out his damned chest to boot—*the swine...*

"...he's extremely hard working, undeniably brave, looks damned impressive in his uniform—"

"Even more impressive *out* of it," he slipped in.

"—and best of all, he's used to doing *exactly* as he's told—"

That brought the smile back to her face and a sidelong, aggravated look from Felix.

"—but for now we'd best leave things as they are. Give everyone a chance to get used to each other, learn, if not to trust each other, then at least not be so suspicious of each other... things will eventually sort themselves out." *I hope—gods, I hope.*

She nodded reluctantly then held out her hand for Anachie. "Anachie...? We need to go now."

He tightened his hold on me.

"Come along; the legate's been very patient with us—he needs his rest."

He promptly buried his face in my side, in the filthy bandage that stank of the drugs Cleander had forced into me by all means at his disposal, stank of rancid sweat, urine and congealed blood, and I couldn't help but wince, startled more than anything else.

Her smile vanished. "Anachie—*be careful!*" She lifted her gaze to give me a very apologetic look.

"It's all right, really—he just surprised me."

She breathed a sigh of relief, replied, "He sorely misses his father and with your coloring and all, you do look like him."

"Father?" Felix asked, as if genuinely shocked Anachie had a father, almost as if he thought babies just miraculously happened... and I suddenly wondered if he *did* know how babies happened. I'd never thought to have that kind of chat with him or any of my men for that matter, assuming they already knew or had figured it out, since most if not all understood the concept of animal breeding... and the hoped for results.

Gods... what if they have no clue? What if they haven't made the connection between animals and people and that having sex with a woman can produce a child?

My men were like that—often unable to extrapolate, to see connections that were patently obvious to anyone else, part and parcel, one could argue, of their still evolving personalities. In all fairness, I wonder how long it took men as a whole to figure it out—I mean it's not exactly a case of do one and immediately get the other, is it? There's nine months separating the two acts. A lot can happen in nine months and as most women will tell you, we men have notoriously short memories. Women, I'm sure, had it figured out from the get go—

"He was killed," she replied softly. "An accident, or so our masters said."

"Oh." Felix cast me a sidelong glance, clearly expecting me to rescue him from his gaffe.

I smiled down at Anachie and gently stroked his head. "And I *very* much miss my son." Damned if I didn't. I looked back at her, added, "Anachie's welcome to visit any time." I desperately wanting to say, 'and you're welcome too,' but instead I said, "And one of my officers, Aetius—loves to make toys—he's really good at it too."

Anachie lifted his head, fixed me with his suddenly bright eyes. "Toys?" He tugged at my elbow as if I could magically produce one.

I smiled. "Really *nice* toys—you ask him; tell him the legate said he's to make you something really special, all right?"

Anachie nodded vigorously.

To his mother: "You *do* have my permission to pass the word on that, all right?"

"Aetius."

"Yes. Resembles a baboon—can't miss him."

"A... *what?*"

"A—oh, never mind. Just ask for him—" I jerked my eyes to Felix. "You did order his recall, didn't you?"

"Of course," he replied, by his tone clearly annoyed I'd questioned his competence in front of a woman he was trying desperately hard to impress—I hadn't meant to—*or had I?* "He and the others returned to camp four nights ago, as well as Duccius and *his* party," he added irritably as if worried I might ask about them as well. *"And* they brought back all the foodstuffs they'd cached." Then to Eithne: "I'll personally escort the two of you to him, or bring him to you, whenever, however you like."

"Thank you." She smiled, again held out her hand to Anachie and murmured, "Come along now."

Anachie looked up at me as if expecting a reprieve from the legate and I found myself wishing just as desperately that I could offer one, but now was not the time, nor in truth, I realized with profound regret, was I the one on which he should affix his attentions. I *had* a wife and son and I still held some hope, infinitesimal as it might be, of returning to them.

Felix on the other hand had no such attachments—and he *would* make a good husband if that's what Eithne was in the market for, and, I suspected, a good father to Anachie, once he got the hang of it.

I motioned with my chin. "Go with your mother."

He stuck out his lower lip in a very Lady Ainiaan-like pout; when that ploy failed to change my stern expression, he let go of me and wriggled off the cot.

She gathered up his hand and started for the flap as Anachie cast a wistful glance back at me. Clearly he had his own ideas on who he wanted—perhaps it *was* simply the similarity in complexion—and I pointedly ignored the beseeching look in his eyes.

"Thank you, Legate," Eithne said, "thank you from both of us."

"*Arri*, please."

She smiled. "Thank you... Arri."

"Tank you, Arr... ee," Anachie echoed in his reedy child's voice and I felt my heart skip.

Felix hurried past her to do the honors and as he pulled the flap aside for her, she stopped and looked at him, then at me. "May *I* come back?"

My hesitation was, thankfully, covered by Felix blurting out, "*Of course!*"

"Good."

"*Soon?*" he asked, pushing his luck.

She smiled, ran a fingertip lightly along his jaw line, his chin, tugged at his lower lip and murmured, "*Very soon, Felix,*" then with one last look back at me, she and Anachie stepped outside and quickly vanished into the bustling camp.

I looked up at Felix. "I think we were just propositioned."

He stared back at me, dumbstruck as he released the flap and it dropped back into place. "Gods, I *hope* so," he moaned, sinking down onto the foot of his cot.

— ii —

Felix was considerate enough to make a lot of noise—coughing, scuffing his feet and the like—before he peeked through the slit in the flap, clearly expecting to find me enjoying Eithne's undivided attentions.

To his obvious dismay I was seated at the table, dressed in my holed and bloodstained woolen undertunic and toying fretfully with a piece of fruit—*alone.*

I looked up, scowled at him as he entered. He was wearing full kit, minus only his helmet, presumably to impress Eithne. "Where the hell have you been?"

"I thought maybe the two of us at the same time might in fact be too much—"

"She's not here, if that's what you mean—*she's not hiding under my cot,*" I added testily as I noticed him giving the tent another quick, and presumably what he thought was a covert look-see.

He shifted his unhappy gaze back to me. "I can see that."

"I mean she never showed up."

"Oh."

"I think you jumped to the wrong conclusion as to her intentions."

"*Me?* You're the one who said *we'd* been propositioned—thank you *so* very much for putting *that* idea in my head, by the way. Do you realize how difficult it's been all day, trying *not* to think about it?"

"I have a vague idea, yes." Of course he didn't have the added burden of feeling intensely guilty each time I visualized making love to Eithne. Hell of a thing to feel guilty about making a grab for some small measure of happiness—even if it was just a few minutes of physical gratification—when your own wife probably had a hand in marooning you on a gods-forsaken planet and leaving you there to die.

And why not? She'd gotten everything she wanted—she'd gotten herself a son by me, a son she could now raise the way *she* wanted without any interference from *me*, raise as a cold-blooded Tuatha who'd treat humans like living dice or worse—another Rasaben presumably; perhaps even a foil to Rasaben's ambitions, a rival for their ancestral lands, once he was old enough. She'd also effectively taken herself off her brother's list of gifts he could bestow on one of his loyal chieftains, tainted as she was by getting herself with child by a vile Roman—again, thwarting Rasaben's plans to recapture what he believed was rightfully his—his seat at the table of the Sidhe Lords—and humiliating him in the process. A win-win for Turan; a lose-lose for Rasaben… not to mention my men and me.

"…but *you've* been in here all day!" Felix was saying, suddenly furious as he began to pace back and forth. "I've been outside, dealing with Borzu—" he shook an angry fist towards the tent flap and the camp beyond, "—*would you believe the gods damned Adraniis were caught stealing food offerings from our gods damned altar?*"

I had no reason to disbelieve it—hunger had the nasty ability to drive people to desperate acts, even one as extreme as risking the wrath of the gods—which begged the question, maybe the Adraniis didn't honor the same gods, maybe they indeed looked upon the Faoimhuir as gods. No matter their beliefs, stealing offerings from an altar *was* a serious offense, one my men and at the very least our gods would be hard pressed to forgive. And since it *was* an altar, one *we* at least paid suitable reverence to, how could it be a 'gods damned altar'? Shouldn't it be a 'gods blessed altar'?

I decided perhaps this was not the time to quibble semantics. Felix was on a roll and in his present supremely frustrated frame of mind I doubted would appreciate me splitting verbal hairs, so, with a sigh, I turned back to him only to find him still in full rant:

"...and dealing with that damned Titivillus and Jotia and Aetius and of course, *Cleander*, each one having nothing but a bellyful of complaints—listening to Rufinius drone on and *on* about the gods damned overflowing latrines as if that's our only gods damned problem!"

He paused to take a quick, wheezing breath before continuing, "Oh, yes, top of that, fighting with Florianus over a rotating schedule for meals so no one feels they got the short end—all the while making damned sure *your* order that the children and pregnant women get enough to eat is carried out to the letter, I might mention, and dealing with all the heated objections *that* raised—and if *that* wasn't enough, playing nice with a bunch of people who see things very differently than we do, who, once they realized *our* animals aren't... sent... sent—" he flailed his arms about, grasping for the word, gave up in obvious aggravation and continued heatedly, "*not intelligent*—meaning like *them* of course, they demanded they be housed *outside our* fortifications—not *them* of course, of course not! Why?—because they claim the animals are dirty and take up too much room, when it's really because they're afraid of them—they're even scared of the damned chickens and the cats—*oh, gods*, one woman flew into a panic when Thisbe walked into her lean-to and began screaming!"

"Thisbe began screaming?" I thought that highly irregular as Thisbe always struck me as a very easy-going feline and so unlikely to fly into hysterics—even at the sight of the interior of an Adranii lean-to. All I can say is it must have been a hell of a mess.

Felix didn't hear my innocent question he was so wound up: "Everyone thought she was being attacked—by one of *us* of course. It almost caused a riot—*and it was just Thisbe!*"

I could understand Leonidas seeding chaos among the priggish Adraniis as he had a tendency to piss all over everything, but Thisbe? I had to bite my lip to stop from laughing at the idea that tiny Thisbe was the cause of a near-riot. In truth there was nothing funny about it. Still...

"They question everything we offer them as far as food," Felix continued after catching another breath, "saying it might make them sick, demanding everything be thoroughly cooked first—even the damned grain! Demanding the water be boiled before they'll drink it—like we have the extra wood for such nonsense—they can drink it lukewarm like us!—who consistently think *we're* in the wrong, *not* them, *never* them of course—the pompous, patronizing bastards!" He threw himself down onto his cot for emphasis and grimaced as his banded armor grabbed him unexpectedly—and you wonder why I stuck to a mailed shirt? It wasn't as impressive, but it was a hell of a lot more comfortable. *"Damn the lot!"*

"Welcome to the wonderful world of command, Primus-Pilus—don't expect any thanks from anyone by the way, not even me."

He eyed me from under a lock of curly blond hair that, like his normally pale, but now sunburnt skin as well as his eyelashes and brows, was noticeably tinged russet with the pervasive ocher dust. Even his polished armor—armor he polished every damned day—had taken on a slightly rusty hue, made all the more so by the amber glow of the hanging oil lamp.

Under other circumstances I would have found Felix's frustrations amusing—fitting justice for him earlier throwing in his lot with the now curiously pompous, patronizing Borzu, as if he was ready for the full and often odious responsibility of command. But I was just too frustrated myself, too angry and yes, too damned confused to enjoy his frustration. Yes, I admit it. I'd spent a *lot* of time thinking about Eithne—thinking of Turan too, remembering with intense longing and equally fervent detail the very few times we'd been intimate on *equal* terms—as if by doing so I was somehow less guilty in my thoughts of bedding Eithne.

All I did was end up wanting them both, desperately—and hating them both for making me feel this way, making me crave things I couldn't have.

So, in an attempt to distract myself from such thoughts, I'd tried, briefly, to add to my diary, update it in fact, since a hell of lot had happened since I'd last made an entry. But instead of losing myself in the events of the past few days, I found myself thinking about Neshoue—was he old enough to learn to read? To me it had only been a matter of a little more than a week I'd last seen him, but that was only a perception on my part, and very possibly a false perception. One thing I'd learned about the Tuatha was that they didn't perceive time as I did, as mere humans did. To them time was malleable—and therefore controllable, so all I knew years might have passed, decades even, or only a few hours. Neshoue could be a grown man, perhaps older than me now, or still a sickly infant.

Would Turan keep her promise and give him the scrolls I'd left behind, scrolls that, in my own words and written by my own hand, held the sum of my life? I found I either had no answers or unhappy answers to my unspoken questions, so I gave up, carefully rolled up the vellum and stuffed it back under my cot, then returned to my chair only to stare furiously at the fabric walls of the tent as if the tent itself was the cause of all my woes.

Looking back, I'd have been far better off if I'd spent the time sleeping, or at the very least, resting—a near impossible task while you have naked women cavorting around inside your head. I'd have even been better off ignoring Cleander's instructions for strict bed rest and going for a walk—working off some of those frustrations with some physical exercise, assuming I would have walked very far without falling on my face… or my ass.

Plus, I knew damned well if I tried, some well-meaning soul would run and tell Cleander and Felix and maybe even Borzu and then I'd right back where I was the night before, the three of them treating me as if I was nothing better than a willful child *instead of the damned legate!*—I was already extremely frustrated; I didn't need to be royally pissed off as well.

So instead I spent a goodly portion of the day squeezing the hell out of a hapless damned piece of fruit as if it was the source of all my mental and physical torment and I was only returning the favor.

"You're really going to wear that undertunic?" Felix eyed the tattered and darkly stained woolen garment; I had indeed brought a spare, two actually, along with an extra set of breeches, as had all of my men—at my insistence—but everyone was reluctant to risk ruining the extras; I mean, it wasn't like any of us could trot down to the local seamstress and have her whip up another. "Carus could repair it—or maybe you want to keep it that way—remind everyone…" his voice trailed off as he caught the look in my eye.

"You mean play on their sympathies?"

He shrugged, unwilling to concede, unwilling to concur, either.

"Carus is a tad busy helping with the wounded. He'll *get* to it. And besides, I haven't left the tent—so, who am I going to remind? *Me?*" I shook my head. "Trust me, absolutely *no* need in that department." And it was so damned true—the throbbing pain just never let up; I couldn't find a comfortable way to sit, and lying down only made it worse. Standing was at best problematic. Breathing in or out only made my side hurt more and I found I had no appetite—even wine didn't appeal, in part because I didn't want to find myself with a full bladder.

Even if I didn't mind using the truly filthy latrines there was no way I could walk unassisted to the closest one. Which meant there was no place to relieve myself except the corner of the tent and I was loath to do that—the hot, stuffy air inside the tent smelled bad enough as it was, made worse by my tetchy mandate to all to keep the flaps down at all times—I was damned if I was going to be on exhibit for any damned passing Adranii. The only other option was to stick it through the slit in said flaps, hoping no one noticed.

Someone would. Bet on it.

"I see you washed up," he grumbled.

"Carus helped me I wash up, yes—*and shave*," I added before he could, as if it was something I needed to justify—it was my long-standing habit to be clean-shaven, a practice most of my men adopted along with the shoulder-length hair, and thankfully lacking the torture—er, I mean *ritual* associated with a visit to a proper Roman barber.

"So, not *that* busy." He eyed the bandage that was clearly visible through the tattered holes in the undertunic. "And Cleander redressed your side—"

"Iulius—he insisted, both on the clean dressing *and* the wash up."

"Well, all I can say is about damned time—you *really* stank."

I squinted at him. "Why, thank you."

"I was going to say something earlier, warn you Eithne might find it more than a bit off-putting, but you were in a *mood.*"

I hurled the now thoroughly bruised piece of—I have no idea, it looked like dried apple when I started tormenting it—across the tent where it hit the fabric wall with a soft *thump* and snarled, "Yeah, stopping a gods damned war and having half my insides blown to bits as a heartfelt thank you did kind of put me in a *mood.* Please accept my deepest apologies for that—and of course my less than immaculate undertunic and, oh yes, let's not forget the gods-awful stink that kept you awake... oh, wait, no, *it didn't!*"

Felix fixed his slitted stare on his knees and chewed furiously on his lower lip.

What followed was a *very* awkward, prolonged and unhappy silence.

Damn. First Borzu and now Eithne. They'd been in our camp only a few days and between the two of them they'd managed to get us at each other's throats, something I would've said was impossible.

I snatched up another piece of fruit and began toying with it, as if I hadn't already had my fill of torturing food. "I've been thinking..."

That elicited a furtive sliding of Felix's still very angry blue eyes.

"Maybe this was for the best."

"What's for the best?" he snapped.

"Eithne not coming back."

He stared at me for a moment, then: "How could this *possibly* be for the best? I think I've rubbed myself raw!"

"Remember what I told her? I said we couldn't accept anything that wasn't freely available to our troops—and I don't recall her mentioning that she was willing to service all fifteen hundred of 'em just so we could bed her and not feel guilty about it..."

"You might feel guilty about it, I'd just feel... well, *intensely* satisfied."

"...so I've decided I will refrain, no matter how tempted I am."

He snorted. "I bet you wouldn't be saying that if she'd actually shown up—you'd've mounted her faster than Wushah with a mare in heat and you damned well know it! You're only saying that because she *didn't!*"

Now it was my turn to eye him. "I *have* a wife, a son, remember?"

"Who you damned well know you'll never see again!" he fired back with utterly out of character brutality.

I blinked, appalled; he jerked his eyes back to his knees, took a steadying breath, looked back at me, all anger having drained from his face, his voice. "Gods, Arri, I'm so sorry—that was a horrible thing for me to say."

I shrugged, tried to sound nonchalant as I fixed my eyes on the piece of fruit I clutched tightly in my hand. *"Truth."*

"Still, I shouldn't have said it."

I shrugged again as my fingers clamped down even tighter, crushing the fruit to pulp—but I kept my voice calm, quiet. "We've all been avoiding the issue—you're right, it's highly unlikely I'll see Turan again, see Neshoue..." I swallowed convulsively then continued tightly, "...*again*... and the sooner I accept that, the better for everyone."

"Including you?"

I didn't answer; I couldn't. Along with thinking of Eithne, thinking of Turan, I'd also spent a lot of time thinking about what I'd suddenly realized the night before, that in reality I was no longer needed, no longer... *necessary.*

While Felix had had a taste of the ugly side of command, he hadn't in fact faltered, hadn't lost his temper and pounded the snot out of Borzu as Aetius would've done. He didn't storm off in disgust, swearing profusely as Rufinius might have done. Felix had dealt with each situation, each grievance, each demand and, according to Iulius, who'd appeared at the doorway with medications and a mandate from Cleander to change the bandages, along with Carus, who'd come to help me wash up, Felix had dealt with each quite effectively. He'd even raised the idea of Gratian 'educating' the Adraniis about our beliefs and Marcus about our four-footed companions, something Borzu had, again according to Carus, heartily agreed to—Gratian too, only far less happily. I didn't ask about Marcus's reaction and Carus didn't offer it—answer in itself.

"Who'd we lose?"

Felix arched a brow, not taken in by my abrupt change of subject but willing to go along with it. This too was a thorny issue, another lingering matter that needed to be dealt with, so perhaps he felt better one than none: "Gnaius Flavius, Marcus Antonius and Aulus Maximus."

I winced as my mind affixed old names with new faces; I'd personally led countless men to their deaths—the original Felix for one, and most had fallen far, far from home, buried, not cremated, with the only the barest minimum of funeral rites, and some—again, like the original Felix, with none, his corpse left to rot in that bog along with the rest of my century, once the Iceni had finished stripping their bodies of anything of value and mutilating what was left.

But for some reason the idea that these three had died *so* terribly far from home and were now buried in truly alien soil troubled me deeply—*unexpectedly deeply*. They'd only been truly alive for a scant few months after spending possibly years trapped in limbo as Kellesuf—had barely begun to grow into their new personalities… and now they were dead—*for what? It should've been me in a grave, not them! I should've died long ago and if I had none of this would be happening—at least not to me and men made from my memories.*

What I'd always considered a virtue—my ability not just to survive everything the Fates threw at me, but *thrive*, to succeed—now seemed a curse, a curse the Tuatha exploited masterfully, just as they'd exploited my extraordinary memory for details not to mention my vanity.

Or maybe I'd been their pawn from the get-go, maybe from birth I'd been marked as theirs. Maybe all of my seemingly miraculous escapes, my incredibly close calls had not been due to luck, to skill, or even to the beneficence of the usually vindictive Fates… but to Tuatha meddling. Without their interference, maybe I would have died years ago.

The abhorrence I felt towards these demi-gods—or whatever they truly were—grew. It had been growing, slowly, ever since we'd arrived; it had intensified as I came to the cold realization that we were going to be left here to die no matter the outcome of the battle—it multiplied as I looked upon the faces of our supposed enemies—terrified and starving men, women… *children*, abandoned by their masters as well and just like us, *disposable*.

It proliferated as I accidentally stumbled upon what was, I now firmly believed, the awful truth behind all of these maneuverings on the part of the Tuatha and the Faoimhuir, and now it gelled into a cold, murderous hatred of these beings who looked upon humanity as nothing more than chattel, who looked upon Earth as something akin to a wheat field to be regularly 'harvested', its rich bounty of living, thinking beings sold into slavery or worse, *as food*. And now, as bait for the Si'aafu.

If I ever return, I grimly promised myself, promised these men who had died, promised the Adraniis who had died, promised all who would die on this cursed planet no matter the cause, *I will personally hunt down Taskim, Rasaben and as many of the Sidhe Lords as I can find*—

"...were given proper burials—I made sure of it..."

I jerked my eyes back to Felix, who, I realized, had been talking the entire time.

"...bathed in oils and redressed in their full armor, buried with their weapons and covered in their scutums—I probably shouldn't have ordered that, but it seemed like the thing to do." He fixed his eyes on me, suddenly unsure.

Weapons and armor were at a premium, but I was not about to deny soldiers about to enter an utterly alien underworld their swords and shields, their armor, nor was I about to question my second-in-command on such a matter. Felix was clearly and profoundly affected by their deaths, the first he'd seen as a former Kellesuf; that he had been left to deal with the matter, a task he'd never faced before—that none of them had every faced before—and at the same time haunted by the fear I might, at any moment, follow them... "I would've done the same."

He relaxed a little, clearly relieved, then turned, fished around under his pillow and produced three amulets. "I did keep these." He tossed them onto the table. "I don't know if you've realized it, but without them we cannot understand the Adraniis nor they us. And they don't have anything like these. So I kept them, just... just in case."

I nodded. And he was right—the simple, yet rather implausible fact that we and the Adraniis could understand each other was something I hadn't questioned—I hadn't even thought to question—or had I? I felt a vague memory flit past, of me wondering if the amulet had a useful range, then it was gone.

I'd worn the snakestone from the moment I'd been captured; in truth it had become as much a part of me as the bead and star necklace and replicate signaculum. My soldiers had also worn theirs, presumably from the time they were taken as well and in light of our vastly dissimilar backgrounds, the amulets were no longer a symbol of servitude but a true necessity.

I'd once been told the dead all speak the same dust-dry tongue—I had no reason to ever question the truth of it; had never had the option to test it for myself. If it wasn't true, then Gnaius, Aulus and Marcus, men who'd trained with each other for months, had lived with each other would find some way to communicate with each other and possibly even the Shades of the Adranii dead, possibly even forge an alliance, just as we, the living, had.

I stared down at the amulets—each different as each man had come from a different Sidhe Lord, fingered the leather thongs which had become stiff with a mixture of dried sweat and blood—

"And while we're on the subject," he said and withdrew his writing tablet from under his cot, "I suggest we use this for any conversations we wish to keep from the Adraniis." He tapped the tablet with his scribe; I raised my brows. "They can't make sense of our writing—I made sure."

My mouth formed an 'O' and I nodded my agreement, surprised and pleased by this ingenious bit of subterfuge on Felix's part, even if he'd stumbled across it by accident—

"Gratian performed all the correct rituals, offered up all the libations—he even did the same for the Adranii dead—after first asking permission from their relatives. Borzu said the families were appreciative of the gesture—who knows if they really were—but none openly refused. All that matters to me is that Gratian said our men were content, grateful for the honors we bestowed upon them, that they would rest easy." He met my gaze, smiled faintly.

"We can hope," I replied tightly.

"We can hope," he echoed, his voice barely above a whisper.

"Before we leave this camp I wish to visit them."

"I assumed you would. As soon as Cleander says you're safe to ride, I'll take you—it's a little distance away; Borzu and I agreed that it would be wise not to bury the dead too close, just in case..." He left the rest unsaid.

Just in case there are *predators about is what you want to say—or maybe you're more worried about what might follow you back to camp and did what any sane man would do and take a zigzagging path on your return?* "No."

He gave me an odd look. "No?"

"You're my second in command. Unless it's to do battle, when one of us leaves the relative safety of the encampment, the other *must* remain behind."

"New rule?"

"*Old rule*—one we should've followed from the get-go, but one that we *will* adhere to from here on out." If I really wanted to adhere strictly to the rule, the two of us would stop sharing a tent—it would certainly improve Felix's chances with Eithne. Hard to woo a woman with your rival seated across from you, especially when that rival was essentially confined to quarters. But Felix wouldn't see it that way. Such a change would wound him deeply and needed to be approached with care; right now things were too strained between us. "Agreed?"

He nodded, albeit reluctantly. This Felix had learned to read me better than the original and he knew I was not telling all—then again, in many ways he *was* me, all of my men were, in some part *me*, my memories of others viewed through the lens of my own perceptions, my own experiences, which of course provided a depth of insight denied the first Felix—denied everyone I'd ever known, including Turan.

"When we find a permanent place to settle, I want to return, retrieve their bodies, and the Adranii dead as well—if their families wish—and rebury them near us." I felt it was the least I could do—not to abandon them on some high, wind-swept desert, to bring them to join us, for them to enjoy regular visits and offerings from their grateful fellows.

"Of course."

I raked my fingers through my unruly hair and squinted at him. "What about the injured? How many and how seriously wounded?"

"Ours? Twenty-two, including three centurions, Rufinius, Baculus and Carbo, but most, including Rufinius and Baculus have been cleared to return to limited or light duty. Four, including Carbo are still being tended to in the medical wagons. Carbo suffered a bad stab wound to the belly and another to the thigh—Cleander said of the four, he's the one he's most concerned about…"

I privately winced—Carbo was a damned good centurion, loved by his men, respected by his fellow officers and rightfully so. He was in charge of the engine crews and a quick study of artillery tactics, taking what little practical knowledge I'd picked up during my very brief, very unfortunate stint as a ballistarii while stationed in Dacia and extrapolated upon that hard won yet very limited expertise with astonishing success; he'd be difficult if not impossible to replace.

"…Tullius Maximus was stabbed in the groin—"

I couldn't help but visibly grimace this time—it was a terrible wound to receive.

"—but Nestor says he's improving... *slowly*. Lollius Gaius suffered slash wounds to the shoulder and arm—some gods damned Adranii almost lopped his arm off while he was trying to defend Carbo after he'd fallen, and Attius suffered a fractured skull and jaw—"

"I thought Attius was hard-headed," I interrupted, making a feeble attempt at a joke.

"Not *that* hard, obviously."

"And the Adraniis?"

"About two hundred of them—those with relatively minor injuries were given over to their families to care for, with regular visits from Nestor and Tigidius, along with the Adranii physician and his helpers. That leaves about thirty or so who've remained under Cleander's direct care.

"Some are pretty damned bad—our boys did their jobs, that's all I can say. Many of 'em probably won't make it—Cleander's not optimistic about their chances, especially if we pack up and move and has said so to Borzu, but he and the others are doing what they can with what we have. Cleander and I have assured Borzu that his people will receive the same level of care as our men—no shorting them on medicines."

"I'll want to visit the injured, too."

"When you're able—nothing to be gained by you wobbling into the medical wagon and falling on one of them."

So, so, so. Felix too felt the need to make a feeble joke.

I replied with an equally feeble smile as I stared down at the piece of squished fruit I still held and suddenly felt exhausted by what lay ahead, by the sheer magnitude of what we were about to attempt. Felix was up to the task—of that I had no doubt—and the same was true of the others; each retained the sanguine, one might even say wholly naïve view that anything was possible, perhaps because none remembered tasting the bitterness of true defeat when captured and enslaved, perhaps because each was keenly aware that he'd been given a second chance—truly a new life in every way—and was going to make the most of it. Maybe after a few unforgiving years they'd realize their folly, but for now nothing was unachievable, even taming an entire planet was entirely doable for men once Kellesuf.

Plus Felix had his eyes affixed on a very worthy prize: Eithne. But in order to claim her, he'd have to succeed in safely leading our men and her people—everyone—to those lusher lands.

I *wasn't* up to the task. I knew it. I suspected Felix knew it too, had known it for some time. I refused to let go of Turan, let go of Neshoue—

let go of Earth. I couldn't, despite telling myself I wanted to, despite tormenting myself by constantly telling myself they'd already let go of me.

I flicked him a sidelong look; he knew what I was thinking and he was scared. Visibly scared. He was also my closest friend. So I did what anyone would do for his best friend—I changed the subject. "I feel up to a stroll—how about you?"

"I just got back from a stroll, I've been strolling all damned day in fact…"

"In full kit?"

"…so much so my feet hurt—*what did you say?*"

"In *full* kit—Carus *did* find the time to fix my shirt." I pointed to the ring-mail garment, draped over the back of the other chair. "Good as new he says. So, how about we show these Adraniis what we're about, eh?" I wiggled my eyebrows. "Give 'em a bit of flash."

Felix grinned, willing to go along, in all senses of the phrase, then just as suddenly sobered. "Are you up to it?"

"That's the damned problem—I've been *up* for it all day."

He laughed—forced, but better than nothing—and rose… then gave me a sidelong, worried look. "What about Cleander—"

"There's simply no hope for him; armor or not, he looks like the rear end of a half-dead mule."

"I didn't mean that. He said bed rest for several days, *minimum.*"

"He didn't mean it."

"He certainly sounded like he meant it."

"He always sounds like he means it."

"Maybe because he does?"

"He just likes to sound important. Trust me, he'll be thrilled to see me up and about."

Felix replied with a decidedly skeptical arch of the brow.

"All right, maybe not thrilled," I amended—that *was* a stretch. "I doubt anything would thrill Cleander. Let's say he will not be overly displeased. How's that?"

"He's going to be pissed as hell and you damn well know it."

"Good. About time he gets a taste of his own medicine… so to speak."

"I don't think this is such a good idea." He began unlacing the chest straps on his band armor.

I crossed my arms. "*I* do and *I* outrank you. Done and done."

He eyed me. "A very short stroll—just down to the main gate and back. Agreed?"

I hesitated then muttered, "Agreed." I knew I'd be lucky if I got half that far. I suspected Felix knew it too, damn him.

"And I assume this means I'll not be hearing any pissing and moaning about the helmet this time?" he asked, pushing his luck.

"Is there a breeze out?"

"Not much."

"Thank the gods for that." The last thing I needed was to be buffeted about and sent staggering sideways by an errant gust of wind. My side was still throbbing painfully—I'd twice successfully sent Iulius away when he'd come to offer me something for the pain by telling him I wasn't hurting in the slightest when in fact I was hurting like fucking hell. On the third visit he wasn't so easily dissuaded from his assigned task, with strict orders this time to change the bandages—or else, and so rather than risk a visit from Cleander—or worse, Nestor—I suffered through the damned dressing change without an outward wince or audible grunt. I did curse a lot—silently mind you while drawing upon my impressive inventory of highly creative of epithets.

It *was* high time for the dressing to be changed as it reeked of drugs and old blood and stale sweat and yes, days-old pee—just the thing to turn a girl's head… the nauseating stench was certainly enough to stir the stomach—even Iulius gagged a few times as he carefully unwrapped me and Carus had the good sense to stand closer to the tent flaps—upwind.

The wounds themselves looked remarkably good—and rather disappointing, if you must know. After seeing the damage the projectile did to my armor and tunics, I was more than just a little apprehensive as Iulius peeled away the last strips of cloth, having first soaked them in water to free them from the underlying and very abused flesh.

There was a hell of a lot of bruising, from shoulder to hip, in fact the entire right half of my body was darkly mottled and yes, there were a shockingly large number of stitches—front *and* back—stitches that would have to come out, eventually, but overall the damage, at least on the outside, didn't look all that bad.

Carus then stepped closer, helped me bathe and shave as Iulius watched and occasionally pointed out spots we'd missed and I worried that this delightful domestic scene might be interrupted by the untimely arrival of Eithne, who I'm sure would have been mightily impressed with the sight of me standing there, buck naked, not to mention black and blue and bristling with stitches while Carus got intimate with a wash rag.

Fortunately, my impromptu and way overdo bath was uninterrupted and once I was deemed marginally cleaner Iulius applied a thick, greasy yellow salve to the wound area then with Carus' assistance, snugly rewrapped my torso in a fresh bandage.

That ordeal over with, he again offered me something for the pain—which I again refused. I was damned well not about to risk being knocked out cold if Eithne did make a return visit, or worse, was so muzzy-headed I couldn't deliver the goods, so to speak. There were many things about a man a woman might forgive, might even be willing to give him a second chance, but being unable to perform when called upon to do so was not one of them—when women were in the mood, you best meet their expectations, even better far exceed them... or forget it.

And in the time since Iulius and Carus had left and now the throbbing ache had not let up—if anything it had gotten worse. So now I was in pain, *serious* pain, not to mention seriously frustrated to boot—and I'd just volunteered to walk the camp in full rig just to impress a bunch of Adraniis, most of whom probably wouldn't give a damn, in hopes of impressing one Adranii, who for all I knew had lied—she'd not kept her promise about coming back after all—maybe she in fact *had* a very much alive husband, maybe even a very jealous husband—and for what? I'd just disavowed any sort of tryst—again!

Stupid, Arri! Stupid, stupid... stupid!

I snatched up my leather tunic from my cot, and after some wriggling and grunting, succeeded in getting it settled into place all by myself, thank you very much, then I happened to glance at Felix. He was already fully armored—and impatiently waiting on me. Of course he'd had a huge head start: he'd been wearing his body armor. All he had to don was his helmet.

"Old man," he murmured then bit back a grin.

I scowled at him as I reached for my breeches. It was approaching dusk and the temperature had already started to drop. Plus this wasn't an all-male, soldiers' camp now, where many had seen fit to go even sans-undertunics, preferring to wear only their underwear during the worst heat of the day. With women and girls about, Felix, according to Caius, had ordered that underwear, undertunics and breeches were now mandatory at all times while in public. Subligaria were notoriously unreliable as far as keeping certain things under wraps, so to speak, and the last thing any of us needed was for a woman or worse, a girl see something she hadn't expected to see and, unlike Eithne, panic.

"Just because I take extra time to look my bes—" I was cut off by the loud, blood-chilling wail of a buccina.

Another one joined it, then a third and a forth and finally a fifth, calling my men to arms.

I looked at Felix; he stared back, wide-eyed as we both gasped, *"Si'aafu!"*

I grabbed my sword and baldric—no time for my armor or helmet, no time even for the damned breeches—and together we dashed out of the tent and into a camp in chaos.

Startled Adraniis had immerged from their lean-tos only to be sent scattering by armed soldiers who now exploded out of their own tents, responding to the ominous chorus of buccinas. Behind us I heard yells and the whicker of horses and glancing over my shoulder saw horses being saddled up in haste and men—many wearing only undertunics and helmets, a few wearing breeches and helmet only—scrambling onto their mounts and snatching lances and shields from their racks as they wheeled their horses around, towards the gate, to meet at a gallop whatever alerted the sentries.

Still others were rolling the onagers towards the same gateway, far too few men at first to maneuver the heavy machines, but others quickly joined them, adding their muscle and the engines began to move in earnest, their wheels' deep rumbling adding to the frenzied yet organized uproar.

My men knew their jobs, damned if they didn't.

Adraniis quickly packed themselves in tight clumps, holding each other, holding on to their children and watching in mute terror as more half-dressed soldiers formed up under the bellowing commands of my centurions.

Satisfied my troops were doing exactly as they'd been trained to do in the event of a surprise attack, Felix and I took off at a run towards the northern-most watch tower, the source of the buccinas' warning blast—and just as suddenly I stumbled to a stop and doubled over, a stitch in my side so agonizing I couldn't breathe.

Felix, realizing I wasn't keeping up, also stopped, wheeled around and started back for me.

"Go!" I hissed, then louder when he grabbed my arm to steady me. *"Go! I'll catch up—go, damn you, that's an fucking order!"*

He reluctantly let go; even more reluctantly stepped back.

"GO!" I gasped with what little air I could get in me.

He turned and kited off, running as fast as he could, plowing through knots of startled Adraniis, his long legs making easy work of leaping over items other Adraniis had dropped in their haste to dodge his onrushing, sword-wielding, snarling charge.

I clutched my side, somehow managed to get a full breath, tried to straighten up—and was caught halfway by another stabbing spasm that left my eyes watering and my mind spinning. It was only through sheer force of will that I kept my hold on my sheathed gladius and baldric.

Out of the corner of my eye I saw movement: Adraniis, who'd dashed back into their lean-tos, or who, in a panic had retreated into the rabbit warren of passageways that snaked their way through the camp had reemerged... and as I watched, struggling for each breath, unable to move, more and more appeared and I suddenly found myself surrounded by a silent wall of their grubby, and now very frightened faces while buccinas continued to wail their spine-chilling warning over the din of bellowed orders, of armed men running, dogs barking, horses whinnying and engines rumbling—even the damned oxen were lowing, adding their alarm to the racket.

The Adraniis' anxiety, their terror bristled back at me tenfold as I glanced around; I wanted to say something—knew I *needed* to say something but I just couldn't get enough air into me to speak.

"What's happening?"—that from a frightened male voice behind me. I managed to half-turn, crab-like, still clutching my side and tried to spot the speaker.

I somehow got a breath, rasped, "I... I don't know. I'm... I'm trying... trying to find out."

More ominous stares while the surrounding camp echoed with the near deafening clamor of soldiers rushing to the walls to defend it—to defend these people who stared at me with expressions that looked less like gratitude and more like murder. Maybe they thought we *were* about to slaughter them wholesale, rather than hastening to their protection. They weren't soldiers after all—this was a totally alien experience for all of them. No wonder they were terrified—and hostile.

"Some... something's... approaching," I forced out. It was a good guess.

Adranii eyes glanced around at the high walls, at the watchtowers and firing platforms now packed chock-a-block with soldiers, each one realizing with dawning relief that all of the weapons were pointing *outwards*.

If I'd been able I would've made good my escape while most were distracted but I was afraid to move for fear my legs would buckle—and by the expressions of those few Adraniis who were keeping their wary eyes on me, rather than the frenetic goings on above them, I was not alone in that estimation. There was simply no point in pretending otherwise.

I swallowed my pride and forced down my own justified fears of these people. They were our allies after all—*grateful*, Borzu said, for our charity, our protection, which was now in full and apparent force. "Can... can someone... help me?"

For a several thumping heartbeats no one moved, no one offered a hand.

I struggled to catch another breath, felt my knees wobbling as I suddenly realized they didn't know who I was. Aside from a handful of Adraniis none had seen me this close up and without my armor, my distinctive helmet, I looked like just another soldier—which might work in my favor...or might not. *"Please...!"*

A young man, barely more than a teenager, very reluctantly stepped away from the rest, but only after being nudged from behind, even more reluctantly grabbed my elbow and steadied me. I nodded my appreciation.

An older woman joined him and cautiously wrapped her arm around my waist, warily observing my sweat-streaked, taut face as she did so. "You need medical care—"

"No!—help me... to that firing platform." I pointed with a shaky, outstretched arm. *"Hurry!"*

The two looked at each other, then back at me, then, to my profound relief they began to help me walk—albeit slowly, excruciatingly slowly but it was the best pace I could maintain. The stitch in my side had thankfully started to ease, but I still felt weak-kneed and lightheaded—anything faster and I had no doubt I'd pass out. I'd been a fool to think I could run, could keep up with Felix—I'd have been hard-pressed even before I'd been shot. I glanced to my right, to the man, then to my left, to the woman, caught them both watching me out of the tail of their eyes and I managed a tight smile.

The woman returned the uneasy smile while the man did not. We walked on, past goatskin tents that had collapsed as their occupants had rushed out, past scattered armor left in haste—but no weapons I noted—past half-eaten meals left by quickly doused fires and I found myself intensely pleased my men had remembered to do this, thus greatly reducing the chances of the camp going up in flames while we were busy defending it.

As we neared the circuit wall and a formation of soldiers, several turned and seeing who approached immediately gave way, elbowing their startled fellows into doing the same. Several, including one of their centurions, Silvanus, hurriedly moved to replace my helpers but I waved them off, murmured, "No. You have your orders," and the men immediately stepped back and watched our passing in silence—in fact the entire camp had fallen into an ominous silence—I hadn't noticed it until just then.

The buccinas had done their job—the camp was on full alert; now it was a matter of waiting to see what had triggered the warning in the first place. I had visions of thousands of Si'aafu approaching from all directions, like a seething mass of scorpions rushing towards us—a nightmare image ripped from a fever-induced hallucination, a terrifying vision that still tormented my sleep.

The woman, aware of the deference given me by the soldiers, gave me a curious look, as did the man. She leaned close, whispered, "Who are you?"

I stopped, slipped my elbow from the man's firm grip then gently eased the woman's arm from my waist as I managed a tight smile. "I'm the legate…"

The man briefly dropped his gaze to my side, to the holes in my leather tunic, put everything together and raised his brows as the woman just stared at me, mouth agape.

"…and I thank you for your assistance. I can make it the rest of the way—best return to your families—urge everyone not to get in my soldiers' way and most importantly, stay calm."

They nodded and as they hurried back the way we'd just come I made my way through a cluster of soldiers and over to the ladder that gave access to the firing platform. I looked up, not at all certain I could make it, but knowing I had to see for myself what we were facing. I managed to get the baldric over my head and settled the sword against my hip, then I reached up, grabbed a rung, placed my foot on the bottom-most, and gritting my teeth, began my climb, each rung gained by sheer force of will.

Almost within reach of the top, two of the men manning the scorpio noticed me, overheard my labored gasping and each scrambled over to offer me his hand up. I grabbed one, then the other and they then lifted me bodily the rest of the way, onto the platform itself. Once on my feet, I grasped the railing with one shaky hand, and mumbling my thanks to the soldiers, wiped my eyes with the other, then looked around for Felix.

His centurion's transverse plume was easy to spot among the helmeted and a few bareheaded men who crowded the platform and pressed against the scorpio, risking their lives if they bumped the primed and loaded weapon just so.

"Legate!" someone hissed, drawing everyone's startled eye.

Felix hurriedly beckoned to me and I made my way through the crush and over to him, only to find Rufinius and Aetius already there, along with Jotia—each in various states of dress.

I swept our surroundings with my gaze—to my immense relief there was no seething mass of Si'aafu rushing towards us from every direction. The desert was remarkably… well, deserted, but something *had* caught the sentries' sharp eyes, something worrisome and unexpected—

"There!" Rufinius pointed north and I squinted into the late afternoon haze, finally spotted what had sent the alarm through the camp: a moving column of ocher dust. Something or someone was approaching—still too far away to be seen, aside from the betraying dust cloud, but it was clearly no natural phenomena; something was kicking up the fine sand as there was only the faintest of breezes, even out on the flats, not enough to create a dust devil of that size. The daily afternoon sandstorm had already come and passed long enough ago the fine dust had settled—and now something *or* someone was stirring it up again.

I leaned against the railing and glanced down the length of the wall to my left, then to my right, to the firing platforms. Crews were standing at their scorpios, the business ends of those truly nasty weapons slanting towards what approached while the watchtowers were thick with bowmen, arrows notched in bowstrings and along the far lip of the riverbed the cavalry had deployed, a solid, bristling semicircle of lances facing north, towards that ominous, billowing ocher column. And just below us, at the base of the hillock stood ten fully crewed onagers along with a battery of ballistas, testament to Carbo's training and I made a mental note to tell him, assuming I had the opportunity, later. Right now any future plans looked rather tenuous.

I had a sudden thought of calling for Wushah, of joining the horsemen—then thought better of it. My presence wouldn't help; in fact it would only be a hindrance as I was in no shape to fight, probably wouldn't even be able to keep myself in the saddle and the cavalry would be torn between confronting whatever was coming our way and protecting me. Yet again I was struck with the bitter taste of my own uselessness.

I leaned heavily against the railing, wiped the stinging, gritty sweat from my eyes and heaved a breath.

Felix glanced at Aetius, at Jotia, then at me, and by the look he gave me clearly wishing I'd remained down on the ground—out of harms way—out of everyone's way. Fortunately for everyone he held his tongue—

"It's Centurion Marcus!"

I jerked my head towards the bellowed voice. Soldiers on the northernmost watchtower were now yelling, cheering, a few whistling loudly and madly waving their arms.

I looked back at the column of dust and sure enough I too caught the eerie, foxfire-blue glint of the low-angled sunlight on armor, the colorful flutter of pennants atop upright lances and I felt my heart slow its breakneck beat: the cavalry unit Felix had dispatched to find a passageway through the mountains was returning at a leisurely canter, rather than a breakneck gallop that might suggest they were being pursued, or worse, a slow, deliberate walk which meant they were returning with serious injuries and dared not risk further harm; I hoped this meant they were bringing good news, something that had been in painfully short supply of late.

I'd even settle for no bad news.

Within a few minutes the glittering bluish-green line became individual horses and their riders. I could even make out Marcus astride his dapple-gray, Belili—and he could see me, too, as he waved, quickly followed by a more formal, fist to chest salute.

I motioned to Jotia, who in turn signaled the men on a nearby watchtower; instantly half dozen polished bronze buccinas rose as one, their mouthpieces pressed to lips, followed by chorus of deep lowing warbles, the signal to stand down, that it was our own who were approaching.

I let loose the breath I didn't realize I'd been holding and glanced up; the sky above had already started to shade to a deep, dusty lavender. Marcus had timed his return perfectly, making it back to our fortified camp just before dark.

I turned to Aetius, who had the best lungs of anyone and gestured to the railing that overlooked the camp. "Better let everyone know everything's all right," and as he turned then carefully eased his way through the crush of men, towards the far railing, I said to Rufinius, "Get that gate open, get everyone inside then get everything locked up tight."

He nodded and started for the ladder just as Aetius cupped his hands to his mouth and staring down at the waiting crowd, bellowed, *"IT'S OUR CAVALRY RETURNING!"*

In reply, a booming cheer went up from the soldiers below.

I turned back to the railing to watch as Marcus and his men joined up with those who'd been hastily dispatched to form the first line of defense and, realizing who it was approaching, had ridden out at a gallop to welcome them back. The shifting mass of men and horses now approached the one safe passage across the riverbed at a trot, ragtag and in small groups, everyone talking, happy to see their companions safely back from their days-long sortie, shared laughter at those who were wearing only breeches or riding bareback, their voices, their relieved chuckles carried up to us on the soft evening breeze, bringing a mood of good humor which quickly spread to those manning the towers and firing platforms: the crews began to stamp their feet in union, the rhythmic beat accompanied by their voices, loudly chanting, *"SPARTOÍ, SPARTOÍ, SPARTOÍ…!"*

I couldn't help but grin at Felix as those around us joined in the general merriment, thrusting their swords skywards and dancing like fools in the cramped space, burning off their nervous energy.

Still smiling, I made my way through the crowd of gleeful soldiers, over to the ladder.

Below, within the camp, the rest of the soldiers had joined the booming mantra of *"SPARTOÍ! SPARTOÍ! SPARTOÍ!"* and added to the general uproar by banging their swords against their shields in time with their voices, all told a deafening racket within the enclosed space, bewildering to the Adraniis, who weren't sure whether they were welcome to join in the impromptu and boisterous merriment or stand back, leaving the raucous welcoming entirely to us.

Felix edged around me, yelled over the din, *"Let me go first!"* and motioned to the ladder.

I reluctantly nodded, and he began to clamber down, but half way he stopped, managed to pull off his helmet one handed and toss it to a soldier below, then he looked up at me, ready to grab me if my leg gave out on me. As I eased myself down onto the first rung, I found I was less worried about my leg and more concerned about my flank which was still throbbing painfully—in fact it had never *stopped* throbbing painfully, only easing off slightly as I was helped by the two Adraniis to the ladder, then re-igniting as I climbed it. Now I was going to have to repeat the maneuver… *in reverse.*

Imagine my joy.

I took another rung, lowered myself and felt for another, got a foothold, then reaching down with a foot, felt for another, each step down taken slowly, with infinite care—I had no desire to falter, or worse, fall—Felix, despite his good intentions, would be hard-pressed to catch me; more likely I'd take him with me.

Fortunately by the time I started my perilous descent everyone's attention had been drawn to the gate—horsemen were now entering to cheers and the continued and thunderous, *THWHACK-THWHACK-THWHACK!* of swords against shields—everyone's attention but one: Felix. He was just below me, one hand dutifully guiding my feet to safe placement on the rungs.

My right foot finally touched down on solid rock, then my left. It took me a moment or so to get my hands to accept that we were in fact back on the ground and in one piece and that it was safe to let go.

I wiped the pain off my face, turned to Felix and managed a husky, "Let's go join the celebration, eh?" then I started off as if nothing was amiss.

Felix wasn't fooled; Felix watched me walk away—or, should I say *shuffle* away and once I thought I'd lost him in the lengthening shadows of dusk and the thoroughly mixed and milling crowd of happy soldiers and anxiously relieved Adraniis, I grabbed my side, hoping that and that alone would ease the stabbing pain that threatened to knock my legs out from under me. I just needed to make my appearance, greet Marcus and his men, hear the news they brought us… and then somehow make it back to my tent… all without falling flat on my face.

By the sidelong looks I garnered as I made my way through the crowd I wasn't giving a very convincing performance, so I clenched my teeth, forced my hand to release its death grip, picked up my feet and *strode* purposely towards the gate, where Marcus still sat astride his gray, talking to Rufinius as Rufinius patted Belili's neck while the rest of the cavalry poured through the gate, in twos and threes and fours, a horde of dusty-faced men and lathered horses accompanied by their grinning fellows.

"Legate!" Marcus yelped and hurriedly dismounted as I stepped out of the throng of people.

"Centurion—glad to have you back—all accounted for I hope?" I yelled hoarsely over the racket of chanting, cheering and happy mayhem that had spread throughout the camp, infecting even the adult Adraniis, many of whom I'd seen smiling—or, even more shocking, *laughing*. Small children—the first to realize this was a shared festivity—were now darting here and there among the throng, giggling and squealing at the top of their lungs.

Marcus glanced over his shoulder as the first engine rumbled back through the gateway, then turned back to me. "Each and every one,

Legate—so good to see you up." He gave me a tentative pat on the shoulder as his eyes searched mine, his relieved grin fading as he realized I might be up, but I was far from fully recovered.

His eyes then flicked to my left and I turned to see the crowd part, giving way to Borzu, Aetius and Felix—who'd recovered his helmet and was again wearing it. Suddenly everyone—the children only at the urging of their parents—fell silent.

I waited until the three joined us, then I said in a voice loud enough to carry even to the men on the far platforms, "What news do you bring us, Centurion?"

The grin on Marcus' coal-black face was back, and telling. "I bring very good news, Legate," he replied in kind, his voice echoing off the circuit walls. "We've found a pass through the mountains—"

A cheer went up, startling the horses—even Marcus's gray whickered nervously and sidestepped, forcing him to give it a quick, sharp jerk on the reins, followed by a reassuring pat on the neck; Felix turned, motioned again for silence.

"It lies to the north, three days march on foot—sixty odd miles I'd judge—and the pass itself is a hard climb, I won't deny that. The smaller wagons and engines can make it, but we'll have to disassemble the larger ones towards the end." Seeing my face fall, hearing the soft groans of nearby soldiers, he quickly added, "But we found grasslands beyond, Legate, just as Duccius said—grasslands as far as the eye can see, and a river—good, sweet water..."

I suddenly found myself savoring the image of a good long soak—even if the water was still freezing ice melt—and rid myself of the ground-in grit that stained everything ocher.

"...the grasslands lie some distance beyond that range," he pointed to the hinter crags, "maybe another two, three days on foot, but still close enough." He looked around, let the news settle before reaching into a pouch tied to a saddle pommel and withdrawing a handful of gray-green grass stalks. "We let the horses graze, including Belili here." He gave his beloved mount another pat on the neck and the horse reached around and began nibbling on the grass as if the intent had been to offer it to him, rather than proof of Marcus' claims. "As you can see, no harm done—I even tried it—"

"Knowing you," Aetius said, "you insisted on trying it before the horses."

The surrounding soldiers erupted into laughter, Adraniis quickly joining in as the soldiers grinned and many clapped nearby Adraniis' backs, making it clear they were truly welcome share in the gaiety—a mass easing of the tension, as if everyone had taken a deep breath and slowly exhaled.

Marcus smiled, shrugged at the undeniable truth in Aetius's remark then continued in a more serious voice, "Since we don't know the seasons here, or even if there are seasons, I suggest we make another sortie beyond the pass, pick out a place to camp, at least temporarily, while the rest of us make our way over the pass, then keep moving south, keeping to the edge of the grasslands—relatively easy going once we get over these mountains.

"From the sketchy map you supplied us, Captain Borzu," Marcus nodded to the man, "south seems to be the best way to go—what we saw confirmed what you remembered from your survey: a series of mountain ranges, valleys with rivers, what looked like a mantle of forest on some of the lower foothills and snow on the higher peaks, with plenty of forage for the horses and oxen along the way—"

"And the goats!" familiar voice shouted from the far back. *"Don't forget the goats!"*

Hardalio. His interjection sent another ripple of easy laughter through the densely packed crowd.

"Then let's all begin our preparations," I said as loud as I could with my hoarse voice. "Plan to move out two days from dawn tomorrow—"

That garnered a collective and startled gasp, mostly from the Adraniis and a sidelong glance from Cleander, who'd appeared at Borzu's side, his goatskin apron stained with old and fresh blood. I fixed him with a stare and he replied with a reluctant nod. Some of the wounded, the weak wouldn't survive the trip—that was a given based on their injuries, their frailty, others who, given time, might otherwise live would also likely die in the move which promised to be grueling even on the able-bodied. But that was the way it was—no one would argue that our injured took precedence over the rest. Better some die en route than let everyone be taken by the Si'aafu.

"The longer we remain here, the worse conditions will become—and the greater the risk that the Si'aafu, when they come, will catch us out in the open. The sooner we get moving, the better. There's absolutely nothing to be gained by delay." I waited, gave everyone a chance to take that in, realize the truth of it, then: "Spend the time deciding what you must take and what you can leave behind, at least for now. When we move, I want to move en mass—*everyone goes.* No one stays behind. If we can, we'll send parties back to retrieve what was left, but I make no promises." I looked at Borzu; the man still carried a bad odor with me, but… well, damn it, it *was* only right that he too address our combined populace—plus my raspy voice was about to give out, a combination of smoke and not being able to get a full breath of air in me.

He nodded then said, "We cannot stay here—as the Legate says, conditions are deteriorating by the hour and we all know the Si'aafu are coming. Gather together what you truly need, leave everything else. I doubt the baggage carts will hold up for a hard slog through the mountains. Despite Engineer Rufinius and his men's gallant efforts to repair and reinforce them they were never built for this sort of work, so pack accordingly—pack only what you can carry, because chances are you'll have to.

"And make it orderly—no need to panic. We're not going anywhere tonight, so I strongly suggest we all relax, get something to eat and get to bed early, yes?" Borzu pointedly sniffed the smoke-greasy air; cook fires that had been doused as a precaution when we thought we were about to be attacked had been hurriedly rekindled, Florianus, his cooks and the hundred or so Adraniis who'd volunteered for the duty had reasonably anticipated a hungry camp, even hungrier riders and had begun preparing the evening meal the minute the all clear had been sounded—by necessity a hasty affair, and simple.

By my decree only the badly injured, the pregnant and nursing women and the children—and tonight the cavalrymen who'd returned from their fatiguing sortie—would go to bed with full stomachs; the rest of us would make do with less, but Marcus had given me, given all of us hope that things might improve, because as he and I well knew where there were grasslands, there were grass-*eaters*, and with luck we'd find the lands beyond the mountain ranges chock-full of game that would fill our cook pots and our bellies.

Of course with grass-eaters came the requisite eaters of grass-eaters, and I made a mental note to speak to my officers—along with Borzu and his officers about how best to set up the column to protect the women, children and the wounded, and at the same time maintain a good speed while keeping the column as orderly and tightly packed as possible—I did not want to be caught out in the open with our people spread out in a scattered, disorganized and impossible to defend train when the Si'aafu arrived—or if we happened across a pack of home-grown predators.

I looked up to a sky which had, in a very brief time, turned from a dusty lavender to a far deeper shade; the whirlpool was already well up and filling the eastern horizon, the massive spiral a ghost of its nighttime glory hidden as it was behind the dusty veil of twilight. Only the bright spot was close to its full, luminous potential, with the azure Remus now nestled in the crags of the western peaks. In a matter of minutes, the star would vanish, tugged down into its bed by the embrace of its much larger opponent... or lover—maybe that was it. Maybe they rose as enemies, sank as lovers, only to repeat the cycle endlessly—

I made a face. *Gods, what a load of crap, Arri! You're getting mawkish in your old age, you know that?*

I dropped my pinched gaze to find Felix, Cleander and Borzu, along with a fourth man, an Adranii, standing a little distance off, talking quietly amongst themselves. I had no recollection of them walking away, leaving me behind, which left me with the distinct impression that they didn't want me to overhear what they were discussing.

I scowled at them—they didn't notice, damn them—so I looked around, hoping for a more attentive response from someone, only to find that Marcus had left, having taken his weary horse and his equally weary men and their mounts with him; Rufinius was elsewhere, probably overseeing the return and proper storage of the engines once the gates were shut and barred, just as I'd ordered. Aetius too was nowhere to be seen—knowing Aetius he'd slipped off the instant the cooks began preparing the meal in hopes of being first in line. My centurions had abandoned me in preference for putting the camp back to rights, their men and the Adraniis following, like a retreating tide.

I thought it all rather rude than no one had thought to ask my leave—they'd all just... *left*. Then again, maybe they had asked for my leave, waited, realized I was staring stupidly up at the sky, lost in my own private musings and they'd graciously elected to leave me to it.

So, I decided to make my own escape while Felix and his buddies were busy colluding and slipped away, into the crowd of soldiers returning to their collapsed tents, their abandoned fires and Adraniis hustling reluctant children back to the familiarity of their shabby lean-tos. My men nodded to me in passing, murmured their greetings, patting me on the shoulder as I made my way through their rapidly thinning gauntlet of happy, relieved faces; Adraniis deferentially stepped aside for me, staring as I passed without, I must add, blatant hostility—some smiled hesitantly, a few even greeted me by title as they respectfully drew their children close and out of my way, but no one stopped me, not a soul followed in hopes of a private chat with the legate. Maybe it was the strained look on my sweat-streaked face, perhaps the worsening limp, or my hand tightly gripping my side. There was no point hiding it now, I was in serious pain and clearly in need of my bed and no one dared keep me—

I suddenly tripped over gods know what—maybe a pebble, maybe air—I was that wobbly—somehow regained my balance—again, gods know how—stumbled on, mind set on my single, unyielding goal: *bed.*

As I made my slow, unsteady, but very determined way through the maze of passageways, back to the command tent, I passed by a number of small bonfires, each ringed by grubby, tatter-clothed Adraniis, fires that had been hastily relit to warm stones that would then be used to warm their beds—a trick they'd learned from my men.

As I passed the altar, I noted it was again bedecked with meager offerings—most non-edible and therefore not a tempting snatch for a hungry child or adult—but here and there, among the scraps of cloth and dark stains of dried wine was a scattering of grain and a few withered but recognizable pieces of fruit. Felix's warning to Borzu had clearly filtered down through the Adraniis. Maybe it was a measure of Gratian's impassioned eloquence in enlightening them, perhaps it was his simple yet thoughtful offer to perform rites over their dead—our beliefs were to be respected even by those who labeled them as backward and asinine, and according to Iulius, some of the more churlish Adraniis, like Isem had, and more so they'd done it openly—while our makeshift altar was sacrosanct even from the immediate and obvious needs that surrounded it.

I was, to my annoyance, forced to circle the perimeter of a large crowd that had formed around one massive cook-fire, its flickering glow catching the glint of armor here and there among the drab, shifting wall of Adraniis—small groups of soldiers had arrived and were now waiting patiently to be fed, while the lengthening shadows cloaked the less savory features of our squalid surroundings—a blessing no doubt: fifty four hundred people, more or less, all crammed into a space fifteen hundred soldiers used to close quarters had found a tad cramped. But thankfully that was about to change—and none too soon.

Rufinius had also clearly, if perhaps only briefly, solved the matter of the latrines as the camp no longer smelled like an open sewer. It didn't smell great, but the air I sucked into my lungs as I stumbled along no longer made my stomach turn with each painful breath.

The murmur of voices followed me, soft, weary voices of people readying themselves for the night after a very long day that had climaxed in a flurry of panic over a feared Si'aafu or gods-know-who attack. Children's overly excited, high-pitched voices mixed with the low, worn-out drone of adults, at times questioning, at times petulant, not at all happy with the thought of being put to bed when there was still plenty of light to play games of tag around the tents and lean-tos: pent up energy looking for an escape and finding none.

I didn't envy their parents.

I finally reached my tent, relieved, in truth sincerely amazed I'd made it all by myself and without serious calamity, but just short of grabbing the nearest flap, I stopped and looked back at the surrounding encampment.

The camp was settling, utterly exhausted truth be told, but thanks to the gods no longer held in the grip of mutual suspicion, of resentment. Soldiers and Adraniis were finally, thankfully, *mixing*. My soldiers had proven themselves and then some to the Adraniis—they *would* protect them, protect their families, risking their own lives if it came to that and the Adraniis knew this now.

The Adraniis in turn had reacted by inviting my men to sit and talk, share the warmth of their small fires, laughter, the company and care of women—with the potential of small flirtations, perhaps even a few assignations. Most of my men, I strongly suspected, were just content to finally feel welcome by these people we'd welcomed into our camp, having never been fully accepted by anyone but me.

But there was more to it than the simple gratitude on the part of the Adraniis, the offer of friendship, more than female companionship and being accepted as equals, as critical as those all were: everyone knew they were going to get something to eat, knew *our* combined supplies *were* going to be fairly apportioned to all—the promise of not going to bed gripped by hunger—that was the key. I could only hope the individual alliances forged this evening over the large, communal cook fires and small, shared campfires, perhaps in the privacy of a few tents and lean-tos, would hold us all in good stead once the food ran out, because run out it would, sooner rather than later.

I shook my head as I drew the flap aside then slipped inside... and stopped in my tracks.

Eithne, bathed in the now guttering glow of the suspended oil lamp, rose from where she'd been seated at the table and flashed me a nervous smile. "Good evening, Legate."

"Eithne...! Uh... what... what are you doing here?" I stammered, my voice gone all raspy, a combination of dust, strain and smoke.

"I was invited, remember?"

"Oh, um... yes," I glanced around, looked back at her. "Felix... Felix isn't here."

When she replied, "Yes, I can see that," I felt a sudden sense of familiarity in the situation and almost expected her to look under my cot, just as Felix had done. But she didn't. Of course she'd been in the tent for some time, alone, plenty of opportunity to check every nook and cranny for herself.

"I... ah... I'm not really sure when he'll be here."

"I'm *sure* he'll turn up eventually—you two are close to inseparable."

I freed myself of the baldric and sword and managed to hang them from the tent pole. "Yes... uh, yes I'm sure he will—perhaps you'd like to sit down while you wait?"

"I was sitting."

I glanced back at her. "Oh, yes... right, of... of course you were."

She managed another tight smile; I clamped my mouth shut. While she was clearly scared, *I* was the one making a stammering fool out of myself—nervous, just like her, every bit as scared as she was, maybe even more, if you really want to know. *Me of all people—scared stupid by a woman.*

I immediately chalked it up to being dog-tired. *Yes, that's it. I'm just extremely tired... didn't expect to find her here—had totally forgotten about her in all the excitement. She took me by surprise, that's all.* And of course the awful realization that one scream from her would ignite the camp—never mind that she had come to my tent willingly—without my knowledge—had in fact been waiting for... me? Waiting for Felix? *Both of us?*—she had, after all, appeared as intrigued by the idea as Felix.

If I did anything to spook her, her fellow Adraniis would no doubt think the worst and all the good will and friendship on display just beyond the walls of the tent would go up in flames and take the camp with it.

I cautiously motioned to my bed, saw her eyebrows lift and suddenly realized she'd taken the gesture the wrong way. *"No!*—I mean that's not what I meant!" *Oh, gods... be careful, Arri!* I took a breath. "I meant is it all right with you if I sit down?"

She nodded, even managed a soft chuckle at my blatantly obvious and intense unease.

I slowly eased myself down, couldn't help but wince as a fold in the leather tunic unexpectedly bit into my exceedingly tender flank.

She noticed and stepped close. "You're in pain."

Eithne had not come here to play nursemaid—but sadly right now I had far more pressing concerns, like getting comfortable, after that...

"Just need to lie down for a while," I replied tightly, "that's all—overdid it—shouldn't have run or climbed that damned ladder." I carefully lay back, using my elbows to slow my awkward descent rather than my abused stomach muscles.

She tucked my rolled up cloak under my head, then helped me get my legs onto the bed. I made no effort to straighten them—they just sprawled and stayed where they fell as I exhaled, suddenly and overwhelmingly weary.

She stared down at me, head cocked to one side, the frown replaced by a look of genuine worry. "I'll get one of your physicians—"

"*No*, please—I'm fine. Really."

She looked skeptical. "Sure?"

"Yeah," I nodded and she seemed to take that as encouragement as she promptly sat on the edge of the cot and began unlacing my sandals. Unlike Cleander, she did it with the minimum of tugging and pulling and once she'd tossed the sandals under the cot she placed her warm hand on my shin.

I jumped, startled.

"You feel clammy—are you *sure* you're all right?"

"Like I said, I shouldn't have run like I did. Really, nothing more."

She sat back, eyed me. "I think you're lying."

I blinked away the unease; replaced it with annoyance at her damnable cheek. It was bad enough to reach my tent, knowing my bed was within my grasp only to find I had unexpected company who clearly had ideas other than napping on her mind, but to then be accused of lying? "I'm just damned *tired*, all right? I need to get some sleep." I pointed at the tent flaps. "Last time I saw Felix he was by the gate talking with your Captain Borzu—"

"I'm sure he'll be arriving shortly," she murmured as she lightly stroked my left foot and ankle, "no need to go fetch him this moment, is there?"

I blinked again. "Uh... no, I suppose—"

"Would *you* rather we wait for him?"

So she was intrigued... Of course my splayed legs might have been taken as a, uh, less than subtle open invitation? I wasn't wearing breeches after all, only my damned underwear under the undertunic, which, as I've mentioned before, is not all that reliable in providing proper, *um*, containment?

"He might be awhile—"

"Then I'm sure he won't mind if we don't wait." Keeping her eyes locked with mine, she slid her hand up my left shin, stopping at my knee and I suddenly wondered what would happen if I screamed—would everyone assume the worse of her?

Un-bloody-likely. "Eithne…"

She raised her brows. "Yes?"

"Felix is quite smitten with you—"

The hand moved higher, stopped as it came across the disfiguring scar that completely encircled my left thigh. Her eyes flicked to it; she briefly grimaced then met my gaze with a questioning stare.

"Got slashed with a sword."

"Oh." She ran her fingertip lightly along the ragged line. "Painful?"

"When it happened? Yeah, hurt like fucking hell."

She again looked at me, sharply this time. "I mean is it painful now?"

I thought about telling her it still hurt like fucking hell—it did always ache, especially so when I'd done something particularly stup—er, I mean *strenuous* like, say, climb a ladder?—and end this, right now, before it went any further because if her hand went much farther up my leg I wasn't sure I'd be able to end it—that I wouldn't *want* to end it despite feeling a deep kinship with the fruit I'd tormented to a pulp earlier. "No, not particularly." I blinked then looked around as if fully expecting to find my twin—a suddenly very horny twin—standing nearby, answering for me. *Why'd I say that?*

Taking that as further encouragement, she slipped her hand fully under the hem of the undertunic; my body responded in ways that were not at all subtle and I glanced around, on the verge of panic. "Where's… where's Anachie?"

"Under the cot."

I sat bolt upright, managed through a startled grimace: *"What?"*

"He's with a friend—so just *relax.*" She pressed her free hand into my chest, gave me a not-so-gentle shove and I fell back onto the cot.

I was sweating now; I could feel it beading on my forehead, my cheeks. "Eithne, I… I *can't.*"

But even I knew it was too late: her hand had slipped through the leg hole and then inside my underwear and was now doing a bit of exploring. "I beg to differ."

I inhaled sharply as she wrapped her fingers around me, then added, "I… I mean I *can*, physically—"

"Obviously," she replied with a sidelong grin while she lightly fondled me.

"—I just… just can't. I want to, believe me—*ooooohhhhhh gods…!*"

She grinned at my protracted moan.

"…I… I do. I just… just… *can't.*"

She relaxed her grip just a little and fixed me with this genuinely perplexed stare because she had all the evidence at, um, *hand*, that that I could. "No one saw me come in your tent if that's what's worrying you—I made sure. So, as long as we don't make a lot of noise, who's to know?"

"I'll know. Felix, if he walks in on us will know. Anyone who strolls by and happens to look through the slit in the flaps will know."

"I could douse the lamp."

"And end up with Felix on top of us?"

She grinned and wiggled her eyebrows. "Isn't that what you wanted, a threesome?"

"I meant he might trip in the dark. He's armed you know, so you might end up with his gladius pommel up your butt instead of something else."

"Oh." She reluctantly withdrew her hand and I breathed a private sigh of relief, foolishly believing this meant she was going to see reason and stop before things got *out* of hand. "What I'm trying to say is that I'm willing, *more* than willing in fact."

"With a gladius pommel?"

She murmured, "Now you're just being silly," and flicked me a sidelong, decidedly wicked look as her hands again slipped up inside my undertunic, this time clearly in search of my underwear's ties. "I just don't see why we need to wait—he could be some time."

"Uh, well…" I began just as I felt one tie go; an instant later I felt her tug the front flap down.

"Ah, much better," she purred as she resumed her fondling, this time two handed and unimpeded by my underclothing. "Now, you were saying…?"

I gasped, gasped again and loudly as one hand went where I hadn't expected it to go, then managed, "I… I c-c-can't think with you d-d-doing that—"

"Want me to stop?"

Of course I didn't and of course she didn't. In fact she took my hesitation as even more encouragement and using the one hand to keep me fully occupied, she half rose and somehow, don't ask me how, managed to get her breeches down around her knees. She wasn't wearing anything underneath and in case you were wondering—don't deny it, you *were* wondering—the shave job did not extend below her scalp. "Do you have any idea just how damned handsome you are?"

I gulped, audibly. "I—"

She roughly wedged her knees between my legs, prying them further apart, flipped aside the leather pteruges on my tunic, pushed my undertunic up, then finished by making quick work of the subligarium's other tie, exposing me completely. She gazed down at me for a moment, grinned, then without further ado she leaned forward, pressed her lips against mine and resumed her fondling and as I gasped again she slipped her tongue into my mouth.

I'm not exactly sure what happened next except that I found myself suddenly on top of her, holding her shoulders down against the cot and kissing her madly, roughly—my throbbing side, the bone-deep weariness instantly forgotten as she opened herself to me.

I couldn't stop myself—didn't want to stop as I began thrusting with no finesse, no decorum, in truth no concern for her needs whatsoever—I was so involved, so fixated on what I was doing, the look in her eyes, her deep moans, the rapid, rhythmic slap of flesh against flesh, so damned eager for release I didn't care if anyone heard and came to investigate. I also didn't watch what I was doing and with one powerful thrust I not only forced myself deeply into her, eliciting a loud groan from her, but I also managed to lock my entire side up, going from pure ecstasy to sheer agony in the space of a single heart beat; I swear I felt my insides rip open. I cried out and as she clapped her hand over my mouth to muffle it, I collapsed on top of her—I think I might have briefly blacked out—the next thing I remember was feeling her struggling to get out from under me and I somehow managed to roll off her, just enough, then tried to curl into a ball.

Heaving for breath I opened my eyes to see her standing over me, grinning and breathing hard herself, her breeches still down around her ankles—clearly thinking the obvious and immensely smug about it—but as she saw the look in my glassy eyes, the smug grin abruptly vanished.

She gathered up her trousers, hurriedly tied them in place then dropped to her knees beside me and touched my clammy face, gently, almost fearfully as she looked me over. *"What happened—are you all right?"*

I was clearly not all right—I was clearly in a great deal of pain, near blinding pain in fact.

"Your side!" She placed her hand on my flank.

I couldn't help but flinch and groan, *"Don't... touch!"*

She jerked her hand away as if burned. *"I'm... I'm so... so sorry! I just couldn't—"*

"It's all right... I'm... I'm all right," I lied, my voice barely above a hoarse, gasping whisper as I very slowly eased myself onto my back.

"You're not all right—*damn it!*—"

"*Keep your voice down!*" I gritted my teeth, angrily wiped my watering eyes.

"You're a fine one to talk—"

"*I'll be all right*—"

"I'll get Cleander—"

"*No!*" Gods, the last thing I needed was for her to go fetch Cleander—he'd ask questions, lots of humiliating questions and next thing it would be all over the camp as Cleander was not exactly the model of discretion.

She stared down at me, arms akimbo, clearly unconvinced and very, very scared. "Felix then. I'll go get Fe—"

"*Please,* no. The... the pain's easing off... just... just give me a moment."

She sighed, shook her head, then knelt and ran her fingers across my sweat glossy forehead, down my jaw as she murmured, "This isn't exactly turning out the way I'd envisioned."

I looked at her out of the corner of my eye. "Thank the gods for that."

She smiled feebly as she discreetly tugged my undertunic down, covering me. What had happened was embarrassing enough. Now it was getting damned chilly—and fine, I can be in agony and still find it in me to be vain at the same time. *Happy?*

"If it's any consolation, it was incredible while it lasted," she murmured as she wiped a sweaty lock of hair from my forehead.

Either she was a liar or she'd never had a skilled lover—I'd gone at her, just as Felix claimed I would given the chance, like Wushah on a mare in heat—I *knew* better, I knew how to make love to a woman, how to touch her in ways that when I finally entered her she was already writhing in ecstasy—it was a very useful, not to mention a highly *profitable* skill. I'd learned from the very best after all.

Finally and clearly thinking the worst was over, she gave me a pat on the arm, smiled again. "Better?"

"*Yeah.*" I wasn't, damned if I was, the agonizing stitch in my side just wouldn't let up, but I felt the sooner I appeared to have recovered from our embarrassing mishap, the sooner she'd find a reason to leave—I was not about to risk a repeat performance.

"Then how about I help you get undressed, make you more comfortable?—and check your side while we're at it, just to make sure."

"I'm used to sleeping in my clothing," I replied lamely—to be totally honest I was really afraid I *had* started bleeding again but I didn't want her feeling responsible for something that was entirely the result of my own incredibly overeager stupidity.

"Up." She rose, offering me her hand. "Come on—no excuses—or I go get Cleander whether *you* agree or not."

I squinted up at her; she clearly wasn't bluffing. So I tried and ended up sitting on the edge of the cot, shaking and gasping for breath, my mind swimming and trying desperately not to heave. She settled beside me and carefully wrapped her arm around me.

I leaned into her, rested my cheek on her shoulder, my eyes squeezed shut, my breath coming in short, ragged gulps.

She stroked my head with her free hand, murmured, "Try to slow your breathing… come on, slower… *slower."*

I focused on her soft voice, the incredibly comforting touch of her hand and her encircling arm as I struggled to do as she asked.

"Slower… yes, that's right. *Deeper* breaths…"

We sat there for several minutes until my head stopped spinning then I very slowly straightened up. Then, don't ask me why, I blurted out: "I shouldn't have done… what I did. I'm truly sorry."

"Why should you be sorry? I'm the one who instigated it—"

"No, no, what I meant is that you should be with Felix, not me—I shouldn't have—"

"You mean you don't find me attractive after all."

"No, that's not what I meant—"

"Then why?"

"Because Felix is a good man, very kind—"

"Meaning you aren't? Arri, I've overheard what you're soldiers say about you—to a man they adore you. You don't garner that sort of fierce loyalty through cruelty and deceit."

I shook my head, immediately regretted it and grabbed it in both hands, mumbled, "I meant he'd be a good husband and a good father to Anachie."

"Anachie preferred you."

Still clutching my head, I looked at her through a gap in my fingers. "Is that why you're here?"

"No, but the fact that Anachie is drawn to you certainly helps."

"Eithne, I *have* a wife, I *have* a son—"

"On Earth."

I slowly lifted my head from my hands as I braced myself for her to say the obvious, that I was a fool for thinking—hoping—I'd ever see them again.

Instead: "I'm sorry, Arri. Truly I am." She kissed me on the cheek and rose, motioning for me to do the same. "Now, let's get you out of that tunic at the very least—nothing more, all right? Then I want you to get some sleep."

I stared up at her. "To be honest I don't think I can stand right now." In truth I wasn't sure I could sleep, either. My side was throbbing in sickening cadence with the pounding inside my skull and my stomach was still debating as to whether I should heave or not. I think it was leaning towards not only because there was nothing to heave up, which would mean a lot of effort for little or no gain.

"Then lie back down."

I didn't need any more encouragement. I sprawled back, this time managed to get my legs onto the bed without help—fine, I was worried if she did help, very recent history would repeat itself with even more disastrous results.

She drew the blanket over me then ran her fingers through my sweaty hair and clearly having second thoughts about leaving, she kissed me on the forehead as she lightly caressed my chin, my lips. "I'm willing to wait."

I'd heard *that* line before, *that* promise and reacted without thinking: "You mean until I give up hope? *Until I see reason?*" I hadn't intended for that to come out quite as bitter as it sounded, damned if I did, but even if I could've, I wouldn't have retracted it. The sooner she understood how I really felt, the better—for everyone involved.

She eased herself down beside my hip and gently wiped the hair out of my eyes, then stroked my cheek. "I don't expect you to stop loving your wife, Arri, or your son, or to stop hoping you'll see them again—it *is* completely reasonable to want that. I still love my husband—and I know with absolute certainty he's *never* coming back.

"It's that very desire that, in part, draws me to you. Here we are, so far from home, and you're still faithful to your wife, you still bleed inside for your son—" She stopped, winced at my wince, "Sorry, bad analogy." Then: "Those are very rare qualities, do you realize that? So, I'm willing to wait for as long as it takes for you to realize—"

She put her finger to my lips as I opened my mouth.

"*Hush.* This isn't a matter of being unfaithful. We have no idea how long we'll be here—maybe the rest of our lives, maybe not, but in the meantime we each have physical needs that can be met—*should be met—*

and I find you *incredibly* desirable. Even now I'm finding it really hard to keep my hands off you. I cannot believe the woman you married would want you to be lonely and unhappy, possibly, I'm sorry to say, for the rest of your life."

"You don't know Turan," I said in a feeble attempt at a joke… that in truth wasn't a joke at all.

"Your wife."

I nodded.

"She'd *want* you to be miserable?"

I shrugged. "Probably not, but…"

"But what?"

I hesitated, not sure how she'd react, then I decided what the hell. "She's Tuatha."

That garnered a slow blink, nothing more, then, "Faoimhuir also take Adraniis as lovers… but I never heard of any who actually married their, um…"

"Property?"

She nodded and shrugged apologetically.

"I call Turan my wife… but we aren't married, officially—it's a private arrangement."

Her mouth formed a polite, silent 'O' as if that explained everything when it in fact only exposed the true depth of my foolishness.

I fixed my eyes on something safe, something other than Eithne's all too piercing gaze, which turned out to be the slit in the flaps, adding, "She loved me, she *promised* me she did—I believed her—I still do. She even had a gods damned son by me, Neshoue—it almost killed her. I almost killed them both by getting her pregnant." I shifted my gaze back to her, hoping for a woman's logic, a woman's mind to tell me what I so desperately wanted to hear. "She wouldn't have done that, wouldn't have risked everything if she didn't love me, would she?"

She hesitated, finally said, "No."

I didn't believe her; worse, I suddenly didn't believe Turan. *I'm a fool, a fool to believe anything—*

"Neshoue. That's a beautiful name—a family name?"

"Yes," I replied angrily, angry at her for trying to change the subject, angry at myself—*gods, Arri, you* are *the complete fool, aren't you? Women have always played you for the fool—*

"Yours?"

I blinked, swiveled my mind and my eyes back to her. "Huh?"

"Neshoue—you said it was a family name. Yours?"

"Her's—her father's name."

"How old is your son?"

I didn't answer immediately. I couldn't, then, hoarsely, "A few months old when I left—I don't know now."

"*Left*. By choice?"

I glared up at her, motioned angrily around me. "*What the hell do you think?*"

"*Shhhh,*" she murmured as she continued to stroke my cheek, gently, undeterred by my menacing expression, my furious tone or the muscles in my jaw that had drawn taut in rage. "I understand why you miss your son, Arri—but explain to me why Turan holds such sway over you?"

"*Why the hell is it any of your gods damned business?*"

Her fingertip wiped the corner of my suddenly watery eye, then lightly touched the old scar just below, on my left cheek. "I want you," she replied softly. "You say no because you refuse to be unfaithful to a woman who even you admit you may never see again, a woman who perhaps knew ahead of time you were being left here to die and if she did, did nothing to stop it—"

"*You don't know that!*"

"—and a woman who, you also freely admit, *owns* you. That gives me every right to know."

"Like hell it does—*out!*"

"Arri—"

"*I said out!*"

She stubbornly remained seated beside my hip but folded her hands in her lap. "Why are you so afraid of being happy?"

I squinted at her and replied indignantly, "I *was* happy."

"When? Tell me the last time you were happy."

"When I woke up and realized I hadn't been killed by that gods damned projectile—I was *damned* happy!"

"Really? Maisoh told me you appeared quite upset."

"*After* she told me she'd poisoned the water she'd just given me to drink, her idea of a joke—I choked on it, thank you, and pissed all over myself. I had damned good reason to be upset!"

"So, not happy."

"Fine. Later then, when I realized Felix was alive."

"Meaning you felt intense relief your best friend hadn't been killed—"

"*Of course!*"

"That's not the same as being happy."

I took a deep, steadying breath. "Then before I came here—not much to be happy about here, is there?"

"So, back on Earth, you were happy—with Turan?"

My thoughts turned inward. *Were* there any happy moments with her? In truth I couldn't remember any. Safe moments, yes. But happy?

"Well?"

"I'm thinking!"

"You're taking too long—doesn't that tell you something?"

"It tells me you won't give me a chance to think about it!"

"You shouldn't *have* to think about it. What about the birth of your son—were you happy then?"

"Turan almost died! Neshoue almost died! Turan was still convalescing when I left to come here—I don't even know if she's still alive!"

"So."

"So, *what?*"

"So you can't recall the last time you were genuinely happy. Here's an easier question to answer: when did you last laugh, and I mean *really* laugh?"

I'd laughed at Isem, but something told me that wouldn't count—

"I don't mean smile because you smile a lot—it's a nervous tic, a reflex, do you realize that? Someone smiles at you—you smile back—granted, you have a dazzling, disarming smile which you use to your advantage, but—"

"Am I smiling now?"

"No. You're evading the question."

I massaged the bridge of my nose with my fingers. "That's because I don't remember the damned question."

"When did you last laugh—a good, hard, from the tips of your toes laugh?"

I stopped my impromptu massage and eyed her. "I've never been one to succumb to side-splitting laughter."

"I don't think you've had much in your life to laugh about, *period.*"

"With the first Felix, Aetius and Rufinius—we used to laugh a lot—mostly at each other."

"But not now."

"As I said, not much to laugh about here."

She cocked her head to one side and squinted at me. "You said the *first* Felix, Aetius and Rufinius—what did you mean by that? First *what?*"

I exhaled forcefully—furious at myself for letting *that* slip and growled, "Look, Eithne, I'm *really* tired—can we *please* continue this some other time?"

She stared at me, clearly not fooled by my less than subtle prevarication, but willing to play along... for now. "Anachie *desperately* needs a father—"

So, we're back to that. "Which I assume is your way of saying no."

"—he doesn't take to strangers, but he took to you immediately; he actually slipped away from me to come looking for you..."

I squeezed my eyes shut and clutched my side. *"Please... go away."*

"...since then he hasn't stopped talking about you—in fact this is the most talkative he's been since his father was killed—everyone's noticed."

Fine—I'll play your game. I reopened my eyes only to fix her with a hard gaze. "Only because I vaguely remind him of his dead father."

"Is there something so terrible about that?"

"No, I suppose not—is that why you're attracted to me as well?" I added suspiciously. "Because I remind you of him, too?"

She ran her fingertips lightly across my forehead. "Honestly? Yes... and no. You do resemble him a little—mostly in your coloring, I'd be lying if I said you didn't, but Tiro was rather... well, I'd say passive, the antithesis of you, but that would be unfair—perhaps the best way to describe him is that like most Adraniis he was content as long as he was left to his work—he trusted the Faoimhuir unconditionally, he truly believed our masters valued him, valued his work."

She looked away, took a breath. "It was that blind trust that ultimately lead to his death—our masters kept urging us to speed up our research, disregard safeguards if need be, worried someone else would make the breakthrough first and claim the discovery as theirs." She looked back at me, eyes glistening. "We were attempting to create a stabilized lattice in phase space—I was pregnant with our second child and wasn't feeling well, so that morning Tiro told me to stay in bed, said that he was just going to run some follow-up experiments to verify our earlier findings, but something went terribly awry—Anachie somehow managed to sneak into Tiro's lab, saw the whole thing, saw his father disintegrate into nothingness..."

I hadn't understood everything she'd said—all right, *fine,* I hadn't understood a damned thing she'd said, but I couldn't help but cringe at the thought of a small boy like Anachie witnessing his father's death by any means. I'd grown up seeing others die, and more often than not in the most gruesome and violent of ways—but Anachie came from a vastly different culture where death was clearly a tidy abstract, not a day-to-day messy reality.

"…at least that's what I was told happened, that it was all just a terrible accident."

"Meaning you think it wasn't?"

She shrugged, "What I thought didn't matter—what Adraniis 'think' never matters to our masters, only that we do their bidding and do it well… or we pay the price." She chuckled, added, "The fact that they rely so heavily on us *thinking*—to create, to develop new technologies, to explore—doing what they are afraid to do, probably aren't capable of doing… yet what we feel in here," she pressed her chest, "or here," she touched her forehead, "means nothing to them."

"Yeah, I know what you mean—to the Tuatha we were means to an end, nothing more."

She nodded, then continued softly, "I miscarried a few days later—much to the annoyance of our masters, I might add, and was told that a new partner would be chosen for me, that 'the best thing for all involved' was for me to get pregnant again as soon as possible. So I was paired with Viri, as he and I were, according to our masters, an 'excellent genetic and intellectual match'—"

"Viri? Wasn't he one of the—"

"Envoys? *Yes.* He volunteered, you know—so did Sallis. Viri was a good man, a good officer—I knew I was incredibly fortunate to have been paired with him." She looked away, took another deep breath. "But Anachie was just starting to talk again—I was afraid, and Viri agreed, that any more changes might set Anachie back. Captain Borzu concurred and interceded on our behalf, hoping to convince our masters to give us a little more time before it became official.

"Since our masters had great hopes for Anachie, believing he had the potential for being every bit as brilliant as his father, they agreed to the delay, but only for half a cycle. I was just beginning to feel he was turning the corner when the *Fihroon* was ordered to make the rendezvous with the Si'aafu—and we ran. That's all we were told—we were running from a Si'aafu ambush, back to Faoimhuir space.

"When we got there, we thought we were safe; next thing I knew he and I were forcibly separated—I had no idea what was happening—no one knew. Then we were told that as crew or immediate kin of crew we were all about to be executed as mutineers. My only hope was that Anachie might be spared, given over to another family to raise…"

She bit her lip, sniffed and wiped her eyes with her trembling fingertips. "But then I learned that they'd separated out *all* of the children for 'safekeeping'—I begged the guards to let me see him—" She suddenly looked away as more tears welled up in her eyes. "After agreeing, after... doing as they demanded they... they refused."

I couldn't help but wrap my fingers around her arm, drawing her strained gaze and what I saw in her eyes made my blood boil.

She forced a wan smile. "While we were held in the pens I could think of nothing else but what he was going through—not understanding what was happening to him, not knowing where I'd gone or if he'd ever see me again.

"I was finally reunited with him the day we were to be herded aboard a Si'aafu transport. I barely recognized him—he was so thin, so frail looking...and he wouldn't come to me when I called him. He just... just stood there, staring at me as if I was a ghost. Viri scooped him up and brought him to me, but Anachie didn't react when I wrapped my arms around him, in fact he tried to squirm free."

She shook her head and absently fingered a lock of my hair. "Can you imagine what he's been through? First he sees the father he worshiped die horribly right in front of him, then just as he's starting to recover from that trauma, he's taken from me and kept from me for over a month—he probably thought we'd never see each other again; maybe he even thought I'd abandoned him—or I was dead, like Tiro.

"I almost lost him, Arri, not once but twice—and when we were dumped here, I fully expected to lose him again, this time for good. I had no illusions he'd survive—he was just too small, too... *weak*. He'd withdrawn into himself and there was no getting him back. Then he saw you and suddenly he's talking again, he's eating... he's even started smiling. So, I ask again, is it so terrible that you remind him of his father?"

"I already said no," I replied defensively.

"Then you have a cultural bias against raising another man's son—I've heard of such foolishness. Is that it?"

Her prying questions left me feeling like I was trial for some heinous crime—such as being steadfastly faithful to my absent wife and son? She clearly wasn't going to leave, let me get some much needed sleep until I explained myself and my unexpected lack of enthusiasm over what she was proposing, in truth an offer any one of my men—Felix in particular—would have jumped at. "I was raised by men, none of whom were my father, so no. Besides, I'm Massaesyli, and it's a Massaesyli's sworn family obligation to raise the orphaned children of relatives as their own."

It was truth… as far as it went.

But I wasn't *adopted* by my kin—what few I had—after my mother's murder, because she was a garrison whore and my father was a Roman soldier, or so she'd told me, not Massaesyli, while my relatives maintained that my sire was actually Massyli—blood enemy of the Massaesyli and as far as they were concerned, I was therefore Massyli. Had I been old enough and stupid enough to press the issue, the best I could have expected was a quick death, the worst… being sold into slavery. As it was I was abandoned in the desert, told to find my Massyli family and left to fend for myself—I'd been maybe five at the time—another kind of death sentence to be sure but without anyone's direct involvement or lingering guilt.

Instead the soldiers from the garrison happened across me on their way back from a patrol and took me in, saying it was the least they could do for my mother, who'd been a favorite among the enlisted men… but not without exacting a very high price for the roof over my head, food in my belly and oh, yes, their *'fatherly devotion'.*

Before my mind could travel very far down that well-worn and painful path, Eithne said, "For the first time in my life I can choose who I want to be with, Anachie can choose—and we both chose you…" She again fingered a lock of my hair, drawing my gaze as well as my thoughts off the still all too real horrors of my own childhood—and she wanted *me* to be a father to Anachie?

She stared at me, really stared. "Where'd you go just now?"

I blinked, blinked again. *"Go…?"*

"Just now. You were here with me one minute… and gone somewhere else the next. Where?"

I exhaled, managed a hoarse, *"Home. I was back home."*

"Not a happy place, either, was it?"

I shrugged.

She continued to toy with a lock of my blue-black hair, seemingly every bit as fascinated with it as Anachie. "Do you do that a lot?—just go mentally wandering off somewhere?"

I shrugged again, having no answer to that, either, at least not one I cared to voice.

"Has anyone ever told you, you have the most amazing eyes?— greenish-gray with flecks of amber-brown."

I truthfully answered, "No," because all of my previous sex partners
had found their attention drawn elsewhere.

She ran her fingers through my hair as she again took me in—all of
me—then she murmured, *"Damn, you're gorgeous."*

I couldn't help but chuckle—just too tired to stay angry, too tired to
stay scared, truth be told. "Let's not get started on that again—didn't end
well the last time, remember?"

She nodded, then leaned down, lightly kissed me on the lips—I have
to admit I braced myself, but to my immense relief she only sat back and
stared at me as if mulling over what to say, deciding which new tack to
take, all in an effort to get me to reconsider her offer. Finally: "I'm
willing... all right, *more* than willing, *whenever* you want it, *however* you want
it in trade for you treating Anachie like a son while we're here—"

"And if I don't want *it*...?"

"Then *that's* the agreement—I won't continue to pursue you. So, no
commitment except to Anachie. Is that so much to ask? He's a really good
boy—smart, eager to please. He won't cause you any grief."

I chewed on that, said, "If I agree to be Anachie's surrogate father,
would you take Felix?"

She sat back, crossed her arms and favored me with an odd look.
"I've never known a man to be so damned eager to procure for another
man."

"Ah. You misunderstand."

"Do I? You've done nothing but try to foist him off on me—no
offense to Felix—since you stepped through those flaps. Why?"

"Just say I owe him—he deserves to be happy, far more than me."

She took a moment to absorb that remark, then: "Very noble of you."

"Maybe once you get to know him better he'll explain our
relationship, and why I feel the way I do."

"Why can't you?"

"I can, I'd just prefer not to. If you ask, and he wants to tell you, then
that's his right—"

"Are you lovers?"

I blinked at her bluntness—even Turan had never openly suggested
such even though she could read my thoughts. Maybe that's why Turan
never raised the issue—thinking thoughts are one thing, acting on them is
altogether different. I'd thought a lot about murdering Rasaben too, but
never actually acted on it.

More's the pity.

"No. We're *not.*"

"So, you want me to bed your best friend for purely altruistic reasons."

"Altruistic?"

"Selfless."

"Then yes—and it's not like it would be an odious task. You yourself said he was extremely handsome."

"And he is—every bit as handsome as you, and at the same time, the antithesis of you."

I raised a brow.

"Light and dark," she fingered my hair for emphasis, "child and adult, openly naïve and… tightly guarded. Like opposite sides of the same coin."

I shrugged—in truth I'd never see us that way, but now—

"And in trade you'll be Anachie's surrogate father for as long as we're here."

I thought about it for a moment. "Felix's a good man, Eithne."

"You've already told me that."

"Which means I can't agree to this. He deserves better—and so does your son. You can't buy affection—" I snapped my mouth shut, instantly regretting I'd said that.

"Turan did," she replied, equally stung. With that she rose, started for the tent flap just as Felix pulled it aside, started to step inside then stopped only to stare, wide-eyed at Eithne then at me.

"Think about it," she said, looking back at me. "If you change your mind, *you* let me know. I *won't* ask again." She turned to Felix, briefly glanced at the bowl he held in one hand, murmured, "Good evening, Centurion," then as he pulled the flap aside for her, she slipped past him and into the gathering darkness.

He turned his bewildered eyes on me. "Now it's Centurion? Not Felix?"

I shrugged. *Better than what she's calling me right now I'd wager.*

He set the bowl on the table, motioned to it, grumbled, "Brought you something to eat," then turning back to the tent flaps, added, "What in the gods' names did you say to her?"

"What I told you earlier. I can't—"

"Oh, gods! You didn't include me in this self-imposed celibacy rule of yours, did you?"

I stared at him; no matter what I said Felix was going to be either mightily pissed off or totally crushed. I figured silence was probably the best route—let him pick the least personally hurtful choice.

"Damn, you did, didn't you?"

I shrugged again.

"You're a right fine bastard, you know that?"

"Yeah. I know." *Believe me, I do.* Eithne had successfully stirred up a lot of ghosts, ghosts who, now awakened, refused to leave me alone. I grabbed my blanket, drew it over me then rolled on my side, away from him and muttered, *"Goodnight,"* while knowing there was little chance of that.

"Like hell!" Felix strode back to the flaps, jerked one aside and stormed out.

— VIII —

Click. *Click. Click… click, click, click.*

I opened my eyes…

Click. Click.

…blinked myself awake…

Click!

…and turned my sleep-gritty gaze towards the odd, repetitive noise, mildly curious as to its source.

Whatever was making the sharp sounds seemed to be close, right outside the tent in fact, hidden only by the fabric wall.

Click, click, click… click.

I'd fallen asleep again, for how long I cannot tell you—I'd been sleeping a lot of late, something that should have worried me; the fact that it didn't should have been another point of deep concern but again, it wasn't. It certainly didn't appear to worry Cleander—he assured me it was my body's response to the massive blood loss that had almost killed me and therefore fully expected; that, according to him, I'd be back on my feet and annoying the hell out of him in a matter of days, if not sooner. But his increasingly frequent and unexpected visits, his sidelong glances at Felix and their whispered conversations when they thought I'd hazed out suggested otherwise.

Click… click. Click-click-click.

I'd refused a sleeping draft the night before—the one I'd insisted on taking the night before *that* had left me muzzy-headed and nauseated well into midday yesterday, unable to muster the energy much less the desire to crawl out of bed and strangely agreeable to Felix's suggestion that I leave everything to him while I slept it off—a plan that went seriously awry with Anachie's unexpected visit—

Click. Click. Click!

—so when Cleander arrived on evening rounds, I'd agreed to take something for the pain but nothing more, saying truthfully I was so exhausted from the excitement of the Si'aafu attack that turned out not to be a Si'aafu attack that I had no need to take anything to aide me in falling asleep. I was tired—damned tired; Eithne's startling and not altogether welcome visit, her insistent questioning, her pointed remarks which for some damned reason I felt compelled to answer, not to mention our aborted effort at lovemaking had sapped the last of my strength—all right, *fine*, it was the damned aborted attempt at lovemaking that had done me in, I admit it.

I knew better, knew it was a really, really stupid thing to attempt, but... damn, it felt *really* good for a moment or two, well worth the agony afterwards, damned if it wasn't. In fact it had felt so damned good I'd had a really hard time not thinking about it afterwards, not entertaining the hope that Eithne would realize she was being entirely unreasonable, make a return visit and in apology, finish what she'd started.

But of course she hadn't, which was probably for the best and I hoped that Felix's failure to return until sometime much, much later had something to do with her failure to revisit my bed to make proper amends. Maybe he'd caught up with her, talked to her and convinced her to give *him* a chance to prove himself worthy without my interference. *Maybe.*

I knew if I could just rid myself of the throbbing pain I'd have no difficulty sleeping through the long Latrunculi night and awaken with none of the draft's lingering and unpleasant side effects. If we were going to break camp in three days I needed to be in full control of my faculties—

Click, click... click. Click.

It hadn't exactly turned out as I'd hoped; the pain killer had begun to wear off part way through the night, leaving me dimly aware of Felix's silent arrival, of him undressing in the pitch dark—the flame from the oil lamp, starved of fuel, having died out not long after Eithne's angry departure, of him easing himself down onto his cot with an exhausted—*frustrated?—satisfied?*—sigh.

And later, once the drug completely abandoned me, of me staring into the darkness, an unhappy audience to the sleeping Felix's truly astonishing range of bodily noises. And as someone who's spent most of my life sleeping in close quarters with other men, I can honestly say Felix's repertoire was truly and staggeringly unique.

That said, I had no desire to awaken him to go fetch Cleander—Felix desperately needed his sleep too; and then there was the niggly issue of the evening before. Felix was pissed at me—seriously and yes, *fine*, rightly pissed. Waking him from a sound sleep—and going by his sharp grunts, gusting sighs and prolonged moans, a seriously erotic dream, with luck a vivid reliving of a very recent experience, but far more likely his mind fabricating what his body had been denied—would just heap insult on top of insult.

Click. Click-click-click-click... click.

And of course once Eithne came to mind—hard for her not to come to mind with what I was forced to listen to, with Felix groaning her name every few minutes—my mind immediately set about dissecting her softly worded but nevertheless stinging accusations, her uncomfortably accurate observations and looking for suitable rejoinders, now far too late to voice them with any effect, and even more irksome, coming up dry. Was I truly in love with Turan? Had I truly forgiven her? Could I be a father to Anachie without betraying Neshoue? What if we *were* marooned here for the rest of our lives?

Had I just thrown away a chance, possibly my only chance at happiness, of having the family Neshoue's birth had made me realize I'd desperately wanted for a very long time?

What would Felix think? How would he react if I took Eithne as mine?

And what if they *had* enjoyed each other's company—and she'd realized he was indeed the better choice?

What if she rejected *me*? How would *that* affect our friendship?

I didn't like my answers, not one damned bit.

Click, click, click....

Cleander had returned, shortly before dawn, found me wake and fretful with my mind full of unpleasant truths and my body full of aches and pains.

He'd insisted on redressing my wound, in the process satisfying both of us that my multiple and escalating acts of stupidity the evening before hadn't done any long-term harm. He'd also insisted that I take another potion—for the pain he'd said.

And it *had* eased the pain—by knocking me out cold. *Again.*

Click, click. Click... click.

Now I was awake, drawn out of a deep, dreamless slumber by the peculiar and very annoying sounds just outside of the tent.

Click... click. Click-click-click-click.

I got my elbow under me, forced myself into a seated position and dropped my feet to the floor, then I angrily raked my sweat-stiff hair out of my eyes while I glanced at the narrow strip of sky visible between the tent flaps. To my vexation what I saw suggested midday, perhaps even later—

Click.

I looked over my shoulder, squinted irritably in fact, and was promptly answered by a taunting,

Click-click-click-click… click!

I rose, unsteadily, clutching my side and stood there a moment, waiting for my dimly lit surroundings to steady. Finally satisfied my legs would support me, I shuffled carefully over to the table, to the folding chair. My leather tunic was where Cleander had left it, draped over the chair back, and under it my ring-mail shirt and chest harness. The bowl was still on the table where Felix had left it—a noticeably empty bowl I noticed. I had no memory of eating whatever Felix had brought, in fact I was sure I hadn't, I'd been too nauseated to eat, which left only two explanations: Felix or one of the cats had decided not to let whatever it was go to waste. My bet was on Felix; he was always hungry, even when he was angry—

Click. Click.

If I was going to make an appearance, especially this hour of the day, the least I could do was to look the part of the legate, look as if I hadn't been asleep all this time while others packed up the camp, but rather seated at my table, plotting strategy and other, equally, critically important legate-stuff—

Click, click, click. Click… click.

I glared at the sound as I grabbed my breeches and after a moment's struggle, got them up around my hips and tied the tie. Next came the leather tunic, which I pulled over my head and angrily tugged into place. I snatched up my mailed shirt and after some wriggling and grunting, succeeded in getting *it* settled into place. Then came the chest harness and the impressive display of phalerae. They were not the usual attire of a Roman legate, but damn it, I was not about to give them up—I'd worked tirelessly and suffered some serious pain for each of them and who was going to argue particulars with me? No one, that's who.

Once I got the harness arranged just so, I ran my fingers over the embossed medallions—Tuatha reproductions to be sure, silvered like our helmets and made of the same strangely iridescent material as our armor, but as I touched each one, the raised and intricate designs instantly conjured up potent memories of now long-distant battles, each a stepping stone in my career.

The Chauci honor, bestowed upon me by none other than Gnaeus Domitius Corbulo himself after I single-handedly thwarted an ambush by the aforementioned Chauci had been damaged by the projectile as it tried to exit my ring-mail—an ominous but otherwise innocuous bulge in neck of the likeness of Emperor Nero that hadn't been there a few days before. The emperor *was* rumored to have an unusually thick neck—now, among his other less than attractive attributes he'd acquired a goiter, something no one else on Latrunculi would think to question.

As I stared down at the damaged medallion, I found myself wondering if *it* would have stopped the projectile had I been hit from the front, or had the metal pellet been slowed enough, after passing through two layers of ring-mail, not to mention my body that it didn't have the velocity to pierce the medal as well?

Something to raise with Rufinius—assuming the Si'aafu carried similar weapons.

Then came the baldric and richly decorated leather scabbard and my equally elaborate gladius—yes, I figured it was time to start wearing it again; with the all-too real threat of a Si'aafu attack looming over us, I was damned if I was going to go about unarmed—if I ruffled a few Adranii feathers in the process, well, too damned bad.

The equally adorned leather belt and dagger followed and I settled the belt on my hips and cinched it into place.

I managed to retrieve my sandals from under the bed using my toe to snag the laces, then I sat down and wiggled my feet into them.

Whatever Cleander had given me had left me with a terrible hangover. Bending over to lace up the sandals, then slip the silvered repoussé greaves into place made my throbbing head swim and my stomach gripe in the form of a few dry heaves, nothing more; I'd committed myself and I was damned if I was going to back out—or, closer to the mark, *black* out now.

With those death-defying tasks done, I straightened up slowly and sat very still until the world stopped spinning anew.

Click. Click. Click-click-click... click—

GODS! That damned noise was enough to drive a sane man mad; my side hurt, my head hurt, my stomach hurt—everything damned well hurt and I was in no mood to deal with anyone demanding my undivided attention yet I knew the moment I stepped out of the tent I'd be bombarded.

But I *was* awake, thanks to that damned racket, I *was* dressed and hell if I was going to stay inside the tent—I needed to be out there, overseeing the packing up of the camp, making sure everything got done and done properly.

While my men shared my memories, I was the only person on the planet who'd ever actually been responsible for packing up a legionary fort and moving it, *in toto*, elsewhere, with the intention of setting up marching camps along the way—that was another fine art: packing up so that only the absolutely necessary items were easily accessible each time we stopped for the night, leaving the rest safely stored, making the packing up the next morning quick and efficient so the train could get moving within a hour of awakening.

It was my plan to make camp each afternoon before the wind picked up, driving curtains of sand and dust before it, get a temporary perimeter set and the civilians settled before dark, then break camp well before dawn and get everyone moving before the heat began to take its toll. That was the plan. I had little hope it would work out that way—

Click!

ENOUGH! I grit my teeth and lurched to my feet, perhaps a wee bit too swiftly as I had to grab the pommel of my gladius in one hand, the tent pole in the other until my head decided it wasn't going to topple off my shoulders.

Satisfied my head was going to remain firmly affixed, I gave my chest harness an annoyed tug here, a yank there, then setting my jaw, I snatched up my helmet and after a quick fluffing of the plume, and an even quicker smoothing of the goose feathers, I carefully tucked it under my arm and strode over to the tent flap and jerked it aside.

It *was* well past midday and the camp was bustling with activity—*well-organized* activity. The packing up was well underway and *yes*, to my shock and chagrin, appeared to be a very orderly affair—on the upside everyone was too busy to notice me. Thank the gods.

To my left, where the make-shift hospital and its canvas awnings and been just two days before now stood a sorry mound of items that were clearly going to be left behind—not much so far. In truth neither side had brought much that wasn't an absolute necessity, now, or in the future. The pile was mostly odds and ends that simply couldn't be used or reused in some other way.

To my right stood a neat row of refurbished baggage carts awaiting their burdens—even the camp itself, surprisingly, appeared a little neater. Perhaps the winnowing down of what could be carried and what simply had to be left behind had gotten people to rid themselves of what was going to be discarded as quickly as possible—as if out of sight meant out of mind as well.

Click… click. Click—

That's it! I donned the helmet, furiously tied the cheek-pieces, started around the tent… and stopped.

Anachie was seated cross-legged on the ground in the shade of the tent, his back pressed up against the fabric wall—as close to me as possible without actually being inside—a purposeful act and one I readily admit left a flutter in my already unhappy gut.

He seemed utterly oblivious to me, oblivious to everything as he patiently built a small stack of pebbles, one-by-one, watched them tumble, then gathered them up and started over again; totally absorbed in the process. *Click. Click… click, click, click…* Repeat. Gods only knew how long he'd been doing it before the repetitive noise wormed itself into my mind and prodded me awake.

…click, click, click.

I pulled my startled eyes off what he was doing and fixed them on his down-turned face. His hollow cheeks were streaked with ocher dust—at first I mistook them for scratches—no, he'd been crying.

I stepped closer. "Anachie…?"

If he heard me, he failed to show it.

Click. Click. Click.

"Anachie, what are you doing?" I squatted in front of him, glanced around, added, "And where's your mother?" The camp was no place to leave a child this young unattended. It was doubtful anyone would do him deliberate harm, but there were plenty of risks about, very attractive risks for a small boy. I reached out, lightly placed my hand on his bony shoulder. *"Anachie?"*

He lifted his grubby face, stared at me with dull, blood-shot and sunken eyes.

"What are you doing here?"

He dropped his gaze and resumed his pebble stacking. *Click, click, click*— the mound collapsed.

"Would you please stop doing that for a moment and talk to me?"

He gathered up the pebbles and began stacking them again, then watched them tumble as if he hadn't expected that to happen.

I glanced around again, worried. "Where's your mother?"

He began restacking the pebbles.

Now I was getting angry—the pain in my side was made worse by my sustained crouch and in full armor no less—and realizing it was tainting my voice I rose, awkwardly, and clutching my side, I stared down at him and tried not to visibly wince as my side spasmed. "Come with me."

He gathered up the pebbles.

"Give me your hand, Anachie."

He ignored me.

"Anachie. *Now.*"

He lifted his head, fixed me with this strange look and shook his head.

I was not used to people disobeying me—and a small boy? And where the hell was his devoted mother, a woman who was willing to sell her body so her son could have a surrogate father, *huh?* Nowhere to be seen, that's where!

I reached down, gently wrapped my fingers around his wrist and gave it a tug. "Up. Come along."

He tried to jerk free, startling me and when I tightened my hold he began to squirm in earnest. I was afraid he'd cry out if I held onto him, but I was equally worried by this strange behavior. Just yesterday he'd eagerly wrapped his arms around me, begged with those same sunken, blood-shot eyes of his to stay with me—and now he cringed from my touch, fought against my hold?

I let go, squatted again and stared at his face as he promptly returned to what he'd been doing as if it was the most important thing in the world to him.

Click... click... click.

"How 'bout I take you to Aetius and he can make you a proper toy. Would you like that?"

That garnered a sharp shake of the head.

Click, click... click—

"Just yesterday you wanted him to make you a toy."

—click... click.

I looked around, anxious, hoping a passing Adranii might explain this behavior, but there *were* no passing Adraniis. Anachie had conveniently plopped himself down out of view of the main camp.

So, I was on my own—unless I wanted to leave him and go find someone, but I didn't want to do that, fearful he might run off while I was gone. So, time to try another approach. I rubbed my belly. "I'm hungry—how 'bout you?"

He stopped what he was doing and looked up at me, unblinking as fresh tears trickled down his grubby, ocher-stained cheeks.

Gods. "Anachie, *please,* tell me what's wrong. If I can fix it I *will*—have you had an argument with your mother? Did you run away?"

"No."

His voice was so soft, so faint I wouldn't have been sure he'd actually spoken if I hadn't seen his lips move.

"Did someone scare you? Were you scared last night with all the commotion?"

He fixed his watery eyes on his filthy hands and nodded, reluctantly.

"Well, just between the two of us," I leaned close and dropped my voice to a conspiratorial whisper, "I was scared too…"

That admission garnered a quick, startled glance, then his eyes returned to his hands.

"…but it was a false alarm—do you know what that means?"

A quick nod.

"And besides, I wouldn't let anyone hurt you—my soldiers wouldn't. They'd protect you. You have my word on that."

A shrug—not so much disbelieving, more not really caring.

"Are you worried about leaving here?"

Another shrug.

"We're going someplace much, much better—over those mountains." I pointed but Anachie didn't look up from his intense scrutiny of his dirty hands and broken fingernails. "Perhaps I'll let you ride with me, on Wushah—would you like that?"

This time he didn't even shrug as more tears trickled down his face.

"What's wrong with you, boy?"

"He overheard our conversation…"

I lurched to my feet and wheeled around to find Eithne standing nearby.

"…last night."

Gods… I turned back to him to find he'd gathered up his pebbles.

Click, click, click.

As I watched him build and then rebuild the mound, I realized this had been a mistake. To have done anything but keep my distance was the wrong thing to do. Anachie had set his sights on me to fill the awful void his father's death had left—desperate to fill the emptiness, longing for the protection a father offered, real or imagined—just as I had done with Gracchus so many years ago. I *knew* that pain, knew the gnawing fear of abandonment, and with it the aching, soul-deep guilt that it had all been my fault, that I'd done something to drive my real father away, drive Gracchus and the soldiers away, damned if I didn't. It had stained my life, made me the selfish, shallow and deeply distrustful man that I was.

I'd been offered an opportunity to spare another small boy from suffering a similar fate and refused out of some stupid, misguided belief that if I'd agreed I somehow betrayed Neshoue—another boy denied a father through no fault of his own. So I'd refused and Anachie had heard that refusal from my own lips.

I should have left things well enough alone. I should have turned around and walked away. That's what I *should* have done.

Of course I didn't. "Anachie?"

He looked up, sniffed then wiping his runny nose on the back of his bony hand, gathered himself up.

I held out my hand and smiled.

He stared at it, stared at me, then turned and ran away. I stared after him, my throat suddenly gone tight, my vision blurring as my hand fell limply back to my side.

I blinked, took a deep breath then steeling myself, turned around to face the adult equivalent, the wounding glare or damning remark from Eithne. Maybe both.

Instead she met my helpless stare, heaved a sigh then shaking her head, walked past me without saying a word, following Anachie, leaving me absolutely nothing to latch onto, no stinging remark, no fierce 'you gods damned bastard' glance—nothing I could justifiably get indignantly angry about, nothing to reassure me I was as much a hapless victim in this as Anachie.

She'd come to me, dammit, unexpected and uninvited—all right, maybe she had been invited, and all right, maybe she had even said 'soon' when Felix asked her when, but finding her in my tent *was* wholly unexpected.

She'd told me her son was with a trusted friend when he clearly found a way to yet again slip away undetected—and I'd just found him all alone, so clearly this was a woman who didn't keep a close eye on her own son; for all I knew she made a habit out of it, just as my own mother did, so, not such a big surprise he'd followed her, especially if he knew where she was going… and promptly overheard our conversation—possibly overheard more than that.

And with what felt like a punch right to the solar plexus I suddenly recalled how *I* felt when I overheard my mother with one of her many customers: confused, frightened… *jealous*.

Perhaps he'd even peeked through the tent flap—only to see me atop his mother doing what to a small child's eyes might appear to be violence… *gods*. I know the first time I'd come across my mother and a client in the act, heard his groans and her cries I thought he was killing her and I began pummeling him with my fists—until he stopped what he was doing long enough to cuff me with enough force to knock me senseless.

When I finally came around I found the man gone and my mother, furious that the untimely interruption had cost her payment for her services, promptly dragged me out of our mud brick hovel by my hair and after telling me she hoped the jackals would come tear me apart and eat me, she went back inside and slammed the door shut, shoving a knife in the jamb to make sure I couldn't slip back inside—I'd spent the entire night curled up against the door, terrified, too scared to even cry for fear that alone might draw the jackals.

For months after that I would hide in the root cellar when ever my mother brought a man home. But soon curiosity overcame fear and I began peer through the gaps in the cubbyhole's crude wooden trapdoor and watch, fascinated and at the same time intensely resentful of the attentions my mother lavished on her male guests, attentions that she could—*should*—have lavished on me. And when they hit her, as they often did, I'd curl up into a ball and cover my ears, too afraid to help, too afraid to run—each time terrified that this time the man would kill her.

And when one of her customers finally did kill her, I didn't realize it until hours afterwards, when growing hunger gave me the courage to lift the door a crack and peek out, only to find her lying face down in a congealed pool of her own blood.

All right, so Eithne hadn't called me a rotten bastard, she hadn't even *looked* like she was thinking I was a rotten bastard. So why did I *feel* like a rotten bastard? And I *did*. I felt like the biggest, rottenest rotten bastard *ever*.

So *that* made me mad. Damned mad.

I jerked my head up, gave my chest harness an angry tug, then spun on my heel and stormed off in the opposite direction.

I ignored the smiles and nods of passing Adraniis, even ignored the murmured greetings of my men as I made my way to the one friend who *would* be happy to see me, who wouldn't make demands of me and who certainly wouldn't tell me to go back to the tent, have a nap and stay the hell out of everyone else's way.

I reached the stable in good time, having worn an expression on my face that warned of serious consequences to anyone who slowed me down—Titivillus, upon seeing me walk by, hurried to catch up, calling, *"Legate!"* with some new issue clearly burning the soles of his feet, but even he stopped short when he saw the look in my eye, his mouth wisely snapping shut.

I stalked on, past the other soldiers who'd turned, drawn by Titivillus' abrupt halt and his curt, deferential dip of the head. I ignored them all.

I was momentarily sun-blind as I stepped under the canvas awning of the stables, waited until my eyes adjusted, then I walked over to where Wushah stood, tethered to a pole and dozing in the stifling heat.

I clicked my tongue and his massive head lifted; he rolled his eye towards me and I swear, if a horse could smile, he would've. Not having that option, he tossed his head and whinnied, his ears flicking forward.

I stepped close, ran my hand over his bronze-coated flank, carefully over the scabbed over wound on his withers as his flesh quivered under my welcome touch—he'd clearly faired better than I had. Then again, he was well over ten times my weight.

I stroked his velvet muzzle and he lipped my fingers, gently, his warm, wet tongue exploring my hand, looking for a treat.

"Forgot—sorry."

He snorted and pawed the ground.

"How 'bout we go for a ride instead?"

He tossed his head again.

I looked around, saw one of the cavalrymen step out from behind his horse, totally absorbed in rubbing the animal down.

"Hannibalianus."

The man looked up, startled at seeing me standing next to Wushah, not to mention that I was in full armor, including the damned helmet. "Yessir!"

"I need Wushah saddled."

"Of course, Legate." He strode over to where the saddles where neatly stacked, grabbed mine—there was no doubt about that; despite someone's best efforts, the light brown leather remained heavily stained with blood—along with the rest of Wushah's tack and walked back, carrying the saddle in one hand, bridle, straps, girth and saddle blanket in the other. This Hannibalianus was a heavy-set man, all muscle and as dark-skinned as Marcus. The original Hannibalianus had been far smaller in stature and lighter complexioned, a man who had declared himself to be not just of Carthaginian stock, but of royal Barca blood no less—a direct descendant of Hannibal Barca himself, a claim many had challenged but none had ever disproved.

This man had taken on the same bearing but in a much bigger and therefore far more impressive package: a slight swagger, a menacing stare and the braggadocio of someone who believes himself to be better than his fellows, having fallen into lesser company through an ugly twist of fate he never gave up hope remedying.

And like his namesake, this Hannibalianus was incredibly brave in battle, a superior horseman who in our mock skirmishes was known to dismount and fight like an infantryman without breaking stride. Had he been among Aper's men who'd hidden themselves in the dry washes, I have no doubt the Adraniis would have suffered far greater fatalities. Once Hannibalianus was ordered to attack, he kept at it until he ran out of enemies; he'd certainly kept our physicians busy in the months leading up to our arrival here by providing them with a taste of what it would be like when we finally engaged in real combat.

I stepped back and he tossed the blanket onto Wushah's broad back, then swung the saddle up one-handed as if it was as light as air. He settled it, hooked the bridle and saddle straps over one of the pommels then set about attaching the girth as Wushah began to dance from hoof to hoof in anticipation.

Felix had assured me that Aper had let Wushah loose in the pen each evening to get some exercise—of a carnal nature, according to Felix—but the warhorse had not been ridden, had not left the camp since the day of the battle and he was clearly every bit as eager to get outside and stretch his feathered legs as I was to escape the stink and noise and demands of the camp. A short ride, to the edge of the salt flats and back, maybe to the temporary cemetery, or to the site of the aborted battle, to pay respects to those who had died there and homage to the gods who'd stopped us from our collective insanity just in the nick of time. I didn't in truth care where we went, as long as it was away from the camp where I could *breathe*.

Hannibalianus punched Wushah in the belly—an old cavalryman's trick—startling Wushah as he jerked the girth tight. Wushah snorted in reply, turned his shaggy blond head and glared at the man.

Hannibalianus grinned, scratched him between the ears as apology, then gave the nearside pommels a hefty tug; satisfied the saddle was secure, he moved on to the breast and breech straps and once they were in place, he slipped the bit into Wushah's mouth and the bridle over his head, quickly and expertly buckling it into place as Wushah held perfectly still for this final step in the ritual.

Hannibalianus leaned under Wushah's head, whipped one rein up and around his massive neck, then straightened up and handed me the other, eyeing me as he did so.

"Just around the camp, Legate?"

"No. Outside."

His wide-set eyes got very round. *"Alone?"*

"Not if you can find me someone who can ride without moving his lips."

"Me." He tapped himself in the center of his barrel chest. "You want peace and quiet, sir, I'm your man."

"Then saddle up—Wushah's waiting."

"Yessir!" He hurried off, got his own horse readied in record time, snatched up his sword and sheathed it, then led the roan mare over to where Wushah and I stood. He bent down and I placed my knee in his cupped hands then I grabbed the front and back pommels.

"Ready?"

"Go."

And up I went.

Once I was settled, I fished around just in front of the saddle for the other rein while Hannibalianus, using a mounting block scrambled up onto his horse.

"Ready, sir?"

I nodded and turned Wushah's head. A light tap of my heels sent him trotting out of the stable, copper neck arched, flaxen tail up, hooves clattering on rock.

Hannibalianus was right behind me, and as we turned towards the gate, he leaned over, grabbed a lance from a bristling rack of the weapons, positioned just for the purpose of ease of snatching from the back of a moving horse.

I knew my planned escape had gone, so far, too damned smoothly and I had little doubt word had raced ahead of us as we trotted towards the gate.

Sure enough, just we rounded one of the medical wagons and the gate came into view, so did Felix, Aetius and Borzu, the three standing directly in my path and Felix had his arms crossed.

I reined in Wushah. "You're in my way. *Move.*"

The three remained where they were.

"Legate," Felix asked, "may I ask what you're doing?"

"I'd think it was pretty damned obvious with this horse under me, but since you didn't notice Wushah here," I patted him on the neck, "I'll tell you: I'm going for a ride."

Felix inhaled through his nose, exhaled the same way as he flicked Aetius a sidelong glance; Aetius only shrugged. Felix turned his eyes back on me. "It's not safe to go out there alone—"

"I have Hannibalianus with me."

Felix squinted at the man, then at me. "Give me a moment to call for Tuzun—"

"Remember the rule?"

"Then give me time to get an escort mounted up—"

"*I don't need a damned escort!*" I snarled and Wushah began to sidestep, rolling his eyes and tossing his head.

"You're the damned Legate!" Felix fired back. *"You can't just go out there with just one man for protection!"*

"You're right, I am the damned Legate—so start treating me like one, Primus-Pilus and you can start by obeying my orders rather than questioning everything I do!"

Felix clamped his mouth shut; for once Aetius knew better than to open his.

"MOVE!" I kicked Wushah in the ribs and he jumped forward; the three hastily got out of our way while the other soldiers who'd gathered nearby to watch the heated exchange in worried silence, likewise scattered.

"OPEN THE DAMNED GATE!" I bellowed and men hurried to swing the heavy gate inwards.

They barely opened it wide enough for Wushah to pass when I gave him another kick and he took the gateway at a canter, Hannibalianus on our tail.

Behind me I heard Felix bellowing orders, heard horses whinnying—he was ordering up an escort, damn him. *Fine.* They'd have to play catch up—I was not about to wait for them.

I gave Wushah another, harder kick and he took off down the sloping backside of the hillock at a gallop and as the pathway flattened out onto the desert proper I gave him his head while I crouched in the saddle, savoring the freedom, the fresh air... even the dazzling sunlight and full heat of a Latrunculi afternoon as Wushah took off, towards the battlefield... towards... *home,* or as near as home was: the place where we realized we were *here* and not *there.*

I heard Hannibalianus' horse running hard behind us, its hooves thundering on the sun-baked sand in cadence with Wushah's, heard Hannibalianus breathing hard. I risked a quick glance over my shoulder, which was a stupid thing to do while wearing a high-crested infantry legate's helmet—no wonder cavalry officers wore more... um, sensible styles in battle—grinned at him as I steadied the helm with one hand and he grinned back and seemingly taking my look as a challenge, kicked his horse and the animal leapt forward, briefly running neck and neck with Wushah and then—*would you believe it*—slowly pulling ahead.

Damn the man! It hadn't been my plan to make this into a race, but if he wanted to get himself badly beaten by the legate, then so be it. I kicked Wushah has hard as I could and he put on a burst of speed, quickly overtaking Hannibalianus and his black-stockinged roan.

Had I known riding was this exhilarating, this damned much fun I would've joined the cavalry instead of the infantry—all those years, walking behind a horse when I could have been aboard one and enjoying the high life instead of marching through shit.

Stupid, stupid, stupid!

Hannibalianus managed to catch up to me, having lowered his lance for better balance and the two of us raced across the desert, horses neck and neck, us laughing like crazed fools and leaving a cloud of dust in our wake, chewing up the distance between the hillock and the battlefield in amazingly quick order.

As the first signs of the aborted battle began to appear in the form of wind-blurred ruts from the wheels of wagons and engines, we fell silent.

I reined in Wushah, Hannibalianus mirroring my actions, dropping first to a canter and then to a trot and as we arrived at the battleground proper I drew Wushah to a stop. In response he pawed at the churned up soil with one massive hoof as if he too knew where we were and was none to happy about it.

Hannibalianus stopped his horse a little distance behind me, sensing I wanted to face this place alone, to look around, to see *everything*.

Everywhere I looked, I saw signs of the terrible but mercifully short mayhem that had come incredibly close to consuming us all—had, in fact, come perilously close to killing me. The hot, dust-laden breeze and daily late afternoon dust storms had yet to completely obliterate the footprints, the hoof prints... or the black pools of dried blood that marred the hard-baked desert floor. A shattered lance, still adorned with its colorful, now wind-shredded pennant lay half-buried where its owner had dropped it. Nearby was the smeared outline of a horse that had fallen and flailed about, its hooves kicking up darker layers of sand. Beyond were tarry pools, some bedecked with tattered bits of clothing that quivered and fluttered in the hot air, then further, the broken yoke of a baggage cart and a crude Adranii shield that had been cleanly split in half.

Around us the desert glimmered and rippled, with far off landmarks brought to life and eeling around within the hot air, making it difficult to determine beyond a certain distance what was real and what was mirage.

I briefly thought I saw a horse trotting along the far bank of an outlying dry stream bed, riderless, its scale armor glittering like embers in the sunlight. Out of the corner of my eye I saw dark, quivering shapes that, until I looked directly at them, appeared to be people moving aimlessly about as if lost: specters held perpetually captive within the thick-aired shimmer. Despite the oppressive heat a cold shiver ran down my spine.

There were no bodies of course—but the presence of the dead was palpable, their ghostly fingers on my bare skin, at the nape of my neck, the back of my knees. I shivered again.

Hannibalianus joined me as if suddenly uneasy—perhaps he'd seen and felt their company as well—but good to his word, he remained silent, his wide-set, dark eyes searching the desert, wary of threats hidden within the glycerin air while his legate was preoccupied communing with the surrounding Lemures and begging their forgiveness.

The sad reunion was short-lived—the stiff breeze shifted, suddenly bringing with it the distinctive sounds of approaching horsemen: the faint, rhythmic thudding of hooves and the accompanying jingle of harness and armor.

Hannibalianus wheeled his mount around to face those who approached as if hoping to stare them down, lance-tip now aloft, its pennant snapping in the stiff, hot wind.

I bid my farewell to the Lemures as they retreated, frightened off by the escort's approach and finally vanishing altogether as the cloud of dust kicked up by the horses' hooves overtook us, briefly concealing us from our unwanted bodyguards.

As the curtain of dust blew on, alternately covering then re-exposing the battlefield, I turned Wushah to face the approaching men.

Felix, like me, did not believe in half-measures. He'd sent twenty fully armored horsemen, lead by Marcus himself.

So much for a quiet, peaceful ride....

— IX —

I glared coldly at the group of riders as they came to an uncertain halt a dozen or so paces from me. Was it so much to ask to be left alone for an hour, to have nothing to worry about but staying centered in the saddle, and for a few blessed, heart-thumping moments forget where I was, why I was here and what we were facing, and then to spend a little more precious time communing with the dead, to assure them they would not be forgotten, to pay proper honor to their sacrifice?

Obviously it was.

Marcus met my hard stare, tipped his head and smiling diffidently, urged Belili forward, away from the perfect line of horsemen. "Legate."

"Centurion Marcus. Funny meeting you here."

He blinked, bewildered as my tone and expression left absolutely no doubt I found nothing humorous about the meeting.

"Go back. I neither want nor need you. I came out for a quite ride, to clear my head if you must know, and pay tribute to our dead. Nothing sinister, I assure you—I'll return within an hour or so."

"Primus-Pilus ordered me—*us*—to stay with you, sir—"

"And I'm the damned legate and I order you to return to camp!"

He chewed furiously on his lower lip as his eyes darted to the equally grim-faced Hannibalianus. Seeing no sympathy for his awkward position in the man's dark eyes—Hannibalianus in the enviable position of having the legate's permission to be with him whereas Marcus did not—he looked back at me. "What if I send back half the men?"

I stared at him, eyes narrowing.

"All but five then?"

My furious squint crinkled into an even more baleful glower.

"Two? Just myself and Auspex? *Please,* Legate."

His voice held the edge of desperation, of worry—of fear that if anything happened to me, he would be held responsible—that he'd hold himself personally culpable if I suffered anything worse than a saddle blister; he was also clearly and deeply disturbed by my behavior, as were his men. I'd been the pillar to them, always rock-solid, always there. Now the cracks that had been there all along were starting to show and it left them unsettled and confused. To press the issue left Marcus no choice but to purposely disobey a direct order—mine or Felix's, an extremely painful position for any soldier, doubly so for a former Kellesuf.

I took a deep breath, exhaled slowly then grumbled, "Can you two keep *quiet?*"

He nodded vigorously and motioned urgently for Auspex to join him; the man tapped his horse with his heels and the thickset sorrel stepped forward only to stop as it came abreast of Belili.

"I want *no* whispering. No sidelong, worried looks. *Nothing*—understand? Eyes straight ahead and mouths tightly *shut.* I want to enjoy my damned ride and not wonder what the two of you are thinking or what you're going to report to Felix or Cleander for that matter. I'm *not* crazy and despite rumors to the contrary I'm *not* suicidal..."

Not at the moment, anyway.

That startling suggestion sent a ripple of disquiet through the already uneasy cavalrymen as if that possibility had never occurred to them... until now.

"... I just need to breathe."

"*Breathe*, Legate?" Auspex said, dark, bushy eyebrows raised, clearly baffled.

"Yes. Breathe. In... out. In... out." I demonstrated basic breathing to him as if he hadn't a clue.

Marcus leaned close to the man seated on the horse next to him. "The legate means he feels suffocated in camp—all the responsibility and such. Whereas out here," he motioned expansively to the desolate and shimmering vastness that surrounded us, "he can *breathe.*"

Auspex thought about it for a moment, then his sun-cracked lips formed a silent 'O'.

I sensed he still didn't get it but was willing to go along so he could come along. This Auspex, like his predecessor, was not the smartest or most insightful man, and clearly never had been, but he was damned devoted to his crazy, suicidal legate, just as the first Auspex was damned devoted to his sane, confident centurion.

"The rest of you—*be off!*" I motioned to the cavalrymen.

With a nod from Marcus, the remaining eighteen men and horses turned as one then quickly formed up into a neat column and began trotting back to the hillock but with a decidedly dejected air about them.

Damn.

I followed them with my narrowed gaze until they were swallowed up by the quivering air with only the occasional flash of sunlight on armor giving their rapidly receding position away. They reminded me of so much flotsam bobbing along while the distant hillock itself appeared like some dilapidated Egyptian barge floating on a sea of liquid air, the ocher stained canvas canopies lending themselves to the appearance of furled sails.

I even could spot movement on those ramparts, the occasional, telltale sparkle of armor, but little else. We had to be a good six miles away and I realized that it had taken longer to reach this spot at a gallop than the battle had lasted.

I looked back at Marcus to find him staring at me, clearly wondering what I was going to do next, perhaps he *was* entertaining serious thoughts about my sanity—and what the hell could he do about that?

"Where's the cemetery?"

He hesitated, taken off guard, then: "This way, sir." He turned his horse's head and started off at a walk, towards the western mountains; I followed with Hannibalianus and Auspex falling in behind. Once we were beyond the edge of the battlefield and having a good idea where we were going, I urged Wushah into a gentle canter and Marcus instantly matched my speed, the two horses abreast as we headed towards a steep scarp at the base of the western range.

The suns were far enough along on their daily path to leave the near-vertical face of the scarp in inky black shadow, its base hidden behind a low dune and also in shadow. As we cantered up and over the dune I didn't immediately see the graves, my eyes still dazzled by the sunlight, but as Marcus reined in his horse and I followed suit, I realized we'd arrived at the spot chosen to be the hopefully temporary resting place of our dead.

I looked around, finally spotted a number of rock cairns deliberately and randomly scattered about at the foot of the scarp, the graves almost indistinguishable from the naturally forming heaps of fallen scree—a precaution to avoid any grave robbing, assuming there was anyone about besides us, and making it difficult for the Si'aafu to find and unearth our dead, presupposing they were so desperate for human flesh they'd forgo the customary prerequisite—and this would be more like human jerky as I had no doubt the combination of intense heat and very dry sand would quickly desiccate the corpses, just as it did in Egypt and of course my native Numidia where it was not uncommon to accidentally unearth a perfectly preserved carcass of an animal or the remains of a person.

I'd been told of cases of bodies, dug up years, even decades after death that were in such perfect states of preservation that the deceased's family could easily identify their kin—even Porsenna, ironically left impaled on a stake and exposed to the desert's dry air, was instantly recognizable when Silva had happened across him. Silva had assumed he'd been dead for only a few days because his body had been barely touched by scavengers, but in truth he might have been dead for weeks... even months, the carrion eaters likely repelled by the rot that had taken hold long before the man's violent death.

I shook off the ugly memory of Porsenna, of his even uglier yet richly deserved death, angry at myself for contaminating this hallowed spot by evoking someone who, to the child Arri, had been the embodiment of evil, and settled my thoughts on those who lay here, quietly, patiently waiting for the day when we would return for them.

I knew Marcus could remount unaided, so with a sidelong look at him, I eased myself from the saddle and removed my helmet. He also dismounted and I handed him the helmet and Wushah's reins, a signal I wanted him to remain with the horses. Then I walked on, into the deeper, cooler shadows and over to the nearest cairn.

There were no markings to tell me who lay at my feet and I couldn't help but glance back at Marcus.

"*Adraniis,*" he murmured. "Our honored dead lie over there." He pointed to a shallow grotto in the rock wall. "Gnaius to the left, Aulus in the middle, Marcus Antonius to the right."

I nodded then carefully picked my way through the ocher-dusted Adranii cairns and piles of scree and over to the naturally formed sepulcher where a weakness in the scarp, a fissure perhaps, had sometime in the long distant past collapsed, forming the high-ceilinged vault and littered the floor with its shattered debris.

I looked up, satisfied myself the roof was stable—I was bareheaded after all; it wouldn't do to be brained by a falling rock—then fixed my eyes on what I'd come to see: three graves arranged in a semicircle within the larger and rougher semicircle of the grotto, but again, placed in such a way that if you didn't know what you were looking for, you'd assume the cairns were just more heaps of scree.

I stepped into the center of the semicircle, into the deep shadows of the grotto, briefly stared at the piles of shattered rock then I slowly sank to my knees to give proper regard for these soldiers who had willingly given their lives in trade for mine.

Gnaius Flavius. A gangly eighteen-year-old infantryman, probably of Germanic stock with sun-bleached, curly auburn hair. He rarely spoke, preferred to listen to his elders but was always quick to grin—and as I stared at his unmarked grave, I suddenly recalled the strange look in his blue eyes as we readied ourselves for battle; perhaps he knew with absolute certainty that he was about to die and had no qualms about it.

Perhaps. Perhaps he was just an idealistic youth who truly believed we were on the side of right—we were defending all of humanity after all, or so the Tuatha had said—and therefore the gods would protect us, protect him. I'd met plenty of that type during my career. They rarely survived their first skirmish, foolishly trusting more in the gods than in their own skills to keep themselves alive.

That said, he was a loyal soldier whose singular desire was to live up to my expectations, live up to the memories of the man who made him, which he had done, and then some.

I shifted my gaze. *Aulus Maximus.* Twenty-six, wiry, with thinning sandy hair, small in stature with keen, feral eyes; one of my elite sagitarii. I'd heard him speak, once, while still Kellesuf and his raspy voice bore the distinct accent of a Greek from one of the more isolated, eastern isles. The last time I remembered seeing Aulus he was atop the firing platform, watching as Isem made his clumsy way back across the desert. At the time his chin bore an ugly scabbed over wound, his cheek badly bruised, injuries suffered from a fall on our way back from reconnoitering the enemy camp.

I shifted my gaze again, to the last cairn, largest of the three. *Marcus Antonius.* Twenty, also infantry; a big man, barrel-chested with powerful arms. He'd been an excellent javelineer, able to throw his pila further than anyone else, and with amazing accuracy not to mention force.

I dipped my head and suddenly recalling a long-forgotten passage from the Iliad, nodded and murmured, *"Far from home he has fallen, dead in a strange land, with no quiet grave. My hand did not help him in his hour of need—now is the world empty of all delight..."*

I closed my eyes and took a deep, ragged breath then, reopening my eyes, bid each a peace neither Achilles nor Patroclus found in death, and promised if we survived to make a permanent settlement we'd return for them. That done I rose, stiffly, and slapped the bits of gravel from my bare knees before they could fall down inside my greaves. I then picked up three small rocks and placed one on the head of each grave as I thanked each man for his sacrifice.

Had I been given a choice, I would have left something more substantial, more meaningful, but as it was, a stone placed by own hand, adding to those already piled over the bodies, was my way of sharing, belatedly in that sorrowful rite. Besides, anything else, especially an offering of food or drink—a common gift for the dead—might draw unwanted attention, encouraging scavengers to dig after tidbits and find more than they bargained for.

I saluted them as I whispered in proper Latin, *"Ave atque vale,"*—*hail and farewell*—then stepped back, pivoted smartly on my heel and walked back to where Marcus stood, between the dozing Wushah and Belili, my helmet clutched to his chest. Hannibalianus and Auspex were still mounted, their horses standing on the crest of the darkly shadowed dune, giving me some privacy and the two cavalrymen an unobstructed view of the surrounding desert while making them difficult if not impossible to spot by anyone or anything out in the dazzling sunlight of the desert itself.

Marcus said nothing as he offered me my helmet. I slipped it on and tied the cheek-pieces. That done, he stepped close to Wushah as I grabbed the pommels and gave me a boost. I settled myself and wordlessly took the proffered reins then, as I waited for him to remount, I cast one last look at the graves of my men and wondered if I would live to see the day when they were reunited with us.

With a sidelong glance at Marcus, I gave Wushah a gentle tap with my heels and turned his head and we left at a sedate, respectful walk until we were well clear of the deepening shadows of the scarp and up and over the dune.

Far to the south—my last link with home—I could see the beginnings of a dust storm; already a number of small dust devils were spinning idly between us and the mountain range to the east, harbingers of the more powerful late afternoon winds to come. It would be hours yet before the storm reached us, but as tempting as it was to turn south, it was also a hard to ignore the message that it was time to return to the relative safety of the hillock. Home… would have to wait.

If Marcus noticed my distraction, sensed my thoughts, he kept it to himself.

I exhaled, then turned Wushah to the north and with a kick to his flanks sent him off at an easy canter, Marcus keeping with me, Auspex and Hannibalianus right behind, a tight four-square of riders kicking up our own cloud of dust, signaling those on the encampment's walls that we were finally on our way back but in no particular hurry.

As we cantered along in silence, I stared at the distant hillock, knew damned well Felix was standing on that wall, and had been the entire time, watching, waiting… and yes, worrying.

It had never been my intention to worry him, to worry *anyone*. But in truth had I been allowed to go alone, I *would* have been sorely tempted to just keep heading south until I could go no further, until Wushah could go no further—desperately searching for that invisible gateway that led back home all the while knowing it was a fool's errand. Had I done that, Felix would've come after me, endangering not only himself but everyone else and he would not have given up until he found me or died trying. *No.* I might be a selfish and self-centered bastard, but I wasn't quite *that* selfish and self-centered.

Get everyone safely over the mountains, get everyone settled in a new, permanent and well-fortified settlement, get Felix married off to Eithne and thus get his single-minded attention fixed on someone far more deserving than me, do battle with the damned Si'aafu if it came to that, then, and only then could I think about myself, think about what *I* wanted—and maybe, just maybe, things wouldn't look so bleak by then—maybe, just maybe, I could let go of Earth by then, let go of Turan and Neshoue.

Maybe I could even convince Rufinius to build me a good, solid Roman bath—with hot and cold water, even a steam room.

Just the thought of soaking in a hot bath, soaking all the aches and pains and age away... *ahhhhh, bliss!* Maybe I'd even find peace, find that elusive happiness I'd briefly tasted today, happiness Eithne put so much stock in. *Maybe—*

A faint cheer went up from the encampment's battlements: my troops had spotted the ocher dust column within the afternoon haze, perhaps could even make us out as individuals and were pleased to see me coming back—intensely relieved I'm sure.

The minute I passed through the gate I'd face sharp looks along with some equally pointed questions, from Cleander, from Felix, but... I suddenly realized I *did* feel better, physically and emotionally. My side hurt, I won't claim it didn't, but it didn't hurt *that much.* And I felt more clear-headed than I had since that morning of the battle, simply because I'd finally been able to *breathe.*

I looked at Marcus, saw him watching me out of the corner of his eye and I managed a thin smile.

Heartened by my expression, as forced as it plainly was, he grinned in reply, his white teeth dazzling against his blue-black skin.

"Come on," I urged then kicked Wushah and we galloped the rest of the way.

— ii —

Felix stared up at me, arms akimbo, his handsome face a rigid mask of absolute calm that perfectly matched his equally composed tone of voice. "Enjoy your ride, Legate?"

My return had drawn quite a welcoming committee, a hefty mix of soldiers and Adraniis—I'm not absolutely sure, but I thought caught a fleeting glimpse of Eithne within ominously silent crowd—some were curious, many blatantly relieved to see me back and in one piece and others, like Felix absolutely furious at what they clearly saw as a stupid, selfish stunt on my part, but pretending to be only mildly put out. I put Cleander in that category as well. And Borzu. And yes, Rufinius, Aetius and… all right, *fine,* the whole damned camp if you insist.

Everyone was pissed as hell at me, pissed *and* scared, with the possible exceptions of Marcus, Hannibalianus and Auspex. To be kind Auspex was too thick to get angry about something like this; as far as he was concerned, if the legate wanted to go for a horseback ride, then that was the legate's affair and absolutely no concern of a simple cavalryman.

Hannibalianus, by being the only man I'd picked to accompany me, had just had his relatively obscure position within the cavalry ranks elevated to something far more important, at least in his mind—'personal bodyguard to the Legate'—even if he'd gotten the plum job strictly because he happened to be in the right place at the right time, a critical detail I had no doubt he'd somehow forget in telling and retelling and of course richly embellishing our daring adventure, so he simply had nothing to be unhappy about.

As for Marcus, he was just intensely relieved he'd gotten me back into the camp without a fight.

I was damned well not going to let Felix or the rest of them know *I* knew just how angry everyone was at me. Hell if I was. So I smiled an impervious smile, replied, "Immensely," then eased my leg up and over the rear pommels and myself out of the saddle—always a delicate and worrisome maneuver, doubly so with an audience. I managed it smoothly and with uncharacteristic grace. Better, I landed firmly on the ground without even a trace of a wobble—thanks to the gods—handed the reins to Hannibalianus, then with a nod to Marcus and Auspex, and a murmured, "Thank you, gentlemen, a most enjoyable way to spend the afternoon," I strode off towards the command tent.

The hushed and hostile crowd parted before me, clearing a path while Felix stared after me, open-mouthed.

I knew his stunned reaction wouldn't last… and I was right. I heard him trotting up behind me, heard his wheezing breaths, and out of the corner of my eye saw him draw abreast of me then match my shorter stride.

"How goes the pack up?"

245 J. E. Bruce

He jerked his baleful eyes towards me but he knew better than to launch into the diatribe he'd been honing to a knife-edge all afternoon, not with the entire camp as an audience. No, he was going to wait until we were inside our shared tent *then* explode, as if the thin canvas walls were magically *scream*-proof.

"Ahead of schedule," he replied coldly. "No thanks to you."

Okay, so that pissy remark just slipped out. I'm sure he hadn't meant to say that in public, but there it was.

So I stopped, turned and smiled at him. "I wasn't expecting any thanks—you're the one who had everything under control well before I left, so you rightfully deserve all the thanks. So, let me be the first to say so. Thank you, Primus-Pilus, for *doing* your *job.*"

He inhaled sharply then exhaled with a loud, strangled wheeze.

My smile stretched into a toothy grin, then I spun on my heel and started off again. It didn't take long to realize that this time Felix was not following—hard to do with a well-honed diatribe firmly stuck in your own gut.

As I continued on my way towards the tent, alone this time, I suddenly realized I was tired, *damned* tired and yes, fine, I *did* hurt. My side had been throbbing all day—not quite as bad as the day before, amazing, when you consider I'd been bouncing around on the back of a frisky horse for a goodly part of an afternoon—but it still hurt, and more so now that I'd *stopped* bouncing around on the back of said horse—go figure. I just wanted to get back to the tent, get out of my armor, call for some wine and something to eat, then sit down and enjoy my meal alone, as I figured, reasonably, that I'd just assured myself that Felix wouldn't be joining me anytime soon.

Granted, that still left a host of other nuisances named Cleander and Borzu and Aetius... and, well, you get the point. I figured I'd deal with them as they came, one by one or as a lynching party.

As I passed by a soldier, I grabbed his arm, gave him my meal order then sent him off to deliver it to Florianus. With luck my meal would arrive just about the time my saddle-weary butt hit the chair because not only was I tired and achy, I was damned hungry—which goes to prove you can work up quite an appetite being a gods damned, self-centered bastard. Who knew? Of course I also couldn't remember the last time I'd actually eaten, either.

I finally reached the tent, hesitated for only a moment as it occurred to me that people had a habit of lurking about the inside without permission and I wondered if I'd find I had yet another unexpected visitor, then with a shrug, I pulled the flap aside and stepped inside.

It was unoccupied and I felt a twinge of disappointment—yes, I admit it: I was hoping to find Eithne seated at the table, or even better, lying on my cot and eager to make amends as the ride, while exhausting, had been equally exhilarating and I was definitely in the mood for some female companionship. Had she been there, I might have reconsidered my 'self-imposed celibacy rule" as Felix called it. Oh, hell—reconsider my ass. I'd have kicked it out the tent flaps and halfway to the damned gate, then shown her exactly what a skilled lover could do—and to hell if the entire camp overheard the result, which, if done properly—which I've already established I planned to do—they would, damned if they wouldn't.

But she wasn't there. In fact it didn't look like anyone had been in the tent since I'd left, hours before: my blanket still lay in a tangle where I'd tossed it and my rolled up cloak on the floor at the head of the cot—where I'd pushed it sometime during the night, preferring the crook of my arm as a pillow.

Had Carus or Felix come into the tent they would have tidied up—Carus because it was his job and Felix because he was compulsive about such things. Perhaps this habit of his was one I should have stressed to Eithne: that he'd make not only a damned good husband but an equally fine wife.

Just the thought made me laugh out loud—

Gods… what's happening to me? I'm genuinely hungry, I'm clear-headed, extremely horny and I've laughed more today than I have in months! Had I known a simple horseback ride would cure whatever was ailing me, I'd have done it days ago… *wait.* I did—and it got me *shot.*

So, maybe not the cure all after all, but I'd take what I could get. As I dropped the flap behind me, I was plunged into darkness until my sun-blinded eyes adjusted.

I lifted the small fire-starting bag from where it hung on the tent pole, just below the oil lamp along with the flask of oil, filled the lamp then withdrew the two flints along with a small wad of kindling, struck the two stones together and on the first strike got a spark which instantly set the kindling alight—but with no dutifully amazed female audience I might note. With a wistful sigh, I lit the lamp, then snuffed out the kindling, using my calloused fingertips.

That job done, I untied my cheek guards, pried off the helmet and placed it on the table then gave my sweat-itchy scalp a good, two-handed scratch—damn, *that* felt good. Next the belt and dagger, baldric and gladius, greaves and chest harness. Then the ring-mail shirt, followed in quick order by the leather tunic—the simple and otherwise trivial detail that I'd been able to strip down to my undertunic and breeches without help and quickly was in fact something of note.

Feeling immensely pleased with myself, I took a deep breath, exhaled then plopped myself down at the table which, I must say, was noticeably lacking a meal, not to mention a mug of wine.

All right, so my usually impeccable timing had been a wee bit off.

I leaned forward, propped my elbows on the table and resumed my two-handed massage of my sweaty scalp—

"Ley-*gate*...?"

I dropped my hands away, straightened up at the unfamiliar, *female* voice and I felt a sudden rush of hope that Florianus might have misunderstood my menu choices and sent what I was really hankering after. I replied eagerly, "Come!" Which of course was exactly what I was hoping was going to happen.

A middle-aged Adranii woman, who I immediately recognized as one of Florianus' volunteer cooks, stepped cautiously into the tent, clutching a bowl in one hand, a decanter and mug in the other and a decidedly uneasy look on her gaunt, sunburnt face.

So, even Florianus was pissed at me—and this woman was his subtle snub in oh-so many ways.

That said, she wasn't to blame for Florianus' pettiness, so I smiled my best smile; she immediately smiled back as she set the offerings on the table—still very ill at ease and now due to my expression, which, I suddenly realized was a less than subtle ogle—yes, I was *that* horny and to make matters worse, she'd instantly reminded me of Boian of goose-grease fame.

Damn, why did I have to remember that?

Now my face was burning; other parts of my body were reacting— thank the gods I was seated at the table. I immediately pulled my eyes off her and fixed them, not to mention my full concentration on the contents of the bowl and what I saw was rather, um, deflating.

Hardtack soaked in wine with a few pieces of dried fruit on the side with a wine chaser. The milled grain, dried meat and root vegetables we'd brought were now being fed exclusively to the children, the wounded and pregnant and nursing women—the rest of us made do with hardtack, fruit, hard cheese and wine, and scant little of that I added to myself as I stared down at the meager meal, at once pleased that I hadn't been singled out for better rations yet irked as I was damned hungry and what I saw didn't look like it would take the edge off that hunger, much less fill my belly. I didn't want to consider that I'd been deliberately shorted just to drive home the point.

I grumbled my thanks and as the woman, still looking like she expected me to force myself on her at any moment, gathered up the empty bowl from the previous evening and made her speedy retreat, I found myself hoping that those grasslands did in fact support game, even if that meant it also supported predators. Loath as I was to admit it, if only to myself, even those shrimp-like creatures were starting to look marginally appetizing. *Meat.* That's what my belly craved. Roasted, boiled, salted and dried—I didn't damn well care. *And women.* I craved them, too. But knowing the fates, I stood a better chance of finding myself with a plate of mounded with shrimp for a late supper than a woman's attentions for the night.

With a very dejected moan, I used my forefinger to mix the concoction into a lumpy paste. That done, I scooped a fingerful into my mouth. It didn't taste *quite* as bad as it looked, but pretty damned close; that being said I'd literally grown up on hardtack and so had never developed an aversion to the staple, unlike many legionaries—to me it had always guaranteed a full belly twice a day, *every day*, something that as I young child I'd never thought possible—of course back on Earth our legions had other foodstuffs to supplement the otherwise bland sameness of our meals: appropriated livestock, wild game, fruit from abandoned orchards… and of course fresh vegetables, goat's milk and everyone's favorite, eggs, that we'd graciously accepted from a farmer in lieu of burning his damned house down.

Here on Latruncŭli there was dry, crumbly cheese, dried fruit… and hardtack.

Thinking back to eggs, I wondered if the hens, unlike the reasonably very confused roosters, had adjusted to their new surroundings and had started laying; last time I checked with Florianus, the answer was a supremely frustrated no—now a couple of cooked eggs, that would be a fine meal. Eggs with onions would be even better.

Thinking of onions, I gave myself a mental punch that I hadn't thought to bring along a few onions. Then again, I'd left Earth not thinking the worst, which was stupid, really. I mean, really, really stupid.

I was going to sorely miss onions, damned if I wasn't. And if the chickens didn't start laying, I'd miss eggs too.

On that bitter thought and ignoring my belly, which had begun to grumble in earnest at the thought of eggs and onions, I refilled my mouth, washed the lumpy, gritty paste down with a healthy gulp of wine, and scooped up another finger-full, the motions carried out by rote, no pleasure here, just a need to get sustenance into me by the most expeditious means. As I again brought the mug to my lips, intent on another swig, I suddenly became aware of the niggly sensation of being watched.

So, as I took a wincing gulp, I flicked the slit in the tent flaps a sidelong glance, suspecting it might be Felix—hoping it might be Eithne—then had to drop my gaze to spot my reticent visitor: *Anachie*. At least I assumed it was Anachie peering at me through the gap in the flaps; the silhouette was definitely that of a small child and since none of the others had shown any inclination to approach my tent Anachie was a pretty safe bet.

I wasn't sure whether to acknowledge him by inviting him in, or pretend that I didn't notice him and maybe he'd find that a reasonable excuse to slip inside.

I opted for the former, figuring the worst that could happen is that he'd run off as he had earlier; choosing the latter risked him thinking I was deliberately, spitefully ignoring him.

I turned, smiled and beckoned with my hand and murmured, "Please, Anachie, come in."

To my immense relief he sidled between the flaps... but came no closer. He just stood there, staring at me. Then I noticed he was clutching a small, carved horse, clearly whittled in haste from a precious scrap of wood and I couldn't help but think back to my first and only toy: a cloth horse, not much bigger than the version he held.

I smiled. "I see you've met Centurion Aetius."

He bit his lip and nodded.

"May I see what he made you?"

He stepped a little closer and held it up.

"That's a *very* fine horse."

He nodded as he again held it to his chest, his lower lip still held in his teeth.

"I went on a ride today on my horse."

He nodded again.

"You saw me?"

Another nod.

"I looked around and didn't see you. If I had, I would have asked if you wanted to come along."

He shook his head, retreated again and for a moment I thought he was going to dart outside. Instead he just backed up against the tent flaps.

"Are you afraid of my horse?"

That garnered a moment of thought, followed by another quick shake.

"Are you afraid... *of me?*"

This time he only stared at me.

I looked away, grabbed my mug and brought it to my lips. I swallowed against the hard knot in my throat, wiped my lips on the back of my hand, said tightly, "Your mother must wonder where you've gotten off to—"

The horse appeared on the table beside my elbow.

I glanced at it, then at Anachie, who was now standing beside me, staring up at me with his huge brown eyes.

"Why are you afraid of me, Anachie?"

He chewed on his lip for a moment then whispered, *"You go away."*

I inhaled sharply, squeezed my eyes shut, then felt him pressing the horse against my arm and I looked down.

"Here, yours—now you'll stay?"

I reached down, gently grasped his bony waist in both hands then lifted him up and sat him on my lap. He immediately wrapped his arms around my neck and buried his face in my chest. *"Don't go away—please."*

"I don't have any plans on going away," I replied as I wrapped my arm around him and with my other hand stroked his downy head. "So you don't need to be afraid of that, all right?"

As he tightened his hold, I felt a slight draft of air and glanced to my right, to the tent flap, fully expecting, almost hoping to find Eithne standing just outside.

Instead I found Felix holding the flap aside, and behind him stood Rufinius and Aetius.

Felix gestured with an open hand, asking permission to enter.

I nodded and he stepped inside, followed by the other two. As Rufinius let the flap drop behind him, Felix said, "I see he found you."

"Yes."

"He was looking all over for you earlier," Aetius added, his voice quiet, leaving his eyes to say what he was really thinking.

"Oh." I looked to Rufinius, but as usual, Rufinius remained silent, in this case his silence every bit as telling as Aetius's expression, every bit as wounding as any angrily voiced reproach.

I'd scared them all, deeply, Anachie worst of all. I looked down at him. "You saw me ride out and thought I wasn't coming back?"

He nodded, answering for all of them.

I whispered, *"Damn..."* then I lifted my gaze to Felix to find him staring at me with the same fearful look as Anachie, unsure exactly what he'd done, what they'd all done to justify this response. "I owe all of you an apology."

Felix eased himself down on his cot and said, "We're just glad you're back," as Aetius seated himself beside him.

"Me too!" Anachie said, then slipped from my lap, snatched his toy horse from the table and trundled over to Felix to show it to him as well. "Look!"

Felix dutifully admired the toy then gave Aetius a sidelong look. "Your work?"

"He asked for his own horse," Aetius replied and met my gaze, "so he could follow you."

I winced.

Anachie immediately crawled onto Felix's lap and once he'd made himself at home, he again held out the horse for Felix to study. As Felix expressed his marvel at the crude toy much to both Anachie and Aetius' pleasure, I shifted my gaze to Rufinius.

He'd remained standing, muscular arms crossed, his black, sullen eyes fixed on me, not quite so willing to let bygones be bygones—not that I could blame him. What I'd done today was only the latest in a series of thoughtless acts towards this man: I'd barely spoken to him since we'd arrived here—I considered it a measure of my confidence in his abilities but he clearly saw it as something vastly different; I'd never acknowledged the camp's impressive fortifications, not to mention the speed at which they'd been erected, I'd never asked about his own wounds and he was still smarting from those oversights.

"Please, Rufinius, sit your damned butt down!" I motioned to the other chair.

He exhaled forcefully, then slipped past Felix, Aetius and Anachie and seated himself stiffly on the other folding chair.

I looked at my three closest friends, all of whom I'd shaken deeply, *hurt* deeply and without once considering how they'd react to my actions. "I'm sorry. *Truly*—gods, it was never my intention to worry any of you."

Felix started to open his mouth but I held up my hand, silencing him.

"I thought..." I looked down at the mug on the table, "I thought you didn't need me any more—how's that for self-pity?" I managed a soft chuckle. "You're all so damned capable—"

"Because of *you*, Arri," Aetius interrupted. "You trained us. You believed in us—no one else did. You made us believe in ourselves."

I nodded at the truth of that, then: "I convinced myself I was useless, with my injuries worse than useless... *an encumbrance.* Everything I said, everything I tried to do was questioned—" I couldn't help but shoot Felix a sidelong glance and he had the good graces to look rather uncomfortable, "—but rightfully so," I added, lessening the sting, "because in truth I was scared—*damned scared.*"

Anachie slid from Felix's lap and hurried over to me then tugged at my arm, asking to be picked up. I scooped him up, again sat him on my lap and he snuggled up against me as if offering me comfort as Rufinius grabbed my forgotten mug and took a deep, wincing gulp of wine. "I wanted to go home. I wanted it more than anything I've ever wanted. I wanted to quit this planet and... *and go the hell home.* And I don't mean back to Taskim's Keep. No. I mean *my* home, back to the Empire—"

"We *can't* go back," Rufinius interrupted heatedly. "If we did the Tuatha would wipe our minds, *again.*" He glanced sidelong at Felix and Aetius, as did I. They nodded.

"I know," I replied softly.

"So, what, you were planning on abandoning us here?" Rufinius growled. "Soothing your conscience by telling yourself we're so damned capable?"

I motioned around me, suddenly every bit as angry as he was. "Have you seen any road signs pointing the way back to Earth? *I haven't! I'm stuck here just like you are!*"

Rufinius' incensed scowl turned into an exceedingly baleful glare. He leaned back in his chair, took another deep gulp of wine then smacked the now empty mug down on the table and crossed his burly arms.

I felt Anachie shift in my lap and looked down to see him staring up at me with fretful eyes as adults argued over matters he could barely comprehend—but 'I wanted to go home' had clearly struck a chord. I took a deep breath, let go of the anger and continued, "As I said, I *wanted* to go home—thought that's where I belonged."

"But you've changed your mind?" That from Felix.

I wrapped my arm tightly around Anachie. "I just needed to be alone for a little while—clear my mind, see everything for what it is, and what it isn't—I freely admit that when I rode out, I wasn't sure I was going to come back—I even gave myself that option, told myself if that's what I really wanted to do, then I should do it—I had to give myself that; I had to prove to myself that if I came back, it was of my own free will—"

"But I sent an escort after you," Felix said.

"Yeah—"

"So you came back… because I gave you no choice."

I stared at Felix long and hard then at Aetius, who looked worried, clearly not sure he wanted me to answer that. Finally I shifted my stare to Rufinius, who still looked angry, *murderously* angry.

I locked my eyes with his. Rufinius was the one I had to convince. Felix and Aetius were ready to believe anything as long it was the response they desperately wanted to hear. "If I'd decided not to come back no escort would have stopped me. Hannibalianus couldn't have stopped me. I came back because I realized *this* is where I belong—with you, with the men out there," I jerked my chin towards the flaps of the tent, "and yes, with the Adraniis. There's no going back, not for any of us." I looked down at Anachie. "So, we make this world ours—we hold it against all who would take it away from us, isn't that right, Anachie?"

He grinned. *"Right!"*

I looked back at Rufinius. "You're going to build us that world, Centurion, stone by gods damned stone—roads, bridges, aqueducts, fortresses… baths, the lot. And Aetius," I turned to the man, "You're going to teach. You have several generations of people who've known nothing but slavery, nothing but living inside of ships and in relative luxury. You're going to teach them how to survive here, how to grow and harvest grain and raise livestock—in other words, how to turn this planet into our home."

His lips twitched in the faintest of smiles.

"And Felix…"

He lifted his chin, met my gaze.

"You're going to train the Adranii men, older boys and yes—any woman who asks—to fight like gods damned Romans."

He blinked, then squinted sidelong at Aetius after a grinning Aetius jabbed him in the ribs with his elbow.

"Any questions?"

Anachie tugged on my wrist. *"What about me?"*

"Ah," I grinned. "Well, you have the *most* important job of all—you're going to be my son."

His eyes got very round then he threw his arms around my neck and hugged me so tight he brought tears to my eyes.

Rufinius was the first to get to his feet; he cleared his throat, stepped close and squeezed my good shoulder as he grumbled huskily, "I'll build you anything you want, you crazy fucking bastard, damned if I won't."

"I want a Roman bath is what I want—hot and cold rooms, a pool, the lot."

"Then you'll have it."

"And I'll keep you to that promise—Anachie, you're my witness."

He nodded eagerly.

"Anachie," Rufinius said, "you're going to help, yes?"

"Yes!" He wriggled, signaling he wanted off and I placed him on the ground, then he turned to Rufinius and held up his hands, asking to be picked up by a man many were rightfully reluctant to make eye contact with, much less approach.

Rufinius dutifully picked him up as I lurched to my feet, Felix and Aetius following suit.

I couldn't help but smile, seeing Anachie now firmly planted on Rufinius' hip, his arms around the engineer's muscular neck. "How 'bout we take a walk around the camp—see how the preparations are going?"

PART THREE: HIC SUNT SCORPINES

— X —

I stepped out of my tent, stretched my stiff muscles and looked around.

It was still dark, or as dark as night ever got on Latruncŭli, with dawn still several hours away. The giant whirlpool was taking up a goodly portion of the western sky with the brilliant spot two hand-spans above the hinter peaks and my surroundings were rimed in their icy glow.

I rubbed my gritty eyes then raked my hair off my forehead.

I hadn't slept—worse, I *felt* as if I hadn't slept. I suspect if asked, not a single adult had slept. Now all pretense at sleep was gone: people were up and wandering around, making last minute checks of what they'd packed, hitching up unhappy oxen who'd enjoyed their work-free days, getting the wounded, pregnant women, the dozen or so elderly Adraniis and the very youngest children properly bedded down for the trip, collapsing tents and lean-tos and getting them securely stored atop already overloaded baggage carts and wagons.

The gate had been taken down sometime during the night and returned to its previous life as the beds of two wagons—while many of the provisions had been consumed we still needed every wheeled vehicle possible. And beyond the now gaping portal I could make out the starlit outlines of several onagers—the rest were presumably lined up beyond, ready to protect the now gateless encampment if need be while awaiting our departure. While I did not look forward to again hauling those heavy contraptions across the one safe crossing in the dry river bank wide enough to handle them, much less on a trek across the desert and over the pass, the onagers, along with the ballistas and scorpios remained our best defense against any Si'aafu attack.

If those strange pellets that had caused me so much personal grief could in fact stop Si'aafu at close range as Borzu claimed, then it stood to reason the same would be true of the ballista and scorpio bolts. I hadn't thought to ask him if he thought our incendiary weapons would be effective against these creatures—that remained to be seen. I suspected at the very least they would scare the crap out of them… *once*. And maybe once would be enough.

I turned at the echo of voices and looked up at the wall—men had been hard at work lowering the scorpios and taking the firing platforms and watch towers apart, carefully salvaging the valuable canvas and handing the wood back to Rufinius's engineers to remake into wagons. Now the work was almost complete with the encircling rock wall bereft of all but one platform and one scorpio.

Cook fires had burned all night, offering up a hot meal for anyone who had an appetite, which few in truth had. Several of the smaller wagons had been set aside strictly as moving feeding stations—people could grab a bite of food or a gulp of water without the entire column grinding to a halt. One of the larger wagons was assigned to pick up people who collapsed from the heat or the strain, or those who began to lag behind. If all went as planned, we weren't going to stop until we reached a site suitable for making camp for the night.

Marcus had said the pass was a good three day's march to the north—but that was assuming we'd keep up a legion's marching speed: twenty miles a day. Even settling for a far less grueling pace was still going to make a very hard first day for everyone—my men weren't used to marching with civilians, and the Adraniis weren't used to marching, *period*. With luck each day would get marginally easier, as everyone learned the routine and adjusted their expectations accordingly.

While Borzu was in charge of his people, especially the children who'd been roused from their beds and were now running around, picking up on the weary anxiety of their elders, I was ultimately in charge of everyone—

"Here," Felix said as he stepped out of our tent, my helmet in his hand, our bedrolls slung over his shoulders. "You forgot something."

I chuckled, accepted the helmet, slipped it on and tied the cheek-pieces then took my bedroll. We'd already packed up the inside of the tent; cots, table and chairs were now safely stored in a nearby wagon. The bedrolls would stay with us, tied to the saddles.

As Carus arrived along with another soldier to take down our tent, Felix and I left them to it and together we walked through the camp, murmuring our good mornings to passing Adraniis and soldiers alike, offering suggestions and encouragement, speaking as if we were all just about to take a casual stroll through a sun-dappled glade rather than embarking on an arduous trek across a furnace-like desert with no certainty of finding safe haven at the end.

My troops were tired but at the same time eager to get going. The Adraniis were clearly scared but willing to trust themselves to our protection—not that they had much choice.

We reached the stables to find the horses saddled. Many of the cavalrymen were already mounted and now leaning on their upright lances and speaking softly to each other as their horses dozed, tails flicking languidly at imaginary flies.

Aetius, Baculus and Rufinius were already there, as were Borzu and Khouri, along with three Adraniis, two men and yet *another* woman, dark-skinned and tall and who, just by her bearing clearly held some sort of import for the others. Borzu, at my pointed stare, introduced them, starting with the woman: Lujaji, the *Fihroon*'s navigator of all things; Jom, whom Borzu explained was his first officer—a rank comparable, he said, to Primus-Pilus; and Birral, an *astro biologist*. I didn't feel now what the time to ask what that was, although I gathered this diminutive, ferret-eyed and twitchy man studied star life, whatever the hell that was.

"We're far ahead of schedule, Legate," Rufinius said. "The camp should be fully packed up and ready to move within the hour."

That was good news; it meant we could actually start off well *before* dawn—while it was still relatively cool but with more than enough light to spot stragglers, saltpans or other problems. I nodded and turned back to the camp.

It now resembled something that had been hit by a sudden, heavy windstorm. Not a single tent or lean-to was standing; most had already been rolled up and were being loaded. Most telling of all, the cook fires had just been extinguished, leaving a low, greasy smear of smoke hanging over the camp. While the Adraniis had no experience at breaking camp they were listening to my men and following their instructions to the letter, which gave me some small hope that this trek to safer lands might not be quite as daunting—or as chaotic—as I'd feared.

I'd toyed with the idea of each horse carrying its rider and either a woman or an older child—then decided against it. The cavalry was our first line of defense against any attack; to mix civilians with them would slow their response to any threat. We'd already agreed to split the mounted soldiers into thirds: the first to lead the march, the second to keep everyone in an orderly column and act as outriders and scouts, and the third take up the rear.

Aper, when Marcus assigned him to command the second group, had griped that it was going to be like herding sheep and something told me he was probably going to find himself not far off the mark. Better than herding cats, I suppose… and speaking of, the cats had been safely caged earlier the previous day—by suggestion of Baculus. The uproar over the Si'aafu attack that wasn't had sent the terrified creatures into hiding and it had taken until the following morning to find all three—and Leonidas, the only male, was found *outside* the walls. All of our animals were now precious broodstock, each a key to our long-term survival and I wasn't leaving even one damned spooked cat behind. But I digress…

Those riders taking up the rear, led by the newly elevated Hannibalianus, were assigned to make one last sweep of the camp, make sure nothing of value was left behind in the confusion, and finally, make sure the fires were out and any useable tinder was recovered before they left to catch up with the column. In truth there wasn't much left within the walls to burn—even so, I was not about to risk sending any sort of signal to any watchers. I'd even considered ordering the dismantlement of the walls—a subtle message that there was no turning back, but I ultimately decided against it—if things went badly, we might have no choice but to return even if by returning we sealed out fate—a grim thought and one I decided not to ponder further.

A muffled but substantial *thump* from behind me drew my distracted gaze: the last scorpio was down and its two-man crew swarmed it, wasting no time disassembling it for travel. Unlike the onagers that were pulled by oxen, or the ballistas that were crewed by four men and drawn by alternating, two-man teams the scorpios were easily parted up and carried by their two crewmen. The firing platform followed in short order and no sooner was the former wagon bed reunited with its wheels and axles than it was loaded and hitched to a team of waiting oxen.

"Time to go."

At my softly worded command Felix strode off to get our horses while the rest left to make sure everyone knew their place in our carefully thought out column: the first group of cavalry led by Marcus and then three hundred infantry led by Rufinius, followed by the medical wagons, then civilians on foot, bracketed on either side by the bulk of the infantry, with the baggage carts and meal wagons scattered among their ranks, then the supply wagons with Hardalio's beloved goats tethered in small, loose skeins to the backs of each, followed by the scorpio crews and then the engines—ballistas first, the ox-drawn onagers following, the last three hundred infantry overseen by Aetius and lastly, the outriders commanded by Aper, who would be temporarily taking up the rear.

Once the train was well out onto the flats, Felix and I would ride to the head of the column, checking for problems as we went, but for now we were staying behind, to help Hannibalianus and his sixty men with their final sweep of the camp.

At least that *was* the plan.

I accepted Wushah's reins from Felix, tied my bedroll to the rear pommels, then with his help got myself up and settled on the saddle. The last man on the wall, standing the final watch, saw me mount my horse and brought his buccina to his lips and gave one long, low warbling blow: signal to form up and get ready to move out, then hooking the horn over his shoulder, he made a quick decent and no sooner had his feet hit the ground than the ladder was pulled and lashed to the side of an awaiting wagon.

A clatter of hooves signaled that the first wave of cavalry was on its way through the gateway, followed by the leading infantry, a moving, swaying and bristling line of men, their armor glittering in the predawn starlight as they snaked their way around the camp and finally out through the gateway. Then the medical wagons began to move, wheels groaning and harness jingling as they fell into line.

Then the moment of truth: the civilians began to form up along with their baggage carts, children in hand, as soldiers quickly took up position on either side, gently urging the Adraniis into a tight formation that, at eight abreast, was going to be hard pressed to squeeze through the gateway. I was relieved to catch a brief glimpse of Anachie, his hand tightly clutched by Eithne, before they took their places in the column. Anachie waved at me while Eithne fixed me with a worried look before turning back to the business at hand. I even spotted Isem among the civilians; he noticed me staring at him but acted as if he hadn't as he quickly melted into the throng.

Right behind them came the supply wagons and soldiers carrying the parted up scorpios along with their packs, all lined up and spiraling around the inner walls, reminding me of a gigantic snake coiled about its lair. The ballistas and onagers, which were already stationed outside would fall in line once the wagons and scorpio crews passed.

As the Adraniis began to move, following the directions of the bracketing infantry and the centurions, Borzu, Jom and Birral abruptly stepped out of line and began talking and gesturing to each other.

Felix looked at me, eyebrows raised; I stared back, then we watched in silence as the three hurried to the very center of the camp and then, to our growing curiosity began gathering up rocks that up until the evening before had formed one of the larger fire pits. They then began placing the stones in strange patterns: large circles intersected by sinuous lines, smaller circles within triangles, triangles within squares and finally, a long, straight line of perfectly spaced stones, like dots.

Marcus led his horse over to where Felix and I now sat astride our mounts, glanced back at Borzu and the others as they worked then looked up at me as if expecting me to explain this inexplicable behavior.

I shrugged, equally baffled and muttered, "Hell if I know."

Marcus swung himself up onto the saddle and favored the three Adraniis with one last quizzical gaze as if expecting their actions to suddenly make more sense from the perspective of a horse's back—of course it didn't or I'd have been able to figure it out.

"A ritual perhaps?" he finally offered.

"Perhaps," I replied, then, "we'll be with you shortly."

"Gods' favor to all of us today," Marcus murmured.

"Gods' favor," Felix and I echoed.

A gentle tap of his heels sent Belili trotting after the deluge of people, animals and equipment that was now pouring through the gateway on his way to the head of the column.

Meanwhile, Borzu and the others hastened to complete their strange task and once they seemed satisfied with the results, Borzu sent his two helpers to rejoin the ranks of the civilians while he walked over to us.

He stopped in front of Wushah and at Wushah's insistence began stroking the warhorse's velvety muzzle as he looked up at me. "A diversion—just in case the Si'aafu come sniffing around."

I raised my brows in begging interest.

He motioned expansively to the strange, flowing patterns. "It's a message that says, in essence, 'We got here first'—in Si'aafu, using a very insulting phrase to get the point across, I might add, akin to saying, 'fuck you'. If any happen across this camp, they might be fooled into believing other Si'aafu beat them to us."

"Oh."

"It might give us a few extra hours, maybe a few days, throw them off our track for a little while."

I stared at the strange patterns then turned back at him. "Thank you."

"No need to thank me, Legate. It was my pleasure as I've been wanting to tell the Si'aafu to go fuck themselves for years—decades in fact."

I overheard several nearby horsemen chuckle, and couldn't help but chuckle myself.

"Captain?" Felix patted Tuzun's broad rump then he motioned to the boulder we'd used as a mounting block.

Borzu grinned and hurried over to the block as Felix turned Tuzun towards it as well.

As Borzu got himself up behind Felix, the cavalrymen began their methodical search as the camp emptied like an ebbing tide and like an ebbing tide, leaving bits of flotsam, in this case discarded pieces of peoples' lives, behind.

I looked around at the now eerily silent and starlit camp, watched as armored men on horseback moved about, each making his own careful search, using lance tips to overturn bits of rubbish, hunkering down on saddles as they ducked into the remains of the stable or the walled off section that had been the now infamous latrines. As each made his pass by the altar, he reined in his mount, saluted or made a sign of deference and farewell, then was off again. A few dismounted to raid the fire-pits of anything remotely useable, stuffing what they found into sacks.

Gratian had earlier gathered up all the prayer ribbons, leaving the altar little more than a heap of wine- and blood-stained rock; those tattered strips of cloth would now temporarily bedeck all the transitory altars along our travels—an enticement, a way of luring the gods into tagging along and hopefully offer their continued protection in trade for our regular devotions, he said. But just in case, he'd also left an entire day's ration of hardtack behind—*his*, to placate any deities who might resent our cheek— where he got these ideas is anyone's guess.

As I've said before, I'm not a pious man and I never put much stock into rituals and piety. I had a sneaking suspicion that Gratian was actually making it up as he went along, richly embellishing on what little I'd imparted to him, which could mean interesting implications for our future society—of course one could argue that most religions are based on carefully crafted half-truths and outright lies, faith verses fact and all that.

Or perhaps he'd *been* a priest in his former life as he did tend to the holier than thou attitude…

Wushah and I made our own slow, deliberate circuit of the camp, him with an air of excitement, me with a mixture of relief and foreboding. The place stank, and probably would continue to stink for days until the heat drank up what little moisture remained. But this hilltop fortress had been our only home on this gods forsaken planet. I felt the same soul-deep twinge at leaving this place as I had leaving our dead behind, abandoning them and it to the elements while we moved on to forge a new life.

I lifted my gaze only to find that everyone who'd remained behind to search was now in the process of gathering near the gateway. As hoped, the search had turned up nothing. I'd feared that in all the confusion a small child might panic and hide and its parents might not realize it until we were well under way. My men had known from the start what—or should I say *who*—they were looking for and had thankfully come up dry.

Just then the soft, predawn breeze that blew through the gateway and into camp unobstructed, spinning small eddies of trash, suddenly turned, bringing me a potent whiff of the latrines.

Definitely time to go.

I clicked my tongue and Wushah began to walk towards the gateway, but at my insistence in a circuitous way: our path first took us close to the altar—there I reined in Wushah, saluted and murmured, *"Protege nos, defende nos,"* and sprinkled a small libation from my waterskin over the mound of stones, just in case—as Gratian suggested—the gods of Latruncŭli were awake at this hour and listening. Then I turned Wushah's head and gave his belly a tap with my heels and he resumed his slow walk, his path now paralleling the pattern of stones. As we passed one of the larger circles, I spat into it, adding my own personal slight to the alien message.

The soldiers, seeing me finally heading towards them, turned their horses and began filing out, in ones and twos, and in absolute silence, as if hoping to slip away without the camp realizing we'd gone, leaving it behind.

Felix, with Borzu seated behind him, followed. I was, by unspoken agreement, the last one out and as I passed through the gateway, I fought the urge to look back. But in truth there wasn't anything to look back to, just as there wasn't that summer morning—how long ago?—when I bade Turan and Neshoue goodbye.

I tapped Wushah into a trot; the others also picked up their pace, like me suddenly eager to rejoin our people, hear human voices, the familiar rumble of the wagons and engines, the comforting jingle of harness and armor and leave the ominously silent camp to its fate just as we left to meet ours.

— ii —

It hadn't taken long, once the suns rose, for the desert to heat up and the air to quiver; worse, the train was kicking up a thick pall of dust that hung over us, making it hard to breathe, even harder to see, to keep one's bearings, especially those towards the back of the column. There wasn't even a whisper of a breeze to dissipate the cloud or fill the gaping mouths of our dragon banners and the soldiers had taken to using their neckerchiefs as dust veils even though it meant their armor would painfully chafe their sweaty, dust-gritty necks.

The Adraniis, following the soldiers' lead, wrapped their heads in scraps of cloth, leaving only slits for the eyes. While they made for easier breathing, they paradoxically added to the panicky sense of being slowly smothered.

Only the presence of the flanking infantry, men who were used to marching under awful conditions and knew to maintain a tight formation no matter what, kept the Adraniis from succumbing to that panic, or becoming disoriented and wandering off—dangerous by itself, but outriders had warned of a wide, loose-walled and rocky ravine a mile or so to our east, the channel of a once rushing river and the wellspring of the deep, narrow gorge we'd been forced to traverse on our way to and from reconnoitering the Adraniis' mountain camp.

Another nagging concern about the dust cloud: it would be visible for miles and while the outriders hadn't reported seeing anything to suggest we were being watched or worse, followed, I couldn't shake the sense that we weren't alone. Felix had admitted a similar niggly twinge between the shoulder blades; Marcus clearly felt the same. Every time I risked a sidelong glance at him as he, Felix and I rode three abreast at the head of the column, I saw his eyes darting here and there, constantly roving, watching for anything suspicious.

To break up the anxious tedium, the three of us began taking turns riding down one side of the column and up the other, checking on progress while looking for possible problems. I was relieved to find that despite its length the train was keeping together, but the pace was far slower than even I had anticipated and by late morning the rate had slowed even further as the Adraniis, especially the children, began to flag in the intense heat.

I kept worrying about Anachie, if he was keeping up, hoping an adult had picked him up—Eithne was too small herself to carry him—and I desperately wanted to turn back, find him and settle him on my lap, but Anachie was only one of scores of children, many every bit as frail as he and who had little choice but to walk. To single him out for special treatment, to ride with the Legate on the Legate's horse, would be a mistake and for once I actually listened to myself.

I couldn't even offer up Wushah's back to someone in need and go on foot myself—I knew my limitations far too well and I was damned if *I* was going to slow down the column. Besides, as legate I needed to remain mounted, visible to all. It sent a very strong message to everyone: they had a leader, a man who knew what he was doing, knew where he was going. They needed to see me astride Wushah, my armor glittering in the dusty sunlight, my face serene—even if the lower half of said face was swathed in my filthy neckerchief and the upper half hidden under my helmet with only my eyes visible—the epitome of the self-confident commander. I was their savior; I would deliver them from this hell—never, ever underestimate the power of power, even if it's all a façade.

We'd been forced out onto the exposed desert, leaving the relative cover of the hinter range behind when we found our path north blocked by a large saltpan that hugged the western foothills, opposite the paralleling eastern ravine and equally treacherous. There was no shade here, no defensible perimeter. If we were set upon, my soldiers and cavalry would be hard pressed to protect the civilians. And of course there was the ever-present danger of a dust storm which would not only make it near impossible to keep an eye on everyone, but would also conceal any natural traps, like quicksand, natron pools… or even dry, rock-strewn and soft-bellied feeder streambeds that could wreak havoc on the wagons, especially those carrying the wounded.

The Adraniis had been told if we were suddenly and unexpectedly overtaken by such a storm to hunker down, not move, wait for the wind-laden sand to pass. In my experience people have a tendency to forget common sense when they can't see their hand in front of their face; it was a constant worry that they'd panic and scatter under such conditions, despite the best efforts of the flanking infantry and we'd spend precious time searching for them and likely never find them all.

That was a hypothetical worry; sand storms were always a much greater possibility in the late afternoon—if our incredibly limited familiarity with the moods of this high desert could be taken as a reliable guide.

But a present and very real worry were the children—they were definitely becoming a drag on the rest of us; adult Adraniis, who in fact were every bit as heat-weary as their children *had* finally resorted to carrying them, in their arms, on their backs and shoulders, but by the looks on their haggard faces as they slogged along, they couldn't keep it up for long. The infantry couldn't help—they were already loaded down with their kits, each pack weighing almost as much as the man who carried it, and of course they were carrying their shields and pila, some carrying the parted up scorpios as well—and oh, yes, all done while in full armor.

I finally ordered the leading cavalry to peel away and turn back, to offer the backs of their equally suffering horses to anyone—child or adult, soldier or civilian—who was in dire need, or help those about to collapse to a space on the already perilously overloaded wagons, but there was to be no stopping—even a snail's pace was better than stopping. That said, I sent scouts ahead, to look for a suitable place to make camp—realizing it was pointless to expect the Adraniis to keep up this pace through the worsening heat of the afternoon that even my soldiers, former Kellesuf, would find demoralizing.

So we marched on... towards shimmering pools of illusory water always just beyond our reach, towards the north, always north as the suns rose higher and higher in the lightening ocher sky and turned the desert floor into a smithy worthy of Vulcan himself.

— iii —

As the suns reached zenith and their rays beat down on us unmercifully, I told myself if we could make another mile, I'd consider the first day a limited success. Then I made the mistake of twisting in the saddle and looking back over the column—the familiar landmark of the high crag that loomed over the hillock was still visible through the dust and above the heat ripples and I judged we'd barely made five miles since leaving the camp before dawn. *Half a gods damned Latruncŭlian day—five miles!* At this rate we'd be lucky to reach the base of the pass in two weeks and the distant grasslands in a month.

And we had less than a week's worth of food, even less water.

As slowly I turned back to face forward, I tried not to let my sense of overwhelming defeat show, tried to convince myself we simply had no choice: to stay meant death from starvation and sickness, meant watching civil order break down, meant murder and rape and suicide and the gods only knew what else. As a foot soldier and later a centurion, I'd entered towns that had been long besieged; I'd seen with my own eyes what happened when supposedly civilized people were put under such prolonged and horrific conditions. It had left me, a seasoned veteran of countless battles, shaken to my core and with a private terror of ever finding myself in such a situation.

To go gave everyone something to keep them occupied and their minds off the fact that we were headed towards total disaster... unless I could somehow increase the pace. The fact that my men could have made the grasslands before our provisions ran out had we not had the civilians only added to my bleak mood.

In short, by offering aid to the Adraniis I'd effectively doomed us all.

I didn't even want to think about what we might or, worse, might *not* find once we reached the grasslands—assuming we reached them. If there was nothing we could find to eat and quickly, we'd have no choice but resort to eating the goats, chickens and oxen, along with the horses, even the dogs, hawks and cats, which would at most stave off starvation by a few days and then we'd be without a cavalry, without the oxen to pull our wagons, goats for milk and cheese, chickens for eggs—at the total mercy of this alien world and the Si'aafu.

Gods...

I pried off my helmet, hooked it over a pommel then untied the neckerchief I'd wrapped around my lower face and used it to blot the stinging, gritty sweat from my eyes and then wipe the back of my neck.

I looked around as I took a deep breath of the sweltering, unfiltered air, hoping by some miracle I would find our deliverance from this hell hole... or at the very least an oasis like those from my far distant home, but there were no verdant islands, no lush stands of date palms, just endless, shimmering desert ahead and behind and the eerie flotilla of floating mountaintops to either side of us.

I combed my sweaty hair off my face, quickly retied the makeshift dust veil then reluctantly donned the helmet—thankful for once that it was Tuatha-forged and not Roman—and tugged it forward to take maximum advantage of its browridge to shade my eyes. Then, as I readjusted my position in the saddle, I fixed my slitted eyes on what lay before us: endless, near featureless desert that shifted and slithered as if turned to liquid in the blistering heat.

So we trudged on, the pace barely more than a slow, staggering walk for most. Even Wushah and Tuzun made no extra effort, just one hoof in front of another, plodding along, heads down, eyes half-closed—

—I felt myself suddenly and roughly jerked back; startled, my legs struggled for purchase on the sweat-slick leather of the saddle and I glanced around, momentarily bewildered, then I realized I'd actually nodded off and Felix had just managed to grab the shoulder strap of my chest harness in time to stop me from toppling forward.

He gave me another shake; satisfied I was awake, he let go and eased himself back into his own saddle and fixed me with a heavy-lidded, humorless look, as if too heat-numb for more. Felix was suffering, truly suffering and if he was suffering, I could only imagine the suffering of those on foot.

Enough.

I held up my hand, reined in Wushah as the signal to halt rippled haphazardly back through the column, horses, wagons and people coming to a jolting, startled stop only to look around as if in a daze.

Marcus appeared beside me as he gave our surroundings a quick sweep with worried eyes, wondering what I'd spotted that would have prompted the unexpected and potentially disastrous order. "Legate?"

"We must make camp—or risk everyone dropping in their tracks."

He nodded wearily as he mopped his sweat-oily face with his grubby neckerchief and looked around again. Nothing suitably defensible presented itself aside from the foothills of the western range, and skirting those rolling hills were saltpans and their natron pools, fed by runoff from the higher peaks beyond. The eastern range was effectively beyond our reach, blocked by the natural moat of the ravine.

"Recall your men—see if they can find a passage through the salt flats."

Marcus put two fingers in his mouth, cut loose a high-pitched whistle and if by magic, outriders who'd been invisible, lost in the quivering air began to appear, at first looking like nothing more substantial than sun-bright shimmers as they converged on the column, but quickly solidifying into armored horsemen.

The first exploratore arrived, breathless, clearly suffering like the rest of us from the intense and unrelenting heat, his helmet-framed face pale and glossy, his mount breathing hard, its mouth agape and foam-flecked, nostrils flared. Then more arrived, each looking no better than the first, some far worse.

"We need to make camp…"

There was a collective mutter of relief from the horsemen.

"…so we must find a way through the salt flats—even if it's barely wide enough for two oxen to pass—get ourselves into those damned mountains. Got it?"

The men only nodded, all too hot and bone-weary to even reply, 'Yes, Legate.' Turning their mounts to the west, they took off at a slow, deliberate canter, fast enough to make good time as they fanned out, but not so fast as to be reckless on what was at best unfamiliar territory, at worst, dangerous ground where any lapse in attention could be fatal for an exhausted man and his equally exhausted mount.

Marcus, on his sortie, hadn't wasted time reconnoitering the western foothills, had in fact made a bee-line for the pass, using the cool of the night to make the one way trip north in the time between sunset and sunrise. Urged on by their happy discovery, he and his men had risked the return trip in the full heat of day, stopping only to water their horses from their bulging waterskins. Felix's orders had been simple and straightforward: reach the pass, determine if it was truly passable, confirm the existence of a river and grasslands and then return. And being former Kellesuf, Marcus had followed his orders to the letter. He hadn't wasted any time scouting for water going or returning or looking for suitable sites for marching camps along the way—a regrettable omission in hindsight; had I not been unconscious at the time he was dispatched, I would have made sure his mission was a little more... um, wide-ranging?

He had reported that there were spots where the foothills gave way to the large scarp that formed the base of the western range, and the scarp itself appeared to be riddled with chasms, most barely more than jagged tears in the rock and briefly visible only at sunrise, but a few were broad and flat bottomed, their true depth hidden in shadow even in the middle of the day. It was my desperate hope one of these could serve as a temporary refuge, if only from the heat.

Keeping that thought foremost, I motioned for the train to turn, to follow, and with a collective heave the column bestirred itself and began to move again, albeit in fits and starts as the civilians, not knowing better than to sit down or blatantly ignoring the grumbled warnings of my men now struggled to get back to their feet using muscles that cramped and joints that had stiffened during the short rest. It was possibly a foolhardy move to get the train to follow when we had no assurance of safe passage through the flats, but it was better than just standing, or in many cases sitting here waiting for word—again, keep people busy, keep their minds on putting one foot in front of the other and they won't start thinking other, bleaker thoughts, won't think about how thirsty they were, how hungry they were... just how damned dog-tired they were—or their odds of surviving the day, much less the journey.

The unexpected change in direction had a positive effect on the civilians who seemed to think this meant the day's trek was fast coming to an end, that camp and rest were only as far as those biscuit-brown foothills that now lay ahead; my soldiers knew better. The foothills, with no solid foothold on the shimmering desert, were farther away than they appeared and once we found a place to stop there was still the job of setting up a marching camp. To come this far and not take proper precautions, no matter how tired everyone was would be a death sentence.

We plodded on as the suns continued to beat down on us mercilessly; even Wushah stumbled a couple of times, too tired to lift his massive hooves over rocks or drifts of burning sand. Behind me the column struggled to follow, people and animals well past their physical limits but too exhausted realize it.

I was beginning to worry where the outriders had gotten themselves off to when out of the corner of my eye I saw a quicksilver flicker within the eeling air: the telltale glint of sunlight on armor. The infantry saw it too and the nearside wheeled towards the metallic flash, pila and shields coming to bear and forming a protective barrier, guarding the civilians' flank, just in case.

As we watched, the apparition divided, first into two, then three… five, six and soon all of the outriders appeared like so many windblown leaves, again at an easy canter, lance-tips pointing skyward—a welcome signal that no trouble followed. Then, drawn to a faint screeching sound, I looked up and spotted two of our hawks wheeling high overhead.

I tapped Wushah's sides with my heels, urging him forward at a very unenthusiastic trot, to meet the approaching riders, leaving the train to follow at a slower pace.

As soon as the first rider got to within easy yelling distance, he called out, hoarsely, *"Water! We found water, Legate!—and a way through the flats!"*

I slumped back onto the saddle, suddenly and unexpectedly overcome by the news, then I quickly wiped my eyes before the approaching horsemen could notice and wonder if their legate had finally lost his grip.

The horsemen quickly swallowed me up, milling around me, their dusty, haggard faces split with broad grins, all looking like they were about to burst while the hawks, at their handlers' whistles, plummeted earthwards, towards outstretched arms.

"Water, Legate!" Aper gasped, breathless, as he held up a fat waterskin. *"Sweet water!"* All, I noticed, were in holding bulging waterskins, their breeches and undertunics still damp and clinging to their bodies.

Another, Arcadius, one of the falconers, added, "A waterfall and deep pool—"

"Full of those 'shrimp' like the sort Quintus found!" That from Pictor.

They all looked like they'd drunk their fill, as had their horses and even the hawks, whose breast feathers, I noticed were still wet. All were tired yes, but no longer gripped by that desperately parched look that still marked the rest of us.

I tugged down the dust veil. "And a safe place to make camp?"

They all nodded, silvered helmets bobbing wildly as Aper said, "Not the most ideal, but defensible—

"Legate," another, Ulpius, interrupted, *"the pool's big enough we can bathe!"*

I laughed at the sheer absurdity of that, a dry, raspy laugh that ended up in a harsh coughing fit. One minute I was battling visions of the entire column succumbing to thirst and hunger before my eyes and now we were talking about taking a bath?

"And it's already in the shadow of the mountains," Papinian, the other falconer added, "much cooler, with a good view of the surrounding desert." He stroked the back of his hawk and grinned—a very proud grin I might add. "Canens here, and Laverna—" he nodded to Arcadius' bird, "—*they* found the gorge, sir. They could smell the water even before the horses did." He gave his horse a pat on the neck and the horse snorted and tossed its head as if acknowledging its lapse.

I eyed the hawk as it balanced lightly on Papinian's leather-clad hand, then the other clutching Arcadius' equally armored fingers, each bird's tiny hawk bells tinkling as the horses beneath them shifted from hoof to hoof, and I *swear* both birds were smirking at me.

So, so, so. No rodents to harry, no hare or fowl to chase—I'd never considered hawks to be water dowsers, never heard of them capable of such, but if true—and going by the grins and nods of the other horsemen it was—then the birds had earned their way and then some.

"We'll have to backtrack a bit," Aper said, drawing my attention back to the immediate as he pointed slightly south, to a promontory that jutted out from the scarp. "But not much."

Food. Water. A defensible site for a camp. My prayers had been answered beyond my wildest dreams.

Now all we had to do was reach it.

I looked up to find Ulpius offering me his waterskin. I shook my head, pointed to the column and he nodded his understanding: offer what you have to the most in need.

"Ride the line, pass the word—*yes?*" I said aloud, giving these men the well-deserved honor of telling everyone of their incredible find. "Encourage everyone to drink, and water the animals too—now we know we can replenish our supply."

They nodded then kicking their horses, took off at a gallop to spread the word just as Felix drew his horse up alongside me and said in a voice barely above a dry whisper, *"Good news?"*

"The absolute best possible news, Primus-Pilus." I heaved a sigh then dropped my head forward and closed my eyes, permitting myself a moment to absorb the simple and yet utterly astonishing fact that we weren't all about to die.

"Arri?"

I lifted my head to find him offering me the now very lean waterskin we'd been sharing, rationing ourselves to an occasional sip and nothing more.

I took it, filled my mouth with the warm water, leaving enough for him to do the same but little else, handed it back to him then arching my head back, I swallowed, washing the grit from my parched throat.

As he filled his mouth, I said, "How does shrimp sound for dinner?"

He swallowed with a startled wince and wiping his sun-blistered lips with the back of his hand, chuckled wearily, "You know, I'd even settle for spider stew."

XI

It was well-past dusk by the time we had ourselves a proper marching camp.

While the lower gorge walls were covered with dry scrub, there was no wood suitable for fortifications. However, the deep, water-cut gorge in which we'd taken refuge had scree in abundance. There was also a back passage through the seemingly impenetrable rock walls of the chasm: a massive fissure largely hidden behind the swirling mist of the ribbon-thin waterfall that dominated the far end of the gorge.

According to the scouts I'd sent to plumb its depths, it wasn't a desperately hoped for short cut to the grasslands beyond—instead it opened onto a narrow and rugged box canyon every bit as desolate and forbidding as the desert. In fact the entire gorge was honeycombed with fissures, barely more than gaping wounds in the sheer rock face but aside from the one behind the waterfall, few were more than a shoulder-span across and none led anywhere. They did, however, provide a rich source of loose rock.

Another plus: the gorge's high walls protected us from the grit-laden wind that, as expected, picked up as the day wore on, sending towering dust devils spinning across the desert floor along with swirling eddies of thick ocher dust into the mouth of the gorge, coating the fortifications along with the engines that were positioned just behind the hastily erected barricade, making them look like natural formations. The wind-driven columns of dust were unable to make the sharp left turn into the gorge proper and so came but no further.

I thanked the gods we hadn't been caught out on the sweltering desert under these conditions, but, on the upside, the dust storm would, with luck, cover our tracks.

The camp itself was also hidden from casual view, tucked well behind the rugged promontory that jutted out into the desert. I'd prayed for an oasis; what I received was even better: a deep defile with a large pool and water-fed grassy ground, with room to make camp. An added plus was that the rock walls, heated during the day, would keep the gorge marginally warmer than the open desert beyond once the suns set. The only downside, and one I kept to myself, was that the floor was not solid rock, at least as far as I could tell. But then again, perhaps the Faoimhuirs'

273 J. E. Bruce

rumored ability to move through anything short of solid rock was no longer of concern because the Faoimhuir themselves were too preoccupied hiding from the Si'aafu to cause us any further grief—or one could hope.

Overseen by Rufinius, every able-bodied man, Roman and Adranii— with the exception of those tasked with sentry duty—had labored all afternoon to build a defensible wall at the mouth of the gorge as groups of women and some of the older children moved along the lines with ladles and buckets of water drawn from the pool—but only *after* the water, at the insistence of the Adraniis, had been boiled—using the dry scrub supplemented by some of our scant supply of firewood for the purpose. We wanted to slack our incredible thirst, not take a hot bath, but Borzu had explained this strange practice away by saying it was a religious custom, akin to our libations and offerings, and one the Adraniis strictly adhered to, pointedly adding that if we expected them to respect *our* rituals, we must do the same for *theirs*.

I recalled Felix had earlier mentioned this practice, and that he, Felix, had decided to allow it, wasteful as it was, believing if he refused, it would only make a bad situation worse—something Borzu heartily agreed to, adding that the last thing our camp needed was an outbreak of *die-sentry*— at least I think that's what Borzu called it—whatever the hell that was. Then, while Borzu was briefly distracted speaking with Jom, Felix added in a whisper that the Adraniis had, at first, also adamantly refused to drink from our waterskins, even *after* it was boiled, appalled that the containers were made of goat bladders. But when they realized it was that or go thirsty, well...

So he'd reluctantly permitted them this seemingly asinine practice, and now I felt little choice but to go along with it, especially when Cleander arrived just in time to agree with Borzu, much to my consternation. But once Borzu, Cleander and Jom left, smugly satisfied by my unhappy capitulation, I found myself facing the sidelong, exasperated looks of my men whose parched throats had to be satisfied by what remained in their lean waterskins. At least we were offered hard tack and dried fruit to fill our bellies while we worked and waited for the Adraniis to conclude this very peculiar and, I must say, *time-consuming* rite.

Other women, under the direction of Florianus and his cooks, had set about assisting in the preparation of the evening meal—there would be absolutely no scrimping tonight—that promise was the only thing that kept the men toiling on the fortifications going, kept everyone going, pushing each and every one of us well past exhaustion.

I could have begged off the physical labor; I have no doubt Cleander, if given a chance, would have demanded I rest, or at the very most limit my activity to supervising the work—but supervising the construction was Rufinius' job; he certainly didn't need my interference—*er*, I mean assistance. So, I made a place for myself in the unskilled work gang— deliberately placing myself among a group of Adraniis, knowing they'd accept my presence without question, even welcome it, whereas my men might take exception—alternately taking then handing off pieces of rock to the next man in the line, leaving the work of actually building the fortifications to the engineers.

Every so often I'd overhear a collective gasp and look up only to realize it was just Florianus and his flints, lighting a fire under yet another cook pot to the continued delight of the Adranii children—just as Felix's lamp-lighting skill had dumbfounded Anachie—children who would then scamper off to find more kindling among the scree in the form of dry grass and bits and pieces of scrub just so they could see his conjuring trick again… and again, and again, oblivious to the fact that they were playing right into his hands.

Even the adult Adraniis remained absolutely captivated by this very basic and life-saving talent, despite all of them being witness to it on countless occasions back on the hillock, and several times I had to elbow the man standing next to me to give me the damned rock he held while his attention was briefly drawn to Florianus's fire-starting sleight of hand.

The horses and oxen had been hobbled, and once rubbed down they were left to graze on the abundant grass on the far side of the pool at the base of the waterfall and drink as they pleased, which they did and with gusto while the goats were allowed to roam free under Hardalio's watchful eye, the dogs and several older Adranii boys who, under Hardalio's willing tutelage, were quickly proving to be natural goatherds. In fact the majority of the Adraniis, to their credit, quickly overcame their initial fear and, yes, disgust of our animals as they too realized that these—to them—strange and smelly creatures, with absolutely no shame or consideration for others when it came to when and where they relieved themselves, were integral to our survival. Even the hawks were released to fly the length of the gorge, up and over and out into the desert, returning only at the beckoning call of their handlers' whistles. The chickens, however, were kept caged as they were just too tempting, not to mention too easy a target for the freed hawks. The cats too remained confined at Baculus's insistence—he claimed they were perfectly content as they were— watching us slave away, and he was probably right.

The rest of the women, along with the walking wounded and the children spent the afternoon splashing around the shallows of the pool, herding shoals of panicked 'shrimp' close to shore and tossing handfuls onto the grassy banks in amazing quantities—so many in fact that no one cared that the dogs, not to mention more than a few of the goats hungrily snatched up any that happened to land nearby, even the hawks managed to swoop down to grab their share—where the shrimp were gathered up and hauled off to the cook fires to be spitted and roasted, or boiled and shelled. Felix had taken the wise precaution of assigning several of our lesser wounded the task of keeping watch on the Adraniis as they chased after our dinners—while most of the pool was waist-deep or shallower, there were a few kettle-holes, largely invisible in the deepening dusk and unlike us the Adraniis could not swim—another life skill I added to Aetius's rapidly growing list of things to teach our companions once we had found permanent shelter.

The women and children's relaxed laughter drew the tired, but smiling gazes of those of us toiling on the wall—of course there was another reason to look: the women's usually baggy clothing was soaked and clinging to their bodies, leaving very little to the male imagination and while it was a distraction, it was also a potent reminder of what needed to be protected at all costs and the net result was a redoubling of our effort on the fortifications rather than a lessening of it.

All in all, we'd created a very effective and efficient division of labor, and one that had the added benefit of allowing every able-bodied person, adult and child, to contribute to our common needs: a safe place to bed down for the night and where everyone, man and beast, would go to that bed with a full belly.

The aromas coming from the fires were truly enticing—Florianus' well known culinary magic at work—so much so I felt a twinge of concern at permitting fires in the first place. Granted, we hadn't seen a scrap of evidence of any living creatures—aside from the aforementioned shrimp, but if there were any predators about, the fragrance of cooking might draw them out of hiding, and with night fast approaching... I made a note to post extra guards, especially on the promontory that provided an unobstructed view of the desert as well as the camp below.

Then, without warning, it was over: the fortifications were built to Rufinius' exacting satisfaction.

We were all stripped to the waist and filthy, wearing either dirty brown Adranii trousers or equally grubby scarlet Roman breeches and as word rippled down the line, ordering us to stop, we staggered back, breathing hard and wiping gritty, ocher-stained sweat from our eyes as we gazed dully at our handiwork.

The dry stone wall was, at its lowest points, ten feet tall and at its tallest, fifteen, just high enough to provide cover, but low enough to look like a natural formation and for the ballistas and onagers, which stood well back from the wall and facing outwards, to easily lob their deadly missiles and bolts at any approaching danger without the risk of accidentally battering down our own defenses. Behind the engines stood the battery of now reassembled scorpios and behind them a defensible space, then the supply wagons, which if pressed would be serve as last-ditch barricades that we could set alight in retreat, and finally the camp itself, with the canvas-covered medical wagons safety tucked against the rock wall nearest the waterfall and the hidden fissure.

So, it was done—every contingency considered, all reasonable possibilities addressed; the last step was the wall and now it that finally complete.

I lifted my tired eyes, spotted Rufinius and managed a weary nod at his startled glance then I happened to notice Felix, Aetius and Borzu, who were standing not far away and also staring at me. The three were stripped to the waist like the rest of us. One look at their dirty and dour faces and I knew they were none to happy to discover I'd been taking part in the physically demanding work, but what could they do about it now? It was done—*bah!*

I shrugged and smiled, then like everyone else I went in search of my hastily discarded clothing. The temperature within the shadow-filled chasm was blessedly much cooler than the desert and now that we'd stopped working, our sweaty skin goose-pimpled in the gathering chill.

Luckily for me my undertunic was near the top of a disordered pile of short-sleeved crimson Roman and long-sleeved dun colored Adranii tunics. Plus mine still bore large, dark bloodstains, not to mention tattered projectile holes, making it easily recognizable even to the middle-aged Adranii who happened across it while digging through the mound looking for his own clothing and who, smiling apologetically, offered it to me.

I'd been late coming to help on the wall—other tasks which demanded the legate's full participation had taken precedence, such as the actual arrangement of the camp, the defenses, and of course the division of labor—a matter I felt best discussed at length with Felix and Borzu, so in fact Felix and Borzu had not labored all afternoon on the wall, either—a point I planned to use against them if they raised the issue, not that it would help much in my defense, I'm sure.

I'd also checked on the condition of the badly wounded and was relieved to find that none were too much the worse for our trek—even the elderly Adraniis, and there were more than a few, along with the heavily pregnant women and infants had come through relatively unscathed. Attius had pleaded with me to permit him to return to duty, to help with the fortifications, which of course prompted Lollius, Tullius and even Carbo into demanding the same thing, all claiming they were recovered enough they could be useful, protesting their continued confinement and to please not leave them to lay about the medical wagon at the mercy of Cleander—worse, Nestor—while there was necessary work to be done.

Carbo was clearly too weak to do anything but complain and even complaining left him pale and shivering. Lollius and Tullius were marginally better off, but one look at Cleander and I nixed any further protests from them.

Attius was another matter. While the burly soldier's head and jaw were swathed in bloody bandages, his arms, legs and body were relatively unharmed. I refused his request to work on the wall, but with Cleander's reluctant approval, I assigned him to help the women and children catch and clean the shrimp and he accepted the humbling detail without objection, pointedly ignoring the lewd suggestions from of the other three as he hurriedly gathered up his clothing and exited the wagon before either Cleander or I changed our minds. I later learned Aetius had reassigned him to lifeguard detail; Attius, clearly of Germanic stock, was one of our strongest swimmers.

Once those pressing tasks were taken care of, I took my leave, in the process leaving Cleander with the mistaken belief that I was going to find some grassy spot to sit down, maybe get some food and water into me and do nothing else but watch—all right, if you insist I in fact *assured* him I was going to find a grassy spot to sit down, grab a bite to eat and do nothing but watch. Instead I eagerly shed my armor, leaving it next to where Carus had placed my saddle and bedroll along with Felix's, and went off to join those toiling on the wall.

What Cleander didn't know couldn't possibly hurt *me*, could it?

Well, all right, maybe it could, so I kept checking my bandaged torso, telling myself if I saw even the slightest bit of seepage I'd stop, but to my continued relief I saw no sign of fresh bleeding. Neither did the Adraniis on either side of me, and they kept looking to the point I found it rather irksome and told them so in no uncertain terms—not that it stopped them, they were just a little more circumspect from then on.

"Ready for inspection, Legate?"

Still tugging my undertunic into place, I turned to find Rufinius, along with Felix, Aetius and Borzu walking towards me. By Rufinius's tone, and the looks on all four men's faces, they'd collectively decided that there was simply no point in telling me I'd been a fool. What was done was done and too damned late to be undone.

I, in turn, wordlessly, generously agreed to let bygones be bygones, nodded, and together we began to walk the fortifications as the men stood around in small groups, watching us, desperately hungry and thirsty and bone-tired but unwilling to leave until the legate himself had pronounced the job done. There was no need to ask Felix if he'd assigned the first shift of pickets—he knew his job, just like Rufinius knew his. Besides, I could spot some of the sentries ensconced in their protected positions high up on the rocky promontory, a task now shared equally by Roman and Adranii—at Borzu's insistence I might add.

So, we walked the full length of the undulating wall, admiring the stonework, the irregularly spaced arrow-slits, noting the careful placement of the artillery, nodding to the exhausted work gangs. As we turned back, I said in a voice that would carry, "This is a damned fine job!" Then I motioned to the awaiting men. "Go get your suppers—go on, off with all of you!"

They replied with weary grins and quickly dispersed.

"A damned fine job indeed," I repeated to Rufinius. And it was. Not only was it a sound barricade, Rufinius and his engineers had fashioned it to look like a naturally formed barrier, possibly an ancient rockfall, nothing more than an extension of the promontory, with deliberately formed irregularities in its height and width as the wall meandered from one side of the gorge to the other. The thick dusting of ocher sand supplied by the dust storm added to the illusion that it had stood in place for millennia, rather than only a few hours. The ocher mantle extended to the artillery as well, coating the engines in a very effective camouflage without hindering their effectiveness if the need arose.

Rufinius only nodded, but a quick, sidelong look at the man revealed a very pleased smile.

"Indeed," Borzu added, clapping Rufinius on his broad shoulder. "Truly amazing work in such a short period of time and with only the materials at hand."

"That's because he *is* a truly amazing engineer," came a vaguely familiar voice and we all turned to find an Adranii leaning against one of the ballistas, arms crossed. "But I'm *just* a woman, so what do I know?"

Woman? I looked back at Rufinius, expecting a very black look in his very black eyes, but what I saw was anything but annoyed. He looked like he was *blushing*.

Rufinius? *Blushing...?* No, it couldn't be—it must be sunburn! He was, after all, as prone to the painful condition as Felix.

The woman straightened up then sauntered towards us with a decidedly, and, I suspected, deliberately suggestive sway to her hips. She stopped directly in front of me and placing her hands on those hips gave me a very slow, head to toe inspection before her icy blue eyes locked with mine. "Legate. So good to see you clearly on the road to a full recovery."

I knew this woman—suddenly realized *why* I knew her—and was sorely tempted to stick out my tongue at her, but I was damned if I was going to lend any credence to her obvious, but totally unwarranted low opinion of me, even though I have no idea why she felt the way she did, or why I gave a damn about her opinion on anything, least of all, *me*. So I replied coldly, "Thank you," when in fact it was clear I was anything *but* thankful.

Felix nudged my elbow, concealing the maneuver within a shift of his weight from one foot to the other, instantly drawing my annoyed gaze. He replied with a sidelong, unhappy glance. It was the same look he always gave me when I wasn't behaving up to *his* damned expectations, *his* damned standards, damn *him*.

The woman couldn't help but catch the silent exchange. "Still nursing a grudge are we?"

"I'm sure I don't know what you're talking about."

"Yes, that's right, you were delirious at the time and thought I was some odious creature called a... *crocodile?*"

I blinked, but before I could think of a suitable rejoinder, she continued, "So, how about we start over?" and held out both hands, palm side up.

I looked down at them, then at her, baffled. Did she expect me to spit on them, slap them, or kiss them? Before I could choose—I was leaning heavily towards the first option—she reached out and grasped my hands in hers, drew them away from my sides and gave them a firm squeeze before releasing them, a very strange custom—if it was indeed a custom and not just her idea of another joke at my expense. "Very nice to finally meet you, Legate. I've heard nothing but *wonderful* things about you from Centurion Rufinius." And that was said in a tone that suggested genuine shock that anyone would say anything positive about me, least of all one of my closest friends.

"Ah… well, nice to meet you too… um…"

"Maisoh."

"Yes, of course. *Maisoh.*"

She grinned—which had a startling, dare I say *miraculous* effect on her hard face, turning it from coldly aloof to something quite… well, not exactly handsome, that *would* be a stretch. How 'bout not completely unappealing?

She then looked around. "Mind if I join you?"

"Not at all!" Rufinius replied enthusiastically.

Now, I must mention at this point that Rufinius was not a man known for his expressions of enthusiasm, unless it was enthusiasm over devising some fiendishly elaborate prank, so I looked at him, looked back at her, then, wondering perhaps if it *was* some fiendishly elaborate prank, I turned my questioning gaze on Felix. He did his best to look oblivious. Aetius for his part deliberately avoided my gaze.

So, not a fiendishly elaborate prank. Something worse. Something far, *far* worse. Rufinius was in love—or at the very least in lust… with a damned crocodile!

I set my jaw and started off again and the rest dutifully followed, Felix, Aetius and Borzu hurrying to come abreast of me while Rufinius and Maisoh fell in behind.

I glanced over my shoulder at the two, then favored Felix with another prodding look and this time he shrugged, but the corners of his mouth twitched into the faintest of smiles, which of course dimpled his damned cheeks.

Well, thanks for telling me, I scowled back at him, then gave my head a shake. *Rufinius and Maisoh?* But if she made him blush when he was being paid a well-deserved compliment—and all right, he *had* been blushing—who was I to say 'what the hell are you thinking, Rufinius—*are you stark raving mad?*' I could, however, *think it,* even if it had been my hope after all that my men would find companionship among the Adranii women and Maisoh *was* Adranii *and* a woman, so she qualified, and, if you believed Borzu, she was an engineer herself, but still… it boggled the mind, damned if it didn't.

And in truth Rufinius, unlike Felix, once freed of his Kellesuf mindset had not had much luck with Taskim's female servants—his forbidding stare and volatile temper always overshadowed his dark good looks and truly impressive physique. Even Aetius had had better luck with the women—a whole lot of luck if you believed Aetius. Simply put, without even trying, Rufinius scared the crap out of most people. So maybe it was not surprising a crocodile found him equally attractive.

I cleared my throat, said, "I think we should stay here at a few days; give everyone, especially the injured and the weak a chance to recuperate, maybe get a little stronger before we make the final push to the pass. Meanwhile we can sun-dry a supply of those shrimp to take with us—"

"Assuming there are any left after tonight," Aetius added, suggestively rubbing his belly.

"Birral said the pool's teaming with them," Borzu replied, "and he's absolutely sure these shrimp are the same species as those your men caught earlier, so perfectly save to eat. Plus Centurion Storax said there's another pool around that outcrop," he pointed, "which appears to be fed by the same source—likely the drain-off from this pool. So, if there are shrimp in one, there should be shrimp in the other—and I was told there are other aquatic creatures... that look like eels? Birral said if your men can catch one, he'd try to determine if it too is safe to eat—"

"Have him feed it to one of the goats," I offered. "In fact from here on out, any potential foodstuffs we come across I want fed to a goat first. I don't want anyone putting something in their mouth unless Birral has first determined its safe."

Borzu looked suitably surprised, and yes, pleased I suddenly put so much trust in one of his officers, and there was a murmur of agreement from the others—only because Hardalio was not in on the plan or I'm sure he would have put forth a host of reasons why the goats should be spared such a potentially unpleasant role. I would have suggested one of the dogs, but we had a far more limited supply of them and they'd already and repeatedly proven their worth so I was not about to risk poisoning one of them. A goat or two we could lose, if it spared the rest of us.

"I'll speak to Florianus about setting up drying racks," Rufinius said. "In this heat, I'd imagine it wouldn't take half a day to dry them to a point they could be safely stored—and I agree, Legate, the benefits of staying outweighs any risks of delaying here a few days," he added, suddenly and for Rufinius, in an *unusually* talkative frame of mind. "But just in case..." He abruptly scrambled up the loosely stacked dry stone wall like some damned mountain goat, then stood atop it, hands on hips and teetering precariously as Maisoh moved close, with upraised hands ready to grab if he fell—not that she could have done much if he had—then again, maybe she wasn't positioning herself to break his fall. Maybe she was taking the opportunity to look up his tunic while appearing to be innocently concerned about his welfare.

Rufinius, unlike the rest of us, was *not* wearing breeches—and either his subligarium had failed in ways I've mentioned of before, or he'd forgone wearing it in glaring defiance of Felix's order—an endowment, so to speak, from the first Rufinius, who like this Rufinius was well enough endowed already and argued that it wasn't natural to confine a man in such a way. Breeches, as far as he was concerned, were for cold weather only, and by cold, he meant *ball-freezing*.

And how do I know he either wasn't wearing anything or what he was wearing wasn't doing its job? Because of the startled yet *very* pleased look on Maisoh's upturned face, that's how. So, she *was* looking up his damned tunic—maybe she'd heard the rumors about his dressing habits, or lack thereof, maybe she'd heard other rumors about him and decided to see if there was any merit to the camp tittle-tattle. Clearly what she saw lived up to her expectations, perhaps even exceeded them.

Leave it to her to take advantage of the situation—she'd done the same with me, after all.

He looked down at us, oblivious to her sly gawking, or at least pretending to be oblivious. With Rufinius, it was often hard to tell. "Perhaps we should add a trench…."

I overheard groans from a few of his engineers still laboring on the other side of the wall, packing small stones into the gaps to stabilize the massive structure.

"Tomorrow," I chided, equally weary and every muscle sore and complaining. "Felix's already posted extra guards, so call the rest of your men back inside—they've more than earned their suppers and their sleep."

He passed along the order then, as the first man scrambled up the ladder and onto the wall, Rufinius dropped down beside us, landing deftly and without a wobble, which greatly impressed Maisoh. Of course I suspected anything Rufinius did at this point would impress her, going by the look she was giving him.

The woman was clearly besotted. And why not? Rufinius was as tall as me, with shoulder-length, curly black hair and very muscular body, and despite his propensity to glower, he was actually quite handsome. Clearly Maisoh liked what she saw, top to—*ahem*—bottom, and as I started off again, I happened to catch her giving the bottom in question a firm squeeze to which Rufinius jumped, then smiled shyly at her.

Borzu too saw the grab, saw the response then looked at me and grinned.

I gave myself a shake, then started through a gap between two onagers, towards the camp. "Rufinius, when you get a chance, ask Jotia if there's some wood we can scavenge from the wagons to make those drying racks?"

Not getting a response, I glanced over my shoulder to find Rufinius and Maisoh suddenly nowhere to be seen.

I turned my now reproachful stare on my remaining companions.

Borzu and Aetius chuckled; Felix grinned and murmured, "I'll speak to Dulcitius, Legate—I believe Rufinius is otherwise... *um*, occupied?"

I'm sure he was—and without so much as a damned by your leave to his damned legate, *damn* him.

Borzu patted my shoulder, drawing my aggravated gaze. "She's a good woman, Legate. She'll make sure he gets something to eat, don't you worry about that."

But not what's on the regular menu, I'd wager. Keeping my less than gracious thoughts to myself, I started off again and we soon found ourselves weaving our way through the camp proper, now alight with dozens of cook fires and children darting here and there, their high-pitched and playful squeals echoing off the surrounding rock walls. An afternoon spent playing in the cool water of the pool and now with bellies full of food had clearly revived them after the strain of the trek—a huge relief, even if it meant the rest of us were forced to suffer their high-spirits.

To my surprise and immense satisfaction the women had gathered up my exhausted soldiers along with their own menfolk and ushered them over to the fires, having realized they were all so tired if food wasn't pressed into their hands they'd just find some place to collapse and worry about eating later, if at all. The women, clearly, would have none of it and for that I was extremely grateful; my troops richly deserved a good fussing over, something only women can do properly—as I'm sure Rufinius would heartily attest.

The men dutifully took the offered food then wearily sank down where they stood or were helped to the ground, to eat in silence as the women and Florianus' cooks moved about, refilling bowls or hands as soon as they were emptied, lightly shaking the shoulders of those who'd fallen asleep the moment their backsides hit the ground, staying if needed, helping men bring food to their mouths if their hands were cramping, tending to the cuts and scrapes and pulled muscles and somehow making each one feel as if he had single-handedly built the wall and therefore had earned the right to be the center of attention.

As we passed by the fires, we were greeted by smiles and offerings of steaming bowls heaped with food.

Felix, Aetius and Borzu happily grabbed themselves meals on the fly while I pointedly ignored the food and trudged on; I was so tired I had no appetite, and all right, now that it came down to it, I wasn't sure I could actually eat those damned creatures, no matter how enticing they might smell once cooked. All I wanted was to find my saddle and bedroll, maybe grab a mug of warmed wine along the way to wash the dust from my parched throat and lay down. Food was an obstacle to that goal and eating at that moment was too damned much... *effort.*

Clearly Aetius, Felix and Borzu harbored no such qualms about the evening's cuisine and ate heartily, munching and crunching as we walked, and after Felix pointed me in the direction of our sleeping spot, he, Borzu and Aetius headed for the nearest cook fire to replenish their now empty bowls.

There were a few, a very few perks at being the Legate—one of them was that I was not expected to do picket duty—*thank the gods*—I'd paid my dues and then some, having pulled far more than my fair share of guard duty as a legionary due, in part, to some minor, and I mean *absolutely trivial* breaches in conduct that some cheesed off centurion used as a pathetic excuse to assign me extra sentry duty. This odious task was now relegated to others—apportioned equitably as I'd trained my centurions to be firm but fair and not to fall prey to the small-mindedness that I'd had little choice but to endure early on in my career—among men who'd already been fed and watered and allowed a few hours sleep while the rest of us toiled on the fortifications in the suffocating heat and dust of the afternoon.

Of course my centurions did have two huge advantages over my spiteful former superiors: first, like them, the men under their command were former Kellesuf, and second, there were no local brothels or taverns to tempt a lonely and thirsty soldier into quietly slipping off for an hour or so without first waiting to be relieved. Everyone did it—I was just the one who always got caught, which again suggests personal grudges at play, which at the time I attributed to petty jealousy on their part and I was never dissuaded from that view.

But I digress...

I staggered over to my saddle, untied the bedroll from the rear pommels with sore and stiffening fingers, grabbed it and shook it out, then barely let it settle before I sank down and sprawled back, using the saddle as an improvised pillow.

Somewhere within the gorge a man began to sing, his deep, clear and singular voice echoing off the rock walls, which was soon accompanied by the rhythmic clapping of hands—it was a common soldier's camp song, an achingly familiar and rather bawdy tune long-popular among the enlisted ranks. Hearing it again instantly brought to mind other nights, other camps, while the shifting firelight conjured familiar ghosts from the gathering dark, their long-dead faces, their dust-dry voices oh-so briefly brought back to life as I found myself silently mouthing lyrics that so well summed up soldier's unhappy lot: sore feet, empty stomachs, perpetually unappreciative superiors, the transitory consolation of a whore's bed—the latter artfully changed to lovers left behind to reflect the mixed company, which briefly threw me off before the singer just as seamlessly returned to the original version of risking death or crippling injury in some far off land by the capricious order of an Emperor few if any had ever seen.

As the singer ended his impromptu solo to resounding applause and calls for an encore, I bid goodnight to my real and spectral companions, snuggled down against the saddle, closed my eyes, took a deep breath and as I exhaled, I savored the sheer, unadulterated pleasure of not moving a damned muscle.

The novel sensation didn't last as I realized four things, each one more annoying than the last and collectively making a quick exit into exhausted oblivion near impossible. *First*, the ground was damned hard and bumpy, despite the bedroll and the underling blanket of the Latruncŭlian version of grass. *Second*, I was going to be stove-up and sore as hell in the morning. *Third*, I *was* hungry, damn it, but just too bone-weary to get up again. *Fourth*, I was cold and my damned cloak was still rolled up and securely tied to the front pommels, effectively out of reach without me rolling over, which required moving, which I wasn't sure I could do at the moment... or, possibly, ever again and all this assuming my fingers could work the pommel lacings. So I opened my eyes and stared straight up, at the darkening sky, framed by the shifting, fire-lit walls of the surrounding gorge and tried to lose myself there instead.

I let my eyes wander the full length of the sliver of visible sky, found that a few of the brighter stars were visible and after few more minutes of search I finally spotted the faint, feathery leading edge of the whirlpool peering over the chasm's eastern lip. In a matter of hours it would be directly over—

"You need to eat *and* drink."

"Huh!" Startled, I jerked my eyes towards the familiar voice and spotted two figures standing not far away and silhouetted against the fire glow; one was clearly a young child, the other was a small, delicately built adult. I didn't need to see the faces to know who my unexpected visitors were.

"Arr-ee!" Anachie squealed with childish delight and dashed towards me, arms out-flung.

I no sooner managed to get my elbows under me than he promptly sprawled across me and wrapped his arms around my neck; I couldn't help but grunt—it hurt, but not as much as I thought it would.

"Anachie," Eithne chided. *"Be careful!"*

He dutifully released his near-stranglehold on me, slid down my side and plopped himself beside my hip. He grinned at me and I couldn't help but grin wearily back.

The singer, at the urging of his appreciative audience, began another solo, this one about the simple wants of any soldier: to live to see his home and family again. It was a haunting tune and lonely, a painfully accurate reflection of a legionary's private fears, his desperate hopes and one that discouraged accompaniment.

"Your man Gratian has a beautiful voice," Eithne said after a moment of listening.

I concealed my own surprise at the man's unexpected gift with a simple, "Yes, he does," as I met her equally uncomfortable gaze.

We hadn't spoken since the incident behind my tent. After all, when she and Anachie were both still smarting from my rebuff. Yes, I'd spotted her occasionally during the pack-up only to have her act like she hadn't seen me when she damned well had, and I thought I'd caught a glimpse of her in the crowd that had gathered to beat—er, I mean *meet* me on my return from my horseback ride. I'd even privately hoped I'd find her waiting for me in my tent, and later, when Anachie arrived, I'd at first assumed—hoped—it was her.

And despite Felix, Rufinius, Aetius and, presumably, Anachie, telling her that I'd told Anachie I now considered him my son, a yielding on principle I thought, at the very least, might have earned a quick visit to thank me, she failed to show up.

So here she was. *Better late than never, I suppose.*

She knelt opposite Anachie and held out a bowl full of those damned 'shrimp'—her idea of a peace offering, I presume—along with a mug which I sincerely hoped was wine. "Here."

I reached back, somehow managed to grab a pommel and tug the saddle closer so I could prop my back against it, then I reluctantly accepted the bowl and mug. Shelled and roasted I could almost convince myself the spiders *were* shrimp. *Almost.*

My stomach let me know under no uncertain terms *it* felt almost wasn't good enough and I tried conceal my less than enthusiastic reaction by taking a deep gulp of—no, not wine, dammit. *Water!* But it did wash more of the grit from my still gummy mouth and throat.

"Something wrong?"

Aside from your frosty attitude? I wiped that thought off my face, lifted my gaze and even managed a sickly smile. "I don't find them very appetizing."

Eithne arched a brow. "Have you tried them?"

"No," I replied defensively.

"Then how do you know?"

"They're good!" Anachie interjected.

Eithne gave me a look, as if to say, 'See? Even a child thinks they're tasty.'

I saw no reason to spoil *her* appetite—despite her demeanor, which was coming across more and more Maisoh-like—or Anachie's with the truth, besides, while we'd been talking, he'd grabbed one, stuffed it in his mouth and smiling at me, began chewing. So I lied. "I don't like what they smell like."

"So, you're a picky eater."

"I didn't say that. I said I find *them* unappetizing."

Clearly Anachie didn't have that problem as he grabbed another and began munching, loudly. I tried not to look as revolted as I felt.

"You'd prefer some of that truly awful hardtack?"

In my books hardtack, even maggoty, moldy hardtack won handily over spit-roasted spider any day—not that I could say that, so I lied again. "I'm really not hungry." I took another deep gulp of water then set the bowl and mug on the ground beside Anachie—if he was still hungry, he was welcome to the rest of them. "Maybe later, all right?" I started to slide back down the saddle, making a futile grab for the cloak as I did so. "Felix is over there," I pointed in the general direction of a nearby fire, "with your Captain Borzu."

"I *know* exactly where Felix is," she replied irritably. "He's the one who sent us, hoping *we* could talk some sense into you and get you to eat something, since he hadn't had any luck."

"Oh." It was at that moment I realized he had been far too willing to let me go to bed without my supper. Now I knew why. He'd set me up, the rat-bastard.

"Close your eyes—"

"I was just about to do that when you showed up—"

"—*and* open your mouth."

My eyes flicked to Anachie, who was happily chomping away, then I looked at her and whispered, "Isn't that supposed to be my line?"

She did not find my attempt at innuendo at all funny. If I hadn't known better, I'd say she was in a *mood*—and not the right kind of mood, either.

"Just *do* it, all right?"

So I did; I figured what the hell, humor her, and maybe she'd repay the favor, but I did it with an exasperated sigh—I felt I was entitled to that. I squeezed my eyes shut and very reluctantly opened my mouth.

An instant later I felt a fingertip on my tongue; my eyes snapped open and I had to stop myself from reflexively biting down—or worse, gagging. *"What the hell...?"*

"Taste."

"Taste?"

"Taste what's on your tongue."

I did—not that I had much choice—all the while wondering what she might have stuck into my oh-so trusting mouth. A whole host of ugly possibilities sprang to mind—

"Taste bad?"

So, it was a shrimp, or at least a taste of what they tasted like—I wasn't sure whether to be relieved or nauseated. In truth it didn't taste that bad, so I answered, *"N-no."*

She reached over me, plucked a chunk of roasted 'shrimp' from the bowl and pressed it to my lips. "Then here. Go on."

I let her place it in my mouth, feeling rather stupid about the whole matter. We were in full view of the rest of the camp, I was able-bodied—and yet here I was, having a woman feed me. Fortunately for me, everyone who was still awake was too intent on filling their bellies to notice exactly how I was filling mine.

Plus I have to admit it wasn't exactly a novel experience. For some reason, women had always felt compelled to feed me, as if I was helpless babe. And under some circumstances it was actually quite enjoyable—sadly this wasn't one of them. Worse, I'd longed for her company—

dreamt of it, dreamt of her and what I'd do if given a second chance. This reunion was not exactly going as I'd envisioned—

"Chew." She tapped the underside of my chin with her knuckle, startling me and setting Anachie to giggling.

So I did; I chewed, then finally and very reluctantly swallowed. And all right, *fine*. It *didn't* taste bad at all, quite good in fact—until I reminded myself I'd just downed a chunk of roasted spider, which of course meant it wanted to come right back up.

She briefly looked away as I made soft heaving sounds, but the moment I stopped she crossed her arms and fixed me with a wholly unsympathetic stare. "If you don't tell me what's wrong this instant, I'll have no choice but to go get Cleander and have him examine you to see if you re-injured yourself working on the wall—and why do I suspect he didn't give you the go-ahead in the first place?"

"He didn't say I couldn't."

"Because he stupidly thought you'd know better. Why he should continue to hold your common sense in such high regard when even by his own admission you've adequately proven you have none when it comes to your own welfare is simply beyond me."

So, she had me by the proverbial short hairs. If I didn't confess, she'd turn me over to Cleander. I jerked my chin towards the bowl, whispered, "Those are spiders, not shrimp."

"Spiders?"

"Creepy crawlies—" I held out my hand, palm side down and wriggled my fingers, imitating one of the scuttling creatures and made a face, "—*bugs.*"

She raised her brows, looked down at the contents of the bowl then back at me. "Who says?"

"Your best friend Cleander."

"So he's an astrobiologist too, along with a physician?"

"No," I replied slowly, "I don't think so…"

"Lieutenant Birral *is* an astrobiologist. He says these are true crustaceans, like shrimp—so, *not* bugs, or spiders if you please."

"He's *absolutely* sure."

"Absolutely."

"Not someone prone to practical jokes?" Gods save us if he was and attached himself to Aetius and Rufinius—

"Birral? Heavens no. I don't think he has a funny bone in his entire body."

I blinked. "A… *what?"*

"It's an expression. Meaning he's *not* joking."

"Oh."

She again reached across me, snatched up the bowl and plopped it on my stomach with more force than was absolutely necessary, eliciting a startled wince from me. "No more excuses. *Eat*. Or I get Cleander."

I glanced at Anachie and with his expert guidance, selected a piece—a very small piece that with a slip of my fingers unfortunately just happened to break in two before I got it to my lips—then at her prompting glare, I put what was left in to my mouth.

No sooner had I swallowed the miniscule fragment with what was, I swear, a totally involuntary grimace than she sighed heavily and shook her head.

"What?" I growled as I wiped my lips with the back of my hand. *"I'm eating!"*

"You take a hell of a lot of work, you know that? Felix is so much easier."

Don't ask me why I suddenly felt so angry—I'd been pushing her towards Felix almost from the moment we'd met—despite my own lustful desires—and she'd been pushing back with equal force. Now I felt as if I'd been knocked totally off balance and I wasn't sure what I wanted—certainly not this diminutive version of Maisoh! Yet at the same time the thought that she wanted Felix more than me, made me want her more and at the same time—*oh, hell!* I was too tired, too sore and yes, too damned confused and hurt to continue this conversation, so I decided to end it by saying, "Then why *don't* you go work on him?" I grabbed another piece, stuffed it in my mouth for spite and chewed furiously, only remembering Anachie after the fact.

I swallowed hard and looked at him. He was no longer smiling. He was staring at me with his large and yes, now very worried eyes. *Damn... damn... damn!*

Eithne touched my arm. "Arri, I didn't mean it the way it sounded."

I exhaled, lifted my gaze to the sky above and for Anachie's sake, visibly let go of the anger. "And I'm sorry I snapped—just really tired." I felt my side, winced for emphasis.

"And really smarting," she added with an apologetic, sidelong look.

I shrugged.

She placed the bowl on the ground next to us, settled down next me and for several minutes we sat in silence while I searched the narrow ribbon of sky as if I was truly looking for something when in fact I was avoiding the touchy issue—still too damned confused if you want the truth—and Anachie, satisfied by our ruse, snuggled down beside me. He yawned loudly, wrapped his arm around me and pillowed his head on my chest.

I smiled at him as Eithne freed my cloak from the saddle, unrolled it then settled it over the three of us. I nodded my appreciation—the temperature was dropping rapidly and my breeches were still damp with sweat—then I glanced around: the spontaneous songfest was breaking up. Everywhere I looked people were preparing for bed; bone-weary and stuffed with food most weren't too particular where they slept as long as it wasn't underfoot.

Then I happened across Felix; he was standing with Borzu and several other Adraniis, not far from a nearby cook fire. While I was loath to rekindle the conversation, worried I wouldn't like the answers, I felt I had no choice but to clear the air, once and for all. "There's someone else who has a stake in this."

"I know."

I looked at her out of the corner of my eye only to find her wistful gaze fixed on him. "Talk to him, Eithne, listen to what he has to say."

"I have—he says all he wants is for you to be happy." She turned to me. "Sound familiar?"

I smiled uneasily and quickly shifted my attention to Anachie, only to find that the long, strenuous day and a full belly had finally caught up with him—he was fast asleep and tucked tight against me.

Eithne, also realizing he was asleep, said, "He's a good boy, Arri—and he's certainly attached himself to you."

I stroked his head and nodded. "Must say I've grown extremely fond of him too." I looked at her, lightly touched her cheek, her lips. "I want you, too, damned if I don't, but—" I looked past her at the sound of approaching footsteps.

Eithne followed my gaze and smiled. "Felix."

"Eithne," he nodded to her, then me, "Legate. Excuse my intrusion, just came to collect my bedroll." He knelt and began hurriedly gathering up his belongings.

"You're not staying?" she asked, as if his actions were wholly unexpected.

He stopped what he was doing and looked first at her, then me, clearly bewildered and very, *very* uncomfortable.

"Stay," she patted the ground beside her.

He turned his anxious eyes on me.

"Stay," I echoed. "Please."

He slowly put everything back as it had been, then trying to look as inconspicuous as possible he began putting his bed together for the night. No sooner had he unrolled his bedroll than he lay down and rolled onto his side, facing away from us, and curled into a ball. If I were a betting man, I'd bet he'd also squeezed his eyes shut in hopes of becoming completely invisible.

I looked up at Eithne; she stared down at me and shook her head then she reached out and placed her hand on his hip. "Felix?"

He didn't move.

"Felix," I said irritably, "we know you aren't asleep."

He lifted his head and looked over his shoulder at us.

"We need to talk." She gave his hip a tug, then another, this one more insistent, and he very reluctantly rolled over to face us. "Actually, the two of you need to *listen* while *I* talk." She kept her suddenly annoyed voice barely above a whisper as she fixed Felix, then me with her reproving stare. *"Got it?"*

I nodded; Felix nodded.

"Good." She folded her hands in her lap, took a deep breath, then: "Each of you has been pushing me towards the other, each with the same selflessly noble rationale: that the other is far more deserving when it comes to being happy—all very gallant, but with the result that we're all very *unhappy*, Anachie most of all. I simply won't have it. Understand?"

This was definitely *not* a question that begged a verbal come back, in fact that was the worst thing to do. I wisely kept my lips firmly locked tight and nodded again; Felix, not being all that experienced around women—especially extremely pissed women—opened his mouth.

"Did I say you could speak?"

He suddenly got wise and snapped his mouth shut.

"Good." She placed one hand on his shoulder, the other hand on mine. "I've spoken to Captain Borzu—"

"What does Borzu…" I began, too late realizing I'd gone one step further than Felix despite knowing better and suddenly found myself in the path of her *very* baleful gaze. So, I did what Felix had done to save himself further embarrassment: I snapped *my* mouth shut.

"May I continue?"

Keeping my lips tightly clamped, I nodded vigorously as did Felix.

"Since he'd studied your culture it had been my hope that he'd have some insight into your customs and, more to the point, your taboos."

I reluctantly held up a forefinger, permission to speak.

She crossed her arms, sighed, *"Yes?"*

"Why didn't you just ask us?"

"Because the two of you were too damned busy convincing me I belonged with the other, that's why."

"Oh."

"But he wasn't much help—so, I'm going to solve this fix we're in, right now."

I looked past her to Felix and he stared back at me; one of us was about to be sent packing and we both strongly suspected it wasn't going to be me.

"As you both well know, men outnumber women almost two to one," she continued, drawing our worried gazes, "which leaves only one logical option: I'm taking both of you."

I blinked, stunned; I have to assume Felix had a similar reaction, but I'll hand it to him, he found his voice, first.

"Both…?"

"As lovers? Yes. Hopefully permanently—it all depends on the two of you."

"But…" I began. *"But—"*

"But what?" You both want me, you both want the other to have me… and I have to say I was incredibly attracted to both of you from start. This solves everyone's problem."

Hell if it does! I shifted my appalled gaze to Felix. While I was hugely taken aback by the whole concept—*two* men, *one* woman? Granted, women *were* physically designed to *accommodate* two men at the same time, three if you really, um, *pushed* the issue, assuming she meant that, Felix was equally shocked—by the fact that he hadn't been rejected after all, far from it.

Now, I'm not naïve, nor do I make any claims at being demure—I was a highly sought after prostitute in my youth after all, and practiced my profession in the Empire's epicenter of debauchery, Carthage; sex with multiple partners, male and female, *at the same time* was definitely *not* an abstract concept for me. And later, as an adult and a soldier, I had little doubt that within a few minutes of me leaving the warmth of a whore's bed I was replaced by another man, and if the whore in question was Oxyrhoë that man was, more often than not, Felix—the first Felix—there were even a few notable times when we enjoyed her attentions at the same time, to everyone's complete satisfaction I must say, but… Eithne was no Carthaginian harlot or garrison town whore. Nor was she a slave or the spoils of war. She was a free woman and from a culture that considered women *equal* to men—which begged the question: perhaps this was not an uncommon arrangement in her society, every bit as accepted, as legitimate as a wealthy man having a wife along with concubines was in mine—

"Have I actually succeeded in leaving the two of you speechless?"

I blinked, met her gaze. "Ah... well..."

"*Well?* Is that the best you can do? I've just given you both *exactly* what you adamantly claimed you wanted. Now you're having second thoughts?" She turned to Felix and caressed his chin, his lips, his ear. "What about you, my sweet?"

"I... uh," he looked around her to me as if expecting me to answer for both of us.

She beat me to it. "Ever since that day Anachie slipped into your tent and the idea came up of, *um*, a threesome, I've been hard pressed to think of anything *but* the two of you—I thought I could choose, but I can't—I *want* both of you. I never thought I'd ever say that—never imagined trying to manage two men at the same time and men as incredibly stubborn as the two of you? I'd say I was crazy to even consider it, but I *have* considered it, *a lot*, and I know we can make this work—I know I can make both of you happy and I have no doubt the two of you can make me *very* happy," she pointedly dropped her gaze, wiggled her eyebrows suggestively, then meeting my stare, added, "but most importantly, you'd both make Anachie happy, give him the sense of security he so desperately craves and richly deserves. But if the two of you just cannot get past your stupid, overblown male pride, well... let's just forget it." She started to get up.

I reached for her at the same instant Felix did, each of us grabbing an arm, keeping her firmly planted on the ground between us; she looked at him, then me. "Well?"

Felix glanced at me, suddenly scared. *Very scared.* I knew what he was thinking and I was just as scared for him. He, like the rest of my men, still harbored stinging memories of being pointedly ignored, or worse, treated as if he didn't even exist. He remembered what it was like to have been rendered helpless to any cruelty, any desire, any caprice of a Sidhe Lord; of being incapable of speech unless directly spoken to by a Tuatha, which of course made Kellesuf equally defenseless against the servants if one had a mind to cause a Kellesuf misery—and sadly, as I'd later learned to my horror and revulsion, many in fact made a practice of abusing Kellesuf, Kyrou in particular, and some who just 'weren't there any longer' as Felix had told me, were in fact the hapless victims of such violence; of the pain and humiliation he suffered at hands of an enraged

Rasaben after my escape attempt, and never once raising an arm to defend himself because as Kellesuf it never occurred to him to fight back unless told to do so.

While Felix was no longer Kellesuf and was now more than capable of defending himself, his body *and* his mind still bore those terrible scars—as Kellesuf he'd been incapable of remembering who he had once been, now he was incapable of forgetting what had been done to him.

It was true that the Adraniis had been slaves themselves, however they enjoyed a certain amount of autonomy—according to Borzu, they crewed their own ships—they were held in high regard, prized by their owners... until the Si'aafu's insatiable gluttony forced the Faoimhuir to choose between themselves and their beloved Adraniis, so, how *would* these former slaves react when they were told the disconcerting truth about my soldiers?

Or should they be told?

Each man had already demonstrated an ability to think for himself, each had grown from the seeds of my memories, flourished under my care and all were well on the way to becoming distinct individuals—even those like Hardalio who'd come late and ended up with only scraps from which to build a personality—similar yet separate from their predecessors. Given time, each would become truly unique, of that I had no doubt, so, was it wrong to keep something of such fundamental importance to my men a secret from people we intended to spend the rest of our lives with? Surely someone would let some reference slip, as I had with Eithne—and then what?

As I stared at Felix and he at me, I realized it was not my decision to make. It was his... and theirs, my soldiers.

Eithne recognized the look in his eyes as well and now she was scared. *"Felix...?"*

"I need to tell you something. I should have said something earlier, but—"

"But?"

"You need to know who and what I am, what... what all of us are, aside from Arri that is—and if you... you want change your mind about me after I tell you, I'll understand, really I will."

She again touched his cheek, his lips. "Felix, whatever you were back on Earth isn't important. All that matters to me is who and what you are here—"

"No!" He heaved back, out of her reach. "You need to know! You need to know everything—*please!*"

I privately cringed at the pure desperation in his voice, in his eyes—Felix was absolutely terrified. I knew that feeling, knew what it was like to live with the constant fear that someone I cared deeply about might actually see the real me and then all would be lost.

I'd *never* willingly told anyone about who and what I really was; Turan knew, but only because she could eavesdrop on my thoughts, could experience my dreams… and Turan ultimately abandoned me, or at least had done nothing to stop what happened; she hadn't even tried to warn me.

Then another hard truth hit me: if Eithne couldn't accept Felix, then how could I accept Eithne? I almost wanted to tell him to shut up, to let it go, but it was too late. She did need to know; better now than a few months, years or decades from now, when the truth, the trickery would cut far deeper.

Eithne settled herself in a comfortable, cross-legged position between the two of us, her right hand tightly entwined with Felix's fingers, her left with mine, and murmured, "I'm listening."

He took a deep, ragged breath and glanced at me and I replied with what I hoped was a reassuring nod.

"I'm… Kellesuf," he began in a calm, surprisingly steady voice. "That's what the Tuatha called us: *Kellesuf,* men of the void, because they'd wiped our minds clean…"

Eithne's lips parted slightly, but she kept the full extent of her shock to herself.

"…I have no memory of who I was, where I came from, if I had a family, a wife—none of us do, none but Arri. He's the only one whose mind, whose memories were left intact."

Eithne risked a confirming glance at me.

"Only because the Tuatha found they had a desperate need for my knowledge of warcraft," I grumbled bitterly.

She looked back at Felix and murmured, "Go on."

He swallowed convulsively but continued in the same even voice, "Who you know as Felix in fact died almost a year ago. He was killed in the same Iceni ambush that almost killed Arri—"

The first Felix." Her startled eyes darted to me before returning to Felix; I nodded.

"—I'm nothing more than a collection of Arri's memories of him. The same's true of the rest of us." He motioned around us to the darkening camp, to the murmur of weary voices, to people settling down for the night. "All of us, each and every one, were Kellesuf. The Tuatha implanted Arri's memories of men he'd known into us—I was fortunate enough to have been chosen to fill the role of one of his closest friends but for no other reason than I looked something like Felix. Same's true of Rufinius and Aetius."

Eithne continued to stare at him and Felix abruptly looked away and biting his lip, fixed his narrowed, glistening eyes on something hidden in the darkness.

"What he says is true," I said, drawing her stunned gaze, not to mention Felix's sidelong uneasy squint, "up to a point. His core personality was created from my memories of the first Felix, but since that time he's grown and become someone totally unique, a soldier I greatly admire and a man I consider to be even closer to me than the first Felix."

Felix blinked, roughly wiped his eyes, then his nose on the back of a very shaky hand.

For a moment Eithne said nothing. She literally held Felix in the palm of her hand; a simple word, even a look would crush him completely—and we all knew it.

She gently tucked a lock of his breeze-blown hair behind his ear, in the process drawing his watery gaze. "I love you, Felix," she said as she wiped his cheek with her thumb. "I love *you*, understand me? Not the first Felix, a man I never knew. *You*. Never, *ever* doubt that."

He managed a tight smile, but he was far from relieved, far from fully believing her. I felt this desperate need to reassure him, tell him she wasn't lying, that she meant what she'd said, but in truth there was nothing I could, or *should* say. This was between Felix and Eithne and only Eithne could provide that reassurance; the only person who could fully accept it as true was Felix.

She looked down at the soundly sleeping Anachie, then abruptly gathered herself up, said, "Come with me," and motioned for him to likewise get to his feet. He looked at me and at my nod, rose awkwardly.

She took his hand in hers then led him away, from our sleeping spot, away from the glow of the cook fires, towards the deeper darkness of the near gorge wall and as I briefly followed the two with my gaze, I found myself also looking inwards.

To my surprise, I felt no jealousy, no anger, only relief, perhaps because I was so damned tired I didn't have the energy to muster up any emotions so fervent...

...Or maybe, deep down inside, I knew it was our only option, *if* we could make this arrangement work—

I suddenly realized in my distraction I'd picked up a 'shrimp' and had been munching away on it: my stomach in its emptiness and left to its own devices was now willing to forgive and forget and while I was preoccupied musing about what Eithne had proposed, it had unerringly guided my hand to the bowl and then to my mouth. And you know, the 'shrimp' actually tasted quite... tasty. So I swallowed my mouthful and picked up another, and another... until the bowl was empty.

Satiated and weary beyond measure, I wiggled down under my cloak and wrapped my arms around Anachie. He responded by wriggling closer and I couldn't help but smile.

No ifs about it—we'd *make* this arrangement work.

Damned if we wouldn't.

XII

The next morning came far too soon as far as I was concerned, and as much as I would have been content just to remain where I was, curled up under my cloak, as legate I had things to do, or, should I say, I had things I was expected to attend to. First and foremost was meeting with my centurions and with Borzu and his officers to map out where we went—literally—from here.

It was incredibly tempting to stay in the gorge perhaps for as long as a week, use the time to collect and dry as many shrimp as we could as well as give the weak and wounded a chance to gain some much needed ground before we tackled what I had little doubt would be the most grueling part of our trek: getting the column safely over the pass. Once committed, I held scant hope we'd stumble across such a spacious and generous sanctuary as the gorge: the gods could be charitable when they chose, but they had their limits.

The constant and all too real threat of the Si'aafu urged me to settle on two days at most before we broke camp. Besides, the gorge could comfortably house us for only so long before it too became little better than the hillock: the supply of shrimp would soon run out and the pools' pristine water would quickly foul under such pressure. Within the space of an afternoon the edge of the pool had in fact already turned to a sticky muck and as I'd passed one of the cook fires the night before, I'd overheard one of the Adranii cooks say she'd been forced to wade out some distance to reach clean water. I was just too tired then, but I made a note to myself that this morning I'd have Aetius show every Adranii who was interested a life-saving trick I'd learned as a young boy and which had reinforced on a near-daily basis as a legionary: find a patch of dry, sandy soil not far from the edge of a pool and dig down until the hole fills with water. It didn't matter how filthy the water source was—it could be little better than a mud wallow; the water that refilled the hole was always clean enough to drink.

It was a time consuming process but one I figured the Adraniis would willingly accept rather than risk drowning in a kettle hole hidden in the eddies of murky water before anyone realized they were missing.

So, intent on delivering that firm message to my centurions and Borzu, I slowly, carefully, eased myself out from under my cloak, got to my knees, raked my sweat-stiff hair out of my eyes and looked around. While the camp was still cocooned in darkness, the sky overhead a deep lavender streaked with salmon pink clouds; only the faintest trace of the whirlpool was visible above the western lip of the gorge.

Many were already awake: a large group of women and girls were squatting by the edge of the pool washing up; further along, not far from the waterfall a goodly number of my men had defied the predawn chill and were now swimming in the plunge pool and splashing water at each other, their good-natured horseplay and laughter drawing the inquisitive gazes of the womenfolk on the shore. Others, Adranii and soldier alike, gathered around cook fires that had been stirred back to life, anticipating the needs of a hungry camp.

Two soldiers stood not far away, both armored and armed, one with his back braced against boulder, the other leaning on his pilum—I assumed they had just gotten off sentry duty as they both looked like they'd been awake for some time. Seeing me up, they immediately drew themselves to stiff attention, then, at my smiling nod, relaxed a bit as they murmured their good mornings.

Felix was already gone, leaving Eithne and Anachie fast asleep and curled up under his heavy cloak, next to me.

I had a vague memory of the two returning sometime during the middle of the night. They'd been gone far longer than I'd anticipated—Felix had been fantasizing about Eithne for days after all and so I'd reasonably assumed whatever she needed to do to reassure him wouldn't take but a few minutes—I remembered Eithne checking on Anachie, who was still tucked in my embrace, the two of us covered by my cloak, of her kissing me on the cheek and me mumbling a sleepy, "Everything resolved?" and her whispering, "Yes, now go back to sleep, we'll talk more in the morning."

I was dimly aware of other muffled voices—soldiers' voices, not Adranii—of Felix asking softly if everything was all right and a voice responding in kind, "Yessir," and then Felix and Eithne rearranging their sleeping arrangements so that Eithne could be next to Anachie with Felix curled up against her back, essentially, Felix and I sandwiching Anachie and Eithne protectively between us—and Felix, I must note, took to his bed with a *very* satisfied sigh.

Now I was awake and just as I feared, I was extremely stiff and sore.

I managed to lurch unsteadily to my feet without waking either Anachie or Eithne, scooped up my leather tunic from behind my saddle then I staggered over to the nearby soldiers.

"Why don't you two go get some sleep?"

"Can't, sir—Centurion Jotia's orders, sir," answered the shorter and slimmer of the two, another Marcus—Marcus Licinius to be exact.

"Order?" I looked to his huskier companion, Fabius Marius.

"Centurion Jotia ordered that you be guarded while you slept, sir," he replied, his pale blue eyes briefly darting to the still soundly sleeping Eithne and Anachie.

I nodded in grudging appreciation while mentally kicking myself. This reasonable, not to mention obvious precaution was something I should have thought of, but hadn't. I quickly chalked up this lapse in my usual cautious nature to being utterly done in by the strain of the day before, but it was still damned embarrassing to be caught with my breeches down, so to speak.

True, it was unlikely any of the Adraniis would do me harm as any attack on my person would go badly for all of the Adraniis and even the likes of Isem had to know that. But while unlikely, it was still a remote possibility and now there was the added complication of Eithne and Anachie: someone with mischief on their minds might instead go for a softer target as I'd just provided two excellent choices.

"Remain with them." I jerked my chin towards Eithne and Anachie. "In fact notify Centurion Jotia I want them to be guarded at all times."

"Centurion Felix already ordered it, sir," Fabius replied. "Said we'd be relived shortly after sunrise and that from now on, the lady and her son were not to be let out of our sight, but to be discreet about it, and to pass that along to our replacements."

"Don't you worry sir." Marcus fingered the grip of his sheathed gladius, clearly proud of his assignment, "we'll watch over 'em but good."

I nodded my appreciation, then turned and tottered towards the nearest medical wagon—managing to gather up my baldric, sword, belt and dagger as I again passed by my saddle, having taken Jotia's concerns to heart. I was loath to ask for one of Cleander's potions but my body was so full of aches and pains I felt I had no choice. The legate couldn't show his age, couldn't let on that the day before had left him stove up and unable to move without grunting or wincing—or both. It would be bad for morale—mine first and foremost.

My fingers were too stiff to unbuckle my belt and I was forced to carry it draped from shoulder to opposite hip like another, shorter baldric, the attached dagger scabbard dangling awkwardly across my chest—I could only hope I wasn't set upon by assassins before I reached the wagon and aid for my aging and abused body as I'd be hard pressed to unsheathe either gladius or dagger, much less wield either with any precision.

As I staggered along, trying manfully *not* to wince or grunt with each painful step, I noticed a new structure, one that hadn't been there the day before: a small altar. Rufinius had made a passing mention of building one once the fortifications and latrines—segregated latrines, at the insistence of the Adraniis—were complete and he'd been good to his word.

Even more gratifying was that in and among the standard offerings of the soldiers—tattered and grimy strips of crimson undertunic scribbled with prayers, small clumps of grain and bits of fruit and cheese were other items: scraps of dingy brown cloth, also covered in writing albeit an unfamiliar, blocky script, here and there a few shrimp, a mug of what I assumed was water or maybe wine, and perhaps strangest of all, several small figures fashioned from dried grass and sticks that instantly— unpleasantly—reminded me of the wicker figures favored by the Iceni and their kin for their gruesome human sacrifices.

I suppressed a shiver at the still very potent memory of coming across the partially burnt remains of one such sacrifice while on patrol a few days before the ill-fated battle in the bog. After one last wary glance at the altar and its odd collection of gifts, I quickly moved on.

A few minutes later I reached the back of the wagon, then peered through the gap between the canvas flaps to find Iulius leaning over the prone, blanket-wrapped Lollius, redressing the man's arm wound by the light of a single oil lamp and I was greatly relieved it wasn't Nestor, or worse, Cleander tending to the injured at this hour. Of course as the two senior physicians, they would've reasonably assigned their juniors the night watch just as legate I'd avoided picket duty, which meant Tigidius was in one of the nearby wagons, probably going through the same motions as Iulius. Maybe the Adranii physician Khouri was up as well, helping out—one could hope.

Finished with Lollius, Iulius straightened up and turned next to Carbo and asked if he needed anything. To my immense relief, Carbo answered—albeit in a thin whisper rather than his usual, deep, rumbling voice, a voice that had rivaled my Centurion's Voice when it came to bellowing orders—that he'd like a sip of water. I waited until he'd drunk his fill and had settled back onto his cot, clearly exhausted by the effort, then I pulled the flap aside and softly cleared my throat.

Iulius jerked his head up, startled as he realized it was the legate himself. Then he put a finger to his lips and looked down at Carbo. Once he was assured the man had lapsed back into sleep, he walked towards me and whispered, "Is there something I can do for you, Legate?"

I rubbed my lower back and grimaced for emphasis. "I… um, well, I think I might have overdone it."

Iulius eyed me suspiciously. "Overdone it?"

"When he blatantly disregarded my advice…"

I winced then turned around to find Cleander *and* Nestor standing not far away. *Fucking wonderful*—

"…to rest and instead he joined the work gangs constructing the fortifications," Cleander finished, fixing me with his far less than sympathetic stare, arms akimbo. "Isn't that right, Legate?"

I squinted furiously at him.

"So, what did you hurt this time?" Nestor asked, crossing his arms and sounding even more unsympathetic, if that was humanly possible.

I considered this attack on my judgment, not to mention my person unwarranted and patently unfair—I mean, three against one?—but I knew if I didn't let them have their fun at my expense I'd only prolong my agony. I looked at him, then Iulius, and finally Cleander and replied with a sickly smile. "My back?"

"And?" Cleander said, knowing I was not telling all.

"My hips?"

"And?"

"My legs?"

"And…?"

"My shoulders, and before you ask, my hands as well." I tossed the leather tunic onto my shoulder, then held out both hands so they could see for themselves the minor cuts, the abrasions and bruises and yes, the swelling—I hadn't noticed *that* before. No wonder my fingers weren't working right. Good gods, they looked like so many fat piglets suckling on their mother's teats—

"In other words, *all* of you."

"Yeah," I started to shrug then thought better of it, "basically."

Satisfied by my capitulation, Cleander motioned for me to follow him over to the next wagon, the one they used exclusively for surgeries, which at the moment meant it was unoccupied. I needed Nestor's help to clamber inside, but once Cleander followed and tied the flaps shut behind him, guaranteeing some semblance of privacy, and Nestor had lit a lamp, I was told to strip down so they could examine all of me and make sure I hadn't seriously injured, or, let's be honest here, seriously *re-*injured myself.

Again, knowing there would be no pain-relieving concoction without doing exactly as I was told, I unshouldered my leather tunic and tossed it in the general direction of the nearest cot, then managed to separate myself from the belt and baldric without whacking myself in the head with my sword or dagger. Those dead-defying acts was followed by a fair amount of grunting, grimacing and wriggling, but the result was that I managed to get my undertunic off all by myself—not that I was offered any help mind you. No. And of course they weren't content with just the undertunic. The breeches had to go as well—*and* the subligarium.

Nestor did the honors of untying the ties as my fingers just were not up to the job—not that he was doing me any favors, oh, no. This was all part of their plan to make this as unpleasant, as humiliating—*and yes, as chilly*—as damned possible, damn them.

I was then forced to endure Nestor picking at and finally peeling the now filthy, sweat and blood-stiffened bandage from my torso and with surprisingly little concern for the underlying flesh which had bonded itself to the dressings with a very effective combination of blood and sweat.

With that over with, I stood shivering as they peered at my flank wound and then each scrape, each contusion, new and old, and *everything* in-between.

It didn't help that Nestor kept making faces—I knew I stank; I didn't need his visual clues, thank you very much—at least I hoped he was making faces because I stank rather than some other reason.

To make matters worse, Cleander had to take advantage of the situation by voicing a litany of complaints about my character while he and Nestor poked at anything they considered of concern, which left little of me *un*-poked. The exam, along with the accompanying and utterly unnecessary recitation of what by any standard would be considered *minor* flaws while I was stood there, stark naked, was damned degrading, not to mention painful, but it was also blessedly and yes, *surprisingly* brief, considering the material they had to work with.

Perhaps Cleander realized he was pressing his luck and decided to quit before he found himself on the wrong end of his deeply flawed legate's temper.

"I think we can leave the bandage off for now," Nestor said. At Cleander's confirming nod, Nestor snatched up a few supplies, gave me one last head to toe appraisal, then departed, presumably now all warmed up and wanting to find some other poor and unsuspecting soul to torture.

I turned back to Cleander to find that he'd produced an all too familiar yellow lozenge: my reward for putting up with their nonsense. I snatched it from his palm and popped it in my mouth before he remembered more personal failings that needed a public airing and grabbed it back.

He offered me a waterskin and I filled my mouth then I handed the skin back to him and swallowed the lozenge.

"Your side *is* healing, Legate—"

"Try not to look so disappointed," I interrupted as I snatched up my underwear; now that the "exam" was over, I wanted to get redressed as quickly as possible—before Cleander thought of something else he needed to poke or look at, or someone happened by the wagon and saw more than they'd bargained for.

"—but you simply *must* avoid any further exertion. Your body has yet to replace the considerable amount of blood you lost, and I understand you've eaten hardly anything since we left the hillock?"

My appetite—or more accurately, *a lack of appetite*—was always of concern to Cleander, and even I must admit it wasn't completely without cause. Mabog had warned him of the life-threatening blows to the gut I'd received at the hands of the Iceni, later exacerbated by Kyrou repeatedly kicking and punching me while I was delirious and oh yes, tied up and unable to fight back. My captors had at first and yes, not altogether unreasonably attributed my refusal to eat or promptly vomiting when I did eat to me being taken prisoner—that denied other more expeditious means, I was trying to starve myself to death. That was certainly the accusation Turan had made and on more than one occasion, one even I had begun to believe was true. Regrettably for everyone involved—especially me—this hypothesis turned out to be utterly *wrong*.

Had it not been for Mabog's timely intervention, I *would* have died. That being said, the lingering effects of delayed care remained a worry, months on, to Mabog and now to Cleander.

I somehow managed to get the subligarium properly placed with everything tucked inside and got its ties retied. Next came the breeches. I tugged them on and as I jerked the drawstring tight I growled, "Who says? I ate last night."

"One tiny bite of shrimp hardly qualifies as a hearty meal—"

I opened my mouth to protest while picking up my undertunic.

"No point in denying it. Eithne told me. She and Centurion Felix came looking for me—"

Before or after, I had to wonder. If I were a betting man, I'd say *after*.

"—they're both extremely worried about you—"

Not that worried or they'd have come to you first and oh, yes, wouldn't have been gone half the damned night—

"—Eithne said you looked to be in some fair discomfort and you had very little appetite. I told them the best thing was to let you sleep if you could; I assured them if you were still hurting this morning, you'd come to me of your own accord—"

So, he *didn't* have that low opinion of my common sense after all. *Will wonders never cease—*

"—not because you realized you'd been incredibly stupid and were now paying a heft price, but so no one else would realize that you'd been incredibly stupid and were now paying a hefty price."

Oh. Scratch that. I scowled at him. Point made, I pulled the undertunic over my head and tugged it into place. That done, I gathered up the tunic, belt and baldric, figuring I could don them later—once I was well away from Cleander.

"Keep this up, Legate, and I guarantee you you'll collapse—or worse." He turned away and began stuffing supplies into his leather satchel. "I'll want to pull those stitches in about a week—do *try* not to scratch at them."

Shit! I had to wonder if the man had damned eyes in the back of his damned head as I immediately dropped my hand away from my side. Nestor's tugging at the sutures had hurt, and now that they were free of the bandage they kept snagging on my undertunic each time I breathed. Plus they itched like hell—I've been told that was a good sign. It didn't feel good—until I scratched them. And now I couldn't even do that. *Shit, shit, shit—*

"Are you feeling a little better?" He turned back to me.

I thought about it and realized I did. Those lozenges were truly miraculous, despite their truly nasty taste and not for the first time I found myself dearly wishing I'd come across a steady supply of them years ago as such a discovery would've certainly made my military career a little bit less... um, painful? "Yes."

He stepped close, placed his hands on my shoulders, startling me and met my wary gaze squarely. "Arri, you really *do* need to do as I tell you— I'm telling you that not just as your physician, but as your friend. I don't want to lose you."

"I'm not going anywhere," I replied, trying but utterly failing to make light of the situation.

He tightened his hold. "You came incredibly close to dying—I mean *incredibly* close and I'd come to the awful conclusion I wasn't skilled enough to save you—even with Khouri's help and he's a hell of a lot more experienced than I am, although not under these conditions. Every time we thought we had the bleeding stopped, it would start up again. I even went so far as to tell Felix he'd best prepare your officers on how best to deal with the news—I figured he needed to know, they all needed to know, since it looked like a damned foregone conclusion and there was the very real risk that our men would turn on the Adraniis and slaughter the lot in retaliation.

"It wasn't until I saw the look on Felix's face that the enormity of what we were facing hit me as well." He abruptly released his hold, cleared his throat then continued, "I'm really sorry to put this burden on you, but to be blunt, you're too damned critical to everyone's survival."

"You far underestimate Felix—you far underestimate yourself."

He shook his head. "You just don't get it, do you? You die and—"

"I'm *going* to die eventually, Cleander. We're all going to die, *eventually,* assuming the Si'aafu don't get to us first."

"*Eventually*. That's the key. Don't you see? None of us were supposed to live this long. But because of you, we have, and because of you, we have a chance of living a great deal longer. But we're only just now shedding our Kellesuf mindset. There's still too much we need to learn, too much we need to experience in order to be what you wrongly assume we are already, and that's *whole*. We won't be whole for years; some of us may never be whole. You're the only whole person among us—and we desperately need you, more than you fully realize."

"You have Borzu for a role model if that's what you mean, not to mention the rest of the Adraniis—"

"None of whom know what we are—how do you think they're going to react when they find out, or figure it out?"

"Hopefully most will react as Eithne did when Felix told her."

He raised his brows.

"Last night. He told her—they didn't mention that to you? No? Well, she was understandably taken aback at first, but once she had time to digest it, she told him it doesn't matter."

He turned away, started to reach for a vial, stopped and stared at nothing in particular. Finally he drew a deep breath, replied, "If only that were so," and resumed stocking his satchel with supplies.

"What do you mean by that?"

He shook his head, grumbled, *"Nothing. Forget it."*

It wasn't like Cleander to be evasive. Something had happened. Something ugly.

I grabbed his shoulder, roughly spun him around to face me and he blinked in genuine shock, unused to me handling him—handling any of them in such a manner. "Did an Adranii say or do something? Tell me, and Captain Borzu and I will deal with them right now!"

He tried to twitch off my hand and getting the message I let go. *"Tell me,"* I added, quietly, but insistently.

He hesitated, then replied, "It's just the unspoken but pervasive attitude that they're all better than us—and that *includes* your Captain Borzu—*and* Khouri, who at first was oh so happy to meet 'fellow physicians' or so he claimed." He waved his hand around. "See him anywhere? See him up before dawn, tending to the *Adranii* wounded, the pregnant women? See him volunteering to take the night shift? *No?* That's because *he's* still asleep."

That galled me as it galled him, maybe even more so—not that I could say so, not as I was staring directly into the distress, the anger in Cleander's eyes.

"That's just the way they are, Cleander. Ask Felix—"

"I have; he agreed with me—if they treat us like this now, how are they going to treat us when they know the truth about us?"

I exhaled and rubbed the bridge of my nose. I couldn't really blame him; he had reasons for his fears. He'd lived the life of a Kellesuf for how long no one knew; he fully remembered what it was like to be treated as something less than fully human, worse, to accept it as his due because he knew nothing else—until I came along and showed him, showed all of them that they had been something other than Kellesuf, once—a truly mixed blessing to be sure.

Even Hanni—an ogre and therefore himself a frequent recipient of anxious stares and hostile whispers—despised and feared Kellesuf and did his very best to avoid them, warning me to do the same.

"They're *not* Tuatha, Cleander. They were slaves of the Faoimhuir—granted, pampered slaves, but slaves nonetheless, just as we were slaves of the Tuatha and they're *damned* grateful we took them in. They'd all have died of starvation by now if we hadn't and they *know* that."

"Sometimes gratitude isn't enough, sometimes it only makes things worse." He turned back to what he'd been doing, which was stocking his satchel. "People don't like being beholden to those they consider inferior to them."

"True, but in this case I think you're dead wrong. Yes, I'm sure you'll find some Adraniis who have an issue with us, like Isem and his ilk, you'll always find bigots like Isem no matter the situation—but *not* because you're former Kellesuf, Cleander. It's because *we* aren't Adraniis. If you don't believe me, why don't you talk to Eithne or Maisoh?"

He didn't answer that. Instead: "Just for once do as I ask, *please?*"

Two can play at this game. "Eithne's taken Felix as her lover—did she tell you that?"

"No, but I'm not completely surprised—I've seen the way they look at each other; you'd have to be blind not to have noticed."

"Shouldn't that tell you something?"

"It tells me that she sees him as exceedingly handsome, which he is, not to mention in a position of power, which he is—women gravitate to men like him—"

And me?

"—and while he's an extremely capable officer when it comes to military matters, and very, very bright, he's also rather naïve, which women also find attractive—"

True—plus, he has dimples, don't forget the damned dimples.

"—but I must say, if asked I'd have said she was more interested in you than Felix."

"What gave you that idea?"

"She was asking a lot of questions about you—about Felix too come to think about it; she thought she was being discreet, but word got back to me—even Borzu mentioned it, as if it was... *amusing,*" he paused to make a face; I must say I felt like making a face too, but I refrained. "But even if I hadn't been told, simple observation would have been enough. She couldn't keep her eyes off the two of you. Had I realized you *were* that blind to notice, I'd have said something—"

"I'm surprised you didn't say something since the two of you have become fast friends."

He glanced over his shoulder.

"With Eithne it's nothing but Cleander said *this,* and Cleander said *that,*" I replied testily. "As far as she's concerned, you are the font of all wisdom—"

"For a woman she demonstrates remarkably shrewdness—"

"—and just for the record, I *wasn't* blind."

He slowly raised a brow. "Then...?"

I braced myself. "She's taken me as her lover too." It was bound to come out after all, and I figured I might as well be the one doing the telling.

"Both of you?" He was genuinely appalled at the concept—and I realized I was seeing my own prejudices through his eyes, which I have to

admit was not particularly flattering. So it wasn't just the Adraniis who could be narrow-minded and wedded to what could only, in our current situation, be described as counterproductive and outmoded views on propriety.

I combed my fingers through my filthy hair. *"Yeah."* Not that I had much choice in the matter when it came down to it. If I wanted Eithne, and I did, damned if I didn't, I was going to have to accept her terms, and her terms included Felix. Her choice certainly could have been worse, *far worse* than my best friend. Her terms could have included Nestor, or, gods' favor to us, Titivillus!

"If you want my opinion," Cleander said huffily, "which I'm sure you *don't*, I think it's a terrible idea. The two of you are the closest of friends... and now you're going to let a woman get between you?" He bit his lip, gave me a sidelong look. "That's not what I meant."

Under other circumstances I would have laughed, but Cleander was serious and *mightily* offended—laughing would not help, not one bit. "It's a done deal." Well, fine. It *was* a done deal between Felix and Eithne; she and I had yet to completely sign off on it, something I planned to address at the first opportunity. "Do the math, Cleander—men outnumber women two to one, a ratio that's not apt to change for at least a generation—assuming the Si'aafu don't intervene and make the whole matter moot. If Felix and Eithne and I can make this work, then maybe others can as well. And we *will* make it work." *It'll just take a little getting used to—oh, all right, it'll take a helluva lot of getting used to.*

"Well, it's none of my business I'm sure."

Which, in Cleanderese, meant that while he didn't approve, was in fact exceptionally scandalized, it did, in a convoluted way make sense even to him—if it hadn't, he would've made it his business.

He again turned back to what he'd been doing, which was clearly just make-work. Cleander was not a man comfortable expressing his personal feelings or his fears and he was clearly *very* uncomfortable... and still *very* afraid. "You really scared us, Arri."

I sighed. *So we're back to that.* "I didn't plan on getting hit with that projectile, you know. It came as a rather unpleasant surprise to me, too—"

"I don't mean that." He looked over his shoulder at me. "I meant afterwards, when you thought we didn't need you any more, when you thought you were... an *encumbrance*..."

I kept my gaze steady, but I did have to wonder how Cleander came to be so damned accurate at times in his sizing up of a situation. I was still extremely touchy about my private thoughts being overheard, and I couldn't help but wonder if perhaps Cleander had a talent he hadn't bothered to tell me about.

"…I didn't tell Felix this at the time, but I was convinced you weren't coming back when you rode out that day."

"So was he. So were Aetius and Rufinius. And I'll apologize to you, just as I apologized to them. I'm sorry, Cleander. *Truly.* I just needed to get away from camp for a while, get some fresh air, nothing more."

"That's not what Felix said—he told me you later admitted you weren't sure when you left that you were coming back."

I exhaled, forcefully, and rubbing the bridge of my nose made a note to speak to my Primus-Pilus about repeating verbatim what I said in private to anyone who came asking. "All right, yes, I did say that."

"Did you mean it?" He angrily grabbed a vial, shoved it in the satchel, then just as quickly took it back out and put it back where it belonged.

"Yes. But I don't feel that way any more."

He glanced back at me, eyes flashing. "Then why are you still trying to kill yourself?"

I blinked, startled. "I'm not!"

"Really."

"Yes, *really.*"

"So, the working on the wall was nothing more than just your way of helping out."

"Of course!"

"Even though you knew damned well it could start you bleeding again—"

"I was being careful!"

"If you wanted to be careful you'd have done exactly as I asked, which was to get some rest!" He turned back to filling his satchel, angrily shoving in things right and left.

"All right, so it was a dumb thing to do! Just like going for a ride was utterly selfish and I ended up worrying everyone! And while we're at it, just like trying to stop a massacre by parleying with the Adraniis was a stupid stunt! So I'm a gods damned selfish bastard—*I never claimed otherwise!* And since we're on the topic, I *never* asked to be dragged out of that bog by the Tuatha and patched back together, I *never* agreed to have my memories torn from my mind and doled out like so much loose coinage among total strangers, I *never agreed to any of this!*"

He turned around, opened his mouth as if to say something but I cut him off.

"And I'm damned scared, Cleander! I'm constantly scared I'll do something, or *fail* to do something that gets us all killed and having everyone tell me at every opportunity that I'm indispensable and that without me everything and everyone would be lost certainly doesn't help one damned bit! There are times I can't sleep without you giving me something to knock me out, times I *can't* eat because my stomach is so tied up in knots… I can't even help on the gods damned fortifications without you or Nestor or Felix reminding me that I'm too damned frail to do anything but rest! So I'm utterly indispensable and at the same time totally incapable. *Satisfied?*"

"Are you still suffering from those nightmares?"

I blinked, taken off guard. *"What?"*

He slowly turned around. "I said, are you still suffering from those nightmares?"

"Uh… well, yes, occasionally," I replied, the wind suddenly gone out of me.

"Every night?"

"No… at least not that I remember."

"Eithne says you just suddenly go off somewhere. Back to that damnedable bog?"

"You and Eithne do certainly find a helluva lot of time to chat about me, don't you?"

"She's been helping with the wounded—so we talk. And she's genuinely worried about you, just like I'm worried about you, and Felix and everyone else to be honest—you should consider yourself very lucky to have so many people who care that much about you instead of bitching about it—now answer the damned question, or I'll just assume the answer is yes."

I shrugged. "Fine. Sometimes—"

"Reliving the first Felix's death, reliving Rufinius and Aetius' deaths."

"That's no secret," I replied defensively. "Watching your friends die, seeing your men hacked to pieces and not be able to do a damned thing about it is the sort of thing that sticks with you—"

"Where, or should I say *what* else?"

I hesitated then answered, "I suddenly recall things that happened when I was really young. Or right after Turan took me captive—they just pop into my head without warning, it's not like I do it deliberately—those are things I'd just as soon forget, *trust* me."

He pursed his lips and I wondered—worried—if I'd revealed something important, said something I shouldn't have without realizing it.

He heaved a sigh, briefly looked away then met my uneasy gaze. "Speaking of... there's something I've been wanting to talk to you about."

I glared at him. "What?"

"I've hesitated telling you—as you say, you have a lot to worry about already, but—"

"Meaning you're going to add to that list—"

"We're *remembering*."

"Remembering...? Remembering *whaa*—" My eyes widened. "You... you don't mean...?"

He nodded. "Bits and pieces—and not everyone, at least not yet. It started a number of days back, right after the Adraniis joined us and while you were still... *um*, indisposed or I'd have mentioned it sooner... men started coming to me—some even to Nestor, awakened by dreams that made no sense, or having a very strong memory of something—or someone that just suddenly came to mind that left them scared and confused.

"Baculus was the first, or should I say he was the first to admit it was happening—he came to me, badly shaken and told me of coming across a little Adranii girl crying after she'd fallen and cut her knee, which prodded loose a memory of him holding a little girl—*his child*, he was sure of it, and him trying his best to comfort her—he said without thinking he picked the child up, tried to comfort her but a nearby Adranii panicked, snatched her from him and he just stood there, unable to move, until another Adranii approached, asking if he was all right, which is when he realized he'd been crying himself.

"Since then others have come, told us about similar things happening to them, invariably prodded loose by some common noise or a familiar smell—at first we assumed it was just some deeply implanted memory of yours that for some reason had bubbled to the surface and prompted by the Adraniis—"

"The first Baculus didn't have a family, at least none he ever spoke about so certainly none I knew about, so it couldn't be a memory of mine—"

"*Exactly*. And what we're remembering is just too personal, too painful to be anything other than a genuine memory, not an implanted one."

"But Turan assured me that once a man's memory was wiped, it was *gone*, permanently."

"I don't doubt she believed that. But her experience was with Kellesuf, not with Kellesuf given new memories. As Kellesuf we couldn't taste, couldn't feel, couldn't... understand anything beyond what we were told. I can't even remember seeing colors—I'm sure I did, but as Kellesuf I couldn't have told you if the sky was blue or the grass was green even on threat of death. And if you'd asked me if an apple you'd given me to eat was sweet or tart I wouldn't have been able to say, but if you told me it was sweet, then it was, even if it truly wasn't—does that make sense?"

I nodded, slowly, as bits and pieces of my very informative conversation with Ainiaan, where she explained how Kellesuf had come to be: she'd said some were insane. She said the Tuatha had wiped their minds, thinking that was kinder than to leave them as they were—

"I remember the first time I saw a sunrise," he continued, drawing my distracted and now worried gaze, "after I'd been given your memories—I... I started sobbing. It was the most beautiful thing I'd ever seen—and at the same time absolutely terrifying."

I stared at him, finding it hard to visualize the usually unflappable bordering on mordant Cleander being emotionally overcome by something so commonplace as a sunrise. I was even more surprised that he'd so readily admit it—and to me of all people—then I realized that what he, what the others had experienced was akin to a prisoner long held in a windowless dungeon seeing the sun again after years of perpetual darkness and being utterly overcome by the sight, perhaps so overcome if given a choice he would've begged his captors to return him to his cell—Felix had told me that he had been so overwhelmed at first, so afraid he'd begged Lady Ainiaan to make him Kellesuf again—

"As I said, none of us were expected to live this long as something other than 'mindless' Kellesuf."

"But you weren't mindless, Cleander. You couldn't have functioned if you'd been truly mindless—"

He shrugged. "*Thought*-less, then. We didn't think—we were incapable of thinking, we reacted and responded only to what the Tuatha said or told us to do—we would've starved to death in front of a table full of food if we hadn't been told to eat *and* told to stop. We even had to be reminded to perform the most basic of bodily functions—" He stopped and fixed me with a sidelong, discomfited look and I couldn't help but wince in sympathy. "So I'm sure the Tuatha never even thought to wonder what might happen after we'd had the ability to think returned to us; they simply didn't care. Our sole purpose was to fight—to defeat the Faoimhuir, beyond that... we were nothing.

"But now sights, sounds... tastes, they're shaking loose memories—*real* memories, *our* memories. And the longer we live... the more it will happen—the presence of the Adraniis, the women and children in particular, are only hastening it. We have no choice but to interact with them, and those seemingly commonplace interactions are prodding loose memories of similar exchanges from our forgotten pasts—remember Mabog saying Nestor and Iulius and Tigidius and I must've been physicians, or at least had some experience with medicine before?"

"Yes."

"We *were* physicians, all of us. I'm sure of it now—after the aborted battle, while the four of us were working alongside Khouri and the other Adraniis like Maisoh who had some rudimentary medical training, trying to patch up the damage, one of us would just suddenly blurt out, 'You should stitch it up this way—less painful, or, that wound's less likely to become corrupted if you pack it with this herb or use that poultice...' and we'd nod and go on as if it was nothing but normal banter between physicians.

"But later, when we had time to think about what had happened, well, we all realized it *was* normal banter—which shouldn't have happened, not unless we'd been physicians before. It's like walking around in the pitch dark, not knowing if you're about to fall off a cliff or bump into someone from your past... someone important, someone you didn't know you'd known until you come face to face with them.

"Mabog taught us how and when to use the medicines we brought along, how to put a needle into a man's vein and run fluids into him to offset bleeding, how to put a man to sleep so he doesn't feel the pain of surgery and then, perhaps even more importantly, how to safely wake him up afterwards—things he called 'advanced combat medicine'. But there were situations we faced in the hours and days after the battle which we hadn't been trained to deal with—like a woman going into false labor, yet the four of us *did* know what to do—and without relying on any of Mabog's drugs or his Tuatha techniques—or Khouri and his Faoimhuir knowledge for that matter, which says to me—says to all of us that these were skills we'd mastered long before we were turned into Kellesuf.

"It would certainly explain why some of us who, well... let's say we don't exactly fit with what the Tuatha preferred when it came to selecting men to be made into Kellesuf and who were purchased for that very purpose. Maybe we possessed rare skills they needed—just like they needed yours and once they'd collected what they needed, unlike you, they wiped our minds."

Because you didn't have someone like Turan protecting you is what you mean. And it was true. I'd been saved from a similar fate only because Turan had taken a fancy to me—or had I? In truth I'd never been able to completely shake the niggly worry that I too had had my memory wiped… and then re-implanted. Or maybe *I* wasn't even the real Arri—maybe the real me really *had* died—*that* was not something I wanted to consider.

Cleander turned back to his now overflowing satchel, shook his head and began removing items and as I stared at his back, I realized what he'd suggested made perfect sense—maybe the Tuatha had picked certain men for their skills—and then for whatever reason, wiped their minds and it did explain the presence of Cleander, not to mention Aetius among the ranks of otherwise much younger and far more physically attractive men.

Tigidius was in his mid-twenties while Iulius in his late twenties and Nestor was in his early thirties. All were physically handsome, so no mystery with them. Cleander, to be kind, was neither young or handsome—I'm sure he'd been young once, but he'd never been handsome, in fact I wouldn't be surprised to learn that he'd been a very ugly baby—and he too was now explainable. Which begged the question: what secret skill or skills did Aetius possess that had drawn the Tuathas' interest? Something told me the ability to fashion children's toys out of nothing but scraps was not a highly sought out expertise for someone condemned to be Kellesuf. He was a damned good centurion, but only because of my memories—or was it?

"Nestor equated it to plastering a rough stone wall…"

I arched a curious brow; Nestor—not to mention Cleander—was not the sort to wax eloquent on anything, much less speak in analogies, so I was curious as to where this was going.

"…you see only the smooth white plaster upon which your memories, a fresco, let's say, have been painted, but the rough stone wall still exists, is still there, underneath. Given time and the elements, the plaster starts peeling… revealing what's been hidden. That's what we're starting to see. We're constantly being exposed to children's laughter, the touch of a woman, the sidelong glance of someone who doesn't quite trust us, the smells of cooking, even the splash of cold water on hot, sweaty skin… sore muscles on awakening. They're like rain and wind, constantly chipping away at that smooth plaster—along with the fresco."

I stared at him, agog, then I recovered and replied, "Nestor said all that?"

He glanced over his shoulder, brow arched and added, "Maybe our Nestor wasn't such a curmudgeon in his past life."

I had no answer to that. But if it was true, then maybe there was hope for the man my troops called Nasty Nestor, often shortened simply to *Nas*-tor.

"Same's happening with others." Cleander grabbed another vial from his overflowing satchel. "At last count, one hundred sixty-eight. And I suspect there are more, far more remembering, but for one reason or another they're afraid to come to us about it."

And suddenly I realized I'd had a prime example right in front of me almost from the get-go and had been utterly oblivious until now: Rufinius. While *this* Rufinius was a brilliant military engineer, the original Rufinius' abilities—abilities that were without question equally considerable—lay elsewhere.

I myself had no experience as an engineer—yes, as a legionary and later a centurion I'd built things, plenty of things, marching camps with their requisite ditches, bridges, aqueducts—even fortresses—but only as part of a larger group and under the direction of someone who knew what the hell he was doing. Like all soldiers, I took seriously the warnings that my life depended on what I was building—while grumbling loudly and nonstop which was also obligatory—and did exactly as I was told to do only as long as it took to build whatever we were tasked to build and promptly forgot what I'd been told to do the minute whatever we were tasked to build was built. So my memories could only have imparted a very insignificant amount of information on such techniques. And when I say insignificant, I mean nonexistent.

I again fixed my gaze, and my full attention, on Cleander. "So what now?"

"You mean, what do we do?"

"Yeah."

"There's nothing we can do, except help each man come to grips with whatever memories surface…"

And maybe that's why Rufinius' surprising expertise hadn't struck me as odd—he wasn't troubled by it; maybe he just assumed his newfound skill set was part and parcel of getting a sizeable chunk of my memories, or maybe for a man who preferred his own company they were a comforting, familiar presence he wisely elected not to question.

"…explain why it's happening, maybe make it a little less frightening or painful, although I doubt there's much anyone can say to make it less painful to suddenly remember you had a child, a family and you have no idea where they are, or if they're even still alive—that like Centurion Baculus, you can't even remember your daughter's name."

Or perhaps worse, I thought, realizing that there was a far darker, far more disturbing side to this matter, *coming to grips with the knowledge that you weren't a respected Roman Legionary in your past life, an accepted member of a tightly knit group, but rather a slave, a prisoner or a condemned criminal, saved by the timely intervention of a Tuatha with a fat coin purse and an insatiable appetite for physically pleasing young men.*

"Nestor and I took the liberty of speaking to all of the centurions— told them to pass the word among their men, and to let everyone know that not everyone will remember, and those who do might only recall snippets… others might take years to tease out whole events from their previous lives and still others might suddenly recall everything—and we're here if anyone needs to talk about what's happening to them."

"I would have done the same."

He nodded, cleared his throat then turned to face me. "Any blood in your urine?"

I blinked, startled, and at the same time relieved he'd moved on to less touchy subjects and by the look he was giving me, he was clearly ready to move on as well. "No."

He looked me up and down. "And what about your appetite? Is it because you truly have no appetite, or…?"

"As I said, sometimes I get a bellyache, but I do get hungry and when I do I can eat the hardtack and cheese and fruit, no problem. I did have a problem with those damned spiders—I just couldn't bring myself to eat them, even though Eithne assured me they weren't spiders—thank *you* so much for putting that lovely thought in my head in the first place, but I did eat some last night, a whole bowl full in fact." I handed him my belt and baldric and quickly pulled the leather tunic over my head—there was a chill breeze blowing into the wagon and my backside was starting to ache again.

"When…?"

I poked my head out of the neck slit of the tunic, replied, "After Eithne and Felix left to… well, spend some time alone with each other," then I yanked the tunic down over my hips. A quick sweep of my hand assured me all the pteruges—front and back—were hanging properly as there was nothing more embarrassing than walking about oblivious that some of the straps were tucked up inside your tunic as people had a tendency to assume you'd just made a hasty visit to the latrine.

He raised a dubious brow as he handed me back my baldric and belt. I slipped the baldric over my shoulder, then I whipped the belt around my leather-clad waist, in the process anchoring the baldric, then I fastened the buckle with a flourish and settled the dagger and sword scabbards into place. *Done!*

Cleander watched the procedure in decidedly unimpressed silence. "Well, I have good news for you, you might not have to eat any more 'spiders'. Duccius managed to spear an eel and Birral force-fed some of it to a goat—Hardalio, when he found out was none too pleased, said he planned on lodging a complaint with you this morning, so be prepared— but if the aforementioned goat seems no worse for its feast by tonight, I'd say we've got ourselves another source of fresh meat—"

"Are we done?" I interrupted, glancing sidelong at my escape route.

Cleander hesitated.

"Good." I spun on my heel, hurried over to the rear gate of the wagon and without thinking, leapt down, onto the hard-packed ground— the jolt up my spine sent my body aching anew—

"Arri…?"

Cleander only rarely used my name and only when he needed to grab my attention—so I wiped the grimace off my face and slowly turned around to find him standing in the back of the wagon, silhouetted against the shifting glow of the oil lamp.

"You need to talk to someone."

"I thought I just did."

"I mean you need to tell them what's really bothering you."

"Right now *you're* what's really bothering me."

He ignored that as he always ignored my less than subtle scoffs. "You need to face your fears—"

"I told you what I'm afraid of—I'm afraid I'll get us all killed."

He crossed his arms, said softly, "Have you always been this unsure of yourself, or are you still blaming yourself for what happened in that bog?"

"Don't you dare tell me it wasn't my fault—"

"I wasn't about to anything of the kind. But what happened, *happened.* We're here now, Arri, none of us can go back and we need you and you need to let go of *your* past as much if not more than we need to remember ours—you *need* to let go of Earth."

"Thanks. First chance I get I'll *do* just that. Right now I have over five thousand people to get over a gods damned pass before the Si'aafu find us." I spun on my heel and stalked away, but not back to where I'd left Eithne and Anachie, not to where I thought I'd probably find Felix, with Rufinius at the wall, looking for any structural weaknesses that might have been missed the evening before. Instead I headed for the promontory, to

the jumbled rockfall that gave our sentries access to the heights above the gorge.

Given a chance I'm sure Cleander would say the climb was far too rigorous for me, that if I wanted a report from the pickets, I should do what any sensible legate would do and order someone else to make the risky climb and gather the information. But I wasn't in search of information. Cleander's remarks had left me decidedly unsettled and I wanted to find something to do to keep me occupied so I wouldn't have to think... about anything.

Something physically demanding, something that would take my full concentration... like scaling an unstable rockfall might be just what the physician ordered, so to speak—if the physician had been someone *reasonable*. Which of course immediately eliminated Cleander. And Nestor. Not to mention Iulius and Tigidius, and probably Khouri too.

I flicked a challenging glare over my shoulder in Cleander's general direction, I even stuck out my tongue—it was still dark enough I doubted anyone would have seen the gesture; moreover I really didn't give a damn if they did.

Satisfied I'd made my point, and without further ado, I scrambled up a large mound of loose scree, managed to clamber up onto the first large boulder, then another, and another... and then stopped, heaving for breath, having suddenly lost both momentum and motivation.

Ahead, the climb was clearly going to be even harder, steeper, the sheer rock face of the gorge marred only by the occasional crack or fissure barely wide enough for a finger or toehold. A year ago I could have managed handily; I'd been an expert climber at one time: trees, cliffs, the walls of a besieged town, you name it, if it was vertical and getting to the top—or bottom—in any way gave us an advantage, I'd climb it—in full armor no less—and often faster than my younger troops... just because I could.

Not now—and since Cleander had put me in a mood to be brutally honest with myself—not *ever* again. The injuries to my shoulder and thigh, while healed, had left both limbs untrustworthy, my damned leg particularly prone to giving out without warning.

But rather than admit defeat, admit that Cleander and Felix and everyone were right, I swiveled around and sat down, as if my intention all along was just to sit atop this damned rock and survey the sights.

I will give the spot its due: it did provide a good view of the still shadow-filled camp, which was now on its way to waking up. The western lip of the gorge was tinged in dazzling red, the first hint of sunrise; it would be hours yet before sunlight lit the grassy floor and pool, but already people moved about; children splashed in the shallows of the pool watched by my soldiers, while Hardalio and the dogs herded the goats over to a patch of grass not far from the waterfall—I could clearly see the all white dog—Aëllo?—darting here and there after her unruly charges who clearly awoke with plans of their own. And by damn... I heard one of the roosters crow!

He'd actually been crowing for a few minutes; I hadn't noticed it at first, it was such a commonplace noise at sunrise it took a while to worm its way and its significance into my thoughts. The first rooster crow: brashly announcing our claim on this world—as affirming as any buccina blast as it echoed off the walls of the gorge.

I did have to wonder how the Adraniis were reacting to hearing one of our roosters doing his damnedest to greet the rising suns in such a comical, strident way. Even more critical, at least to me: how the hens reacted? And the other roosters? Maybe there'd be eggs aplenty in the coming days, and I made a note to myself to remind Florianus that as legate, I should be at the top of the list of recipients of the hens' favors. I didn't like pulling rank, but these were eggs we were talking about and I do so love eggs.

But... eggs were days away, at best, so I patted my happily rumbling belly and shifted my narrowed gaze to the fortifications. I was right: men were already at work, shoring up spots, adding a bit of height here, widening it there. I felt a twinge in my gut, realizing I should have spoken to Rufinius first thing, warned him there was no point in making the wall substantial enough to last a millennium. In two days time we'd be knocking our own hole in it, leaving it and the gorge behind in hopes of finding something better, something safer on the other side of the mountains—

Gods, let it be true—

A second rooster suddenly joined the first, and then a third and finally, a fourth. Horses too took to whinnying. They knew food and water were to be had, and had in abundance and were demanding to be released from their nighttime tether lines. And as if not wanting to be left out, I heard the occasional bark from a dog and responding annoyed bleat from a goat, followed by a sharp whistle, presumably from Hardalio or one of his apprentices.

I grinned at the cacophony of such mundane, Earthly sounds filling the gorge below; clearly a full belly followed by a good night's sleep had done wonders for everyone, man and beast alike.

I swept the gorge again with my gaze and was suddenly struck with the memory of staring down on the Adraniis' camp that night—*how many days ago?*—seeing what I thought were thousands of campfires, and feeling utterly done in by the sight. And now here we were, all one *very* big, 'happy' family... and still playing hide and seek with the enemy, a common *un-human* enemy—

I heard footfalls behind me and the sharp clatter of pebbles sent scattering by a misplaced step, accompanied by a telltale *wheeze... wheeze... wheeze.* I was tempted to look over my shoulder, but in truth there wasn't any need.

A moment later Felix carefully eased himself down beside me as he flicked me a sidelong, worried look. "You all right?"

"Never better."

"So what are you doing up here?"

"What does it look like?"

"It looks like you're hiding from someone—now," he tapped his forefinger on his chin, "let me guess... *Cleander?*"

"I've already had my morning dose of Cleander."

"Titivillus then?"

"Nope again—but an excellent guess." I had to concede that, because it was an excellent guess, although in truth Titivillus hadn't entered my black thoughts, which, considering the prominent role the man usually played in my tempers, was surprising.

He hesitated. *"Me?"*

I flicked him a look.

He sighed, *"Me."*

I shrugged; the same thought had occurred to me as well.

"You should have had her, first."

I eyed him, annoyed by his damned impertinence. *"What the hell makes you think I didn't?"*

He blinked, taken aback, but whether it was due to my response or my tone I can't tell you. Knowing Felix, it was probably the latter.

"Oh. When?—I mean, if you don't mind me asking."

So I was wrong—it was the former. And I did mind, but... "Remember when you walked in on us?"

He stared at me then his eyes got very round. *"Oh...."*

"Oh indeed." I exhaled, let go of the anger. This was Felix after all— my best friend and clearly just as ill at ease about this novel arrangement as I was. "Maybe I should clarify. We *tried*—almost made it too, but I got a little overly enthusiastic and didn't watch what I was doing and my side locked up, thought I'd ripped it open to be honest... kinda lost all desire after that."

"Ow," he winced in sympathy. "Sorry, Arri."

"Not your fault. I did exactly as you said I would, given half a chance."

"And what was that?"

"I went at her like Wushah on a mare in heat."

He fixed his narrowed gaze on the goings on below us. "So did I," he finally confessed, adding, "not that she seemed to mind, in fact she rather encouraged it."

She hadn't seemed to mind with me, either, *and* she'd been the instigator.

I pursed my lips, let my gaze wander the full length of the gorge, then: "You know it's really strange, sitting here, the two of us discussing having sex with the same woman—a woman, if we're lucky, that we'll spend the rest of our lives with." And it was; damned if it wasn't.

"Yeah," Felix nodded solemnly, then, after another moment of thought: "I wonder if women—you know, like concubines and whores— discuss having sex with the same man?"

I knew they did—or should I say whores did. I'd been schooled by prostitutes after all, grew up among the whores of Carthage, male *and* female, and as such had been privy to their conversations—in fact had often taken an active part in the conversations—which were rarely complimentary to our customers. But rather than say so, and possibly Felix asking how I knew so, I replied, "I bet they do, and I bet they laugh a lot when they do."

Felix replied with a sickly smile, and: "Does this mean we're Eithne's concubines?"

I eyed him—sometimes Felix's leaps of logic truly amazed me. Of course his choice could have been worse. Still... "I can't speak for you, but I'm damned if I'm gonna consider myself subservient to a woman, any woman, even if that woman is Eithne."

He looked uncomfortable, muttered, "Neither do I, but..."

"But what?"

He began picking at his tunic. "I did exactly what she told me to do— last night."

I bit my lip and let my gaze wander the full length of the far gorge rim before I answered irritably, "That's different."

"How?"

"It just *is.*"

He heaved a sigh and thankfully let the matter drop just as I hoped he would.

For several minutes we sat in silence, our gazes and our attention fixed on the goings on below.

"If it's any consolation for your side locking up," he said suddenly, "I got a rock up my ass."

I blinked, then ever so slowly swiveled my eyes towards him. "A rock up your...?"

"*Ass.*"

"Dare I ask how?"

"It's embarrassing."

"I can't see why," I said straight-faced. "Getting a rock up your ass while having sex is quite common, or so I've heard."

He stared at me, lips quivering then he burst into laughter.

I joined him and slapped him on the knee. "Damn, Felix, how the hell'd you get a rock up your ass?"

"Well, uh, we—just how detailed do you want me to be?"

"*Very detailed.*" Hell, I was damned curious on so many levels—can you blame me?

"I, uh, I was on top..."

"And? I still don't see where a rock could possibly get involved." Actually, I could, but this Felix was rather naïve when it came to sex, and Eithne knew he was naïve, and so I seriously doubted either would have thought to be that adventuresome—that would, ahem, *come* later.

"Not then. Later—"

See? I told you.

"—you *said* you wanted details."

"Of course I did—*please*, go on."

He took a deep breath, continued, "So, after we were done... and we rested a bit, she asked if we could do it again."

"A reasonable request," I replied amicably as it boded well—for all of us.

"And of course I said yes."

"Of course."

"But this time she wanted to do it differently."

And you didn't believe me. "*How* differently?" I was intrigued. *Very intrigued.* In-depth knowledge of Eithne's sexual preferences would come in very handy, later. Yes, we're talking *that* 'later'.

"Her on top."

An image instantly popped into my head of the two of them going at it, an image that was very difficult to uproot, in fact one I wasn't at all sure I wanted to uproot as it was quite... well, enjoyable and gave me all sorts of ideas. "Well, it certainly makes getting a rock up your ass a little more likely, I suppose, still—"

"I kinda got carried away."

I arched a brow. "In what way?"

"I managed to stand up with her... well, still... um, *firmly affixed?*"

I blinked. I'd *never* tried that. *Ever.* It certainly had possibilities, although in truth I wasn't sure I could manage it, not with my bad leg, which I suspect meant I'd have no choice but to leave the love-making gymnastics to Felix and settle for impressing the hell out of Eithne with my technique, a technique that, I'm proud to say, drives women wild and begging for more. "I still don't see—"

"Things kind of got out of control after that and, well, it was really tight quarters and at the worst possible moment I stumbled..."

"Oh." I couldn't help but wince in manly sympathy.

"...and sat down, *hard.*"

I grimaced and through my clenched teeth said, "Which is where the rock came into play—so to speak."

He squirmed a bit. "Yeah. Problem was, Eithne was... well, she was unaware of my situation—considering her reaction I think she thought I'd done it deliberately, you know..." he paused, then continued, "and well, I couldn't just stop—neither one of us was... um, quite finished." He flicking me a worried glance. "You won't tell her, will you?"

"You mean she *doesn't* know? How could she *not* know?"

"You think I'm going to say, 'hey, would you mind pulling this rock out of my ass?' to the woman I just made incredible love to, not once, but *three* times..."

Three? I raised a brow, at once amazed and yes, a little intimidated. All right. A *lot* intimidated. Twice in relatively short period of time I could, ah, manage—*but three?* That was just plain showing off.

No wonder they were gone so long...and no wonder Felix went to bed with a big grin on his face... along, I must surmise, with a *very* sore ass—

"...what would she think?"

"That you got a rock up your ass?"

He stared at me, dubious. "I think that would have killed the mood."

"I would have thought a rock up your ass would have killed the mood, but then again, I've never had a rock up my ass, so what do I know." Sure, I'd had other things up my ass, but these were objects designed for the purpose and no, they hadn't killed the mood, quite the contrary, but a rock? One does have to draw the line somewhere.

He bit his lip, fixed his gaze on the camp below.

I hesitated then whispered out of the corner of my mouth, "Is it still up your ass?" It was a reasonable question. Felix was my best friend, and friends help friends, even if it means winkling said rock out of said friend's ass.

"No."

"Well, that's a huge relief."

"Tell me about it. Took me forever to get it out, and of course I couldn't just make my excuses and go off and get the damned thing out."

I eyed him. "So you…?"

"Waited until she fell asleep. Problem is—she really took it out of me."

"You're not speaking of the rock."

He scowled at me. *"No.* I fell asleep. When I woke up I went off and got it out."

"You slept with a rock up your ass?"

"I was *exhausted."*

"I can see why, but I think I'd have taken the time to get a damned rock out of my ass, no matter how damned exhausted I was."

He shrugged. "It was more like a pebble. A *small* pebble—but kinda sharp. I think it might have broken off something when I sat on it."

Well, that explained why he was up and gone before I woke up. Still… "Why didn't you have Cleander take it out?"

"Cleander?"

"When you and Eithne stopped by to tell him how worried you both were about me."

"Oh. He told you."

"This is Cleander we're talking about. He couldn't keep a confidence to save his life."

"And you wonder why I didn't ask him for help?"

I nodded solemnly. "Point taken."

Felix again fixed his narrowed stare on the camp below, as did I.

Finally he said, "Are you truly all right with this… arrangement?"

I looked back at him. "Are you?"

"I asked first."

"You're my closest friend, Felix, the closest friend I've ever had."

"Which is what worries me. I love Eithne, Arri, truly I do. At first I thought it was just pure and simple lust for both of us, but... well, after last night...I realize it's a lot more than that. Gods, Arri, she's amazing—what she did... I mean, *three times!* And each time was more fantastic than the last. But it was more than that. She kept telling me she loved me—*me*, not the first Felix, *but me.*" He chuckled softly, but there was little mirth in it. "And I love her too, absolutely and unconditionally—when I told her that, she started crying. And when I asked why she was crying, had I done something to hurt her, she just wrapped her arms around me and told me to shut the hell up—did I do or say something wrong?"

I shook my head and smiled. "Sounds to me like you did and said everything just right—aside from the rock."

He exhaled forcefully, ran his suddenly shaky fingers through his pale blond curls. "I don't remember ever feeling like this towards a woman..." He glanced at me, managed a lopsided grin and a shrug. "Of course I wouldn't, would I? Still, that said, I don't want to risk our friendship—nothing's worth that, Arri, not even Eithne."

"I love Eithne too—it won't be easy, but I agree with her, I think we can—we *have* to make this work. Not just for the three of us and for Anachie, but for the others—fifteen hundred unattached men, far less than half that number of available women."

"And Eithne assured me this isn't a totally unheard of arrangement among Adraniis," he added hopefully.

But we aren't Adraniis—a thought I kept to myself, but one that would occur to both my men and the Adraniis I'm sure once word got out. I'm sure it had already occurred to Felix.

"Still," he continued, "it's going to be rather... well, strange."

"Stranger than sleeping with a rock up your ass?"

He grimaced and shifted a bit. "Hopefully not."

I patted him on the knee. "We best get back to camp..." I started to lurch to my feet; he beat me to it and offered me a hand up.

I gratefully grabbed it—in the short time I'd been seated, my joints had stiffened up—and he jerked me to my feet. "Got some bad news to deliver," I added, dusting myself off.

He eyed me. "Bad news?"

"I've decided we break camp day after tomorrow."

He thought about it for a moment as he swept his gaze the length of the gorge, from wall to waterfall. "Bad news indeed, but I agree—any longer and it'll be well-nigh impossible to get the Adraniis moving." He started off, absently rubbing his backside, then stopped and looked back at me. "Coming?"

I smiled feebly. "I think I might need some help climbing back down."

He grinned and held out his hand. "Come on, old man."

— ii —

As expected Borzu and his officers were not particularly happy with my plan, but they did agree we'd be risking the ire of the Fates if we stayed put much longer. So, after Marcus had drawn a crude map of the pass and what lay beyond it in the damp sand at the edge of the pool and we'd hashed out the details, he and the others dispersed to spread the word among the Adraniis as Felix, Aetius and Rufinius left to relay the news to our men.

Soon everyone was hard at work preparing and with a shocking lack of grumbling on the part of the Adraniis.

The women and youngest children gathered more shrimp, having become quite expert in catching the creatures, then they placed them on any rock surface that faced the suns; we'd quickly found that worked far better, and faster, than drying racks made from our scarce supply of wood.

Some of my archers set about hunting eels in the plunge pool at the base of the waterfall, having first tied strings to the arrows. It made for easy work retrieving the valuable arrows, not to mention their squirming victims.

A number of the infantry, taking up Duccius' successful technique and unwilling to stand by and let the *sagitarii* grab all the glory, stripped down to their underwear—at Baculus' authorization I must note. He rationalized that the humble undergarment in fact had a very long and honorable history among fighting men, deemed suitable for gladiators to wear in the arena and it was the hands-down choice of attire of soldiers while exercising—and while hunting eels didn't rise to the level of gladiatorial combat, it was a form of exercise, wasn't it?

How could I argue with that logic? And if it increased my men's chances with the womenfolk, well… so much the better.

So my men, attired only in their underwear, waded out into the center of the pool and using their pila, began spearing the fast swimming creatures that fled the *sagitarii's* arrows and were seeking refuge in the shadowy kettle-holes. Some of the older Adranii boys were quick to offer their help in bringing their catch to those tasked with cleaning the eels, but soon their true intentions were revealed: they were fascinated by the weapons and were eager to learn how to use them with the same finely honed skill displayed by my soldiers.

A large number of the older girls likewise eagerly offered to help only to linger, striking up conversations with the scantily-clad soldiers, who, not unexpectedly, found female attentions far more rewarding than spearing eels, and only continued their work as a means to impress their giggling and appreciatively grinning audience with their hunting prowess, not to mention their physiques which were conveniently on full display. Between flexing muscles and sopping wet subligaria that left little to the female imagination... well, the Adranii men simply didn't stand a chance.

I figured it would be wise to catch, gut and dry as many of the eels as possible—and while the socializing between my soldiers and the younger Adraniis was an obvious distraction, it provided a chance for them to freely mingle while under the guise of honest preparations—something even the more suspicious among the older Adraniis couldn't openly question.

Meanwhile, other preparations were taking place: a dozen mounted scouts, led by Hannibalianus this time were dispatched in hopes of finding a course closer to the foothills, one that would keep the salt pans to our right, in the process adding the natron pools and even the desert itself to our defenses while Rufinius and his engineers began a thorough inspection of the wagons, starting with those that carried the wounded.

Men and women alike scrambled up into the scree fields to gather the scant amount of scrub that remained, along with every bit of dried grass, which could be used as fodder as well as tinder—assuming we found any wood along the way that would serve to fuel campfires. I considered this unlikely and not altogether necessary as the provisions we were taking with us could, and most likely would be eaten without being cooked. More grass, fresh grass, was harvested and tied in bundles to the sides and on the canvas roofs of the wagons, even to the sides of the engines, which had the added bonus of providing camouflage and some added protection from the suns' heat.

It would be lean fare for everyone, including the animals until we reached the grasslands, but with proper rationing what foodstuffs we would be carrying with us would last—they would have to last.

The same was not true of water. We didn't have enough water wagons, waterskins or barrels to lay in an adequate supply for the entire trip; even converting a large number of the baggage carts to carry nothing but water using some of our dwindling supply of oiled canvas, which

Rufinius suggested and at Borzu's go-ahead began to implement, wouldn't help much, adding at most a day to what was already no more than a two to three day supply and that was only if we limited everyone, with the exception of the smallest children, the pregnant and nursing women and the badly wounded to a few precious sips a day. The animals would, by necessity, face the same inadequate rations as the rest of us.

Under such circumstances I would have far preferred to travel at night, taking advantage of the cooler air that would make the trek marginally less grueling for everyone, but Marcus's description of the route made that option far too risky.

As the day wore on and the suns' full intensity filled the gorge, people stopped working, sought shade where they could or just walked out into the large pool and sat down, which to me seemed the best idea of all.

Then Rufinius brought word that he and his engineers, having little else to do now that the fortifications were complete and the wagons and baggage carts had been repaired or refurbished, had taken it upon themselves to wall off part of the smaller pool that was already partially hidden from the main camp by the promontory, providing a private bathing area. The water there was shallower, sandy-bottomed and much warmer, and for me now blessedly almost absent of shrimp as those that had populated the pool were the easiest to catch, having fewer places to hide.

I assigned Felix and Eithne the job of overseeing a schedule for bathing—while a thankless task, I figured it would give them more time to get to know each other and better, be seen with each other. It also meant Eithne had extra protection—just in case someone took exception. Rufinius, along with his second, Dulcitius and Maisoh had taken over watching Anachie—not that it had taken any arm-twisting of anyone involved. Anachie had shown a remarkable interest in how things were put together, like fashioning a new wheel for a baggage cart from what materials we had on hand, or how and why to reinforce the stone barricade.

Rufinius, according to Maisoh, was already bragging to his engineers that he'd found himself a very talented protégé—and it wasn't surprising, she added, when one considered Anachie's father's interests. That clearly and deeply pleased Eithne, which in turn pleased me. It also freed me up to concentrate on other matters, knowing that both Eithne and Anachie were as safe as safe could be.

Felix and Eithne decided that women, girls and young children were to be first, with a few of my men posted within earshot but out of direct view, just in case someone got into trouble, then the Adranii men and older boys, and lastly, us, with our numbers broken up into three groups, so the camp remained fully guarded at all times. Each group was permitted an hour to bathe, to wash their clothing, even just sit and soak if that was their preference.

When they finally got their chance, my men made good use of the time with their razors and scrapers, clearly with hopes in mind of impressing the womenfolk with their polished appearance. We'd quickly discovered the Adranii had no analogue to these grooming tools, which left me—and probably most of my men—privately wondering what they *did* use to cleanse their skin and what the men used to shave—assuming they kept themselves clean-shaven. They certainly weren't now.

Spending the hottest part of the day bathing or just relaxing was a small luxury and well earned, one which everyone took full advantage, but as Romulus touched the western edge of the gorge and inky shadows began to slide down the rock face, people wordlessly resumed their work on preparations.

I'd been among the last group of bathers and as I trudged back into camp, wearing my freshly washed undertunic, subligarium and breeches that like everyone else's had been left to dry on the surrounding rock while we bathed, I found myself surrounded by truly enticing smells emanating from the now crackling cook fires.

I stopped and placing my hands on my hips, looked around. One more day for everyone to eat and drink and rest as much as possible… I could only hope it would be enough—

"Legate!"

I turned and quickly spotted Aetius, who stood with several Adraniis, adults and children, next to a cook fire; he eagerly motioned to me and as I approached, he grinned. "Care for some grilled eel, sir?"

I pointedly sniffed the fragrant air and smiled. "Is that what I smell cooking?"

The woman who was clearly in charge of this particular fire nodded and held out a platter piled high with chunks of steaming, bright blue meat. I have to admit I was rather put off by the startling color. "I assume it's safe to eat?"

"Gods, I hope so," Aetius said and patted his belly.

"Lieutenant Birral gave his go-ahead, Legate," the woman replied, eyeing Aetius, "Not that that would have stopped the Centurion here—he's already polished off one platter all by himself."

"Can I help it that you're a damned fine cook?" he countered, grinning at the woman. "A *damned* fine cook…"

If it was his intention to flatter her, he succeeded. She smiled, granted, a clearly nervous smile, but a pleased smile nonetheless.

"…who also happens to be *very* easy on the eye," he added, wiggling his bushy eyebrows suggestively at her.

He should have stopped when he was ahead. The woman's shy smile instantly disappeared and the other adult Adraniis fixed their now unhappy bordering on hostile stares on him.

Aetius blinked, his own broad grin evaporating as he turned to me, presumably hoping either for rescue from his unintentional gaffe or an explanation. As I think I may have mentioned before, Aetius was not a man blessed with good looks. While he wasn't as butt-ugly as his namesake, he wasn't… well, particularly handsome. But what he lacked in physical attractiveness he more than made up for in bravery and resourcefulness—perhaps those traits alone explained why the Tuatha had taken him—not to mention kindheartedness and his skill at making toys and storytelling, a legacy of the first Aetius.

This Aetius had quickly become well known among the very youngest Adraniis. It was rare to find him without a gaggle of children following his every move. Even now he had the usual entourage that hovered around him, grubby faces upturned, some even clinging to the pteruge-fringe of his leather tunic. That being said, what I sensed in this woman was not a less than positive reaction to his looks, but rather to who and what he was. Meaning, he wasn't Adranii and therefore his polite advances were wholly unwelcome.

Aetius cleared his throat then looked down as if not realizing he had a retinue. "Oh, my! I promised you all a story, didn't I?"

The group of small children giggled and nodded excitedly.

"Then a story you shall have—come, let's go find a comfortable place to sit." He scooped up one of the smallest, settled the child on his hip and walked away, the rest happily following as if bewitched.

I watched him leave then slowly rolled my eyes back to the woman. She was still holding the platter and as I turned to her, she again offered it to me as if nothing was amiss.

I glared at her, growled, "I'll pass—wouldn't want to risk befouling *your* food." I then pivoted smartly on my heel and stalked off.

I'd gotten no more than a few paces when a voice called, *"Legate! Please… wait!"*

I stopped and slowly turned around. One of the Adranii men who'd been standing with Aetius was now hurrying towards me—and that man was none other than Jom, Borzu's first officer.

I crossed my arms and set my jaw. "What?"

"It wasn't Laatao's intention to insult you, sir—"

"I'm sure it wasn't," I replied icily. "She did, however, *intend* to snub Centurion Aetius."

He bit his lip and fixed his gaze on the fire, on the woman, Laatao, who now had her back to us then he looked back at me. "She didn't mean it the way it came across—"

"Really? Centurion Aetius was paying her a compliment. He meant no harm, and he certainly wouldn't have taken it any further. My men *know* the rules. None will touch any woman without that woman's willing consent—have any of your womenfolk complained of being bothered by my soldiers?"

"No, sir, but—"

"Or looked at in a way they find threatening or demeaning?"

"No, not at all, but—"

"Then her reaction was altogether unwarranted, not to mention ungrateful and if this was an isolated event I'd just chalk it up to a personal failing on her part. But others have told me of similar, offensive treatment—"

"I'm sorry, sir, I didn't—"

"We've willingly shared *our* food, *our* medical supplies; we've offered you *our* protection, since you clearly cannot protect yourselves, and at great risk to us I might add—"

"I understand that, sir, and we're very grateful, but—"

"—and there's a far better than even chance I've doomed my soldiers by taking your lot in—and this is how your people react? We're *not* your inferiors and you are certainly *not* our superiors. The sooner your people understand that the better for everyone." I glared balefully at him. "Pass this along to your Captain Borzu: the next time one of my men is treated as *anything* but an equal by an Adranii I will personally mete out what I consider to be adequate punishment to the offending party and I don't give a damn if it's a woman, a man or even a child *if* that child is, in *my* estimation, old enough to know better. And if this is in any way unacceptable to you and Captain Borzu then I see no other choice than to part company—*do I make myself clear?*"

He swallowed hard and ducked his head. "Yes, Legate. Perfectly."

"Tell him. *Now.* And tell him I expect his answer by nightfall—that way if he finds my terms unacceptable, it will give my men time to pack up so we can move out before dawn." I spun on my heel and stormed off, still seething, intent on calling a meeting of my officers—and mine *alone*.

I'd made no idle threat. The look on Aetius' face, the tone in Cleander's voice, the fears Felix had had to face down—were simply *intolerable*. Had I a mind to do it, I could enslave the Adraniis. Or, I could simply order my soldiers to kill the men and take the women by force, using the children to keep the women under control. I'd been ordered to do such many times as a centurion and had followed those orders. I could do it again—and, I realized, I might just have to do it again.

I had no doubt that my men and I could survive on this planet, but life would be better if we had women, even if they were unwilling partners. The Adranii men weren't absolutely necessary to that survival— hopefully Borzu and his officers would realize their rather precarious position and stop acting like condescending jackasses—

"Arri?"

I stopped and glanced over my shoulder to find Eithne standing not far away with Anachie beside her, holding her hand. And behind them, two fully armored soldiers. All were staring at me in obvious worry, although the soldiers were doing their damnedest to look like they'd just happened to be walking in the same direction as Eithne and had stopped rather than intrude on our conversation. One even plopped himself down on a large rock and began cleaning his nails while the other leaned on his pila, the two seeming engaged in a private chat of their own.

"What's happened?"

I wiped the murderous look off my face, turned and replied blandly, "A simple misunderstanding."

She squatted beside Anachie. "Centurion Aetius is over there." She pointed to where Aetius had set up shop as a storyteller atop another water-smoothed boulder, not far from the edge of the pool, "I'm sure he'd love your company."

Anachie looked at me.

I nodded and smiled.

He then looked back at her, not at all taken in, but willing to go along, then at Eithne's urging—a gentle swat on his rump—he trotted off.

One of the soldiers, with a sidelong glance at me, and my answering nod, murmured something to his companion, and casually walked off... by pure happenstance in the same direction as Anachie.

Eithne rose, slowly and walked towards me, the remaining guard remained where he was, still pretending to be fully absorbed in cleaning his nails with the tip of his dagger, while his eyes, hidden in shadow by his helmet's brow guard, began to roam, searching for possible trouble.

"Now tell me the truth."

"Truth? Here's the truth: I'm royally fed up with your people treating us like we're less than they are—*less than human!*" I snarled, suddenly unable to contain my rage.

She bit her lip and glanced around, clearly concerned my voice had carried to the group of nearby Adraniis. It had certainly carried to her guard as the man briefly met my angry stare with a startled one of his own.

If the Adraniis overheard, they wisely didn't show it, but grudgingly taking her hint, I lowered my voice to a furious whisper: "That's why Felix was so gods damned scared last night. You simply have no concept of how he and the others were treated by the Tuatha—they suffered terrible injuries that were left untreated because they didn't have the capacity to speak unless spoken to, didn't even have the capacity to understand why they were in such pain, any more than a horse or a dog can understand pain, they just accepted it!

"Felix walked around on a badly broken leg for well over a week until someone noticed and did something about it, but only because it interfered with his ability to do his Tuatha master's bidding, otherwise he would have been left to suffer until the injury healed on its own, or it killed him—that stab wound in his throat?"

She nodded.

"I've long suspected it was the work of a Tuatha, or maybe one of their servants—Felix claims he doesn't know what happened, but I think he does, I think he damned well remembers exactly what happened—in many ways the servants were even worse because they too had to suffer the Tuathas' cruelty, but then they could always go after a Kellesuf and beat the hell out of him or worse. Notice how most of them are extremely good looking?"

She again nodded, slowly, reluctantly, as her eyes darted to the nearby, now impeccably manicured guard—he fit the bill perfectly.

"That wasn't by chance," I added, drawing her uneasy gaze. "They were bought from slave markets all over the Empire, or so I was told, picked out based on two criteria," I held up one finger, "one, that they were in relatively good shape, physically—and two," I held up a second finger, "if possible, they were *attractive*. But why should their looks matter?

They were going to be made into Kellesuf after all, men who couldn't speak and who'd do *exactly* as they were told to do."

She winced, having come to the same awful conclusion I had.

"And the worst part of it?"

She visibly braced herself.

"They do *remember* most of what was done to them as Kellesuf—and you wonder why they're so damned, one might even say *fanatically* devoted to me? Because I'm the only gods damned person who's always treated them as if they're human, every bit as human as me and you, and not Kellesuf! I'm the only one who's ever cared a damn about them!"

She glanced back at her guard and he replied with an unhappy, confirming nod. She then wrapped her fingers around my arm and began guiding me away, out of earshot of the Adraniis as she whispered, *"But my people don't know they were Kellesuf—"*

"No, they don't, but it hasn't stopped them from treating them as if they're inferior and simply put, I won't have it!" I looked away, fixed my furious gaze on something inanimate: a small pile of scree, and using all my strength, tamped down my rage. Eithne knew, and Eithne had fully accepted Felix—Eithne in fact *loved* Felix every bit as much as she loved me, of that I had no doubt.

I took a deep, ragged breath and looked back at her. "I should warn you, I just gave Jom an ultimatum to deliver to Borzu. The degrading attitude stops, *this instant*, or your people and mine part company… *tonight!*"

Her eyes widened and her lips parted in shock, rapidly turning to horror.

"I'll take along any of you who want to come, but from here on out, I refuse to let my men risk their lives to protect a pompous lot who think they're better than we are."

She took my hand in hers and gave it a squeeze. "I'm so sorry—"

"I'm not the one who's been treated like shit, Eithne." My eyes flicked to Aetius, who appeared to be totally engrossed telling in some wild yarn to the utter delight of his young audience, the earlier matter forgotten—but I knew Aetius. The look Laatao had given him was burning its way through him. "I'll give your Captain Borzu and the rest some credit—they're *not* stupid. They treat *me* as an equal—at least to my face—but only because they're keenly aware of the fact that *I* hold the key to *their* survival—"

—Which promptly raised another issue: what *would* have happened had I died as Cleander and Felix had feared? Assuming my soldiers didn't massacre the lot in retaliation, would Borzu have been able to manipulate Felix, manipulate my officers, my men into doing his bidding? He was clearly making inroads when I finally came around and was quite adept at playing Felix and I off against each other.

Then it hit me like a punch to the gut: Cleander's greatest fear, Felix's greatest fear, in fact the greatest fear of all of my men was that I *would* die and as a result, they *would* be at the mercy of the Adraniis, a position little better than Kellesuf—no wonder Borzu had been so eager for me to make an appearance, prove to my men I wasn't dead or dying and at the same time stand beside me, visibly and physically supporting me, thus gaining their trust, or at least dispel some of their very reasonable qualms.

Naïve, that's what Cleander had said of Felix. And he was; they all were. Worse, they all knew it.

And I was the most naïve of all, because I'd fallen for Borzu's act as well, and of anyone *I* should have seen through it. No wonder my men were scared—

"Let me go speak to Aetius," Eithne said, stepping away from me.

I made a grab, caught her elbow. *"Leave it."*

She looked up at me.

"I said leave it."

She sighed, ran her finger down my jaw, then wrapped her arm around my waist and gave me a firm hug, mindful of my side. "We're not bad people, Arri. Truly we aren't."

"You and Anachie aren't, I know that. But right now that's as far as I'll go."

"Fair enough. And we'll go with you, if it comes to that, of course we will—but I don't think it will come to that."

"And I don't like the idea of leaving a bunch of defenseless civilians behind for the Si'aafu, but I will if I have to."

"I know." She pressed her fingers to my lips and smiled faintly. "I love you."

I took her hand in mine, kissed her fingertips. "I love you, too." Then I jerked my chin towards Aetius and sighed, "I suppose he could use some help—he's drawn quite a crowd." And indeed he had. What had started out as six children, seven with Anachie, had quickly swelled to over twenty, with more on the way.

Eithne knew a dismissal when she heard it and released her hold on me. "And you?"

"I need to speak with my officers—let them know what's happening. Things could get ugly."

She nodded then started towards Aetius.

"Eithne?"

She stopped, looked back at me.

"Anachie looks like he could use an early night—have Aetius and his friends walk you two back to our sleeping area, all right?"

She nodded and started off again, her guard pausing a moment before following, trying to look as if he wasn't—that had been Felix's order after all: discreet protection, but that had been before, when the precaution was nothing more than a case of being prudent. Now that I'd made my threat, chances of it rebounding was very real.

I waited until she'd joined Aetius, knowing if things did get ugly, she and Anachie would be as safe with him as they would be with me—but just in case… I looked around, caught the eye of another nearby soldier, Libius who clearly had just come off duty and was on his way to his supper and made a quick hand-signal for his eyes only: guard them.

Libius dipped his helmeted head in understanding, concealing the acknowledgement in a languid stretch then he ambled over to the edge of the pool not far from Aetius. He cleared his throat, in the process drawing Aetius' gaze, pointedly flicked his eyes to Eithne then back to Aetius and lightly gripped the pommel of his gladius as if he was doing nothing more than pushing the sword aside, after which he knelt, removed his helmet, then began to splash water on his face and the back of his neck, looking for all the world as if that had been his sole intention.

In turn Aetius looked pointedly at the other two guards who were now seated among the children, acting as if they too wanted to hear a story. In fact it wasn't uncommon to find my men as part of Aetius' appreciative audience, often as not with a child in their lap. This time the band-armor and weapons these two wore quietly discouraged it.

Satisfied, I turned and walked in the opposite direction, towards the fortifications, having a good idea I'd find Rufinius there, possibly Felix and Jotia as well.

— iii —

I lifted my gaze at the sound of approaching footsteps, the soft, repetitive crunch of dry sand under multiple feet.

Rufinius, who'd been seated beside me and vigorously sharpening his sword, lurched to his feet, as did the other grim-faced officers around our small campfire: to my left Felix, Jotia, Cleander and Aetius—he'd joined our meeting late and only after he'd placed Eithne and Anachie under the watchful eyes of Pictor and Auspex, relieving Libius and the other guards;

to my right: Rufinius, Titivillus, Marcus, Aper, Florianus and across the fire from me, my senior infantry centurions: Silvanus, Baculus, Germanus, Duccius, Petronius, Storax, Lupus, Dulcitius and, despite his injuries, Carbo. He'd insisted on attending—demanded in fact and Cleander, surprisingly, had relented.

I remained seated, my own unsheathed gladius resting crosswise on my lap, the translucent Tuatha blade glittering menacingly in the shifting firelight along with my ring mail shirt and silvered phalerae.

"Captain Borzu," Felix said as the man, along with his officers, Jom, Maisoh, Birral, Khouri and Lujaji stopped not far away, at the edge of the shifting fire glow.

"Centurion Felix," Borzu replied then turned to me. "Legate. May we approach?"

I placed my sword on the ground next to me then rose and fixed my hard stare on the man, pointedly ignoring his companions. "Well?"

"It won't happen again," Borzu began and looked at each of my officers in turn. "All I can do at this point is apologize, to each and every one of you and to your men as well. I'd like to say I was blameless, but… in thinking back over my interactions with all of you over the past days I realize I've been just as patronizing as everyone else."

My officers stared back, utterly expressionless and silent, once again Kellesuf to outsiders, each one clearly feeling more comfortable fully armored in that ugly familiarity, a reaction, a reflex that pained and angered me deeply.

Borzu turned to me, hoping, I presume, for a more welcome response but if that was his hope, he was sadly disappointed. "'We're *not* children', you said to me. 'We're just not you—not only that, we don't *want* to be you. Fail to grasp that simple fact at your peril.'"

"Yes, I did," I replied in a calm voice that belied look in my eyes.

"And we did just that."

"Yes. *You* did," I replied pointedly then happened to notice that Carbo was now visibly wobbling despite Dulcitius' steadying hand cupping his elbow, the centurion's fire-lit, sweat-glossy face having gone suddenly quite pale.

I immediately eased myself back down on the ground, motioned everyone to seat or reseat themselves around the fire. Maisoh, I couldn't help but notice, seated herself next to Rufinius, wedging herself in between him and Titivillus as the two men shifted to make room—a clear message to her companions.

I met her gaze, briefly, tipped my head in acknowledgement then again fixed my eyes on Borzu. "So, now what?" I deliberately left off the 'captain' in my reply and my omission wasn't lost on him.

"So now we try to regain the trust and goodwill that we've effectively lost," he answered in an appeasing tone.

As he spoke I heard an all too familiar jingle of empty promises—a sweet sound that left a very sour taste. "*We?*" I picked up my own sword, leaned forward and used the tip to angrily stab at the coal bed. "Again, you mean *you.*"

He opened his mouth but I stared him back into clamp-lipped silence. Point made, I sat back and listened to the blue-green crackle and watched as a spiral of cinders rose high into the night air, briefly rivaling the myriad of stars overhead.

As the last one winked out, I dropped my cold gaze back to Borzu. "We leave before dawn, day after tomorrow—*as planned*. Any of your people who wish to come with us are welcome. Those who prefer to take their chances on their own…we'll leave what foodstuffs we can spare, but I'll warn you now, it won't be much—my sole concern from here on out will be the welfare of my men and those who willingly choose to accompany us; I care little for fools who elect to remain behind and besides, there's still food to be had…" I jerked my chin towards the pool, "for those willing to work for it."

Borzu replied, "We'll pass the word." Realizing there was nothing else to say, he rose, motioning to his officers to do likewise and with a nod to me, he turned and walked away.

The others quickly followed suit—all but Maisoh that is. She remained seated beside Rufinius, her fingers firmly intertwined with his, her other hand on Titivillus' knee.

She looked around the fire, at the faces that stared back—faces that were not altogether friendly. "I'm going with you," she said, as if there'd been any doubt. "Most of us will. The smart ones will. But there'll be some who'll refuse—they've been waiting for any excuse to say, 'See? They're nothing but a bunch of barbarians and we'd be better off without them.' Trouble-makers, the lot."

"I assume Isem is among them?" I asked, drawing her gaze.

"He's their spokesman." She looked around again, making eye contact with each of us, her gaze lingering worriedly on Carbo before moving on. "I am *truly* sorry. And just so you all know that I mean it, Rufinius told me about… well, about you being former Kellesuf…"

There was a ripple of disquiet around the fire; glittering eyes darted to me, briefly to Rufinius and then back to Maisoh.

"...and I don't blame any of you for resenting our treatment of you. But just so you know, I haven't said anything to anyone. I figure it's up to you who you tell and who you don't, but I will say this: it won't matter a whit to most of us. You've all treated us very well, far better than we deserve considering how we've treated you, and I for one am very grateful."

"Think you could find us a few more women who are equally grateful?" That was Florianus and several others made rude noises—including Carbo—instantly lessening the tension.

"Fifteen hundred would do, and do *very* nicely," Germanus added, rubbing his hands together, to which the others nodded their hearty agreement. Even Carbo managed a hopeful smile.

Maisoh laughed, a genuine, warm laugh, not at all offended and watching her, I began to understand what Rufinius had seen in her; maybe she wasn't a crocodile after all. "I'll do my best." Then she sobered and turning to me added, "If Isem and his followers insist on remaining behind, Legate, please *don't* try to dissuade them—"

"Believe me, I *won't*. In fact I've been trying to think of some way that isn't too obvious to encourage them to do just that."

"We could sneak away without telling them," Marcus offered helpfully.

"A possibility," I replied. "Can you imagine Isem waking up to find he was all alone—aside from the ring of Si'aafu standing around him, plates at the ready?"

That garnered a few chuckles—*uneasy* chuckles.

"We'd all certainly be better off without him and his ilk," Maisoh replied. "Some... well, they did things to some of the women, the girls too. Awful things." She lifted her gaze to Aetius. "Laatao was one of them, Centurion. She honestly didn't mean to offend you—she's still deeply traumatized by what happened to her—the men with her, Jom and the rest of her close kin, they meant no harm either, they're just protective of her."

"*Who?*" Aetius replied quietly, his thick fingers toying with the grip of his sheathed gladius.

"Who's responsible you mean?" Maisoh shook her head. "I don't know, Centurion, truly. She won't say—none of them will."

"Give her a message from me," he growled, "ask her to point out who it was and I'll make sure he won't bother her again, *ever.*"

Silvanus added, "Same goes for the rest of us—just point and we'll take it from there." That was followed by an ugly murmur of agreement from the others.

"Just make sure they understand it will go equally bad for them if they falsely accuse someone," I added. Fair's fair after all.

"Of course." She looked around her, at the ring of somber, fire-lit faces that stared back but this time with far less hostility. "And thank you, gentlemen. I'll tell her; I'll tell the others. I doubt any will take you up on your offer—but I'm sure they'll appreciate the gesture."

"Because the perpetrators were never properly dealt with," I added.

"It was... *agreed* that it would only make matters worse. And I'm ashamed to admit I thought that was true at the time. I don't now."

"Assure the women they and their children *are* safe with us. Once your people came under my protection, they also came under my brand of justice and any such abuse will *not* be tolerated."

She nodded.

I motioned around me. "These are my officers. Carbo is on the far right," I said by way of introduction, in the process drawing everyone's attention to the man's sweat-streaked and strained face.

"This is the first chance I've had to say thank you for tending to my injuries," he said in a weak and raspy voice that sounded nothing like him.

"You were a model patient, Centurion," Maisoh replied as she smiled warmly at him, to which Felix muttered,

"Unlike someone else."

I pointedly ignored the comment and the muffled but clearly forced chuckles it garnered as I flicked Cleander a sidelong glance; he responded with a shrug as if to say, 'You called for an officers' council, what do you expect?' Then I continued, "and next to Carbo is Dulcitius, who you also know, then Lupus, Petronius, Duccius, Germanus, Baculus and lastly, Silvanus on the left."

Maisoh pulled her own worried gaze off Carbo, nodded to the others and said, "Good evening, gentlemen."

They murmured their good evenings in return.

"And you're welcome to join us anytime, Maisoh," I continued. "In fact I encourage you to join us when we discuss plans. Your input and insight would be most welcome." I expected to hear at least one gasp, but everyone remained politely silent and while perhaps inwardly aghast at the idea of a woman being a part of our officers' council, none were willing to voice it openly. Maybe it was Maisoh—with her publicly defiant stance against her fellow officers she'd certainly forced me to revise my opinion of her upwards. Perhaps the same was true of the others.

Then again, maybe it was Rufinius. No one who knew Rufinius wanted to cross him and offending his ladylove would be a one-way trip to his *very* wrong side.

I looked around at the fire-lit faces of my officers, my friends. "We still have much to do, and only one day left in which to do it, so I suggest we all get something to eat, then get off to our beds—Carbo, you're to return to the medical wagon…"

I expected him to protest, but he surprised me when he replied hoarsely, "Yes, Legate," and then with Lupus and Dulcitius' help, lurched unsteadily to his feet.

With nods and smiles, everyone rose then the group began to disperse—Rufinius and Maisoh heading off in a direction opposite to that taken by the rest, while Carbo, with Cleander and Lupus' assistance, staggered towards the nearest medical wagon. Within a few minutes only Felix remained—along with two soldiers who had, as if by magic, appeared out of the gathering darkness, our guards for the night.

I looked at him.

He stared back, said, "I think it might be prudent to post extra sentries around the supply wagons, the medical wagons—just in case someone decides to do something stupid."

"Agreed."

He motioned further up the gorge. "Eithne and Anachie are over by that cook fire—how 'bout you join them for dinner? I'll set up the extra patrols."

What he was offering went beyond the obvious. In truth I wasn't in the least bit hungry. I was far more interested in sleep. But I knew if I didn't at least put in an appearance and ate something, I could plan on a lecture from Eithne followed by a visit from Cleander. So, I smiled and nodded and headed for the cook fire as Felix headed off in the opposite direction, each soldier attaching himself to one of us.

Eithne, Anachie and the soldiers who'd gathered around the fire greeted me with warm smiles, the few Adraniis present also murmured their good evenings, but with a little more circumspection—clearly word *had* already spread. Whether their reticence was over my threat, or that Eithne and I were now definitely a couple I cannot tell you, and to be honest, I really didn't give a damn—fact was fact and I was that tired, that achy and in no mood to make excuses.

An Adranii tending the cook pot offered me a bowl of boiled shrimp, which I took and ate, if not heartily, than at least enough to satisfy Eithne and please the cook. And once I'd had my fill, a soldier handed me a mug of fire-warmed wine, which I drained completely.

I'd hoped this meant I could make my excuses and slip away, back to our sleeping spot, but the cook insisted in engaging me in light conversation as she and her two elderly helpers served up steaming bowls to crowds of hungry soldiers just coming off watch, along with a scattering of Adranii men—her way of easing the awkwardness I suppose and making me feel welcome.

In turn I answered her questions politely and complimented her cooking, having no desire to add to the perception that I was little more than petty, barbarian tyrant. In the process I clearly pleased Eithne by my good behavior, but I was tired, damned tired and both Eithne and the cook were beginning to realize that; now that I had some food and wine in me if I lingered much longer I'd fall asleep standing up—and I wasn't the only one. Anachie had already taken matters into his own hands and had curled up at my feet.

"I think I best get you two to bed before I have to carry both of you," Eithne murmured in my ear.

Salvation! I nodded and as she said her goodnights, I managed to scooped up Anachie without waking him. Together we walked back to our sleeping spot, Anachie cradled in my arms with Eithne's arm around my waist, offering comfort, not to mention guidance as I was suddenly so muzzy-headed, I'd forgotten exactly where we'd left our bedrolls. Our guards dutifully and silently followed.

I knelt, carefully placed Anachie on the blanket beside me, leaving room for Eithne as well, then I sprawled out beside him, suddenly and overwhelmingly exhausted…

…and stood there, paralyzed as I watched Cerialis and his officers flee in panicked retreat, leaving the rest of us behind to die for their folly.

I shook myself out of my shock and began bellowing orders to regroup—

"ARRI!"

—I wheeled around, towards Felix's frantic scream, only to confront the full horror of our situation: Iceni were pouring out of the surrounding forest en masse, screaming at the tops of their lungs—

"Arri—"

I flinched from the voice, from the spear driven into my shoulder with enough force to send me staggering and my mind reeling.

"Arri…!"

I gasped and my eyes snapped open—only to find Eithne leaning over me, her worried face frosted with starlight.

"Are you all right?" she whispered, her fingers tightly clutching my bad shoulder.

Still panting, I lifted my head and glanced around, wild-eyed in my panic.

"Arri?" She released her hold on my shoulder, ran her fingers down my jaw and I jerked my eyes back to her. *"Are you all right?"*

I knew where I was now; more importantly, I knew where I'd been: back in that accursed bog, watching my friends, watching Felix die.

"Arri, I said, are you all right?" she asked as she gave my shoulder a gentle, but insistent shake.

I swallowed convulsively then managed, *"Yeah... yeah, I'm all right."*

I must have sounded less than convincing, going by her doubtful expression.

After a moment she said, *"That was a truly terrible nightmare."*

I felt my heart, which had just begun to settle, start to race again—could she eavesdrop on my thoughts, my dreams, just like Turan? *"What... what do you mean?"*

"You were thrashing about, groaning... it sounded as if you were in terrible pain." She hesitated, then asked, "Are you sure you're all right? Should I send for Cleander?"

I shook my head, briefly relieved, then another thought, equally worrisome and I glanced around me. "Where's Anachie—"

"With Felix." She glanced over her shoulder and I peered into the star-lit night to find Felix on his side, fast asleep and facing us, Anachie safely ensconced in his arms, also sound asleep. I fixed my eyes on Felix, on his relaxed face, watched his flank rise and fall as he breathed, listened to his familiar wheezing snore... satisfying myself it *was* just a dream; that I was in fact staring at a very much alive, albeit sound asleep Felix.

Just not the same Felix I'd just seen die—had seen die so many, many times.

I turned my anxious attention back to Eithne. "I didn't strike you, did I?"

She shook her head. "Just scared me."

"I do that—ask Felix. I don't mean to—"

"I'm sure you don't, but point taken."

I struggled to sit up; Eithne slipped her arm behind me, helped me the rest of the way then I dropped my head into my hands and took a deep, heaving breath as she stroked my sweat-soaked back.

After a few minutes I lifted my head and ran my shaky fingers through my equally sweat-drenched hair.

She lightly stroked my cheek, murmured, "Want to talk about it?"

"Rather not if it's all the same to you."

She sighed, then: "Think you can get back to sleep?"

"Not... not this moment, no."

She produced a mug. "Water. Drink—all of it."

I took it and downed its contents in two loud wincing gulps, then handed it back to her.

"Hungry?"

This time I only shook my head as I squinted up at the sky. The whirlpool was directly overhead, which meant I'd been asleep for hours... and I didn't even remember falling asleep.

She wrapped her arm around me and I leaned into her and exhaled wearily.

"What am I to do with you?" she whispered into my ear as she combed her fingers through my hair.

I eased myself out of her embrace and favored her with a sidelong, arched look.

"I have an idea," she said and pressed her lips to mine and as I responded tentatively—I had no idea where she was going with this but I was also suddenly, desperately in need of this kind of comfort—I felt her slip both hands up under my tunic; she made quick work of my breeches' lacings, followed by skillfully undoing the near tie on my underwear, then withdrawing one hand, she slipped the other down into my loosened clothing.

"Lie... down," she murmured between kisses.

I didn't have to be asked twice, but quickly realizing she wasn't planning on just a quick grope, but intent on completing the act, I stammered, "We... we need... need to... to find a place—"

She very reluctantly lifted her gaze to meet mine, murmured, "Are you telling me you're shy?"

"No, I'm just not a damned exhibitionist..."

"It's dark—no one can see us," she replied as she continued her fondling, unmoved, which is more than I can say for me.

"Not that dark, and Anachie—"

"Is sound asleep, as is Felix. So as long as we don't make a lot of noise—"

"Oh, gods," I groaned.

"Shhhh!" She hissed but didn't stop what she was doing—what the hell did she expect? Damn the woman—I'm just flesh and blood!

"Hard n-n-not to... to make n-n-noise with y-you d-d-doing that."

"Want me to stop?"

Hell if I did. "I... I find it m-m-more en...enjoyable... if we s-s-sat... satisfy each... e-e-each other at the... t-t-the s-s-same... same time."

That got her attention and she stopped doing what she'd been doing long enough for my tongue to untie itself.

"What do you propose?"

"What the hell do you think?"

"Then let's go for a... stroll." She got to her feet and offered me her hands.

"Stroll?"

"Yeah, around the pool."

I eyed her as I quickly retied my clothing, then I grabbed her proffered hands and with her help lurched to my feet—and immediately regretted my offer to take care of her needs while she took care of mine. Parts of me that needed to be stiff suddenly weren't any longer and other parts that needed to be loose *had* stiffened up.

She wrapped her arm around my waist. "A stroll, first, remember?" As if reading my thoughts added, "That'll loosen you up," as she gave my butt a not-so-gentle squeeze, then, tugging my hand, she led me away from our sleeping spot and towards the pool.

As we began our "stroll", arm-in-arm, and caught the eye of soldiers coming from or going on picket duty, Eithne and I nodded and murmured our good evenings and to my great surprise, and yes, to my mounting chagrin, I saw knowing smiles, even encouraging grins in reply; even the handful of Adraniis we met looked intensely pleased rather than resentful. It was if they were all in on the seduction of the legate—and hell, maybe they were. Maybe they realized I needed an anchor just as desperately as they all needed me to be theirs—or more likely hoped such a union would go a long way to repair the damage done to our nascent and still very fragile alliance.

We walked by the medical wagons and overheard the soft murmur of voices from within—my physicians still at work tending to the wounded. To my immense relief I overheard Khouri's distinctive voice politely arguing a point with Nestor of all people and even more shocking, Nestor being *civil* in return—while I wondered where we were going.

Eithne clearly knew but had no intention of telling me. Within a few minutes her destination became obvious. She steered me towards a cleft in the rocks not far from the large fissure and waterfall and well beyond the reach of the shifting glow of the nearest campfire.

Within the cleft was an even smaller hollow—she let go of my hand just long enough to step closer and peer around—and once assured it was unoccupied, she again grabbed my hand and drew me inside. It was more than big enough for a couple to take care of what needed to be taken care of and in complete privacy with the rushing sounds of the nearby waterfall masking any complimentary but completely involuntary noises. There was even a large scrap of canvas, already laid out on a thick, but noticeably flattened bed of recently cut grass.

I looked down at her, and slowly arched my brow.

"We're obviously not the first—"

"Obviously."

"—in fact I think once this spot was found, it's been in almost continual use." She grinned again, patted my arm. "It's a *good* sign, Arri—a very *healthy* sign—everyone's starting to come to the realization that we might just make it and they want to affirm that in the most basic way possible—and I include a goodly number of your soldiers in that observation."

So, the day's fishing *had* netted more than a few eels....

She gave my wrist an insistent tug, murmured, "Come along, no more stalling," and drew me deeper into the small fissure. Once we were hidden from view, she wasted no time in disrobing. I watched, transfixed then, at her prompting sidelong glance, quickly followed suit, tossing my hastily discarded clothing on top of hers.

The combined cold glow of the whirlpool and starlight washed over her pale skin—it made her appear as if she was a statue carved from the finest alabaster, until she moved, until I felt her warm skin against mine.

She smelled of sweet grass; I smelled of sweat—

"Maybe I should go wash up."

She grinned, jerked me tight against her. "Later."

So, well. If she wasn't put off my body's less than pristine condition, who was I to argue? I pressed my lips against hers and eagerly fondled her breasts, her buttocks—she inhaled sharply, which of course only encouraged me.

"Down," I managed between passionate kisses.

She didn't have to be asked twice.

I immediately followed and using my knees, my hands, I wedged her legs as far apart as was comfortable for her then I sat back on my haunches. I took her in, savoring the moment, planning my attack while she watched me, her chest rising and falling in irregular gasps. It was incredibly tempting to do what she expected. It would certainly have satisfied me, and maybe, if I could last long enough—a *big* if—it might satisfy her, but that was *not* the plan. This was my chance to do it right and proper, just as Felix would once he'd exhausted all of his pent up energy—and I made a note to myself to speak to him, to make sure he knew to always take care of her needs as well as his and if he was smart, as I was, to take care of her needs, *first*. And maybe, if asked I'd even teach him a thing or two. And speaking of…

I gave her the lightest tickle with my fingers, just so. Her eyes widened, her mouth parted. I explored her, ever so slowly, front to back, probing gently, savoring the sudden dampness. Meeting her gaze, I slipped a finger into her and got as my reward a shudder and low moan of delight. Two fingers, then three, as deep as I could go.

She grabbed fistfuls of the blanket as she groaned and ground her hips.

Her suggestive hip motion and her moaning had the desired effect on me as I continued to slide my fingers in and out. She was panting now, her skin glistening with sweat, her hands clenched. She was staring up at me in intense anticipation.

I grinned, slipped my hands under her and lifted her hips up, urging her to wrap her legs around my neck then I proceeded to show her *exactly* what I'd been taught by the harlots of Carthage.

Only after I'd thoroughly satisfied her and then some did I take care of my own needs, which in truth didn't take long—I was more than primed after all—after which I eased myself down beside her, both of us utterly spent.

"That… that was incredible…" she managed, breathing hard. "I've never—I mean, where… where the hell'd you learn to do that?"

"From the very best."

"I would say so."

I rolled onto my back and she wrapped herself around me. Resting her head on my shoulder, she reached across my belly and slowly ran her hand down the row of stitches on my opposite flank. "They're quite… prickly."

"You should feel them from the *inside.*"

She lifted her head, looked at me and made a face. "Ugh!" Point made, she again rested her head on my shoulder and while she toyed with the beads on my necklace, the amulet and signaculum, I stared up at what was visible of the massive whirlpool and savored the feel of her warm body entwined with mine.

Then it hit me: I belonged *here*, on Latruncŭli, with the Adraniis and my men, with Felix, and most of all with Anachie and Eithne—best of all I *knew* my feelings were well and truly *mine*—not urges, emotions imposed on me.

I wanted to make this world ours and ours alone, hold it against all who would take it away from us—yes, I'd said those words before, to Felix, Aetius and Rufinius, and I thought I meant it. Now I *knew* I meant it—now I had a damned good reason to want to hold it, at all costs, against anyone who might try to take it from us—or us from it.

And something else, something equally important: the grip Turan had on me, the grip Earth had on me, the grip that cursed bog had on me suddenly loosened, then, as I fully realized what was happening, all abruptly let... *go*.

I thought it would hurt and instinctively tensed. But in fact the sensation was no more than a finger-light touch that slid across my bare skin and then was gone—

"Arri...?"

I blinked, refocused my watery gaze on the whirlpool, on the brilliant spot of flotsam.

"Arri?"

I slowly turned my head, my eyes locking with Eithne's as she levered herself up on an elbow to stare down at me.

"Are you all right?" She lightly touched my lips, my jaw.

I rolled over on top of her, suddenly possessive. "Never better."

She kissed my lips then ran her fingers through my hair as I eagerly nuzzled her breasts, but her voice, when she spoke, was still clearly worried. "One of these days I hope you'll feel safe enough you can tell me where you go."

I lifted my head to meet her gaze. "Go?"

"Just now—you were somewhere else. And earlier—that was no run of the mill nightmare."

"I'm sorry." And I was, truly; she deserved my undivided attention when we were alone. She'd get it from now on.

She ran her finger down my cheek then tugged at my lower lip. "I love you."

I smiled, kissed her on the nose. "I love you too."

Her full lips drew back in an intensely relieved smile, as if I'd just handed her the world—maybe in some ways I had—and kissed me firmly on the lips.

It was so damned tempting to take her again—so I did. And a little later, I did again. And sometime after that... well, it was getting late; Felix might have awakened, wondered where we'd gone—no, he'd have a damned good idea what we were doing, if he didn't know exactly where we were, but knowing Felix, he'd start to worry and then he'd come looking. In many ways it was like having two children to worry about now.

I reluctantly got an elbow under me, said, "We'd better get back before Felix mounts a search party." Besides, I'd matched his record. No need to best him—it wasn't like we were in competition or anything.

"The guards know exactly where we are," she replied as she managed to get to her feet.

Guards? I looked up at her, my shock clearly written on my face.

"You mean you thought we came here unaccompanied?"

I staggered to my feet. "You... you knew?"

"You mean you didn't? You're the one who felt the need for bodyguards... and one could argue what better time to spring an attack than when two prime targets are, um, fully occupied?"

I gave myself a shake. "I hope they plugged their ears."

She grinned as she lightly ran her fingers over my naked body. "You didn't make *that* much noise."

"But you certainly did."

"And how is that *my* fault?"

I smiled, a decidedly smug smile. "Point taken."

She giggled at that.

I looked down at myself then at her—just looking at her naked body sent fresh thoughts racing through me. "How about a quick rise off in the waterfall?" While a quick wash up sounded like a good idea, it was actually the chilling effect of the mist and water I was after.

"Let's make sure you didn't pop open, first." She turned my injured side into the frosty starlight and peered at the scabbed over wounds while she again carefully palpated the still lividly bruised area. "You've healed remarkably well."

"You sound just like your best friend Cleander."

She lifted her gaze to meet mine. "Meaning?"

"Meaning you sound surprised."

"That *was* you working on the fortifications, wasn't it? It *was* you who went galloping off, who knows where a few days ago… and it *was* you who climbed that ladder when we thought we were being attacked?"

"Yes," I replied slowly.

"I rest my case."

"So do I."

She chuckled and taking my hand in hers, she led me over to the cave opening. A quick glance around satisfied us both that wherever the guards were they weren't visible—to us. But they *were* nearby, of that I had no doubt. On the upside, their presence certainly guaranteed that another couple with similar plans wouldn't have interrupted us.

She then drew me out into the open and quickly over to the pool at the base of the waterfall.

Even the mist was bracing and I was shivering by the time we actually stepped under the narrow ribbon of the waterfall proper, but it still felt wonderful—even better when Eithne took it upon herself to scrub my skin, my hair, using her hands, her fingers to do the job.

Finally she stepped back, looked me up and down, nodded her satisfaction then motioned to me, as if to leave, to reclaim our clothing.

I had other ideas.

I grabbed her, pulled her, giggling, back under the waterfall, then I wrapped my arms around her and as she buried her face in my chest, I rested my chin on the top of her head and closed my eyes, my body shielding hers from the sting of the water. And as the thin stream pummeled my shoulders and back into an all over and decidedly delicious numbness, I realized that for the very first time in my life, I was utterly, completely and blissfully… *happy.*

XIII

"Arri…?"

"Enough, Eithne," I mumbled irritably and buried my face in the crook of my arm; the damned woman was insatiable! "I can't manage it again…"

A hand gave my shoulder a quick, determined shake then immediately let go. "Arri…! Dammit, wake up!"

Felix? My eyes snapped open at his urgent, whispered voice.

"Are you awake?"

I lifted my head and glanced over my shoulder. It *was* Felix, and Aetius was with him. *Gods…*

I covered my embarrassment with a growled, "I am now."

Felix replied softly, "We have a problem."

His tone of voice sent a shiver down my spine. If I hadn't been fully awake before, I was now, damned if I wasn't.

I rolled over, managed to sit up—careful not to wake Eithne or Anachie as the two were curled up under my cloak—and angrily raking my hair out of my eyes, glanced around.

The camp was dark; the mirror-still water of the pool aglitter with a thousand stars, the surrounding grassy slope dotted with hundreds and hundreds of wheezing mounds—the sleeping forms of our people.

"Problem?" All looked peaceful, but as I well knew, looks can be deceiving—

"Something just flew overhead."

I jerked my worried eyes off the camp, my unease at what mischief Isem and his buddies might be up to and looked skyward, my heart suddenly in my throat. "What?" I gasped, matching Felix's strained whisper.

"One of our pickets spotted something—the Adranii with him said it looked like a ship of some sort—too high to definitely identify it as it passed over, but whatever it was, it was big—"

Warned by the faint, metallic hiss of swords being slipped from scabbards, I glanced back at my bodyguards, found they were now holding their swords at the ready, then followed their pointed stares: two men were moving quickly but quietly towards us, threading their way through those fast asleep on the grassy slope. As they neared us I recognized them as Borzu and Jom by their builds alone.

At my hand signal, the guards returned their weapons to their scabbards, but remained tense, ready for any unexpected move on the part of the Adranii captain and his second.

Borzu nodded warily to the guards then squatted beside me. "Felix tell you?"

"Yeah." I took Aetius' proffered hand and he jerked me to my feet as Borzu likewise rose. Once standing I motioned for everyone to step well away from the sleeping Eithne and Anachie, to keep our voices to a whisper as I turned to Borzu. "What do you think it is?"

"If we're lucky it was just a shooting star our startled sentries mistook for something else."

"And if we aren't... 'lucky'?"

"It was a low-flying Si'aafu scout doing recon."

I flicked the otherwise tranquil night sky another anxious and now furious glance. *"Shit—"*

"Legate," Borzu interrupted, "if you'll permit me a suggestion?"

I nodded unhappily; I'd be a fool to ignore any guidance about creatures I knew little about, even if that advice was coming from Borzu, a man who'd yet to redeem himself in my eyes, a man I didn't trust—

"We need to stay put and out of sight for the time being. If it was indeed the Si'aafu, they'll be hard pressed to spot us in this deep gorge and even at this hour the surrounding rock is still putting off enough heat to mask our presence unless they look directly down on us, which is pretty unlikely—but, just in case, I've sent Birral and several of our men to douse the coal beds, and until we're sure they've moved on in their search, I'd strongly advise we not light any more fires."

"According to the sentries," Jom added, drawing my sidelong scowl, "our trail has been obliterated by the sandstorms—so, if it is the Si'aafu, they won't know which direction we took. For all they know, we might have gone east, back to our—meaning Adranii—campsite and then maybe deeper into those mountains."

It would have been a reasonable choice; the Adraniis' camp did have a known water source after all. And maybe some of their foot tracks, the wheel ruts of their baggage carts as they left the valley on their way to do battle, even bits of refuse left behind might still be visible in wind-protected spots, more clues to throw the Si'aafu off our track. It was, after all, one of the reasons why I chose *not* to go in that direction.

"Or they might fall for our ruse," Borzu said with a smug smile, "believe the message and go in search of their fellow Si'aafu."

I glanced at Felix, at Aetius and I had little doubt the same worry had occurred to them: what if *this* was indeed another ruse by Borzu, one to fool *us* into thinking the Si'aafu were near and on the hunt, forcing us to stay here, rather than decamp as planned and leave some of their number behind. The timing, if nothing else, was highly suspicious.

I crossed my arms and gave the sky another careful sweep with my narrowed eyes as I chewed on my lip, mulling over our options—*my* options. What Borzu said made sense—assuming he was telling the truth and had no hand in the 'sighting'.

"So," I began glumly as Birral, Lujaji and two other Adraniis as well as Rufinius, Maisoh and Rufinius' second, Dulcitius silently joined us, "we stay here, at least for now, but I want the wagons pushed up against the walls of the gorge—and gather more scrub to cover them completely—the engines as well, break up their outlines—"

"And tether the animals out of sight," Borzu interrupted, "inside the fissure if possible—that'll certainly throw off any heat signature."

I looked at him and as I did so I came to the disheartening realization that at least for the near term I had no choice but to rely on this man's admitted limited expertise on the Si'aafu to keep everyone safe and at the same time deal with the persistent, niggly feeling that he very well might be manipulating us. I knew we'd be no match for the Si'aafu if or when they came, even with our engines, our cavalry. Lady Ainiaan had told me they employed advanced technology—just like the Faoimhuir but with none of those pesky restrictions imposed by treaty—and possessed weapons that were simply beyond my imagining. "Is that good or bad?" I replied irritably.

"Good, Legate," Birral answered. "Definitely good. The Si'aafu will try to locate us using our body heat. But between the suns' heat, absorbed by the surrounding rock by day and given off by night, and keeping the animals behind the waterfall... it'll make it that much more difficult for them to home in on our heat signal."

"Maybe we should move the wounded, along with the women and children into the fissure as well," Felix suggested.

"And make sure the other entrance is properly barricaded, just in case," Rufinius added.

"But no so as to slow our escape if it comes to that," Felix countered as I again looked up at the sky.

Two-thirds of the whirlpool was now behind the western lip of the gorge, which meant we were only a few hours away from dawn. I'd seen the inside of that fissure myself, was loath to trust the women, children and the wounded to its crumbling roof, its leaning walls—it could just as easily become a death trap as an escape route of last resort. I looked at Borzu and found it extremely galling to ask, "What do you suggest, Captain?"

"I agree with Centurion Felix. Get the wounded, along with the women and children into the fissure—if it is the Si'aafu, it's unlikely they'll employ concussive or explosive weapons that could accidentally collapse it. They want us alive—"

"Of course they might not realize over half our number is in that fissure," Aetius interrupted, "and believe they're only blocking off our escape route, trapping us here... sir."

"True," Borzu said, turning to me, "but if given the choice, Legate, and as truly terrible as it is, I'd rather our people die in a cave-in than be taken by the Si'aafu."

It was indeed a terrible choice, which was in fact no choice at all.

I took a deep breath, exhaled slowly as I looked around me. "I agree."

For the brief time I'd spent alone with Eithne the evening before I'd forgotten just how truly precarious our situation was; we'd found food, water and shelter—more than any of us could have hoped for. I'd even permitted myself the rare indulgence of thinking about a life with Eithne, of watching Anachie grow up, of fathering lots of children, Felix too, of having a future, a family—and now we were facing what we'd all feared: the Si'aafu.

Real or ruse, it didn't matter; just the threat was enough to send my heart pounding against my ribs.

As if reading my thoughts, Borzu said, "We're incredibly fortunate to have left the hill camp when we did—had we remained there, and if this is indeed the Si'aafu, we'd already be in their grasp—we're all still alive and that's entirely due to you, Legate."

Aetius nodded, placed his hand on my shoulder and gave it a squeeze. "Indeed."

The others immediately echoed that sentiment, not that it brightened my black mood, not in the least. As far as I was concerned, all I'd done was delay our grisly fate a day or two.

"What's happening?" That from a new voice, a sleepy *female* voice: *Eithne*. She appeared beside me, wrapped her arm around my waist and reached for Felix's hand then looked up at my bleak face, at Felix's.

"Scouts believe they saw a Si'aafu craft fly overhead not long ago," I replied, matter-of-factly.

She tightened her hold on us as her now very frightened eyes searched the sky above.

"We're going to move all the women, children and the wounded into the fissure," Felix said as the other men silently backed away as if they suddenly had business elsewhere, "at least for the time being. You and Anachie will be safe there—understand? *Safe.*"

She dropped her gaze to him, then me and managed a thin smile. "What do you need me to do?"

I kissed the top of her head then slipping from her embrace, murmured, "Start waking people up—tell them not to light fires, to make as little noise as possible, stay near the walls of the gorge and for the women and children to start moving into the fissure. No need for panic."

"Cleander will need help with the injured—"

"I'm sure he will, but you're to stay with Anachie, stay with the rest of the women and children. You can help with the wounded once they've been moved."

Her smile vanished, replaced by a tightening of the lips.

"Just do exactly as I—" I glanced at Felix and at his nod, dropped my gaze back to her, "—as *we* tell you—all right?"

She continued to stare up at me. "Is this the way it's always going to be? Two against one?"

"We're at war—you expected it to be different?" I replied, perhaps a little more harshly than I'd intended.

"Right now we need to focus our attention on what needs to be done to protect everyone," Felix said, and to my chagrin far more gently, "the last thing Arri or I need is to be distracted by worrying about where you and Anachie are."

"But—"

"Want to rethink your decision?" I interrupted. "I wouldn't think less of you if you did."

"Are *you* having second thoughts?"

"No, *absolutely* not," I answered firmly.

"No," Felix echoed as she turned to him, shaking his blond head for emphasis. "But we want you to fully understand what you're getting yourself into, getting Anachie into. If the Si'aafu attack, Arri and I will be in the thick of it—"

"I wouldn't expect you two to do anything but lead the charge if it comes to that."

And I suddenly did feel those second thoughts—because she was right, which meant she had picked two men who each had a much higher than average chance of being killed in any confrontation with the Si'aafu.

It was tempting to order Felix to take charge of the wounded, the women and children—keep him as safe as Eithne and the others, but one look at his face and her's and I nixed the idea. In truth none of us were safe; if I failed…well, no need to state the obvious.

"Let's hope it doesn't come to that." I motioned with my chin towards the silent group now standing some distance away. "Captain Borzu says this is a huge planet. The dust storms have covered our tracks and we're very well hidden in this gorge. Chances are, if that was a Si'aafu ship, they didn't find what they were looking for and have moved on—with luck they won't be back."

"Do you honestly believe that?" she replied.

I shrugged, smiled feebly. "No, but I was hoping you would."

She stood on tiptoe, kissed me on the lips then without warning, without even any damnèd provocation, she punched me in the gut, not hard, but enough to leave me blinking and spluttering in surprise.

"Wha-what the—!"

"Always tell me the truth, all right?" She wheeled on Felix, her small hand still balled into a fist. "That goes for you, too. You can bend the truth with Anachie while he's young, but *only* to protect him. You two *always* tell *me* the truth." She turned back to me. *"Got it?"*

"Are you going to hit me again?" I whined, guarding my belly with my hands.

"I will if you don't agree, only this time it'll be a *lot* harder and I'll definitely aim *lower."*

I instinctively backed up a step.

"Agreed?"

I exhaled. "Agreed."

She looked sharply at Felix.

"Agreed," he replied with a hasty nod.

"Then come here." She pointed to the ground in front of her and we both dutifully stepped close and she wrapped an arm around each of us, drawing us even closer. "I love both of you with all of my heart—always remember that."

"I love you too," I replied, "and you damned well better not forget it."

"Yeah, same goes for me," Felix said.

She briefly tightened her hold, then released us and looked over her shoulder at the camp, said, "Best start waking people up," and began to walk away.

I swallowed hard, took several steps after her, said, "Eithne?"

She stopped and looked back at me.

I fished around inside my tunic, withdrew the bead necklace with the raw silver, four pointed star and slipped it over my head. "For you, and when he's old enough, for Anachie."

She took it from my outstretched hand and looked into my eyes, her own suddenly aglitter.

"It's always kept me safe."

"Hadn't you ought to keep it then?" She tried to hand it back.

"I want… I want to give you something. Aside from my armor, that's all I have—in fact it's all I can claim is truly mine—I've worn it since I was a boy. Now I want you to have it."

She hesitated.

"Please."

She stared up at me, nodded and I immediately plucked it from her hand and draped it around her neck, the crudely made star settling against her tunic, between her breasts and twinkling as she breathed. She touched the star, touched each of the beads, murmured, "It's beautiful," and again stood on tiptoe and kissed me on the lips. She then walked back to where Felix stood, empty-handed and clearly unhappy about it and kissed him with equal passion then hurried back to where she'd left the sleeping Anachie.

— ii —

The day passed without any further sightings but the strain took a heavy toll on everyone: while the previous two days had drawn to a close with full bellies and the happy chatter and squeals of children, this day ended as it had begun, with oppressive silence and furtive glances skyward; of the Adranii men densely crowded into the gorge's many narrow side clefts— the very same clefts that had served as trysting spots now provided cover for their ragtag ranks, each man tightly clutching his sword or spear as if he'd prove a credible opponent to the Si'aafu; of the womenfolk and children occasionally peering out from the darkness of deep fissure, the entrance and exit now thickly guarded by cavalrymen, temporarily bereft of their sequestered mounts.

The engine crews had suffered the worst of all, spending the entire day hunkered down next to their machines under the makeshift camouflage of ocher stained canvas and bits of dry scrub, while our archers kept themselves well-hidden within rockfall of the promontory. The bulk of the infantry had spent the long hours pressed up against the gorge's steep walls, a single, snaking line that ringed the base of the overhanging walls of the gorge, effectively as invisible as the rest, unless someone looked directly down on us.

Aside from the cavalry, none of the soldiers wore armor—not even helmets, only their leather tunics but this was no concession to the suffocating heat. I was not about to risk a metallic glint drawing unwanted attention, but their armor was within easy reach, hidden under bedrolls that in turn were covered in clumps of soil. The only movement among the ranks had been that of water buckets and food baskets passing down the line, a regular necessity for anyone forced to endure the full intensity of the strength-sapping heat for hours on end.

It would have been impossible to keep soldiers at the peak of readiness for such an extended period—even former Kellesuf had their limits—so by mid-morning and at Felix's order, men began taking turns catching a nap: every third soldier sat down, tucked himself up against the rock wall and dozed for an hour, then they'd the switch—a ripple that passed down both sides of the gorge, all done in complete silence and with almost mechanical precision.

Borzu, who had been standing beside me and next to Felix had watched the first change off, clearly fascinated by the seamless perfection as the changeover moved down the ranks, then he cast Felix a questioning stare; Felix explained it away by saying it was just another example of Roman military discipline. This appeared to both satisfy and deeply impress Borzu, but the moment he shifted his attention to something else, Felix flicked me a worried look.

I nodded my understanding, made a quick, subtle hand gesture only one of my soldiers would understand—'we'll talk later'—then I turned back to the business at hand, and that business was a day—a very *long* Latrunculi day—spent in fretful, sweat-drenched immobility with only the occasional dry mouthful of hardtack, chased down by a gulp of warm water to keep our bellies from cramping too painfully against the ceaseless tension.

Now the day that had seemed endless was in fact drawing to a close, the late afternoon ushered in by an unusually powerful dust storm, which for several heart pounding minutes left us utterly blind and buffeted and unable to hear anything above the wind's abnormally high-pitched and warbling shriek, but it finally moved on and once the dust settled, the desert looked even more polished and pristine and I looked upon the approaching night with a mixture of weary relief and gnawing unease. What if this had all been as a result of a false alarm… or worse, a poorly considered and desperate ruse on the part of the Adraniis to keep us here? Such a concept gave me a sharp twinge in my gut and added to the already painful throb behind my eyes.

I rubbed my belly and then my eyes in response. For now all that really mattered was that a temporary reprieve from our physical woes, in the guise of nightfall, was fast approaching.

The floor of gorge behind us was already cloaked in darkness, the waterfall and its swirling cloud of mist cooling the air while cleansing it of the lingering haze and grit of the storm—a blessed relief for everyone—while the desert beyond was rapidly turning from an eye-dazzling orange to deep amethyst as inky shadows cast by the rugged mountains behind us slowly stretched outwards, eager to snatch the land from the searing light of day.

Only the very tallest spire among the distant eastern peaks still burned with the eerie light of Latrunculi's twin suns and as I stared at it I was suddenly reminded of the Pharos of Alexandria.

After I'd murdered my wealthy benefactor—a desperate act of self-defense I must stress—I'd escaped from Carthage aboard the merchant ship *Aequitas* bound for Egypt. And it was aboard the *Aequitas* and while still quite far out to sea that I first experienced the marvel that was the Pharos—I'd assumed it was a low-riding evening star it was so bright, but the ship's cook, Niger, assured me it was no natural phenomena or the act of a god, that it was in fact the handiwork of man. I didn't believe him at first; Niger was well known to tug at the legs of the naïve after all—I was about as naïve as they came when it came to seamanship and he'd hoodwinked me on countless occasions.

But seeing the Pharos up close, in the clear light of a balmy autumn morning as the *Aequitas* sailed into Alexandria's teeming port and realizing it was just as Niger said it was did not diminish its magic, in fact the fact that it was built by men made it even more astonishing in its ability to cast light far, far out to sea.

Later, as a teenager in the house of Lady Ilissia I'd spent many a night gazing at the Pharos from the open window of my apartments and as a soldier aboard troop ships coming from or going on deployment, I found myself regularly passing under its watchful, incandescent eye, but in all those years it never lost its magic, its power.

Pharos, I thought as I gazed wearily at the distant peak. Aside from what my men and I had agreed upon as names for this world, its three small moons and its mismatched suns—names the Adraniis had gone along with in the belief that they were well-established names rather than the results of our gallows humor—it had no place names, and if we were going to make Latrunc̆uli fully ours, it was only right that we should stake our claim by bestowing landmarks with names.

Pharos. It was fitting—Romulus had set and Remus was following close behind, now almost fully hidden behind the western mountains, yet Pharos was still a luminous cyan against the backdrop of the deep violet sky streaked with saffron clouds, a terrestrial guidepost that, for these few precious moments at twilight briefly rivaled any royal jewel or the dazzling flotsam caught by whirlpool—not to mention the original Pharos...and then it was gone, the light abruptly extinguished, the spire instantly plunged into darkness, the whirlpool now taking its rightful place, a celestial diadem dominating the eastern skyline, signaling the end to this awful, uneventful day.

Felix, Borzu and I had spent the entire time not far from the northern end of the wall, behind a grass-camouflaged ballista, alternately standing and squatting in a slight hollow in the rock face, a place that offered no protection from the burning morning sunlight, intense afternoon heat or the sting of the grit-laden wind. It did, however, provide an excellent view of the desert and our voices, our commands would carry all the way back to where the cavalry stood watch. Fortunately, we had not been called upon to use the gorge's natural acoustics to call the camp to arms.

While Borzu and I had whiled away the sweltering hot hours of the afternoon in a game of latrunc̆uli—he and many of the other Adraniis had picked up the rules from the soldiers while we were encamped on the hillock—Felix had occupied himself by weaving an elaborate wristlet out of dry grass cautiously plucked from the nearby ballista masquerading as a tussock, his homespun offering to Eithne to offset the gift of my necklace. Borzu and I were suitably impressed with the result and said so, which briefly brightened Felix's otherwise bleak mood.

Now night was approaching and the sun-baked rocks, according to Borzu, would take over some of the duty of defense, effectively concealing our presence with their radiating heat, the very same warmth that would keep the desert chill at bay, just as the slight bend in the gorge had kept the worst of the dust storms at bay.

Borzu said he'd never heard of the Si'aafu launching a nighttime attack—although he added the caveat that in the unfilled places between worlds there was in fact no nighttime, no daytime which I readily admit made absolutely no sense to me—however he believed we were still at risk of detection from their "over-flights"—as he called them, that in fact they might prefer to search at night, using a variety of means while using the semi-darkness to their advantage.

In other words, it was no time to relax our guard or loosen the restrictions on unnecessary movement within the gorge, which meant another hastily swallowed meal of hardtack and dried fruit—no fires, not tonight, maybe not for many, many nights to come. Worse, it was too great a risk to fish the pool to keep our food stocks supplied: in daylight the activity might be spotted; at night and without the aid of torches, there was little chance of seeing anything much less catching it. I could only hope our limited provisions would last while we remained out of sight. What we'd set aside for the hard push over the pass was now at risk of being consumed before we ever set foot outside of the gorge—all that work, all that preparation....

I heaved a sigh at the grim options before us: we'd run out of food if we stayed—even the pools' supply of shrimp and eels wasn't limitless, not with fifty four hundred mouths to feed, and the horses, goats and oxen had already cropped most of the grass. If we stayed much longer we'd have nothing to sustain us on the trek over the mountains, and if we decided to make a break for it, it would be little better than a nonstop dash in the full heat of day, using the suns light to dazzle the eyes of any watchers, in the process having no choice but to leave behind anyone who couldn't keep up.

I looked around and shrugged, feigning indifference. *Better some of us survive than none*—or so I tried to convince myself. But we were out of painless options. In fact there hadn't been a single pain-free option handed to me since we'd arrived here—if I wanted to be totally, brutally truthful with myself, there hadn't been a pain-free option handed to me since that fateful day in the bog.

I leaned close to Felix, whispered, "Why don't you go get something to eat and some sleep—take Borzu with you. I'll take first watch."

His bright blue eyes flicked to the flush-faced and profusely sweating Adranii captain, who'd faired the worst of us, then back to me. "How 'bout I take first watch?"

"You were awake before I was."

"And you're the Legate."

"That's right. I *am*. So I'm giving you a direct order to stop arguing and go get something to eat and get some damned sleep!" Fine, I admit it:

the heat and strain had made me a wee bit testy, in fact it had made us all a wee bit testy.

Felix favored me with a sidelong and very baleful squint, followed by a formal salute then he spun on his heel and stalked off, keeping as close to the rock wall as possible. See? Testy.

Borzu watched him leave then turned back to me and growled, "Am I supposed to follow him?" And there again, more testiness.

I slowly slid down the rock face and into a crouch then wiped the sweaty grime from my forehead and the corners of my eyes. "I'd wait a bit if I were you."

— iii —

I lifted my head from where it had been nestled in the crook of my arm and peered muzzily out at the starlit desert, my burning, gritty eyes making yet another search for any movement, any telltale glitter… *anything*, from my perch atop the wall.

Once darkness had fully engulfed the gorge, I'd moved up onto the wall, along with a handful of the engine crews who were eager to abandon the suffocating confines of their canvas and grass hides. We'd quickly found that the most comfortable—not to mention most stable—position was seated with knees tucked up against the chest, one arm wrapped around the legs, the other doubling as a pillow for the occasional catnap.

If the Si'aafu were out there, they were doing just as we were doing: lying low. The night sky was full of nothing more sinister than the occasional shooting star—real shooting stars as Borzu's second, Jom had explained the difference to us—not a Si'aafu ship arcing high overhead, thank the gods.

I shifted my gaze to the muffled crunch of approaching footsteps below, accompanied by a familiar, *wheeze, wheeze, wheeze.*

A moment later Felix, laden with supplies, scrambled rather ungracefully up onto the wall, sending small pebbles and bits of scree clattering and pinging as they bounced down the fortifications, and eased himself down beside me. He pressed a fat waterskin into my hands and I immediately brought to my lips and began gulping down its wonderfully cool contents. My thirst slackened, I squeezed more over my head, soaking my hair, my shoulders then I squeezed more into a cupped palm, which I then used to wash my dusty face and throat.

Finished, I handed the still very plump waterskin to the soldier seated next to me, who promptly repeated the ritual before handing the skin on.

"Compliments of Eithne and Anachie," Felix murmured and handed me a bulging sack he'd had slung over his shoulder.

I took it, opened it to find it full of dried fruit, dried eel and chunks of hard cheese—more than a meal for all of us. I snatched up a handful, stuffed my mouth, dumped another handful into my lap then again passed it along to the eager grin and whispered thanks of the man beside to me.

"I'll take over," Felix said as I chewed and motioned to the camp, adding pointedly, "Eithne's waiting for you."

I stopped chewing long enough to shoot him a sidelong glance then through my mouthful muffled, "Manage to get any sleep?"

"Yes," he replied coolly as he fixed his eyes on the starlit desert and I realized he'd taken my question in a way I hadn't intended. *Or had I?*

This arrangement was going to take some getting used to. It was just too damned easy to say something that could raise hackles, causing offense where none had been meant—then again, we were all working on a very short leash.

I swallowed with a loud and wincing gulp, gathered up what was left in my lap and tossed that into my mouth and quickly reduced it to a swallowable size, then I grasped his shoulder; he jerked his eyes back to me.

"I'll need help getting up."

He nodded, rose and just as he offered me his hand someone further down the wall hissed, *"Something's out there!"*

I twisted around as Felix dropped to his belly beside me, our eyes, like everyone else, now frantically searching the flat expanse of starlit desert.

I leaned close to the soldier next to me, Ocelus was his name, a man who, like Hardalio had been one of Lord Tistriya's Kellesuf, and whispered in his ear, *"Ask what he saw... pass it along but keep your voices down."*

He nodded and leaning to his right, whispered into the ear of the man next to him. And so my message moved down the line; a moment later, the reply rippled back to me as the men, like us now flat on their bellies on top of the wall shifted and leaned close, whispering to each other.

"Lusius says he saw something move..." Ocelus pointed, *"out there, on the far side of the flats. But whatever it is, it hasn't moved since."*

I squinted into the crisp starlight that rimed everything in the deceitful look of hoarfrost. It would be easy for exhausted eyes to see something shift within that faint sparkle, but Lusius had begun his watch only a short time before Felix arrived, having somehow managed to catch an hour's nap while still under the canvas cover of his engine. And Lusius, like all former Kellesuf, tired or not, was not prone to flights of imagination—quite the contrary. If he said he saw something move, then he *saw* something move.

"Tell everyone to take position," I whispered to Ocelus; and to Felix: *"Return to camp—warn the others—have Duccius use those goat legs of his to get word up to the sentries."* I motioned to the heights that almost fully surrounded us; maybe the pickets had also seen what Lusius had seen—with their altitude they certainly had a better angle on the far stretches of the desert—perhaps one was already clambering down as fast as he could safely manage to warn us. It was equally possible they hadn't seen anything amiss, but realized something was afoot when they saw those below scattering, some to the engines, others to the weapons caches and had wisely dispatched one of their number to find out what the hell had caused such a stir. Once we were off the wall, they were going to be our only eyes and I wanted to make damned sure those above were fully aware of the potentially ominous turn of events.

"And you?"

"I'm staying with the engine crews. You're to command the infantry—"

Felix opened his mouth to protest but I cut him off.

"—and get word to Marcus—he and his men are to stay with the civilians no matter what. Tell Borzu to keep his men in reserve—"

Felix made a face; I fully agreed. The Adraniis would be, in our estimation, little more than a snack on the run for the Si'aafu.

"—with luck we won't need them but I damned well don't want them underfoot."

He rose to a crouch, whispered, *"I'll have someone fetch your armor,"* then he startled me when he firmly grasped my shoulder. *"Gods' favor to us, Legate."*

I grabbed his wrist that held me, gave it an equally firm squeeze. *"Gods' favor, Primus-Pilus."*

We both let go and Felix, without a backwards glance, leapt off the wall, landing deftly on the uneven ground below.

I watched him scurry off, keeping close to the rock wall, passing the word as he went, leaving men to rise quickly but stiffly and shake off their sleepiness as they snatched up their weapons and, this time, their armor.

Ocelus got to his knees, then, like Felix to a crouch and wordlessly offered me his hand up. I accepted the help, got my feet under me then hunkering down, followed others as they scurried over to the end of the wall, where the rock face provided some footing and a less risky way down than jumping, leaving behind two men on the wall and those high up on the promontory to keep watch and give warning.

Crews were already hard at work uncovering the ballistas and onagers, all done as quietly as possible, some men assigned to gathering up the hastily shed and highly combustible camouflage of dry grass and canvas and getting it safely stored well out of the way while others set about preparing the engines themselves, checking the tension in the ropes, the chocks on the wheels, while still others had scattered to the strategically placed supply dumps and began to assemble the carefully stockpiled and now needed supplies—a deadly mix of naphtha, sulfur, oil and saltpeter that would provide the onagers with the weapon I hoped would send any advancing Si'aafu into a panicky retreat as it had done with so many human armies: incendiary missiles that would explode on impact, splattering the enemy with the burning liquid that would cling to anything it touched.

It was a shock tactic I suspected would work only once, but once might be enough—

"Do you believe that?" I heard Eithne's dubious voice echo in my mind and I couldn't help but reflexively tense my stomach. I *didn't* believe it, not for a moment. The best I could hope is that we'd singe the eyebrows off a few Si'aafu—assuming they had eyebrows—give 'em a little what for and royally piss 'em off in the process before they overran our fortifications—

—my stomach spasmed again, this time into a painfully tight knot. I'd given an order to Marcus, one only he knew, but others, like Felix, Cleander, Rufinius and Aetius probably suspected: he and his men were to kill the women, children and wounded rather than let them fall into the hands of the Si'aafu, then slaughter our livestock and lastly, turn their weapons on each other.

If the Si'aafu did indeed prefer to butcher their own meat, then the least I could do was to deny them that. It would be a small victory, and one, if it happened, I would not be alive to savor, but a victory nonetheless.

XIV

The attack came at second sunrise, just as the dazzling azure Remus peeked above the far peaks only to hurl blazing shards of light across the desert already stained a vivid vermilion by its companion, Romulus.

Hundreds of Si'aafu appeared to boil out of the very sand itself at the far edge of the desert, clearly hoping to take advantage of the suns' combined glare to blind us while they rushed the gorge mouth and wall: an undulating and high-pitched chittering gray mass that surged towards us, unstoppable. Their numbers were briefly and densely packed and their advance slowed as they were funneled by the surrounding saltpans, but once past that bottleneck they again spread out and came at us with surprising speed, their low-slung bodies carried on multiple legs that churned up the dust, masking whatever followed first wave.

I'd insisted on returning to the wall well before dawn, unable to wait with the engine crews, totally reliant on the eyes of the sentries high above to give warning. So, to that end, I was again lying on my belly on top of the fortifications, Aetius beside me this time, also flat on his stomach and both of us in full armor. The sight and sounds of the charging Si'aafu, along with the blood-chilling wail of the buccinas from above, was enough to get me to my feet in one quick scramble—absolutely no help needed this time.

I'd wanted to see for myself what we were facing when the assault came and what I saw sent a shiver of pure terror down my spine. Lady Ainiaan's nightmarish description of an un-Earthly martichora with the same gluttonous preferences paled in comparison to the reality: the Si'aafu were indeed massive, at least twenty feet long, their wide, spatulate bodies covered in overlapping, articulated scutes with wedge-shaped heads and multi-jointed, spindly legs covered in what looked like spines—spines that rippled as they moved as if the spines themselves had a mind of their own.

If they had eyes, I was hard-pressed to recognize them. They certainly had chelae—huge, bristle-covered pincers snugged close to their broad, plated chests, with massive, segmented tails that whipped back and forth as they raced towards us, looking less like scorpions to me and more like a truly grotesque mix of crocodile, centipede and spider—and you know how I feel about *them*.

I motioned to Aetius to move out of the direct line of fire and I followed as fast as I dared, my eyes darting between the onrushing Si'aafu and the loose scree beneath my feet—fearful a misstep might find me on the unhappy side of Rufinius' wall. I stopped a short dash from the relative safety of the gorge's northern wall yet still in clear view of my troops and held up my hand; it would be close—it *had* to be close.

Behind me I heard the telltale groan of rope, the rapid *click-click-click* as wooden gears turned, ratcheting up the tension, of engine crew-chiefs barking commands as crews filled the onagers' missiles with the incendiary, while others stocked the scorpios and ballistas with their deadly bolts. High above scores of pinpoint fires now dotted the cliffs: *sagitarii* preparing to add their bitumen-tipped flaming arrows to the hail of weapon fire.

But in order to do the most damage, we had to wait until the last possible moment—until the first line of charging Si'aafu were within thirty feet of the wall—as I said, it was going to be close.

Real damned fucking close.

And no chance in hell for a do-over.

I risked a quick glance over my shoulder.

Felix and two thirds of the infantry were ready, pila upright, a bristling mass with scutums to the fore, a solid shield wall that paralleled the stone fortifications, seven men deep. On Felix's signal, the soldiers would form a testudo and rush forward, to surround the engines, pila poking up through the narrow gaps in the 'roof' of scutums. Any Si'aafu who managed to scale the wall and foolishly leapt in a way to avoid the burning fire-bowls of the onagers would instead find itself impaled.

The rest of the infantry under Rufinius' command, along with the bulk of the *sagitarii* were standing back, barricaded now behind overturned supply wagons and forming the third line of defense at the narrowing of the gorge, just before it turned to the left, with a space of a hundred paces or so separating us: a killing ground for the archers and javelineers. Further back, on either side of the central pool stood the Adranii men and their puny weapons, and behind them, the waterfall, the fissure and my cavalrymen, led by Marcus.

Back there, tucked away behind the waterfall, deep in that fissure was Eithne and Anachie... along with almost twenty five hundred others, terrified yet trusting us to protect them... and in a matter of a few minutes they all very well may be dead, hacked to pieces by *my* men—on *my* order.

I swallowed convulsively, felt my upraised hand falter as I quickly swiveled my head back to the approaching Si'aafu.

I spread my fingers, signal to mark.

Then I silently counted down, one finger after another curling into my palm: *five... four... three...two... one*—no sooner had my thumb followed the rest than my now clenched fist and arm sliced down.

I immediately dropped back to my belly and instinctively covered my helmeted head with my hands; Aetius did the same and for a moment it must've appeared to those below that we'd been consumed by the combined volley of fire that leapt over the wall like a massive wave curling just before crashing ashore.

The burning liquid drenched the leading line of Si'aafu and they began shrieking as their bodies, now ablaze, writhed, engulfed by flames that fed off their scutes, which buckled and curled and smoked like the orange-glow edges of vellum set alight.

I stared, agape: the Si'aafu didn't just *burn*. Once the incendiary mixture peeled back their scutes, which it did with astonishing speed, the underlying flesh promptly *exploded*, lobbing balls of flame and burning body parts every which way, including into the crush of those who followed—the ear-splitting shrieks, the loud popping and crackling from the immolating Si'aafu and the concussive, *THAWUUMP!-THAWUUMP!-THAWUUMP!* of the battery of onagers as they launched their deadly, flame-trailing missiles in rapid succession was enough to shake even a seasoned veteran like me to the marrow of his bones—

"*SHIT!*" Aetius yelped, also totally unnerved by the sight and the near-deafening racket.

It was as if the entire desert had been set ablaze and the two of us were at the very center of the hellish maelstrom. Si'aafu who could were now retreating, many alight, scrambling over or knocking down those behind them, but their chaotic retreat wasn't fast enough. Another barrage of incendiaries pin-wheeled over us, whistling and squealing ominously, to impact amongst the panicking Si'aafu. To my shock, to my utter amazement, recognizable chunks of Si'aafu were launched, spinning, high into the air by the force of their own exploding bodies only to come crashing back to earth... further spreading the inferno and terror within their fleeing ranks.

A hail of bolts arced high overhead, followed in short order by volley after volley of flaming arrows, loosened by *sagitarii* high on the promontory along with those behind the supply wagons.

While it was a truly amazing sight to witness from the height of the wall, I also realized Aetius and I were now not only a rallying sight for our side, but the Si'aafu as well. I grabbed him by his mailed collar, dragged him back to his feet. Together we stumbled the remaining length of the rock wall's sinuous spine, ducking and weaving and desperate not to lose our precarious footing while wave after wave of bolts flew just above our helmeted and plumed heads, the weapons warbling shrilly as they sought out their fleeing targets.

High-pitched screeching from the Si'afuu followed each volley, drawing more artillery fire from the scorpio and ballista crews who took their lead from the archers and using those high on the promontory to guide their attacks. The result was pinpoint accuracy, as the *ballistarii* followed the trail of the flaming arrows with a nonstop barrage and the accompanying, thunderous, *THAWUUMP!-THAWUUMP!-THAWUUMP!* chorus of the onagers that almost drowned out the hoarsely bellowed orders of the engine crew-chiefs and centurions.

Roiling clouds of acrid smoke now filled the gorge, adding to the general confusion and concealing the exact positions of the artillery as the engines continued to lob their deadly volleys—not that there was any fear now of the Si'aafu mounting a counter-attack, oh hell no. They were in full panicked retreat, each Si'aafu for himself—herself—*itself?*

I could only imagine the Adraniis' collective terror at the thunderously booming echoes that reverberated off the gorge's high walls, the truly awful sulfurous stench of the incendiaries combined with the stink of the burning Si'aafu and the swirling gray miasma that was regularly lit from within as the onagers launched volley after flaming volley—and having no idea who was winning, who was losing, if they were about to be set upon, set afire... or set free.

Once Aetius and I had reached the northern face of the gorge and flattened ourselves against it, I stopped, breathless and turned to watch, wide-eyed, the truly horrific inferno I'd unleashed as I struggled for air in the suffocating murk.

"You... y-you c-c-can let... let go... now," Aetius wheezed. *"P-p-please...?"*

I jerked my eyes towards him and realized my fist still held a wad of his mailed collar under his chin, making it even harder for him to breathe, so I convinced my fingers to release their near-stranglehold, then the two of us watched as the *sagitarii* and *ballistarii* found fresh targets among the rapidly scattering and dwindling ranks of Si'aafu.

I could have called a halt, saved what remained of our weaponry and incendiaries in case the Si'aafu had a mind to come at us again. I could have ordered my soldiers to stand down, to regroup.

Instead I waited until the wind shifted, briefly clearing the smoke from the mouth of the gorge then I yanked my gladius from its scabbard and using the tip to gesture at the retreating enemy, bellowed at the men below: *"BREACH THE WALL! WE'RE TAKING THE BATTLE TO THE SI'AAFU!"*

A booming cheer went up, every bit as deafening as the onagers lobbing their missiles and as the exhausted engine crews stood back, every one breathing hard, scores of soldiers rushed forward, to the preplanned weak spot in the fortifications and using muscle alone, gave a great, collective heave and managed to topple the section.

Felix and his detachment of infantry were the first to scramble over the tumble of scree, roaring as they went, followed by the rest, who'd happily abandoned the overturned wagons in preference for giving chase, a living, screaming and armored tide surging through the breach, each man hell-bent on butchering as many Si'aafu as possible—you've gotta love 'em for their gleeful enthusiasm if nothing else.

Aetius and I followed, managing to clamber down the wall before being swept into the deluge of men pouring from the gorge and out onto the desert.

The same pools of natron that had been such a barrier to us now worked in our favor by forcing the fleeing Si'aafu into again bunching together, making them even easier targets for our *sagitarii*. Those few who dared the glistening natron quickly sank up to their bellies in the blistering liquid and unable to free themselves writhed in agony, having doomed themselves to a far more prolonged and hideous death than that delivered by our weapons—too damned bad.

I accepted a pilum from a soldier on the run and once beyond the gauntlet of natron pools we fanned out, hacking and stabbing at anything that moved and running down any Si'aafu who had somehow managed to escape the firestorm that had consumed their fellows. I quickly lost count of how many I killed—just shove the blade between the overlapping scutes, give it a twist to pry the flexible plates apart, shove the pilum in as far as it would go then swizzle it about. It was in fact far less effort than shucking oysters, with similarly unhappy results for the Si'aafu.

I was so involved in the wholesale and thoroughly enjoyable slaughter of these creatures that had caused humanity so much misery, so full of bloodlust my bad leg and shoulder never once failed me despite me running full out and in full armor, stopping only to gleefully dispatch yet another Si'aafu and with more sword-thrusting gusto and pilum-swizzling enthusiasm than was probably absolutely necessary to get the job done— *gods, it felt good!* I'd quickly gotten the technique down as had my men, and the surviving Si'aafu, despite their size, their massive chelae and their speed, were truly no match against a legion of human berserkers.

Isem had been wrong—in this case, *dead wrong*. Swords and pikes were, in fact, more than a match for the supposedly redoubtable Si'aafu— and goes to prove the old adage that the best weapon of all is the one your enemy least expects you to use. The Si'aafu had been mightily surprised; of course I was equally stunned that our tactics had actually *worked* and worked so far beyond my wildest imagining.

The total rout was over with in an incredibly short space of time and as I found myself standing next to Felix, both of us heaving for breath in the quivering early morning heat of the open desert, I saw not a single Si'aafu still standing—of course neither Felix or I were entirely unscathed. Felix had suffered several puncture wounds on his arms along with a deep cut on his cheek and a nasty gash across his left thigh that had sheathed his entire leg and greave in blood, mementos' from a dying Si'aafu's thrashing tail; I had a profusely bleeding wound on my upper right arm, not to mention a bloodied nose and one hell of a headache, parting gifts from the same damned Si'aafu's tail, along with a scattering of burns that were rapidly turning to blisters on the back of both legs and the back of my right arm, painful reminders to never turn my back even on a dead and smoldering Si'aafu until it had entirely burned itself out.

Minor wounds, considering the carnage we'd inflicted.

What had, only an hour or so before been flat, pristine ocher sand was now be-smudged with long streamers of soot and littered with hundreds upon hundreds of Si'aafu corpses, some whole but little more than burnt-out husks, many more in pieces large and small and still smoking, a few still actively burning—the cloyingly sweet stink of their cooked flesh mixed with the sulfurous stench of the incendiaries was nauseating and at the same time *intensely* satisfying, as if something stolen from me had finally been restored and I couldn't help but grin as I looked around.

What few Si'aafu were still moving feebly only drew the businesslike attention of my troops who were walking about, using their pila to finish the job and everyone flinching at the occasional loud 'POP!' as yet another Si'aafu exploded and flaming bits briefly became airborne, this on top of the continual background sizzling and snapping of the sizable chunks that lay scattered all around us.

I peered into the smoke-greasy, morning glare and to my utter amazement realized we were in fact a goodly way out into the desert, more than half way to the eastern peaks, the mouth of the gorge barely visible despite the western range being awash in sunlight and evident only because a trail of dead Si'aafu led right up to it, like macabre and smoldering stepping-stones—the Latrunculian version of the Via Appia perhaps? *Via Scorpiones? Naw*, I shook my head. It wouldn't catch on as few would see the humor in it.

The familiar muffled jangle of approaching armor drew my attention: Rufinius was jogging towards us, casually zigzagging his way through the obstacle course of smoldering corpses, his soot-rimmed mouth drawn back in a decidedly satisfied grin and like us, splattered head to toe in the tarry, greenish-black blood of these supposedly unstoppable monsters, which, as it turned out, weren't quite as formidable as advertised—*gods' favor to us indeed!*

"Report, Centurion," I said as he came to a stop in front of us.

He jabbed his pilum's butt-end into the sand, braced his shield against it, then, placing his hands on his hips, he caught his breath as he glanced around. "Not a single Si'aafu escaped, Legate." He untied his cheek-pieces, pushed his helmet back as he turned back to me and wiped his gore-covered brow with the back of an equally gore-covered hand. "We're still moping up, but what few are still alive won't be shortly."

I braced myself for the bad news. "And our casualties?"

He pointedly eyed me, eyed Felix before replying, "Some seriously broken bones from those who foolishly weren't watching where they were going and tumbled down into a wash or got their legs knocked out from under them when they were struck by a Si'aafu's tail, stab and slash wounds," he added pointedly and with another sidelong glance at Felix, "but the most common injuries are burns from being splattered by burning Si'aafu…"

Fortunately for me I was facing him. His tone suggested he harbored little sympathy for those so painfully afflicted and I figured now was not the time to point out that his legate had the dubious, not to mention quite painful distinction of being a member in good standing of this honored albeit singed company.

"…but no more than a hundred I'd label as badly injured." He tugged the helmet back into place, retied the cheek-pieces. "No deaths—and *everyone* has been accounted for."

I blinked, dumbfounded that the worst we'd suffered were burns and broken bones, then I rolled my eyes to Felix to find him angrily and repeatedly stabbing his gore-covered sword into the fine ocher sand to clean it.

"They didn't put up much of a fight," he snarled, punctuating each word with a vicious stab and sounding rather put out by it all, not that I could really blame him. He'd been itching for a fight since the day we arrived, had spent months training to do battle and was greatly looking forward to testing himself against a worthy opponent, thus proving to himself that he was every bit as capable as I said he was.

It had to rankle.

"Most didn't put up *any* fight," I replied and it was true; a handful did but only when they were surrounded or cornered and they were quickly dealt with. Then it struck me why: "They wanted us alive"—Borzu's words uttered by my tongue.

Rufinius nodded as he squatted beside his shield and carefully wiped his own sword free of its sticky coating of Si'aafu blood. "Clearly they didn't expect anything other than passive resistance—"

"Which is exactly what they would have gotten from the Adraniis," Aetius muttered as he joined us, barely recognizable under a truly impressive coating of Si'aafu blood, sand and soot—if I didn't know better, I'd swear he'd deliberately rolled in it, but since I did know better I assumed he'd just slipped and fallen in it, then was forced to roll around order to get out of it.

And it certainly didn't help that a flaming bit of Si'aafu had fallen on his helmet's transverse horsehair plume, sticking to it and singing the hair and leaving it still smoldering, which left him bearing a striking resemblance to a just doused candle with a whiff of acrid smoke spiraling upwards from his head.

Rufinius also clearly saw the similarity and flicked me a sidelong, bite-lipped glance.

"Notice not damned one joined the fight?" Aetius continued, oblivious. "They all stayed behind, probably cowering behind their womenfolk if truth be told." He spat on the ground for emphasis then happened to notice Felix and me. His eyes widened. "What the hell happened to you two?"

"What does it look like?" Felix snapped, blotting his wounds as best he could with his already blood-soaked neckerchief.

"That some Si'aafu did fight back?"

Felix eyed him and his smoking helmet plume disdainfully. "You're not exactly one to point fingers—"

"At least none of this is mine!" Aetius fired back, motioning to the greenish-black gobs of goo liberally splattered on his band-armor and helmet that made him look as if a dragon with a severe head cold had just sneezed on him...

So perhaps he *had* been doused after all—

"—do you realize your helmet's plume is on fire?"

Aetius squinted at him as if not fully trusting Felix, cautiously reached up and touched the smoldering crest—then yanked off the helmet, tossed it to the ground and began kicking sand on it as he snarled, *"Thanks for telling me!"*

"We thought you knew," Rufinius replied, straight-faced.

Aetius snatched up the helmet, did his best to fluff the badly singed and now sand covered horsehair back into something resembling its former glory, then fixed Rufinius with a cold look as he replaced the helmet on his head and angrily retied the cheek-pieces.

"Besides," Rufinius continued, picking up the previous thread of conversation exactly where it had been dropped, "the Adraniis would've had to get past Marcus to do it." He rose and reequipped himself with his shield, adding, "And if I were them, I'd pick an army of Si'aafu over Marcus alone any day."

Aetius scowled at him. "So would I, but that's beside the damned point!"

"If I remember correctly," Rufinius said, thoughtfully tapping his soot-smeared chin with his equally blackened forefinger, "it was Felix's job to train the Adraniis to fight like Romans." He turned to Felix, eyebrows raised. "So, Primus-Pilus, what happened?"

Now it was Felix's turn to scowl. "Been a wee bit busy—"

"So I've heard," Rufinius replied, wiggling those same eyebrows.

"And you haven't?" Felix snapped.

"A gentleman never discusses such matters," Rufinius said as he resheathed his sword with a flourish.

"You don't *need* to discuss it—everyone could hear the two of you going at it—gods, Rufinius, *must* you cry like a little girl?"

Rufinius' black eyes flashed as he yanked his pilum's shaft free of the sand. "At least I didn't get a damned rock up my ass while I was 'going at it'!" He emphasized the remark by a quick upwards jab of said pilum.

Felix blinked then turned his suddenly appalled gaze on me.

I shrugged, smiled feebly. "It just kinda slipped out."

"Unlike the rock," Rufinius added, elbowing Aetius, who promptly roared with laughter.

Felix just stood there, sooty lips working furiously but not a sound coming out.

"*Gods, Felix,*" Aetius gasped. "Here I thought Arri was just pulling our legs—did you really get a rock up your ass?"

"If you must know," he replied coldly, "*yes.*"

Aetius and Rufinius looked at each other, then at Felix, still agog.

"*Intentionally?*" Leave it to Aetius to ask.

Felix's glare turned positively baleful. "*What the fuck do you think?*"

Aetius shrugged and looking innocent, replied in a deeply aggrieved voice, "Just asking," then he walked over to a nearby Si'aafu corpse and kicked its still smoking head, which promptly detached itself from the charred body and rolled a little way away, leaving a trail of tarry blood and soot. He followed, kicked it again, harder, like a fretful child kicking a ball. "Bet it came as one hell of a surprise—"

"To Felix or the rock?" Rufinius replied an instant before I could stop him with a sidelong, warning glance.

"I *meant* the Si'aafu," Aetius replied and gave the smoldering head one last, powerful kick that sent it spinning like a top across the hard-packed sand, spewing globs of congealed blood and bits of burnt brain as it did so and scattering soldiers who found themselves in its pin-wheeling path. "But now that you mention—"

"*Legate...!*"

We turned as one to the hoarse, gasping voice, only to find Carus trotting towards us, an odd, dare I say very worried look on his soot- and gore-smeared face.

"What is it?" I asked.

"We... we found something down in that deep ravine over there." He pointed as he stopped in front of me and as I squinted into the smoke-haze and heat ripples, I could barely make out the telltale, shifting gleam and glitter of armor within the miasma: men were milling about, presumably at the lip of said ravine—the same deep, soft-walled gully that had served as a very effective barrier to the eastern range.

I glanced at Felix, then Rufinius and lastly Aetius, who'd rejoined us, having lost interest in his game of kick the detached Si'aafu head and see what comes out.

It was the same general area where the flicker of movement had drawn Lusius' eye the night before; one look at my companions confirmed they'd all made the same worrisome connection.

"*Something...?*"

"Yes, Legate," Carus replied, still trying to catch his breath in the smoke-thick air.

I started towards the ravine at an easily sustainable trot despite the heat, the smoke, and my now aching muscles, Carus abreast of me, Rufinius, Aetius and Felix following along with a number of soldiers who'd overheard and, like us, were curious, not to mention nervous as to what Carus and his companions had stumbled across.

"Centurion Silvanus and a group of us were running down a handful of Si'aafu—*we got 'em all*," Carus quickly assured me, "but then we wondered what prompted them to run in the direction they were headed as they never stopped and turned to fight once they realized we were after 'em, they just kept running, so we thought we'd best investigate, see what they were all so desperate to reach."

I nodded my approval as I gave him a sidelong look, extremely relieved that he'd survived what was, by anyone's definition a massacre unscathed—young, overconfident soldiers were always at great risk of being killed while chasing after a panicked enemy in chaotic retreat; Carus had, thanks to the gods, beaten the odds… unlike Gnaius.

He looked at me, smiled nervously, unsure whether his find would please me immensely, or royally piss me off. I was really hoping for the former, but suspecting it was probably going to be the latter.

We jogged the rest of the way—zigzagging through heaps of dead Si'aafu, with only the rhythmic and familiar jangle of our armor to keep the eerie whistle of the dust-laden desert wind and the occasional loud *POP!* of exploding Si'aafu from rubbing our already frayed nerves raw.

I slowed to a winded and wincing walk as I neared the milling group of soldiers at the crumbling rim of the ravine, then, as they flicked me anxious glances and hurriedly stepped aside, I stopped and looked down.

My eyes widened.

Felix joined me and visibly flinched in astonishment; Aetius appeared at my other elbow and uttered a protective oath while Rufinius peered over Aetius' shoulder and, like Felix and me, only stared in stunned silence.

More and more soldiers arrived, drawn out of curiosity, fear or perhaps a yet unquenched desire to find something else to kill… and like us, cautiously approached the lip of the deep, water-carved gulch, swords, shields and pila at the ready and clearly expecting to find more Si'aafu.

Instead they were confronted by the sight of a massive and ominous looking dull gray, flattened cylinder that almost filled the ravine, wall-to-wall, dwarfing the handful of soldiers, Silvanus with his centurion's helmet visible among them, who were walked around it, poking and tapping at it with their pila; it pinged in response, sounding to my ears like metal on hollow metal.

All around me I could hear more whispered oaths as soldiers called upon the protection of gods who had, most likely, totally forgotten we even existed once they assumed all the excitement was over, or perhaps they were just as curious as we were and were expecting us to satisfy their interest, despite the risks—*to us.*

"What the fuck is that?" Felix gasped, finally finding his voice.

"Their ship," Rufinius replied quietly but with such absolute sureness it sent a chill racing down my spine and a ripple of unease through the two hundred-odd soldiers who like us now stood, shoulder to armored shoulder along the lip of the ravine.

All eyes swiveled to him.

"Maisoh," he continued, his intense black eyes taking in every bit of the peculiar looking thing with intense curiosity mixed with equally intense worry, "she told me about their ships—this fits her description perfectly."

"A ship?" Felix replied, hands on hips. He jerked his chin towards it. "Where're the damned oars? The mast?"

"Not *that* short of ship, Primus-Pilus," Rufinius said in a regrettably patronizing tone.

Felix scowled at him. "So a ship that just moves about all on its own?" He made exaggerated swimming motions with his arms; several of the soldiers chuckled—and promptly shut up the instant Rufinius' furious eyes sought them out.

Satisfied he'd made his point, Rufinius turned those piercing eyes back on Felix. "In a word, *yes*—again according to Maisoh."

"Who's now the ultimate expert on ships," Felix sneered. "A *woman.*"

Rufinius' black eyes flashed. "And *you* are, Primus-Pilus?"

Felix stabbed his finger at it. "I know that damned well couldn't float!"

"It's not supposed to."

Felix arched his soot-smudged brow, having no suitable retort for that. I really wanted to say that Rufinius' remark had let the proverbial wind out of Felix's sails, but I doubted my attempt at humor would've found an appreciative audience, so instead I cleared my smoke-raw throat, drawing their gazes. "Speaking of, how could it have gotten here without us noticing? The pickets saw nothing, and it couldn't have been here all along or the outriders would've seen it, certainly." And they should've—

there was no way they could've missed this hideous behemoth. Besides, had it been here any length of time I would've expected its surface to have a thick coating of sand, at the very least. As it was, its hull was barely dusted in ocher.

Rufinius stared at me; Felix stared at me, then they stared at each other, clearly hoping the other had an answer and would offer it up before the silence became *really* awkward.

Aetius broke the brewing stalemate with an exhaled, "Hell if I know."

"Maybe Maisoh knows," Felix added snidely, "since *she's* the expert."

Rufinius fixed him with a sidelong, squinty-eyed glower and opened his mouth to say something rude but I cut him off with: "Could there be more Si'aafu inside?"

That truly frightening possibility drew everyone's startled attention not to mention our worried eyes back to the looming matter at hand.

We'd only just come to grips with the stunning reality that we'd slaughtered every last Si'aafu and now… maybe we hadn't? One wholly unexpected and utter trouncing of the enemy I could accept, but two? That would be pushing our luck—not to mention the favor of the gods— a wee bit too far in my estimation, and going by the looks on my companions' faces, they were in full agreement.

So if there were more Si'aafu holed up inside, we might not find it such easy going this time—they'd be cornered, they'd know now what sort of mayhem we were capable of unleashing, and of course there was the always looming threat of advanced weapons—weapons the Si'aafu hadn't employed earlier because they wanted to capture as many of us alive as possible, something I suspected would no longer be a high priority among any survivors. Revenge, in my experience, often trumps all other motivations, even a severe case of the munchies.

Clearly they hadn't expected us to fight back, had in fact come at us largely weaponless—if you discounted their massive chelae, which, as it turned out were little more than decorative. I'd witnessed one of my junior infantry centurions, Ammianus, being grabbed by the pincers of a desperate, but up to that moment uninjured Si'aafu, and before I could I rush to his aid he'd easily wrested his armored torso from its grip as then plunged his sword between two of the large, flat scutes that covered its belly, exposed when it reared up, hoping, I assume, to use its height to intimidate Ammianus, which, as this Si'aafu—like many of its companions—realized too late was a really, I mean *really* poor choice of tactics.

Others too, including Rufinius, Titivillus and Aetius had come up against these seemingly formidable weapons and had lopped them off with ease and without breaking stride. I'd even seen one man, none other than the infamous Quintus of 'shrimp' fame, happily wreaking murder and mayhem among the Si'aafu while seemingly oblivious to the fact that he had a set of severed pinchers still affixed to his middle.

Felix looked sidelong at Rufinius. "I think that means the legate expects us to find out, Centurion."

"I think you're right," Rufinius replied, Felix's snub of Maisoh seemingly forgotten. He pointed to a low spot along the ravine's lip that looked to be a marginally less treacherous way to reach the bottom, in fact was clearly the route taken by Silvanus and his men. He grinned, bowed then motioned, "After *you*, Primus-Pilus."

So, *not* completely forgotten.

Felix squinted at him, then irritably motioning for the other soldiers to follow, he trudged over to the spot and without further ado began his precarious descent, using an appropriated pilum like a walking stick to help steady him as he negotiated his way down exposed rock and loose sand that made up the ravine wall. Clearly a Si'aafu's multiple legs were, at least in this situation and despite their spindly appearance, far superior to our two not so spindly legs as they'd had no problem racing up the crumbling sides of the ravine on their way to meet their doom.

"Be mindful of rocks this time," Aetius offered helpfully, not realizing his voice would so easily carry and was forced to smother his laughter as Felix stopped abruptly and fixed him with a very annoyed stare.

Point made, Felix resumed his descent.

The rest dutifully trudged after him and following Felix's lead, used their pila as walking staffs, with Rufinius wisely taking up the rear. I was tempted to join them, but if there were Si'aafu inside, well... no point in belaboring the point. 'The rule' *definitely* applied here.

Instead I turned to find that a large number of my troops had gathered nearby, awaiting my pleasure. "Bassaeus." I beckoned to the soldier I'd picked only because I could instantly recognize him as he'd removed his helmet to give his sweaty scalp a good scratch and his blond hair stood out among the shifting throng of smoke-blackened helmets, soot-smudged faces and gore-covered armor.

He promptly stepped forward and saluted smartly. "Yes, Legate?"

"Get word back to the camp—tell them what's happened, that they can stand down and then get Marcus, have him mount up and bring the

Adranii woman, Maisoh, here as quickly as possible. Tell her we're in need of her expertise…"

Bassaeus blinked then favored his equally shocked companions a sidelong glance but wisely said nothing.

"…Captain Borzu as well, but only *if* he asks. And we need some way to transport the wounded back to camp—tell Cleander I leave how that's done up to his discretion. Tell him about a hundred or so have been seriously injured—but no deaths."

He saluted again, replaced his helmet, turned and took off at an easy lope across the now quivering sand, weaving his way through the still smoldering, snapping and popping carnage that lay all around us.

"Legate!"

I wheeled around and looked down into the ravine to find Rufinius now standing in the shadow of the odd craft, close enough to touch it, his hands cupped around his mouth.

"We've found what looks like a hatch!" He pointed.

I saw nothing that resembled a hatch, then I realized it was probably closed and in shadow and at my distance invisible.

At my nod—meaning I recognized his discovery, nothing more—he reached out for something.

"Gods, don't open it!"

He stopped, looked up at me and held out his hands in question.

"I've sent for Maisoh!"

Felix, who was standing next to Rufinius, punched him in the shoulder and said something to which Rufinius replied and punched him back but with a little more force, enough to send Felix staggering back several steps.

"Stop it!" I snapped as Felix raised both fists, my sharp voice echoing off the ravine's walls and the 'ship' and the two jerked their suddenly innocent, albeit filthy faces towards me. I exhaled explosively, shook my head then remembering the rest of my troops, turned to them. "The rest of you—retrieve as many of our bolts and arrows as you can find, even the damaged ones. *Go!*"

They wisely scattered; even Aetius scurried off.

I rubbed my burning eyes, made a cursory effort at wiping the drying blood from my upper lip and chin, stupidly took a deep breath of the smoke-fouled air, coughed explosively then looked around. I had nothing else to do until Bassaeus returned with Marcus and Maisoh, so I joined my soldiers in gathering up arrows and bolts.

Many of the arrow shafts had been broken, but the feathers, arrowheads and bolts were salvageable and, at least for now, irreplaceable. Granted, most had to be hacked out of their victims, but my men didn't seem to mind the gruesome job, in fact they appeared to take particular relish in the task, as if they hadn't had enough impromptu butchery. The bolts had faired better and were easily pulled from the corpses, or snatched up from the blackened and blood-sticky sand.

We'd collected quite a pile by the time I overheard the approaching jingle of harness and the restive whinny horses and I turned to see Marcus, aboard Belili, along with two cavalrymen, Ulpius aboard his sorrel and Sisenna on his piebald, trotting towards us, the warhorses nervously picking their way through the smoldering and sputtering corpses with Maisoh seated behind Marcus, Borzu behind Ulpius... and Birral clinging, one-armed, onto Sisenna's band-armored waist as his head wildly swiveled this way and that, his free arm gesturing excitedly, all the while speaking rapid fire.

Sisenna appeared utterly disinterested in what the man was babbling on about—*no*. More than disinterested. *Utterly exasperated*. Birral's jerking and twisting about was making it difficult for both men to keep their seat aboard the equally excited horse, yet Birral appeared entirely oblivious to their shared peril.

The horsemen reined in their mounts and I stepped forward to assist Maisoh in dismounting—immediately thought better of it and motioned for Rufinius' second, Dulcitius, who happened to be close at hand, having just dumped an armload of arrows on the ground not far away, to do the honors. Birral hastily slid from the rump of Sisenna's mount, then with an impatient nod to me, hurried to the closest, largely intact Si'aafu corpse; Sisenna followed him with his contemptuous squint, then looked at me and slowly shook his head.

Maisoh gratefully accepted Dulcitius' help, eased herself into his arms and he pulled her from Belili's back and set her on the ground, then Marcus dismounted, handing the reins to Sisenna, who, like Ulpius, remained mounted, lance-tips pointing skyward.

Borzu also managed to dismount, but not quite as smoothly as Birral, then he dusted himself off and looked around, as if having a hard time fully coming to grips with what lay all around him—what we 'bloodthirsty barbarians' had accomplished.

"I hear you've found one of their ships?" Maisoh said as if she'd fully expected nothing less than a total massacre and we hadn't disappointed her, which in a strange way was the ultimate compliment.

"Over there," I motioned to the ravine.

As Borzu joined us, we started towards it, Dulcitius, Marcus and a handful of inquisitive soldiers trailing behind—their curiosity this time raised by Maisoh and why their legate clearly held her views in such high regard. "We're not sure if anyone is still inside. We hoped you might assist?"

"Of course," she replied, grinning at me.

I grinned back as Borzu, who hurried to keep abreast of us, kept looking around, an expression of utter incredulity on his broad face. I flicked him a sidelong look, asked innocently, "Something wrong, Captain?"

He turned his wide eyes on me as he nervously licked his lips. "Never in my wildest imagination did I think this," he swept his shaky hand around us, "was possible. A landing force of Si'aafu—utterly destroyed, no, *slaughtered*, by... by humans—"

"By Roman legionaries," I corrected, prompting a winking grin from Maisoh.

"—it simply boggles the mind."

"Bet you're glad we preferred to parley, huh?"

He briefly jerked his eyes back to me, agreed heartily, "Indeed, Legate, *indeed!*" before his dumbfounded eyes again took in the battlefield.

Satisfied I'd made my point, I turned back to Maisoh. "Rufinius thinks he's found a hatch—"

"He didn't try to open it, did he?" she gasped, grabbing my forearm as she flicked Dulcitius, who was now walking beside us a sidelong, anxious look. "Dulcitius, tell me he didn't try to open it."

He replied with a vehement shake of his head and, "No, ma'am—the Legate stopped 'im."

"*Good,*" she breathed, turning back to me. "Si'aafu are known for booby-trapping their ships."

"As I suspected," I replied. The Germanic tribes, not to mention the Iceni, were infamous for employing such cowardly tactics. We Romans *never* stooped to such... well, all right, fine. *Hardly* ever, and only when we'd been undeservedly provoked, which meant in our case such tactics weren't cowardly but heroic, if not downright brilliant.

We stopped at the lip of the ravine, Maisoh and Borzu to my left, Dulcitius and Marcus to my right.

Maisoh placed her hands on her very female hips—something the accompanying soldiers had noticed too, going by their lingering glances— stared at our find and announced, "It's a troop transport," to which Borzu added his confirming nod and to my ears and eyes neither appeared altogether pleased by the discovery.

"And...?"

"I wouldn't be at all surprised to find a skeleton crew still aboard, and if that's the case, then they've probably already warned their fleet."

I looked skywards and swallowed, hard, as Dulcitius muttered, "Well, shit."

"Which means more Si'aafu," I replied, dropping my pinched gaze back to her.

She nodded. *"Lots more."*

I slowly sank to my haunches and dropped my helmeted head into my hands, suddenly and utterly exhausted. So, it wasn't over. This *was* the bill come due, and just the beginning—a taste of what was to come. Next time I doubted the Si'aafu would repeat their mistake of coming at us unarmed. The old proverb about revenge being a feast to savor suddenly took on a whole new—and decidedly unappetizing—meaning.

Maisoh squatted beside me, placed her hand on my shoulder and eyed me worriedly. "Legate, what you and your men did today was... well, *beyond* amazing. Don't think for one moment it wasn't."

I lifted my head and squinted at her. "But it won't stop them from coming back and this time finishing the job."

"Probably not, but not for a while. You dealt them a blow that will shake them to their very core. Si'aafu aren't accustomed to *anyone* hitting back—even the Jaglavak go to great lengths to avoid antagonizing them."

Of course we'd done a lot more than just antagonize them, which meant—

"I agree with Lieutenant Maisoh." Borzu drew my defeated gaze. "It'll take the Si'aafu quite some time to regroup—time enough for us to do the same."

I sighed, peered down at the ship, at my men who stood about waiting for me to tell them what to do. And I didn't know what to do, what to say to be honest—I'd thrown everything I had at the Si'aafu only to find it wasn't going to be anywhere near enough.

They'd be back. Count on it, and next time they'd come bearing a grudge *along* with a hearty appetite—

"And besides, now we have one of their troop ships," Maisoh added smugly.

I shifted my gritty, burning eyes back to her as I wiped my cheeks, my chin with the back of my hand. *"So?"*

"So we can fly it—well, the captain and Jom can."

We all looked at Borzu.

"I've never actually piloted one," he replied admitted while shooting Maisoh a glance as if not entirely pleased she'd let this heretofore unmentioned yet very germane expertise slip, "neither has Jom, but we've trained on simulators and—"

"Fly it?" I flicked Dulcitius a sidelong, startled look and he stared back at me, equally wide-eyed.

Maisoh nodded enthusiastically. "To anywhere on the planet—it's big enough we can take everyone in six, maybe seven trips, including the animals and even the wagons and engines—*everything.*"

I glanced at the ship, back at her. "You're *not* serious."

"I'm deadly serious, Legate," she replied, getting back to her feet and dusting herself off. "No grueling trek over the mountains in hopes of finding something better—now we can go anywhere, land anywhere on the planet and within a matter of hours, rather than weeks, months or even longer."

With Marcus's help I rose, wincing as my leg cramped from the sustained crouch, then I looked at Borzu, hoping, I suppose, to see some glimmer of sanity in his eyes.

I was sadly disappointed.

He nodded eagerly, clearly quite smitten with the idea now that the truth was out about his heretofore-unknown piloting skills. "This planet has many areas that are far more inviting—far more *human-friendly* than anything within many months' walking distance of here." He pointed south, in the general direction of the abandoned hilltop camp, the hinter crags, both invisible within the shimmering and smoke-greasy air. "There are some large, forested islands we spotted on our survey that lie far off the southern coast. They're uninhab—they'd be ideal for a permanent settlement," he corrected himself, "with rich soil, temperate climate and plenty of fresh water, but without this ship—any ship for that matter—well beyond anyone's reach, certainly our reach for the foreseeable future."

I looked at Dulcitius and Marcus and what I saw in their eyes confirmed what I was feeling. Not a good feeling, not at all, because Borzu was clearly not telling all. *Uninhabited.* That's what he'd started to say. Meaning there were other parts of this world that *were* inhabited, but by who? What?

"What's wrong?" Maisoh asked, touching my arm and drawing my unhappy gaze. "This is *good* news, Legate."

"Is it?"

She blinked, taken aback. "But—"

"Perhaps we should first see if anyone's inside," I said crossly, "and if they're willing to hand their ship over to us without too much…" I looked around at the still smoldering battlefield, "…untidiness."

She nodded, but was still perplexed, greatly worried now, like us, although for vastly different reasons.

"Over there," I pointed, "a way down."

She and Borzu started off, then just as quickly she stopped and looked back at me. "Coming?"

"No."

She stared at me for a moment then with a quizzical shake of her head, she hurried over to the low spot and quickly descended, Borzu following but with far less grace.

"If I were a Si'aafu," Dulcitius said softly, thoughtfully tapping his forefinger on his chin as his eyes pointedly flicked to Birral, in the process reminding me and Marcus that there were Adranii ears about, "I'd wonder where my pretty ship went and go looking for it… starting with," he shot me, then Marcus a sidelong look, "I dunno, far more human-friendly locales?"

I nodded; the last thing we wanted to do is go where the Si'aafu would expect us to go—and oh, yes, there was that lingering, niggly feeling that Borzu was deliberately withholding information critical to the discussion. I shot Birral a glance—he was clearly a weak link, not to mention the supposed expert on star life, and I made a mental note to speak with him, later, and in private where there would be no interference from Borzu.

While there was little risk of him overhearing us as he was fully occupied in studying the dead Si'aafu, Marcus followed Dulcitius' lead and whispered, "And if I were an Adranii, I'd come up with some excuse to leave us behind—*temporarily*, mind you, and just 'forget' to come back, with the hopes that the Si'aafu would come looking for us where they last found us rather than some far off island."

I crossed my arms, nodded and massaging the bridge of my nose, replied in kind: "Maybe even scuttle the ship in deep water… you know, the sort you'd find far out to sea. That's what I would do *if* I were them."

"Yeah," he sighed.

"But we're *not* them," I replied.

"Thank the gods for that," Dulcitius muttered disdainfully, watching Birral out of the corner of his eye as the man poked and prodded incautiously at the corpse. Dulcitius didn't have to wait long for his reward: a muffled *pop!* followed instantaneously by a startled expletive from Birral.

A broad smile spread across Dulcitius' soot-smeared lips as he turned his satisfied gaze back to me.

"Then again," I said, squinting at the ship, "it might not be such a bad idea…"

Marcus and Dulcitius raised their eyebrows in begging interest.

"…let all the Adraniis who want to go, *go*—people like Isem and his kind, you know, the ones who think we're less than they are."

"It would certainly solve one problem," Marcus agreed.

"Let 'em go just where the Si'aafu would expect us to go." I kicked at a clump of sun-hardened sand as I scowled at nothing in particular. "And it wasn't like we hadn't considered the idea of splitting up—"

"Gods' favor—I don't believe it!"

I wheeled towards Sisenna's startled outburst, jerking my sword free of its scabbard, expecting the worst; Marcus and Dulcitius mirrored my reaction, both bringing their weapons to bear as the unarmed, unarmored Birral wisely stepped closer to us—well, let's be completely accurate: he hurriedly stepped *behind* us. The man might be reckless when it came to handling dead Si'aafu, but clearly he wasn't entirely stupid.

"Look!" the cavalryman added, pointing back to the gorge. *"There!"*

I shielded my eyes with my hand, squinted into the glare… and finally spotted what had drawn Sisenna's attention: multiple flickers of movement within the shimmering air that quickly solidified into scores of Adraniis. Many were managing makeshift litters, others were pulling refitted baggage carts—laden with medical supplies, water and food… I could only guess—which would have been far easier to get over the collapsed wall than one of the medical wagons, and leading this ragtag column was none other than Cleander, Iulius and Nestor—the three conspicuous in their crimson tunics and notably pristine band-mail armor and helmets against a drab backdrop of Adranii brown and tan.

A personal note here: given my druthers, our undertunics and breeches would have been white, or as close to white as conditions permitted as white held an unexpected boon over other colors: it was obvious when it was soiled and we legionaries, as a whole, are disinclined to enter into combat wearing filthy clothing. Not only does slovenly attire reflect badly on the ranks and give one's superior officers good reason for making your life hell, it's widely believed among the soldiery that if you just happen to have the misfortune of being stabbed during combat, *clean* fabric going in the wound along with the weapon doing the stabbing, as opposed to dirty fabric, reduces the risk of corruption to the wound, later. I can honestly say I've never seen an example of this. In my experience, if you get stabbed in battle, you're in for a very unhappy time, corrupted wound or not.

But in this case the choice of undertunic and breeches color was not left up to me. It was another of Lady Ainiaan's fancies. She said white was the color of cowards, of household servants, while crimson—the splendid hue of fresh blood—was absolutely, positively the most manly of shades.

When my troops heard that, there was nothing I could do but agree. Crimson it was. Besides, it matched our shields and as everyone knows, there's nothing more demoralizing to a soldier than a color-coordinated adversary.

But I digress…

Not unexpectedly, Cleander had found a unique way to fulfill my orders and then some. I couldn't help but smile and shake my head, wondering what incentive—or, knowing Cleander, what *threat*—he'd used to pry the Adraniis from the bastion of the gorge.

Nestor topped my list of possibles.

My troops reacted to the welcoming sight with a loud, albeit hoarsely voiced cheer as they wearily thrust their swords and pila skyward, then, at Nestor's bellowed command the Adraniis dispersed, those carrying litters hurrying to where small groups of our wounded sat or lay, patiently waiting for aid and guarded by their fellows. Nestor, Iulius and Cleander also split up, each heading in different directions, drawn to the worried summons of those who'd been tending to the most seriously injured.

Several carts also peeled off, to follow the litter-bearers and our physicians while others continued to slog onward, pulling the converted water and food carts—no easy task with the bone-dry sand chewed up underfoot and sizable pieces of Si'aafu strewn about—until my troops shook themselves from their own stunned amazement and began to converge on the carts like ravenous locusts; within minutes every cart was surrounded, but true to their Kellesuf nature, there was no pushing, no jostling among the ranks. Every man waited his turn, those in the worst shape were urged to go first and each was given the chance to slake his thirst before he stepped aside, opening up a space for the next man, but not before an Adraniis pressed a handful of dried fruit and cheese into his hands.

Men stumbled away, clutching their meager meals, found out-of-the-way spots then began to eat, some wolfing down the food as fast as they could manage, others taking one piece at a time and bringing it to their mouths as if they were so hot and tired it was almost too much effort to eat.

I urged Marcus and Dulcitius to go, to get something to eat and drink, and they did so without any further encouragement, hurrying over to the nearest cart and getting in line with the rest—no pulling rank here—while I started back to the lip of the ravine to check on progress.

"Ley-gate?"

I stopped and turned to find an Adranii woman holding a water bucket in one hand, a ladle in the other—*no*, not just any Adranii woman, but none other than the woman who'd publicly rebuffed Aetius: *Laatao.*

She smiled nervously as she stepped closer, realizing I recognized her and was none to pleased to find her here, then she dipped the ladle into the water bucket and offered it to me.

I accepted it—I was that damned thirsty—downed the water in three loud wincing gulps then handed it back only to find her looking me over, taking in the dried blood that caked my face, my throat and arms, not to mention the burns that had begun to blister.

"You're injured." She met my narrowed gaze with a worried stare as she raised her hand as if planning to touch my face.

I jerked my chin up, out of reach, then grumbled, "Nothing serious," as I roughly wiped my blood-crusted upper lip and nose with the back of my hand. I had no doubt I looked a total mess, close to done in, my helmet, armor and phalerae blackened with drying gore not to mention a goodly amount of my own blood. To someone unused to such I probably looked fatally wounded.

Getting the message, she dropped her hand back to her side and sighed as she fixed her gaze on a nearby cart and the silent, orderly crowd of heat-weary soldiers then her eyes slowly took in the devastation of our surroundings before turning back to me. "Saying thank you for saving us, yet again, saving our children doesn't seem to be enough, does it?"

And it was then, as I saw the look of poorly concealed horror—and yes, blatant revulsion—mixed with guarded relief in her eyes that I realized that for her, for all of the Adraniis, the carnage that encircled us was utterly shocking, incomprehensible in its unconditional and primal savagery; for us it was, well… *quotidianus.*

And in the mood to make *that* distinction clear, I angrily motioned around and replied in an equally angry voice, "This *is* what we blood-thirsty barbarians do—we *kill.* So absolutely no thanks necessary." I was tempted to add that we'd thoroughly enjoyed doing the killing too, but

391 J. E. Bruce

even in my current frame of mind, that seemed just a tad gratuitous, even if totally true.

Laatao looked suitably discomfited, but whether it was in response to my words or my tone I cannot tell you. But dammit, I was hot and tired, my bad leg and shoulder—not to mention the blisters—were really starting to throb. Oh, yes, I had one hell of a splitting headache, so I was indeed in what Felix would call 'a mood'. Her superior attitude and the hurt she caused Aetius still rankled, damned if it didn't. And as I glowered at her nakedly earnest yet deeply aghast expression, I was, yet again, struck with the yawning gulf that separated us, Adranii and Roman, and yet at the same time the intimate ties that bound us inexorably together as humans. Would we ever fully understand the other? More to the point, did we want to?

She abruptly broke our uneasy staring match to look around again, this time with an obvious target in mind, then turned back to me and asked hesitantly, "Where's... Centurion Aetius?"

"Worried he's going to pay you another unwelcome compliment?"

She winced, said, "I deserved that, yes, I did most certainly." She wet her lips, again met my hard gaze and continued, "I wanted to apologize, to him *and* to you, Ley-gate. Maisoh told me of his offer—the offer of your officers—I'm sorry, I *truly* am—I never meant to hurt his feelings, never meant to hurt anyone's feelings..." she abruptly looked away, hastily pulled a filthy rag from her baggy breeches and roughly dabbed her eyes.

There. You've made her cry, Arri—proud of yourself? I dropped my now ashamed gaze to my gore-splattered feet and bit my lip. *Damn—*

"He's a very kind man, your Centurion Aetius," she said softly, drawing my sidelong stare. "A *good* man—I know now he meant me no harm." She sniffed again, wiped her nose on the rag and turned back to me, her eyes glittering and her haggard, sunburnt face smudged with an unflattering mixture of soot and tears. "I wasn't prepared and I... well, I just panicked." She bit her lip, dabbed her eyes again before adding, "Is there anything I can do to make amends?"

She wasn't pretty, this Laatao. I doubted she'd ever been pretty but there were hints that her now withered body had probably been quite voluptuous—before she and the others had been dumped here with hardly anything to eat and even less understanding of how to survive, before the Faoimhuir decided their cosseted Adranii slaves were going to pay for their masters' greed and stupidity, before the strain had taken its inevitable toll on those most unable to defend themselves even against their own kind. Despite the gaunt face, the sunken and shadowed eyes, the dirt and loose skin that hung from now prominent bones Laatao still retained a look of softness about her, as if she'd never known hardship and now she found herself in the hardest spot imaginable and was utterly baffled by it all.

Aetius had seen something in this woman that he found appealing; maybe it was simply that she could cook—the man did love to eat—maybe she reminded him of the original Aetius' long dead wife, maybe it was her obvious and genuine helplessness that urged him to offer his protection. Or maybe this Aetius had had wife too; maybe those memories had started to bubble to the surface.

I took a deep, calming breath—still not having learned my lesson—coughed, then said in a smoke-raspy voice, "Last time I saw him, he was over there." I pointed and she peered into the greasy, eye-stinging haze of smoke. "Here," I added, "I'll help you find him." I took the heavy bucket from her fingers then offered her my free hand.

She was clearly surprised but to her credit she didn't shy away from drying gore that caked my sword arm from fingertips to shoulder, in fact she grasped my hand firmly and together we started off in the direction I'd last seen Aetius. As we walked, she glanced up at me occasionally, out of concern but also now clearly curious. I smiled as I felt her tighten her hold on my fingers and responded in kind, which elicited a shy smile from her, too.

Knowing Aetius' predilections and priorities as I did, I suspected the moment he realized food was on offer he probably left the collecting of arrows and bolts to others and headed towards the nearest cart, which is why I ended up taking Laatao on a roundabout walk that took us past the majority of the carts. In truth I hoped we'd find him hard at work doing something... well, *manly*, something suitably impressive and perhaps cause Laatao to revisit his tentative advances and this time in a positive light.

A short time later we did find him, and not, thank the gods, in line at a cart, or worse, leaning on his scutum, stuffing his grimy face. He was in fact squatting beside a Si'aafu corpse, struggling to free a deeply buried and badly bent pilum shaft from the creature's largely intact torso and grunting and swearing loudly with the effort of it—not exactly the impression I'd hoped for, but marginally better than other possibilities.

Oblivious to our arrival, he continued his litany of grunts alternating with snarled obscenities, which were becoming louder and more creative with each futile tug on the gore-slippery shaft—until I coughed, loudly, startling him and he lost his precarious grip on the shaft and fell back only to sit down, hard.

He swore again, this time explosively as he swiveled his head around to fix his furious squint on the perpetrator—I suspect he suspected it was Rufinius, maybe even Felix, but realizing said perpetrator was me, and far more importantly that I'd brought genteel company, he scrambled to his feet and tried his best to dust himself off—hard to do when you're covered in a gooey mix of sand, sweat and gore—then he stood up straight and saluted smartly. "Legate." He shifted his still startled, blue-eyed stare to Laatao and dipped his helmeted head. "Ma'am."

She smiled thinly as if suddenly wondering what the hell she'd gotten herself into, not that I could blame her. Aetius certainly looked worse than me by a long shot; in fact he was barely recognizable—had it not been for the singed horsehair plume I might have walked right past him in my search.

"Please, call me Laatao. And may I call you Aetius or would you prefer *Centurion* Aetius?"

So, so, so. Someone had been schooling the woman in proper Roman etiquette, or maybe she had better sense than she'd shown earlier. Taken off guard, perhaps, just as she said.

"Aetius is fine," he replied with a deferential dip of his helmeted head as he fixed his pointed gaze on me.

Getting the hint that my presence was no longer needed—*or wanted*—I made my feeble excuses, handed him the water bucket and left the two to figure things out on their own. A desert battlefield strewn with smoldering, smelly and occasionally exploding corpses is not at the top of my list of places to woo a woman but this was Latrunculi after all and if Aetius could win over Laatao amidst the stink and carnage and loud popping sounds, well... it boded well for the rest of my men, each and every one having the right to claim they'd had a direct hand in saving the Adraniis from the slavering jaws of the rapacious Si'aafu. Any doubters need only to look around... and speaking of, I had to wonder if Isem was among the Adraniis who'd brought us succor.

An inner voice warned me not to waste my time looking for him—so I didn't.

Instead I made my limping way back to the lip of the ravine, in the process passing several of the improvised food carts that had been emptied of their original cargo and were now being filled with the recovered arrows and bolts. Enough time had passed and I was curious as to what had transpired in my absence, trusting Maisoh at least would keep her wits about her... while keeping Rufinius and Felix from doing something stupid—or going for each other's throat.

I reached the crumbling lip to find Felix, Maisoh, Borzu, Rufinius, Birral and Silvanus, along with a handful of soldiers now milling around next to the ship and beside a gaping hole in its otherwise featureless hull—presumably the now open hatch. No one looked the slightest bit ruffled so I had to presume the ship had been empty of crew. Good news… as far as it went.

As Marcus suddenly and wordlessly appeared beside me, leading Belili, I cupped my hands to my mouth and bellowed, *"HOW GOES IT?"*

Belili shied and Marcus, clutching the reins, stumbled back as the startled horse side-stepped while everyone below flinched violently and swiveled their heads towards me as my voice echoed off the walls of the ravine.

Felix yelled back, *"ALL CLEAR!"* then he motioned for everyone to climb out of the ravine. Maisoh touched something on the side of the ship and the hole abruptly vanished—leaving Marcus and me blinking at each other in astonishment—then she and Rufinius followed the soldiers as they headed for the low spot in the ravine with Felix and Silvanus bringing up the rear.

We watched as the small party slogged their way up and out of the crumbly-walled rift and back onto the desert proper, then as Felix, Borzu, Rufinius, Maisoh and Birral started towards us, Silvanus and his men, at my approving nod, hurried off in search of what remained of the food and water, some grumbling loudly that no one had bothered to come fetch them while the pickings were better.

As the five stopped beside me, Felix gestured to the abandoned ship, said hoarsely, "Perhaps they were all so eager for a hot meal, no one wanted to stay behind and risk missing out on the feast?"

"A reasonable assumption," I replied, suddenly and uncomfortably aware of Rufinius' enthrallment with the vessel: he hadn't taken his eyes off it during the entire return trip, causing him to stumble several times. "Rufinius, are you all right? *Rufinius?"*

He reluctantly tore his gaze off the ship, fixed his enraptured eyes on me. "It's *huge* inside, Arri—it could carry everyone and everything, including the wagons, in a few trips—we could go anywhere on the planet!"

"Yeah," I replied unenthusiastically. "So I heard."

"Even back to Earth," Borzu added, grinning at me.

I blinked then shifted my startled stare to Felix; he stared back, his now expressionless face speaking volumes. I then turned back to Borzu, replied, *"Earth…?"*

"Assuming you'd want to go back," Maisoh added quickly, with a sidelong, annoyed glance at Borzu.

"Wait until you get a look inside!" Rufinius continued, oblivious as his eyes flicked back to the ship. "You'll be amazed, simply amazed! I could spend a lifetime just figuring out how the plumbing works!"

I couldn't help but smile thinly at Rufinius' grinning excitement. It took a lot to get the man this animated—*but Earth?*

Clearly the gods hadn't forgotten about us, forgotten about this real life and death game of Latruncŭli. They'd just changed the rules *and* upped the ante.

I followed his gaze back to this hideous looking thing that offered so much promise—and pain. If this was true, if I could choose to return, would I? Would I order my men to come with me or let each one decide for himself? What if Felix chose to take his chances here, what if Rufinius and Aetius likewise wanted to remain? And if I—*we*—could return to Earth, that meant the Adraniis could potentially return to their feckless masters, assuming they could find them. If given the chance, would they? Would Eithne choose to go with them?

And assuming everyone wanted to leave, some would, by necessity, have to remain behind at least temporarily, and with each successive trip we'd be leaving a dwindling number of people who'd be at the complete mercy of the Si'aafu and for who knows how long. And each trip would be fraught with danger—there was always the possibility that those left behind would be marooned here as had been the original plan, but in far too few a numbers to have any meaningful chance at survival. The same was true if only a handful elected to stay.

All of my hopes for a future free of the Tuatha and the Faoimhuir, a future built around Eithne and Anachie, my men and the Adraniis seemed in serious doubt now that we had a *choice* to stay or leave, rather than making the best of what we had.

I found myself staring—glaring at the ship. Along with transporting the Si'aafu, it had brought along a host of possibilities, chief among them our collective doom.

I exhaled, glanced around to find everyone staring at me, clearly worried, prompted into thinking along the same lines by my grim expression, so I cleared my throat and forced a smile as I turned to Marcus. "Return to camp—let everyone know the danger's passed... *for now*, but not to relax their guard. We still have company," I jerked my thumb upwards. "And speaking of, set up a rotation of picket duty, starting with your cavalry along with those *sagitarii* and *ballistarii* who remained behind taking the first shift—the infantry's more than earned a few hours rest—not to mention a bath," I added, eyeing Felix's filthy armor and face as he eyed me with a similar, less than impressed impression.

Marcus nodded as he gathered up Belili's reins and reached for the nearside pommels, then stopped and looked back at me. "How 'bout I leave Belili here for you, Legate—I can ride with one of my men." He motioned to the mounted Sisenna and Ulpius.

"I ran out here," I replied. "I think I can manage to walk back."

He looked worriedly at Felix, then back at me and reluctantly nodded. "The rest of us will be along shortly," I continued as he mounted with annoying ease. "Tell Florianus he's got a lot of very tired, *very* hungry men to feed—and we damn well won't settle for more dried fruit and cheese."

"Speaking of… pity to let all this cooked meat go to waste," Marcus remarked, surveying the battlefield from the height of Belili's back, and for a moment everyone thought he was serious and reacted accordingly—until he turned back to us and grinned, his white teeth dazzling against his sloe-black skin. "Turn about is fair play, right, Legate?"

I played along in his well meaning, but rather obvious effort at lightening the mood and motioned to a nearby corpse. "Be my guest, Centurion."

"Me? Not just no, sir, but *hell* no!" He shook his head and wrinkled his nose. "I'll stick with those shrimps if it's all the same to you, sir."

I chuckled, said, "See you back at camp," and motioned for him to take his leave.

He saluted then turned Belili's head and with a click of his tongue sent the warhorse trotting away; Sisenna and Ulpius joined him and once well free of those on foot, the three urged their mounts into an easy canter.

"What about the ship?" Borzu asked.

I eyed him. For just an instant I'd forgotten about the damned ship and all the troubles it brought and let my annoyance show in the tone of my voice. "What about it?"

"You're going to post guards, aren't you?"

"Guard it from what? I don't see anyone about who wants it—aside from you, that is."

"But what if the Si'aafu come back for it?"

"Not long ago you suggested they wouldn't be back for some time—now you think they'll come back tonight?"

"Not tonight, no, but—"

397 J. E. Bruce

"That vessel is going to be the least of my concerns if or when the Si'aafu return, Captain. But since you seem so concerned about it, I'll supply you and any other Adraniis who volunteer to remain behind with what weapons we can spare. I'm not leaving any of my men out here to protect that thing—as far as I'm concerned, if the Si'aafu want it they can have it."

"But—"

"Have everyone form up," I turned to Felix and Rufinius, effectively dismissing Borzu and his demands, "I want it neat and orderly mind you—let's get the hell out of here."

My order was greeted with a very frustrated huff of breath from Borzu, which drew my equally irked gaze.

"I'll see what I can do, Legate—since *you* obviously fail to grasp just how critical this vessel could be to our mutual survival." With that he stalked off; Birral gave me an odd look then hurriedly trotted after his captain, every bit the loyal dog.

I followed the two with my bemused gaze then turned to Maisoh, expecting a similar reaction. She only shrugged and smiled faintly, as if in apology for Borzu's wrong-headedness... or grudging acceptance of mine.

I promptly shifted my irritated gaze to two of my three senior centurions—Aetius being noticeably absent, a point not missed by either Felix or Rufinius. Rufinius eyed me and sensing something was up, glanced about. He finally spotted Aetius... and Laatao, grinned and elbowing Felix, whispered something in his ear.

Felix followed his pointed gaze and smiled; Maisoh looked downright smug.

I was suddenly too weary to ask if she'd had a hand in the whole matter. The flush and excitement of the rout had quickly evaporated under the furnace-like sunlight and the nauseating stink of the Si'aafu dead hung over us with not even the faintest of breezes to disperse the thick smoke-haze that burned eyes and throat alike.

My bad leg throbbed, my bad shoulder ached and yes, I still had a near-blinding headache—definitely time to quit the field and return to the relative safety and comfort of our camp and the well-earned attentions of our grateful Adranii charges... not to mention a nap and wash up.

I looked down at myself, plucked unhappily at my gore-sticky chest harness and grimaced. Yes, *definitely* a wash up—*then* a nap. Everything else, including what to do about the Si'aafu ship, could damned well wait.

XV

I'm pleased to say that what greeted us on our triumphant return was indeed a proper heroes' homecoming, a suitable and befitting tribute to my men and what they'd accomplished—by any standard a truly astonishing feat for us, an equally astounding *defeat* for the Si'aafu.

By design and for maximum impact the Adraniis entered the camp first, bringing the wounded, some on litters, most walking but only with help and once within the walls they were swarmed by those left behind and promptly whisked away to the medical wagons.

Next came the baggage carts overloaded and wobbly with our recovered weapons along with the armor and shields of the injured... and finally we made our entrance: centurions and signifers to the fore of each century—Cleander having had the forethought to bring our standards along—leading wyvern glinting in the smoky mid-day sun, my men marching four abreast in perfectly cadenced formation, scutums drawn close and pila tips pointing skyward, helmet-framed faces wiped clean of any hint of strain as they marched through the cleared gap in the wall, a soot-smudged and scarlet procession that eeled its way into the gorge and through the rapidly parting yet silent throng of Adraniis—and in case you're wondering, not a single Adranii, not even Borzu, elected to remain behind. The moment he and his volunteer guards realized I was deadly serious about quitting the field and taking all of *my* soldiers with me, he and they wasted no time in quietly rejoining their fellow Adraniis. Huge surprise, eh?

Felix, Rufinius, Aetius and I had elected to take up the rear, in part to watch for stragglers, in part so my worsening limp wasn't so apparent to my troops and especially to the Adraniis on the return trip and no sooner had the four of us passed through the wall than a booming cheer went up, first from our cavalry and *ballistarii* along with the *sagitarii* still stationed high above, but quickly joined by the Adraniis, the collective, overjoyed and yes, thoroughly welcoming outburst reverberating off the high rock walls.

Jotia, Storax and Baculus had been at the head of the column and the instant the cheers died down Jotia turned and hoarsely bellowed the long awaited order to halt.

It had been an exhausting march and in the full heat of the midday and as the soldiers came to a lurching, staggering stop, most wobbled despite their best efforts to not to look utterly undone by the morning's events. To their credit the entire column maintained order, standing stock-still, although in truth many were leaning heavily on their shields or pila and heaving for breath, awaiting their legate's pleasure, despite the enticing aromas that surrounded them, despite their overwhelming fatigue and thirst.

I should have maintained discipline; these men would do without question anything I ordered them to do. I should have ordered them to clean their armor, to bathe, to have their wounds tended to and only after those critical chores were done could they seek food and drink and then a well-deserved rest, or rest then food and drink, whichever they found most appealing. But I was every bit as heat-weary as they were, every bit in desperate need of something to eat and drink, shaky in fact with my vision blurring, not to mention in equally desperate need of a few hours uninterrupted sleep and maybe a soothing salve for the blisters—and it was barely past noon, which also meant that the Si'aafu would have to wait another day to plead their case before the gods of Latruncŭli if they decided to question the legality of the massacre... my pathetic attempt at a private joke about a particular quirk in the infamously labyrinthine Roman legal system that fell flat even with me.

Feeble joke aside, it *was* barely past midday and that meant those who chose to could bathe and clean their armor *after* they'd got several hours of well-earned sleep and still be able to get those crucial tasks done well before it got dark when the camp needed every able-bodied soldier armored up and alert, just in case Maisoh and Borzu *had* wildly overestimated the lasting shock-value of the Si'aafu's stunning defeat and subsequent slaughter.

So, at my signal the centurions gave their centuries leave and the precise line quickly disintegrated: Adraniis rushed the column, helping those clearly about to collapse over to the nearest cook fire or medical wagon, while those still able to move under their own power stumbled after any Adranii who beckoned to them, promising food, water and probably first and foremost in the minds of my exhausted men, a place to sit or even better, lay down.

And behind us a team of Adraniis, under the watchful eye of Jom, hurried to rebuild the wall as the engine crews went about repositioning their machines, again, just in case. While Aetius claimed he was going off to find something to eat we all suspected he was actually going in search of Laatao.

Felix, at my grumbled urging hurried off to find Eithne and Anachie, to assure them we'd both survived... relatively unscathed.

Rufinius and I remained behind to watch the rebuilding of the wall—me out of surprised appreciation, Rufinius out of concern that the job be done right, and within a short time the wall was again a solid rock barrier and to Rufinius' liking no less, cutting us off from the desert—and the desert from us.

At his voiced approval, I smiled, clapped him on the back and said, "Maisoh's waiting for you, my friend."

"And you?" he asked, wincing as he pried off his helmet.

"Bath. I want a *damned* bath." I did, desperately so, but now that I'd recovered from the march back to the gorge, foremost in my mind was everything the Si'aafu ship represented, good *and* bad, and I wanted to confront each of those possibilities, at least for now, *alone*. There'd be time enough, later, to discuss the matter with Felix, Rufinius and Aetius, Eithne—everyone, yes, even Borzu.

With that I walked—all right, fine, *staggered* towards the small pool we'd designated as the public bath, but first I made a quick detour to our sleeping spot. I managed to strip down to my filthy undertunic and breeches then I limped the rest of the way, stopping only briefly to accept the damned gratitude of every damned Adranii I passed, along with gulping down the mugs of water they insistently pressed into my hands. While the water was welcome—although given a choice I'd have preferred wine—couldn't they see that their heartfelt expressions of thanks could wait?

Obviously not.

I also wondered just how long this undying appreciation would last. A day? A week? Given my admittedly limited experience with them, I put my money on the moment they learned there was an alternative to a grueling trek over the pass—or a way back to their spineless masters.

Keeping that thought foremost, I managed to break through their grinning and backslapping gauntlet and stumbled on, through the man-made gap in the rockfall and into the finger chasm only to find the smaller pool deserted—clearly my men had opted for food and sleep first. And while the once pristine pool was no longer quite so pristine after being used as a communal bath by almost fifty five hundred people, it was still incredibly inviting and I wasted no time in wading over to a waist-deep spot next to a large boulder.

I looked around once more and satisfied I was indeed alone, I peeled off the undertunic, gave it a vigorous scrub—well, fine, as vigorous as I could manage—followed by an equally vigorous swish in the water then I tossed the marginally less filthy garment across the boulder to dry. My equally grimy breeches and underwear followed in short order.

Those chores done, I sank down, savoring delicious the feel of cool water that came up to my chin and soft, fine sun-warmed sand under my bare butt. I scooped up some of that sand and used it to scrub my skin while I still had the energy to do it—the combination of cool water, hot sunlight and aching muscles was rapidly sapping what little strength I had left.

In truth I didn't even have the energy to do what I'd come here to do: confront the Si'aafu ship and everything it represented. Instead I just let my exhausted mind wander and it happily trundled off to ponder far more appealing topics, such as what Florianus and his cooks had been up to; the aromas that had met us when we returned, triumphant, and which followed me here were certainly enticing. My stomach concurred and grumbled, loudly.

I patted it. *Patience is a virtue, belly—so be quiet.*

I found I didn't even mind the occasional tickle of curious shrimp, drawn, I presume, to the nasty crud that was now slowly sloughing off of me, staining the water around me a sickly greenish-brown. It was only fair after all, as I imagined I'd be nibbling on quite a few of their fellows in short order—of course the idea that I'd be eating something that had been eating us—or should I say eating our cast-offs did make me briefly rethink my meal selection…

Satisfied I'd gotten myself as clean as I could manage, I pressed my back against the warm, water-smooth boulder, closed my eyes and allowed my aging, aching and thoroughly battered body to finally relax.

Ah, bliss…

I was so relaxed I shrugged off the niggly feeling that I was no longer alone by assuring myself one of my men had come to his senses and realized he'd sleep much more soundly if he washed up—and that washing up might in fact dramatically increase his chances of not sleeping *alone.* Perhaps it was Felix; like me he was always a stickler for cleanliness, and besides he was still desperate to impress Eithne—and dried blood and gore was usually not high on most women's aphrodisiac list—although I've known a few who were hugely smitten with gladiators fresh, so to speak, from the arena, and the gorier the gladiator the better. I'd heard rumors of one wealthy matron—some even went so far as to claim it was the Empress herself—who had an insatiable predilection for dead gladiators and paid handsomely for discreet deliveries to her private villa; what she did with the corpses after that was anyone's guess, and as you can imagine, quite a few did guess, each suggestion more bizarre than the last.

But I digress…

Maybe whomever it was thought I was in fact dozing and wisely didn't want to disturb the legate and so was being as quiet as humanly possible.

Maybe he'd even elected to wait for his bath and had left me to my well-deserved soak in total solitude.

Maybe...

After a moment and not hearing any splashing, not hearing anything—suddenly remembering that I'd recently found damned good reason for bodyguards—I slowly opened one eye a crack and gave my surroundings a surreptitious look-see.

If there was someone about, they weren't readily visible—by accident or design—and sore muscles that had only just relaxed instinctively tensed up.

I was weaponless—unless you counted my sopping wet clothes, which I suppose one *could* use to whack an assailant upside the head—and I began to silently curse my exhausted stupidity—*and* my equally inane assumptions that the expressions of heartfelt gratitude I'd heard on my way here were truly heart-felt and extended to *all* of the Adraniis.

Isem *had* been noticeably absent from the welcoming committee after all. And I certainly wasn't at the top of Borzu's current best buds list.

I reached up, slowly, and began to tug the undertunic off the boulder—it was closest and hey, it was better than nothing—while I dug my fingers into the sand. My cunning plan was to wallop whoever it was with the sopping undertunic, hurl the sand in his eyes then dive underwater and make for the deepest part of the pool. Adraniis couldn't swim, so as long as my visitor wasn't armed with pila or bow and arrows—or, gods forbid, another of those nasty projectile weapons—I could keep him at bay until my men came running in response to my manly scream for help—

A tiny pebble bounced down the boulder and splashed into the water not far from my left hip, scattering a cloud of tiny shrimp that had been feeding on my castoffs—

To hell with subtly! I grabbed the undertunic, lurched out of the water and wheeled around—

—only to come fist to face with a grinning Anachie.

I pulled my punch just short of making impact and gasped, *"Anachie—!"*

"Arr-ee!" he cried and leapt off the boulder, trusting me to catch him; I did, barely, then stumbled back, into deeper water, almost losing my grip on him as he squirmed around, trying to get his arms around my neck, giggling and splashing and not at all afraid.

I finally got my footing, got a better grip on him and wiping my wet hair out of my eyes, spluttered, "What... what are you doing here?"

"I was *worried,*" he said, suddenly serious, his large eyes taking in my bruised and battered countenance as he clung tightly to my neck.

"Does you mother know you're here? Did Felix tell you to sneak up on me?" I glanced around while trying to surreptitiously wash the crusted blood off my nose and upper lip—if true, I was going to have words with both of them but as far as I could tell, we were alone—which sent a fresh wave of panic through me as I realized how easily he could have drown and I made a mental note to post at least two guards at the pool at all times while we remained here, modesty be damned; it would be an unspeakable tragedy to have saved everyone from the Si'aafu only to have an overly curious child—or even an adult—drown in this pool that had been deliberately walled off for privacy—and why hadn't I thought of this before? Maybe Felix or Rufinius or Aetius had—and hadn't thought to mention it, assuming I trusted them to deal with such everyday details. One could hope.

He shook his head vehemently. "No!"

I hugged him tightly, said, "Never, *ever* come here alone, never get near *any* water—not until Felix or Aetius or Rufinius or I teach you to swim, agreed?"

He stared at me, his lower lip held in his teeth.

"Promise?"

"Yes, Arr-ee."

I nodded, gave him another hug then looked around for my clothing. Startled by his unexpected leap of faith, I'd let go of the undertunic in order to grab him and now the garment floated some distance away; my breeches and underwear were even farther, still drying on the boulder. I'd have to swim to reach any, taking Anachie with me because I didn't trust him not to follow me.

"I need to grab that," I said, gesturing with my chin to the floating island that was my undertunic. "You come with me, all right?"

He grinned. "You're going to teach me to swim?"

"Not right now. I'm really, really tired—*sleepy*, understand?—later, all right? Now, wrap your arms around my neck and hold on."

He did as I asked and I carefully kicked off the sandy floor of the pool, then using my legs and one arm, keeping the other arm firmly wrapped around his waist, I swam over to my undertunic, grabbed it, handed it to him, then turned around and swam back to water shallow enough Anachie could stand on his own feet with his head and shoulders just above the surface.

I then quickly donned my undertunic and once clothed, I stood up, took his hand in mine and we walked out of the pool and directly into the path of Eithne's worried stare, Felix's too, along with, I noticed, two of my *sagitarii*. So, my bodyguards had followed me and reasonably assumed Anachie posed no threat, not realizing that I might have seriously hurt him by accident—as I had come very close to doing.

"Hi," I said feebly, using my fingers to comb my wet hair out of my eyes.

Eithne looked at me, at the equally drenched Anachie then blurted out, *"We've been searching all over for you!"*

Anachie tried to slip behind me, but I grabbed his shoulder, drew him back out to face his mother's anger and Felix's fright.

"Anachie," Felix said, squatting in front of him and placing his hands on his small, bony shoulders. "You really, *really* scared us—don't go running off like that again, *please."*

"But I wanted to see Arr-ee!"

"I know you did," Felix flicked me a reproachful look that said, 'you should have come with me.' I also noted he'd found time to wash and his wounds had been dressed—at Eithne's insistence I'm sure.

"I'm sorry, Anachie," I said, dropping to my haunches so I too could stare him square in the eye. "I just wanted to get cleaned up—I *should* have come seen you first. I'm sorry. Will you forgive me?"

He stared at me, all solemn, lower lip held out in a pout. "Maybe."

"How 'bout I give you a ride on Wushah? Will that make up for it?"

"Maybe."

Felix rose with a sidelong glance at Eithne then turned to Anachie and said, "I was told Florianus is making something extra special for the evening meal and wants *you* to be the official taste tester."

Anachie glanced back at me, clearly torn between such an honor and me.

"You'd best not keep Florianus and his creation waiting—I'll be along in a moment. I need to speak with your mother in private."

He nodded then reached for Felix and Felix hoisted him up onto his shoulders. Anachie waved at us then hung on as Felix dodged and darted back and forth, leaving Anachie squealing in delight as the two made their zigzagging way back to the main camp.

As I followed the two with my eyes I realized that Anachie clearly hadn't puzzled out our rather unorthodox relationship with his mother, but he'd clearly decided upon his relationship with us: I was unquestionably his father now, a role, a responsibility I both savored and feared, wanting to be everything to him I'd so desperately craved at his age, yet having no suitable model to go on; Felix was now his elder brother, playmate and protector, a role for which Felix was supremely suited. Hopefully, by the time Anachie was old enough to realize Felix was something else to his mother our situation would have become the norm.

As the two vanished behind the rockfall that separated the finger chasm from the gorge, I smiled and shook my head, then turned my full attention to Eithne while the two archers, taking Felix's departure as a clue, discreetly melted back, to guard the only entrance. "I'm sorry I didn't come with Felix; I should've, I didn't think—"

She pressed her fingers to my lips. *"Hush.* No harm done." She looked me up and down and slowly shook her head as she fingered the freshly scabbed over gash on my arm and my now lividly bruised nose and cheek. "But speaking of harm—are you all right?"

"Never better." I jerked her tight against me, realizing I wasn't *quite* as tired as I thought I was. It had been my intention, now that we were alone, to raise the matter of the ship, get her reaction to the matter—yes, to reassure myself she'd want to remain with us, regardless of whether we decided to stay or return to Earth. But now we were alone—relatively speaking—other thoughts, more immediate thoughts took hold.

"Perhaps you should see Cleander, let him—"

"I have a better idea. Much, *much* better."

She raised an intrigued brow.

"How 'bout we let *you* be the judge." With that I drew her, now giggling, back into the shallows of the pool and around behind the boulder, out of sight of the guards—in order to retrieve my breeches and underwear. Honest.

— ii —

I set the empty bowl on the grassy ground beside me, sighed contentedly then grinned at Felix only to find that despite the fact that he was seated upright and cross-legged with Anachie cradled in his lap, he was now fast asleep, as was Anachie, the two swaddled in Felix's heavy cloak, their faces bathed in the flickering light of a nearby campfire.

In fact the entire camp had collapsed into an exhausted silence as the extraordinary events of the day finally caught up everyone—not even Gratian, who'd fought has hard as any of my troops, was up to treating us to a song. Many had already bedded down; those who hadn't now formed small groups, seated or standing around the larger fires that kept the gathering chill at bay, speaking in smoke-hoarse whispers if speaking at all. Night had fallen and the sky above the fire-lit gorge walls was ablaze with stars along with a goodly portion of the whirlpool—yes, despite the risks, I'd given the go-ahead to keep the fires lit, perhaps out of the age-old human want to keep the night—and those who might use it to their advantage—at bay. Besides, the Si'aafu knew where to find us if they had a mind to come looking for more of the same.

I truly must have been getting soft because I'd also—although in my defense *very* reluctantly—agreed to arming a group of Adraniis who foolishly insisted on returning to the ship before it got dark, 'to protect it', Borzu steadfastly maintained, as if Adraniis could protect anything but their own damned self-interests, which, I suppose you could say, the ship personified. And yes, within minutes of our triumphant return the entire camp knew all about it, but surprisingly the Adraniis as a whole hadn't reacted as I'd expected them to react: wildly enthusiastic relief that salvation was near at hand. In fact their muted reaction had been quite the opposite, so much so I'd been utterly unaware that word had gotten out—at first.

While I'd been occupied soaking away my aches and pains, Aetius had been equally busy strolling from cook fire to cook fire, sampling what was on offer, and in doing so happened to notice a large gathering of Adraniis not far from the waterfall. Curious, he quietly joined them only to find none other than Borzu the center of attention as the captain made his unofficial 'official' announcement of our discovery, in order to take full credit and hopefully shape camp opinion more to his liking. But, again according to Aetius, most of the assembled Adraniis absorbed the news in silence, or like Laatao, who appeared at his elbow as Borzu continued to boast of 'his' good news, with poorly concealed worry.

Clearly irked by the general lack of interest, Borzu insisted right then and there on returning to the ship, alone if need be—until the rest of us came to our senses—with the presumption that his act of selfless heroism would shame his fellow Adraniis into recognizing their shortsightedness.

His timing, however, could have been better. For most Adraniis the realization that they were still alive, that we, their self-anointed protectors had in fact protected them, had in fact utterly destroyed the Si'aafu was more than enough excitement for one day—everything else, even a potential way back home, could wait. There were, of course, fools who agreed with Borzu and a few who, emboldened by their captain's remarks, loudly voiced their view that *I* was in fact the fool—all done, I might add, while I was conveniently out of earshot.

It didn't help my frame of mind that Aetius and Laatao came to warn me of what was going on, in the process interrupting Eithne and me at a very critical moment. I'd *earned* a few minutes alone with her, damned if I hadn't, but the duties of the legate always took precedence over personal needs, and someone stirring up trouble was definitely a matter that needed the legate's immediate attention—but not before I sent Aetius and Laatao off to find Felix and Anachie while I escorted Eithne back to our sleeping spot.

Once Aetius and Laatao rejoined us, bringing Felix and Anachie with them, Eithne, Anachie and Laatao as well were left under the watchful gaze of the *sagitarii* while Aetius, Felix and I left to deal with Borzu, and by *deal* I mean I offered him exactly what I'd offered him out on the desert: what few weapons we could spare but not a single soldier. Take it or leave it.

So, just before dusk as the desert cooled and the last of the afternoon dust devils lazily spun itself into nothingness, twenty-odd volunteers led by a publicly very indignant Borzu and armed with their own puny weapons plus a few pila we couldn't really afford to lose but which I was now obliged to provide, scrambled over the wall and headed for the distant ravine.

As you might imagine, I hadn't bothered to walk with him to the wall, to formally see him and his companions off. Neither had any of my officers. As far as we were concerned the moment they set foot beyond the scree wall they were on their own—a fact I'd made *very* clear to Borzu, prompting him to snatch a proffered pila from a rather taken aback Germanus without so much as a thank you before storming off to join his 'guards' in their absurd mission. If they got into trouble that was too damned bad and if—gods forbid—the Si'aafu did sneak back to reclaim their property, well... let's face it, Borzu and his buddies would be little better than a celebratory snack.

The over-the-shoulder look Borzu gave me as he stalked away to rally his fools—er, I mean *fellows* suggested he'd come to have serious second thoughts and had assumed I was going to offer him a last minute, face-saving way out.

You'd have thought he would've known me better by now.

I had other, far more important matters to attend to than waving him a fond farewell, first and foremost our wounded. By design I'd given my physicians time to assess, inventory and treat the damage before I came calling and I must say I was greatly relieved and heartened by Cleander's report that while many of the injuries sustained in the Si'aafu rout were serious and painful, none were life threatening. He also had one bit of surprising news: the woman I'd spotted days before, heavy with child, had gone into labor—the stress of the Si'aafu attack he said—and shortly before we returned to camp she'd given birth to a boy, mother and baby doing as well as could be expected, which in truth wasn't all that well.

So, on a day full of so much death, there was also a tiny spark of life. My men reacted to the news of the birth as if this was an omen, a sign that the gods truly favored us—the unexpected and total massacre of the Si'aafu having already been consigned to ancient history. Such was the thinking of former Kellesuf who had reasons, damned *good* reasons for not wasting time reminiscing. To them only the future mattered; the past was just too painful to contemplate.

Felix and I spent time with my troops, taking the time to tell each man how proud we were of him and we were immensely proud, while I savored the simple fact that all had survived the day; we did the same with my centurions and over fire-warmed mugs of wine, Felix and I oversaw the arranging of shifts for picket duty.

By now Felix was noticeably wobbly, almost asleep on his feet, so I sent him off to our sleeping spot under the pretext of checking on Eithne and Anachie while assuring him I'd join him shortly. He didn't argue but instead nodded dumbly before stumbling off into the darkness—followed discreetly by a far more alert soldier, while I, along with my equally vigilant bodyguard, made the rounds of the crowded cook fires. The matter of Borzu's angry departure required some delicate diplomacy with the Adraniis, and the sooner I dealt with the matter, the better.

To my immense relief everywhere we stopped we were greeted with friendly albeit tired smiles along with platters heaped of food, which my guard happily accepted, in fact he managed to consume a truly astonishing quantity of food while still keeping a wary eye on our surroundings. I was just too damned worn out to be hungry—or wary for that matter—but I nevertheless grabbed a bite here and there, lingering at each campfire only long enough so my Adranii hosts wouldn't take my leave-taking with offense and further exacerbate the very problem I was trying to resolve. Thankfully, any further discussion about the ship itself and what to do with it appeared to have been shelved, at least for tonight, by unanimous, albeit unspoken consent.

When I finally staggered over to our sleeping spot, I found to my surprise that Felix, Eithne and Anachie had waited up for me. Well, that's not entirely true. Eithne was wide-awake. Felix and Anachie... not so much.

Eithne smiled, then held up a bowl of roasted shrimp and eel, along with a mug of wine as she said, "We were starting to wonder what had become of you."

"Proving to everyone that I'm not a petty tyrant took longer than planned."

"Had we known that was your plan," she flicked the decidedly droopy-eyed Felix a sidelong look before turning back to me, "we'd have assumed you wouldn't be back before sunrise... if then, and not waited up."

Felix managed a soft grunt, which I assume was his attempt at a chuckle, rather than him agreeing with Eithne.

I replied by sticking out my tongue at her. She grinned and wiggled her brows suggestively.

Normally I would have responded in kind, but I was too tired even for that—too tired even if Eithne did all the work. Instead I eased myself down next to her with a long and weary sigh, accepted the proffered the bowl and mug, took a deep swig of wine, then at Eithne's prodding stare, I began to eat.

And now, as I'd swallowed the last bite, Eithne, who'd been curled up beside me, wrapped in my cloak and gazing at a nearby fire, lifted her eyes to mine and patted my belly. "Full?"

I nodded.

"Now how 'bout you get some sleep? You look utterly done-in."

"I'm too tired to sleep." And it was true. I was *that* bone-weary and worse, still full of aches and pains—so much so I'd briefly thought about asking Nestor for one of those miraculous lozenges even if it meant risking him demanding I undergo a complete exam first—I was the legate after all and needed to be clear-headed and well-rested to face whatever the next dawn brought, to deal with the matter of the ship first and foremost, but as I'd walked among the wounded, the newly injured, murmuring words of encouragement, of praise and painfully aware that we had a finite supply of the medicine, I lied when he asked if I needed anything.

I wasn't exactly regretting my decision, but I wasn't anticipating a restful night either. Felix, on the other hand, and going by his now totally relaxed face and intermittent, grunting snores clearly wasn't suffering the same afflictions, damn him—

"Come on," Eithne urged, tugging at my elbow.

I lay back and she drew the cloak over both of us then as I wrapped my arm around her, she snuggled up against me, carefully, using my bad shoulder as a pillow—I didn't mind, not one bit. She was warm, soft… she still smelled of fresh grass—and she was *alive*.

Everyone was alive.

Not a single death on our side—and one birth.

I wanted to savor that—savor the sheer magnitude of what we—what my men had done. And yes, what *I'd* done. Yet again, I'd overcome incredible odds, some might even say impossible odds and I'd not just survived but had come out victorious.

"What are you thinking?" she whispered in my ear.

I smiled, knowing she had no idea just how much those four words meant to me: that my private thoughts were once again truly mine—*and* private. And as much as loved her and wanted to share my life with her, I needed that, needed a place to retreat to, to be alone with myself. So I replied with four words I hoped meant as much to her: "That I love you."

She hugged me tightly, kissed me firmly on the lips, murmured, "I love you too," and then startled me by thumbing me in the ribs. "Now, *go* to sleep."

— iii —

I was startled out of a sound and dreamless sleep by a very strange noise: a deep, dull hum that seemed to come from the sky above, from the surrounding gorge and the ground beneath me—even from deep within my own bones. An instant later, the hum was joined by the alarming wail of buccinas from high above.

I tossed the cloak off me, uncovering a now equally wide-eyed Eithne in my haste and grabbing my gladius I scrambled to my feet only to find the rest of the camp likewise awakened. If the strange hum and the warning blasts from the buccinas wasn't enough to throw the camp into turmoil, our animals joined the uproar, whinnying, lowing and barking in terror.

By now everyone was either on their feet or in the process of rising, heads snapping this way and that, many fearfully looking up at the encircling rock walls as if fully expecting them to come crashing down on us as the deep hum intensified—setting the mirror-still water of the pool to quivering as tiny pebbles, cast from the chasm's heights that overhung the waterfall, peppered the pool's surface.

Felix appeared beside me, having handed off a frightened Anachie to Eithne and raking his hair out of his eyes snarled, *"What the hell?"*

Before I respond with, *"Hell if I know,"* a startled yell behind me—from the mouth of the gorge—caused everyone to turn as one then stare in gaping shock at a massive black *something* that had engulfed a goodly portion of the star-filled, eastern horizon.

"SI'AAFU!" someone screamed, shattering the instant of horrified paralysis.

Adraniis panicked, grabbed their children and scattered, some back to the relative safety of the fissure, others towards the closer but smaller cracks in the gorge walls, clearly preferring the risk of the rock collapsing on them than the Si'aafu, while my men, equally unnerved but for vastly different reasons scrambled to snatch up their weapons and armor.

The shape began to rise higher above the gorge, now visibly wobbling as the deep hum rapidly turned to a high-pitched, ear-numbing whine that muffled the screams of the women and children, the terrified whinnying of the tethered horses, the hysterically barking dogs and the bellowed commands of my centurions.

As the Adraniis bolted for cover my soldiers ran the opposite way, for the wall, for the engines. Those high above wisely hunkered down, having realized very quickly that whatever it was, it was too high and too huge for their arrows to reach, much less wound.

I grabbed my leather tunic, pulled it on, snatched up my mail and managed to get the shirt over my head and settled then as I snatched up my helmet, I yelled at Eithne, *"GET ANACHIE TO THE FISSURE!"*

She grasped my chin, kissed me on the lips then, grabbing Anachie's, hand the two fled.

Felix, dressed in his leather tunic was still struggling with his banded armor—yet another reason I've always favored ring-mail: easy *off*, easy *on*.

"LEAVE IT!" I barked and nodding he tossed the lorica aside, grabbed his helmet and sword and together we joined others running pell-mell for the wall.

To my surprise I suddenly found Jom running abreast of us.

I flicked him a sidelong, acknowledging glance, and, to his credit I noticed he was clutching an Adranii pike.

Even more shocking was that more Adraniis soon joined us—men *and* women, Maisoh, Birral and Lujaji among them—likewise armed and we reached the wall to find the engines fully manned and loaded, their crews awaiting orders to fire… but at what? A spreading darkness?

I scrambled up onto the wall, finding the footing precarious as the scree that made up the wall was being shaken loose by the intense vibration, Felix, Maisoh, Birral, Lujaji and Jom following, only to find Rufinius, Jotia, Titivillus, Marcus and Aetius already there, staggering like drunkards barely able to keep on their feet.

Rufinius turned his wild eyes on me, yelled over the din, *"IT'S THE SHIP!"*

And it was.

The Si'aafu ship had indeed risen out of the ravine like some hideous specter from its grave, an ominous and rapidly enlarging black *nothingness*. There was no reflection of starlight on metal—it was as if the ship was consuming the sky itself, swallowing stars whole and growing with each massive bite.

Jom grabbed my shoulder, leaned close and yelled: *"IT'S NOT THE SI'AAFU!"*

I stared at him as if he'd gone mad. *"WHAT? BUT—"*

"IF IT WAS THE SI'AAFU THEY'D HAVE TAKEN OFF OR ATTACKED! IT'S GOT TO BE—"

"BORZU!" I fixed my now enraged glare on the ship as my fingers instinctively tightened their hold on the grip of my sword. *"THAT GODS DAMNED FUCKING BAST—"*

"NO!" Jom gave my arm a vicious jerk to reclaim my full attention but in the process came perilously close to costing both of us our balance. *" DON'T YOU SEE?—THEY'RE CLEARLY HAVING PROBLEMS FIGURING OUT HOW TO FLY IT! THE CAPTAIN CAN'T BE AT THE CONTROLS! IT'S GOT TO BE ISEM AND HIS LOT!"*

Isem! I hadn't seen him with the others who left with Borzu; of course I hadn't seen them off, either. What seemed like a suitable slap in the face at the time now appeared to be a serious, possibly fatal oversight—on my part.

I swallowed hard, fixed my still fierce gaze on the rapidly enlarging pool of black now almost directly above us and suddenly wished it *were* the Si'aafu we were dealing with. Si'aafu I could understand: their motives were utterly unambiguous.

I swiveled my furious eyes back to Jom. *"THEN DO SOMETHING!"*
"WHAT WOULD YOU HAVE ME DO?" he fired back with startling ferocity.

I started to open my mouth but instead grimaced, tried to cover my ears—hard to do while wearing a helmet—the noise, the intense vibration, was reaching a crescendo—

"OH… SHIT!"

I followed Jom's horrified stare just in time to see the ship suddenly drop, kicking up a thick cloud of dust, then lurch sideways as if it was about to smash broadside into the gorge. We all instinctively ducked, not that it would have done us a fat lot of good, but just short of impact it abruptly gained ground and suddenly sped off, leaving a glowing trail that briefly lit up the dust cloud and desert floor as well as the far distant eastern peaks as it again swooped low then arced high into the sky—

—and was *gone…* leaving behind a silence so profound it was as if we'd all been rendered deaf.

I stared after it, my body numb from the intense vibration, my skull pounding in rapid cadence with my thumping heart. I knew better than to speak. No one would be able to hear me. So I waited until my abused ears started picking up on familiar noises, like my own labored breath, Felix's gasping wheeze and the high-pitched ping and clatter of pebbles dislodged by the shaking still tumbling down the gorge's rock face.

I glanced around at my centurions and saw my own stunned incredulity mirrored in their slack-jawed faces.

I'll give Marcus his due; he was the first to find his voice with a simply worded, if badly shaken, "One problem solved."

Of course in solving one problem, Isem had birthed a host of new ones.

"We need to leave," Jom said hoarsely, accompanied by unhappy nods of Maisoh, Birral and Lujaji, "get the hell away from here and quickly."

I whole-heartedly agreed, having no desire to linger myself, to see what else Isem's reckless actions might shake loose. "Get back to camp—Marcus, Jotia, Maisoh, Lujaji, Birral and Titivillus—go with Jom. Order everyone to pack up—I want to be ready to leave by dawn if not sooner."

One by one they edged around me, around Felix, Rufinius and Aetius, then hurried off, scampering down the wall then one-by-one leaping into the darkness below.

"Now what?" Rufinius asked, trying but failing utterly to look and sound unperturbed.

I scanned the seemingly tranquil night sky then dropped my gaze to my three closest friends. "Now we hope the Si'aafu chase after Isem while *we* go to ground."

— iv —

While a mixed contingent of infantry and Adraniis toiled to clear a path through the dead Si'aafu wide enough for the wagons to pass, a unit of cavalrymen tasked with reconnoitering the star-lit desert happened across Borzu—or, should I say they happened across his body, not quite half way between the ravine and the gorge mouth.

Cleander, Nestor and Khouri, after examining the corpse agreed he'd been badly beaten before being pushed, still alive, out of the ship. This matched reports from the archers high on the promontory who reported seeing a flash of light, like a door opening and closing just before the ship sped off. By the scrapes and bruises on his badly broken knuckles, he'd clearly put up a good fight but it was the fall that had actually killed him. So, he died as he'd lived, trying to protect his crew and their kin, first from the Si'aafu, then the Faoimhuir and finally, paradoxically, from his fellow Adraniis.

I freely admit I never liked the man, never trusted him—never shook the sense that he'd tried to manipulate Felix and my officers while I was conveniently incapacitated, playing on their Kellesuf naïveté and almost succeeding, then he repeatedly tried manipulate me and that despite him claiming otherwise, he'd never fully overcome his belief that we were somehow inferior. That being said, he also tried to do his best for his people and for that I could muster up some grudging respect—but he'd also been a fool and been played for a fool, assuming men like Isem could be trusted.

The badly shaken Adraniis insisted that their beloved captain be given a proper burial before we decamped and they collectively agreed on a spot not far from the waterfall; I, in turn, insisted it be a quick and simple affair.

It wasn't until I was about to preside over the interment that I learned that Borzu had a wife, along with two adult sons, who, along with their wives and children had, as closest kin, the misfortune to accompany him to this world. He'd never mentioned their presence to me; perhaps he assumed I knew, or felt it wasn't critical to our discussions—or maybe he didn't want me to know, fearing I could use them against him.

I must say I'd never thought to ask, either.

So, after speaking privately with his sons, offering them my condolences—expecting condemnation but surprisingly receiving only their gratitude for my genuine concern and my willingness to delay our departure in order to give their father a proper burial—and trying my best to comfort his grief-stricken widow, I officiated over the torch-lit funeral; all of my officers and a goodly number of my men were present and in full kit no less, an impressive demonstration of respect Borzu's family and the Adraniis appeared to appreciate. And so after Jom murmured the Adranii version of burial rites over the canvas wrapped body, after his widow and sons were given a moment to say goodbye and Gratian made the requisite offerings, Captain Borzu, late of the Faoimhuirian survey ship, *Fihroon* was hastily buried, the gravesite covered in a large cairn of rock cannibalized from the now redundant fortifications. Within the hour, the last of the campfires were doused, the wet wood recovered and bundled up and lashed to the sides of the wagons where it would dry in the heat of day and then, with a single blast of a buccina, the column moved out, through a wide gap in the dismantled scree wall.

It was a sad leave-taking for the Adraniis—most if not all had never known anyone other than Borzu as their captain, their leader. They'd put their trust in him to deliver them from this nightmare they'd found themselves in—and now he was gone, killed not by the Si'aafu, by some of their own. His widow was inconsolable, at first refusing to leave his gravesite, but finally, and at my urging, her doting sons placed her under Cleander's care and she was bedded down in one of the medical wagons.

Jom was now the Adraniis' de-facto leader—a role not disputed by the rest of the Adraniis as Isem had not only taken away any hope of escape from Latrunculi, he'd also effectively robbed them of any well-organized resistance to my overall leadership. If any remained who shared his views, they wisely kept their feelings to themselves as the growing outrage over Borzu's cold-blooded and brutal murder would likely have been vented on them.

Not surprisingly Jom was very uncomfortable with his new role, still grieving for his captain, just like the rest and uncertain of my motives yet having little choice but to put his trust in me and my men to get us all to safety. But the Adraniis needed a leader of their own, even if that leader deferred to me on all matters of importance, something I stressed to Jom, as well as the rest of Borzu's command staff and who were now, by necessity, members of my command staff: Maisoh, who'd already proven her worth to me and then some, Khouri, the fierce-eyed Lujaji and yes, even the always twitchy Birral along with a dozen or so others I knew only by name, and whose posting aboard the *Fihroon,* not to mention their expertise meant nothing to me.

So, just as the bright spot of flotsam within the whirlpool touched the western rim of the gorge, we decamped en mass, using the same order we'd employed on our march here: a third of the cavalry led by Marcus, then three hundred infantry, the medical wagons, civilians on foot along with the baggage carts and bracketed on either side by the bulk of the infantry, then the supply wagons, the engines, the last three hundred infantry and finally the rear-guard cavalry with the remaining third of horsemen already out on the flats, acting as outriders and scouts. Leaving before dawn had an added bonus: the pearly glow softened the heaps of Si'aafu dead, leaving the impression—if you didn't look too closely—that the mounds of corpses were nothing more menacing than boulders.

Sadly, the still night air did little to lessen the stench and mothers kept their children close, trying to hide the carnage that lay all around us. The bracketing infantry, sensing the need to protect the youngest and the women, did their part by turning their shields outwards, providing a near-solid, moving barrier to inquisitive eyes.

Just like when we left the hillock, Felix and I remained behind with Hannibalianus and a handful of horsemen to make one last sweep on foot of the fissure behind the waterfall, the finger gorge and all of the many smaller cracks and crevices that riddled the deep chasm we'd briefly called home, using torches to probe the deeper recesses.

Satisfied we'd left no one and nothing of importance behind in our haste, we each in turn doused our torches in the pool before tying the precious bundles of sticks to our saddles and mounting up, hoping if there were any gods up and about at this ungodly hour, they'd understand that this miserly offering of fire was the best we could do and was by no means a snub.

As the last flaming torch-head hit the water, the gorge was plunged into darkness, with the mouth and the yawning gap in the wall silhouetted against the starlit desert. Beyond, I could plainly see the moving column; the bulk of it had carefully snaked through the perilous gauntlet of natron pools—no safe passage had been found between the pools and the foothills, so we were again forced out onto the desert proper—and had already turned north, the flash and glitter of armored horses and men leading the way.

And just like the last time, I was the last to leave this temporary refuge, but this time, as Wushah walked through the gap, I did look back, to bid Borzu peace and assure him that as long as I lived, I'd take care of

his family and people as if they were my own, because they were now—
Isem had very effectively seen to that.

XVI

We reached the base of the pass in amazingly good time: *three* days.

I'd like to say the Adraniis had learned to keep pace with us, but in truth it was more the constant, prodding fear of the Si'aafu that kept them walking without serious complaint and maintaining a decent speed while they were at it. No one, as it turned out, wanted to linger—not even Isem's distraught wife, whom he'd kindly left behind, along with his three small children, to explain his inexplicable actions to a less than understanding audience. The other men—nineteen in all—the ones who'd gone with him, had no families and if camp rumors were true, unlikely to find willing wives among the womenfolk—perhaps reason enough for their eagerness to abandon their fellow Adraniis.

So, everyone was up and ready each day, hours before dawn with meals eaten in haste, eager to get moving, to reach the desperately hoped for safety of what lay beyond the mountains no matter the temporary hardship.

True to his laconic Kellesuf nature, Marcus hadn't exaggerated the daunting character of the pass. It was going to be, in a word, grueling, for man and beast. As I looked up at the distant and still sunlit defile that cleaved two massive crags—the ancient and weather-worn breach he and his men had twice traversed without serious mishap—I privately wondered how many of our company we'd lose by the time we reached the other side. Marcus, his men and their horses had been in good shape at the time, well rested and well fed. That was not the case now, for any of us.

If the gods still favored us, we'd lose only a precious a few of our number, those too weak, too young or too badly injured to survive no matter what. But if the gods callously chose to forsake us just as Isem had capriciously abandoned his wife and children, well...

I glanced over my shoulder, to the heat-weary, ocher-dusted column of soldiers and civilians, wagons and their drivers, horsemen, engine crews and infantry, all patiently anticipating my order to start the climb as soon as the recalled outriders rejoined us. Some had taken the brief respite to grab something to eat or down a gulp or two of water. Most just stood where they'd stopped, simply too exhausted to do anything else.

I took a measured swig from my waterskin and swallowing with a wince, looked straight up. The sky above was dazzling pink shading to deep bluish-lavender, harbinger of approaching dusk; inky shadows had already begun to seep down the western range only to pool in the shallow valleys of its rolling foothills, while the eastern mountains had taken on the look of burnished copper. Pharos was only one of many held in the clutches of the low-riding suns, but all too soon its summit would, yet again, briefly burn blue-bright, rivaling Remus and the whirlpool that now lurked behind it at the edge of visibility, veiled in the dust-thick and quivering late afternoon air—

Someone nearby rudely cleared his throat, breaking my maudlin train of thought.

—and now that I was aware of it, I realized whoever it was had been repeatedly and insistently clearing his throat for some time, the noise finally worming its way past my distraction. So I dropped my slitted gaze to the perpetrator, who, as it happened, was sitting astride his horse next to me and mine.

In reply to my annoyed stare Felix raised his russet-tinged blond brows, clearly wondering like everyone else if I was going to give the command to move out, to go as far as we could while there was some daylight left, or if I was going to make camp here, give everyone a few extra hours of rest before the final big push.

It was extremely tempting to move on, to get the column up into the foothills at the very least, less exposed than the open desert and hope we'd find someplace safe to stop and bed down once night fell. It was just as likely we'd be forced to spend the long Latruncŭli night hunkered down and spread out along the winding path of a powder-dry creek bed or worse along the bare, exposed switchback spine of a foothill.

I twisted in the saddle, again looked at the silent column—even the children were too dog-tired to make a sound, to move unless they had to; they just stared back at me with sunken eyes devoid of all expression.

Enough.

I turned to Felix, said simply, "Make camp."

He nodded, turned Tuzun's head and with a click of his tongue sent the warhorse trotting wearily down the line to pass the word.

The Adraniis had learned the hard way not to just sit down where they stood no matter the temptation; they'd learned to help set up a proper marching camp before anything else, no matter how tired, thirsty and hungry they were because anyone who was able-bodied and didn't help didn't eat. Simple.

And I'll give them credit, it didn't take very long for them to catch on and to accept tasks allotted to them by my centurions and without any grumbling: the younger boys hurried off to help the wagoneers tend to the needs of the oxen, assist Hardalio and the dogs with the goats, or feed and water the caged chickens while the older boys and men muscled the massive medical wagons into the center of the camp, followed by positioning the supply wagons into a loose ring around them while the women, girls and all but the very youngest children, under the watchful eye of Florianus, set about preparing the evening meal, which by necessity was always a simple affair. In fact after two days practice, the Adraniis had gotten quite adept at their respective duties—so good that this third camp was set up in record time.

There was of course no wood to spare for fortifications, not even enough loose rock to build a barricade of any consequence, so, just as for the past two nights, the onagers, ballistas and scorpios served as a makeshift and rather porous semicircle just beyond the ring of supply wagons and tethered horses and oxen, the engines' menacing faces pointed outwards, towards the desert—as if the desert was our only concern. Marcus hadn't seen any sign of recent life during his sortie over the pass, nevertheless the barren foothills did offer a marginally more hospitable landscape and in my own experience as a child of the desert I knew that wildlife would grab any advantage it could get. So, if there was such life about, it was lurking out of sight in those hills. Another reason not to push on past dusk, when all advantage would go to those familiar with their surroundings.

Of course there was simply no protection possible from the sky above, a fact everyone was painfully aware of and so saw no reason to mention it.

So, we took what we could get and hoped the gods aided our sentries' sharp eyes and ears and kept watch over us from on high while we took a well-earned rest.

But just to increase our odds… I called for Gratian as I did each time we made camp in hopes he could again bargain with the gods, eloquently plead our case as he had before and yet again convince them that if they just continued to cooperate, they'd be handsomely rewarded down the line—in truth a *lot* further down the line.

That said, in my very limited experience with the divine I've found scant few deities willing to take *anything* on faith—which, when you think about it, is exceedingly hypocritical. Most demanded currency up front, be it blood, coinage or both. Usually both, and both in abundance.

Still, Gratian could rightly argue astonishing success when it came to being persuasive, because, as he reminded me at every opportunity we were all still alive due *entirely* to the gods' continued favor—a claim I felt prudent not to challenge, at least not aloud, despite plenty of evidence to the contrary. I never did ask precisely *which* gods he was referring to as it didn't seem particularly relevant. Divine favor *is* divine favor—who was I to question whether they were Roman, Adranii or those indigenous to Latruncŭli?

Gratian did his best with what little we had to offer, I'll grant him that. No pure white ox this time, not even a damned dirty white goat. This evening's offerings were little better that the previous two nights: a small, hastily lit pyre appropriated from our meager supply of firewood upon which he cast one whole dried eel, albeit a small one, along with a carefully measured number of shrimp—only he understood how to calculate such things—to the wisely silent dismay of the watching Adraniis and hungry, lip-licking stares of my men, followed by the requisite, and to me *overly* generous libation of ritual wine.

As I stood beside our soldier-priest as he preformed these rites while murmuring the proper incantations I found myself pondering how in hell my impious memories had produced someone so devout—perhaps he *had* been a priest in his previous life, or maybe con man? To me the only difference between the two was that a priest could, with the blessing of the emperor, fleece you, whereas a con man risked his life each time he helped himself to your hard-earned wages... unless, of course, the con man in question *was* the emperor. He could rob you of everything you owned with impunity.

Oblivious to my less than flattering musings, Gratian continued to murmur his incantations while many of those gathered around the pyre cringed as the crackling fire greedily consumed perfectly good food, not to mention a better than average wine.

I too couldn't help but wince—and sincerely hoped the gods would be sympathetic to our continued stingy displays of piety and not take them as the slight they might appear to be, or, worse, as the last, desperate act of fools.

As I made a quick sweep with my gaze of the surrounding ring of grubby, sweat streaked faces, of Felix, Aetius and Rufinius, Jotia, Baculus, Silvanus and Cleander and a silent audience made up mostly of my centurions and soldiers, but with a healthy scattering of Adraniis, men and women, children and adults, I saw my worries mirrored in their weary eyes—harsh reality was starting to rub even former Kellesuf raw...

Gratian ended his invocations as the tiny pyre, now satiated, collapsed in on itself and everyone present turned his or her attention on me. And dutiful to my part in what had become a nightly ritual, I said, "Off with you—we break camp before dawn," and yet again, like some cheap conjurer's trick, it sufficed to disperse the crowd.

Gratian and my senior centurions remained, staring at nothing in particular, having nothing to say that hadn't already been said and yet each reluctant to take his leave.

Beyond, the now well-banked fires of dusk left the eastern peaks awash in a deep and eerie greenish-blue glow; only Pharos gleamed bright and as I stared at that familiar landmark, I suddenly realized that within a day, two at most, this strangely familiar twilight phenomena would be lost from my sight, possibly forever. I felt a twinge at the loss.

Annoyed with myself, at my growing ease at slipping into such overly sentimental thoughts, I shifted my gaze from Pharos to my silent companions. By their sidelong, uneasy expressions it was obvious they too had been following my intense stare, curious perhaps, or worried as to what had so absorbed my attention yet loath to interrupt their crazy legate's private musings.

"Do I have to make that a damned order?" Okay, that came out a wee bit cranky, but I was too damned tired and hungry to be polite.

My officers wisely and hastily departed—even Felix hurried off, to seek out Eithne and Anachie as he had the past two evenings, to share a meal and their company while I joined my unattached officers. While Eithne's relationship with the two of us had matured past idle camp gossip, not all of the Adraniis were fully accepting of it and we'd all agreed it would be impolitic for me to spend time with them while we were on the march. As legate, I was supposed to keep my mind solely on the objective of getting everyone safely over the pass; as far as everyone was concerned anything—or, more specifically *anyone* else was an unjustifiable distraction.

That being said, it didn't seem quite fair that it was perfectly fine with everyone if Felix was distracted... not to mention Rufinius or Aetius and at least—at last count—a hundred or so of my men.

Which left me and the dying fire—a fire that taunted my own painfully empty belly by sending up fragrant wisps of smoke that smelled deliciously of roasted eel and I found myself glancing here and there among the coals for any morsel not fully consumed—surely the gods wouldn't mind... or would they?

Probably.

Damn them.

So, rather than tempt the fates—or myself—I left in search of safer, more earthly fare even if that fare was little more than a gritty paste of hardtack and a truly mediocre wine.

— ii —

Dawn arrived, accompanied by a bitter wind that blew down from the towering heights that loomed over us.

We'd been on the move for several hours, using the chill radiance of the whirlpool to guide us safety into the barren foothills, following the trail of cairns Marcus had placed every half mile or so—cairns that were dismantled by the last of the infantry as they passed as I felt no need to clearly mark our passage to anyone or anything that might follow—and now, as the stars winked out and the whirlpool faded, we were confronted with a taste of what was to come: a biting cold that eddied around us as if probing for weakness among our ranks and finding plenty.

I drew my heavy woolen cloak tight around my goose-pimpled throat and hunkered down in the saddle, thankful for the protection my helmet offered my neck and cheeks; even Wushah folded his ears against his neck, shook his massive head and snorted irritably, protesting this latest affront. The rest of the column did what they could to bundle up; everyone knew that while we might have a brief respite once the suns rose, it was only a temporary reprieve. From here on out, it was only going to get colder; we had to keep moving.

Suddenly, a shaft of ruby light snagged the highest peak above us, then ever so slowly began to spread, hopping from crag to crag and trickling down the mountains and with it came a welcome breath of warm air. *First sunrise.*

I glanced over my shoulder, smiled thinly at the overfed Romulus as it lazily peeked over the eastern range and in between my teeth chattering, quietly urged it to hurry the hell up—

"Fuckin' cold—reminds me of that damnedable Germania," I overheard Felix grumble from within the folds of his cloak as he struggled to get his bare calves under the heavier fabric while maintaining his seat on his saddle.

A moment later he lifted his helmeted head, just enough to peer at me, blood-shot eyes barely visible between helmet brim and cloak. "I mean I bet it reminds *you* of that damnedable Germania."

I couldn't help but laugh at that, adding, "It'll be warm enough soon enough…"

The rest of his helmeted head immerged from the swaddle of his cloak, looking rather like a tortoise extending its neck, lured by the mere promise of warmth.

"…and knowing you, you'll find cause to bitch about that, too."

He glowered at me as he jerked his cloak tight under his helmet's neck-guard, around the cheek-pieces and his goose-pimpled throat.

I chuckled again and fixed my gaze on what lay ahead. Romulus was well on its way to clearing the eastern range and spreading not only its ruddy light over the creased and folded foothills but its welcome warmth as well.

I tapped Wushah's flanks with my heels and clicked my tongue and he picked up his pace, Felix and Tuzun, along with the rest of the column, dutifully, albeit unhappily following. I'd known from the start that today we'd be lucky if we made half the distance we'd made on the flatlands. While the climb wasn't steep—for now—Marcus warned me that it was still going to be arduous, and he was right.

Soon we were zigzagging our way through a massive boulder-field—both treacherous and worrisome, as it was the ideal site for ambush, with most of the column hidden from sight at any given time. This nerve-wracking yet thankfully uneventful passage was followed by a painfully slow and equally precarious trip over a series of castellated ridges that rocked and jolted the wagons to the point of loosening joints and threatening to shatter spokes along with the legs of our horses and oxen.

After a brief rest—time enough to water the animals and check for injuries, we pressed on, only to find a powder dry, sand-filled riverbed blocking our path. Marcus and his horsemen along with those on foot found it little more than a slow slog, but it was a quagmire for wheels, so Rufinius decided to remove the wheels from the ballistas, onagers and wagons and drag them across like sledges, but we quickly discovered that the heavier wagons still needed to be fully offloaded otherwise they just plowed into the sand and stuck fast.

Even emptied of their cargo, it took multiple ox teams, not to mention scores of men to get them safely to the far bank. Ferrying the wagons' contents across by hand or horse, or in the case of the wounded by improvised litter, was an equally time consuming process and by the time everything and everyone was reloaded and the ox teams rested it was approaching midday.

The far bank offered no suitable campsite, so we pressed on, and ended up winding our way up, over and down a succession of spalled humpbacks that further strained the already sore muscles and frayed tempers of man and beast alike.

And we were only in the foothills, I reminded myself. What would it be like when we reached the mountains proper? While we knew from the outset that eventually the larger wagons would have to be completely disassembled and packed, piecemeal, over the pass, Marcus had assured me the smaller wagons, engines and handcarts could make it intact, but every time I risked a glance upwards, I found my doubts rising as well.

At least a dozen of the Adranii carts just couldn't stand up to the nonstop abuse; they were cannibalized of everything of possible use before what was left was carefully buried under loose rock—again, I was not about to leave any obvious evidence of our passage. Twice the entire column had to stop while Rufinius and his men hastily repaired a wagon's broken axle and finally gangs of men again had to add their muscle to that of the oxen to get the large medical wagons safely up and over two hillocks that otherwise blocked our path. The alternative was to spend precious hours of daylight backtracking then searching for a safer route around them with the possibility of finding none.

By mid-afternoon we were well into the mountains and while the going was harder, at least the air was a little cooler, with a light and welcome breeze that was thankfully free of dust. Florianus, his cooks and a number of Adranii women had taken to moving up and down the length of the column with water buckets and bags of dried fruit and hardtack, while Marcus and his men, along with Hardalio and his Adranii goatherds-in-training offered the horses, oxen and goats mouthfuls of water-moistened fodder. The end result was that the column kept moving, albeit at a much slower speed.

Late afternoon found us part way up the pass proper, and chasing the last rays of Romulus' vermilion light along with the lingering warmth of the day. Cloaks and blankets that had been hurriedly tossed into baggage carts and wagons, rolled into packs or tied to the backs of saddles had been just as hastily reclaimed and now everyone was bundled back up, trudging along in determined, gloomy silence as if it was my mad plan to march all night and there was simply nothing to be gained by arguing about it.

My men went where I went and the Adraniis knew if they wanted to survive they had little choice but to keep up with us. The chilly breeze that nipped at their heels didn't hurt—everyone was painfully aware that sore muscles and a cold night awaited us where ever and whenever I chose to make camp, so perhaps it was those thoughts, rather than fear of risking my ire that kept urging them on.

As Remus neared the highest peak, I ordered our resident mountain goat, Duccius, along with a handful of scouts and their dogs to hurry ahead of the column in hopes of finding some place, any place suitable for a camp. Footing that was dicey in the full light of day became down right perilous in the dark and so it was with no small relief for everyone that just as Remus followed Romulus behind the crags above us, plunging us into a premature dusk, Duccius and his companions returned with word that not more than five hundred paces ahead the trail narrowed as it passed between two massive boulders, then it took a sharp turn and beyond was a wind-protected and relatively flat expanse. While far from ideal, it was judged suitable for a marching camp, albeit an *extremely* crowded camp.

That news—that a meal and a place to sleep—were close at hand urged everyone on and by the time it was truly dark, or as truly dark as it ever got, we'd yet again settled down for the night in relative safety, sheltered from the mountain cold by a large promontory, and the natural bottleneck, along with our always-manned scorpios that ran the length of the passageway, from boulder to boulder provided some measure of security—at least against any who might have followed us.

It was far from a comfortable locale, but no one complained and after another cold meal—by my order absolutely no fires this time as at this height they'd be clearly visible for miles—the exhausted Adraniis bedded down, along with a third of my equally exhausted troops.

Soon the entire camp fell silent—even the horses, oxen and goats were too tired to grumble about their half-empty bellies and the dogs, now tasked with guard duty alongside the pickets, went about it in a thankfully quiet, businesslike way. The chickens, having been bounced around inside the confines of their coops all day, had the good graces to keep their clucking to a petulant mutter, and the cats, who were now housed in one of the medical wagons had nothing to complain about aside from the fact that like the chickens, they were securely caged and would remain so until we found at least a temporary place to settle. According to Tigidius, the cats proved a surprising, but welcome distraction to of all people Borzu's widow, Aostre, who, still grief-stricken, found solace in their company and spent the long hours of our trek seated beside their crate, murmuring comforting words and enticing them with tidbits to eat, as if they were her own babes.

I spent time with the wounded, as I did each evening and then again, each morning before we broke camp and this evening, just as with previous evenings, I found myself seated beside Carbo, helping him get down a slurry of hardtack and watered wine. He managed to grumble half-heartedly about the meal, about the lack of proper accommodations, and of course about Nestor, but it was all a feint. Carbo was failing—my physicians knew it; I knew it. Worst of all, Carbo knew it but doggedly refused to concede to the inevitable.

He asked how long before we reached the summit, he asked me to tell him again about the grasslands and the forests beyond, and leaning against me and closing his eyes, managed a thin smile as I repeated what Marcus and Duccius had told us, repeated what I'd told him the night before, and the night before that and the night before that and in fantastical and imaginary detail, of endless steppe rolling before the wind like any vast sea, and again assured him there would be game aplenty to hunt and that I was depending upon him, we were *all* depending upon him and his expertise at tracking to bring down something that we could sink our teeth into.

I assured him that the women would see him as a wonder, a hunter of incredible prowess and he'd have his pick of the youngest and loveliest, each and every one clamoring for his attentions, begging him, the ultimate provider, to take as one of his many wives. He grinned at that, his eyes bright with fever, but the weak grin all too quickly faded.

Only after I was satisfied he'd finally lapsed into sleep, desperately hoping I'd helped him enter into a dream of those promised grasslands, or of being surrounded by young, pretty girls, where he was once again well and strong and capable, and at Cleander's urging and assistance, I eased him back down onto his pallet.

But rather than leave as I usually did, once Carbo had fallen asleep, this evening I lingered, perched on the edge of his cot, to watch in silence as Cleander and Nestor went about their business tending to the badly wounded who were housed in the same wagon, soldiers and Adranii alike packed onto narrow cots that were stacked from floor to canvas covered ceiling with barely enough head room for each person to breathe. It was so cramped Cleander and Nestor had to continually squeeze around each other—not to mention around me—as they moved from patient to patient, tending to their wounds, offering sips of broth and lozenges to ease the pain.

Surprisingly, neither urged me to leave; they didn't even flick me a disapproving look. That said I *was* in their way and realizing I had nothing to offer aside from my earnest sympathy for their patients' suffering and admiration for their dedication, I rose, stiffly, then went in search of my own belated supper.

And so our first day climbing the pass proper ended, and ended without serious calamity—gods' favor *indeed*. Which meant that I no sooner washed down my last mouthful of hardtack with a gulp of wine than I called for Gratian and asked what we needed to do in order to guarantee continued divine protection. He smiled and said he'd already taken care of it while I was with Carbo. I was just as bone-weary as everyone else, which meant I was too damned tired to ask what he meant by that, trusting he hadn't made promises we couldn't possibly honor, and after thanking him and patting him on the back, I bade him goodnight and as he stumbled off to his bed, I made my unsteady way to mine.

I awoke only once during the night, bumped in the shoulder by Felix's elbow as he tossed and turned in his sleep, and unable to fall back asleep, I grudgingly rolled onto my back and stared up at the spectacular sky. But rather than admiring its unrestrained splendor, I found myself looking for any betraying flicker of movement within the glittering and glimmering expanse. After several minutes of search and finding nothing worrisome, I settled back and allowed myself a few minutes of sheer extravagance, of giving the now benign night sky its due: the air was cold, thin and sparklingly beautiful with the icy spirals of the whirlpool directly overhead and seemingly close enough to touch.

Finally, feeling the familiar and welcome tug of sleep, I bade the gathering of stars a heart-felt goodnight, snuggled back under my cloak and without further ado, reclaimed my well-earned slumber.

— iii —

The next day started out promising enough. The dawn air was crisp and clear—my goose-pimpled flesh and the shiver down my spine instantly conjuring up memories of Cisalpina in autumn, of pursuing deer through stands of flame-headed maple and copper-clad beech, of the frosted breath of my companions as they paced me, their winded laughter and directional whistles that echoed off the surrounding crags, the thrill of the hunt… and the bone-deep chill of evening chased away by fire-warmed wine, roasted venison and the camaraderie…

I couldn't help but flick Felix, who was riding next to me a sidelong glance and wonder if we'd share similar experiences in the years to come, of Carbo now fully recovered and leading the chase—assuming Latrunculi proved as bountiful and hospitable as Earth. *Gods, I hope so—*

He noticed my preoccupied gaze and answered with a quizzical arch of the brow.

I smiled in reply then fixed eyes on what lay ahead.

With a light breeze that kept the dust at bay, we kept up a remarkably good pace—in hindsight a reckless pace over unfamiliar and exceedingly treacherous territory. As the column snaked its way along the wide, sunlit rim of a shadow-filled ravine, what appeared to be solid rock suddenly gave way beneath one of the smaller wagons—the wagon toppled then tumbled down into the pitch-darkness of the ravine, taking its terrified and bellowing ox-team with it.

The driver managed to leap clear at the last possible instant and was pulled the rest of the way to safety by several quick thinking Adraniis. By the time Felix and I reached the scene, the driver, Pacha, had stopped shaking uncontrollably, but his normally swarthy face had yet to regain its color and he was close to inconsolable over the loss of Pultuce and Kastur, his beloved oxen, not to mention the wagon and its irreplaceable contents of grain, dried meat, several spare axles and spare canvas.

A quick look-see over the crumbling lip squelched any thought of retrieving anything of value: what we'd all assumed was a steep slope cloaked in shadow was in fact a near-vertical drop off, the ravine's true depth hidden in inky darkness. Just to make sure, I tossed a stone into the abyss then began to count, slowly. I stopped at thirty, not because I heard the faint, telltale-echoing clack of the rock hitting the bottom, but because that in itself told me all I needed to know.

My heart-felt reassurances that no one was to blame, that it was nothing more than a tragic accident did little to comfort Pacha or, for that matter the equally shaken Adraniis who'd rushed to his rescue and were now coming to grips with the reality that their spur-of-the-moment, life-saving actions almost cost them *their* lives. Adraniis, as I might have mentioned before, are not the bravest people. But in their defense perhaps in their previous lives as pampered Faoimhuir slaves they had little reason, much less opportunity to be brave.

The frightening incident served as a stark reminder to all just how precarious our position was and as a result the entire column ground to a sudden and uneasy halt: Adraniis were clearly afraid to keep moving for fear more rock would give way beneath them and yet were equally afraid to retreat to seemingly safer ground for fear we'd leave them behind. Wagoneers too clearly feared for their teams, not to mention their own lives and of course many of the wagons carried our wounded, the weak and the sick.

It would have been impossible retrace our steps, even if I'd wanted to: there was simply no room to turn the larger wagons, not to mention the onagers, around. So, if we retreated, we'd have no choice but to abandon the wagons and the onagers—equipment that might mean the difference between life and death on our trek to find permanent sanctuary.

We had scant provisions as it was—even less now—we couldn't afford to lose anything more, much less abandon anything, yet if our progress was slowed to a crawl as I reasonably assumed it would, we'd have that much less, if anything to eat or drink on the way down the other side and of course no assurances of finding anything edible once we got there.

I could have ordered everyone to keep moving. My soldiers would have followed without question, albeit with far more attention to the ground beneath their feet or the wheels of their wagons and engines. But the Adraniis were another matter. They were scared—terrified in fact and virtually frozen in place, firmly convinced we were doomed no matter which way we went.

In truth there was simply no choice *but* to keep going and the Adraniis needed to be convinced, cajoled into it. Ordering them to follow, demanding or forcing them at sword-point to do as I commanded had the potential for making a very bad situation even worse. They needed to truly believe they had an equal voice as to whether we kept going or we backtracked.

So, I called for a meeting of my centurions and the Adranii officers, while at the same time I sent Duccius and his scouts ahead again in the slim hope of finding a safer route to the summit. Marcus had made the climb, had searched for the safest path with the limitations of our column foremost in his mind and this was all he had found, so I wasn't too optimistic, but I figured what the hell. If anyone could find a better route, it would be Duccius. Plus, we had some time to waste while we held this meeting to discuss our "options"—all of it little more than a carefully orchestrated effort to reassure our jittery Adranii companions that we all weren't about to plummet to our deaths.

After some heated discussion which included some damned clever maneuvering and manipulating on my part—skills I'd learned from the very best, chief among them Silvanus Vulso—Jom, Lujaji, Birral, Khouri and Maisoh found themselves agreeing wholeheartedly that we must keep going the way we'd been going, but at the same time it was just too dangerous for the larger wagons to continue, even if Duccius found a safer path; they would have to be disassembled here, their precious contents, including the wounded, not to mention the parted up wagons themselves carried by man, ox, horse and the smaller wagons and baggage carts until it was deemed safe enough to reassemble them, which common sense said was only after we were well down the other side.

I left it up to the onager crew chiefs to decide if they wanted to take apart their machines, but none took me up on the offer. Once the larger wagons were dismantled and their loads doled out, there would be few free hands or backs left to carry anything else and none of the crews were willing to leave their prized engines behind. They had, after all, proven their worth against the Si'aafu and no doubt would, in the future, prove their worth again.

There was an added bonus to the decision to take apart the wagons: it gave everyone something to do and take their minds off all the reasonable worries we all had, while we awaited Duccius' return.

Even Wushah was drafted and ended up no better than a pack mule, his back burdened with heavy sacks of grain and topped with rolls of precious canvas and bales of grass and wood. Undignified for a warhorse, yes, and he let me know it by stomping a feathered hoof, rolling his eyes and tonguing his bit. Of course this meant that I was on foot like everyone else and like everyone else, I was expected to carry my fair share of the load.

Six hours—six precious hours of daylight later and two hours after Duccius and his companions returned safe but luckless in their search, I cautiously shouldered a heavy pack filled with foodstuffs, grabbed Wushah's bridle to steady myself, then gave the whistled signal to move out. As I looked back at the column I saw every able-bodied person, including the all but the very smallest children, laden down with supplies; I saw oxen with wheels, yokes and wagon boards strapped to their broad backs and a few had the extra burden of our caged chickens and cats; I saw our cavalry horses carrying babies, young children and pregnant women along with bulging sacks of supplies; I saw litters carrying our injured and dogs carrying packs—I even saw a few of the larger goats with waterskins now lashed to their backs—and I was suddenly struck with a childhood memory, of seeing a long line of ants scurrying along, carrying leaves.

I turned back and clicking my tongue, started off, Wushah plodding alongside and looking supremely disgruntled about his rapid change of fortunes. I was also keenly aware that I would be setting the pace along with an example for the rest. With that thought foremost, I squinted at the ankle twisting and backbreaking path ahead with the unhappily realization that pain was afoot.

Felix, who was carrying his own heavy pack and leading a similarly laden down Tuzun, leaned close as he followed my pinched gaze. "We don't have to make the summit today—remember, everyone's on foot, including most of the children."

I flicked him a sidelong look. *Nice try*. It wasn't the children he was worried about, or, should I say, the children's welfare wasn't foremost in his mind. He was worried about me. As well he should. *I* was worried about me. What lay ahead would test the mettle of the fittest man, and I wasn't keen on the idea of putting my own physical limitations on full display for the entire column to see, not when everyone was looking to me to lead them to safety.

My fears—not to mention Felix's worries—turned out to be unwarranted. While the natural trail that wound its way through sunlit rockfall and shadowy clefts was demanding, it wasn't exhausting. In fact now that we were no longer encumbered by the limitations of the larger wagons we actually maintained a decent speed—when someone had to stop to tend to stone-bruised feet and blistered hands, or adjust the load carried by a horse or ox, they would step out of the column so others could pass—and if we kept up this dogged pace, I figured that at worst we would add a day, two at the very most to the time it would take to reach the summit, fair trade for increasing our chances of making the summit with our numbers largely intact.

I did order the column to make camp when we reached another relatively flat, wind-protected cleft, marked by yet another cairn of rocks. Marcus and his men had camped here on their way to the grasslands and on their way back, and according to Marcus there wasn't a better site reachable before nightfall. To me it was more than suitable, not to mention sizable—the entire column was able to fit, albeit again very snugly, within its steep walls—walls that would effectively conceal the glow of firelight while keeping the warmth of those fires contained, and the winds at bay. Yes, tonight I would permit cook fires—and to that end sent word to Florianus to get the pots cleaned of their days' long accumulation of dust and the firewood readied. Despite it being only late afternoon, it was already quite chilly and everyone was in dire need—and richly deserving—of a hot meal. But before anyone could enjoy that meal, the horses and oxen were to be rubbed down, then they, along with the goats and dogs were to be fed, watered and checked for injuries. Our continued survival depended on our four-footed companions and their needs took priority.

And then there was the matter of all of the parted up equipment, which needed to be carefully stacked so as to make it easier and faster to redistribute everything in the morning, yet not be in the way if we had need to defend ourselves—or make a hasty escape. Neither was likely, but I was not willing to take any chances.

While everyone was busy getting the camp set up, I walked the length of the cleft, from deepest recesses to its mouth, offering genuine praise to the weary Adraniis as they tended to the animals and the injured or assisted in stockpiling the supplies and wagon parts, and words of encouragement to my troops as they, under Rufinius' watchful eye, set up the requisite defensive perimeter.

But the walk wasn't just for everyone else's benefit: I needed to keep moving. The moment I sat down, my abused bones and muscles would exact their painful and prolonged revenge. And for once I was glad of the long night ahead: time for everyone to rest, to gather the energy needed to resume the climb once the suns rose. I privately winced at the thought as I shifted my narrowed gaze to the object of everyone's single-minded fixation: the summit.

Duccius, who'd twice reached that lofty goal in his constant hunt for a better route and returned safely assured me if the column kept up the same pace, we'd reach it by this time tomorrow, at worst the day after and then...

As I stared at that massive cleave in the mountain, I felt a twinge in my gut. What if what lay beyond offered no more promise than what we'd left behind? What if I too had put my trust in those same fantastical tales I'd used to such effect on Carbo? Yes, there was grassland to be sure; Duccius had seen it and Marcus had actually reached it, but unlike the horses, goats and oxen, we couldn't survive for long eating grass. What if that's all there was? What then?

I flinched violently as an arm eeled around my waist and I looked down to find Eithne staring up at me.

Her face was grimy and sweat-streaked, and her downy hair and clothing was still coated in the ocher dust from the desert far below, but as our eyes met, she smiled and suddenly she was beautiful again, as beautiful as the first day we met, as desirable as the first night we made love, or, should I say, attempted it. And as dog-tired as I was, and as much as my bones and muscles ached, I suddenly found myself wanting to take her, right then and there.

My expression must've given me away; she grinned then tugged at my lower lip. "Wait until dark—if you're still... *uh*, up for it, come find me."

"*Where?*" I asked a wee bit too eagerly. It had been several days—several very long days, and *equally* long, lonely nights—since I'd enjoyed her attentions.

She motioned with her chin. "Over there." Then she slipped away, leaving me to stare after her with, I realized to my chagrin, very obvious intentions written all over me. I say that because no sooner had she made good her escape when I overheard some stifled giggling. I looked around and quickly spotted a group of Adranii girls nearby. They were favoring me—*the damned Legate*—with sidelong and decidedly pointed looks while whispering to each other. Worse, several of the older ones were clearly intrigued and just as clearly wanted me to know it, which of course didn't help my current state one bit.

I gave my ring-mail shirt a hard jerk here, an angry yank there then I stalked off. I'd like to say I went in search of my supper, but in truth it was my dignity that had suddenly gone missing.

— XVII —

The next morning our luck—or, as Gratian would insist, *the gods' favor*—ran out. Gods are notorious for being fickle after all, and on this day they proved that and then some.

Long before we started what I knew would be a dangerous ascent, I told myself we'd be incredibly fortunate if we only lost a few along the way—the badly injured and the ill, the weakest among us, or through the sort of accident that came close to claiming Pacha. I thought I'd truly accepted these deaths as inevitable and that when—*not if*—they occurred, they would be a small price to pay if it meant the rest of us reached what lay beyond the pass.

So, one could argue that Carbo's death was *expected*—in fact each evening, as the camp settled and I made my rounds, checking on the wounded, I'd found myself surprised and intensely relieved that he was still with us; even Cleander found himself at a loss and finally, grudgingly—at Gratian's insistence—attributed his continued survival to divine protection. But I alone knew the truth to his tenacity: Carbo desperately wanted to live to see the grasslands—the real Carbo had, after all, come from the high steppe, far to the east of distant Parthia, and I had begun to suspect the same was true of *this* Carbo. Perhaps this alone explained why he'd picked the memories, the personality he did.

So, drawing equally from his Kellesuf mind-set, my memories and maybe his own, he steadfastly refused to succumb to injuries using a simple yet powerful goal: he wanted to live to see home again.

Each morning as I rounded again, he would ask me in a desperate voice barely above a breathless whisper how much further before we reached the summit, as if that was the ultimate goal rather than just the first in a long line of hurdles we'd have to overcome in order to survive on this world. But it wasn't the summit he yearned for; it was the sight of an inland ocean of grass rippling in the wind, the smell and feel of that sun-warmed grass underfoot.

But each day he grew visibly weaker as the trek got harder, the air colder and the unavoidable jolting and jostling of the wagon got rougher, and rougher still when the injured were transferred to litters with little protection from the harsh sunlight and the biting wind. During the long hours of the night, and despite being given a sleeping draught, he would twitch and moan softly, or worse, feebly thrash around and mumble incoherently, caught in the grip of a fever that failed to yield to Cleander's potions.

So, on this portentous morning, less than one day's hike from the summit, less than one day before he could see what he had so desperately wanted to see, he simply failed to wake up.

As my grief-stricken officers gathered around the body to give their heart-felt respects I overheard Tigidius whisper to Nestor that his death was a blessing.

Nestor, for his part wisely kept his feelings to himself, as did Iulius and Khouri. Cleander, uncharacteristically, blamed himself, believing he'd misjudged the previous evening's dose of the sleeping draught.

Perhaps he had; but then again, perhaps even Carbo couldn't fight Orcus forever, couldn't stop Morta's ever-sharp blade from cutting the thread of life—his life. Perhaps it *was* a blessing, albeit a very bittersweet one.

My troops and especially the artillery crews took his death every bit as hard as Cleander did, every bit as hard as my officers and I did, and the Adraniis, sensing this was a deeply personal loss we didn't wish to share, wisely kept their distance and a respectful silence as Gratian performed all the requisite—and yes, *time-consuming*—rites. While Carbo's death was, as I said, not wholly unexpected, it was an unwelcome and very painful reminder of the lingering suspicions, the unspoken yet palpable resentments that still simmered just under the surface of our otherwise seemingly cohesive company.

The cleft in which we'd taken refuge had scree in abundance and we could have built a suitably impressive cairn over his body with an equally impressive view of the mountain-ringed desert far below. But I knew this place wouldn't have been his choice for a tomb, his crews knew it, and so with my blessing, Cleander and Iulius prepared the body for travel, gently wrapping it in precious canvas then placing it on an awaiting litter with the same care they'd have shown if Carbo still breathed—and if the Adraniis objected, or wondered why a lowly artillery centurion was being accorded the honor of accompanying us when their beloved Captain Borzu was not, they wisely kept their objections and their questions to themselves.

By the time we finally broke camp, the mismatched suns were several hand-spans up in the sky, yet despite the late start, and the final leg of the climb being some of the hardest, we still reached the summit by early that afternoon and as Felix and I, along with our heavily laden mounts stepped aside to allow the rest of the column to begin the long-anticipated descent, I found myself staring out at those much-heralded grasslands and yes, the forested and snow-capped peaks far beyond.

The air was certainly different: instead of the cloying dust and strength-sapping heat of the desert or the chill of the pass, the mild breeze that blew up the eastern slope of the range brought with it the sweet smell of water, of grass and sun-warmed earth. The sky above was full of scudding, fat-bellied clouds and in the constantly shifting gaps between them, angled and fast-moving shafts of sunlight streamed down, leaving the rolling, gray-green steppe alternately bathed in sunshine and shadow.

And far to the north-west and towering above a jagged range of mountains, more clouds: these thick and dark and threatening rain—*rain!* Wushah and Tuzun confirmed what I saw by tossing their heads, pawing the ground and whickering softly—they could smell rain. Just the thought of feeling rain on my upturned face again brought a broad smile to my sun-cracked lips.

"It's beautiful," Felix whispered as Aetius and Rufinius joined us, awe-struck by the view, just like the rest of us, and it was—it was everything Marcus and Duccius had said it was and more; it was everything Carbo had dreamt it would be—everything I'd promised him it would be.

"Indeed it is," Aetius replied and the always-laconic Rufinius nodded his agreement, his bright and wonder-filled eyes speaking volumes.

I could imagine his thoughts, of aqueducts and bridges, of farms and fences and *baths*—all awaiting his skilled hands—and couldn't help but grin at the prospects.

In fact as the column passed by us, I noticed that each and every person, soldier and civilian, adult and child alike paused briefly to stare, slack-jawed out at the verdant and inviting landscape spread out before us and then, realizing they were holding things up, each eagerly resumed his or her descent, smiling and in some cases laughing, their weary and dusty faces suddenly alive again, alight with the warm glow of the afternoon sunlight. I even spotted the days-old baby among the throng, carried in his mother's gaunt arms as his father walked alongside, stoop-shouldered and laden down like the rest of us.

I caught the man's eye and nodded, pleased that our tiniest member had survived and now, perhaps, had a chance to thrive; he smiled and nodded his gratitude in return.

Gods' favor indeed.

Then Carbo's canvas wrapped litter appeared, carried not by his fellow centurions, but by four of his engine chiefs: the still recovering Lollius, his injured arm wrapped in filthy bandages, Geta, Burrus and

Eugenius. Carbo's crews had rotated in the task of bearing the litter this day just as they had every day, and whether Lollius' turn just happened to take place as we crested the summit and began our descent or it was by design, I was relieved to see him up and walking, glad for him he was well enough to participate, even briefly, in what was a very personal rite for the crews.

The four stopped briefly to take in the view and I overheard Lollius murmur to their silent burden that he was almost home before they continued on and were quickly swallowed up by the flow of the weary but cheerful column as it shuffled its way along. Then I spotted Borzu's widow, Aostre, accompanied by her sons, along with Laatao and Isem's wife and their combined horde of children. I dipped my helmeted head and murmured my respects as they passed and each nodded in reply. Aostre even managed to smile and Laatao... I swear she winked at the grinning Aetius.

Eithne and Anachie soon joined us, along with Jom and Maisoh, and as Rufinius hoisted Anachie up onto his shoulders for a better view, Eithne wrapped one arm around my waist, the other around Felix's and tugged us close—not an easy task with each of us carrying a heavy pack, but somehow we managed. Maisoh embraced Rufinius, then roped in Aetius with her other arm and Aetius promptly draped his free arm over Jom's shoulders and we grinned at each other like a bunch of exhausted, giddy fools.

We'd made it—and by the looks of things, we had a good chance of making Latruncŭli not just a place to eek out a meager existence, but our *home*.

"Hic sunt scorpiones," Jom muttered distractedly as he gazed out at the grand and inviting panorama spread out before us, in the process drawing our collective and curious sidelong stares.

"You think we're going to find scorpions here?" I asked; then a horrible thought: *"Si'aafu?"*

He turned to me and smiled. "No, Legate. Captain Borzu once told me that it was something written on old Earth maps to denote the unknown. *Hic sunt scorpiones...* here be scorpions, meaning here lies unexplored territory and who knows what you'll find. Apropos, don't you think?"

I looked at Aetius, at Rufinius and Maisoh, Eithne, Felix and Anachie, and seeing the looks of eager anticipation in their eyes, I grinned and said, "Let's go find out, shall we?"

www.ingramcontent.com/pod-product-compliance
Lightning Source LLC
Chambersburg PA
CBHW050021030726
47506CB00001B/61

* 9 7 8 1 6 0 2 1 5 1 8 7 1 *